THE ISL...
THEIR F...
THEIR F...
THEIR TRIUMPH

SARAH
Scarred by a tragic love, her pride soared over the petty tyranny of her enemies to create an unshakable dynasty

HORATIO
He would amass a huge fortune through his talent for exploiting the island's countless treasures . . . but his children were doomed to destroy it

VERONICA
Her blood raced with the twin needs of power and passion . . . but the hungers of her heart were haunted by a past that could never let her forgive

SAM
A rich playboy who lived only for pleasure, he discovered the one great love of his life . . . only to see it perish before his very eyes

ROBERT
Brutal, dangerous, and uncontrollable, he set off the tragic chain of events that would topple his family's empire

Other Avon Books by
Neal Travis

CASTLES
MANSIONS
PALACES
WINGS

Island

NEAL TRAVIS

AVON
PUBLISHERS OF BARD, CAMELOT, DISCUS AND FLARE BOOKS

ISLAND is an original publication of Avon Books. This work has never before appeared in book form.

AVON BOOKS
A division of
The Hearst Corporation
1790 Broadway
New York, New York 10019

First Avon Printing: August 1986

AVON TRADEMARK REG. U.S. PAT. OFF. AND IN
OTHER COUNTRIES, MARCA REGISTRADA, HECHO
EN U.S.A.

Printed in the U.S.A.

K-R 10 9 8 7 6 5 4 3 2 1

Author's note: This is a work of fiction, but many of the events recorded here did happen on the island of Bermuda; most of the others could have happened on Bermuda and its adjoining islands. As the early mapmakers wrote of Bermuda, "Here be Devils."

Contents

Chapter One
(1919–)

Sir Horatio Fleet stood with his back to the somber boardroom and looked out on the bright blue waters of Hamilton Harbor; a cluster of His Majesty's Navy ships were anchored there—already seeming out of place, unwanted. The Great War was over at last and with it the Navy's role of protecting Bermuda. It was time for them to go, to be replaced by the trading vessels of a dozen nations and the gleaming white passenger liners of The Fleet Company.

Fleet lowered his gaze to Front Street, busier than ever, horse cabs and carriages competing for right-of-way with brightly dressed shoppers, stiff-suited businessmen, urchins and stevedores. Sir Horatio found the view from the boardroom pleasing. The early Fleets had chosen the site for their headquarters well: The Fleet Company occupied the best and biggest premises on the main street, owned the finest docks and the largest warehouses. Sir Horatio liked to look out on all the things he owned, and now the good times were about to return to Bermuda.

A discreet cough behind him heralded the entrance of Pennyworth, the company secretary.

"Good morning, Sir Horatio. The board members are in the anteroom. Shall I show them in?"

"Have my sons arrived?"

"No, sir."

"Then we'll just have to wait, Pennyworth. They're board members too, now. And heroes, home from the war. We must be indulgent. They'll soon be here."

Robert and Sam. In other times he'd have taken the whip to them if they'd dared be late for an appointment with their father. He smiled. Getting soft in his old age. But it must have been the devil of a war for them—as it had been for everyone.

The big cedar doors of the boardroom crashed open and Horatio spun around in annoyance as Sam tumbled in like an overlarge puppy, all gangling arms and legs. Grinning broadly, Sam said, "Sorry, Father. Didn't mean to keep you waiting on The Big Day."

"Good God, young man! You might at least have dressed for the occasion. If the tailor hasn't completed your new suits, you should have worn your uniform."

Sam Fleet glanced down at his brightly striped blazer and white tennis flannels.

"Sorry, Father," he said again. "But I've got a tennis date at noon with Ginny Winders. At the club. This meeting won't take long, will it?"

"It will take as long as needs be," Horatio said. "We have a great deal of important business to decide. We're not meeting only to confirm you two boys to the board."

The others began filing into the boardroom, all his old associates, men of the other first families Horatio had grown up with. They nodded and murmured greetings and moved to take their accustomed places around the oak table.

In the rear of the crowd came his eldest son, Robert, pale, emaciated-looking like all the Fleet men, but also displaying a strange moroseness that had worried his parents all Robert's life. At least, Horatio thought, the fellow was suitably dressed in a dark blue linen suit.

"You two take those seats at the bottom of the table," he said, moving to the high-backed captain's chair traditionally occupied by the chairman of the board.

Sir Horatio glanced around the table. "Well, gentlemen, you all know my sons. I'm sure you're as pleased as I am to have them home safe and assuming their places at this table."

"Here, here," someone called out and there was a round of polite applause.

"I'll take it from that they are confirmed," Horatio said. "Pennyworth, we'll dispense with the reading of the minutes and all that. There's a lot to be decided today." He fumbled for his pipe, filled it and watched the cloud of smoke rise up to the sturdy beams of the dark ceiling. Six generations of Fleets had presided over meetings in this very room; it was a comforting thought.

"The biggest decision facing us today," he said, "is whether we have faith in Bermuda's future. These past years have been hard, but I believe a great economic recovery is about to begin in our biggest market—America. We had fewer than two thousand visitors last year. I think that figure will increase by at least a thousand percent this year and continue to grow at incredible levels. We have the ships to bring the people here and will construct more as the demand warrants. But the urgent need is for a grand new hotel, something to put the existing ones to shame. We have the perfect site for it on the hill behind us, and labor will be plentiful again as the men come home from doing their duty."

"What kind of money are you talking about, Horatio?" Steven Lapin asked. "My bank would want to finance it, of course, but we really haven't got access to the vast funds we enjoyed before the war."

"At a guess, to the order of two million pounds." There, that set them back in their places. "But money is no problem," Horatio said. "You will remember at the start of the war, in the full flush of patriotism, we turned over our ships to His Majesty for troop carriers. At the time it seemed wrong even to discuss compensation." He relit his pipe. "Now, though, I've had our London agents make representations to HM's government. We shall be receiving a check for three and a half million pounds, plus the King's heartfelt thanks."

"Bloody marvelous!" Lapin shouted. "Bring on the next war at once! We've made more money out of this one than we ever would have from carrying cargo and tourists."

Down the table Sam winked at Robert, but his brother stared stonily ahead, the pale blue eyes showing no emotion. Sam shrugged: at least he was still able to see the funny side of things.

"Full-steam ahead then, Horatio," cousin Jamie Baseheart said. "If we get a quick start, it might even be completed in time for your sixtieth birthday celebrations. A fitting tribute."

Horatio nodded. He did want the hotel finished in time for his sixtieth birthday celebration. It was so rare for a Fleet male to reach that grand an age; the occasion warranted particular notice.

"What's wrong, Sam?" he asked down the table. The boy was squirming around in his seat, trying to see out the window. "Do you have some comment on my proposal?"

"No, Father. It sounds a wizard idea. I was just looking at the sky. That blasted tempest must be moving closer. I hope I get my tennis game in before it hits."

Primrose Odlum slowly moved the telescope in a wide half-circle, surveying the other great houses around the sound. Primrose enjoyed spying on the neighbors; what she saw through her glass was so different from the starched fronts perpetually maintained by the leading citizens of Bermuda. Why, if the world—or even Mr. Winders—knew what Mrs. Winders did with her butler in the master bedroom . . . Primrose chuckled.

"Do stop snooping, darling," her mother said. "I bought you that telescope to encourage an interest in astronomy, not to turn you into a Peeping Tom."

"Good morning, Mother," Primrose said without taking her eye away from the telescope. "I didn't hear you knock."

Julia Odlum crossed the room and gave her daughter a gentle swat on the behind.

"Since when do I need to knock to visit with my daughter?" she asked. "Anyway, the door was wide open.

Really, Primrose, I do wish you wouldn't spy on our neighbors. It's not at all nice."

"But it's fun," Primrose said. "It's the only thing that stops me going mad with boredom. Oh, I wish all the boys would come home. I even miss my brothers." She focused the lens. "The Fleets' house flag is coming down and they're running up a storm warning. The blessed thing must be getting closer. At least it will break the monotony."

"If you're so bored, darling, you could always lend a hand down in the laboratory. You know how short of chemists we've been. The factory is crying out for new product lines. Your father's so busy with the House of Assembly in session, and you know I'm hopeless around the lab. I agree with you about wanting the boys home. We need some help about the place."

"Kosmos runs itself, Mother. The shops in London and Paris take all the perfumes and cosmetics we can produce. And I'll be involved soon enough. Can't I have a little fun for now? I'm only just eighteen." She grinned at her mother and was rewarded with a smile. They were good friends. "I notice the Fleets didn't have any trouble getting their sons back early from the wars. I hear they bought them out of their regiments the moment the truce was signed. Why didn't we get Jeff and Cable home the same way?"

"Because we don't do things that way. We're Odlums." A frown crossed Julia's face. "Sometimes, darling, I wish we didn't have to live up to the Odlum 'creed.' It's hard being holier-than-everyone all the time. I pleaded with Jonas to keep one of the boys, at least, out of the war. But you know your father—everything has to be done by the book, no privileges just because we have money and influence."

"Not like the Fleets," Primrose said, gesturing to the mansion across the water. "They say Sir Horatio even bought his knighthood. Gave Queen Victoria a frigate for her Navy."

"That's just gossip," her mother said firmly. "The

Fleets have done a great deal for Bermuda and for the Crown. Horatio deserved his honor, I'm sure."

"But surely you don't *like* the Fleets, Mother? All my life I've been hearing about the blood feud between us and them."

"It's all old stuff, dear, from back in the dark days of the colony. Leave it buried." She joined her daughter at the window. "Perhaps the new generation of Fleets will be different. Bermuda is too small a place for old grudges to be allowed to live on."

"Young Veronica's okay," Primrose said. "We were quite good chums at school. But those older brothers of hers! I can see why our ancestors wouldn't have liked that bunch. I hope the war's improved them."

"The Fleets have done it hard, for all their vast wealth. There was a time old Horatio would have traded every ship in his line for one healthy son to carry on the family name. At least Robert and Sam survived the war all right. Maybe the Fleet luck has changed at last."

"I'll bet they only survived because they wheedled themselves into nice safe desk jobs," Primrose said. She tossed her long, black hair; her brown eyes sparkled. "I'm only teasing you, Mother. I'm not really such a hard girl."

"For all our sakes, I hope not. The times ahead for Bermuda are not going to be easy. We will all have to pull together if the colony is ever going to recover from this dreadful war."

She watched his bare torso, brown and sweating, the muscles rippling as he let out the jib to catch the switching breeze and get their boat around the point into the sandy cove where they would picnic. He tacked once, got a clear run on the beach and pulled up the centerboard; the dinghy slid through the warm blue water and crunched onto the pink sand of the deserted beach. He jumped out of the boat and stood ankle-deep in the water, his white drill pants sloshing around his calves.

"If madam will allow me to lift her ashore," he said

with a mock bow, "madam will not have to get her dainty little feet wet."

Veronica laughed and poked at him with her parasol but allowed him to gather her up in one strong arm and swing her onto dry land. The touch of him, his bare chest against her silk blouse, felt good, exciting; the long, dark curls, so unfashionable—almost common—gave him a raffish, piratical air.

"You're such a clown, Tom Jepson," she said, laughing, kicking sand at him. "If you're going to treat me like the lady of the manor, why not tug your forelock when you greet me? That's what the serfs used to do."

"If there's any hair to be pulled, it will be yours," he said, dragging the boat farther up the beach and taking the picnic basket from it. He reached out a sunburned hand and snatched at the blue bow; it came away and Veronica's long, white-gold tresses tumbled free down her back.

"You beast," she giggled and fell on him, pummeling him. They tumbled on the sand, playful as children but wrestling hard enough to bring a film of moisture to her forehead. She flipped him over and straddled him, not caring that the maneuver had pushed her skirts up above her knees.

"Give in," she demanded. "Give in or I'll put you in a hammerlock."

"Okay," he muttered, suddenly awkward. He could feel his huge erection pressing against her and was terrified she would feel it too. That was the trouble with the games they had been playing together for the past three years, since they were fourteen. She was still a tomboy, but he had all the stirrings and lusts of a man. At nights, sometimes, when he thought of her, Tom was ashamed of himself. Now he tried to edge out from under her, away from the tantalizing feel of her slim thighs locked around his hips.

"Say 'Uncle' first," she insisted. "Admit defeat."

"Uncle," he croaked, and as she climbed off him he rolled sideways in the sand to conceal the bulge in his pants. He watched as she busied herself unpacking the

basket, spreading chicken and bread and salad on the
blanket, pouring cool lemonade from a big stone pitcher.
As always, Tom was stunned by her beauty. Where most
of the male Fleets were pale and sickly-looking, Veronica's bloodlines had been excessively generous to her. She
was pale blond, thin but gracefully proportioned, with
light blue eyes gracing a long, proud nose and elegant
cheekbones.

As she worked, she concealed her smile. Poor Tommy,
so infatuated with her. Her own Great War casualty—
because she knew if the war had lasted one more year
and Tommy had gone off to fight, she would have given
herself to him. That was a girl's duty. A pleasant duty,
she suspected, if the boy was like Tommy, so handsome
and fun to be with and so in love with her. But now the
war was over and life had to go on and she was a Fleet
and different things were expected of her. Watching him
now, scrunched up in the sand so she wouldn't see his
thing, she was sorry the war had ended. Veronica knew
she was very close to being in love with Tom Jepson.

"We better keep a close eye on the weather," he said,
staring at the horizon. There was a scatter of thin, wispy
clouds. "They posted a tempest warning in St. George's
this morning. But it's still way out in the Gulf."

"I wish summer could go on forever," she said. "But
every year when the tempests threaten, you know summer's over and winter's coming."

"We don't do too badly," Tommy protested. "Even
winter's easy to take here. Imagine living in America or
Europe! People freeze to death in the streets. No thanks!"

"America has other attractions. Great cities, art gal-
leries, the opera . . . all of which we haven't got in poky
little Bermuda."

"I thought you loved Bermuda. Haven't we always
sworn to each other we would never leave here?"

"I do love it, Tommy, but there are other places." She
frowned. "I might as well tell you now. I'm going to
America next month, to college. Daddy's got me into
William and Mary, at Williamsburg. I didn't want to

mention it earlier, and spoil our summer together." The shock in his eyes hurt her, but also pleased her.

"What do you mean? Just for a semester, or something?"

"No, Tommy, I'm going there full-time, get myself a degree in the arts. Daddy wants me to be educated so I can take my place in the company."

"What about us?" he cried wretchedly. Her heart went out to him. "I won't see you."

"I'll be home on some holidays, and for the long break next summer. And we'll go sailing again, and dancing and tennis. It'll be fun."

"No it won't," he said. "You'll meet other boys, men, at college, and when you do return here all the fellows back from the war, all those Forty Thieves families, will be rushing you and I'll be left out. After all, I'm only a Jepson. The fact that we were making sails for your family three hundred years ago doesn't make us eligible."

She put down her cup and crawled over the blanket to sit beside him. There was no point in denying the truth.

"It's not fair, is it," she said. "The families that made all the money all those years ago—now their descendants think God's chosen them to run the place. But that's the way it is. I have to do what Daddy expects of me. You see, he hasn't much faith in my brothers. Robert's even stranger since he came home from the war and Sam . . . well, Sam's in training to be a playboy, Daddy says." Tom wasn't listening. She reached out and touched his cheek. "Tommy," she whispered, "do you want to kiss me?"

She lay back on the blanket, hearing her breath come fast and feeling the great bulk of him moving over her. And then his lips were locked on hers and his bare chest pressing down on her. She felt her heart flutter and a warm, dangerous sensation deep inside her. She kissed him back, fiercely, and shivered when his hand tentatively moved to her breast. His fingers fumbled with the buttons of her blouse, and then he was inside her brassiere and it felt very different from when she touched herself there.

"Oh, Tommy!" she gasped as her nipple rose to his fingers. She could feel his thing hard against her thigh, and then his hand was gone from her breast and stroking her bare knee, inching higher until it brushed the down through her silk panties. She would stop him in a minute. She felt her legs part and his hand was inside her, a little pain and then moist warmth. She didn't know if she wanted to stop now, didn't know if she could.

The first drops of cold rain fell on her hand where it lay on his back. She felt the goosebumps rise on his shoulders as the wind came gusting in from the sea. She opened her eyes and saw the clouds rolling in, high up but menacing.

"The tempest, Tommy," she whispered. "The storm is almost here. We've got to go." She heard him groan, felt his hand slip from her; for a moment she felt longing, a chance missed. But it was better this way. She must have been mad, taking such a risk.

John Clay could see the hull of the rowboat high above him; down here the water was clear and green, a world seen through bottle glass. A pair of inquiring parrot fish swam up to him and he pushed them away as he continued to pull the conch shells off the rocks. You had to dive deeper and deeper these days to get the best conch. The pressure was on his lungs now, and Clay lifted the wire basket of shellfish off the seafloor, pushed down hard and sent himself knifing toward the surface. He emerged a foot from the boat, gulped down fresh air and tossed the basket to Billy Youngblood.

"There's got to be a better way to scratch out a living," Clay said as he clambered over the side of the little boat. "There's only enough there to make six pies. Used to be we could get ten times that amount in a single dive."

"Lobsters'll be starting soon," Youngblood said. "And it looks like a real good season. We can make some money then. Meanwhile, the conch keep us eating."

Clay shivered and picked up a burlap bag to rub over his ebony skin. He looked up into the sky, saw the clouds coming in and felt the cold wind on him.

"Storm's coming," he said. "We better call it a day."

The two young men took an oar each and the boat raced across the chop for the shelter of the North Shore cove. They made a good team, tall and strong and tuned to each other's rhythm. Clay was broader across the shoulders than Youngblood, but their athletic contests usually ended even. They grounded the boat and pulled it up the sand to the makeshift boat shed and flopped down under the entwined palmetto fronds. Clay dug in the sand and produced the rum bottle.

"Ah," he sighed as he took a long swig before passing the bottle. "That's more like it. Suddenly life doesn't look so bad."

The rising wind rattled the palmetto shelter; Billy Youngblood also drank deeply, then corked the bottle.

"Well," he said, "let's get these conch home to the cooking pot. Quicker they're in a pie the quicker we can sell them at the market. Except, if the storm really gets up, there won't be a market."

At Billy's house—just one room, really, a tiny stone cottage painted brilliant pink—they threw wood on the fire and set the big iron cooking pot on it. John, clad only in damp shorts, shivered again and moved closer to the blaze.

"I wouldn't mind another drink," he said. "Warm me up inside."

"You know Momma won't have that stuff in the house. She's dead-scared the police will come in and find it and we'll all be off to prison. Like when they raided the Jollimonts last month." He dropped the shellfish into the bubbling water and followed them with three big, sweet Bermuda onions. "We'll have ourselves a beer later, over at Rodney's bar. Get this job out of the way first, though. Momma's only doing a half-day over at the Winders' house and I want to be gone before she gets back here." A smile split his handsome face. "I love her dearly, but I can sure do without another lecture on how I should be out searching for a real job."

"Yeah. My father's getting worse like that. All right for him. He's been driving that horse cab all his life. But where in hell are the likes of you and me going to get a job? God knows we've both tried." He scowled. "If they'd thought we were fit to serve the King, I'd have been the first man on the island to sign up. But no place for a black man there. And now the damn war's over, anyway. Sometimes, Billy, I don't think emancipation was all it was cracked up to be. Seems like the only freedom our people got was the freedom to starve."

"Things will get better." Billy laughed. "War's over means the Americans will start coming back. The tourist dollar, all those tips your daddy's always talking about."

"So we'll carry their golf bags for them, maybe put on a white jacket and fetch their drinks. But we still can't vote, can't drink, can't go into any of their places unless we're working as servants. The schooling they allowed us wasn't good enough, and if you get sick you're on your own. Things need to get better."

"It's not so bad," Billy insisted. "A little garden plot, fish in the sea . . . we're all surviving."

"It's fine for you," John said, playfully thumping his friend in the shoulder. "You got Amy Johnson to divert your attention from the sorry world. I had a girl like Amy, I'd be an optimist, too." He peered into the pot. "I guess they're done. I'll make the pastry."

"I've been thinking, if I could get a job I reckon I might marry Amy. She's sixteen already, and she'll soon start getting impatient."

John put down the dough and crossed the room to Billy. He put his big hands on his friend's shoulders and gazed into his eyes.

"You can say it's none of my business, Billy, but I think you're crazy to talk about marriage with Amy Johnson. She's beautiful, sure, and a real nice nature. But, man, she's black as the ace of spades, black as I am. While you, that old white blood in your veins, you could almost pass. You have to marry yourself another mixed blood; you'll have children so pale they can go to Harvard."

"But I love Amy. Anyway, someday it's not going to matter the color of a man's skin."

"That won't change, not in Bermuda, least not in our time."

Later, pies delivered to the market and the tempest still holding back, they repaired to Rodney's bar to drink near beer enlivened with shots from a concealed rum bottle. Enid, the girl behind the bar, gave them both the eye.

"That's what you should be going after," John said. "A sassy mulatto girl like that one. You have kiddies by her, they'd all become members of the House of Assembly."

The drumming of the rain on the tin roof had increased, almost drowning out their conversation. They both looked up when the door crashed open and two sodden, laughing figures spilled into the little room. They quickly lowered their eyes when they saw who it was.

"Any port in a storm, Ginny," Sam Fleet shouted, removing his dripping blazer from her shoulders. "Sit yourself down and I'll get us a drink while the old man fixes the carriage wheel." He was half drunk already from all the champagne cocktails that had replaced their washed-out tennis match. Sam strode to the bar and demanded of Enid she fetch Rodney, the owner.

"We need a drink, a proper drink," Sam ordered when the wizened old man appeared from his recess in back of the bar. "I bet you've got some rum stashed away somewhere. Just make sure the glasses are clean."

"Yes, sir," Rodney said, his head bowed. "I got some rum for medicinal purposes. And I squeeze some limes and make you and the lady a real fine potion."

Sam went back to the table and awaited the drinks. He glanced around the gloomy little room; all eyes dropped when they encountered his stare. God, how awfully these people lived. They should be out bettering themselves instead of sitting in here drinking. But they were all bone-lazy. As a teenager, before the war, he and his pals had sometimes invaded the black bars like this one to get the liquor they were not allowed in their par-

ents' clubs. The blacks had been a shiftless lot then and
apparently they all still were. Bloody Bermuda. Nothing changed. The drinks came and he gave old Rodney a
florin, receiving a grateful, shuffling thanks.

"I'm so wet, Sam," Ginny Winders giggled, downing
her drink. "I'll catch my death of cold." She too was tipsy.
"Look at my lovely skirt. It's ruined." She lifted the
white tennis skirt which was clinging to her long brown
legs and flapped it in a drying motion. Then, abruptly,
she smoothed it down and grabbed Sam's arm.

"Those boys, those two blacks there," she said loudly.
"Sam, they were looking up my dress!"

"Oh hell, so what, Ginny? That dress of yours barely
covers your knees. Everyone at the club got a great sight
of your knickers today."

"That's different," she huffed. "They weren't blacks.
I want you to do something about it."

"Like what? You want me to horsewhip 'em? Or send
for a lynching party? Forget it, Ginny." But he saw she
was really angry and supposed he'd better go through the
motions. He pulled himself to his feet and ambled over
to the table where John and Billy sat staring down into
their beer mugs.

"You fellows were gawking at the lady," he said easily. "You better apologize or I'll kick your black arses."

John saw Billy's muscles tense and reached out a hand
to still him.

"We're real sorry, Mr. Fleet," John said. "We sure
didn't mean any offense to your lady."

"Okay," Sam nodded. "Just keep your place in future." He turned his back on them and went back to Ginny. "Your honor's satisfied," he said. "And the carriage
should be fixed. Let's get out of this dump."

They watched the couple leave and sat in silence for a
moment. Billy was still tense with anger. John poured
them each a big tot of rum. And then he punched Billy
in the shoulder and laughed.

"Goddamn it, Billy, I wish you wouldn't invite your
relations in here! Those Fleets are always causing trouble."

* * *

Cable Odlum pulled on the starched white mess jacket and adjusted his black tie, studied his appearance in the mirror of the cramped bathroom and stepped back into the cabin. His brother was lounging on a bunk reading a novel.

"Hurry it up, Jeff," Cable said. "Can't be late for dinner on the last night out of Bermuda. And Captain Smutters has promised a special menu with the finest French wines."

Jeff regarded his elder brother with amusement.

"Good old Cable," he said. "You really love all this dressing up for the captain's table, don't you? You're going to miss your Medical Corps uniform, all the trappings of an officer. Won't be much glamour in your future, being just another family doctor."

"Don't I know it," Cable said. "That's why I'm trying to milk every last moment." He sleeked down his dark hair. "I think I'll go up to the bar ahead of you. I told Mrs. Benbridge I might see her there."

"Watch out for that one, Cable. Apart from the fact that she's old enough to be your mother—"

"She's only thirty-nine. What's fourteen years difference?"

". . . she's a Forty Thieves wife. Those chaps don't appreciate their women having it on with anyone else, no matter how handsome he happens to look in his uniform."

"Old Roy Benbridge must have been mad to let a beautiful creature like her sit out the war in New York, You know he only visited her three times in the whole period?"

"So tonight you aim to ease her frustrations. Loosen her up for old Roy, so to speak?"

"Don't be coarse, Jeff." He grinned. "But if I leave the signal on the door—"

"I'll find somewhere else to bunk for the night, okay."

Captain Henry Smutters glanced around his table at the primped and gowned women and formally dressed

men. Quite a change from the years of ferrying troops,
when you never knew who would be at your table. Soon
the *Pride of Pembroke* would be refitted and they could
all get back to the normal business of transporting well-
heeled tourists from New York to Hamilton. Smutters
caught the ardent looks being exchanged by Faith Benbridge and the Odlum boy and smiled to himself. Before
the war, Faith had been a regular passenger on the *Pembroke* and had broken a heart on every trip. Gossip
among the officers was that her husband was impotent,
old and unable to satisfy her. But he owned the colony's
oldest-established law firm, Amberley & Benbridge, and
he paid for Faith's expensive tastes, so between voyages
she stayed with him.

"A perfectly marvelous trip, Captain," old Mrs. Trump
shouted at him from the foot of the table. "And no sign
of those dreadful storms we get at this time of the year."

"There was quite a bad one last month, ma'am," he
replied. "You'd have known about it if we'd been sailing
through that tempest."

"Excellent wines, sir," Major Dale said, nodding to the
steward for more of the burgundy. "I pity our American
cousins. They'll not be enjoying such vintages for a long
while."

"Why ever not, sir?" Jeff Odlum asked. "Surely even
the Americans can appreciate a good wine."

"You haven't been reading your newspapers, Lieu-
tenant," Dale said. "Congress this month passed the
Volstead Act. Come the new year, America will be totally dry. Prohibition."

"It's all nonsense," Mrs. Trump announced. "They
tried it in Canada but now they've gone back to normal.
I'm sure the Americans will reject the experiment just
as quickly."

"No danger of the *Pride of Pembroke* going dry, eh
Captain," Dale said, draining his glass. He felt a twinge
of gout and a pang of regret as he took yet another refill;
tomorrow the glory days of the war would be over for him
and he would be returned to the dreary, ill-paid job of sub-

Inspector in HM's Constabulary in crime-free Bermuda. "Bottoms up," he said and quaffed the glass.

There was dancing after dinner, causing Jeff Odlum to retire to the cozy first-class bar. On previous nights he'd been embarrassed at having to refuse the good-hearted entreaties of matronly fellow passengers trying to get him onto the dance floor. He could cope with the artificial leg in most situations—only three months after the land mine at Ardennes, he'd even talked his way back to duty with his regiment—but he didn't think he was ready for the foxtrot. From the bar Jeff could see his brother gliding around the floor with Mrs. Benbridge, cheek to cheek. He guessed the warning signal would be posted on their cabin door tonight. Good old Cable; he always got the women, always succeeded at anything he attempted. Jeff felt no resentment toward his older brother. They were good friends, could almost have been twins, sharing as they did the fine-chiseled Odlum features, tall and strongly built. It was just that Cable did everything a little bit better—he had sailed through his medical studies, then honed his skills as a surgeon in the terrible theater of the battlefields. Cable was now fully equipped to realize their father's ambition for him. Jeff, at twenty-one, had no idea what he would do with the rest of his life. But something would turn up, he felt. There was plenty of time.

"Have one with me," the major said, easing himself onto the next bar stool. "I'm not up to the dancing, not with this bloody gout." He coughed, suddenly embarrassed. "Sorry, old chap. Gout's not something to talk about, compared with your problem. Two pink gins, thank you." He forgot his gaffe when the drinks were before them. He wanted to talk. "Funny to be home tomorrow. Bit of an anticlimax for me, you know. Keeping the coons in line instead of harrying the Hun. All right for you, though, young Odlum. I suppose you'll be going into the family business."

Jeff laughed. "Not a very exciting prospect, Major Dale. I'm not sure the cosmetics business is what I want. I'm afraid Bermuda is going to seem awfully confining."

"But the money, my boy, the money. That's all that matters. You chaps, members of the Forty Thieves families, you have your futures assured."

"I wonder if that's enough."

"It's a damn sight better than the alternative."

Later, Jeff went below to check the cabin; he smiled when he saw the silk handkerchief looped over the door handle, and limped back to the upper-deck lounge. A steward brought him a blanket and he settled down in a leather armchair for the rest of the night.

He woke at dawn and stood on deck, a warming mug of beef tea in his hand, as the islands of Bermuda slowly emerged on the misty horizon. His home, the home of his family for three hundred years. There was a lump in his throat as Bermuda grew closer, long and low and green in the brilliant blue sea. He stayed there on deck as Captain Smutters expertly guided the vessel through the jagged coral reefs; a school of dolphins accompanied them, circling the ship and performing their repertoire of tricks. The sun was full up now, warming him. October could be a very nice month in Bermuda. He wondered if the gentle climate and the embrace of family and friends would be enough for him.

Cable laid his head between her small breasts and let his hand caress her smooth thighs. She parted for him and he entered her again. He had never known anything like making love to Faith Benbridge; her body was at once taut and yielding, responding to his as if an electric charge ran between them. He felt a goofy pride when she climaxed again; this was what it was all about, satisfying a woman, a real woman. He groaned in ecstasy as his own peak came, then fell away from her in the narrow bunk, sweat plastering his dark hair to his high forehead.

"Time to go," she said, springing up. She was unconcerned by her nudity, fully exposed in the shaft of sunlight coming through the porthole. She stood there a moment, rumpled dark hair, grinning green eyes, the triangle of fur on her smooth white belly. "That was quite lovely, Cable." She dressed hurriedly, and he sighed as the magnificent body was concealed from him.

"Can we be together in Bermuda?" he asked. "I don't want this to end. You're wonderful, Faith."

"You won't need me in Bermuda. The handsome, rich young doctor home from the wars. You'll need a stick to beat the girls off. But," she said, placing her hand on the doorknob, "if you ever need an older woman's shoulder to cry on, I'm sure we will be able to get together discreetly." She blew him a kiss, slipped through the door and was gone.

Cable lay back in his bunk among the tangled sheets, feeling the sweat of love dry on his body. Then, guiltily, he remembered Jeff somewhere out there wandering the ship. He jumped up and removed the handkerchief from outside the door.

The police band was on the dock playing Sousa as they berthed; every ship in the harbor set off its whistle and streamers came floating up from the crowd. It seemed all of Bermuda had turned out to welcome home the first big contingent of returning heroes.

Primrose stood between her parents, scanning the decks of the ship.

"There they are," she shrieked, leaping and waving. "Cable! Jeff!" They were coming down the gangway. She had willed herself not to cry, but the tears were flowing. Her mother was crying, too. Only her father managed to keep his habitual reserve, and even he—Primrose noted—was swallowing rapidly. Now the band was playing "Rule Britannia" and all around them people were crying and embracing. Cable reached them first, then Jeff, favoring his leg.

"Thank God you've come home," Julia Odlum whispered as her sons embraced her. Beside her Jonas stood erect and proud; he offered his hand to his sons. And then they were kissing Primrose, joshing her for her tears.

"See how she's grown, Jeff," Cable shouted. "Whatever happened to the little snotnose we left behind? Almost a lady now."

Just down the dock from them, Mrs. Benbridge, surrounded by steamer trunks, pecked her husband on the cheek. Roy Benbridge blushed and busied himself with rounding up porters. As always, he felt overwhelmed in the presence of his beautiful young wife. She seemed too exotic a creature for his fusty world.

"You look tired, my dear," he said. "A rough voyage, I suppose. I can never get any sleep at sea."

Major Dale brightened a little when the bandmaster snapped to attention and saluted him; perhaps it wouldn't be so bad, being home. If he got his inspector's bars, and the better accommodation that went with the job . . . his wife was going on about how hard it had been to manage on his allotment. The whine in her voice came back to him across the years. That, at least, had not changed. He burped, and the taste of strong red wine came back to him. Now it would be warm beer and cold pork pies. He looked across to the Odlum group. They had it all, he thought enviously—power and money, three handsome children. All the riches Bermuda had bestowed on those lucky enough to have been in on the founding of the colony.

"So what are your plans?" Jonas Odlum asked, pushing back his chair and looking around the big dining table. "Cable can buy into Dr. West's practice; it's all arranged. But Jeff, I don't know. I think you had better come into the family company."

"Jonas!" his wife protested. "The boys are only just home. There's no need to rush things." She smiled at him fondly. He was a good man, always firm with the children but loving, too, and fair. He worked so hard at everything he did; sometimes he didn't understand that young people needed time to find themselves. Particularly dear Jeff with his dreadful injury.

"Well, I will have to find something." Jeff smiled. "I'm afraid my tennis-playing days are over." He saw the pain in his mother's eyes. "I'm only teasing. The leg is no bother, really. But, Father, I do want to take some time to think about the future, make sure I choose the right path."

"Of course," Jonas said. He cursed himself for his inability to tell the boys how proud he was of them, how much he loved them. "Didn't mean to rush you. Just wanted to get you thinking about civilian life. You take all the time you need, both of you. You deserve it."

"The only important thing," Primrose said, "is the welcome-home ball next week. Everyone will be there. It's going to be the first great party since the awful war began."

It was as if they were shouting at him, all through the never-ending dinner, the voices crashing into his brain. He felt the sick headache pounding behind his temples, easing now that he was in the sanctuary of his room, the brandy bottle beside him. But he could still hear his father; blustering, domineering, demanding. The old bastard, setting himself up as some paragon of virtue. If the world knew the skeletons in this family closet! He took another glass of brandy and crossed to the window overlooking the Great Sound. It was pitch-black out there, no moon or stars. A sudden flurry of rain struck the glass. He shrugged off his dinner jacket and dress shirt, replacing them with a black sweater and a seaman's rough jacket, then started down the back stairs of the mansion. The stables were dark but he needed no lamp to find his horse, saddle it and lead it silently out through the mounting yard. It was not until he was on the road, pounding through the wet black, that the headache finally left him. Faster, faster he raced through the night down the hard narrow lanes. Once he heard a scream and caught the white flash of a mouth wide open in terror as his huge black hunter hurdled someone on the road. Across the causeway, sparks flying as the horse's hooves struck stone, the beast was as caught up as he was in the mad gallop, froth flying back from the horse's mouth, foam soaking its withers. At last the lights of St. George's were coming up beside them and he slowed the horse to a canter and then a walk. He dis-

mounted on the edge of the town square and led the horse
to the trough beside the Fleet Fountain; he tied it there
and waited until they had both stopped trembling before
crossing the square to the bright lights of the Seahorse
Tavern.

The tavern was warm, a fug of smoke and sweat and
wet clothing mingling with the fumes of stale beer and
harsh spirits; the noise level was high, but it did not
bother him as the table talk in his own home had done.
He kept his hat low over his eyes, shouldered a way to
the bar through the press of sailors and local white trash
and growled an order for rum. He stood there drinking
for two hours as the tavern gradually emptied out. The
rum went right through him, hot and exhilarating, like
fresh blood in his veins.

He had been watching the serving girl since he'd entered the tavern; young, perhaps only sixteen, slim and
pretty, he thought, for a black. Twice she had brushed
against him as she brought her sloshing tray back to the
bar. Now, as last orders were called, she was next to him
again. He reached in the pocket of his jacket and laid a
five-pound note on the wet bar. She swept it up, shoved
it down the front of her low-cut blouse and nodded toward the tavern door.

She joined him in the square a few moments later.
Only a few lights remained on; they could hear the
shouts and curses of the last drinkers making their way
back to their ships. He took her roughly by the arm and
led her along the wharves to a low, open-walled shed. A
street lamp provided just enough light to lead him to a
cluster of bales in the center of the shed. He pushed the
girl down on her knees and leaned back against the
rough sacking, unbuttoning himself. His member sprang
out, stiff and gleaming in the faint light until she closed
her mouth over it; he forced himself into her, ignoring
her gagging, clutching her hair to prevent her pulling
away. She was gasping for breath when he finally pulled
back and dragged her up onto the bales. He threw her
skirts up over her head and held them there with one
hand, effectively silencing her as he plunged between her

legs, ploughing and ripping and tearing at her, only just able to hear her sobs of pain. Her tattered underwear was in shreds, and he thought he saw blood there as he continued to penetrate her.

"Whore! Whore!" he heard himself cry as he finally exploded inside her, felt the skinny young body shaking with pain. She was sobbing softly when he pulled out of her and flipped her over on her stomach. She had no strength to fight back as he stuffed the scarf in her mouth and bound her hands behind her back with the belt from around his waist.

He pulled the riding crop from his boot, his hands trembling and wet as her thin buttocks quivered before him. The whip came up and made a hissing sound as it lashed her, biting into the flesh, raising a new line of blood droplets at each blow. The more she struggled and jerked away from the blows, the harder he thrashed her; the roaring was back in his head and the blood on her buttocks in his eyes. She had long fainted before he was finished, before the mad urgings had left him. But at last he was spent, wiping the crop on her skirt, untying her hands and removing the gag from her mouth.

"Let that be a lesson to you," he muttered. He pulled down her skirt to cover the obscene wounds. He heard her moan as she slowly regained consciousness. "Here," he said roughly, "here's another twenty pounds." He pushed the notes at her and felt her trembling hand close over them. He began to back away, wanting to be far from this place. "You just forget about what happened tonight." He thought he saw her nod as he slipped out of the shed and moved across the dark square to where his horse was tethered.

Back inside the big house, Robert Fleet eased himself into his bathtub; the hot water washed over him and the tension subsided. But still a shiver ran through him. Tonight was closer than he had yet come to totally losing control. But he had had his release, and his head was calm now. The demons had been expelled for the present.

* * *

The Fleet family carriage ground up the drive to Government House; the area was already crammed with coaches, and their driver had to inch the four-horse team between them to reach the great steps leading up to the main hall.

"I told you we were running late," Joanna Fleet complained. "I don't know what the new Governor will think of us."

"I don't think any Governor of Bermuda minds the Fleets being late," Sam laughed. "Just so long as we appear. Surely the King still consults you about the appointment, Father?"

Sir Horatio glared at his son. "Young man, I do not like flippancy. In fact, I don't like your whole attitude since you've been home. You haven't been near the office; you lie in your bed all day then go out carousing God knows where at night. It's not good enough, sir!"

"Please don't fight," Veronica begged. "I'm hoping this is going to be the most glamorous night of my life. My first ball. Don't ruin it by having another of our family spats."

"If you'd only been ready on time . . ." Joanna repeated.

"For Christ's sake, stop nagging, Mother," Robert snapped. His cold, pale eyes swept the interior of the carriage. "All of you shut up! This is a farce, playing 'happy family.' None of us can stand the other. This constant pin-pricking only makes it worse."

They all fell silent. Robert had them intimidated, his moody silences and sudden outbursts of rage impossible to plot. The carriage door was opened, and the steps dropped down and Sir Horatio and Lady Fleet alighted gratefully. Veronica was next. As she placed her hand on the arm offered her, she looked up into the solemn face of Tom Jepson. Color came to her cheeks.

"Hello, Tom," she said, favoring him with a smile. "Moonlighting as a valet? I'm surprised they could find a uniform to fit you."

He said nothing, fixing his gaze on a spot just above her head. It had been weeks since he'd seen Veronica, and his heart ached all the time. He had supposed her off in college in America, but here she was. The realization that she had been home in the big house or at the club—forbidden territory to him—while he was missing her so terribly, intensified the pain.

"Veronica," her mother hissed, pulling at her arm, "you're delaying us."

"I'm sorry, Tom," she said. And then she moved away with her parents.

"That was the Jepson lad," her father said as they moved up the steps. "Damn fine sailmakers, that family. But you shouldn't be speaking to him, Veronica. You must remember your position."

"Daddy, he was my playmate for years. I'm not going to snub him just because—"

"That was when you were a child. You're a young woman now and you'll conduct yourself properly."

Thank God she would be leaving next week, Veronica thought as she waited on the receiving line. Her family was driving her mad. Sam was the only one with any humor about him, and he was never there, always off with Ginny Winders, the two of them acting as if they had some great secret.

The Odlums at their table watched the grand entrance of the Fleets, personally escorted by the Governor. Primrose and Veronica exchanged smiles as they passed but the senior Fleets stared straight ahead.

"Horatio's looking well," Julia Odlum said. "He must be getting close to sixty. Some kind of record for a Fleet male."

"Poor devils," Jonas said. "But the boys look well. Perhaps the Fleets' fate has changed at last."

Later, on the balcony taking a cigaret, Jeff Odlum found himself standing beside Sam Fleet.

"Bad luck, old man," Sam said, clapping Jeff on the shoulder. "The leg, I mean. But I must say you're getting about well. Apart from that, did you have a good war?"

"I'm in no hurry to go to another one." Jeff smiled. "Although," he said, dropping his voice, "I am finding

Bermuda a bit restricting after the past few years. Nothing seems to have changed here."

"I know. They expect you to go off on a great adventure as we did, then come home and settle into a desk in the family company." They took champagne from a passing waiter. "My father thinks I'm a layabout, just because I'm not in there every morning punching the clock."

"Me too. Father doesn't say much, but I catch him looking at me, wondering what the devil he's been saddled with. The leg is keeping him off my back for now, but it won't do as an excuse for much longer. They're so proud, our fathers, of what they and their blessed ancestors have achieved here. You haven't the heart to tell them there's a bigger world than Bermuda out there."

Sam studied the younger man. Here was an Odlum who wasn't all that different from a Fleet, at least from this Fleet. He recalled all the stories, spelled out like legends around the tables of his childhood; the Odlums were their mortal enemies, never to be associated with. A lot of bunk.

"You sail, don't you, Jeff? I've had them restore my grandfather's cutter for me and it's great sport. I took Ginny out the other day and she complained about getting a wet arse. She's more the type for grand motor yachts. But maybe you'd like a sail with me."

"I'd like nothing better. I've just taken up golf, and it seems a stupid game. I'd be much happier, getting back into sailing."

"How about tomorrow, then? The boat's at the Yacht Club dock. Meet me there about eleven."

Cable had dutifully danced with a string of eligible young women; now he figured he could safely approach Mrs. Benbridge. He nodded to her fat old husband and felt a wrench in his guts; it was obscene to think of a fellow like that in bed with the woman Cable loved.

"Would you care to dance, ma'am?" he asked, bowing. She took his hand and they joined in the waltz. He put his lips close to her ear. "Faith, I've missed you so this past week. I must see you."

She smiled at someone dancing by. He thought she had not heard him. But she moved a fraction closer to him, and as their bodies brushed she smiled again.

"Far too dangerous," she said as if discussing the weather. "Roy would shoot me if he thought I was carrying on with anyone here in Bermuda. It's only away from the islands I am allowed my freedom. And there is nowhere here we could safely be alone. All these gossips." She saw the hurt in his eyes and laughed. "My poor young man. Perhaps when you have joined Dr. West's practice I shall become your patient. That would be a safe way for us to meet."

Steven Lapin was the most prominent banker in Bermuda because, apart from all the expected talents, he made it his business to know everyone else's business. He liked the leverage that knowledge gave him: if a man was gambling heavily, or drinking too much, or keeping a mistress, Lapin knew. In such circumstances he might make a loan, secure it with the man's property, and foreclose when the crunch came. Lapin's Bank of Oceania had acquired many of its major assets through such dealings.

"So, Dimity," he said as their carriage rolled home through the night, "when I see Sam Fleet and Jeff Odlum acting like old chums, I take note. If the Fleets and Odlums were ever to forget their old feuds, settle their differences and join their fortunes, a great merchant empire would be created. And the man who acted as broker for such an amalgamation would do very nicely."

"You'll never get the Fleets and the Odlums together," his wife said. "The hatreds go back too far. And the patriarchs are too different. Horatio is a ruthless old bastard while Jonas is just too decent to be true. No, you'll never see those two families come together."

"There was a time when my own family were sworn enemies of the Fleets," he said. "That passed. Now a Lapin sits on the Fleet board of directors. Anything's possible, Dimity."

Primrose threw a stick for her setter and watched the fluid red shape bound across the green hilltop. She continued on across the field, delighting in the perfect autumn day, loving the orderly pattern of her Bermuda laid out below her. At times like this she adored her country intensely, knew she would never leave it and felt only pity for those who did not understand it. She came to the clump of bracken, pushed it aside and—the red setter snuffling ahead of her—sank down in the entrance to her cave. It was her secret place, the one she had been coming to since she was a little girl, the hideaway where she could be alone with her thoughts.

Today she was thinking about her family and all the changes that were taking place. Cable, besotted by that woman. No good could come of it. And poor Jeff, bravely ignoring his handicap but obviously scarred by it. He was still the laughing boy who had gone off to the war, but now his cheerfulness had a desperate note to it; he gave no sign of wanting to settle down. Primrose had seen her father's despairing looks at the boys, her mother's brave attempts to demonstrate that nothing had changed. Snug in her cave, the dog's wet nose in her lap, Primrose promised herself she would not let her parents down. If she was the perfect, dutiful daughter, then there would be less pressure on the boys. It was like having a vocation, she thought; she felt good about her resolution.

Chapter Two
(1612-)

He had waited three days for her to come to him in the
hidden cave high above the bustling town. Sometimes he
could hear the sounds of St. George's borne on the trade
wind; the thunk of the adze against timber at the boat
ramp, the raucous shouts of men at the grog shop, the
shrill laughter of women doing laundry at the village
pump. The workaday buzz stabbed at Jonas Odlum as
sharply as the gangrene eating at his shattered right leg,
sharper than the hunger pangs in his empty belly. Jonas
tilted his head and let a few drops of water fall from the
limestone roof of the cave into his mouth, then pulled
himself out into the sunlight onto a bed of bracken. It was
better in the hot August sun, on the cliff top with the
longtails winging over him and the bright, blue Atlantic
below. It was worth the risk of discovery. After three
years as a fugitive he might almost have welcomed capture and the harsh embrace of the hangman's noose. But
now there was Sarah to live for, and the baby soon to
come.

Jonas Odlum let the sun and the fever take him for a
while into a painless world of dreams: he and Sarah and
their child, free and happy in the new colony, all sins for-
given, united with the other brave settlers to build a future in Bermuda, the Somers Islands. His dreaming
obliterated the dreadful day three years before when
he'd been forced to fight the brutal bosun, when a des-

perate lunge with a rigging knife had pierced the giant
bosun's heart. Dreaming let Jonas forget his flight into
the rugged, unexplored country beyond the cleared area
where Sir George Somers's party was building a ship to
continue the voyage to Virginia. Perhaps they wouldn't
have hanged him; Sir George was a fair man. But scut-
tlebutt had it that Sir Thomas Gates thought Somers too
soft on his men, and had been looking for a showdown.
Jonas, whose parish schooling in Devon had equipped
him to think for himself, reckoned he could be made the
scapegoat.

So he had fled into the cedar forests and hidden, sometimes sneaking back to the edge of the undergrowth to
observe his former shipmates as they finished building
their ships. On the day the two ships, *Patience* and *Deliverance,* finally set sail for Jamestown, nine months
after the tempest east them ashore, Jonas Odlum
watched from the cliff top and cried; no one had ever felt
as alone as he, one man on an uncharted island on the
edge of the New World. He survived on gulls' eggs, fish
and berries, but he could not stave off the terrible pangs
of loneliness. When, in his second year on the island, colonists arrived, Jonas wanted to rush down to the shore
and embrace them. But reason told him he was a killer
and a deserter, and would surely hang. So he stayed a
fugitive, sometimes skulking near the new settlers like
a wary fox circling a fowlyard. Sometimes when his
loneliness drew him too near St. George's he would be
spotted, and the authorities would make a desultory
search for him; but for the most part the colonists were
too busy establishing themselves to worry about the fugitive Jonas Odlum. Time to hunt him down when they
were settled; certainly, there was nowhere he could flee
to from this rocky chain of islands in the middle of a vast
ocean.

And then she had found him: tall, gaunt, austere Sarah Jessup, moving as silently through the forest as he
did, coming upon him as he bathed in a concealed pond,
unafraid of him even when he rose up out of the water

naked and threatening. He advanced, shaking his fist, but she stared him down.

"You have nothing to fear from me," Sarah Jessup said. "I know who you are. I am more on your side than on the side of those who have forced me into exile in this terrible place."

The words were heavenly music to Jonas, not for their meaning but simply because they were words spoken to him. In his isolation he had kept inside himself a thousand emotions, a million words. With Sarah's coming, no matter the risk, he let it all flow out. He put himself totally in her trust, and she never betrayed him. They began to meet regularly, on the half day a week Sarah was free from her duties as housemaid to the Magistrate's family. With joy they discovered each could read, rare in the colony. She brought him a Bible, as well as food scraps and threadbare clothing she stole from her employer.

"I am already convicted of a 'crime' I did not commit," she told him firmly, when he protested at the risks she was taking. "They gave me the choice of prison or transportation and indentured labor because I dared speak out against the corrupt mayor of our town. So anything I can provide you with, Jonas, I have already paid for a hundredfold."

Their love was quick to bloom but slow to be acknowledged. It wasn't until the bitter winds of December had turned the island almost as cold as their longed-for England that they came together. It was the Sunday before Christmas and almost dark under the storm clouds when Sarah stumbled down the wooded slope to the rude lean-to Jonas used for his winter quarters. He watched silently as she unwrapped her gifts; a scrag end of pork, some weeviled biscuits, a jar of fat rendered from a shearwater. And then, her strong brown eyes sparkling, she reached into the basket again and produced a bottle.

"Sherry, dear Jonas," she said gleefully. "His Worshipfulness drinks it by the barrel and will not miss this small amount. I thought it might warm you in your cold and lonely refuge." She pressed the bottle on him.

"Drink. For a few moments, we will forget where we are, ignore the betrayals of fate, and imagine ourselves in a better place than this."

The rich, red wine was the most marvelous thing Jonas had tasted in years; it coursed through his body and banished the cold and wet and isolation, bringing vivid visions of home and warmth and loved ones. He carefully wiped the lip of the bottle on his rough sleeve and passed it to Sarah. As the wind howled around their shelter and the darkness closed in, a great intimacy enveloped them. When he moved to her side and placed an arm around her, it was a natural thing and neither was surprised.

In her twenty-two years Sarah had never been touched by a man. Jonas's only sexual experiences had been with dockside trollops. But their bodies, each starved of love, showed them the way. Her heavy skirts and his canvas trousers were flung aside, and they joined swiftly, longingly, creating a warmth that spread all over them and kept the evening cold at bay. They moved in rhythm, the tall, proud cedar trees sighing above. They found release together as the waves found the rocky shore all around the island. For both of them it was the only sublime moment in their bitter exile.

"Ah, Jonas," she murmured when at last they lay quietly, the sweat drying cold on them, "I have often wondered what it would be like, the coupling. I never imagined it would be as violent as the tempest, yet soft as the summer breeze."

He could not speak, overcome with love and amazement that something so wonderful could happen in his wretched life. Instead he again placed an arm around her strong shoulders and kissed her.

Later, when she had stayed too long for safety, Jonas escorted her through the black forest to the outer edge of St. George's. They kissed again and he watched her receding figure before stepping back into the trees and heading for his shelter. He knew every step of the terrain, but the day's events had made him careless, or there was a new spring in his step; whatever, coming down the final slope he hooked his bare foot into a tree root and fell over a ridge onto a rocky outcrop. He felt the leg break, heard the snap of the bone and lay stunned as the pain washed over him. But even at its worst, the pain was nothing compared to the joy in him; Jonas gritted his teeth and crawled the rest of the way to his lean-to. He made a splint of a cedar branch. It would heal, he told himself; but because of today, he, Jonas Odlum would never be the same.

Now, as he daydreamed in the summer sun, Jonas tried to ignore his fears. The leg had never mended; since the gangrene had set in, Sarah had managed to come to him every day, to bathe him and administer the potions she knew. And to share with him the joy of their approaching child. Eight months now and she was apparent: if her master had not treated her with such indifference, he would have noticed. The consequences . . . Jonas did not want to think about the punishment that would be meted out to his Sarah for falling pregnant. If only his fever would subside, if the sickening canker in his leg would vanish, if he had time to plan . . . If he were well, he would build them a boat and they would escape this place, sail for the Americas or the Indies, somewhere they could be free.

The sun was too hot and he hauled himself back into his summer cave. He fell into a fevered sleep, dreaming of what might lie ahead of them, longing for her to come to him.

The heavy wooden yoke of the stocks pressed down on Sarah Jessup's neck and shoulders, but so long as she was still, the pain was bearable. She was thin and bony, but the years of domestic slavery—toting water from the pump, scrubbing crude stone floors, washing and polishing—had made her strong and nearly impervious to pain. It was not the constriction of the stocks or the heat and dust and flies of St. George's Town Square that hurt her or made her fearful. It was fear for the baby moving in her, and her longing to be with Jonas, tending his wounds. She was frantic when she thought of him, less than a mile from her, lying weak and helpless, probably thinking she had abandoned him. Her other emotion was anger—a pure, searing rage directed against the society that had put her in the stocks, the people now passing before her, jeering at her humiliation. Bastards! she thought. Greater bastards than our love child. What a cruel term to apply to a tiny, unborn baby; as cruel as the terms they applied to her Jonas.

It was Mistress Owens, wife of her owner, who had noticed Sarah's condition.

"That hussy is with child, Silas," the woman snapped as Sarah huddled in the rough lean-to that served as her room. She could hear them easily through the earthen walls. "I told you she would bring scandal on us, her with her airs and graces, thinking she's too good to be a servant girl. Who is the father? That's what the whole village will want to know. And what I demand to know—right now. Because I have long withdrawn my favors from you, did you think you had a charter to dawdle with a servant? Answer me, Silas!"

"Not I, dear one," Magistrate Owens protested. "I would never stoop so low, nor risk your good name—"

"You would if you thought you could get away with it."

"No, my dear," he pleaded. "Please, do not even suggest such a thing."

The magistrate, Sarah thought wryly, was a tyrant when he had his wig and bench to protect him. But when lashed by his wife's tongue, he was humble as any poor felon.

"Then we must learn the name of the fornicator," Mistress Owens said. "And he must be brought to book and punished, just as the harlot herself will be. Come, we'll demand the truth."

Sarah heard them coming and steeled herself. They must never know she had had contact with Jonas. Any serious search mounted for him would surely flush him out, sick and vulnerable as he was now. The lamplight fell on her from the open door and she pretended sleep.

"Get up, you slut!" Mistress Owens shouted, striding forward and grabbing Sarah by the hair. "We'll have the name of your bastard's sire, thank you, miss." She forced Sarah's head back. "Are you going to tell us, or shall we beat it from you?"

Sarah wanted to strike out at the shrew, to spit at the man cringing behind her. But she knew her only hope was to remain silent and seem as servile as she could.

"Cat's got your tongue, eh?" Mistress Owens hissed. She was enjoying the scene. "Hold her arms, Silas, and we'll see proof."

Sarah kept her head down as she was roughly forced into the circle of light. The little magistrate's arms gripped her tightly; she felt a tremor run through him as his body pressed against hers. Then shame flooded over her as Mistress Owens pulled up Sarah's shift, exposing her nakedness in the lamplight.

"See? See the belly? She's almost full term, Silas." The woman let the shift drop, and in the same movement struck Sarah a stinging blow across her face. "Who did this, girl? Who was it you spread your limbs for, who was so glib you would bring shame on us who've been so good to you?"

Sarah stayed mute, hoping she looked humble and scared, not furious.

"Still not talking? Silas, fetch the whip."

The two women stood still, the mistress glaring, Sarah downcast, as Owens hurried from the room. In a moment he was back, a coach whip in his hand. Sarah felt tension mounting between the couple.

"Hold her over the stool, Silas." The woman's voice was husky and she was breathing heavily. Sarah allowed herself to be forced face down over a high wooden stool. She shut her eyes as she felt her shift lifted again; she tried to shut her mind.

The first blow only stung, but then Mistress Owens established a rhythm, and the thin whip began to cut deeper and deeper into Sarah's buttocks. Owens tightened his grip on her shoulders, meanwhile forcing her head against his groin. Even through the pain Sarah felt contempt and loathing for him and his wife and the twisted pleasure they were taking. The beating went on until Mistress Owens's arms tired. Then the couple changed places and the magistrate himself took to thrashing her with gusto. Sarah gave them nothing: not a tear or a moan, and certainly not the name they wanted. They were still beating her, and blood flowed freely between her thighs, when she passed out.

And now it was her third day in the stocks. The magistrate had decreed, and the colonists concurred, that she would stay in the stocks until she revealed the name of the father. As far as Sarah was concerned, she would stay there until her child was born—right here in the stocks, or in the prison cell where she was placed each night. She raised her eyes and looked out over the dusty square to the bright blue water of the harbor. How promising this new colony had looked, even to her, arriving in unjust servitude. A new beginning, indeed! All the colonists had done was bring the worst of old England with them: the snobbery and unfair class systems, the brutal justice of the stocks, ducking stool, whipping post and gallows tree. If only she had been transported to Jamestown—perhaps in the Americas there would have been the chance of a new and fair life. But then she would not have met Jonas, would never have known love. She sighed in silent anguish for him and the child.

The affected drawl, the infuriating tone of the upper class which had treated her so unfairly reached her before the two figures came into her field of vision.

"The Jessup wench is holding up well," Thomas Fleet said to his companion. "Many more days in the stocks, though, and she'll never walk upright again." He stood squarely in front of her, and she felt his arrogant eyes on her swelling breasts, revealed to all by the gaping sack-cloth shift she wore. "Not a pretty sight, Sam," he said to his companion. "It would appear the town's urchins have been aiming true with their mudballs."

"At least she's made her little mark on our history, Thomas," Sam Cobcroft replied. "Already she holds the record for time in the stocks, established in just one session. If she survives the birth of her bastard, she'll have a whole lifetime to add to her tally."

"And then there's the ducking stool." Fleet laughed. "Perhaps she could try for a record there, too. Though God knows there are enough other rogues and slatterns in our colony to give her fine competition."

"You should not joke about such matters, Thomas," Cobcroft said, careful to keep his tone light. Fleet was above him in station, and he dared not risk offense. "I think it a matter of great concern that our young colony already has the reputation of a lawless place, a haven for scum even the Froggies and Spanish wouldn't give shelter to. We must have law and order, Thomas, and tame the populace. We did not leave dear England to come live in another Barbary."

"You are so right, Sam." Fleet raised his walking stick and gave the side of the stocks a resounding whack before turning away to continue his stately stroll. "This woman should remind us of the depths we can sink to if we're not careful. I hope she holds out for many days yet."

The blow of the cane sent reverberations through the stocks and set Sarah's head ringing, but that was nothing compared to the rage she felt at the two self-important dandies. The others of their class were no better. She heard their laughter as they moved away, and bile leaped into her throat.

Fleet and Cobcroft had already forgotten the unfortunate woman. They moved slowly in the August heat, sweating in their velvet frock coats but determined not to show it: *noblesse oblige,* the price of being above the common herd.

"Now here is our real future, Sam," Fleet said. They stopped before the slipway where the latest of the Bermuda-built ships was taking shape. Fleet raised his silver-topped cane and tapped the cedar skeleton. "A sound ship, and many more of them to come. Long after we've exhausted the agricultural possibilities of these islands, we'll still be prospering from the sea. Abundant cedar, and the craftsmen to turn cedar into great ships. And men to sail them on the seven seas. Carrying the riches of the Indies back to Europe, perhaps even a worthwhile trade with Virginia if that godforsaken place ever recovers from its dismal beginnings. Yes, long after the abundant resources of the islands have been exhausted, we will still be taking a fine living from the sea."

"I'd feel better about all the sea surrounding us if there weren't so many pirates roaming free," Cobcroft said. "I've heard all the tales of sea monsters out there, but they do not worry me as the two-legged monsters do. Thomas, we are wide open to attack here. Any marauder could sail into our harbor and plunder this colony. Such soldiery as we have—I think the English Army was pleased to be rid of those men. The dregs!"

"You are right to be concerned about pirates," Fleet said. "But I think there is a solution to the danger in which we have been placed." He lowered his voice. "I have the Governor's ear, as you know, Sam, and I've put a plan of action to him. I want us to have a man-o-'war based here, under the command of one of the great captains, and he shall sally forth and wreak havoc on the pirates. Fight fire with fire! Let them know we are strong and they will avoid us."

"There could be some handsome prizes as well." Cobcroft smiled. "No need to restrict our captain to going after pirates. The passing Spaniards and French are loaded with treasure. Imagine the trading possibilities if we could waylay a cargo of spices, or tobacco! Tobacco is bringing three shillings an ounce in London now. A man could get very rich if he owned a shipful of the stuff."

"Good thinking, Sam. Of course, we must always aver that our purpose is solely to hound the pirates out of our waters . . . but I do not see why there can't be a profitable sideline to it. After all, we will be paying the piper—so we shall call the tune."

"You mean the Company will be paying?"

"No, Sam," Fleet said patiently. "I had it in mind a few of us would put our capital together, hire the skipper, pay for the boat and keep the proceeds."

"But Thomas, it would be one thing to have a protective warship sailing under the Virginia Company's flag, and quite another to have it operating for mere citizens. Would we not then simply be privateers?"

Fleet laughed. "For a young man, you do worry, Sam. By the time my scheme comes to fruition, I shall have cloaked it in respectability. You will see: in this place, no one will care how you make your money, just so long as you make it. Back home in England, they think of us as brave adventurers. They're behind us. Well, morally behind us, if not backing it up with men and money." He clapped his companion on the back. "It seems we're already celebrated in verse. My sister writes that a traveling company of players was in Plymouth performing the latest work by that Shakespeare fellow. *The Tempest.* It's a salute to the *Sea Venture* and her arrival here on the wings of a hurricane."

"William Shakespeare writing about us? I bet he got it wrong. Those penny-a-line scribblers always do." Cobcroft glanced across the square at the rotund figure advancing on them. "Here's one of them now, the odious Mr. Piggot, hunting for gossip for his pamphlet. Better he should restrict himself to shipping notices and the Governor's proclamations."

"Piggot's nothing to worry about. Just a fat little man trying to ingratiate himself with his betters. Actually, his weekly journal might become useful to us," Fleet said. "Ah, good day, Piggot! I trust you have prepared an essay on the evils of adultery and the punishment it brings."

"Why, yes indeed, my good sir," Jeremy Piggot gushed. "The next issue of the *Clarion* will sound the message loud and clear. Although," he added, nodding across the square, "I suspect the ordeal of that strumpet will not deter many from dalliance."

The other two turned and looked toward the stocks. A small crowd had gathered; there was some kind of disturbance.

"I am afraid, Sam," Fleet exclaimed, "our good wives

have arrived and are meddling. Come, we must put a stop to this."

Jessica Fleet's bright red lips were pursed as she held the pannikin of water to Sarah Jessup's mouth. Beside her, Hilda Cobcroft, holding a sponge, gently wiped the caked dust from the prisoner's brow. The crowd watched at a respectable distance, muttering their disapproval. Neither Jessica nor Hilda noticed the arrival of their husbands.

"Come away at once, my dear," Fleet commanded. "Leave this wench to suffer her punishment. She must tell the truth before she can be set free, yet she gives us only silence."

"This is barbaric!" Jessica snapped at him. "This poor woman will die if she is not released from these stocks. And why is she here? Because she has been caught in something almost all the worthies of this colony engage in. If we placed all Bermuda's adulterers in this woman's position, we would have to strip the cedar forests to build enough stocks!"

"Mind your tongue, my dear," Fleet said, glancing at the editor beside him, who appeared to be enjoying the scene. "The woman will go free as soon as she reveals the name of her seducer."

"I don't give a damn if it was Magistrate Owens himself," Jessica said. She was flushed with anger, and with her shining auburn hair and near six foot height, she was a daunting sight. Fleet, normally so sure of himself and his position, felt almost helpless before her.

"Why don't you intercede, Thomas?" demanded Hilda Cobcroft. She was small and fair, but no less daunting than Jessica. A pair of firebrands, Fleet thought grimly.

"Yes," said Jessica. "That silly little Magistrate will do anything you tell him, Thomas. Everyone knows he only serves on the bench at the pleasure of colonial leaders like you and your cohorts."

"This is not the place to be discussing such matters," Fleet said, noting the crowd eagerly listening. "Come with us now. We will take a drink on the Mayor's terrace, then go home and escape the heat."

The two women allowed themselves to be led away to the cool depths of the Town Hall; they had done their best to comfort the poor woman, but in the end, it was men who made the laws and ordered punishments. There was nothing they could do about it.

Thomas and Jessica Fleet tumbled in their new four-poster bed, the first in the colony. Even the Governor was still making do with a camp stretcher. But then, Fleet thought smugly, the Governor didn't have a wife like Jessica to pleasure him, so why would he need the finest bed? He caressed Jessica's splendid jutting breasts beneath the silk sleeping shift. She responded to him instantly, plunging her tongue into his mouth and stroking his inflamed member through his nightshirt. Her passion in bed more than compensated, in Fleet's mind, for her fiery spirit. Freed from the layers of heavy clothing so unsuitable in this climate, the stays and petticoats cast aside, Jessica in bed was a wild thing, with no inhibitions, and a fierce desire to give and get total satisfaction. She pulled him hard against her, and he reveled in the pressure of her strong, lithe body, shivering with anticipation as he heard the low growl in her throat. It was so good to have this cottage to themselves, to have the luxury of privacy when others were still forced to share accommodations. He remembered the stormy five-week passage from England and their aching frustration; there was nowhere in the cramped ship for them to make love. Well, no restrictions now, Fleet thought as her long fingers closed on him and her smooth legs parted. His lips found her nipples as he mounted her. Wonderful sensations joined them. It was too good to let finish, but when it did they were both consoled by the sure knowledge that the next time would be just as perfect.

Hilda Cobcroft lit a night candle and looked across to the bed where Sam lay, hands behind his head, smoking a long clay pipe. She noted the contentment on his face; baby Amanda was, for once, sleeping quietly in her crib

at the end of their bed. It had been so hard since the girl's
birth; Hilda had not been able to hire help of any kind,
and certainly no wet nurse. The one-room cottage sometimes seemed like a prison, and often Hilda found herself wondering just what they were doing in Bermuda
instead of Virginia; she did not believe all the horror stories she had heard about Jamestown and how it had almost been abandoned. Virginia, she was sure, would be
much grander than these islands. But Sam was doing
well here and she would stick it out with him until they
had made their fortune.

Hilda checked the net surrounding the crib. The mos-
quitoes had been bad this month, and she suspected they
might have something to do with the new fevers raging
in the islands. Satisfied the baby was all right, her back
carefully to Sam, Hilda swiftly undressed and enveloped
herself in a long, heavy cotton nightdress.

"I'm well pleased at the way things are working out,"
Sam said as she slid in beside him. "We may not have
much yet, but at least we have established our place in
the community. Back home in London I would still be
just a clerk. Here, as Harbormaster, I have every chance
of becoming a man of substance. And look whom we have
for friends! The Fleets would never deign to know us in
the Old Country. I am most grateful to you, dear Hilda,
for pursuing your friendship with Jessica. She has a
sharp tongue, and sometimes I wonder why Thomas
doesn't take a whip to her. But it is good you two are
close, as Thomas and I are."

"I like Jessica for herself," Hilda said firmly. "She is
a thinker, someone who, if given the chance, will see to
it that Bermuda becomes a great colony and not just a
cheap copy of what we all left behind."

"Leave the thinking to us," he said. "Don't concern
your pretty little head with the affairs of men. Just raise
our child well and prepare to shed a tear when we marry
her off to one of Bermuda's new gentry."

"I would hope by the time Amanda's of marrying age,
we will all be back in London, Sam. I can't contemplate
living in this outpost forever."

"It will not be an outpost long," he said. "Why, Thomas told me today we've already had a play written about us and performed on the English stage. Makes us out to be most heroic, brave pioneers. The fellow who wrote it, Shakespeare, you remember, is very prolific. The most commercial of the London playwrights."

Hilda sat up quickly.

"A play about us! How wonderful! Sam, I have a grand idea. We will obtain a copy of this play and perform it here. Bermuda's first cultural event. That would be such a feather in my cap, in our caps."

"There's no demand for culture here, and no time for it. All the people need is to be able to count to a hundred, read the Bible, and sign their names." He laughed. "I know Shakespeare is for the masses, but even he would think twice about having his work performed in a place like this. A good whipping is all the culture these people can appreciate."

She bit her lip. There was no point in arguing with Sam. He saw their needs, and the needs of Bermuda, so simply. Hard work and the grasping of every opportunity; the exploitation of the land and the sea. This was Sam Cobcroft's creed, and there was no room in it for anything except essentials. She sighed as she felt his hand touch her breast and was again disappointed at her failure to respond. If the baby weren't lying so close to them, if their surroundings had been a little more comfortable, if Sam would just work at arousing her . . . As he prepared to mount her, she reached beneath the pillow and found a silk handkerchief to wrap around his member. The last thing they needed right now was another child.

The sun was already high and hot when Jonas Odlum, the fever coursing through him, began his painful descent to the town. The crutch he had fashioned from a tree branch was of little help; every forward movement sent waves of agony through him as his useless leg struck the hard ground. But Jonas was driven on, beyond pain and fear of the fate awaiting him, by worry over Sarah.

When at last he was on the outskirts of St. George's he slipped into the shadows of a narrow alleyway. He was close enough to the town square to hear the hubbub, the raucous laughter and occasional jeer. He sat propped in a doorway for half an hour, waiting for strength, pondering his next move. He had to make contact with Sarah. Perhaps the baby had arrived already, or the birth had been difficult.

A boy entered the alley, kicking at a stone and humming to himself. He was a small, frail child dressed in ragged calico, and he gave a cry of fear when Jonas shot out a long arm and clutched his collar.

"Be quiet!" Jonas said. "I shall not hurt you."

The boy shivered and tried to twist away from the grip of this wild-looking creature. He was sure he was in the clutches of one of the devils who dwelled in the rugged hills beyond the town.

"Hush," Jonas said. "Tell me what I need to know and you can go on your way." He gave what he hoped was a reassuring smile, but the bared teeth, broken and yellow, only increased the boy's terror.

"I am seeking Mistress Jessup, maid to Magistrate Owens. Point me in the direction of the house and then you can go."

Some of the boy's fear subsided. Hadn't he just been with the other urchins flinging mudballs at Sarah Jessup? There could not be much to fear from this tangled creature if it was the whore in the stocks he was seeking.

"Give me a copper and I'll take you to her," he said, all cunning and confidence now. His captor suddenly squeezed his arm so hard he cried out loud.

"Tell me at once, you little guttersnipe," Jonas hissed, "or I'll rip your arm off."

"She's in the square . . . in the stocks," the boy gasped. "Four days now, and she still won't tell who's father of the child. The square." He pointed with his free hand. "Straight down there."

Jonas released the boy and saw him dash like a hare for the entrance to the alley. He did not feel the rock the boy flung at him as it bounced off his cheekbone. Jonas

slowly pulled himself up in the doorway and began to
hobble toward his target; the pain burned in him as
brightly as the sun in his eyes, but he stumbled on
through the twisting streets, past the crude cottages,
until he emerged on the edge of the town square.

He came up behind the twittering crowd, and his presence was like a cloud passing before the sun. As the idlers
on the outskirts saw him, they fell silent and pressed
away from him, opening a clear path to the pathetic figure slumped in the stocks.

Jonas saw her and stopped dead. He lifted his head and
bayed like a wounded animal. The crowd scurried farther from the wild giant.

"Sarah, Sarah," Jonas sobbed, lurching toward her,
dropping his crutch. "What have they done to you?" He
flung himself in the dust before her and kissed her dirty,
stained face. "Sarah," he implored, his huge hands cradling her head.

Sarah slowly realized it was not another of the hallu-
cinations she had known in her cruel captivity. She focused her eyes on him and tried to smile, to speak. But
her lips were cracked and her tongue swollen and she
could only croak.

"Water! Bring water, you bastards," Jonas screamed.
But the crowd only backed farther away. Jonas slowly
pulled himself up, towering over all of them. He placed
his hands on the crosspiece of the stocks and flexed his
muscles once, twice. Straining mightily, he wrenched
the instrument of torture apart. The crowd gasped at this
feat of strength—none but a devil could have ripped open
the iron-bolted cedar trap—but Jonas didn't hear them.
He had Sarah in his arms and carried her tenderly to the
pump where he scooped water from a pail and brushed
her lips.

"My poor darling," he whispered. "That I should have
caused you this suffering." He put his lips against hers.
His hand brushed her belly. "And the child, our child.
What kind of people would do such a thing to you both?"

"It's all right now, dear Jonas," she gasped, "everything is well now you are here." Delirious though she

was, she could feel his strength flowing into her. She felt
him stand again, lifting her with him.

"I will take you away now," he said, cradling her.
"Back to our home in the woods, far from these demons."
He started slowly across the square, and no one moved
to block his path. "I shall build us a little ship, Sarah,
and we will sail away to a place where we can be free,
proud. We shall live, Sarah, the three of us." He continued to stare down into her face as he walked. The broken
leg was forgotten, although it was grotesquely twisted,
the foot flapping sideways. He paid no heed to the two
figures who entered the square and positioned themselves between him and the exit.

"What the devil!" Thomas Fleet exclaimed.

"The wildman," Sam Cobcroft muttered. "Making off
with the Jessup woman," Sam exclaimed.

Fleet stood his ground and let the lumbering giant
come to him. "Put the woman down! She is a prisoner of
the Crown."

Clutching Sarah with one arm, Jonas swung the other
arm out in a wide arc, smashing in the bridge of Thomas
Fleet's nose and sending him sprawling. It was the action of one brushing away a fly. All Jonas wanted was to
be away from this place; he had no desire to hurt anyone.
He continued, a great wounded beast heading for sanctuary. Sarah's head was on his shoulder and she looked
behind her to Fleet, now being helped to his feet by a so-
licitous Cobcroft. She saw Fleet apply a handkerchief to
his bloody nose, then reach into the belt beneath his frock
coat.

Thomas Fleet was white with anger and shock. There
was no fear in him; fear was for the ignorant peasants
who were standing around in quaking silence. He primed
his pistol and started after the giant. Now they were only
a yard apart and he could see Sarah Jessup's eyes looking into his own, imploring him. Their eyes held for a
moment. He raised the pistol; the barrel almost touched
the shaggy hair at the back of the giant's head. The noise
of the shot rolled around the silent square until it gave
way to Sarah's long, keening scream. She crumpled to

the ground with Jonas, his blood and brains spattered
over her.

She fainted before the eager crowd rushed forward to
congratulate Fleet and kick at the lifeless body of Jonas.

The Governor was pleased to bestow a reward of
twenty guineas on Thomas Fleet for his heroic capture
and killing of the deserter, murderer and fornicator Jonas Odlum. Thomas would have liked to keep the money,
but Jessica thought that was common, so they directed
that the reward be used to build a public drinking fountain in the square on the spot where Thomas had shot
the fugitive. When the Governor unveiled the Fleet
Fountain, he predicted its water would always flow sweet
and clear.

Sarah Jessup was not put back in the stocks. She was
allowed to crawl to the house of Mary Fletcher, the midwife, who for reasons unfathomable to the entire populace, had taken pity on her. There, three weeks later,
Mrs. Fletcher delivered Sarah of a fine, strong girl. At
first Sarah wanted nothing to do with the child; her grief
at losing Jonas was such that her only wish was to join
him. But the baby was bright and beautiful and she had
Jonas's eyes. Sarah came to love it. She called it Prudence Odlum, and the authorities, reluctantly, recorded
it as such in the parish register.

Uplands Cottage,
St. George's, Bermuda.

8 June 1613

My dear Lord Marley,
Humble apologies for the delay in this latest report;
I cannot use official channels for these dispatches be-
cause the Governor, who is suspicious of everyone, cen-
sors all messages. Thank God we are soon to be rid of
him! In the meantime, I am sending this to you in Lon-
don in care of Midshipman Cornelius, who is known to
my family and is, I am sure, reliable.
The news that the Virginia Company is selling us out

to the Somers Island Company has caused a furor here, not least among the aspiring leaders of our society who see all their toadying gone to waste and a new government to be wooed. Lord Cavendish, it is to be hoped, will prove more reasonable than the man he is to replace, at least on that matter which is of such great interest to you and your associates, namely the employment of black and Indian slaves. The fierce debate about importation of this labor continues: a couple of the lesser churches oppose on moral grounds. At least our own church is, as always, happy to do whatever the Establishment wants. But the real opposition is widespread in the community and is based on the fear of being overrun by Negroes. "There were no natives here when we arrived; why then import a potential problem?" is their argument. They point to the devilish problems Virginia is having with its Indians. One could reply that Virginia is, however, having no trouble at all with its slaves, said to be a docile and hard-working lot.

I think it best if we hasten slowly. Already there are a few colored servants on the island, the slaves of Virginia-bound families who have stopped over here for various reasons. As these gentle creatures are seen going about their duties in total subservience, the general fears will abate. And the demand will grow as the colony wives want to know why they should still have to make do with the services of some Irish trollop when Madame X down the street has a brace of strong and silent blacks to do her bidding. I would imagine the climate will be right by perhaps the end of this year to bring in a small number of slaves, hand-picked for desirable qualities.

I am, of course, most conscious of the vast rewards awaiting you and your associates if a monopoly of this colony and, subsequently, the Americas, can be established. Perhaps if you were to have a word to Cavendish before he sails to take up his new position . . .

You might, my Lord, also whisper in Cavendish's ear what a loyal and trustworthy aide-de-camp I have proved to be. I'm sure the outgoing Governor will not recommend me. The man is almost contemptuous of me, I who have given him nothing but support through these hellish three years! I would hope you would agree it is to all our benefits if I can remain in this position and keep a close eye on our interests.

On other matters, Thomas Fleet continues to push the barrow of deploying a privateer here. I cannot quite tumble what his game is. The Hon. Fleet is only interested in schemes to line his pocket. He continually warns of the danger of pirates invading us. I think we have more to fear from land-based pirates like Fleet and his ilk! Whatever, he has much of the community convinced we need protection although none of them is willing to pay for it. I shall keep a close eye on this for you in case he has some devious notion of getting into the slaving trade himself.

Day-to-day life here remains dreary beyond belief. Still less than five hundred souls, most of them ill-bred and believing their journey here entitles them to a new start in life. We suffer the most primitive conditions. It could indeed be a paradise, I suppose: the climate, except when winter bites or the tempests rage, is benign. Most things will grow if the colonists take the time to plant them. But for the most part the Bermudians would rather reap than sow. It is quite alarming to witness the denuding of large stands of forest and the decimating of the wild hog packs. Even the wildfowl, at first so plentiful, appear to be giving our islands a wide berth. The fact that more than a thousand of them were slain to provide ersatz pigeon pie for His Excellency's recent celebration dinner could explain this.

No, for too much of the time the people here are content to rape the land; there is no forward planning, no attempt to improve housing, no thought to deepening and widening the inadequate harbor, nor of moving the settlement from this end of the island to the choice area on the shores of the Great Sound.

About the only thing in which we can take heart is the progress being made with shipbuilding. The people who have settled here have proved remarkably adept at *fashioning sound vessels from the islands' cedar. Others of the settlers are fine sailors. I think Bermuda will find its real future plying the sea lanes.*

There is little evidence of a sense of community developing. The people of the lower orders, who include press-ganged wharf rats, pathetic serving girls and common criminals, are as lazy, undisciplined and unpromising as you would expect. But their supposed betters are, for the most part, jumped-up tradesmen. These people are already giving themselves airs. They refer to themselves as the Forty Families. Forty Thieves, more like it!

The colony needs discipline and vision. Religion and the lash in equal portions, I think. Instead there is fornication at all levels and the liberal use of rum. I hope Cavendish lives up to his reputation as a hard man.

Well, my Lord, the ship is making ready to sail and I must seal this and entrust it to Cornelius. I will write again after Lord Cavendish's arrival when, I hope, I will be well established in his trust.

> *I remain, your obedient servant,*
> *Nathaniel Pike, ADC.*

Chapter Three
(1921–)

They passed the Montauk light, sailed into Long Island Sound and waited an hour, riding easily at anchor in the light swell. They were waiting for the signal. Jeff Odlum dragged his leg along the foredeck as he scanned the shore. The cold sea air did nothing for him. On nights like this he could actually feel the missing limb, the sensation of a tensing muscle, an itch between the toes. But he liked the discomfort and he liked the danger; it made him feel he was a whole man doing man's work. A footstep sounded and he whirled around; Sam Fleet approached.

"Come on back in the cabin," Sam said. "It's cold as a witch's tit out here. The crew will tell us when they're ready on shore."

Jeff nodded and followed Sam back down the dark bulk of the ship. It was their sixth run and promised to be the most profitable yet. Jeff grinned in the night. His father would have a fit if he knew what these voyages were all about. So far the old man had accepted his story that he wanted to learn all about the shipping trade so Kosmos could eventually become independent of carriers and do its own exporting in its own ships. Jonas Odlum would be struck speechless to know that his younger son was a bootlegger.

Back in the watchcabin Sam produced two glasses and a bottle of Napoleon brandy. He poured them each a stiff slug and they settled down for the wait. Sam hated this part of it, the dangerous, vulnerable time when the booze was in the lifeboats ready to be taken ashore and they were at the mercy of everyone from the Coast Guard to their own crew to the hoodlums they had to deal with on shore. He envied Jeff's grace under pressure. The fellow treated these times like great adventures. He acted more like a Fleet was supposed to than Sam did; not like a land-based Odlum.

"I reckon we should be looking at chartering a second ship," Jeff said. "Mr. Finkelstein says he can take all the booze we can supply him with. It's the only premium stuff getting into New York just now. And Prohibition won't last forever, Sam. We could double our profits with another ship."

"I don't think my father would go along with it," Sam answered after a moment. "While we keep the operation small like this he can pretend he doesn't know about the extra cargo. But the old fellow would be mortified if what we're doing ever came out. He was a rogue in his day, so now all he wants is respectability. God, he's so thrilled about the Prince of Wales coming out to open his new hotel!" Sam shook his head, smiling at Jeff over his glass.

Jeff nodded and poured himself another brandy. All the parents of all their contemporaries were like that— terribly respectable, ignoring their ancestors and the swashbuckling origins of Bermuda.

"You know, Sam, I've never really thanked you for bringing me in on this scheme. Damned if I know what I'd be doing if not for you. I just can't face settling down in the family company. And, hell, they don't need me there anyway. Young Primrose is all but running Kosmos now and making a great fist of it. Cable's happy playing the good doctor." He shrugged. "There's no slot for me, not one I'd be happy in."

"It wasn't charity, Jeff. You're great at handling guys like Finkelstein and the suppliers. I've no head for that stuff. All I know about is getting the ship from one place to the other." He laughed. "It's a kick, though, isn't it?

The two of us working together? Just goes to show you don't have to be bound by your family's past."

A crewman knocked on the cabin door and Sam turned down the lamplight before calling him in.

"The light's showing, Mr. Fleet," the sailor said. "We're all ready to go ashore. You want to check the list?" He passed a typed manifest across the table; a hundred cases of Johnnie Walker were in one lifeboat, a hundred of Beefeater in the other. At $5 a bottle net to Sam and Jeff, each would make $6000 off tonight's run.

Sam handed back the list. "Maybe you're right about a second ship," he murmured to Jeff. "Talk to Finkelstein about it tonight. This money's too good to pass up."

"You're not coming ashore?" Jeff asked.

"No, I'll stay in the lifeboat until the deal's completed. You're better at dealing with those guys than I am."

"For God's sake, pay attention, Robert." Sir Horatio Fleet glared at his son who was slouched in his chair and gazing out into the spring night. "If you're going to help run the hotel you have to know what makes it tick. I intend the Tropicana to be something we can all be proud of, the beginning of Bermuda's greatest tourist boom. Veronica says the foyer colors are all wrong."

Robert feared a headache was coming on. He pressed his fingers to his temple and tried to concentrate on the old man, then looked across the library table and fixed his cold blue eyes on his sister.

"Down from college a week and already finding fault," he said. "Really, Veronica, I wish you'd talk to me before running to Father with your tales. That was only the undercoat you saw in the foyer. Another week and it will be finished and you'll all be happy."

"Don't speak to her in that tone," Horatio snapped. "I asked the girl to look everything over and give me her opinion. I'd trust Veronica's insights before yours, or Sam's."

"Please," their mother said, "please don't quarrel. I'm sure Robert has everything under control. And I'm sure Veronica will have lots of useful suggestions. There's no

need for us to fight. Let's just be happy for a change."
She heard her husband snort in derision, and Joanna
sighed. They were always at each other's throats, the
boys and their father. If only Sam would settle down and
stay home, and if Robert were not so surly, so . . . dangerously unapproachable. She smiled at Veronica. At
least *she* was sweet and loving, and keenly interested in
the business. What a pity she hadn't been a boy; she
could take over everything then, and her brothers might
do as they pleased.

"Yes," Veronica said, "it would be nice if we all made
an effort to get along. I'd particularly appreciate it during the opening celebrations. You see, I'm going to have
a guest down from New York, someone I met in college.
If that's all right, Father." She studied her hands. "It's
someone who's rather special to me. A man."

"What's all this, Joanna?" Horatio demanded. "No
one told me about Veronica getting serious. Is he a Bermudian? Do we know him?"

"I haven't told Mother about him," Veronica said. "And
no, he's not a Bermudian. But he has . . . links . . . with the
place. So with your permission I'd like him to stay with us,
meet you all. I know you're going to like him."

Who could fail to like John Chester? she thought. From
the moment she met him on campus two years ago, Veronica had had the feeling he was the one for her. It was
freshman year and her first sorority party; she was feeling awkward and provincial among the American students, who all seemed so sophisticated. They were
dressed more smartly, appeared actually to like the taste
of bathtub gin, knew all the new dance steps. She was
beginning to think her coming to college might have
been a dreadful mistake.

"It's all pretty terrible, isn't it?" he said, standing beside her on the crowded landing above the dance floor.
"I've been watching you. You don't fit here. A real out-
doors girl." He bowed. "I'm John Chester, law school.
Would you like me to take you away from all this?"

"Veronica Fleet. Arts. And I think I should stay."

"Your accent. English?"

"No, I'm from Bermuda. I only just got here, and I'm afraid I'm feeling quite out of my depth."

"Bermuda. I should have known. My family came from Bermuda. We must have lots in common. Let's go find somewhere we can talk."

She had surprised herself by agreeing. John Chester was so reassuring, a senior, tall and handsome, but not stuck up like so many of the older students. They drove off into the crisp Williamsburg night and parked on a rise above the town; she found herself talking on and on, telling him all her hopes and fears. It was quite late when she finally ran down.

"You must think I'm awful," she said nervously. "Prattling on like that. I'm so sorry. It's just there's been no one for me to talk to. And I'm such a country mouse here."

"No," he said softly, "you're a welcome change from the girls here, all trying so desperately to be sophisticated. Will you have dinner with me tomorrow night?"

He drove her back to the dormitory and didn't even attempt to kiss her good night. Veronica was disappointed. He did kiss her on their third date, and she was relieved to find him just as passionate as she was. If he'd tried, she'd have let him go further than Tom Jepson had.

It was not until they had been going together for more than six months and his graduation was looming that they finally surrendered to the desire that had been building in them night after night. It happened in his car, and all she could really remember was a scramble of garters and panties and a door handle pressing in her back and a sharp pain when he entered her. But afterward they felt so tender and close. He asked her to marry him.

"I will, John," she said, tears of love in her eyes. "There's nothing I want more. But we will have to wait. I'm only nineteen and my parents would not agree to it yet. But we can be engaged in secret."

Last summer had been dreadful for them both. He could not come to Bermuda to be with her but had to sit in a steaming office on Wall Street, seeking to put into practice what he had learned at William and Mary. She would have gladly forgone her vacation at home but her parents had been outraged at the suggestion of her going to New York and she hadn't pressed the point, nor told them about John.

It was better when she returned to college. John managed to drive down once a month: the visits were spent making wonderful love and planning their future. And now, at last, he was coming to Bermuda to meet her family and bring their romance out into the open.

The family meeting was breaking up. She watched Robert slouch off; her mother moved around the room straightening things, then pecked Horatio on the cheek and patted Veronica on the shoulder.

"Don't sit up too late, you two," Joanna said and left them alone.

Her father poured himself a port and settled across the table from her.

"Sorry about Robert," he said gruffly. "There's something wrong with that boy. Boy, hell, he's thirty-one years old. But he doesn't have any common sense and he's got a mean mouth. And Sam." He sighed. "Sam is just a damned fool. He'll never amount to anything."

He looked so sad, as if all his great achievements had been for nothing. Veronica felt all her love for him well up. He had always been a stern, distant father, but she knew how much he cared for them all, how much he wanted them to take pride in the Fleet name.

"The boys will settle down, Daddy," she said. "Why, any day now I'm sure they'll be getting married to nice girls and starting their own families . . ." The thought of marriage brought a flush. " . . . and then you'll see they're all right."

He shook his head. "No, dear, I've watched them for years and I don't think either is ever going to be worth a damn. It's the curse of the Fleet line—weak menfolk. Thank God we have strong women." He drained his port. "That's what I want to talk to you about, Veronica. When you're through university, I hope you'll be equipped to take over everything from me. You've always been very interested in the business, anyway, and there's a loyal staff to help you. I'll be around a few years more to guide you.

"I'm raising the issue now, rather than later, because of the young man you mentioned tonight. Don't get too serious. Or if you do, make sure he knows what lies ahead of you. A lot of men wouldn't be able to cope with their wives' presiding over an empire of the kind I'm offering you."

"I don't know how John would react," she said. She smiled at her father. "This is all a bit sudden. I've always assumed the boys would be running things."

"No," he said. "I've known for a long time that you would be my successor. That's why I insisted you go to university. So. Is it serious with the young man?"

"Yes, Daddy. You'll see why when you meet him." She got up, ran around the table and embraced her father. "With your approval, we want to announce our engagement while John's here, perhaps at your sixtieth birthday party and the Tropicana opening. I'd rather like that, the Prince of Wales at my engagement party."

"Who is he? You said he had links to Bermuda?"

"His name is John Chester. He's a lawyer who was at William and Mary my first year and . . . and he's wonderful. I know you're going to love him." She paused. She had been going to save the next part for a surprise, but it might be wiser to tell him now. "Actually, Daddy, John's family went from here to the U.S. one hundred fifty years ago, so there are no close ties anymore."

"Chester? No, I don't recall any Chesters in the colony."

"When they were here, they were Odlums." She saw him flush but hurried on. "John's mother married Eric Chester. Her father was one of the American Odlums. I think he was some kind of naval hero in the Civil War." Her father was clutching his throat as if choking. The red in his cheeks was now deep purple. Before she could get around the table to his side, he had toppled from his chair.

She cradled his head in her lap while tugging frantically at the bellpull to summon the servants. His forehead felt cold and damp, and his chest was heaving, his limbs twitching. She dragged on the rope again. Where were they all? Was he dying? His lips were moving and she put her ear near his mouth. The words were strangled but she could not mistake them.

"His grandfather killed my father. John Odlum killed Davis Fleet." His eyes rolled back until she could see only the whites; his mouth gaped open and he fell into unconsciousness. And then the butler was in the room, followed by her mother. Veronica fainted.

The unloading of the boats onto the shore at Sag Harbor and into Finkelstein's waiting trucks took two hours. While the process was being completed, Sam backed the lifeboats a hundred yards out into the bay; he didn't like being trapped close by the shore. Police and Customs men could swoop down on them too easily that way.

Jeff stood in the lee of the first truck talking quietly with Finkelstein as tarpaulins were lashed down over the precious cargo. The huge wad of hundred-dollar bills nestled inside Jeff's shirt.

"It's okay for you," Finkelstein said. "Your part of it is over. I still have to get the stuff back to Manhattan, dodging the law and hijackers. At least your Bermuda booze is worth the extra risk and worth the price. My customers—"

A half-dozen dark shapes slipped out of the trees. Jeff heard Finkelstein swear under his breath.

"Don't anyone move," one of the shapes said. They came closer, and Jeff could see the machine guns leveled at Finkelstein's party. "All lie down flat. We're taking the trucks. We want the delivery money, too."

Jeff's hand went to the bulge over his ribs. He was damned if he would give up all that money to a bunch of thugs. As he sank down beside Finkelstein, he rolled under the truck and out the other side. He would spring down the beach and hide until Sam could come in and

get him. The hijackers wouldn't wait around too long.
They wouldn't dare.

He got a head start, but the leather straps on his artificial leg snapped. He crashed onto the gravel: they
were almost on him by the time he was back up on his
one leg. Jeff plunged into the bushes and began working
his way along the shoreline. The first burst of fire was off
to his right; the second closer, the bullets whipping
through the bushes, sending twigs and leaves flying.
There was silence for a moment, and he heard the lifeboats' engines start up. Sam was coming in for him. But
as he crouched there, he realized the engine noise was
moving away from the shore. Fear gripped him, fear of
being abandoned, crippled, in this hostile country.

"Sam!" he screamed hoarsely. "Sam! Wait for me!"

The next burst of fire homed in on his voice; three bullets unstitched his chest. Jeff Odlum was dead before the
hijackers reached his body.

News of the tragedy did not reach Bermuda until four
days later, when Sam and his ship slipped into St.
George's. Sam had been drunk the whole time, trying to
blot out the memories of the dreadful night and his
friend's cries for help. There was no point, he knew, in
swearing the crew to secrecy; there were too many of
them, and the death of a prominent member of the tight-
knit community was something they would all talk
about.

He didn't think he could face the Odlums, so in the end
he wrote the family a brief note telling them what had
happened to their son without going into any more detail than necessary. He avoided any mention of his sailing away from the shore while Jeff was being pursued.

He was almost glad for the tragedy that hung over his
own home. With his father hovering near death, Sam
was not questioned too closely about what had happened
on the voyage. His mother was distraught, sitting at Horatio's bedside around the clock. His sister was pale and
silent. It was left to Robert to explain what had happened.

"Veronica got herself involved with some fellow and wanted to bring him down here to announce their engagement," his brother said. "She told Father all about it, then dropped the bombshell. The chap is an Odlum. The old man threw a fit, literally." He laughed. "Isn't it rich? While you were killing one Odlum, another Odlum just about finished off our father."

"What's Veronica done about it?"

"She wrote to the fellow and canceled everything. She seems quite cut up about it. But she's thrown herself into organizing the hotel opening. You'd think she was the eldest son instead of me," he added peevishly. "But Father seems to think you and I aren't worth a penny."

"Maybe he's right," Sam said. He was sick of trying to cope with it all, his family, his responsibilities. If little Veronica wanted to shoulder the burden, that was fine with him. Sam had lost any desire to compete.

Jonas Odlum mourned in silence. The loss of his son was a terrible grief to him, but he refused to let his emotions show. And he kept to himself the belief he had long held, that no good could have come of Jeff's association with the Fleet boy.

"The poor man," Julia said. "He loved that boy so. If he would just break down and cry as we do."

Primrose nodded. "It's such a waste. Jeff came through the war, even if it did cost him a leg. And he had such a wonderful future. He would have settled down soon, I know he would." She was crying again. "What are we going to do, Mother?"

"We are going to be strong. Jonas was still hoping Jeff would take over the business, despite all the signs to the contrary. Cable's got his own career. So it will have to be you, Primrose. You're well-equipped to do it." She touched a hand to the girl's cheek. "I'm sorry all this is being thrust on you. At your age you should be having fun, meeting people."

"It's all right, Mother. I'll do whatever I have to."

John Clay and Billy Youngblood, dressed in their crisp new porters' jackets, watched the ceremony from the bell

captain's station. All afternoon the lobby of the Tropicana Hotel had been jammed with sightseers hoping for
a glimpse of the Prince of Wales. Now there were only
invited guests in the lobby, the movers and shakers of
Bermuda, stiff in tails and cocktail gowns, listening intently to His Highness tell them what a man of vision Sir
Horatio Fleet was, and how unfortunate it was that he
could not be with them to see his latest dream unveiled.

"I wish he had less vision and more generosity," Clay
whispered. "The wages are so bad here. Pray God the tips
are big. My woman thinks I'm crazy to have taken the
job."

"At least we've got jobs, John. We're better off than
most. They say the hotel's booked solid for the next four
months. All the Americans are flocking back here, and
they're big tippers." Actually, Billy was trying to convince himself. He needed desperately to make enough
money to rent a cottage for himself and Amy. They
couldn't go on living with his mother now that a baby
was on its way.

"If we had some kind of union, they couldn't get away
with paying us slave wages," John whispered to his
friend. "Maybe that's what we should do—organize all
the staff here and threaten to strike."

"Don't talk crazy. The Forty Thieves won't let the
white workers form a union, let alone us. They'd kick our
asses out of here so fast . . . and there'd be a hundred
other blacks lining up to take our jobs."

"You're turning into a real coward, Billy."

"Only facing facts, John."

Steven Lapin listened to the clipped English accent and
studied the back of the Prince's head. He wondered if it was
true, that the fellow would hump anything in skirts. A lot
of the flowers of Bermudian womanhood would be willing
to find out. He frowned as he looked at Veronica Fleet sitting at the Prince's right. Since the old man's stroke, she'd
been pushing herself into the limelight a bit too much for
Lapin's taste. Of course Horatio was crazy, thinking he
could install his daughter as chairman. As soon as Horatio

was actually dead—which wouldn't be long, judging by appearances—Lapin would get the rest of the board together and vote her out. Robert could have the job in Veronica's place. He was handleable, with the evidence Lapin had of his perversions.

Ah, the Prince was finally finished speaking, had unveiled the plaque, and they could all head to the ballroom for a drink.

"He's rather handsome, isn't he?" Dimity Lapin said as they rose from their seats. "I'm looking forward to meeting him." She patted her long dark hair and fished a compact from her evening bag. Checking her makeup, she concentrated her hazel eyes in the glass, frowning.

"I'm sure the pleasure will be all His Highness's," Lapin said. "You look quite ravishing, my dear. I hear the Prince has an eye for beautiful women."

"He's quite young."

"Not *too* young, Dimity. He's twenty-six."

"You wouldn't mind then? I mean, if it's true what they say about him and he takes a fancy to me . . . ?"

"My dear, it would be a feather in both our caps. It's almost your patriotic duty to bed the future King." He let his hand rest a moment on her trim bottom. Young Eddy would be in for quite an experience if he got off with Dimity.

He watched her wend her way through the crowd, plotting a course to bring her alongside the Prince.

"A very successful opening, Steven," Jamie Baseheart said as they met by the bar. "Horatio was correct, as always. The Tropicana has come on the market at just the right moment. By next season we'll be back to prewar tourism numbers."

"Such a tragedy Horatio can't be with us," Lapin told his fellow director. "I visited his sickbed yesterday and I'm afraid there's no hope. He's quite gone in the head. It'll be a mercy if God takes him quickly."

"All we can do is carry on the company the way he would want us to," Jamie shrugged. "But I'll miss his leadership."

"We all will. However, Jamie, I wouldn't pay much

heed to the decisions he's been making since his stroke. This nonsense about the girl taking over from him. Really! We should prepare to nip that scheme in the bud. I've spoken with some of the other directors and they are all appalled, of course, as I am."

"It's very awkward for me," Baseheart said. "Being a cousin, I mean. I can't get embroiled in family squabbles. If Horatio wants Veronica to succeed him . . ."

"He doesn't, Jamie. He's a sick old man who doesn't know what he wants," Lapin said patiently. "It's up to us to protect his achievements. We can't let the whole enterprise bog down because of some misplaced ideas of family unity." He grinned. "Anyway, I propose keeping it all in your family. There must be a Fleet at the head of the company. I thought Robert would be the ideal cnoice."

"Better than Sam, certainly. But perhaps we won't have to make any move. Maybe Horatio will recover."

Lapin shook his head.

Across the crowded room Veronica stood with her mother; she had been watching the meeting between Lapin and Baseheart and she had a fair idea of what they were talking about.

"They don't like it," Veronica said. "They've all made it very clear to me they think Daddy's mad, pushing me forward to run the company. Sometimes I wonder if they're not right. I could go back to college, finish my degree. That's the normal thing to do."

"Your life will never be normal, darling," Joanna said. "Already being a Fleet has cost you so much." She knew what giving up the young man had done to Veronica. "You might as well enjoy the power that goes with the sacrifice. And you've promised your father."

"I know. I just wish it hadn't happened so suddenly. And I wish . . . I hadn't been the one who crippled Daddy."

"You weren't, dear," her mother said patiently. "Doctor says anything would have brought the attack on. He says it was a miracle your father functioned for so long.

You've got to be strong and do what we always secretly believed you would—keep the company going."

"But it's such a slap in the face to the boys. I guess Sam doesn't care one way or the other, but Robert . . . Robert looks at me as if I engineered the whole thing."

"Your father engineered everything, just as he always did. If Robert has any complaints he should address them to him. He was his own undoing, a long time ago. The same with Sam. We tried so hard with the boys, but we both knew they weren't working out. So we put all our faith in you. I know it's going to be rewarded."

Robert was at their side in a moment. His blue eyes flashed danger, and Joanna took note of the large glass of bourbon in his hand. He did not appear drunk, but seemed to be hovering on the brink of some kind of outburst.

"If the Fleet women are taking over the company," he snapped, "it would be a help if they took care of our guest of honor. At the moment the Prince is firmly in the clutches of Dimity Lapin. I think someone should display the family flag. Bloody Sam hasn't even bothered to show up. What about you two going over and making yourselves pleasant to the man."

"Quite right, Robert," Joanna said. "We were engrossed in talking about Father. But he would want us to do our duty. Come, Veronica."

"I hope the grand opening is going well," Primrose said. She was standing by the open window at home, looking across to the lights of Hamilton, brighter than ever tonight with the sweep of the searchlights installed around the Tropicana. She and her mother were still in black, and would not have attended the party even if they had been invited.

Their lives were slowly returning to normal. All of them continued to grieve for dear Jeff, but the world had to go on. Bermuda's history was founded in centuries of sudden and bloody death.

"I'm sure it will be fine," Julia Odlum said to her daughter. "Getting the Prince to stop over on his way

home from Canada was quite a coup for the Fleets and
for Bermuda." Julia was sitting at her desk sifting
through papers. "The Governor wanted us to come for
cocktails with the Prince tomorrow, but of course we
can't. He was very understanding." She sighed. "Primrose, I don't think your father's going to get over the
tragedy."

"I know. I tried to talk to him last night. He seems so
. . . defeated. He still cares about the Assembly, but not
much else." She turned away from the window and went
to stand beside her mother. "Isn't it ironic, he and Sir
Horatio Fleet struck down at the same time? It's as
though our two families must always be linked in both
triumphs and tragedies."

"There have been few enough triumphs and far too
many tragedies," Julia replied. "You must be tired, dear.
You were in the laboratories all day."

"I've got an idea—it's probably mad, but I've been
watching what the new crop of tourists are doing, and
listening to them," Primrose confided, her voice excited.
"It's suddenly become fashionable to have a suntan. I
mean, fashionable for women. No more the deathly pallor to indicate you don't have to go out in the sun and
work. All these wealthy, fashionable New York and Boston women are actually lying out in the sun without hats,
trying to become brown. It's the new status symbol, to
show you've traveled to tropical places. But no one is
doing any cosmetics to go with the new bronzed look,"
she explained, almost elated. "I've been playing around
with a whole new range; products to protect your skin
while still letting it tan, products to show off the tan. If
I'm right, and the trend of staying out in the sun continues, we could be on to something big. I want to call it The
Bermuda Line."

Steven Lapin lay back in his bed, well pleased. The
Prince had been immediately smitten with Dimity and
invited the Lapins to join a small group at Government
House after the formalities at the hotel. No one minded
when Steven begged off, claiming another appointment.

He'd left the carriage with Dimity and spent a few hours
at the club, lobbying two more Fleet board members.
Now it was midnight and he was keenly anticipating
Dimity's return. If they had hit it off together, if she became one of the bachelor Prince's women, doors would
open to her and her husband all around the empire. It
was a scarcely kept secret that all the single Royal males
were taken in training, so to speak, by well-bred women.
It was the ultimate compliment to a husband for his wife
to become a royal mistress.

Steven heard the carriage coming up their drive, got
out of bed and twirled the bottle of Krug he had placed
in the ice bucket.

Dimity was glowing—there was no other word for it.
She came dancing into the bedroom, eyes flashing, the
color in her cheeks owing nothing to rouge. She flung
herself into Steven's arms and waltzed him around the
room.

"I'm dancing with a girl who danced with the Prince
of . . ." Steven sang his own version of the popular music
hall ditty and they both collapsed on the bed, laughing.
Steven let his hands roam over her body, hiking the silk
cocktail dress up to her waist. He touched her core; she
was moist and yielding. It gave him a thrill close to an
orgasm, knowing who had brought her to this stage. He
moved off the bed to the champagne bucket and poured
them each a glass while looking down at her sprawled so
wantonly before him.

"Tell me all of it," he said huskily. "Every little detail."

She wriggled around on the bed, revealing all of herself to him through the thin veil of French silk knickers.
She motioned for him to come sit beside her.

"I couldn't have planned it better," she said, licking
her full red lips. "The others only stayed for one drink.
Then they got the message and left us alone in his drawing room. He was so polite and a little shy. I made small
talk and fussed over him, filling his glass and making
sure he got a fine view of my bosom. He was still hanging
back, so finally I took the initiative and asked him if he

would show me his bedroom. I practically had to drag the poor boy in there, but once he realized I was serious he got quite excited." She leaned forward to sip her champagne. Her eyes sparkled as she remembered; she placed her hand under Steven's robe, feeling him rock-hard. "He started kissing me—my God, Steven, his nose is so long it got in the way—and undressing me. Suddenly I didn't have a stitch on and he was nuzzling my breasts." She began to stroke her husband.

"I had to get him out of that ridiculous uniform—all those buttons and ties and toggles and things, no wonder they need valets—and at last, there we were. Except," she paused, "except the poor chap wasn't ready. Not like you," she said, squeezing him. "We lay on the bed and I waited for him to do it to me and absolutely nothing was happening. I could have screamed! He got quite depressed then and said it had to do with how tired he was, all the traveling and everything. He kind of turned his head away, ashamed, and then, listen to this, Steven. He muttered something about how, despite his reputation, he hadn't been able to satisfy any ladies. So," she said, "I was suddenly inspired. I did this to him." She put her mouth where her hand had been; Steven was enveloped in her lips, cold at first from the iced champagne, then hot and pulsing on him. It took a supreme effort of will to control himself, and he was almost pleased when she sat up again. "Suddenly he was hard as a rock and so proud of himself. He clambered on me, and at last we did it. It was as if it was the first time for him. I kept him going for ever so long until he started moaning. Then I felt him bursting inside me."

Steven was nearly bursting himself. He swung himself over Dimity, pulled the silk aside and plunged into her. She continued to talk, voice thick, as they rode together to the climax.

"He said no one had ever done that to him before. Fancy that! My lips were the first." She giggled. "What a secret! If I passed that secret on to some other woman and she used it right, why, she could marry the future King of England!" She moved her hips faster and faster, catching up with Steven and passing him. It was, she exulted, the greatest night of her life.

Later, they lay exhausted in each other's arms. She spoke again.

"I deliberately didn't take any precautions, Steven. And he didn't use anything. What if I'm pregnant? Do you think I'm too old to have another child?"

"Of course not," he murmured. "Not at thirty-eight. And just imagine if you are! What a secret we would have! And it would put us in the charmed circle of intimates at Court. You're a wonderful girl, Dimity, and I hope to God you're pregnant."

Roy Benbridge raised his fat hands in despair, letting the pile of papers scatter over the table. All morning he had been going through the Articles of Association of the company, records going back three hundred years, and now he was back where he had begun.

"Joanna," he said wearily, "you know I would do anything for you, anything in my power. But the Articles are absolutely clear. Even if Horatio were fit and well, he couldn't change them. It would take a unanimous vote of the board and he wouldn't get it, not for this proposal. Veronica can be his proxy on the board, but until she is twenty-one, a legal adult, that is all she can be. The moment he . . . he passes away . . . his stock is suspended. Until his heir is of age."

"And in the meantime Lapin and his cronies, aided and abetted by our sons, can do what they like with the Fleet empire," Joanna said. "Damn it, Roy, there must be something we can do. I am determined Horatio's wishes be carried out."

"The only way they can be is if he stays alive until Veronica reaches her majority." He dropped his eyes. "And, sadly, we know that is most unlikely. The poor man. It's all such a tragedy, such a loss to you and the company and to—"

"Yes, Roy," she said, cutting him off. "I have pretty well done my grieving for Horatio, you see. Now I am looking to the future—the company's future. The company must be in Veronica's hands."

"Perhaps if I talked with the boys, persuaded them to go along with their father's wishes?"

"You know Robert and Sam! They're as ruthless as all the Fleets are. They're not going to sit back for five months and let their little sister take over all that power. No, I'm going to have to find a solution."

"I wish you well, my dear," he sighed, "but I fear the situation is hopeless."

Long after he was gone, Joanna sat and thought; the sun came in through the long windows of the library and struck the ancient portraits of Fleets lining the library walls. There were no Fleet women represented there, she mused, and yet often it had been the Fleet womenfolk who had saved the company from disaster. Joanna walked to the windows and looked out onto the sound; the *Pride of Pembroke,* having just discharged a load of American tourists, was resting at anchor. She returned to the table, scribbled a note on embossed paper and rang for a footman.

"Take this at once to Captain Smutters on the *Pride of Pembroke,*" she told him. "Go in the carriage. The captain will be returning here with you."

Cable Odlum helped the old lady into her coat and bid her good night. He slumped back in his chair and looked around the surgery wearily, wishing he could prescribe something for his own depression, something like the morphine tonic he had given his last patient. But Cable knew of too many doctors who couldn't get by without morphine, who were quite addicted to the wonder drug.

All he really needed, Cable thought, was a change of pace. He had come home with such high resolve: he would hone his skills, be a great surgeon, perform lifesaving operations. Instead he had become just another pill-pusher, tending to the mostly imagined illnesses of the well-to-do. His brother's death still weighed heavily on Cable; sometimes he thought he heard Jeff's laugh and for a moment was cheered. Then the gloom returned. Perhaps, he thought, he should get away from this place; Bermuda was confining him.

"Is that it for the day, Louise?" he asked as his nurse came in. "I'm exhausted."

"Not quite, doctor. Mrs. Benbridge just arrived." Poor Dr. Odlum, thought Louise. He worked so hard, and there were always people like Mrs. Benbridge demanding more and more of his time. Louise had checked Mrs. Benbridge's medical records and couldn't see anything wrong with the woman, certainly nothing to justify all the visits she made.

"Okay, show her in," he muttered, "and then take yourself home, Louise. I'll lock up." Tonight he would tell Faith it was all over between them. Their affair was going nowhere and he felt increasingly guilty about playing around with another man's wife. There had been a time when he was sure he was in love with her, but as the months passed and her visits to him became more frequent, he had realized it was only a sexual attraction and bound to do him no good.

"Hello, Faith," he said, rising to greet her. He kissed her cheek. "You look lovely, as always."

"Fix me a drink, Cable. I've had the most awful day. That dreadful women's committee. Four hours debating whether to have a red or a white theme for the club ball. And our cook is still sick and Roy's complaining about having to take his meals at the club. It's all getting to be too much like work. I want to play."

He mixed them a martini in the specimen bottle he kept for the purpose; she was a damned attractive woman, he thought as he handed her her drink. He would probably kick himself when the affair was all over.

"Ah, that's better," she said, getting an instant lift from the astringent drink. She flopped into the consulting chair, kicked off her shoes and placed her silk-stockinged feet on his desk. She knew she had magnificent legs and enjoyed showing them off; she rubbed her left foot along the back of her right calf and saw his eyes follow the movement. He had been just a little bit casual toward her lately; tonight she would make it a very spe-

cial performance. Faith passed her glass across for another drink, then went and sat on the examining table,
swinging her legs. "It's funny," she said, pitching her
voice low, "doing it here in your surgery. There's an element of . . . I don't know, forbidden danger. Like doing
it in the kitchen, or something, when you know the servants are around?"

"You and Roy making love in the kitchen? I find that
hard to imagine."

"I find it hard to imagine Roy and me making love
anywhere," she said. "I was just talking." He was standing close to her now, and she began to gently rub against
him. She could feel his arousal. In a few minutes, he
would not be casual.

Henrietta Baseheart was pleased to see the surgery
lights still on. She thought it might be too late, and her
elbow was quite sore. She wanted badly to be able to play
in the mixed doubles tomorrow. If Dr. Odlum could give
her a shot of some kind, she was sure she would be fit
enough.

Henrietta strode through the empty outer office,
knocked lightly on the surgery door and breezed straight
in.

For an instant she thought she had burst in on an intimate examination, and made to retreat; but as she took
a good look at the scene before her, she understood. There
was Dr. Odlum, stark naked, flat on his back on the table
and Faith Benbridge mounted on him, her shoulders
thrown back and her sharp breasts swinging in the soft
light. And the expressions frozen on their faces!

"Good Lord!" exclaimed Mrs. Baseheart. "I see I've
barged in on a physiotherapy session." The laughter
came then, in great bursts which she could not control.
They looked so ridiculous, the pair of them. Faith Benbridge! Henrietta would never be able to face her across
the tennis net again without recalling this sight. She
backed slowly out of the room, still gasping with laughter, the pain in her elbow forgotten.

* * *

If only his father did not look so defeated, Cable would not have minded so much. But poor Jonas seemed to have shrunk before his eyes; such a scandal, coming after Jeff's unsavory death, had all but destroyed the once-proud head of the Odlums. The study was dark, but Cable could see the pain in his father's eyes.

"It is the ultimate disgrace," Jonas was saying. "A doctor found in adultery with his patient. I cannot believe you would do such a thing. I must blame myself. Somehow I failed you in your upbringing."

"No, Father," Cable protested firmly. "I was just weak. I—"

"I cannot bear to speak about it," Jonas said, his voice a whisper. "Benbridge has been to see me. The scandal is all over the colony. Benbridge says he will ruin you for this. He proposes reporting the matter to the British Medical Association. You will surely be struck off if he does that. I have tried to convince him no good will come of making the sordid affair public, and he has made one concession: if you leave Bermuda forever, he will make no formal complaint. He intends to remain with his wife, anyway, so I think he will be satisfied if you are removed from the scene. The *Pride of Pembroke* sails in two days, for New York and then London. I have secured you a passage. Good-bye, Cable." He lowered his head to conceal the tears.

Joanna and Veronica piled the rugs around the figure in the wheelchair; it was a cold dawn on the passenger wharf, but they had wanted to be at the ship before any of the other passengers began to board. Joanna watched as her trunks were hoisted aboard, hoping no one would notice there was only a Gladstone bag for Horatio. Captain Smutters fussed over them and waved away a pair of stewards. Smutters would personally wheel Sir Horatio to the stateroom he and Mrs. Fleet would occupy for the next six months.

"It's not worth it, Mother," Veronica said again. "Let

the boys have the company. I don't care. Anyway, someone will uncover your scheme."

"It *is* worth it," her mother said fiercely. "Because it's what your father wanted." She smiled. It was the kind of audacious plot Horatio had thrived on all his life. "Captain Smutters can be trusted, and no one else but you and I will know. Your father will be just as comfortable in the ship's freezer as in the cold ground for the next six months. And when I bring him back, only just passed away, at sea, you will be of age." She kissed her daughter. "Just stick to our story that Horatio insisted on this long ocean voyage rather than staying in a sickbed. No one can prove otherwise."

Cable too wanted to get aboard without being exposed to the other passengers. He kissed Primrose and his mother good-bye, wishing they wouldn't cry. He strode away from them toward the gangway, passing the little knot of people around the man in the wheelchair. Though he kept his eyes down, he couldn't help glancing at the invalid. Old Horatio Fleet. To Cable's expert eye the fellow appeared quite dead.

Chapter Four
(1615–)

It was stifling hot under the marquee, but they ignored the temperature; for the socially prominent ladies of Bermuda, the Governor's levee was the first occasion to parade their new season's gowns brought from London. The levee had been switched to early evening to accommodate them, but still the heat was intense, the tenth straight day the glass had moved over ninety degrees. It was even worse in the small, steamy kitchen where a flock of specially recruited women sweated over the preparation of food and plunged their red arms into the greasy washing-up water. The genteel sounds of a string quartet drifted into the kitchen to mock the women working there.

Elsie Tropp straightened up from the tub and eased her aching back. She pushed back the lank hair plastered to her forehead and looked around at her fellow laborers.

"A shilling for working in this sweatshop!" she said. "We must all be mad. I don't know why they're still debating slavery—they've already got it."

"If you don't want the money, there's plenty others who do," snapped Miss Vance, the Governor's housekeeper. "If we let the slavers have a free hand here, there'll be no work for any of you. No money to pay for porter for your idle husbands."

"At least we've got husbands, Miss Vance," Elsie re-

plied, then glanced at Sarah Odlum, silently scrubbing
utensils on the other side of the tub. "Sorry, Sarah," she
muttered, wishing she'd bitten her tongue to silence.
They all felt a vague sorrow for the gaunt figure, battling on so bravely, bringing up her bastard child alone.
Sarah Odlum knew how to cure their children—deliver
them, even, when the midwife wasn't on hand—and was
always ready with a potion or a draught when anyone
was sickly.

Sarah shrugged. In the three years since Jonas had
died in her arms, her grief had exhausted itself; now it
was just a dull, constant ache eased only by her love for
their child. She thought of Prudence alone in their cottage; she hated to leave her, but they needed the money.
Every penny counted if she was ever to obtain books to
teach Prudence about a world not bounded by the stric-
tures of Bermudian society. Sarah had no regular employment; the mistresses of the wealthy homes had been
told she was rebellious and untrustworthy. And her
ministerings to the poor returned her little except garden produce or game, no coins. She sank her arms back
into the tub and shut out the babble around her.

Lord Cavendish was feeling the heat, too. The dog days
of August were the only times he regretted leaving England for this great adventure. He mopped his brow and
slumped back in his chair set on a platform above the
sixty men and women who were milling about before
him.

"They're all enjoying themselves, Nathaniel," Cavendish said to the aide-de-camp standing beside his
chair. "A chance to dress up, parade their finery, gossip
and flirt. Although," he added, running a finger around
his high collar, "I wish we could all forge some new conventions about dress. These outfits are damned uncomfortable in this climate."

"I am sure if you gave a lead, my Lord, they would
happily throw off all their clothes and dance naked,"
Pike murmured. He enjoyed the blush his remark
brought to the Governor's cheek. Pike liked teasing the
old booby, enjoyed just skirting the bounds of insolence,

showing all the others that he, Nathaniel Pike, had the Governor's ear. "At least," he added, "I am assured by certain ladies that they have come to terms with the climate." He placed his mouth near the Governor's ear. "None of them wear those damned pantaloons here!" He grinned as the Governor's color deepened. "Perhaps we should have the musicians play a polka, set their gowns flaring."

The Governor was relieved to see Thomas Fleet bearing down on them. At least Fleet wasn't always teasing him like this damned Pike. Fleet could be just as annoying, however, constantly trying for some advantage or other, always pushing some barrow. Still in all, Fleet was of excellent stock, and would be a Lord himself if his elder brothers continued to get themselves killed off in wars and hunting accidents.

"Ah, Thomas," he said, gesturing for Fleet to sit beside him, "do you think it is all going well? It's so important, I think, to keep up standards."

"It's going very well, sir," Fleet said, easing himself into the chair. "Quite the most fashionable gathering we have seen in Bermuda, and a worthy punctuation to the civilizing influence you've been on all of us."

"We try, we try," the Governor murmured smugly. "We are still such a small settlement."

"And not capable of any growth, not here in St. George's," Fleet said. "I must show you the site for the new capital one of these days. I've had my men peg out the streets around the waterfront. There we can build something quite grand, something befitting the importance Bermuda will someday enjoy in the world of commerce."

Pike suppressed a smile. From all the papers that came across his desk, he knew that Fleet and his associates had been quietly buying up land shares to obtain the finest sites in the proposed new town. Pike had been doing the same thing.

"And where is the lovely Jessica tonight?" Cavendish asked, peering out into the crowd. "I have not seen her.

It was, you know, only for the chance to feast on her great beauty that I consented to this affair at all."

Fleet scowled. "My wife could not attend," he said. "The boy has croup, and she insists on staying by his bedside. God knows, Septimus has enough nannies and maids to care for him for a few hours. But Jessica will trust no one with him. The child has quite disrupted our lives!"

This too Pike knew. He had his spies everywhere, and they informed him all was not well in the Fleet household. Since the birth of their child, Jessica Fleet had moved in with it; Fleet, they said, had to take his pleasure with one of his servant girls.

"Do tell her I missed her," the Governor said. "I hope the boy is soon well."

"At least we have the consolation of your protégé's wife," Pike murmured. "Hilda Cobcroft becomes more pretty by the day. She looks such a fragile English rose, yet she thrives in this climate."

The three men watched as Sam Cobcroft and his wife moved toward them through the crowd. If Cobcroft the Harbormaster still had a certain diffidence about him when in the presence of those he perceived as his betters, his wife Hilda radiated assurance. Tonight she was gowned quite daringly in blush-pink taffeta cut low to reveal her high, full breasts. Her blond hair was pulled back and flowed free down her bare shoulders in the latest style from Paris. Spots of rouge, only just in fashion in London, highlighted her cheeks, and her blue eyes sparkled.

"Straighten up, Sam," she hissed as they approached the dais. "You need not cringe before the Governor; he knows what a fine job you are doing for the colony." She made a curtsy to Lord Cavendish, knowing the three men were enjoying an unrestricted view of her ample bosom.

"A wonderful party, my Lord," she said. "Who would have thought our tiny settlement could produce so many handsome men and beautiful women? Truly, this group would not be out of place in the finest London salon."

"None is more beautiful than you, my dear," Caven-

dish said. Her ripeness almost overpowered him; he
quickly switched his attention to her husband. "Well,
Cobcroft, I see your port is busy today. What is that large,
untidy vessel that came in on the afternoon tide? Didn't
look like a regular merchantman."

Cobcroft resisted looking at Thomas Fleet. He felt his
palms begin to sweat.

"The captain seemed a good enough fellow, my Lord,"
Cobcroft said. "He said he'd just taken a cargo of salt up
to Jamestown and is here to see if there are any goods
for transport to Plymouth."

"He should find a cargo easily," Cavendish said with
satisfaction. "I have been pleased with the colony's output. The hogs may not be the biggest of beasts, but
they're plentiful, and all manner of vegetables flourish
here now. If only we could get a healthy tobacco crop. I
hear Virginia is having great success with the leaf. It
would be most humiliating to have those fellows in
Jamestown cornering a market as lucrative as tobacco."

Hilda quickly switched the subject; everyone knew the
Governor was hell-bent on creating a tobacco export
trade, and no one was willing to tell him that all the signs
pointed to Bermuda's climate and soil never yielding
good tobacco.

"Our carriage detoured through the Square on our
way here," she said. "Signs of revelry were everywhere.
I think it was so generous of you to provide free porter
for the common people, my Lord."

Cavendish beamed at her, keeping his eyes on her face,
no lower.

"It wouldn't be right for us to be here enjoying ourselves and those poor wretches left out," he said. "We
must always remember we need their strong backs, their
sweat and toil, to progress. I'm proud of every one of them
for the way they have adapted to this place."

Pike raised his eyes to the canvas roof in mock exasperation and Fleet suppressed a grin. If the old buffer
would just listen to them and approve wholesale importation of slaves, there would be no need for any white
man or woman to sweat out in the sun. No wonder the

Virginians were already ahead of Bermuda in the race to produce trade goods.

Captain Harry Monserat stood on the darkened poop deck of his ship and surveyed the twenty of his crew who were allowed abovedecks. He motioned to his first mate.

"Let the others come up now," Monserat ordered. "And tell them to be damned quiet about it. We go ashore in fifteen minutes." He listened to the scurrying below and watched as forty shadowy figures emerged on deck breathing in the fresh night air after their hours in the confining hold. If the townspeople had seen these desperadoes on the *Mary Helene* when she sailed into St. George's that afternoon, they would have had every reason to be nervous.

"One more time," he cautioned the mate. "Tell 'em again what my orders are. It is not to be a complete sacking of the town. Just grab what they can carry and race back here. No prisoners. And no killing if it can be avoided. The soldiery is all up at Government House, but it will only take them a short time to realize what is happening."

The mate nodded. He had been with Monserat long enough to know what happened to men who disobeyed him. The plank was well worn by the reluctant last footsteps of such. Monserat, big and black-bearded, had been a privateer until the peace with Spain. Rather than lose his trade, he had become a pirate and now felt free to prey on anyone. But on this occasion, for the lightning raid on Bermuda, he was imposing strict limitations on what the crew could do. The mate didn't understand it all, but he would see the men complied.

They went over the side and into the longboats and rowed ashore with muffled oars. There was little need for caution; raucous laughter and singing from the tavern spilled out over the waterfront; flares outside the bar left a circle of deep blackness where the pirates came ashore, cutlasses in hand.

Even when fifteen pirates burst into the tavern, no one paid them heed at first; the Governor's free grog was the center of attention. One of the pirates had to leap onto a table and brandish his cutlass to get some attention.

"All lie down on the floor!" he shouted. "You are prisoners of Captain Harry Monserat!"

It was the name that got through to them. Monserat, as ruthless as Bluebeard, cleverer than Morgan.

They fell groveling on the floor, all but Tom Winders, drunker than the rest and suddenly caught up in a dangerous flush of bravery. He stumbled toward the pirates' spokesman and reached out to drag him off the table. But even as his hand stretched out, the pirate raised his cutlass and severed Tom's hand at the wrist.

A low moan of terror passed through the suddenly sober villagers as they saw the hideous, bloody hand twitching on the sawdust-covered floor. Winders fainted.

The pirates moved swiftly behind the trestle table and began passing out gin and rum; three of their number manhandled six barrels of porter out through the door and down to the docks. There was no attempt to rob the tavern patrons: these were clearly men with nothing worth stealing.

The rest of the pirates had split up into small gangs and were moving through the town, smashing down the doors of the more prosperous residences, plundering anything of value. They met little opposition: almost all the houses they entered belonged to the gentry who were up at Government House; the servants had nothing to gain by resisting.

Monserat himself led two of his most trusted men on a foray to the big house on the point beyond the town. He consulted a rough map before striding up the driveway and putting his shoulder to the door. A servant girl tried to block his way, but he brushed her aside and marched toward the rear of the house. As he pushed open a door he heard the servant cry out behind him. Then, from the four-poster bed inside the room, he heard another female scream. A lamp burned beside the bed and the pirate could see the couple, frozen in shock. Monserat strode forward and pulled away the tangled sheets. She was a real beauty, he thought, eyeing her long nakedness; hair

tousled and damp on her high forehead, eyes bright with
lust and fear. The man with her was pale and trembling,
a thin, weak-looking wretch. Monserat glanced over to
the chair by the bed; clerical vestments were strewn
across it. Why would a beautiful creature like this be
tumbling with a skinny little common cleric? He ran his
eyes over her again. If only he had the time . . . But he
couldn't breach his contract that way, anyhow. Monserat began to laugh, a deep rumble from down in his ample belly, a sound every bit as terrifying as his shout. He
swept the tricorne from his head and bowed low over her
nakedness, a lank of his long, greasy hair brushing her
breasts.

"Madame Fleet, I presume," he chortled. "I was not
expecting to find you in. The parson's call must have
been an unscheduled one." He pushed out his cutlass and
prodded at the quivering young man, who rolled himself
up into a ball, his pale buttocks exposed. Monserat
swung wide and brought the flat of the blade down hard.
The parson screamed and fainted as a broad red welt
sprang up on his skin. Monserat motioned his men into
the room.

"You may cover yourself, ma'am," he said. "Or else
these wretches will stand all night looking at you—as I
would love to do." He directed his men to a pair of
candlesticks and a set of pewter vessels. "And the silk
curtains too," he said. "And that will do us. It's time we
were back to the ship before the soldiers come down to
investigate all the noise that's starting up outside. Good-
bye, ma'am. I suggest you revive the little preacher fellow and send him on his way. I'm sure your husband will
even now be hurrying here to make certain you are safe."
He looked at her again, laughed and bowed, and left the
house.

Minutes after he was gone, Jessica was still shaking
with humiliation and fear. She was not afraid of Thomas
bursting in on them: since Septimus's birth he had become cold and distant to her. He was interested only in
advancing himself, always scheming to corner yet another sector of the market, always looking to add to the

chest of gold sovereigns in the cellar. She reached across
the big bed, the same one she and Thomas had so happily
romped in when things were still good.

"Stop sniveling and get dressed, Rodney," she commanded. "If my husband finds you here he'll treat you
much more roughly than our visitor. He may not love me,
but I am one of his most prized possessions."

The Rev. Rodney Haggard scrambled into his clothes,
his trembling hands making hard work of the buttons
and ties. He cursed himself for a fool for taking such
risks; as a junior minister in the church, he was in Bermuda at the pleasure of its leaders. Their patronage
could be withdrawn at any moment for something as
simple as sermonizing against what they saw as their
interests. If he were caught in adultery with one of their
wives. . . . The fit of trembling nearly overcame him.

"This has all been too much for you, Rodney," Jessica
mocked him from the bed. She threw back the sheet and
exposed her magnificent breasts. "Feast your eyes, Rodney, for the last time. I suppose I shall have to find another lover now. A pity. For a little man, you were quite
accomplished."

Up at Government House, the tumult from the village
had finally been recognized as something more than
drunken revels, and a platoon of soldiers was dispatched
to investigate. By the time they arrived on the scene, the
pirates were back aboard the *Mary Helene* and moving
out on the tide. As they left they torched a ship at anchor, but as it belonged to a Frenchman, no one on land
was concerned about putting out the blaze. The raid, all
agreed, could have been much worse.

"But," Thomas Fleet argued at the Assembly the following day, "we can take no consolation in getting off
relatively lightly. This attack proves what I have been
saying for years now. We cannot rely on the occasional
presence of a ship of His Majesty's Navy to protect us
from pirates. As our prosperity grows, we will become an
ever more attractive target. Next time they may drag off
our wives and daughters, burn our houses and slaughter

our cattle. It is obvious what we have to do: we must protect ourselves."

He listened to their mumblings. Stupid, shortsighted
tradesmen and shopkeepers, elevating themselves to
leadership in Bermuda, patently ill-equipped for the
role. And determined not to spend a penny.

"You need not concern yourselves with the cost of protection," Fleet informed them. "As we have offered in the
past, a group of us are willing to finance a ship and crew
whose sole task will be to keep Bermuda and the nearby
shipping lanes safe and free." He bowed to the Governor,
presiding over the Assembly. "My Lord, in the past you
have opposed this scheme. I would hope the dreadful
events of last night, and the worse fate awaiting us
should these brigands call again, will have caused you
to reconsider."

Cavendish patted his brow and regarded the tall figure haranguing him. There must be a fortune in this for
you, Fleet, the Governor thought. Protection indeed. I
hope it's not your private navy we'll all be needing protection from. He nodded wearily. It had been a long
night, inspecting the damage, soothing the colonists, in-
suring that the soldiery was on guard for any return visits. How dared they have chosen the night of his levee
for their assault? It was too damned arrogant of them.

"I have listened to your arguments, Honorable Fleet,"
the Governor said. "I have long opposed the setting up
of private militia, but this raid has demonstrated how
exposed we are on these far-flung islands. I am now determined to accept your generous offer. This Assembly
will grant you a charter to operate an armed ship and
will guarantee you all the facilities needed to operate
her."

A buzz went through the Assembly. Bloody Fleet! He
always got what he wanted. A few of them wondered if
it was too late to offer Fleet their support and buy into
the privateer. Others cursed themselves for not thinking of the scheme first. Because everyone knew the
charter to operate a warship was a license to steal.

* * *

"Sam is thrilled to be in the ship syndicate with Thomas," Hilda Cobcroft said. She was sitting on Jessica's shaded porch looking down on the dockside activity in St. George's. The afternoon was hot and the two women moved languidly; a servant girl brought lemonade and cool towels. "Though how we are going to afford our contribution, I don't know."

"You can always borrow," Jessica said. "Thomas is certain there's a fortune in the venture. And if there's one thing my dear husband is good at, it's making money." She frowned. "It's all falling into place very neatly for him. Too neatly, perhaps."

"What do you mean? Thomas has been promoting his scheme a long time now, and if it wasn't for silly old Cavendish he would have been granted the charter years ago."

"It was something that dreadful pirate said when he burst into the house," Jessica said. "He knew my name and knew I wasn't supposed to be home. And the fact that they took so little from our house . . . almost a token to demonstrate that the Fleets had suffered along with the rest of the town."

"Don't even think like that, Jessica. Thomas would never . . . No, I won't even put your thoughts into words. So the pirate knew your name. It means nothing. But thank God you were alone, and no one else heard him. There would have been gossip."

"Yes," Jessica said. "It was lucky there was no one there to hear him address me."

Jeremy Piggot finished cutting the stencils for the latest issue of *The Clarion*. He had labored long and hard over his news selection: the pirate raid deserved more, as did the granting of a charter for Thomas Fleet's long-discussed warship. But there were all the usual government proclamations to be fitted in, the shipping news, the tides and weather. Piggot sighed over the omissions he had been forced to make. Always a feast or a famine with the news.

Piggot loved news, the sense of power he got from

knowing just what was going on in all the big houses of
the colony. In another era he would have been the consummate gossip columnist; already in Bermuda he had
established a string of informants who peddled him the
secrets of their employers. Most of it he could not use—
Piggot knew his tenure was shaky, that he was only allowed to publish *The Clarion* at the Establishment's
pleasure—but he happily paid out coppers for the back-
stairs intelligence. And what a little cesspit the young
colony had become! While they punished commoners for
making love out of wedlock, many of the Forty Thieves
were happily bed-hopping and scarcely bothering to conceal the fact from their spouses. Piggot had heard all
about the pirate Monserat catching Jessica Fleet naked
in bed with the Reverend. He'd paid sixpence for that
juicy item. Of course he could never use it against the
Fleets themselves. They were too powerful. But it might
be useful if he ever had to put pressure on the Rev. Haggard, whom Piggot did not need to fear. And it was interesting that the pirate had known whose house he was
in, yet another sign of how far and fast Fleet's fame was
spreading. And now Fleet was to have his own privateer!
Piggot could only admire a man with such unswerving
avarice, such drive to be ever more rich and powerful.
With the ship, Fleet could easily plunder the French and
Spanish fleets which passed Bermuda; the peace was
only on paper and, as long as he didn't touch British
ships, Fleet would be thought of as just a dashing free-
booter instead of an outlaw.

Piggot was reading by lamplight in the room he occupied at the back of the printshop when the knock came.
It was very late, but then his informants usually called
after midnight when there was less chance of being seen.
He opened the door a crack and peered outside.

"Mr. Piggot, sir," the fat old woman whispered from
the darkness. He recognized Polly Farmer, a washer-
woman. "I might have something for you." He waited,
impatient. They always tried to extract payment before
passing their information and he always refused. He

made as if to close the door and the woman began her story.

"My boy Freddy, the one that's a bit slow," she said. "I managed to get him cabin boy on an American trader three months ago, as they were strangers here and didn't know about Freddy's handicap. Anyway, they sailed down to Jamaica, then up to Jamestown and back here two weeks ago. They put Freddy ashore here and wouldn't pay him what was owing, on account they said he was more trouble than he was worth." She sighed. "It's just not fair. He's a good boy and does his best. It's just he doesn't understand things unless you tell him slow."

"I don't give a damn about your idiot child, woman. Get on with your story."

"Yes sir. Well, Freddy was standing around by the harbor front when the pirates came ashore the other night. They couldn't see him hidden away among the bales of cargo. He got a close-up look at their leader, Monserat. And he'd seen him before, on the same ship in Kingston harbor."

"Who cares?" Piggot snapped. "The world knows all the pirates have a safe harbor in Jamaica where they rest up, drink their criminal profits and cock a snoot at lawful authority. A nest of pirates is Jamaica. That's not news."

"No sir, I'm sure. But Freddy said the man on the bridge of Monserat's ship in Kingston, talking and laughing and taking rum with him, was Thomas Fleet. He's real sure of that. Of course, no one else in Freddy's company knew who Fleet was, but Freddy did. He's got very good eyes, has Freddy, even if he isn't so bright." She waited expectantly. "Well, Mr. Piggot, is that story worth something to you?"

Piggot thought fast. He had to handle this carefully.

"No, Mrs. Farmer, I'm afraid it's old news. The Assembly knows all about it. Fleet was down in Jamaica trying to get an undertaking from the pirates to leave us alone, to buy them off. As we all now know, to our great regret, he failed. I think you and Freddy had best forget

about it. Fleet is most unhappy about his failure to buy
those rogues off. He would not want it to be common gossip in the marketplace, being such a proud and prominent man." He sensed the woman's disappointment; he
had convinced her. "Here, though, is a penny for your
trouble. You keep up the good work and always come to
me when you think you've got something interesting. It's
no fault of yours if your tidbits are already known to me."

He watched her move off into the night, then closed
and bolted the door and sat down to think of how he could
use this dangerous knowledge to best advantage. Thomas Fleet and his cronies hiring Monserat to scare the colony into granting Fleet his privateer's charter! Damn it,
you had to admire the cheek of the man. And you'd better handle him with kid gloves.

Sarah Odlum painfully worked the whalebone needle
through the rough hessian; the agony in her fingers increased, just as the pile of sacking waiting to be stitched
seemed to. She did not mind the pain too much but, from
her reading, she knew the disease causing it was degen-
erative. In a few more years, perhaps, she would no
longer be able to sew, or cook, to take in laundry. There
would be no way to insure little Prudence's future. The
child had to be given a chance in life, and Sarah was the
only one who could provide it. There was no free schooling, no medicine, no food and clothing for the poor of Bermuda. They were, in so many ways, worse off than they
would have been in feudal England. At least back home
there had been squires who took some responsibility for
their tenants, and there had been the common land
where crops could be grown. In Bermuda such arable
land as there was had been claimed by the Company, and
only the well-to-do could purchase shares to create homes
and farms. But Sarah did have title to the one-room cottage on the outskirts of St. George's. It had taken her two
years of working at every task available, while doing a
full day as assistant to the midwife in return for room
and board for her and the baby, to save the five pounds
to buy the cottage from Miz Fletcher. It had been worth

the trouble, she told herself as she looked through the
single window to the yard where Prudence was playing.
She loved the child so, for her happy disposition and
shining smile, for her quick intelligence—she could already spell several dozen words and count to a hundred—
and for her companionship. Because Sarah had been
completely alone from the day of Jonas's death. A few,
like Midwife Fletcher, had offered her a little kindness
but she had turned away from them. She blamed them
all for what had been done to Jonas, to her and to the
child. It didn't matter that the other poor people were
under the yoke of the Forty Thieves, the Army, the Company, the Constabulary and the Governor, just as she
was. The others had not paid the terrible price extracted
of Sarah Odlum. So Prudence was her only friend and
confidante, the only person she could take in her arms
and love. Her hatred of Thomas Fleet, personally, had
somewhat abated. She no longer saw him as the one who
murdered Jonas; they were all, collectively, guilty of that
crime and she loathed them all, and Bermuda, equally.
But she did not want her daughter to grow up with bitterness in her, and she tried to teach the child love and
caring and compassion. Even if only once, for that one
fugitive year, she had ever felt such emotions herself.

The sun was sinking fast and shadows darkened the
yard. She called for Prudence to come inside; the Novem-
ber chill, though not as damp and dreary as England's,
had a real bite to it and the croup was common. Prudence
came tumbling into the cottage, rosy-cheeked and
laughing, to hug her mother's legs. Sarah stroked the
child's fine brown hair and pulled her closer. For a few
moments, standing in the fading light, Prudence warm
against her, Sarah Odlum forgot about her circumstances and dreamed of the way it could have been: her and
Jonas, braving tempests and the great Gulf Stream to
reach America in their own boat and start a life together
with their child. Surely everything would have been fine
in America. She brushed her eyes with her sleeve.

"Don't cry, Mama," Prudence said, squeezing her. "Be

happy like me. We live in a beautiful place and we have each other. What more could anyone ask for?"

It was after midnight when Sarah tumbled from her bed to answer the banging on her door. She turned the night lamp up, pulled on a shawl and called softly, "Who's there?"

"Eileen, Miz Odlum, from the Fleet house."

Sarah looked over to Prudence who was sleeping peacefully in her trundle bed. She moved quietly across the earthen floor and opened the door.

"Be quiet," she cautioned. "You must not wake the child. What is it you want at this hour?"

"The mistress sent me to fetch Doctor, or failing that, Miz Fletcher. The baby, little Septimus, is very poorly. But Dr. Samuel has gone out to one of the ships to tend a seaman and the midwife is birthing Nancy Pheland around the other side of the island. So I thought I'd ask you to come."

"Did you, now. And why would I be going out on a night as cold as this to tend a child of the Fleets, or any of their kind? Those people don't want to deal with someone like me."

"I know, Miz Odlum. But, please, the boy is awful sick. And everyone says you are as good as the midwife and both of you better than the old sawbones."

Sarah shrugged. She would attend the boy and charge them fairly. It didn't matter what his name was.

"Where is he sickly?" she demanded. "I need to know what potions to take with me."

"His chest. He wheezes and cannot breathe. And he is hot and sweating."

Sarah began to pack her bag with the compounds she thought she might need. Then she gathered up the sleeping Prudence and wrapped her in a blanket.

"The child must come with me," she said. "You can put her in a warm place in the kitchen while I do what I can for the boy." She stroked her daughter's forehead. "At least I'm sure the Fleet hearth will be a warmer one than mine."

They trudged through the sleeping village and up the rise to the dark bulk of the Fleet home. It was an impressive place, Sarah admitted to herself grudgingly. While most of the dwellings in Bermuda had an air of impermanence to them, Fleet had constructed a large L-shaped dwelling using the local limestone and polished cedar. It was, she guessed, at least five rooms and still growing. For Bermuda, a veritable mansion. Another of the house servants let them in and took them straight to the nursery where Jessica Fleet, pale with concern, knelt by her baby's cot. She glanced up eagerly when Sarah entered, then her face fell.

"Where is the doctor?" she demanded. "Is he on his way, Eileen?"

"He's not available," Sarah said. "You'll have to make do with me tonight. But you need not worry. I think I know as much as he or Mistress Fletcher about treatments. Although that's not saying much for any of us."

"Don't dare make jokes at a time like this," Jessica snapped. "My child is dreadfully ill and needs the best attention."

"I wasn't joking," Sarah said. "Let me look at him." She knelt beside Jessica and placed a hand on the baby's tiny, damp forehead. He was burning up. She opened the heavy blankets in which he was swathed and felt the chest, straining to breathe, and heard the fluid sloshing around his lungs.

"It's the flux," she murmured, more to herself than to the frantic mother beside her. She reached into her bag and began to remove the materials she would need. She was stopped by a hand savagely gripping her arm.

"I just realized who you are," Jessica hissed. "You're the crazy woman with the child by that wildman my husband killed. I will not have you laying hands on my boy. You would kill him in revenge." She stood up, dragging Sarah with her. They were each as tall as the other and for a moment stood eye-to-eye. Then Sarah reached out and twisted Jessica's hand away.

"It does not matter who I am, ma'am," she said, all emotion removed from her voice. "Tonight I am all you have, and the boy needs treatment now. I think I can cure him, but I know I cannot if you continue to stand in my way. Leave me with him now or I shall depart."

Jessica wanted to order her from the house. It was crazy to entrust the treatment of her darling son to this woman, this figure of odium in their community. But she had no one else to call on. Thomas was out God-knew-where and the boy's condition had been worsening all evening.

"All right," Jessica said finally. "Do what you can. But if any harm comes to him from your witches' brews, you will pay, do you hear me!" She glared at the woman and swept out of the room.

The bitter years in Bermuda had taught Sarah to hold her tongue; now she contained her temper and focused all her attention on the sickly child. She called for hot water and prepared a poultice of ground mustard seeds, wrapped up in muslin. The child gave a gasping cry as she slapped it onto his bony chest, but Sarah continued to press the poultice down, forcing the heat inside the fever-wracked little body. Six times she repeated the process over the next two hours, alternately sponging the boy with a cool, damp cloth. By the time she was finished, the baby and his bedclothing were soaked with sweat.

"Tell your mistress she can come in now," she told Eileen. She unbent her joints and pulled herself up off the floor as Jessica swept into the nursery.

"My baby!" she said, rushing to the child's side. "How is he? What have you done?"

"He will be all right if you do as I say," Sarah said. "Tomorrow you can have the real doctor attend him, but by then the crisis will have passed. I have poulticed him and broken the fever. Now he needs to be kept warm and fed gruel and all the liquids he can take." She glanced at Jessica. "Is he still on your breast?"

"Of course not," she snapped. "There is a wet nurse."

"It would have been better if you had nursed him yourself," Sarah observed. "There is nothing like a mother's milk to protect a baby from the ravages of a climate like this. But that is your affair. I must go now. I have my own child to think of."

"I suppose I must pay you, then. But I repeat, if anything happens to Septimus, the wrath of God and my own will fall on you." She fumbled in a purse tied to the belt of her robe. "Here," she snapped, "a shilling for your trouble." But just then little Septimus reached out his hand and clutched her fingers; it was the first sign of recognition from him in all the long night. Jessica touched his cheek and most of the heat had gone; his breathing was easier and he seemed on the edge of normal sleep. Jessica felt tears of relief come into her eyes.

"It seems you have given him some easement of his fever," she said. "Perhaps I should better reward you. Here," she said, burrowing again into the purse. "A sovereign. And you may keep the shilling as well. A guinea for a few hours' work! We should all be so well rewarded." Jessica was blabbering; she wished she had not been so rude to the woman earlier.

Sarah would have liked to fling the coins in the woman's face, but she had learned what mattered in Bermuda—money. The guinea would procure so much of what she needed for Prudence. It was more money than she had possessed at any one time, a fifth of the value of the cottage she had paid off at a shilling a week. So she folded the heavy coins in her handkerchief and made to depart. But she could not resist a remark.

"I remember you well, Mrs. Fleet," she said. "When I was in the stocks, you argued for my release, most volubly. Not for long, to be sure, but at least you spoke up for me. My, how you have changed."

Jessica flushed. How dare this strumpet speak to her like that. She would complain to Thomas, put the baggage back in the stocks . . . except she felt Septimus still clenching her finger, the life flowing through him. And for just an instant, she felt humble.

"I am sorry, Mistress Odlum," she said. "This place has changed us all."

* * *

Thomas Fleet groaned in ecstasy as the warm lips of Hilda Cobcroft fastened to him again. He watched the trim blond head moving in the lamplight and felt her strong fingers stroking up his groin. The night had been all he had imagined, and more, and he smiled to himself as he thought how well he had planned this campaign of seduction. Poor silly Sam sent off on the morning tide to purchase cannon in Jamaica for their privateer; Thomas just dropping in on Hilda after dinner, to see she was safe and well. Then the glasses of wine and the teasing conversation, her flirting with him all the time, even when she pretended to swoon when he pulled down her bodice and at last fastened his mouth on those beautiful orbs he had so long admired. There'd been no swooning once they got down to it; he had ridden her with gusto and she had returned his lust, almost the way it had been with him and Jessica before things soured. It must be very late, he thought as she tried to bring him to one more climax. He should be going home. Not that he worried Jessica would say anything. She did not concern herself with his movements anymore. But it would not do for one so prominent as Thomas Fleet to be observed strolling home at cock's crow. He reached down and drew Hilda up to him. She was a pretty little thing and—he realized now—had always been his for the having. Because she and her husband needed his patronage; he was their ticket to riches and respectability. He would send Sam away more often.

Jessica was not in her bed when Thomas, a last cognac in his hand, entered their chamber. He felt a spurt of anger: if she was not in the house at this hour, it could only mean one thing. But surely she was too sensible to risk their good name. And certainly she no longer displayed any passion for him or, so far as he could tell, anyone else. He crossed the center hall to check on the boy. Septimus had looked poorly before the wet nurse put him down. He eased open the door and was surprised to see his wife stretched out on the floor beside the boy's cot. His presence in the nursery awoke her and she sat up, blinking in the dim light.

"So you have decided to come home at last, Thomas," she said. "I do not wish to know who she was. I am sure a great man like you can have his pick of the women of this colony. But you are lucky, my dear. Your return tonight could have been the most awful tragedy. Our son was gravely ill and neither doctor nor midwife was available. It was thanks only to the ministerings of Mistress Odlum that his crisis has passed."

Fleet crossed to the cot and looked down at the small figure asleep.

"He looks fine to me," he said. "And if all it required to cure him was a visit from that witch Odlum, there couldn't have been much wrong to begin with. You coddle this child, Jessica. I don't like it. I want him to grow up a man, a gentleman, not some mama's boy."

"Just shut up, Thomas! I will raise Septimus as I see fit. If by being 'a man' you mean you want him to grow up like you, I'll do my damnedest to see he doesn't. Look what you have become here in Bermuda—a ruthless, grasping tyrant always looking only to advance yourself. You and most of the menfolk here, you make me sick! You have been put down in what could have been paradise and you despoil it."

He had advanced on her while she spoke, and she wondered if he would strike her. She really didn't care.

"And as for your whoring around," she continued, "I suppose you think it makes you a gay blade. It doesn't, you know. It makes you a figure of fun in the community. 'Here comes the almighty Thomas Fleet with his cock straining at his codpiece.' That's what they think of you, Thomas. I could tell them so much more, of what a poor and inconsiderate lover you became after the child was born. All I needed was a little time and understanding, and you gave me neither. I think you were just looking for the excuse to go and graze in new pastures." She blinked back tears. "And so you ruined a marriage that was good, just as you would ruin an island that could be great. Go now, back to the bed we once so lustily played upon. Dream of all your conquests and all the ones to

come. I shall stay here and care for our son and pray he
does not become a model of his father."

Thomas Fleet stepped down from his carriage and
stood in the warm May sunshine gazing on the almost-
completed hull of the good ship *Protector*. She was the
biggest construction yet attempted in the St. George's
slipway, seventy-two feet from bowsprit to stern, and
the shipwrights had responded nobly to the challenge.
Fleet let his eyes wander over the sleek lines not at all
blemished by the eight bays down each side where the
cannon would be mounted. The strong cedar beams had
been securely caulked, and *Protector*, even without her
three masts and rigging, looked as if she wanted to be
out on the high seas.

"You are making good progress, Master Johns," Fleet
said when the foreman approached him. "There will be
a bonus for all your men for every day she is completed
before August thirty-first."

"It will be costing you a pretty penny then, sir. At the
rate we are proceeding, she'll be completely fitted out at
the end of July."

"Good, good. It is vital we have her out at sea defending our colony as soon as possible. I hear rumblings that
the 'peace' London sued with the French and Spaniards
is a fragile one. Either of those treacherous nations could
tear up the treaties at any moment, and we know exactly
which jewel in the Crown they would swoop on. Our precious Bermuda! But they'll think twice about it if con-
fronted with *Protector* bristling with guns and manned
by our own brave seamen."

Johns nodded. It wasn't, he thought, Europeans who
would have to think twice once Fleet had his warship
prowling the Gulf Stream. Any vessel not flying the
British Ensign would be a potential victim for Fleet. He
was a ruthless man, and the officers and crew he had already recruited were all brave and greedy. Johns wished
them well in their privateering: it was every man, and
every colony, for himself these days, and Bermuda could

surely use the spoils, no matter from where they were acquired.

A discreet cough heralded the arrival of the rotund Piggot, who stood sweating and nervous until Fleet acknowledged him.

"Ah, Piggot, come to inspect the most exciting project in Bermuda, have you? And to tell your eager readers all about it," Fleet said. "It's a pity *The Clarion* has such a restricted circulation. I wish every seadog lurking in each Caribbean sanctuary could read about the *Protector.* They would then give us a wide berth and my ship could be used for only peaceful purposes. But I'm sure after we have handed out a lesson or two her prowess will be known throughout the oceans and we will at last be left alone by marauders."

"Indeed, sir, I intend to publish a special supplement on this mighty vessel's launching," Piggot said, falling into step with Fleet as he moved away across the square. "I pray you will spare me some of your valuable time to explain to the readers your vision, to give them a glimpse of what it takes to be such a daring and forceful presence in our humble community."

"It would be my duty to do so, Piggot."

"There's another thing, sir," Piggot said, dropping his voice. "I was wondering if you might have room for one more shareholder in *Protector.*"

"Subscriptions are all but filled," Fleet said. "Of course, for someone of distinction there might be a place, not that we need any more money. Whom did you have in mind?"

"Me, sir," Piggot said, keeping just the right note of humility in his voice.

Fleet burst out laughing. "You, Piggot? Come, man, the smallest share costs five hundred pounds. I doubt a humble scribbler could put his hands on a purse of that magnitude. You are joking, surely."

"No, sir. What I had in mind was I could pay for my share over a fixed period. And the profits of the venture are going to be so great, I'm sure, my dividends would amply cover those repayments."

"Really, Piggot, that's enough nonsense. I am a busy man. I'll be glad to talk to you about the project but I'll have no more of jesting."

"It is no jest," Piggot repeated. He felt his palms go damp. He had to make his move now. He'd had such vivid visions of riches, of acceptance among the Forty Thieves, of being "someone" after his miserable life of kowtowing to others. "I thought, sir, you would wish to include me in your syndicate because I have such a close knowledge of how it came about."

Fleet said nothing. He waved a hand at Piggot, dismissing him.

"You see, sir, I have learned of your meeting with the pirate Monserat in Kingston Harbor," Piggot said. Now that he was playing his cards, the terror left him. "It has always seemed to me the pirates must have had help ashore. How else could they pick the one night for their raid when all the troops were on parade at the Governor's levee? And why should they have been so gentle with our community? No raping or killing, not a great deal stolen. And then I learned that when they entered your house—which was all but spared—Monserat knew your name and that of your wife and was surprised to find her at home."

"These are dangerous slanders," Fleet said very slowly. There was no expression on his face but his mind was racing.

"I could publish them in *The Clarion* and turn them into libels," Piggot replied. "And then we could have a trial and let the people decide where the truth lies."

"You would do that, Mr. Piggot? You, an insignificant editor, are not afraid of me, Thomas Fleet?"

"I'm afraid of you, all right, sir, but I'm more afraid of just going on in my present miserable circumstances."

Fleet laughed. "Well said, Piggot. There's a depth to you I had never imagined. Of course your story is ridiculous, but it does show you are a man of imagination and not a little courage. I think perhaps it would suit the syndicate to have a pamphleteer involved. You will be able to explain our exploits and marshal public opinion behind us. Yes, I think I can accommodate you, Mr. Piggot."

It had all been so easy, Piggot thought as he watched Fleet stroll across the square to the Harbormaster's office. It didn't matter how rich and powerful they were; back them into a corner and they responded like any timid peasant. Piggot was a happy man, visions of great prosperity dancing in his head. He repaired to the tavern to partake of a five-course lunch.

Fleet looked happy, too, as he entered Sam Cobcroft's office, but the smile vanished when the two men were shielded from the gaze of the three clerks working at their tall desks.

"We have a problem, Sam," Fleet said. "The detestable Piggot knows you and I organized Monserat's little visit. Actually, he thinks it was you acting on your own, and he wanted to expose you in *The Clarion.* But I prevailed on him to remain silent by offering him a share in *Protector.*"

Cobcroft's face paled.

"But Thomas," he gasped, "I had nothing to do with recruiting Monserat. I was aghast when you told me—"

"Sam, we're in this together," Fleet said. "It doesn't matter who set things up. Piggot thinks it was you, and I have bought his silence. For the moment. But we know blackmailers always become greedy. There will have to be a more permanent solution to this problem."

"What can we do? Oh dear, things are getting out of control. I feel I am in deep waters."

"Keep calm, Sam. I will find an answer to Piggot."

It was the simplest of plans and appealed to Fleet, but it struck terror in the heart of Cobcroft. Suddenly, from his safe and respected position as Harbormaster, he was involved in intrigue and now he was to be an accomplice in murder. But there was no way out: Fleet made that very clear. The fact that his assistance in doing away with Piggot would bind Cobcroft even more closely to Fleet only added to the appeal of the scheme for Thomas.

"But won't Piggot suspect something?" Sam argued.

"To suddenly be invited sailing on the Great Sound with us—he must know you would never consider socializing with the likes of him."

"I have talked with him this morning and he fairly leapt at the invitation. The little toad is now all puffed up with his own importance. He thinks it only natural that you and I should share his great opinion of himself. Just the three of us out on the sound, far from prying eyes. It will be quite safe, Sam."

Indeed, Piggot suspected nothing. He basked in his new status as he rode between the two men at dawn the next day. There was no one stirring as they left town and trotted through the sleeping countryside to the slip where Fleet's handsome pinnace awaited them.

"We must do a lot of sailing together, Piggot," Fleet said when they had stowed their food and wine aboard and made ready to go out on the calm water. "We will show you the ropes. It wouldn't do to have one of our syndicate a total landlubber. Eh, Sam?"

Cobcroft grunted. As the dread task approached, he was beginning to feel awfully ill. Fleet pretended not to notice his pallor, and continued to joke with Piggot as they sailed out on the sound, heading for a group of deserted islands, far from prying eyes.

About noon they dropped anchor in a secluded cove; it was one of the prettiest spots in Bermuda, a sheltered pink sand beach surrounded by lightly wooded hills. The sun was high and hot and they were grateful for the shade of the sail.

"Let us see what my housekeeper has provided," Fleet said as he placed the hamper between them. Two roast chickens, a leg of mutton, bread and cheese, preserves and a jug of wine emerged. Piggot's eyes bulged at the richness of the repast, but he restrained himself from falling on the food. Instead he ate delicately, keeping an eye on his companions to make sure he did not offend them in any way.

"Most excellent, sir," he told Fleet when he at last wiped his lips. "And the wine is remarkably good. Not English, I would wager."

"No," Fleet said, "it's from France. For all their faults, the Froggies do make the best wines. And you shall be drinking them by the barrel when the profits start flowing from our ship, Mr. Piggot." He raised his glass to the fat man. It was the signal, but Cobcroft didn't move. Annoyed, Fleet raised his glass again. "Your health, Mr. Piggot, and prosperity for us all."

Piggot beamed, burped and drained his glass.

"Ah, Sam," Fleet said softly, "it seems you have no stomach for this." He stood up and suddenly pointed to the shore. "Look, Piggot! That strange bird on the beach. What could it be?"

Piggot stared intently at the shore but could see nothing. Instead, there was blood in his eyes and he could hear the bones in his skull crushing against each other where the heavy iron spike had slammed down. He pitched forward onto the deck and felt the warm, smooth wood against his cheek. He wondered what was happening to him, and then the pain swamped him and he could think of nothing else.

"Here, Sam," Fleet ordered, handing the spike over. "Finish him off at once."

Cobcroft thought he was going to vomit. He looked down at the spreading blood and the broken shape of Piggot's head. He gazed imploringly at Fleet but the older man would not let him off. Cobcroft raised the spike and brought it crashing down, once, twice, three times. Bones and blood and wisps of hair flew around the cockpit, but he went on raining blows. It was only when Fleet's hand stopped him that he saw the carnage he had created. Cobcroft threw down the spike, hurried to the side of the boat and was violently ill.

Fleet watched the heaving shoulders and nodded approvingly. Sam Cobcroft would not forget this day and the deed; he would be an even more loyal follower and that much easier to manipulate. Fleet slowly gathered the ropes and canvas and iron pieces he had stowed in the locker and began to bind and weigh down the still warm body of the editor. When he was finished, he called

to Cobcroft to lend a hand; they wrestled the form over
the side and watched as it sank into the deep blue water.

"The sharks and barracuda will pick him clean," Fleet
said. "There will be no more editorials from the pen of
Mr. Piggot." They washed the blood from the deck with
bucket after bucket of seawater; the bilges ran red. They
then sailed home, saying nothing to each other.

Everyone turned out for the launching of *Protector;* the
Governor made a speech, cut a ribbon and they all
cheered. For, despite the widespread belief in the community that the ship was just another way for Fleet to
get richer, it did inspire confidence in them all. Surely
now Bermuda would be safe from marauders and she
would have a chance to share in the treasures being
transported from the Indies to Europe. All the young
men of the colony, too, welcomed the chance to get away
from the dead-end land jobs. The thirty permanent crew
were considered the elite of the young colonists, and their
fortune and future seemed assured.

The Rev. Rodney Haggard was at the launching,
wearing his new hat as editor of *The Clarion.* His vicar
had had to argue long and forcefully before Haggard had
taken over from the vanished Mr. Piggot: it was, the
vicar said, a chance to spread the word of the church in
the community newspaper. And to curry favor with the
people who ran Bermuda and who had not, so far, displayed any great interest in the pursuit of godliness, not
if it got in the way of profitability. Haggard took copious
notes on this day, not missing a word of his vicar's blessing that fulsomely praised the vision and generosity of
newly knighted Sir Thomas Fleet who had endowed this
Christian ship and its Christian sailors; he also scribbled descriptions of the gowns the colony's leading ladies had selected for the grand occasion. The words ran
together when they came to Lady Fleet; she was so beautiful, so striking, so imperious, that Haggard could not
believe he had ever shared her bed. Jessica herself had
put the affair quite out of mind and she looked through

Haggard as though he were not there. Which to her, he wasn't.

"Parish Notes"
From the Royal Bermuda Clarion,
August 14, 1622

After the recent King Tides many objects of interest have been cast up. The fisherman Eugene Gower presented to the authorities part of a human skeleton at the place in the Great Sound known as Paradise Cove. Some remnants of rope were still affixed to the bones, giving rise to the belief the unfortunate one may have been a pirate who fell out of favour and was cast into the Sound. It is known that before the coming of English civilization to these islands, pirates did occasionally put into the Great Sound to shelter from tempests. The bones were placed in a hole in the ground without ceremony as there was no means of knowing whether they were of a Christian or otherwise.

The Governor has decreed all water for human consumption must henceforth be boiled. His Excellency's decision is sparked by recent isolated outbreaks of the Yellow Plague. There is some reason to believe the Plague may be spread by unclean drinking water piped from too close a proximity to the nightsoil dumps. A plague of a different kind, the most ferocious and fearless rats, is also reported. The Governor has decreed a bounty of three pence will be paid for each dozen rat bodies delivered to the Old Customs Shed at St. George's. Harbormaster Cobcroft has ordered all ships docking here to place shields on their lines to prevent more of these vermin coming ashore.

A Ball was held recently in the new Mansion of the Hon. Nathaniel Pike, to celebrate his appointment as Agent General. The Mansion was much remarked on, built as it is on a rise above the Great Sound and enjoying a finer outlook and more gentle breezes than any *house in St. George's and its environs. Many who attended were overheard to remark how suitable this new area would be for a second town in Bermuda. Port facilities may be even more felicitous than those existing at St. George's. A most honored guest at the Ball was Lord Marley, who made the long journey from Plymouth to personally congratulate the new Agent General and deliver him of a gift: two fine blacks already trained to serve in the house. Lord Marley, who has extensive shipping interests, will stay in the Colony for several weeks as a guest at Government House.*

Sir Thomas Fleet announced the commissioning of his eighth vessel, the Septimus, *described as a merchantman for the developing salt trade out of South America. Sir Thomas, who continues to demonstrate his great faith in the future of trade for Bermuda, intends to institute regular routes between our Colony, the Virginias and Europe. He has the stamp of approval of Lloyds of London, impressed as they are with the absence of harassment suffered his ships due to the commanding presence of Sir Thomas's armed escort vessels.*

There was a great commotion in St. George's ten nights ago when rumors were spread the Spaniards had landed in the hills behind town and were marching to sack the settlement. These malicious rumors caused panic among the townspeople and it was stilled only when the supposed invaders staggered into the town and were revealed as some drunken British sailors who had purloined a barrel of rum and consumed it in the hills. They were all whipped and returned to their ship in irons. The Governor repeats that there is no need to walk in fear of the Spanish invasion. The Colony's own forces and those at her disposal through the good graces of Sir Thomas Fleet render Bermuda unassailable. Rumormongers are warned of the whip-

*ping penalty awaiting any who spread consternation in
the community.*

*The Government has made an Order prohibiting the
taking of Sea Turtles or their eggs. This has been done
because the valued sea creature has all but vanished
from our shores. It is believed they will return in abun-
dance soon and the conservation Order will then be reviewed.*

Chapter Five
(1925–)

Primrose Odlum spotted the tall figure of her brother standing in the crowd on the dock; she waved her silk scarf until Cable saw her, then hurried down to the first-class gangway to be among the first ashore. When she was finally in his arms she found herself crying unstoppably.

"Dear Primmy," he said, patting her head, "I thought you were supposed to be the tough business lady, and here you are, blubbering like a schoolgirl." But he held her tightly and had to blink back a tear himself.

"Oh, Cable," she said. "It's been so hard, coping with everything. Mother's old and tired; you and I are the only ones left. It seems only yesterday we were a happy family, a whole family."

He summoned a porter for her bags and they moved out into the West Side sunlight to the waiting cabs. The noise, the crowds, the harsh smell of the autos almost overwhelmed her, and she clutched his arm. She had read up on New York but the reality was so much more than she had imagined.

"It's a little scary at first, after quiet Bermuda," he said, helping her into a taxi. "And your visits to London won't have prepared you for this city." He leaned back, hands behind his head as they jolted off through the teeming traffic. "But it's the greatest city in the world, Primrose. Anyone with a little capital and a lot of gumption can make a fortune here."

105

"Is that what you're doing, making a fortune?"

"Heavens, no. I make a very comfortable living at the hospital and I'm happy." He grinned at her. "And I don't have to worry about piling up the millions, anyway. You've turned Kosmos into a gold mine."

"I don't think Daddy would have approved of all this rapid expansion," she said. "He always liked to think of it as a nice little family company that accidentally made money. And now we've got a hundred employees in the Bronx factory alone."

"I'm glad you've finally decided to make a visit to New York. I'm sure the people running the operation for you are fine, but they're not family, are they?"

"They're doing a wonderful job, Cable. The figures, since we launched the Bermuda range, are fantastic. We'll gross ten million this year. All because the women adore our suntanned look." She gazed out the window at the crowded sidewalks. "I'm such a provincial! I still can't get used to girls showing their knees. And all the makeup they wear! No wonder we're making a fortune."

"Are you really happy running Kosmos? I feel guilty sometimes, being able to lead the life I want while you're stuck at home minding the family treasury. Up here life seems so full and rich. And as an Odlum, particularly in my profession, you can do no wrong in New York. West Side General has an honor roll of Odlums who've been resident surgeons."

"Yes, I'm happy. I like doing the kind of things they think a woman can't do. If I didn't run the company I'd be expected to marry, give tea parties and play tennis."

"What about marriage? There must be so many suitors. You're an awfully pretty girl, Primrose."

"There's no one." She shrugged. "I'm too busy for romance, and even if I weren't, there isn't exactly a wide field to choose from in Bermuda." She patted his hand. "Don't look worried, Cable. I'm only twenty-four. Plenty of time to avoid being an old maid. But tell me about your own family."

"Muriel's wonderful. You'll meet her tonight. I thought we'd just have a family dinner, give you a chance to recover from the voyage. And the children are allowed to stay up past their bedtime to meet you. They're very excited—an aunt from Bermuda sounds quite exotic to them."

The cab deposited them at the Waldorf-Astoria, and Cable accompanied her up to her suite. She'd insisted on staying at a hotel rather than with him and his family; she had a lot of business to conduct and, anyway, she wanted to be independent on this trip. The suite was big and airy, facing onto Park Avenue. There were flowers, chocolates and French champagne from the management.

"I thought you were under the dreaded Prohibition," she said, twirling the bottle in its ice bucket.

"Prohibition's just a joke," he said. "They'd repeal it now, but everyone's having too much fun with it. It's amazing what tastes good when you're drinking in some little speakeasy. Forbidden fruits, you know. The public even vicariously enjoys the violence associated with it all. They figure bootleggers only kill each other." His eyes clouded for an instant. "You and I know better. Poor bloody Jeff. It still hurts."

When he had left her to rest up for the evening, Primrose ran a bath and let the hot water relax her; she was very nervous about this trip, the first time she had stepped outside the safe confines of Bermuda since she had taken over the running of Kosmos. It was all right at home—just the family name was enough to insure things were done as she wanted. But New York was a different story entirely.

Cable came for her at six P.M. and they took a cab for the brief journey to his house on Beekman Place. The family car and driver, he explained, always stayed at the Hudson River estate; parking and maintaining a car in Manhattan was quite impossible. It made her feel a little smug about Bermuda, where automobiles were still banned.

Even to Primrose's untutored eyes, the Beekman Place house established that Cable was doing very well indeed. The house, tall and narrow, was of soft white stone, glowing in the evening light. There was a butler and three maids, and everything had the same air of genteel elegance she had remarked on in London. Here, overlooking the East River, the rough vitality of New York was not allowed to intrude.

Primrose liked Muriel from the start. Cable's wife was a lively young woman with dark brown lustrous hair. She was the youngest daughter of a prominent Boston family, now happily devoting her life to her husband and Tom, the three-year-old, and now Frances, the baby.

"I'm so glad you finally made it here," Muriel said, hugging her. "I felt terrible that we couldn't come when your father passed away. But Cable works so hard at the darned hospital, and you know how long the trip to Bermuda is."

Primrose gave Cable a quick look; at least he had the grace to blush. His wife apparently didn't know of the disgrace concerning his departure from Bermuda, and the threat still preventing his return.

"One of these days they'll be flying airplanes down to Bermuda," Muriel went on, "then we'll be able to visit as often as we like."

There was another guest that evening, but he too was family. John Chester and the Odlums decided they were second cousins. He was a lawyer—thirty, successful and absolutely charming.

"But you must come to Bermuda," Primrose told him as they chatted over dinner. "Bermuda's in your blood. You're an Odlum."

He shrugged. "I almost did make the journey four years ago. I was in love with Veronica Fleet and was heading down there for the grand announcement of our engagement. Out of the blue she canceled everything—no explanation. I suppose it was something to do with the family feud. She and I used to laugh about it when we were in college together. I guess it wasn't all that funny."

"Family feud?" Muriel asked. "How quaint. I thought they only had those kind of things in the boondocks. The Hatfields and the McCoys."

"My dear little Boston princess," Cable said, smiling.

"How protected you Americans are. Your families, quite correctly, put aside passions and spent the past three hundred years making money. In Bermuda we are more European in our outlook; our hatreds still run deep. John was a victim of our family passions."

"Poor Veronica," Primrose said. "You know she's thrown herself into running the family empire? She had to defeat her brothers before she could take over the job, but she's making a great fist of it."

"You see each other, then?" John Chester was longing for news of Veronica and didn't mind showing it. "You're in similar situations, each running the family enterprises. How is she?"

"She's not married," Primrose said smoothly, "and as far as I can tell she likes what she is doing. But I don't really know Veronica. We nod when we meet, but there is still this dreadful gulf between us. The Odlums and the Fleets," she shrugged.

It was, she decided, rather nice dealing with Americans. They didn't act as though it was impossible to take a young woman in business seriously. David Bendrodt, her New York managing director, had lined up a succession of appointments for her, and she was impressed with the way everyone got straight to the point. The agency people, the distributors, the franchisers—it wasn't like doing business in Bermuda or London, where half the day was devoted to niceties.

"Just one more and we can call it a day," Bendrodt said as he tidied papers on the desk in her suite. "This one is Richard Billings, the guy I wrote you about. A Wall Street hotshot, made fortunes for all his clients in the market." He laughed. "I know that's not very hard these days, the way the market's gone through the roof, but Billings is something special. He's been doing a profile of our company and wants us to go public, figures there'll be a heap in it for you without your surrendering any control."

Richard was another pleasant surprise; she was expecting a money hustler but got a charming young man

in his late twenties, who quickly and wittily stripped
away all the jargon of stock brokering and laid out for
her a plan whereby Kosmos New York could be floated
on the market while leaving her Bermuda company intact and independent.

"The market's got at least a few years of steam in it,"
Billings said. "It would be a shame for a growth company like yours not to take advantage of it. Your Bermuda Line is the right product at the right price at the right
time. If the money you raised going public went into expansion, you could have an empire stretching across the
U.S."

David Bendrodt nodded enthusiastically, then continued to scribble figures on a legal pad. Primrose listened
some more, understanding the proposition but, for now
at least, not seriously considering it. Because something
was happening to her, a sensation she had never known
before. She watched the way his lips moved, the tilt of
his head, the lock of his curly fair hair falling over his
forehead. And then her dark eyes met his blue ones and
their gaze held. Bendrodt looked up into the silence.

"Are you okay, Primrose?" he asked. "You look
flushed. I'm afraid I've loaded you down with too much
business your first full day in New York." He glanced at
his watch. "Anyway, I've got to get back to the office.
We've got a sales meeting." He stood up. "Can I drop you
anywhere, Richard?"

"Please stay awhile, Mr. Billings," Primrose said. "I'll
order tea. I want to hear more of your proposal."

When they were alone she felt awkward, girlish. But
he continued to talk easily, as if he could not feel the
electric current running between them. Was it only her?
She knew so little about love, yet was so certain this was
what she felt. Then the expression in his eyes when their
glances met . . .

"Anyway," he was saying, "I don't want to weigh you
down with too much detail at this stage. It's a very big
decision. But, if you do go along with the scheme, my
company would be honored to underwrite the whole
thing." He listened to himself and marveled he could still

discuss business in such a rational tone. Because the whole time in the suite with her, his pulse had been racing. She was beautiful, yes, but there was much more to her than beauty. Feminine but strong, so in control despite being a young woman in the world's most testing city. She seemed different from the girls he'd known, the silly, vapid creatures of the Jazz Age. Love at first sight. Not him. He stood up to leave but the wrong words came tumbling out.

"Look, I don't suppose you're free for dinner tonight. I'm sure you've lots of people to see in the city. But if you were at a loose end . . ." He blushed. "Oh, hell, it was just a silly idea."

"Why, that would be delightful, Mr. Billings," Primrose said. "I had resigned myself to having something sent up by Room Service. I'm not nearly confident enough to go out into the streets of New York on my own."

"Please call me Richard," he said. "And may I call you Primrose?"

He arranged to come for her at eight o'clock and she needed all that time to prepare. She was glad now she had packed the pale blue silk from Paris; it set off her light tan. She piled her hair high and held it with a diamond clip and studied her reflection in the glass. She grinned suddenly. She was going on a date with a high-powered New Yorker. She should be worrying about what to say, how to conduct herself; instead, all she could think of was seeing Richard Billings again.

They had dinner at the Algonquin, the year's most fashionable spot, and she relaxed in the dignified atmosphere and attentive service. Around them was a warm hum of conversation, tuxedoed men and gowned women all looking handsome, confident and wealthy. She gazed through the candlelight at Richard, dashing in his white tie and winged collar.

"I feel like I'm in the center of the world," she said. "New York makes Bermuda so small and quaint." She watched the waiter deftly boning her quail. "It's funny, when you think my home was settled fifty years before there was even a village on Manhattan; and here you are, the world capital of finance and communications and the arts. I don't know how I'll ever settle down again."

"Don't be fooled," he said. "We lucky ones move in a rarefied world. For most of the people every day is a struggle. The city has grown too big too fast." He grinned at her. "But for now, it's the most exciting place anyone could be."

After dinner they walked up Broadway, mingling with the emerging theater crowds, then on to a jazz club on 54th Street. They drank martinis from coffee cups; sat enthralled as the rich chords of "Rhapsody in Blue" washed over them; danced close together on the tiny floor. She didn't want the night to end, but suddenly it was two A.M. and the tables around them were emptying.

"Do you want to come in?" she asked as she fumbled for the key to her suite. She knew she was breaking all the rules but she didn't care.

"No, I'd better not," he said. For the first time since they met there was sadness in his eyes. He took her hand and raised it to his lips. "We both have busy days to-morrow. I just want to say this has been the nicest eve-ning of my life."

She watched him retreating down the wide corridor to the elevators.

"Will you call me tomorrow?"

He turned and waved. "Just try and stop me."

Sam Fleet stumbled over something on the bedroom floor and suppressed a curse; in stockinged feet he edged through the dark to the sanctuary of his dressing room, where he snapped on the light and examined his rav-aged features. God, he looked like an old man already. Have to cut down on the boozing, he told himself as he found the bottle of cognac and poured himself a stiff one. There was lipstick on the collar of his dress shirt and he pulled out the studs and cast the evidence in the laundry basket. There were enough fights with Ginny without giving her ammunition. He finished the brandy, stripped off the rest of his clothes and turned off the light before

silently going back into the bedroom and feeling his way
between the sheets. He gingerly explored the rest of the
bed with his foot; she wasn't there. He smiled in the dark
and clambered from the bed, the need for silence gone,
the advantage his for once. Sam pulled on a silk dressing
gown, turned on all the lights and fetched his bottle.

It was an hour before Ginny appeared, at first trying
to slip noiselessly into the room, then defiant when she
saw him sitting there waiting for her. She pushed back
a lock of hair from her forehead, smoothed her dress
down over her long legs and made to step around him.

"How thoughtful of you to wait up for me, Sam. But
I'm quite exhausted, so if you're looking for a row it will
have to wait until morning. I'm just going to slip into the
bath . . ."

He grabbed her roughly by the arm and his other hand
snaked under her dress to find the nakedness there.

"You forgot your knickers," he growled. "Did you
leave them with someone as a souvenir?" He twisted her
arm harder. "Which of your dashing young men was it
tonight, you whore?"

He was really hurting her now and she tried to twist
away. Then she slashed at him with her long, red nails
and he had to release her as blood sprang from his cheek.
For a moment they faced each other, breathing hard. She
watched his pale blue eyes and waited for the slap as his
open palm rose up.

They fell on each other, kicking and scratching and
biting, rolling around on the plush carpet. He was on top
of her, forcing her down, his robe open and his weapon
big and hard. She heard her dress rip as he plunged into
her brutally, and she fought back, wriggling her hips
away from him. But he had her pinned down and he resumed the assault, battering an entry, grunting as he
found her core and driving on to a furious climax. She
heard her own cries as she raked his back with her nails
and her hips began to move against the crushing weight
of him.

At last they rolled apart and lay on the floor, panting.

"That dress was a Paris original, you bastard," she said.

"I'll buy you a new one," he said. "Do you want a drink?"

"Why not," she said, not bothering to cover her nakedness as he climbed to his knees and crawled across to the side table where bottle and glasses rested. God, his back was a mess. It would be days before he could show himself in a bathing suit. But the violence was the only way they could rekindle their lust these days; only physical and verbal abuse brought them to a peak anymore.

"We're a strange pair, aren't we," she said as she accepted the brandy. She touched her cheek. "I hope there won't be a bruise there in the morning."

"Ma'am, I'll not be responsible for this dangerous voyage," Henry Smutters insisted. "Sure, we have to broaden our trade now the American market is closed to our produce. And shipping fine wines from Europe to Canada makes good sense. But not in that ship and not with the crew your brother is insisting on."

Veronica Fleet sighed. Smutters was her senior captain, but he didn't understand the family pressures she had to cope with. Robert, always smarting over the fact that he wasn't company chairman, had demanded the chance to run the cargo division. His duties at the Tropicana were not arduous, they all admitted. The hotel was a roaring success and ran itself.

"You can't deny him this, Veronica," her mother had said. "Perhaps the challenge of organizing new routes and new cargoes will be the making of him. You know how I worry about the boys."

Joanna Fleet was old now, and frail. Veronica wouldn't have done it, but she owed her mother this. Joanna had secured the chairman's job for her, enduring the macabre months with Horatio's body in the ship's freezer until Veronica had reached her majority and the body could be brought home and the death announced. Yes, she owed her mother.

"You are *not* responsible, Captain Smutters," she said now, rising from the desk and standing beside him at the big office window overlooking the docks. "Robert has charge of the cargo division and the responsibility is his and, in the end, mine. I appreciate your counsel but I cannot act on it even if I wanted to."

Slowly, he nodded. There was no point in arguing with Veronica Fleet; she could be even tougher than old Horatio. Smutters had a great admiration for the plucky young woman; it wasn't her fault the cargo division was in a mess and losing money. It was just bad luck, the kind you always had to expect from time to time if you made your living from the sea. But it was wishing bad luck on yourself to send the worst ship in the fleet, with the least trustworthy captain and crew, on such a crucial voyage. The cargo alone was worth a hundred thousand pounds.

"The insurance is all taken care of, I trust?" he said carefully.

"Mind," she laughed, "that you don't put a hex on the ship. But yes, the *Pride of Sandys* has just been revalued and is carrying adequate coverage. Thank God we enjoy such a good reputation with Lloyds. They didn't require their own survey to be done."

"Lucky for us. I wouldn't even sail in the *Sandys,* much less insure her."

"Come now, Captain, it's not that bad. And after this voyage we'll put her in dock for a complete refit."

"She needs it."

She could see Robert now, down on the docks with Brian Johns, the *Sandys'* skipper. They would be sailing in a couple of days, loading the wine for Canada at Marseilles and general cargo for America at London. She watched the tall, thin white-haired figure of her brother and sincerely wished him well. It was so hard, running this giant operation on her own; if poor Robert could finally pull himself together and succeed in this venture, she would use him more, bring him back into the company as a full family member. And then she'd go to work on Sam.

For a moment she was heartened by a vision of them

all pulling together, all Fleets, proud and prosperous.
That was the gift she wanted to give her mother while
there was still time. Joanna had suffered so much by
marrying a Fleet. Old Horatio had been a stern, difficult
man to live with, and the boys had been sickly when
young and a disappointment to their parents when they
were grown. So if Robert could make a go of it . . . Well,
she figured, it was unlikely Sam would ever be worth a
damn. Marrying Ginny Winders and securing a proxy
over the Winders' shares in the Fleet company was about
all they could expect Sam to contribute.

The ship's clock on her wall struck noon, and Veronica
suddenly decided she would be like the rest of Bermuda
and celebrate this holiday, Somers's Day. The streets of
Hamilton had been deserted all morning, with most of
the populace away to St. George's to see the East End v
West End cricket match. She hadn't been to one in years
but recalled how much fun they had been when she was
a schoolgirl; she ordered her carriage brought around to
the front and told her driver to take her to the Cup
Match.

"You put your money on the East End," Jethro ad-
vised her as he closed the door of the carriage, giving her
a toothless smile. The old black man had been driving
her family for decades. "That Billy Youngblood, now,
you count on him to make a century. And West End's got
no bowlers to speak of." She listened to him chatter on
as they rolled out of town and onto the narrow road
winding through cool, green palms and flame-colored hibiscus. It was good to be out of the office. Her island was
so beautiful, but lately she'd been cooped up inside. She
must make more free time for herself. For an instant she
felt a wave of self-pity. Here she was, amid all this
beauty, alone. No one to share it with, no one to make all
the striving worthwhile. She never let herself think
about John Chester and the months in which she had
known love. But it was always there in her heart, just as
the horror of realizing what she had done to her father
was always there.

She cheered up when the carriage rolled onto the edge

of the neatly clipped cricket ground; it was just as she
remembered Cup Match—the bright marquees provid-
ing shade, the ladies of the colony comfortable in lawn
chairs, their menfolk in bright blazers and white flannels standing at the bar and occasionally acknowledging a well-played stroke on the field. Across the other side
of the ground, in rough, temporary stands, were the
black spectators whooping and cheering, sometimes
running onto the pitch to press a reward—a chicken, a
pitcher of beer, a handful of coins—into the hands of a
player who had done something particularly skillful.
Veronica had always thought the Negro side of the
ground had more fun than the white preserve.

She moved through the shaded tables, nodding greetings, and accepted a seat with the Basehearts. Their butler brought her an iced glass of punch and a plate of cress
sandwiches; for an instant she felt half her age, just another of the trilling young girls dashing among the tables. Before the war, before everything had started to
change.

"It's been a jolly good match so far," Jamie Baseheart
said. "These fellows get better at the game every year."
There was polite applause under the canopies and a roar
of approval from the black side of the ground as the red
leather ball went sailing over the boundary rope on the
full. Play stopped as Billy Youngblood, the batsman, was
mobbed.

"That's his fifty runs up in even time," Baseheart said.
"He and his family will have a lot of goodies to take home
tonight." Veronica watched as the batsman's wife and
children carried off the spoils and the match resumed.

"He works for us, doesn't he, Jamie?"

"A porter at the Tropicana," he said. "Good stamp of
boy, too. Not like some of the black bastards, always
causing trouble. They're still making noises about a
union, you know. All the hotel workers. But," he added
hastily, "don't you worry your pretty head about that
stuff. Robert's got his finger on it."

She would have snapped at him for the remark; like
most of her fellow directors, he tended to patronize her.

But it was too nice a day to get into a quarrel with her cousin, who was really quite a dear old booby.

"Where *is* Robert?" he inquired. "I didn't think he'd miss a Cup Match."

"Working with the *Pride of Sandys*," she said. "There's a lot to be done to get her ready for such a long journey."

"We all have high hopes for it. And Robert's just the chap to pull it off," Baseheart said. "I'm sure he'll soon have the cargo division profitable."

Veronica let her eyes roam the perimeter of the cricket ground. Off to her right was the area where the working-class white families gathered; like the black stand it was much more raucous than the Forty Thieves' dignified enclosure. Some of the young men, she saw, had actually removed their shirts and were sunning themselves in blatant defiance of social custom. She couldn't miss Tom Jepson: his massive torso glowed brown in the sun, his long hair curled down his shoulders. She saw him quite often around the docks. Since he took over his father's business, he had achieved a lot of success as the maker of fine racing sails; Tom's sail loft was employed by sportsmen from as far afield as Newport, R.I. When they did meet she always nodded and Tom touched his cap. He seemed to understand and accept the distance between them. But Veronica, watching him now, his muscles rippling as he horsed around with his companions, could not forget their youthful days together, the wrestling in the sand . . . she shivered in the heat.

Billy Youngblood took stance as the bowler came thundering in at him from the other end of the pitch; the ball carved through the crystal-clear air at some seventy miles an hour, but Billy's sharp eyes easily tracked its course. He went forward, driving hard with his heavy willow bat, and the ball crashed through the fieldsmen for another boundary. He straightened up, wiped the sweat from his brow and waved his bat to acknowledge the new round of cheering from the grandstand. His batting partner, John Clay, strolled down the pitch to confer with him.

"When are you going to give me a chance to score a few runs?" John laughed. "You're going to win this match single-handed, the way you're going. Give me a chance to impress the ladies."

"Okay. We'll just run a single off the next ball and you can have a shot at them," Billy said. "This fellow bowls very fast but he's got no guile. Just hit him with a straight bat."

Billy was feeling very good. He loved the adulation in his son's eyes each time the four-year-old trotted out onto the pitch to join the other supporters congratulating him. Matthew needed someone to look up to; God knew there were few enough heroes for a young black boy in Bermuda, Billy thought. He could feel the banknotes and loose change in his pocket pressed on him by those who had bet he would get past fifty runs; Amy would have plenty of food for the pot for days to come, what with the chickens and lobsters and roast pork the fans had presented him with. Billy Youngblood stood tall and proud on this one day of the year when white Bermuda paid any heed to its blacks. He smiled as John smote a ball to the boundary. At this rate they'd have the match over in another hour and they would all adjourn to the church hall for feasting and singing and the discreet consumption of Jamaican rum. It was a pity he had to work the midnight shift at the Tropicana, but it couldn't be helped; he would just be very careful he didn't drink too much in the post-match celebrations.

Robert Fleet sneezed; it was hot and dusty in the wharf shed, the sun beating down on the tin roof and raising the temperature inside to over one hundred degrees. He preferred to have their meetings at night, but the afternoon of Cup Match was such a perfect time for them to get together without worrying about being discovered. He looked around the shed at the dozen men gathered there. Not an inspiring lot, Robert thought, but soon their numbers would grow. There were a few missing members and they would be reprimanded. At least these men who were willing to give up the delights of a public holiday were like him; they could no longer stand watching a bunch of niggers showing off, strutting, on the noble field of cricket. Robert sneezed again and brought the meeting to order.

"Vigilance!" he snapped, pounding the tally clerk's desk in front of him. "We must be vigilant at all times. Ian Smith was vigilant last month and saw a Negro from St. David's jostle two white children in Front Street. As you know, we tracked that nigger down and gave him a sound whipping. But there is still much escaping our notice. A cow was stolen from Brown's Farm and has still not been traced; intimate garments were taken from a lady's washing line in Paget; three windows were smashed at the Oceanic Club. All this was the work of the Negroes and they must be made to pay for it. Soon, the way they are breeding, they will outnumber the white and Portuguese residents of these beautiful islands. They must be constantly reminded of their position." He produced a canvas seabag. "I have received a new collection of literature from our friends in Georgia. I want you all to study these tracts. They are the way to salvation for Bermuda."

The men crowded around the desk, leafing through the poorly printed pamphlets. They were particularly taken with the line drawings of hooded men around burning crosses.

"Why can't we dress up in white sheets, Mr. Fleet?" Cyril Arkwright whined. "It would scare the hell out of the niggers, when they see us riding through the night dressed up like these fellows are."

Robert regarded young Arkwright with barely concealed loathing. He was a wharf laborer, unwashed and uneducated. Not far removed from a nigger himself. Robert wished he didn't have to deal with such lowlifes. Speed the day when more of the leading citizens realized the cancer that was in their society and joined up with Robert's band.

"I have explained before," he said impatiently, "that Bermuda is not Atlanta. If we started lumbering around in costumes—no matter how much terror they would strike in the blacks' hearts—we would attract a great deal of attention and would be quickly identified. It is essential we remain anonymous for now. There are too many misguided people in our community." He smiled. "Why, only last week Inspector Dale approached me with a rumor he'd heard of some secret society being established here to attack the Negroes. The idiot was carrying on about how law and order must be maintained, no one could take the law into his own hands, et cetera, et cetera. He asked me to pass on to him any information I might receive from my workers about such a society. Of course I promised him full cooperation. But, you see, that is the kind of attitude we are up against. When we mete out punishment, it must be done in a way to attract the minimum of attention. Our mission is to subject the blacks, not turn the whites against us."

After the meeting broke up, Robert walked along deserted Front Street and up the rise to the Tropicana. The marble lobby was cool and empty but for a handful of staff who snapped out of their mid-afternoon lethargy when they saw him. Robert went to his office, turned on the overhead fan to get the sultry air moving and began to study the accounts for the past weeks. But one of his headaches was coming on; the ledgers of neat handwriting swam before his eyes. He slammed the books shut and reached into the bottom drawer of his desk for the bottle.

He would rather think about the brilliant prospects of the voyage of the *Pride of Sandys*, anyway. An event that would really show them all what Robert Fleet was made of, show his mother how wrong she had been to back Veronica against him.

The New York summer was at its steamiest, and no one, family or business friends, could understand why she was staying on in the city. Certainly there was little business to be done: the decision makers had fled to Newport or the Hamptons for the season; the streets were given over to tourists. But Primrose would not leave because the thing happening between her and

Richard Billings was growing more intense each day and she was willing to ignore all her duties to let it have time to bear fruit. He hadn't said anything yet, and neither had she, but she knew: they loved each other.

Even the grand hotel had an empty feeling this late, hot afternoon as.Primrose moved around the suite preparing for his arrival. His knock came as the first roll of thunder broke over the city, and the next flash of summer lightning caught her eye as she ran to open the door to him.

"What's wrong, Richard?" She already knew him so well it was obvious to her something was wrong. Even in his seersucker suit, white boater in hand, he had a winter look about him. "Has something happened?"

"Nothing I couldn't have put right a long time ago," he said, moving into the suite but avoiding her gaze. "These weeks together, Primrose, have been wonderful for me. But I've been living a lie all through them. I should have told you the very first night—remember, 'Rhapsody in Blue'?—but I didn't have the guts to. I *wanted* things to go further, to get to know you better. I was dreaming, I guess. Anyway, I have to come clean now because my wife's been having me followed and she thinks there's something going on between us." He forced a smile but Primrose did not see it.

His wife. Of course she should have known there was a wife somewhere; he was too sweet not to be married. But she had convinced herself their budding relationship was normal, that he was like her and just hadn't had time to collect the usual appurtenances of a successful young career man.

"I guess it sounds like a lot of baloney," he said, "but Doris and I fell out of love years ago. I can't leave her because of the children. They're only tiny. She doesn't much care for them, but of course she'd get custody if I walked out on her. We had a sort of truce operating for the past couple of years. I lived in my apartment in town through the week and went home to Larchmont on the weekends. And then you came into my life and I guess Doris could see the change in me. I was so happy, she couldn't stand it. There was a hell of a fight last night. She had all the details of where you and I had been. . . . She made it all sound so sordid."

"Would you have told me about her, anyway?"

"I don't know." He shrugged. "It's meant so much to me, being with you. I didn't want to risk that."

She sat down on a couch by the window. The summer storm was at full force outside, flattening the garden plots of Park Avenue. She too was being buffetted. She studied him, standing in the center of the room, his head bowed, and made her decision.

"So she thinks we're sleeping together?"

"Yes. And she says I have to stop seeing you or she'll file for divorce."

"It would be impossible for us not to see each other if Kosmos goes public. And I've decided it will." She stood up and crossed to him. "And since I'm branded an adulteress, I might as well find out what it's all about." She reached out and touched his face. "Richard, take me to bed now, please."

She had always wondered what it would be like when she finally gave herself to a man, but nothing in her wildest dreaming had prepared her for this. He undressed her slowly, reverently, then stripped naked himself in the stormy afternoon light. She shivered when she saw how big he was, shivered again when his fingers gently touched her breast. Her own hands explored his body, feeling the hard edges, the firm maleness of him beneath his smooth skin. His lips brushed her nipples and his hand found her glowing center and at last they joined together. There was none of the pain she had expected, just a shaft of pleasure running through her, faster and faster, heading for a crescendo almost terrifying in its intensity.

"I love you," she said quietly as they lay together, exhausted. "I know it's wrong, but it doesn't matter. If I have to share you, I shall learn to live with that." She felt him slip from her and the sense of loss was great.

"I love you, too," he whispered. "I've loved you from the moment we met. Did you sense it?"

She nodded. "It was mutual. I knew this day would come. I've longed for it. There are no regrets."

"But what happens now?" he asked. The misery was back in his eyes. "I can't have you, but I can't be without you."

"We'll make it work somehow." She felt older and wiser than he, absolutely sure of herself. "We have to see each other from time to time on business. We'll just have to learn to be discreet. And maybe in a few years . . . maybe the situation will change."

Long after midnight the revelers were still in the bars and lounges of the Tropicana; the color and spectacle of the Cup Match had put the tourists in a party mood and they were reluctant to let the day end. None of them realized the handsome young man in porter's uniform was the hero they had applauded a few hours before on the cricket field. Billy was glad of that: he had always found it best, safest, to be anonymous when around white people.

It was two A.M. before the lobby was finally silent, and Billy could consider sneaking a nap behind the bell captain's desk. He was so tired after the day of heat and excitement, so proud of himself for coming through on this one occasion when a black man was allowed to shine. His head was nodding when the telephone on the desk gave its soft ring.

"This is Mrs. Simmons in 402." The voice was slurred, or sleepy. "I want someone to come up and fix my window. It's stuck and I need some air. It's so hot tonight."

He moved quickly to the staff elevator and went up to the fourth floor, glad to have something to do on this usually uneventful shift. He moved down the long, silent corridor and tapped on the door of 402.

"Come in," she called. "It's not locked."

Mrs. Simmons was a small, plump, blond American in her early forties. And she was almost naked. At least, that was the impression Billy got before he hastily dropped his eyes.

"The window over there, open it," she commanded.

The window opened easily, and soft jasmine-scented air flowed into the room. Billy, eyes fixed firmly on the carpet, started for the door. They had all warned each other about situations like this.

"Just a moment, young man," she said. "I'll give you something for your trouble." She fumbled in her purse and came up with a bank note. "Here's a pound for you."

It was a very big tip, equal to a week's wage, and Billy was forced to look up and acknowledge it. He saw she was wearing some kind of filmy nightgown, quite transparent.

"Thank you, ma'am," he mumbled, preparing to make his exit.

"Don't be in such a hurry. I can't sleep. I need someone to talk to." She sounded sad and desperate. "I'm down here to get over my divorce and I'm so lonely." She was standing close to him now, her breasts shining through the material of her nightgown. "There's plenty more money for you," she said huskily. "Just stay with me."

"I can't, ma'am," he said. "I have to get back to my station. Other people—" He shivered and jumped back. Her hand had touched his groin. "Please," he said, "you'll get me in trouble." She was close to him again, rubbing up against him. He felt around behind him for the doorknob.

"Just a little while," she crooned. She undid the tie at her neck and the gown dropped from her. She clutched at him again and he shoved her hand away, more roughly than he'd intended.

Two spots of red appeared on her cheeks, and her soft, seductive voice suddenly changed. Her hand came up and the nails raked his cheek. He had to push her off him before he could get the door open.

"You black bastard," she hissed. "You'll be sorry for this."

He heard her scream as he ran down the corridor; the first doors had opened before he reached the elevator and he saw the white, sleepy faces looking at him with horror. He felt the blood on his cheek and he began to shake all over. He knew he was in terrible trouble, and all he could think to do was escape to the safety of home, to Amy and the children. The lobby was still silent when he got out of the elevator, and Billy hurried through it, out the staff entrance and onto the back lane. He started running through the warm night, just wanting to be far away from the hotel.

Inspector Dale wriggled in his chair; his pajamas chafed under his blue uniform jacket and he had rushed out without his pipe and tobacco. He yawned and blinked at Robert Fleet, who was pacing the floor of the manager's office.

"No, sir," Inspector Dale repeated. "The lady does not want to press charges. I assume you've seen incidents like this before, Mr. Fleet. A lonely woman late at night, a member of the staff summoned to her room . . ."

"It's disgraceful, Inspector!" Robert was still shaking with anger that something like this could happen in his hotel. "This poor woman, molested by a black. I want him punished and punished most severely. The rope is the only course."

"I don't think that was the way it was," Dale explained patiently. "I think the lady made a play for your fellow and he wasn't having any of it. She just wants to forget the whole thing."

Robert glared at him. The man had obviously gone soft on the blacks. Well, they would see about that. He would speak to his superiors about an early retirement for Inspector-bloody-Dale.

"So you're not going to do anything about it?"

"No, Mr. Fleet, there's nothing I could do about it."

Robert remained in the office brooding long after he had sent the inspector away; the incident was a personal affront to him and a general indicator of how the situation was getting out of hand in Bermuda. It was time for action. By nine A.M. he had sent out messages to his little band of followers to assemble that night.

"You didn't do anything wrong, Billy. You've nothing to be afraid of." Amy stroked her husband's face. Under the light brown skin he was gray; now, hours after he had stumbled in the door of the cottage, he was still shaking, his eyes wide with fear. The poor man, after a day of such triumph in Cup Match, to be reduced to terror by some silly American woman. She made a face at the children, and little Matthew and Annie ducked behind the door; they had first welcomed their father home with joy, then confusion and fear had set in when they saw how distressed he was.

"I'll fix you some food, then you rest awhile," she said. "I'll ask around and find out what's going on at the hotel. I'm sure it will be all right."

John Clay brought the first news, when he had finished his day shift at the hotel. It was okay, the police weren't after Billy. The woman had all but admitted she'd made the whole thing up. The bad news was their boss man had told John that Billy was fired. Mr. Fleet was hopping mad about what had happened and it would not be wise for Billy to appear at the Tropicana again.

"That's not fair!" Amy said. "He didn't do anything. And if he's fired from the Tropicana, he'll never get a job in any other hotel here. I'm going to go see Mr. Fleet, put this thing right."

"Don't be crazy, woman," Billy said. "There's nothing you can do. It's just the way things are. It could be worse. I could be in jail, or at the end of a rope."

After John left they sat in silence, Amy brooding over the injustice, Billy still jumpy and scared. The children, finally cowed into silence, had been sent off to bed right after supper.

Billy was sleeping when he heard the crash of the cottage door being kicked in. Six of them crowded into the room. By the light of their flares he saw that all were masked. One of them carried a coiled rope. Billy heard Amy wake up, suck in her breath, preparing to scream. He clapped a hand over her mouth.

"You should have stuck to nigger women," one of the invaders snarled. He was tall and thin and the mask did not conceal his shock of death-white hair. "Now we're going to teach you a lesson, one the rest of your brothers won't forget. Take him."

Amy was struggling under his grip as the men moved forward to capture Billy, and he had to release her when one of them struck a stinging blow on his forehead. Amy screamed; in a moment the children would come into the room and be exposed to all this evil. Suddenly, Billy rolled out of bed and launched himself at the ring leader. He struck the man, putting his full force behind his fist, and felt bone crush under the black mask.

The attack took the men unawares, and there was a gap between them. Billy shot through it and out the door into the night, running faster than he thought possible, running through the rough lanes of the black ghetto, running down past the waterfront and up into the hills behind. He ran until he could no longer hear their shouts of rage, could no longer see, over his shoulder, the flame of their torches.

He ran until he collapsed in an overgrown garden behind a darkened house. There was a buttery at the bottom of the garden and he crawled inside, sprawling on the cool stone floor. There was nowhere else to escape to; he lay there through the dark hours, and just before dawn fell into a fitful sleep.

"There's a man in the buttery, Captain Smutters," Hilary said. "In his nightclothes. Gave me such a scare! He's asleep."

"Probably a drunk," Smutters said, "or one of your suitors, Hilary." He laughed as his housekeeper blushed. "I'll just finish my coffee and go down and see him off."

He strolled through the dew-damp garden, cautiously opened the buttery door and looked down at the bedraggled figure. He prodded the man, then turned him over, face toward the light. He saw fear in his eyes as they blinked open, and the man groaned with despair.

"You're Billy Youngblood, right?" Smutters said. "Come on, man, on your feet. You can't sleep here."

Billy slowly focused on the huge figure standing in the doorway.

"Captain Smutters, sir," he said, climbing to his knees. "I'm most sorry to have bothered you. I'll be on my way—"

"Hold on a minute, Billy. You were involved with some madwoman at the hotel the night before last. But I heard you were innocent. The Inspector said it wasn't any of your fault. Is that why you are hiding here?"

Billy figured he had nothing to lose. The whites were all the same. He might just as well tell his story to this one, before they came to take him away. He let it all spill out, the words tumbling over each other, knowing he would gain nothing by silence. He slumped back against the wall, then, and waited to hear his fate.

"You're in a lot of trouble," Smutters said when the account was finished. "And not of your own doing." He stood a moment, thinking. "You just stay here for the while, Billy, and I'll see what I can do. I'll have food sent down to you. Don't budge until I get back, though."

Smutters rode into town later that morning. He called at the coffee house and a couple of taverns, and by noon he had a good picture of all that had occurred. Besides which, he'd learned, Robert Fleet had fallen down some steps and was in the hospital with a severely broken nose.

He strolled along the waterfront and went aboard the *Pride of Sandys;* the captain and first mate were ashore, completing the paperwork before their sailing that night. But it was Fairweather, the bosun, he was looking for. The man was no better than the rest of *Sandys'* crew but he had one virtue: he was terrified of Smutters, and had been ever since he'd served as cabin boy under the senior captain. Smutters walked him aft, away from the other seamen.

"I'll be putting a man aboard tonight, Bosun. A black, but he's light enough to pass. Keep him out of the way of the captain and tell the crew to mind their own damn business or they'll answer to me. I'll see he has all the right papers. That's all you need to know."

Back in the buttery Smutters handed Billy a seabag containing clothes, papers, and food enough to sustain him until they were well out to sea. He gave him ten pounds as well.

"After you've gone I'll get a message to your wife and tell her you're all right and will be in touch," Smutters said. "You could stay and fight this, but you'd never win, so why chance it? That was Robert Fleet's nose you smashed last night. He'll not rest until you've paid for it. So, young Billy, what you are going to do is sail in the *Sandys* and be my eyes and ears. There's something funny going on with this voyage and I want to know about it. You'll be off to Europe first, then Canada to unload liquor, then general cargo in Baltimore. You can jump ship in Baltimore and send me a message about everything that's happened to date. You can write?" Billy nodded. "Good. When I get your report, if it's satisfactory, I'll send you some more money and arrange to get your wife and kids shipped up to you. Don't let me down, son, and I'll look after you."

It had been a difficult birth; the doctor joked about the boy's big nose and ears. Dimity forgot the pain when she saw her son and knew for certain. They called the boy Edward David, and Steven Lapin was every bit as proud as his wife. Of course they couldn't actually tell anyone, but now the boy was growing and a few would guess and that was enough for the Lapins.

Primrose took the tray from the housekeeper and stepped out onto the wide, sun-drenched balcony. For a moment in the strong morning light, her mother appeared to be as reassuring a presence as ever; she sat stiffly upright in the wheelchair, looking out over the Great Sound, undisputed mistress of the big house and all she surveyed. But when she turned her head and smiled at Primrose, the tiredness showed in her eyes.

Julia Odlum knew her time was near and she was resigned to it. Since breaking her hip in the fall she had been confined to the chair, and she didn't like being an invalid. Too much time to think about the sadnesses in her life. Jonas gone and, worse, young Jeff taken before he had a chance to know life. Cable in exile in New York. Julia made a silent prayer for Primrose: God, let her, at least, have true happiness. She deserves it.

"Good morning, Mother," Primrose said, kissing her cheek. "Another lovely day." She laid out the cups and poured tea for them. "I should be down at the office, but work can wait. I wanted to spend a little time with you."

"That's nice, dear. You work much too hard. At least your trip to New York seemed like a nice long break." She stole a glance at her daughter. "You've been ever so cheerful since your return."

"That's something I want to talk to you about." Primrose sipped her tea while she tried to compose the words. "I met someone up there, a man. I'm in love with him."

"Wonderful! I'm so happy for you, Primrose. I know you're only twenty-four but I was starting to worry you'd never meet anyone, what with being so tied up with the business. So when am I going to meet your young man?"

"Richard Billings." She loved saying his name here, in her own home. It brought him closer to her. "He's arriving next week. Richard's the man who's handling the Kosmos float for us. He's quite brilliant, one of the most-quoted men on Wall Street. And I guess he's going to make us even more millions."

"That's only on paper, dear," her mother cautioned. "I admit I don't quite understand this 'going public,' but it certainly looks very good at this stage. Your father would be embarrassed at all the riches pouring in. Still, it's all just paper assets at this stage; it's the products we make and sell that really measure our worth."

"Of course, Mother. I'll never lose sight of that." She smiled fondly. Her mother was—and her father had been, for that matter—so old-fashioned about the family business. They would have gone on running it like a little corner store. But thanks to Richard's brilliant scheme, Kosmos looked like it would become America's biggest cosmetics manufacturer within a year or two. "Anyway, Richard's coming here officially on Kosmos business, but I want you to meet him. You'll love him, too."

"So what's the problem, Primrose? I can tell there *is* a problem."

"He's married." She let it rest there between them for a moment. "He can't leave his wife because of the children. There's been nothing between him and her for years. It's not as if I broke up their marriage or anything."

"He's married," Julia repeated. She sighed. "Poor Primrose. Even in these modern times . . ." Her hand shook, rattling her teacup. "I don't know what to tell you. There weren't such problems when I was a girl. The only thing that mattered was that there never be a breath of scandal. I suppose we missed out on a lot because of our sense of proprieties." She was glad Jonas wasn't here to confront the situation. He had been a loving husband and father, but his sense of doing the right thing had outweighed all other emotions. Cable's disgrace had been even more wounding to him than Jeff's death.

"I'm sorry this is upsetting you, Mother. I didn't plan for things to work out this way. It just happened and there was nothing I could do about it." She stroked her mother's hand. "Please, try and give me your blessing. I don't know what's going to happen to us, but I know I must see it through because I love him."

Richard Billings tried to concentrate on his cards but his mind was wandering. He willed the ship to travel faster, to cut through the seas and get him swiftly to Bermuda and Primrose. He longed for her, and the longing grew more intense every day. He didn't care how much he was risking for her; he could blot out the icy hostility his wife had displayed over this trip. He was in love and it canceled out everything else.

"Damn it, man! We've gone down again. That was a ridiculous bid." Masters, his bridge partner, was flushed with anger.

"I'm sorry," Richard said meekly. "I can't seem to pay attention tonight. Let's go to the bar and I'll buy the champagne to make up for my stupidity."

Masters was still grumbling, but Jones and Fren-

cham, their opponents, were happy to call it a night with
twenty dollars won.

"Your first visit to Bermuda?" Frencham asked Richard as they stood at the card-room bar. Richard nodded.
"You'll enjoy it," Frencham said. "A most beautiful
place and an ideal escape from the pressures of Manhattan. I was there briefly before the war. I don't think it
will have changed very much."

"This is strictly a business trip," Richard said, hugging his secret to himself. "I shan't have time for the
tourist bit."

"Oh, it's business for me too," Frencham said. "But in
Bermuda there's always time for pleasure as well, Mr.
Billings." Frencham pushed up his horn-rimmed spec-
tacles and rubbed his eyes, then ran his hand over his
gleaming bald head. "I'm looking forward to the break.
It's such a hectic pace in New York these days."

"It's a wonderful time to be in business, isn't it," Richard enthused. "We're going through the greatest economic boom in the world's history. There seems no end
in sight. More champagne," he said to the steward. Richard felt wonderful, and in his joy had compassion for the
rest of the world's citizens who would never know emotion such as his. For one mad moment he almost confided
in Frencham his real reason for the trip: it would be good
to bring some romance into the poor chap's life. But he
restricted their conversation to the everyday things of
businessmen—the market, politics, and the fortunes of
the Yankees now that Babe Ruth was hitting everything out of the ballpark.

Billy Youngblood had done his job well. He had
blended in with the crew of the *Sandys,* been accepted by
them, and was able to observe most things that happened in the ship. Over the months they had loaded general cargo in London, then case after case of fine liquor
in Marseilles. The liquor was in unmarked containers,
but Billy had slipped into the hold and scratched a tiny
cross on each of the crates. He wasn't sure what he was
supposed to be watching for but it seemed obvious to him

that the precious liquor was the most important thing
aboard. The cargo was certainly worth a lot more than
the *Pride of Sandys* itself. The ship was only just sea-
worthy.

It was the bosun who told him of their change of course
and presented him with a dilemma.

"We're going into Baltimore first, then on to Halifax,"
the bosun said. "I don't know what the skipper thinks
he's up to, calling into an American port with all that
liquor aboard. Mr. Fleet will string him up by the balls
if he loses that cargo to the feds."

Billy didn't know what to do. Captain Smutters had
told him to jump ship in Baltimore, *after* they had called
at Halifax and unloaded the liquor. He didn't make his
decision until, standing by the hatch covers and watching the cargo being winched out on a cold Maryland
morning, he saw that each of the containers bore his own
carefully marked cross. He went ashore with the liquor,
saw it safely placed in trucks and grinned to himself
about Fleet's audacity. A massive bootlegging operation
carried out in broad daylight. The rich people on the
Eastern Seaboard would be drinking the right stuff for
a change.

He got himself a room in a waterfront boarding house
and a job as a porter at the Hotel Baltimore, all in the
first day. There was no hurry to write his report to Captain Smutters; he wouldn't be expecting it for another
week or two. And he wanted to think about the report
because, if it satisfied the captain, Amy and the children
might soon be on their way to join him.

When he read the paragraph in the Baltimore *Sun,* he
was glad he had waited. All it said was that a Bermudian ship, the *Pride of Sandys,* had foundered in heavy
seas off Nova Scotia. All hands had taken to the lifeboats
and safely reached Yarmouth. The cargo of "precious
spirits and wines for the Canadian market" had been lost
with the ship.

"I think, Mr. Fleet, it is in your interests to cooperate
with me." Frencham rubbed his bald head and gazed

across the desk. "If you let me into the room, I'll get my evidence with a minimum of fuss and without disturbing your other guests. We would not want them all to know adultery is being committed under your roof, would we?"

Fleet nodded. It was a damned impertinence, an American guest in his hotel engaging in lewd conduct with a young woman. He was grateful to the private detective for bringing it to his attention.

"And you say they're up there now, in broad daylight?" Fleet asked. "It's scandalous!" He took the master key from his desk. "We will go and unmask them now."

She lay in his arms, feeling the afternoon breeze from the open window cooling them. Happy shouts rose up from the swimming pool four floors below. Primrose sighed in contentment and snuggled closer to Richard, her lips resting on his bare chest and her long legs holding his body to hers.

"That's nice," he whispered as her tongue traced patterns on his skin. His hand moved over her breast and she snuggled closer. It was their third stolen afternoon, hour after hour of ecstatic lovemaking, a precious time when they could forget their uncertain future and just live for their glorious present.

"What the—?" She felt him jerk away from her, saw the flash of light brighter than the sunshine coming through the billowing lace curtains. She looked up and screamed as the bald man took another photograph of them; she pulled a sheet up over her as she saw Robert Fleet's pale eyes raping her.

Richard was half out of the bed, swearing and struggling to free himself from the tangled sheets.

"Sorry about this, Mr. Billings," Frencham said. "I'll be going now."

"Get out, you bastards," Richard yelled. "I'll kill you for this. I'll sue. I'll—"

"You will vacate this hotel at once, sir," Fleet snapped. "I don't know what you Americans call it, but here in

Bermuda adultery is still a crime. Get out and take the woman with you." God, the Odlum girl had a wonderful body. He wondered if Frencham might let him have a copy of the photographs. The detective was tugging at his arm, and reluctantly he left the lovers to their shame.

"We Smutters have been captains for the Fleets for a long time."

"Of course I know that," Robert Fleet said. He tried to conceal his annoyance with the big, bluff seafarer who was lounging in an office chair and making no attempt to come to the point. Henry Smutters always made him feel awkward; the fellow had an air of insolence. And now Robert was due at the board meeting to discuss the aftermath of the sinking of the *Pride of Sandys*. "The two families have had a long and happy association," Robert said.

"Mostly happy, Mr. Fleet. But not when I see my ships being sunk from under me."

"What are you talking about, man?"

"The scuttling of the *Pride of Sandys*," Smutters said, swinging his feet up onto Fleet's desk. He was enjoying this. "Don't bother to deny it. I know you got the booze off at Baltimore before you had Brian Johns sink the ship. I know Lloyds is convinced the booze went down with the ship and has agreed to pay the insured value. If I want to prove it was an insurance job, I've only to wave my fist under Johns's nose and he'll tell all. He's weak as piss."

"You're talking nonsense. I don't have to—"

"You do have to, if you don't want to go to jail for fraud. You have to do exactly what I say, Mr. Fleet."

Robert felt the black rage rising in him; that a man who worked for him, just a jumped-up seaman, could speak to him this way. But his intelligence told him to keep calm. The situation was fraught with danger. The members of Lloyds would throw him in prison and bring down the house of Fleet if they knew what he'd done. And his own board of directors would stand guard at the cell door.

"What do you want?" he demanded.

"I figure you've made at least fifty thousand pounds 'losing' the cargo of liquor. And the company has come out well ahead on the sinking of the *Sandys*. She was over-insured. So, first I want a cashier's check for ten thousand pounds." He saw the hatred in Fleet's eyes. "It's not for me, but you won't believe that and I don't give a damn about you, anyway. I don't give a damn for the poxy underwriters at Lloyds, either, so I'll still leave you with a handsome profit. The other thing I want from you, Mr. Fleet, is going to cost you a lot more. I want an understanding that you will give up any idea of running the shipping side of your family's business. I'm happy to work for your sister, but I'm damned if I'll be senior captain for a man who scuttles ships." He stood up; he was the same height as Fleet but seemed to tower over him. "You won't understand, Mr. Fleet, but to me the sea is the most important thing. I'm proud of who I am and what I do. The first Smutters in Bermuda was a cabin boy who rose to be a captain. I won't have anything besmirching my family's traditions."

"How do I know you won't come back to me with further blackmail demands?"

"You don't. But it's not blackmail. Look on it as a fine for being caught out. And I'm doing you a favor, getting you out of the shipping side of the business. You're not suited to it."

Fleet stepped backward and studied the man; no, threats wouldn't work. Better to just recruit someone to deal with him on a dark night in some foreign port's back alleys.

"All right," he said. "You can have your check tomorrow. And the other thing—I'll do it. I don't want to spend my time messing about with a clapped-out shipping line, anyway. I've bigger plans than that."

"Fine," Smutters said. "But don't think of having me set upon by that feeble band of thugs you've formed. Or anyone else. I've taken precautions so that if anything happens to me, chapter and verse of what you've done will come out."

* * *

The board meeting was quite cheerful, considering they had recently lost one of their ships. Of course, they had all seen the figures and knew Fleets was well ahead on the deal. Still, this voyage had been Robert's great scheme and he owed them some excuses.

"Before the recriminations begin," Robert said, "I'd like to make an announcement. Madam Chairman"—he bowed to his sister—"I trust you will give me the floor."

She nodded. Ever since the *Sandys* had gone down, she had been feeling for Robert. Sure, they had fought each other for control of the company, but he *was* family and no Fleet wished to see another fail. She just hoped he could recover from this setback and carry on as a member of the team.

"I've decided," he said, "in view of my misplaced effort to beef up the cargo division, to face facts. I am not cut out for the shipping business. And acting as a glorified desk clerk at the Tropicana isn't my idea of business satisfaction, either."

She wanted to reach out to him, tell him their battles didn't matter. Don't humble yourself like this in front of outsiders.

"So what I am going to do," he said, "is give you all first option. My shares in the Fleet company are up for sale to any bidder. I am going to cash up and go my own way." He watched his sister, saw the angry flush on her cheeks. That surprised you, you bitch. You thought we'd stick together for the family name, that you could humiliate me but still count on my Fleet loyalty. Well, not so. He looked around the board table, truly enjoying himself now, the humiliation of Smutters's demands forgotten.

"You, Jamie," he said, sneering at the pale Baseheart, "you've always thought yourself as good as the main branch of the family. Here's your chance to grab a big block of shares and prove yourself. My holding's for sale for four million pounds. Think you can run to that much, Jamie? A lot of people in London will consider it a bargain-basement entry into a great company like this." He cast his glance around the table again. Smutters had actually done him a favor. He had these people in total confusion. "What about you, Steven?" he demanded of Lapin. "Wouldn't you like to buy a Fleet out and get control? Finally establish your legitimacy in Bermuda. All you have to do is come up with the cash. I don't care whom I sell to."

Steven Lapin listened to Robert's diatribe. The fellow had finally come unhinged; it was only to be expected. Damn, though! If he'd known Robert was going to crack at this point he wouldn't have sunk all his available capital into the Kosmos float in New York. Perhaps he could use some of the trust funds to pick up Robert's holding and worry about reconciling the books later.

"Robert," Veronica said grimly, "we all know you're upset about the loss of the ship. It's not your fault. You don't want to sell up your heritage. Let's move on to other business for now, and you and I will have a talk later."

"No," he said. "My proposition is on the table. If none of you is interested, I'll offer it in London." For a moment he felt unsure over what he was doing. The oldest son of the current Fleet generation, throwing in the towel. But he remembered the implacable Smutters: he was out of the business, anyway, thanks to that bastard, so why should he care if he took his bloody sister out with him?

"I don't think there's much point continuing with this meeting," Veronica said. "My family will want to talk this over privately. Nothing like this has ever happened before." She looked around the table, noted the gleam in Lapin's eyes, the confusion in Baseheart's, the sympathy in Benbridge's.

Henry Smutters explained it all to her again, the details of the sailing, how Billy would be on the dock in New York to meet her and the children. And the fund he had set up with Fleet's money to allow the Youngbloods to live comfortably and educate their children.

"It's too much for me to grasp," Amy said. "Why are you doing all this for us, sir?"

He shrugged. "Maybe I just like causing trouble. Or I feel it's time to redress some of the wrongs committed in Bermuda. It doesn't matter, girl." In truth, he didn't know why. Perhaps, he thought, his whimsical decision to give this family a break was a reaction to all that had happened to his own family in the history of Bermuda, of generation after generation clawing its way to respectability but never to acceptance into the class which ruled the islands. "Just see the children get a good education," he said. "The day is coming when we're going to need some black professionals here."

The Bermuda newspapers were much too aware of their place in society to publish anything about the divorce; they existed by the grace of the leading families, and no scandal about them would ever be printed. But copies of the New York papers—the tabloids had a field day with the affair, what with a Wall Street giant, a beautiful young Bermuda tycoon and a "tropical love nest" being involved—filtered down to the colony, and everyone lapped up the sordid details. Primrose held her head high; her one real regret was the pain she knew the scandal was causing her mother.

"Don't worry about me," Julia said. "Look out for yourself. You are bearing up well but you are under a great strain." She studied her daughter. "I just want you to be happy, my dear. If you end up happy, today's unpleasantness will have been worthwhile."

"It's almost over now, thank God," Primrose said. "Richard's going to lose everything, of course. He's had to resign from his company, too. The worst thing for him is the children. They were all he cared about." She sat down in front of her mother and took her hands. "I'd better tell you everything. I'm pregnant—and I'm glad."

Julia managed not to wince. She had wondered about it, anyway; hoped the girl wasn't, but prepared to love her just the same if she was.

"So you and Richard will marry as soon as he is . . . free?"

"The very instant." She smiled at the prospect and the

haunted look left her eyes. "Thank you for standing by me. I promise you it will all work out and you'll not have to feel ashamed of me."

"I don't feel ashamed of you, darling."

She accepted Captain Smutters's invitation to join him on the bridge for their entry to New York Harbor, and her excitement mounted as they rounded Sandy Hook and passed through the Verrazano Narrows; in an hour or so she would be in Richard's arms again. Smutters glanced across at Primrose hugging herself in the dawn cold, and he smiled. She was a nice girl, he thought, and brave the way she had shrugged off the stares and whispers of the other passengers.

After the tug had them in tow and they were edging into the pier, he spoke to her.

"If you go down to the first-class salon now, you can be at the head of the line to go ashore. I guess you're in a hurry."

"I am, Captain," she said, flashing him a smile. "Thank you for everything. It's been a wonderful voyage."

Smutters stayed on the bridge after docking. He studied the crowd through his binoculars and picked out the tall figure of Billy Youngblood on the dock. Then the third-class passengers were coming ashore and he saw the ecstatic reunion of Billy with Amy and the children. Smutters smiled, put away his glasses and went below.

There was obviously something wrong in the first-class salon; the rest of the passengers were gone but Primrose Odlum was still there, close to tears as she argued with two immigration officials and tried to avoid the flashing cameras of three pressmen.

"What's the trouble here?" Smutters demanded, moving to her side.

"They won't let me ashore, Captain," Primrose said. "They say I'm denied entry to the U.S.; I'm not a fit person."

"What rubbish!" Smutters turned on the officials. "I

can vouch for Miss Odlum. Her family is one of the most
respected in Bermuda."

"It's not a matter of vouching for her, Captain," the
more senior of the officials said. "She can't come in.
She's guilty of moral turpitude."

Primrose burst into tears then; they had succeeded in
making her ashamed at last. She felt desolate and alone,
the more so because Richard would be out there on the
dock waiting for her. The cameras went on flashing; it
was Page Three for sure, even One on a quiet news day.

"You'll have to keep her aboard and take her back
with you," the official told Smutters.

"No," Primrose sobbed, "I'm not going back. Can't I
appeal to someone?"

The official shrugged.

"Sure you can, lady. But it'll mean sitting on Ellis Island until they decide, and I don't think you'd care for
that."

"I don't care what it's like," she said. "I've got to stay."

It became the longest day of her life. She was taken
ashore in handcuffs, rushed through the gawking crowd
without glimpsing Richard, then placed in a launch and
transported to the forbidding island. It was bedlam
there, thousands of would-be immigrants milling around
in vast halls, trying to make themselves understood to
overworked and cross officials. First Primrose was taken
to a cold, echoing ablutions block where a grim matron
ordered her to strip and enter the communal shower. At
first she refused.

"We've got a smart one here, girls," the matron called
to two of her fellows. "Won't take her clothes off." The
three of them surrounded her and roughly pulled off her
garments. Their hands were all over her, touching and
pinching and prodding. The matron squeezed her breast
until Primrose cried out in pain. Then they forced her
under the shower of freezing water.

Later, feeling defiled and defeated, she huddled in a
corner and listened to the sounds around her. Babies
crying with their mothers, people arguing and pleading

in a dozen tongues, a man singing a lonely love song. And no one came near her. She had ceased to exist.

It was dusk before an official at the barred windows called her name; she forced her way through the clamoring crowds and saw her brother standing in the doorway to freedom.

"Oh, God, Cable," she sobbed when she was finally released into his custody, "it was awful. I thought they'd never let me out of there."

He kept his arm around her as he guided her onto the ferry. She was shivering violently and he wrapped her in his topcoat.

"I had a fur," she said vaguely. "It was with me when they put me in there."

"Do you want to go back and look for it?" he asked.

"No! Leave it. I never want to see that place again."

On the ride uptown, Cable told her of their efforts through the day to have her released from Ellis. Richard, he said, was back at Cable's house still working the telephone trying to find someone who would act.

"In the end I got onto cousin Spencer Odlum," Cable said. "He's something big in the State Department. I had to browbeat him some, but he finally came through and rang the right person. Richard will be relieved; he's been going crazy." He hugged her to him. "We're quite a pair, you and me, Primrose. We can really pick our lovers. I hope Richard's going to be worth all the trouble he's caused you."

"I've talked to him again but he won't budge," Joanna said. "He wants out. He just laughed when I appealed to his sense of family loyalty. It's as if he has just been waiting for the chance to punish us." She sighed, feeling her age in every bone. "If Horatio were here, Robert wouldn't dare attempt something like this. But Robert has only contempt for you and me."

"He's a bastard," Veronica snapped. "In one way it'll be good to have him out of the company. But we can't have such a large block of shares falling into the hands of strangers. Then it would only need for Sam to do something similar and we'd lose control of Fleets."

"Maybe we've got to accept losing control. It's not going to be any kind of life for you, dear, running the company on your own. You're young and beaiful and should go after your own happiness."

"Don't talk like that, Mother! I'm a Fleet before I'm anything else, and I don't intend letting my rotten brother put an end to the empire our family built." She meant it. In the past few months, Veronica had realized she didn't care about abstract notions of love and gentleness; she was not a prisoner of her sex. "I'm going to run this company successfully and make it bigger and better than anyone ever dreamed of. I'll be more ruthless than any of the male Fleets ever were if I have to be."

Joanna studied her daughter, saw the fierce determination in her eyes and the defiant set of her chin. For a moment she wished the gentle child she had raised would return, but she knew this could never be; for better or worse Veronica *was* a Fleet and, like all of them, she would trade anything for power.

"I want you to call on Mrs. Marsden," Veronica said. "Tell her I'll marry Rupert on condition he buys me my brother's shares."

"No! Don't speak of such a course, even in jest. Rupert Marsden! He's forty years old, ugly as sin, a namby-pamby who's ruled by his mother—it's no wonder he's never married."

"The Marsdens are almost as rich as we are," Veronica said. "Okay, they haven't got any class, but I don't care. All the first families had to start somewhere. So the Marsdens are only grocers—they're awfully successful ones. If Rupert marries me, he'll move up about ten rungs on the society ladder. His mother will be able to die happy."

"No," Joanna said again. "You can't sell yourself to that awful little man."

"Don't try and stop me. I've made up my mind."

* * *

Primrose's marriage was a quiet affair, family only, at the Hudson River estate. It wasn't, she thought without bitterness, what she had dreamed her wedding would be: her pregnant, both she and Richard in public disgrace. But she stood proudly before the justice and held Richard's hand fiercely as they were pronounced man and wife. She kissed him and repeated the marriage vows in her head: she would have to protect him, she knew.

He had been quite shattered by the chain of events. The loss of his children and his career had changed him deeply. He loved Primrose more than ever but felt himself less worthy of her love; he had dragged her down with him. He accepted Primrose's suggestion he come and work with her at the Bermuda end of the Kosmos operation simply because there was nothing else he could do.

"I think I know what you must be feeling, darling," she said to him in their bedroom after the subdued wedding feast. "Please, don't let it get you down. We have each other now, and that's all I've ever wanted. And soon there will be the baby, our baby. I know the price you've paid for loving me and I swear I will do everything I can to make you think it was worthwhile."

He held her close so she would not see the tears in his eyes.

"It would have been worthwhile if I'd only been allowed to know and love you for a day," he said. "My regret is that it could have all been perfect if we'd met long ago and no other lives had been damaged by our love."

"Oh," she laughed, "you wouldn't have liked me when I was very young. And I didn't have any interest in men. So even if you had showed up in Bermuda, we would have passed each other by." She stroked his cheek. "Forget about what might have been, Richard. We must live for the future, our future."

Veronica's wedding was a grand one, even if half the participants were violently opposed to it. Robert attended and glowered through the proceedings; her mother wept more copiously than a mother should at a wedding; Sam got very drunk and sneered at everyone.

Veronica held her head high; she knew their friends had
taken to referring to Rupert Marsden as "the Fleets'
poodle," but the day she decided on this course of action
she steeled herself against public jibes and private regrets. She heard the great organ of the cathedral strike
up, and started back down the aisle with her husband at
her side, he almost trotting to keep up with her, his shiny
bald head coming just up to her shoulder. So they made
an odd couple, she thought; they also made damn good
business sense and she would do everything in her power
to see she did not jeopardize their pact.

The marriage had been pathetically easy to arrange.
His mother, all her jowls trembling, had spoken for Rupert in the negotiations. The four million pounds for
Robert's shares was no hurdle, but Mrs. Marsden, who
knew where every bag of rice was in the family warehouses, had insisted on a prenuptial agreement whereby
the sum had to be repaid if the marriage did not last a
minimum of five years.

"So five years and you can be free of the odious little
man," Roy Benbridge had told Veronica. "I still think it
too high a price for you to pay to keep control of Fleets,
but at least you know it's not forever."

"I intend it to be forever," she told the lawyer. "A
marriage of convenience, but a marriage nonetheless."
She meant it. She had known love once and it had
brought disaster to her; with Rupert she would be civil,
dutiful and distant.

The reception at the Tropicana was a nightmare for
her, though. The guests, fueled with an unending supply
of the finest champagne, became more bold as the evening wore on and were openly condescending to her and
patronizing of Rupert. Dimity Lapin was among the
worst offenders.

"Such an *odd* choice, Veronica," she said. "He hardly
comes up to your waist, the mother's an ogre, and the
whole family has only just brushed the flour off their
hands. We all expected to see you marry one of the Forty
Thieves."

Veronica looked across to her husband standing alone

with a bemused look on his plump pink face. For a moment she felt sorry for him and angry at these pompous, self-important people.

"The Forty Thieves hardly have impeccable credentials, Dimity," she replied sweetly. "Why, Steven's own family got their start running a high-class brothel."

"But don't you see the difference?" Dimity said. "At least the Lapins were here, almost from the beginning. It doesn't matter what the forebears did, so long as they did it early enough."

Robert bumped into her late in the evening, his pale eyes smarting from the smoke of a hundred Havanas, but awash with hatred.

"I didn't think you'd go through with it," he hissed. "Sell your body to that gnome just to defeat me one more time. You're a Fleet, all right. Father would have been proud of you."

"And you, Robert. You are a man after his own heart. Just don't squander your blood money. Horatio never believed in spending capital."

"Don't worry about me, sister dear. Look to yourself. I hear the grocer gets his money back if you don't satisfy him in bed."

Upstairs in the honeymoon suite she undressed and slipped into the four-poster while he was in the bathroom. She had been dreading this moment and wanted it over with as quickly as possible. She watched him enter the bedroom and wanted to giggle, or cry. He was wearing a long, flowing nightshirt and looked ridiculous. And he was carrying a small blue-wrapped parcel, which he hesitantly offered her.

"Open it, please," Rupert said. "It's from Tiffany's. I had them send it down for you. If you don't like it . . ." He watched anxiously as she tore open the wrapping. In the box was one perfect diamond, big and glowing against its dark blue velvet rest. It was the most expensive purchase of his life—apart from the price of the bride herself—and he desperately wanted her to approve of it, to accept it as his personal tribute to her. For Rupert

Marsden was under no illusions about why she had married him.

"It's quite beautiful," she said, putting it beside the bed. "Thank you." She didn't mean to be blasé about the gift, but precious gems meant little to her; Veronica was more interested in the realities of life, like ships and hotels.

If she had been enthusiastic about the gift, Rupert felt later, he would have had more confidence. Instead, as he switched off the light and edged into the bed with her, he felt weak and impotent. But Rupert knew what his duty was and he tentatively reached out a hand to touch her on the shoulder. He heard her sigh and almost stopped.

"Is there something wrong, my dear?" he whispered. "Perhaps the day has been too much for you. I had them put a couch in the sitting room. Perhaps you'd prefer me to sleep there."

There was nothing she would prefer more, but Veronica too had a sense of duty. She rolled onto her back, undid the bodice of her silk nightgown and felt for him in the dark.

He trembled as he moved beside her and his hand found her breast. It was too much to believe, that he was finally here in a marriage bed with the girl who was the fairest and most desired in Bermuda. For a moment he put from his mind how he and his mother had bought this position. He felt himself harden and he gently raised the hem of her gown and put his hand on her secret place. She did not move but he would not have expected her to. Slowly, gently, afraid of hurting her, Rupert lowered his body onto hers and found the entry; it only lasted a minute and she lay still throughout. He climaxed, withdrew and fell back in the bed, nervously wiping the sweat from his forehead.

"I hope there was no pain," he whispered. "I tried to be gentle with you."

She lay there saying nothing, feeling nothing. Because if she let herself feel, she would hear her heart crying out for John Chester and the real love she had once known. It was too late for feelings. She had chosen her bed and would lie in it and no one would ever know how much she hated the choice.

Inspector Dale shoved open the door of the native bar and peered into the fog of smoke; the acrid fumes of marijuana assailed his nostrils and the sounds of the steel band assaulted his eardrums. Drugs and music were all these people needed, he thought, to keep them in their places. So although the drugs were officially outlawed, the inspector and his force were prepared to turn a blind eye in that direction. Because Dale was in the front line every day, he knew the misery in which the blacks lived and was quite happy to let them enjoy the weed as long as it kept them quiet. He walked through the crowded room as legs were hastily pulled back to make a path for him. He found the proprietor behind the bar and waited silently while the old man fished around in a drawer and produced the brown paper parcel. He would count it back at the police station, but no one would dare shortchange Inspector Dale.

"One of these days you niggers are going to realize I've been right all along," John Clay said as he watched the inspector leave. "We are going to have to organize against these bastards, show them we have the numbers and the strength. Until then they'll just go on ripping us off and using our women."

"You be careful what you say, John Clay," Jerome Butters said. He took another drag of the fat cigaret and passed it to the next man. "The police ain't no problem, so long as they get paid, but you have to watch out for Mr. Fleet and his night riders. They near to whipped the hide off Danny Tester when they caught him up in Tucker's Town the other night."

"I'm not scared of Robert Fleet," John insisted. "He's crazy and that'll be his undoing. Those night riders are just a bunch of stupid fucking whites with no support in the community. We can handle them. It's the rest of the people, the ones who think of us as cheap labor and nothing else, we have to convince. The union, man, that's going to be the answer to our troubles."

"Have another joint, John. The only union we're going to get is the union we feel right here."

Billy Youngblood had bought his position as a Pullman porter, but he never regretted the price. The tips were good, and with the money he got each month from Captain Smutters's trust he could keep Amy and the children in a comfortable apartment on 115th Street. Billy couldn't wait until Matthew was in real school for real education. Because despite what was done to the Negro in America, he thought, there was real opportunity here, much more than in the tight little community of Bermuda. Billy read everything he could about the founders of the union movement: Gompers was his hero, and Bill Green, the new boss, would have got his vote if the union were open to blacks. If Matthew ever did want to return to his roots in Bermuda, Billy decided, he would go back educated and equipped to start a union and get justice for them all.

In the meantime, though, Billy envied no one. He was happy in his ordered life. The only person he felt he owed, apart from taking care of Amy and the kids, was Captain Smutters. The captain could call on Billy for anything, he vowed.

Henry Smutters was sorry the honeymooners weren't enjoying their Caribbean cruise; the purser gave him the gossip every night and he knew all about the tenseness in the owner's staterooms, the heavy drinking by the bridegroom. And Veronica Fleet herself had spent a lot of her time with her senior captain, keeping up with affairs of the company. Smutters was sorry she wasn't having a better time of it, because, while he didn't much like the Fleets as a family, he had a soft spot for Veronica. She never should have married the little worm, he thought. But, then, she never should have been born into such a God-awful family.

Smutters completed his log, blotted it dry and called for his First Officer.

"I didn't want to bother you, Captain," Farris said.

"But the latest weather report's just come in and it's looking bad." He passed the cabled message across the desk. "I think maybe we should be changing course. It looks like a real bad blow."

Smutters read the report and nodded. "A pity. I thought Mrs. Marsden would enjoy visiting Havana. But you're right, First. We'll head over to Ocho Rios instead and miss the worst of it."

The weather deteriorated through that day and the next; the storm was spread across the Caribbean and was impossible to avoid. Most of the passengers took to their bunks and lay groaning as stewards dispensed beef tea and dry biscuits.

"I think I'm going to die," Rupert Marsden moaned as he felt the ship lurch under him. He had always been a terrible sailor in the best of waters; the tempest roiling the ocean now was more than he could stand. He peered around the stateroom and saw Veronica by the porthole, working a tapestry. "Hold my hand, my dear," he implored her. "I feel it is the end."

She frowned; she had no sympathy for those who suffered seasickness. Because she didn't, Veronica suspected it was all in the mind. But she put down her needlework and went to her husband's bedside. His clammy hand reached out and clutched hers.

"If I do die," he said, "I want you to remember me fondly. You have already made me so happy, dear Veronica." He shuddered along with the ship. "My only wish is that I could have made you happy. If I survive this dreadful journey, I shall devote the rest of my life to that end."

"You're not going to die, Rupert," she said, not bothering to keep the impatience out of her voice. She looked down at him, mottled, ugly and helpless. A pity he wasn't as sick as he felt; Mr. Marsden's early death would be a blessing to her. She took a cold cloth and patted his forehead. "Take some sleeping tablets now, and by tomorrow the worst of it will be gone," she said. "I am going up to dine with the captain but will look in on you during the evening."

It was good to be out of the confines of the stateroom.
She had the ship almost to herself now, and as she moved
through it she felt the ownership and power her name
conferred on her. The first-class dining saloon was deserted, but a steward gave her a message from Smutters
that they would be dining in his quarters if it suited her.
She found him in the dark, masculine cabin, the air
heavy with pipe smoke.

"Still the perfect sailor, Mrs. Marsden," Smutters said
as he steered her to a chair. "I thought even you mightn't
be up and about tonight."

"How bad does it look?"

"Bad enough. The *Pride of Pembroke* can take it,
though. It's the passengers I feel for."

"Yes. My husband is laid low." The wind was stronger
up here, high in the ship. She listened to its howling, felt
the force of it. Now the ship climbed one wave and
plunged down into the trough before the next one. She
loved the sense of battling the elements. She was a Fleet,
and Fleets had been defying the sea for hundreds of
years.

"I think, Captain, I would like a brandy before dinner," she said. It was a night for strong spirit. She took
the glass from him and watched as he filled his own. She
had never really studied him as a person before; he had
always been there, and before him his father, as their
senior captain. Now she saw a ruggedly handsome man,
hair and skin burnished brown by the sea; big, powerful
shoulders, dark eyes with just a hint of humor in them.

"Yes," she said, "I'm glad it's not the *Sandys* we are
out in tonight. She did not survive a gale one-quarter as
fierce as this one." She continued to watch him. "I still
wonder about the loss of that ship. And our great good
fortune in having her so well insured." Now he would
not meet her eyes. "You, of course, counseled most
strongly against the *Sandys'* voyage. I suppose you were
quite pleased with yourself when your caution was vindicated."

"The loss of a ship gives no sailor any pleasure,
ma'am." The gleam in his eye now was an angry one. "It

reflects badly on all of us: on Bermuda, on the Fleets and on me."

"It didn't bother my brother," she said, "at least not at first. Then, suddenly, he said he was throwing in his hand and getting out of the family business. I wonder what caused his change of mind." She took more of the brandy. "There were rumors. I heard them and I'm sure you did too. Most of the crew didn't know what caused the disaster; the captain swore she sprang some plates and foundered very rapidly."

"I guess that's what happened then," he said. "The *Sandys* wasn't in too good shape."

"Stop fencing with me, Captain," she snapped. "The *Sandys* was scuttled on my brother's orders, wasn't she?"

He fixed her with his gaze and stood in the center of his cabin, swaying easily with the pitch and roll of the ship. He did not speak for several minutes.

"Never repeat that charge," he said finally. "Fleets would be out of business if it was ever spread around such a thing might have happened. I could have killed your brother for what he did. Instead, I forced him out of the shipping business."

She nodded. It was what she had suspected.

"And in so doing you forced me into marriage with Mr. Marsden. Do you realize that? You should have come to me, Captain. I would have handled Robert."

"I had to do what I thought fit. It's a captain's responsibility to make tough decisions. I'm sorry if it caused you . . . difficulties."

Neither of them was surprised their talk was centering on such intimate matters as her marriage; there was a bond between them, owner and captain, at sea in the raging storm.

Later, after stewards had cleared away their dinner, they drank good port and talked more general business. The wind howled on and the seas raged and the cabin was a sanctuary from it all.

"I suppose I should go and see how my husband is," she said as the ship's clock struck midnight. Their eyes

met and held. It was not right or wrong she was considering, but the risks involved. She stood up. "I believe I
can trust you, Captain Smutters."

He moved across the cabin and held out his hand to
her and they went through to his sleeping quarters.
Wordlessly they undressed and clambered into his bunk.
It was for each of them purely a physical encounter,
linked to the storm outside. She used him to vent the
frustrations of her sterile marriage, pulling him deep inside her as she rode him to a series of climaxes, then falling exhausted beside him. He took her then, raking and
plunging into her yielding body, not stopping until every
drop was wrung from him. Afterward they did not speak;
she dressed and left his cabin and went down in the ship,
through the empty companionways to the stateroom
where poor Rupert Marsden tossed in a drugged sleep
and groaned at the misery of his dreams.

The tempest had long gone when they reached Jamaica, and Rupert was solicitious as ever of his wife,
guiding her ashore and into a gaily striped carriage for
the tour up into the mountains. The night before, they
had both dined with Smutters, and as she had fully expected, the captain was polite and respectful. Like the
storm, their night of lust was receding in the memory;
there were no traces left of either event.

Joanna Fleet died in her sleep three nights before the
Pride of Pembroke returned from Veronica's honeymoon
cruise. Her daughter buried her in the family plot in the
little graveyard in Devonshire Parish. Now Veronica felt
totally alone in the world; it suited her. She had only one
ambition—to be the most successful Fleet in history, and
she wanted no emotional ties to restrict her.

Chapter Six
(1626-)

In the early evenings, in the time between finishing work and the setting of the sun, the people of St. George's promenaded in the town square, exchanging pleasantries and gossip and, slowly but surely, reestablishing the patterns of life they had left behind in their English villages and towns. Now, fifteen years after its founding, they could feel real pride in what they had achieved. A solid little town; the houses nestling up to each other were no longer shanties, and cobbled streets just the width of a carriage fanned out from the square. A too-close imitation of England for some of the inhabitants.

"God knows, this is a boring place," George Morris grumbled to his companions. There were three of them sitting on the seawall, sharing a jug of ale. George Morris, Ewen Staley and Will Acton. It was the opinion of some of those who passed them that the trio of twenty-year-olds were n'er-do-wells. The trio didn't think too highly of the passersby, either.

"Yes," Ewen Staley said, "I can see us sitting here night after night, drinking warm beer, until we are old and gray. And by then there will be a new generation of young men to whistle at the girls or complain of boredom."

"At least we won't be saddled with nagging wives and snot-nosed children," Morris said glumly. "With our lack of prospects, we'll never be bridegrooms. It's a circle, isn't it? If we had money we could buy shares of land; but until we own land we'll have no money."

"To the devil with becoming a peasant farmer!" Will Acton said. "Our parents may be satisfied with re-creating all the faults of England here. But for me, I expect Bermuda to offer a new start, not to be a land where the old order operates and we stay stuck firmly in our place."

The others did not jeer at Acton. He was not as physically strong as they—he was tall and thin and deathly pale, with bone-white hair and faded blue eyes; almost an albino and totally unsuited to the hot sun of Bermuda—but he was a deep thinker and they respected his intelligence.

"There are few opportunities for the likes of us, though," George said. "That we can read and write—that gets us nowhere. The few clerical jobs have all been spoken for."

"We have to make our own opportunities," Will said. He gestured to the slipway where yet another ship for Sir Thomas Fleet was taking shape. "As Fleet did. He and his cohorts have tens of thousands of guineas in their coffers and adding to it daily. And why? Because he had the gumption to become a semi-legal pirate." He stood up and started pacing the foreshore. "We three should build our own ship," he said. "Use the little money we make when there's work on the docks, plus our knowledge and the free cedarwood here for the taking. A small ship first, just to ferry people and their goods around these islands. There's a great demand for such a service, now that people are starting to move to the outlying areas."

Ewen was taken aback by the audacity of the proposal. Shipowning was for the upper classes.

"We wouldn't be allowed, Will," he said. "They'd say we were getting above our station."

"Bugger them! There's no law to say we can't in our own time and with our own hands build a little boat." Acton's white cheeks were highlighted now by a flush of red. "There's no need for anyone to know we intend to become traders; let them think our ship is just for fishing." He found a stick and knelt in the sand and began drawing shapes. "See, a sturdy, broad little boat along these lines with the three of us as crew could carry maybe half a ton of provisions to the outlying settlements."

Ewen and George looked at the marks in the sand and felt Will's enthusiasm flowing into them. A ship of their own: freedom at last and the chance to be as good as the next man. They were in a new land and Will was right—it was a time for new strategies.

"With the money we would make from this one," Ewen enthused, "we could proceed to build another, bigger. Someday this is going to be the most important port in the Atlantic, with all America's trade passing through. We could be part of that trade, be men of substance! With fancy wives and fine houses."

"Why, even Mrs. Odlum might approve of you, Will." George grinned. "Surely a shipowner would be considered good enough for her little Prudence."

Will pretended annoyance, but he liked being joshed about Prudence. It made him feel there was some future for them; so far, though, his courtship had been restricted to shy glances exchanged during church. The formidable mother was making sure none of Bermuda's young layabouts got close to her beautiful little girl.

"Who'd want that dragon for a ma-in-law?" George asked. "As bitter as hemlock, that one. And as for the late father: the day he come down to town, he looked like a wild man, all matted hair and dragging one leg. He grabbed me in Pie Alley and scared the daylights out of me. I saw Fleet kill him, and it was the best day's work Sir Thomas will ever do, no matter how many Frogs and Spaniards he sacks."

"Yes," said Ewen, "it is amazing two like them could produce such a beautiful delicate creature." He clapped Will on the shoulder. "So we'll pitch in and build a ship so you may win the daughter."

Will hoped Ewen was right. He ached with love for Prudence and even felt sympathy for her mother. But time was running out; most girls of Prudence's age had been promised in marriage already. He had only her shy glances to reassure him she was interested in him. But all the booklearning she had—that wasn't a good sign. A girl intending to marry didn't bury herself in books.

As the sun set, the three young men started for their homes, each dreaming new dreams, all determined to make them come true.

Prudence had been coming to the cliff top every day for a week, standing in the breeze and gazing forlornly out to sea. Sometimes there were other young women there, like Prudence, waiting for their men to return. Today she had the vantage to herself: the only Bermudian ship at sea was that of Will Acton, who had been expected home a fortnight ago with a cargo of Virginia tobacco. His partners, Staley and Morris, told Prudence not to worry: Will might have continued up to Halifax, or gone down into the Caribbean. Will would go anywhere there was a pound of cargo to be carried. But she did worry, dreadfully. She knew how hard the partners had to drive their ship if they were to compete with the established lines; the day Will returned, either Staley or Morris would take the ship out again with no time for routine maintenance, much less slipping and recaulking.

"He'll be all right," her mother had reassured Prudence before she set off for today's vigil. She touched Prudence's fair cheek. "He's got too much to look forward to. Just a few weeks to your wedding. You should be finishing your trousseau instead of moping around on the cliffs." Sarah was fiercely protective of Prudence, and it had taken her a long time to accept Will Acton as a suitor. But he had proven himself a diligent worker, turning one little coastal trader into a respectable, oceangoing merchantman. And he was a polite and courteous caller who obviously loved Prudence. And the girl was seventeen now; time she flew the nest. At least, with Acton's long absences at sea, Sarah would still have plenty of time with Prudence. Prudence was Sarah's whole life, her only friend, her one link with Jonas.

Now Prudence lay back on the grass and let the sun

warm her. She made a daisy chain and daydreamed of
her and Will and their children, and dear Mama, all living happily ever after in a nice house on a hill like this;
of a time when Will would no longer have to go out on
the sea, risking his life to secure a future for them.

There was another daydream, too, one that brought a
flush to her cheeks and set her heart pounding. The day,
two months ago, when on the eve of Will's departure she
had finally given herself to him. The first time for both
of them, so fumbling and timid as they explored the secret places of their yearning young bodies. She could still
feel his hand on her breast, the hardness of him between
her legs, the blissful pain as they came together. And afterward, lying damp together in deep embrace in this
very field. She shivered and came hastily out of her rev-
erie. While she had been dreaming, the clouds came racing in from the ocean and a bitter wind was suddenly
howling about her. Just a squall, she thought, not a tempest. Please God there would be no tempests while Will
was on the high seas. The cold rain was beating down on
her and she needed shelter. Prudence remembered the
cave her mother had shown her long ago, the cave where
the father she had never known had waited for her
mother to come and ease his pain.

Prudence dashed across the field, the wind and rain
buffetting her, to the stand of trees and bracken con-
cealing the cave mouth. She found the entrance after a
brief search and crawled inside, the dusty dryness making her cough, the darkness enveloping her. As her eyes
adjusted, she detected a tiny glow coming from a pile of
sticks in the rear of the cave; she crawled over to them
and blew on the fire, bringing it back to life. She wondered who else knew of this hideaway; whoever, she was
grateful to them for leaving her some warmth. She
hugged herself and edged closer to the flames while outside the wind increased its scream.

Her own scream was lost in the storm. When she saw
the three men crawling toward her from the recesses of
the cave, she tried to flee; but one of them, moving crab-
like and swift, clutched her ankle and dragged her back.

She could see them all clearly in the firelight, three dirty, desperate men. She guessed they were the Navy deserters who had been seen periodically in the hills behind the town foraging for food. She began to tremble.

"Please," she said, her voice shaking, "please don't hurt me. I won't tell anyone you are here." She wondered if they could hear her over the noise of the storm. "I'll bring you food and clothing!" she shouted. "Just let me go and I will help you."

The three just looked hungrily at her. She saw red in their eyes as the flames flared. And then the one who still grasped her ankle began to pull her toward them. She reached out instinctively to push her skirts down, but one of the others grasped her hands and pinned her to the ground. And then they were all over her, ripping and tearing at her clothes, beating her savagely when she tried to resist. It was as in her worst nightmares, these wild beasts defiling her, and she screamed again and again until she had no voice left. And still they attacked her, grunting and snarling.

"Will! Will!" she cried as she passed into a merciful faint. And she thought she saw him there, battling through the storm to reach her and save her. She clung to the dream throughout the hours they used her; it saved her sanity through the outrage, and numbed the pain of her poor bruised body.

She did not let herself come to until they were finished with her; she heard them talking as they flopped back against the cave walls, debating what to do with her. She kept her eyes closed tight and managed not to shudder at what they said.

"Kill her now and dump the body over the cliff while it's dark."

"No. I will want more sport soon. Keep her awhile."

"Yes. Keep her. Six months since I had a woman and God knows how long until there will be another. They are going to hang us anyway, so what is there to lose?"

"All right. We will rest awhile, then have her again, then over the cliff with her. Mozes, you keep an eye on her while we nap. Though she'll be too sore to be going anywhere."

The fire had subsided, and it was almost dark in the cave; outside, the storm still howled. If she could just reach the entrance she knew she could lose them on the cliff top. Prudence held her breath and tried to hear her attackers; as best she could tell, they were all asleep. She began to move, an inch at a time, toward freedom. One of the trio stirred and grunted and threw out his hand, brushing her leg, and a wave of nausea swept her. But she continued, edging to the entrance and away from the horror in the cave. At last the cold night air was on her face and the driving rain mixed with the blood on her cheek. She dived through the opening and ran blindly out into the night, the bracken ripping at her tattered clothing. There was no sound of pursuit but she did not slow, running all the way down the hills, through the storm to the safety of her home, tears blinding her, pain pulsing through her body. She was close to fainting when she at last fell against the door to their cottage and called for her mother.

Sarah Odlum cried out in anguish when the lamplight fell on Prudence. The girl was bloodied and bruised; her clothes were falling from her and there was terror in her eyes. Sarah gathered Prudence up and carried her into the little house, bundled her in blankets and laid her in her bed, all the time making gentle, soothing sounds. She heated water, undressed Prudence and bathed her. One glance at the young body told Sarah what had happened to her daughter. She quickly ascertained there were no broken bones or serious physical wounds, and soon she had Prudence in a warm nightgown, a bowl of hot soup clutched in her hands.

"My poor darling," Sarah said at last. "You have been cruelly treated. Don't talk about it now. Just lie still and I will hold you until the pain and shock have gone."

"No." Prudence's voice cracked but she was determined to pour out her story, to purge herself of the horror. "I went to Jonas's cave when the storm came upon me. There were three men there—the English deserters, from what I heard them say. They fell upon me and ravished me. Over and over again. They beat me and did unspeakable things to me, as if I were not a living creature. And when they were spent, they slept. I escaped then."

"Are they still in the cave?"

"I think so. They did not hear me go and did not pursue me. And it is black as pitch up there on the cliffs. I do not think they will be able to leave the cave until it is light."

"I shall kill them, then."

"Yes."

Prudence watched as her mother took the huge fowling piece from its stand beside the fire and double-loaded it with black powder, shot and iron filings. The piece stood almost as tall as Sarah, its barrel thicker than a man's arm. It was an ancient but deadly weapon; it had been her father's and was the only keepsake Sarah had brought with her from England.

"Rest quietly," she told her daughter as she hefted the piece. "I shall be some time, but no harm will come to you here. When I return you will have been avenged."

Mother and daughter looked into each other's eyes. Prudence nodded once and her mother was gone into the night.

It was a long and arduous trek up to the cliff top, and Sarah, weighed down by the gun, was panting when she stopped fifty yards from the cave mouth. She was sheltered now from the worst of the storm, and she removed the oilcloth that had been protecting her weapon. She began to crawl forward, silent and sure of her way. At last she was only a foot from the cave. She placed the weapon on a flat rock, its muzzle actually inside the cave.

"Help! Help!" she cried, cupping her hands about her mouth for the sound to reach them inside. "I am lost in the storm. Lead me back inside with you and we will have more pleasure together."

She could just hear their voices and the shuffling sound as they edged toward the low entrance. She could not see them, but could picture them in her mind, bent double, shoulder-to-shoulder, squeezing their way out of the cave to recapture the fair prize that had fallen into their hands.

"Are you all there?" she cried. "Are you coming for me?"

"Oh yes, indeed," one said. And she heard two others laugh.

The flash lit up the night for a second, just long enough for Sarah to see the three of them kneeling a yard from the end of the gun. Then the awesome roar in her ears as the sound of the gun bounced off the cave walls and rushed back on her. Followed by their screams as the metal ripped and tore at them. She wished she had more light to see their agony; she could only imagine how the shot would have all but cut them in two.

Sarah lay there awhile, her cheek resting on the heavy iron gun barrel. She listened to the sobbing moans dying away, and when all was silent again she took the knife from her waist and crawled inside the cave. In the darkness her hands slipped in the blood that was everywhere before she clutched on to the rough cloth of a jacket. She located all three of them, still warm and pulsing, and carefully slit each of their throats before dragging them back into the furtherest recesses of the cave. She did her work swiftly, emotionlessly, and within minutes she was standing outside again, lifting her face and hands to the night sky and letting the rain cleanse the blood from her. There were tears coursing down her face now, mingling with the rain, and she did not move until the worst of her grief had washed from her. But then she knew she must hurry home and tend to Prudence. She gathered up her weapon and started back down the hill.

Prudence lay four days in the darkened room, semiconscious. Sarah tried to protect her from prying eyes and malicious tongues, but in a tight-knit community of only some one thousand people privacy was a luxury enjoyed only by the very rich and powerful. Soon all kinds of stories spread about the nature of Prudence's suffering: she had been captured by sea devils, had had a spell cast on her by witches, been ravished by a band of pirates who had come ashore to shelter from the tempest. Finally, Sarah called in the Rev. Rodney Haggard and put a stop to the gossip. She told the editor all that had befallen her daughter; her only departure from the truth was to say the three attackers had fallen from the cliffs and perished as they chased Prudence when she escaped from them. And there was no mention of Jonas's cave.

It was a good, stirring story for *The Clarion,* and Haggard made the most of it. Prudence's ordeal was a metaphor for what awaited the whole colony, he wrote, God's warning of what happened to people who were idle instead of industrious, who wandered daydreaming in the green fields instead of tending their garden plots. Haggard freshened it all up for his Sunday sermon by adding that the provocative dress adopted by the women of the colony—influenced as they were by the salacious French fashions—naturally aroused the beast in men.

After the sermon Hilda Cobcroft and Jessica Fleet dismissed their carriages and strolled home, accompanied by Hilda's daughter, Amanda, and Jessica's son, Septimus. It was a bright lovely day, but the two women were engrossed in the events of the black night on the cliffs.

"How can Haggard attach any blame to the girl?" Hilda asked. "Even if she were a strumpet, is she not entitled to walk in a field? Will there always be people like Haggard sitting in moral judgment on women?"

"Of course," Jessica replied. "And their judgments will always be as sound as their morals. Haggard is a hypocrite, a blusterer and a coward." She smiled as she remembered him years before, quaking in her bed, behind bared for Monserat's spanking. "They will always try to make scapegoats of us women." She glanced around to see if the young people were out of earshot. "Take Thomas the Grand, the preening Sir Thomas Fleet. He is incapable of lovemaking now, his member limp and useless, the result of recent flush years in which he has every day grossly overeaten and fallen into his bed in a drunken stupor. But does he blame himself for the loss of his virility? Of course not! It is *my* fault. It's I who have rendered him impotent, either because I demand too much in bed or, alternatively, coldly reject his advances. The contradiction doesn't bother him. He is a man, and a leader, so there is no arguing with him." She slyly glanced at Hilda. "I'll wager he can't even get it up with you anymore."

Hilda blushed and pretended to stumble on a stone in the lane. This was the first time her friend had revealed that she knew of Hilda's long-ago liaisons with Fleet.

"I don't know what you mean—"

"Nonsense, Hilda. I knew about every one of his conquests and it soon ceased to matter to me. I raise it now only to make the point: men will always attempt to blame us for their own failings." She stopped for a moment, waiting for Amanda and Septimus to overtake them. "Perhaps we can teach our children better ways, though I doubt it."

"Teach us what?" Amanda laughed. "After the Reverend Haggard's lesson today, it would seem the only thing a young woman need learn is to stay indoors and shroud her beauty. I think he was most unfair on that poor girl. Why, it could have as easily been me abducted by those swine!"

Hilda reached out to take her daughter's hand. The girl was so handsome and sure of herself; Hilda sighed as she remembered what it had been to have all the world ahead of you.

"If anyone ever did anything bad to you, Amanda," Septimus Fleet piped, his voice breaking embarrassingly, "I would . . . I would kill the perpetrators with my bare hands." He fell into a blushing silence as the three women laughed at his fourteen-year-old bravado. But he suffered a fierce puppy love for Amanda and each night prayed to the Lord to keep her for him, just a few more years until he had grown up and made his mark and the age difference between them would no longer matter.

"Such outrages are not committed against people like us," Jessica told him. "And when they are suffered by such as the Odlum girl, they are not of such great import. When you have no name to lose, you are not so vulnerable to shame."

There was only one piece of news, Sarah knew, that would raise her daughter from her bed; and when it came she ran all the way home to announce it.

"Will's ship is arrived and is standing outside the bar," she said. "As soon as the tide turns he will be here. You must prepare yourself."

Together they worked to erase the marks of Prudence's ordeal. Her fine hair was washed and combed and piled high on her head; gentle color applied to her pale cheeks; her one best dress was brushed and pressed. There was nothing to be done about the dark rings under her eyes or the blue-black bruise on the side of her chin, but Sarah was at last satisfied her daughter was ready to meet her fiancé.

"Go to the docks now," she said. "And hold your head high. You have done nothing to be ashamed of." She opened her arms and enfolded Prudence. It was an awkward, unfamiliar gesture. Sarah could not easily show affection. But for a moment they held each other and love flowed between them; then Prudence mustered her courage and stepped purposefully out into the bright afternoon light and, ignoring the glances and whispers, started down to the docks.

She saw him at once, standing tall on the bridge, waving frantically to her as his ship edged alongside and sailors scurried to get lines ashore. The signs of a long and hard voyage were everywhere, but to Prudence it was the most magnificent vessel afloat. There was a lump in her throat and tears in her eyes as she watched Will come sprinting down the gangway to her.

She watched his long white hair swaying in the sunshine and saw his washed-out blue eyes shining; when at last his arms were around her she knew, finally, she would survive. Everything would be all right.

"My darling Prudence," he cried, not caring about the stares they were attracting. "Every day I have whistled for a wind to speed me home to you, begged the great Gulf

Stream to flow faster. It has been so long that I despaired
you would wait for me."

She snuggled into his arms and felt his body yearning
against her. The fear returned: would she be able to love
him again, physically, after what had been done to her?

"I have missed you sorely, Will," she said, content for
now just to feel the rough cloth of his jacket against her
cheek. "I have paced off the days you were away, particularly these weeks you have been overdue."

"It was worth the delay!" he shouted. "Wait until I tell
you what I have achieved on this voyage. I have found
new ports, fresh cargoes—the best voyage I have done.
When the profits are in, there will be more than enough
for us to be married and live handsomely. We are going
to be rich, Prudence, and bow our heads to no one in Bermuda." He held her at arm's length then and studied her
face. Some of his elation vanished. "What is it, my dear
one? You look so pale and desperate. Your face, your
beautiful face . . . it is as if someone has struck you."

"Come, Will," she said. "Walk with me away from
these curious eyes. There are things to tell you, dreadful
things."

And as they moved down the dock, away from the other
women welcoming their sailors home, she began to de-
scribe to him what had happened up on the cliffs. She
could not meet his eyes and told her tale in an abrupt,
cold manner, her face cast to the ground. She did not consider what the telling would do to him; it just had to be
all revealed as quickly as possible. When she had finished, she continued to walk, feeling his arm drop from
around her shoulder. So that was that and she could not
blame him.

But suddenly Will was in front of her, dropped to his
knees, his arms encircling her hips and pressing her to
him. She could not hear what he was saying, and slowly
she raised his chin to where she could see his face. It was
drenched with tears.

"My darling," he sobbed. "My poor beauty. My heart
breaks for you. But it loves you even more for the agony
you have endured. The things those animals did to you

. . . it does not exist for us, except in the suffering it has cost you. The pain and the bruises will fade, but my love for you will continue to grow." He pulled himself up and kissed her full on the lips. "Take no notice of the cheap sharp tongues of this village," he said. "We are above them. And now I am a man of substance and we are going to be married."

They stood together for a long time, Prudence taking strength from him. She had been given back what she thought she had lost forever. The love of this good, gentle man. Her God had not deserted her. She wondered, wryly, how her God coexisted with the God the condemnatory Reverend Haggard prayed to.

"You are a brave man, Will Acton," she said at last. "I promise, every day of my life, I shall repay your faith and love. I will make you a good wife and bear you fine children and watch you go from strength to strength. I swear you will never regret what you have done today."

"Stop talking like that, Prudence. It is I who is filled with thanks to God to find you here and waiting for me. What happened could have been so much worse. If you were dead, then I would fling myself from those same cliffs. There would be nothing to live for without you." His hand was around her waist and he led her back to the docks. "I will collect my papers, then call upon your mother," he said. "There is a great deal for us to discuss."

At that moment they were so happy, they could ignore the stares and the whispered comments. They were sure nothing could ever change the way it was for them.

The Governor had a most severe headache; despite his failing eyesight, he had been compelled to spend the morning with the Bermuda Company's Official Visitor going over and over the depressing production figures for the Colony. The Official Visitor had been blunt, rude even. The Governor sighed and rubbed his eyes. The Official Visitors were always blunt with him—they did represent the people who appointed the Governor, after all, so they felt no need to mince words—but this latest was particularly obnoxious. Now the fellow was pacing the Governor's office and ranting about what had to be done. The Governor knew it all: it wasn't he who had to be convinced, but the settlers.

"Every crop you people have attempted has been a disaster," the man repeated. "Corn, peas, cabbage . . . even the humble potato. And now it is apparent the tobacco will let us down again. I tell you, sir, it's not good enough. Our investors have been patient, but we must have some return on our capital or they will abandon us. And then we will abandon you. Like that!" He snapped his fingers, a gesture that further irritated the Governor. "And what will Bermuda be then? It will revert to being a cluster of rocks in the middle of a vast ocean, just as it was when the Spaniards and the Portuguese discarded it as worthless for anything but a dry place for shipwrecked sailors. Damn it, this should be a Garden of Eden, a place of abundant crops. The climate is gentle and we have provided every plant and seed you requested. So where are the cash crops, the dividends? It's humiliating to us, to see the riches the Virginia Company is beginning to reap. Those fellows laugh at us, saying they sold us a pig in a poke when they sold us Bermuda."

"My dear fellow," the Governor said wearily, "it's not as simple as you would paint it." He'd been through all the excuses with all the other impatient Official Visitors. "The soil is not so fertile as it appears. There is a very thin covering of earth, and that is stripped away when the tempests come through. Beneath us is limestone and beneath that salt water. It may look like a land as green and plentiful as England, but it requires a very different approach to agriculture. One we have not yet discovered. And the colonists themselves—generally they were not farmers selected to come here, but townspeople. I doubt they could have farmed England; certainly they can't succeed here."

"They might have some success if they labored harder. From what I have seen, they are a spoiled lot, content to live by what falls out of the sky or leaps from the sea."

"I'm afraid a lot of us came here with false hopes," the

Governor said. "All the talk of a new paradise. Now, already, our natural resources are becoming exhausted and—as you so firmly point out—the things we have introduced have generally failed. What we need are some new colonists, handpicked for their ability to farm difficult terrain. We need terracing to halt the erosion caused by tempests, irrigation to spread our scarce water supply, new crops which can thrive under our conditions."

"You can forget about new blood. There's no money left in the company to ship more settlers here, and those who could pay their own way have already heard what a disaster this place is. Now the Americas are all the rage and you are just a pimple, an irritating one, on the map of the Empire."

"We have had some successes," the Governor said. Despite all the problems, he had come to love Bermuda. He did not like this London fop's denigrating it. "Our merchants are proving to be astute and there are quite fine shops here. And our ships and seamen are gaining renown all along the Gulf Stream."

"Shopkeeping and seafaring may line the pockets of the people but they return no dividends to London," the Visitor sniffed. "The only income the Company has seen lately is the royalties Fleet pays us for his charter. Imagine! A great company like ours relying on the tribute of a man engaged in what we all know is piracy. And even that source could dry up at any time. There are misguided fools in the Parliament who would put a stop to such activities. They say the peace is endangered." He smiled for the first time that morning. "The peace, of course, is a sham. We will all soon be back to declared war on those European bastards. Then perhaps your rocky outpost will again have some significance." He made a great show of inspecting his fob watch, a big, heavy object of beaten silver. "Noon already. I am due to lunch with Fleet. Perhaps I can screw a greater royalty from him so my trip will not have been totally in vain."

"I wish you well," the Governor said. He did not attempt to hide the bitterness in his voice. "Sir Thomas and his cohorts are all about making themselves rich.

Only so long as Bermuda serves that purpose are they loyal to it."

"You could say the same about the Company. None of us is a charitable concern."

The Governor saw the Visitor out the French doors to his carriage. He poured himself a large brandy from the decanter on his desk, settled back into his chair and let himself slip into a dream in which he was strolling the gentle hills of the Cotswolds, his faithful dogs gamboling at his heels.

The bird had been scouring the island since early spring, getting ever closer to the settlements as it searched for a mate. It dimly understood the danger of approaching the creatures who now dominated the islands, but fear was not enough to deter it. Because there was a worse fear, the fear that it was totally alone. Now it lumbered through the trees at the edge of the green lawn and paused, staring shortsightedly at the two creatures sitting there.

"I'll be damned," Sir Thomas said. "It's a boobie! Haven't seen one in ages."

"What is a boobie?" the Official Visitor asked.

"See, there at the edge of the lawn. That big, stupid-looking bird. There are thousands of them at first, funny creatures who were too stupid to know fear. They would let you walk up and pet them. They were a great source of food, though none too delicate on the palate." Fleet called to the tall, white-liveried servant standing at a discreet distance from their table. "Jimbo! Go fetch that bird and bring it here for our inspection."

The black slave moved swiftly across the lawn to where the bird waited, trembling but resigned to whatever would happen. Jimbo reached out and grasped the bird by its neck, gave it one sharp twist and carried its rapidly dying body back to his master.

"A most odd creature," the Official Visitor said, studying the sad mass of feathers, soft beak and liquid brown eyes. "I don't think I would relish eating one." He picked up his fork and returned to the poached fish as the last

boobie on Bermuda, sole survivor of flocks of hundreds
of thousands that had been in the islands for five hundred
years, died.

They were both nervous, lying together in the hidden
sandy cove. Will and Prudence had been uncertain of
each other since his return; the ordeal she had been
through was a wall between them. He was hesitant to
make love with her, imagining as best he could how
threatening all men must now seem to her. Prudence too
was afraid of how she would respond to the man she
loved. The scars were still too fresh for her to truly remember the way it had been before the outrage. But she
knew she must help Will and herself to get past the barrier. She cradled his head against her bosom and felt him
stirring; his hand tentatively touched her ankle, then
moved up her calf. She suppressed a shiver and willed
herself to respond to him. When they kissed she opened
her lips and met his tongue; she felt his hand between
her thighs and did not flinch; she welcomed his weight
on her. But she could not stifle a cry when he entered her,
so great was the hurt.

"Do you want me to stop?" he whispered. She shook
her head, and then Will was swept up in the passion of
the moment, plunging deeper and deeper into her, trying
to dispel all his own fears and doubts, wanting to purge
himself of suspicion.

At last Prudence felt herself responding to him, forgetting the pain and letting her body find its own
rhythm. She could see the blue sky through his pale hair,
feel the warm sun on her hands as they clasped his
shoulders. She felt him quicken as he built toward release and she prepared to welcome a flood of him inside
of her. She suddenly wrapped her strong legs around
him, pulling him even closer.

"Did you do that with them? Did you? Did you gasp
and cry like that?" His voice was cracking with anguish,
confused with lust, laden with fury. He finished his climax and fell away from her, facedown in the pink sand.

Prudence lay there in despair, the words he had spoken still battering at her senses, the fleeting passion she had felt now sickening her. She knew there was no hope for them. She turned her head and saw his shoulders were shaking and she heard his sobbing.

"Forgive me, please forgive me," he cried, pressing his face into the sand so he would not have to meet her poor, hurt eyes. "I did not mean it—the words came from somewhere else. My sweet Prudence, I would cut out my tongue if it would bring those terrible utterances back."

"It's all right, Will," she said, patting his heaving shoulder. "I understand how you must feel. You need time to adjust to all that has happened." She continued to comfort him when all the time her own mind and body were crying out for comfort and understanding.

"I don't need time," he muttered. "I know what happened was not your fault. I love you and I am going to marry you. It's just . . . oh God, it is so hard to accept. I am trying, Prudence."

They adjusted their clothing and walked home in strained silence, Will ashamed of himself for his evil suspicions and determined they would never surface again, Prudence numb in the knowledge that the wall was still there between them and now more solid than ever.

"I will try, Prudence," he said as he held her hand outside her cottage.

And he did try. But his own doubts were fueled by the cruel gossip of the town. He began to believe they were all sniggering at him; he read contempt in every glance or, at best, pity.

"You must snap out of this, Will," Ewen Staley told him. They were sitting in the tavern, waiting for news of George Morris and their ship's current voyage. George had undertaken their most ambitious trip yet, shipping a cargo of nutmeg and cinnamon from the Spice Islands to Portsmouth. He would return—if he returned; seven Bermuda ships had been lost already this year—with bolts of cloth, crates of tea and a swag of other goods in demand in the colony. Everything was going well for the three young men, except for the mental state of Will Acton.

"I can't help it, Ewen," he said. "It eats at my belly, as if there is a rat inside me gnawing his way out. I know I am wrong to feel like this, but there is nothing I can do about it. I love her, but when I look upon her my imagination runs riot. I am as bad as all the vicious old biddies of the town who say when a thing like this happens to a girl she must have done something to bring it on." He drank deeply and banged his mug down on the rough bar for another. He knew he was drinking too much these days but he could find no good reason to stop.

"Time will heal all, Will. You know Prudence; you know what a fine girl she is. What happened was none of her fault. And after you are married the gossip will stop. They will find some other innocent target for their idle tongues."

"I know you are right, Ewen, and I know Prudence is innocent. It is I who am at fault. I am not mature enough to accept what has happened. Instead of sympathy and understanding, I give her jealous ravings, vile accusations. I try, but I have not the moral strength needed in a situation like this." He drained his fresh mug. "I think I will take the next voyage of our ship. Perhaps a spell away from this confining little town will clear my head." He was quite drunk now and nauseated. He pushed himself off his stool to make for the stinking trough at the back of the tavern and bumped heavily into a huge man clutching three tankards of ale.

"Watch where you're going," James Stannard growled. Stannard was the blacksmith, the strongest and meanest man on the island. It was wise to avoid him at all times but particularly when he was in his cups.

Will tried to mouth an apology, but suddenly all the bile in him came spilling up. A fountain of porter and vomit spurted from him and hit the blacksmith fair in the chest. The big man looked puzzled for a moment, then shook his head and let out a great roar.

"You turd!" he cried, dropping his tankards and swinging his massive fist, sending Will sprawling against the bar. "You jumped-up peasant, thinking you're better than us because you have yourself a scruffy little ship." He advanced on Will and picked him up by the scruff of the neck. "What are you going to do about this mess, eh? Maybe get your 'fiancée' to wash my clothes clean? I don't know I'd want that, though. I hear she has the pox herself, so many men she's been with."

Will's drunkenness was swept away by a red tide of fury. He scrabbled behind him on the bar and felt a heavy pewter mug in his grasp. Still suspended by the smithy, he swung his hand in a wide arc and brought the mug crashing into Stannard's face. It was all in slow motion, the edge of the mug biting into the bridge of the big man's nose, the flesh opening, the bone crunching, the torrent of claret-red blood gushing forth.

Stannard dropped him to the dirt floor and slowly raised his hands to touch his nose. He gazed at the blood covering them and reached down to Will. As Ewen started forward to help it was already too late. Stannard pulled Will's head in close to his mouth and bit his left ear off. He spat the sorry scrap of flesh onto the dirt floor and ground it in with his boot.

"You are lucky I don't kill you," Stannard snarled, shrugging off Ewen, who had sprung onto his back, and still holding Will off the floor. "I will let you live for your slut's sake. There's no one else would be desperate enough to marry her after she has spread her legs for all of the fleet." He let Will drop then, wiped some more blood from his face and strode out of the tavern.

Slowly the other patrons edged back from their refuge around the walls. They regarded the bloody, earless side of Will's scalp with awe. The tavern keeper, experienced with the results of violence, took a grubby cloth and soaked it in gin, then slapped it on Will's wound.

Jepson, the sailmaker, fished in his dilly bag and found a bone needle and a length of catgut.

"Hold him still," he ordered Ewen and a couple of others. He took a fistful of the loose flesh on the side of Will's head, pulled it together over the gaping wound and roughly stitched the whole mess together. He bit off the

catgut with his teeth, knotted the ends and stepped back
to admire his work. "Not pretty," he announced, "but it
will stop your brains leaking out."

Ewen put his arm around Will and supported him out
of the tavern into the cool, dark night. He pretended not
to hear Will's sobs as they stumbled to the low seawall
and flopped down.

"Jepson's right, Will," he said, striving to be hearty.
"It will heal clean. And no one needs two ears."

"It's no good," Will said. He was talking only to himself. "It will always be like this. I will always be the object of jibes and sneers and I am too proud for that. I
intend to be someone in this damned place and I cannot
have them all laughing at me or pitying me." He pushed
himself to his feet, staggering as a new wave of pain
swept him. He shook his head and a few spots of blood
splashed on Ewen's upturned face. "I will leave you now,
Ewen," he said. "I must go home to rest, and to think."

Prudence gasped in horror when Will appeared at her
door the next morning. The side of his head was a grotesque mess of blackened blood and she reached out to
touch it, to comfort him. But he shoved her hand aside
roughly, and staring somewhere over her head began to
speak.

"I cannot marry you," he said. "You are forever
marked, the object of scorn and gossip. A scarlet woman.
It matters not whose fault it was. That is the way things
are. Good-bye." He turned stiffly and strode away down
the narrow lane. It was done and he felt no more sorrow
for either her or himself. He did not look back, so did not
see Sarah Odlum holding her daughter to her, did not
see Sarah's eyes burning into his back. And of course he
did not know this was the day Prudence had finally accepted that she was pregnant.

They fought about the baby until it was too late to
abort it; Sarah only wanted to save Prudence from bearing yet another burden, the unwanted issue of the wild
men in the cave. But Prudence, silent and withdrawn,

would not hear of ending her pregnancy. It did not matter to her how the child had been conceived. She wanted it for herself, to be hers alone. Because Prudence, only just in her eighteenth year, already knew she was destined to spend her life without a partner to love and protect her. She let herself dream about raising her child to be someone, to make the name of Odlum something more than one to bring a sneer from the well-to-do. Her dreams kept her sane during the final, long months the baby was growing inside her.

Sarah delivered Prudence of a child late one cool spring night. The tallow lamp flickered as the boy gave his first cry and was washed and placed in swaddling clothes. In the soft light Sarah and Prudence regarded the infant: the snow-white hair and pale, pale blue eyes, the skin so fair—it could only be the child of Will Acton.

"You didn't tell me you had gone with him," Sarah said as she placed the child in Prudence's hands. "This changes everything."

"No, Mother, it changes nothing. I had hoped the child would be his rather than one of those men who attacked me, but it would not have altered my feelings. I want nothing from Acton. In the end, he will be the one who lost, for I am determined this boy will grow up strong and proud. And he will be an Odlum, not an Acton."

The next day, though, Sarah sought out Will Acton. She found him at the dockside haggling with a group of merchants, and she had great difficulty gaining his attention. The past months had not been kind to him. The ravages of strong drink showed in his face and unsteady hand; the obscene scar where his ear had been pulsated when he was angry or excited. It was pulsating now as he tried to brush off the big, gaunt woman demanding his attention.

"I am busy," he snapped at her. "Get out of my way or I'll have the sheriff to you."

"I had hoped to keep this private, Mr. Acton," Sarah said, "but if you prefer your linen aired in public then so it shall be. My daughter, Mr. Acton, to whom you were betrothed, gave birth to a boy last night. It is clearly your child and I would be obliged to know what you intend to do about it."

All talk stopped as the men standing about regarded Acton. Shock showed in his eyes, and just for a moment, compassion and hope. A son, his own son, he thought. And he remembered the love he had had for Prudence. Perhaps . . . no, it was too late.

"So your daughter has produced a bastard and you would like to lay it at my door, Mistress Odlum," he said, his voice rising. "That is one of the disadvantages of being a man of property. Ambitious mothers would marry their daughters off to us. I expect there will be dozens more like you. I should be flattered. I will get a reputation as a great stallion." A few of the listeners laughed. "But, mistress, I think you would be better spending your time at home caring for your daughter and the child. You will get nothing from me."

"In that case, Will Acton, I will give you something." Sarah's voice was low and cold, and those nearest drew back. "I give you a curse, that all your children and all their children, your whole male line from this day on, will be sickly and miserable. Everyone will know an Acton by the misfortune that dogs him. The child you have just rejected will be the only one of strong blood and he will not be burdened by the name of Acton, anyway. You will forever rue this day."

Acton shivered in the sunshine. He was as superstitious as any man, and this woman did have a reputation for knowing strange herbs and potions. But wasn't he, Will Acton, someone to be reckoned with? A shipowner, a man of means.

"Take your curse and get out of my presence!" he told her. "You will get nothing but the taste of my whip if you continue to harass me." He took a step toward her, his fist upraised, but the cold hatred in her eyes stopped him. He turned on his heel and hurried away from the docks, heading for the sanctuary of the tavern and the bottle awaiting him.

Cliff Cottage,
Paget,
Bermuda.
September 1635

Dearest Sister,
    *The news that you will visit us next year fills me with
joy. I despair sometimes of ever making the trip Home—
Sam always has one excuse or another as to why it is
not "practical" for him to undertake the voyage and
why I cannot go alone. To have you here in the Colony
will be a great consolation. Sam at least promises to secure you a superior berth in one of our ships. Plan to
come at Easter when our climate is at its most gentle,
and stay through the summer which, while hot by your
standards, is quite bearable. I will write you later about
what clothes to pack, but generally dress as for a summer in the country at Home. We DO dress for dinner,
but it is accepted that only two or three different gowns
are needed.*
    *So much has happened since my last letter. Sam is
prospering mightily, his fortune reflected in his growing girth. He is, between you and me, Angela, an exceedingly dull man whose total ambition is to be
comfortably wealthy and accepted here socially. Both
of these things he has achieved and would now rest on
his laurels if not for my nagging. Good Lord, I don't
know what we would have to talk about if Sam did not
have his shipping interests: he is, despite his wish to re-
linquish the post, still Harbormaster and that gets him
out of the house during the day. The money, of course,
comes from his partnership with Tommy Fleet and that
operation goes from strength to strength. It is funny
when I look at Tommy and remember how "close" we
once were. Sometimes I discreetly tease him about it, but
he is so pompous now he pretends to remember nothing. Maybe he doesn't. Remember, I mean. Goodness,
Angela, I am forty-five years of age now and have difficulty recalling what passion was. How cruel life is, to
be almost over before one had the chance to experience*

it to the full. Perhaps you are lucky, having never married; you have nothing to regret.

Speaking of marriage, it appears Amanda is close to that step at last. She would need to be: at twenty-five she is very close to being on the shelf and there is nothing in this community for a spinster to occupy herself with. The fellow in question is not the type we would think suitable anywhere except in Bermuda. He has dragged himself up from humble beginnings and now owns three quite respectable ships. This really is the kind of place where anyone can succeed.

Anyway, Amanda's suitor has good prospects, even if he is ugly as sin with his strange pale coloring and grotesque missing ear. He did rather endear himself to Sam and me by the way he defeated his partners in shipping and claimed the whole operation for himself. A masterly scheme! He arranged for the partners, Messrs Staley and Morris, to be guarantors for a shipment from London which vanished on the high seas. When they were required to pay up, they had to sell their shareholdings to Will Acton or else go to debtors' prison. After it was all done, rumors began that the ship was not lost at all. Acton diverted it to the Indies where the cargo was sold and he and the captain split the takings. That was the source of the money with which he so generously bailed out his erstwhile partners! He will go a long way in Bermuda, our Mr. Acton. There might even be a merger after he marries Amanda, though his shipping line is nothing to compare with the vast enterprise Tommy and Sam now control.

I had, as you know, hopes of marrying Amanda off to the Fleet boy. But, though he still moons around after her, she will not entertain thoughts of him as anything more than a little brother. A pity. Young Sep isn't the brightest or best looking, but he will inherit a vast fortune, and one that is already interlocked with our own. Jessica and I have done our best to bring the two of them together but time is running out for Amanda and it appears she will only settle for the opportunistic Mr. Acton.

*Lest you think it is all plain sailing for us, you will
see (if you pursue the Admiralty Reports, which I am
sure you don't) that Tommy and Sam have been chart-
ing a risky course of late. One of their privateers bailed
up a ship out of America in June. It tried to make a run
for it and of course had no chance against our speedy
Bermuda ship. Anyway, they shot it up rather badly
and at last drove it ashore here. Well, you can imagine
the embarrassment when it turned out to be a British
merchantman! The Board of Enquiry was handled well
but there were some sticky moments and we were forced
to return the cargo of tobacco we had captured. Thank
God the Board accepted the evidence that the ship never
broke out the ensign, and gave appearances of being a
fugitive pirate. And thank God we had the Enquiry here
on Bermuda. If it had been at the other end, among
those dreadful Americans, I am sure they would have
hanged our men as pirates.*

*Do not expect too much when you eventually arrive in
Bermuda, dear Sister. It is still a small and rather
crude outpost of Empire. I am sure you will find us figures of fun after the sophisticated people you know in
London. I am still undecided about this place; on good
days, when the sun is shining and the warm wind
comes in off the Atlantic, it seems like the prettiest place
on earth. But I feel so isolated here, cut off from Home
and all I hold dear. You will realize on your long voyage just how far away we are from anything. Sam
grandly offers to send me on a holiday to Virginia because it is relatively close, but who would want to go
there? Jamestown's only slightly larger than St.
George's and every bit as rough. What will be familiar
to you is the look of our town—it could be any English
village by the sea. I cannot fathom why we should have
come so far to such a different place and climate, then
duplicated what we left behind. But St. George's is all
tiny, cramped stone cottages built flush onto narrow alleys, huddled cheek by jowl as if there wasn't room to
spread out. At least my nagging Sam has paid off in
that respect. Cliff Cottage is now complete and I am*

quite pleased with it. I think some of the locals laughed behind their hands as the cottage took shape but now a few of them are copying us. The cottage is large and airy and very pretty, built of Bermuda stone with cedar doors and supports. And the roof is a thing of practicality and beauty—stone again, terraced to collect the rainwater into cisterns, and whitewashed. It is a most distinctive look, and it means we are the only house that does not need to have water carried up. I have a garden around the house and have got Sam's officers into the habit of bringing me plants when they return from their journeys. As I write to you I can look out and see the vivid blooms of Hibiscus framed by the green fronds of our young banana plantation. At least all kinds of tropical flowers flourish when introduced here, which is more than can be said for the sorely needed cash crops.

I should not complain, should I? Here I am talking about lush tropical growth, hearing birdsong in the trees, fanned by the trade winds. And there you are, reading this on what will surely be a bitter cold October day. I should revel in all this but I would swap it easily for time in my beloved England, sleet and snow and rain regardless.

I must caution you of one thing when you visit. In your past letters you have expressed some doubts about the practice of Slavery, which is now quite entrenched in all parts of the Empire (and you will understand why when you see how difficult it is for any white man to work out of doors in these climes). Slavery is a de facto business here—so far there are only a handful of blacks working in the leading houses. But the leaders of the community are determined to greatly increase the number of Slaves after first overcoming the fears of the general populace. Our Agent General, Nathaniel Pike, privately swears he will see full-scale importation of slaves before he dies, and of course Sam and Tommy back him totally as they foresee a great trade in bringing the Slaves here, then shipping out the produce they will reap from the fields. So do not let your misguided missionary zeal rule your tongue in this matter while

you are here. I have enough arguments with Sam al-
ready, thank you.

  Anyway, in a few short months we shall be sitting
here together, taking tea and talking and talking. I
can't wait! I miss you so, dear Angela. God speed.

> *All my love,*
> *Hilda.*

"Hold my hand, Prudence." Sarah's voice was weak in
the darkened room; she felt her strength slipping away
and she needed to conserve it, to have these last minutes
with her daughter. Sarah had not given up easily to the
plague sweeping the islands; she had tried every one of
her potions and powders. She had even consented in the
end to having the doctor bleed her with leeches. But she
had seen so much death, and she knew, when the time
came, there was no point in defying it further. She felt
the cool, firm grip of her daughter's hand.

"I am going now, my dear," Sarah said. "I do not want
to leave you. I am sorry I have not been a warmer mother.
Often I wanted to take you in my arms and hold you and
protect you from the world. But I always knew this time
would come, when I would have to leave you all alone.
So I tried to make you strong and independent, as I was.
I think I have succeeded in that, though at a terrible
price to both of us." She stroked Prudence's hand. "I have
loved you dearly, every day, and longed to show it."

Prudence felt the tears spilling onto her cheeks. It was
hard to accept that this strong, brave woman was not im-
mortal. All the years of hardship and pain . . . Prudence
could recall her childhood clearly, and Sarah's exhorta-
tions to stand tall and proud, be brave, ignore the taunts.
It had always been the two of them together against this
smug little community, the stern, gruff mother and the
silent, wary daughter.

"I know you love me, Mother," she said. "We are two
of a kind, in that we have no need to show affection and
would find it difficult to do so. But I have always loved
you, too, and we have plenty of time left to prove it."

"Don't be silly," Sarah snapped. "I have taught you all I know about medicine and you can see that I am sinking fast. This is no time for pretense. What I want to tell you now is to look to your future and to that of young Jonas. There is no point in living with old hatreds. I learned that a long time ago. Hate did not bring my Jonas back. For years I had bile in me. I loathed these people who destroyed the man I loved. But then I began to live again through you. When Acton betrayed you, hate enveloped me again. But in these past ten years I have buried it. It has been a happy time, here with you, watching the boy grow big and strong and wise. He has it in him to be a good man, Prudence, but he must not be filled with old hatreds or saddled with scores to be settled. In the end, I realize that we are now of Bermuda, no matter how we came here or what Bermuda has done to us. Jessica Fleet once told me this place had changed us all. She was right, except that she meant it had changed us for the worse. There is no need for that. It doesn't have to be a bad change. You and the boy will be well here."

"No," Prudence said. She didn't want to argue with her mother but she would not pretend, either. "I cannot forgive these people. You ministered to them when they were sick, delivered their babies, bound up their dead. And all the time they acted as if you did not exist. Now they do the same to me. I am a leper except when they need the skills you have taught me. If I had the means, and someplace else to go, I would take Jonas and leave here forever."

"Then I am glad you do not have the means. Bermuda is your home now and will be even more the boy's home." She laughed. "Why, your father was the very first settler here! No, Prudence, times will improve and the lot of the Odlums will improve with them. Someday, an Odlum—" A coughing fit wracked her and she tightened her grip on Prudence's hand. "Stay with me a minute more. I will be gone soon," she whispered. "Say good-bye to the boy for me. I do not want him to see me like this." A shudder ran through her body then and Sarah Odlum died in the bed in which her daughter had been born.

Prudence buried her in the little cemetery at St. Steven's. Jonas, already tall and strong, stood beside her. The only other person present was the new young vicar, just out from England. He talked about Sarah's pioneering spirit and her great good works for the community. Prudence allowed herself a bitter smile.

"So the old devil is dead," Will Acton grunted. "She was lucky it wasn't on the gallows, the trouble Sarah Odlum caused people. My God, I cannot understand why the community put up with the likes of her, the harridan!" He puffed on his pipe, scowling into the blazing log fire that warmed the big, handsome living room of his mansion. "Maybe now my luck will improve."

"I heard she did a lot of good down in the town among the poor people," Amanda Acton said, peering at her embroidery. "And what is wrong with your luck? I remember seeing you when I was a little girl. You were one of the crowd of roughnecks always by the harborfront. Father used to say you should all be pressganged into the Navy. Look at you now—a fleet owner, a man of substance almost of my father's class."

"Almost! That's the point. Your father and the rest of the Forty Thieves will never think people like me are as good as they are. Just because they got a head start on me . . ." He scowled at his wife. "Well, I don't give a damn anymore what your father or Fleet thinks of me. I have a scheme that will make me richer than either of them. One of these days, I'll buy them out."

"Perhaps you should be content with what you've got," Amanda said. "When Father dies I shall inherit from him, and I might be prepared to look at a merger with you." She tried to tease him out of his gloom. "But I'd never merge with a grumpy old man, so you had better get a smile on your face."

"You think it is my fault, don't you," he said. "That I'm too old to give you strong sons. Three stillborn and one sickly wretch surviving day-to-day. I see you looking at me and I can tell that you despise me. Well, if the truth were known, it is more likely that your bad blood is the

cause of our misfortune. Your father never managed to
produce more than you. Nor did your mother, despite, I
hear, trying to with half the gentry."

"You are a tiresome person, Will," she said. "I am used
to your drunken ranting, but I will not hear you speak
ill of my mother." She watched him defiantly spill more
brandy into his goblet and wondered yet again what she
had seen in him. Of all the people she might have married! She had been infatuated with his grim, pale looks
and vivid scar, seeing him as a daredevil sailor. The
scandal of his affair with the Odlum girl and his despic-
able treatment of his naive partners had all added to the
sense of delicious danger she felt when she was around
him. But the years had dispelled all of that; now he was
just a self-pitying drunkard. And all she had to show for
her years of marriage were a big house and poor little
Richard, at seven her only surviving child.

"I'll say anything I damn well please in my own
house," Acton said, sprawling down in his chair and
splaying his long legs out. His heavy boots scratched the
gleaming floor. He flung a hand out, sending his crystal
goblet crashing into a thousand pieces against the floor.
"That Odlum woman!" he ranted. "It's all her fault. The
curse she put on me has come true. I am stuck with you
and that poor excuse for a son."

"The Odlum curse!" She laughed aloud at him. "Will,
the bottle has got to you even more than I realized. Any
curse you bear is of your own making. You are a mean-
spirited man, and your ugly demeanor flows into everything you do. You poison yourself as you poison all
around you. Every day I give thanks that Richard does
not have your nature, even if he must bear the burden of
looking like you." She gathered up her embroidery and
moved swiftly out of the room. If she stayed, he would
probably strike her. It had happened often enough. If she
got out of the room, he would remain there and drink
himself into a stupor. Later the servants would put him
into his solitary bed.

Amanda tiptoed into Richard's room and gently
brushed the pale hair from the boy's brow; at least he was

breathing more easily tonight. It had been weeks since his last bout with fever. Perhaps now he was past the worst of the childhood sicknesses. Poor little boy, she thought, gazing down at him: for all the riches in your family, there is no love except the love I have for you.

For once, Acton did not drink himself insensible. His anger and frustration kept him just on the right side of sobriety, and he continued to plan his next great coup. It would be even more daring than the way he had taken stupid Morris and Staley and embarked on his fortune. This time he was going to leave bloody Fleet and Cobcroft, and that snake Pike, gasping at his audacity.

The idea had come to him with the arrival of the French family, M. Henri Lapin and his wife and her two sisters. The Lapins would have caused comment in any event. Fresh from the exotic island of Haiti, they were young, handsome and elegant, quite unlike the general dour English settlers. But when they came ashore, it was their entourage that caused the most talk; four tall, strong, blue-black servants, so vastly superior to the usual run of slaves in Bermuda. The Lapins' slaves had elegant manners. They were suitably subservient, but they seemed proud to be in the service of their family. In the two months the contingent had been in the colony, their presence had done much to remove fears about introducing significant numbers of blacks to Bermuda.

Lapin himself, a friendly fellow eager to get to know the colonists, had invited Acton up to their rented house for good French brandy and conversation. When Will remarked on the quality of his slaves, Lapin laughed.

"You should have seen the ones we had to leave behind," he said. "They are what make Haiti—for all its heat and fever—a fine place to live. We French are wiser than some others. Instead of taking just anything, we handpicked our slaves on the theory that we were going to have to live with them and their descendants. Almost all of them are from the Cameroons, so they are physically and intellectually a cut above the type of slave the slavers now capture. And, my dear Acton, if I may say this without sounding too proud of my home country, we took the time to teach them our culture, our manners, our cuisine. In consequence, we have a large, stable and happy band of blacks at our disposal. In fact, we have many more than we need, so rapidly have they bred in what is, to them, an ideal environment." Watching Acton's eyes, he saw the gleam of avarice. "In my short time here I've come to understand something of your situation. You people are fearful of being overrun if you bring in the black masses. I think if a fellow with an empty ship were to make a run over to Port au Prince and buy himself a hundred or so of our housebroken blacks, he would make a fortune bringing them back here and auctioning them."

"I'm sure you are right, M. Lapin," Acton said, the brandy and the prospect before him sending his pulse racing. "But this colony has had so few dealings with your people in Haiti. A man would need connections, references."

"I could arrange all that. The man would be doing us something of a favor, taking our surplus off our hands, if you see."

"I might," Acton said cautiously, "be interested in such a scheme."

In the ensuing weeks he had had more talks with the charming Lapin, and he was almost ready to proceed with his daring scheme. He would show Amanda, and her father, and the superior Sir Thomas Fleet. They were still waiting for official sanction to get their great slave-trading scheme under way. Will Acton didn't wait for anyone. He'd steal a march on them all, slip out of harbor to Haiti with a chest of gold and return with a holdful of beautifully trained slaves. Three thousand pounds profit at least, he reckoned. The top people of Bermuda would be cutting each other's throats to have one of Will Acton's slaves. He would be looked up to as the man who'd made it all happen, respected as a man of vision.

He found a new goblet and poured one more drink. Respect, that was what he wanted, even more than riches. Respect would make up for all of what was lacking in his life. He could not remember now when it had all begun to go wrong for him. Coming home to discover that his fiancée had been conducting herself lewdly: that had been a turning point. He felt a stab of real pain as he remembered Prudence before it all went bad. And bitter sadness as he thought of the boy, Jonas Odlum, he sometimes saw in the town. Damn, he had fathered one fine-looking boy. Why couldn't Amanda give him the same? Of course it was nothing to do with the Odlum woman's curse; Will Acton didn't believe in all that nonsense. Still, he was glad she was dead. Now his luck would change. And the daring voyage to Haiti would be the beginning. You made your own luck, Acton reminded himself, thinking back to the day when he had first decided to build himself a ship.

But that was more bad luck. He had been right to destroy Ewen Staley and George Morris; they were not real men of vision. The company would never have got anywhere if he had been saddled forever with them as his partners. But his coup, while widely admired in the community, had not earned him respect. Instead, it became harder and harder to find anyone who would do risky business with him, and nearly impossible to have anyone who trusted him and whom he could trust. Acton clutched the brandy decanter in a shaky hand. Well, damn them all. He'd come this far on his own and he would keep going, to Haiti and beyond. He raised the decanter to his lips and drank deeply, took two faltering steps backward, and collapsed into his chair.

Nathaniel Pike was drinking brandy, too, but a better brandy and in more reasonable quantities than Will Acton. The Agent General was the guest of honor—actually, the sole guest, to his surprise—at dinner at the Lapins. And a lavish affair it was, far surpassing anything he had yet been privileged to attend in Bermuda. The food and wines were exquisite and the service from the slaves immaculate. But most of all, Pike loved the company. Lapin himself was quick-witted and urbane, probably still under thirty but well read and full of wicked gossip about the French court and the colony

from which he'd just come. And the women! Madame Lapin—Josie, as she insisted Pike call her—was a striking
creature, all breathy laughter and flashing eyes, much
younger than her husband but quite as wise. Her black
hair hung down in ringlets around rouged cheeks; when
her red lips parted they revealed pearly white teeth and
a flash of pert pink tongue. Pike was quite enchanted by
her, and by her sisters, Angelique and Jeanne. The evening was stimulating, a bittersweet reminder of the life
he had left behind in London so many years ago. Pike
found his emotions swinging wildly between nostalgia
and long-forgotten lust as he gazed on the incredible dé-
colleté of his hostess. Her bosoms were like perfect, ripe
melons and her gown was cut so low that Pike could see
the upper ring of her nipples. Oh, that he could have
known such a woman when he was still capable. Pike
sighed.

"What is wrong, Mr. Pike?" Lapin asked. "You look
sad. We wanted so much to make this a happy evening
for you. You are our first guest of substance in Bermuda
and we are anxious to make a good impression on you."
He poured a generous measure of brandy into Pike's
glass. "My family adores your island and would like to
settle here, but we worry we will not be accepted. The
stupid differences between our countries, you know. One
year we are at war, the next we're allies. I would hope,
out here in the New World, that nothing counts except
what kind of people we are."

"It is nothing, Lapin," Pike said. "Just a middle-aged
man suddenly sad to be surrounded by so much youth
and beauty." He flinched as Josie reached forward and
placed a sympathetic hand on his. Good God, he could see
her nipples, rouged like her cheeks and straining forward at him. He drained his brandy. "But you are right,"
he said, patting his lips with a crisp linen napkin. "There
is too much mistrust among us all. I believe we are all
pioneers and should leave old hatreds behind us. Why,
before I accepted your gracious hospitality tonight, I discussed it with the Governor. He was most anxious I
should attend your table. 'Find out what they want here,'

he said. 'Maybe they're spies. Can't trust those Froggies.' The Governor is a most conservative man," Pike
said. "I think I am his only link to the real world."

"I had been told of your influence on His Excellency,"
Lapin said, smiling. "That was but one of the reasons we
were so keen to have you join us this evening." He smiled
again. "Another was that my ladies made dire threats
against me if I did not produce for them someone who was
dashing and gay and worldly-wise."

"Oh, yes," the delectable Josie said. "I told Henri he
had to invite someone distinguished, someone who would
remind my sisters and me of all we left behind in Europe
when we came to the outposts of civilization." Again the
hand on his; Pike flushed and felt a stirring in his loins,
a sensation that had vanished years before. "You do not
think we are spies, surely?"

"No, no, madame," Pike spluttered. "A ridiculous
suggestion and typical of the insular thinking in this
place. I shall tell the Governor what a delightful family
you are, how lucky we are to have you, and that my only
fear about you is that you will quickly tire of us and depart for more stimulating locations."

"You are too kind, Pike," Lapin said. He clapped his
hands, and two of the liveried blacks appeared. "We shall
take coffee outside under the stars. Your climate, Pike,
is so much more conducive to outdoor living. In Haiti we
hide behind nets and fans once the sun sets. Josie, take
our guest in hand while the girls and I repair to the
kitchen and try, yet again, to instruct our staff in the art
of brewing good coffee. You see," he said to Pike, "while
our servants may appear quite skilled, there are still
many social graces they have not learned. Coffee is new
to them. But they will learn."

Pike felt her moist little hand in his as Josie led him
out onto the wide terrace surrounding the house. It was
a clear, moonlit night and they could hear big fish jumping in the sound. A warm breeze kept the insects away;
the only other sound was the chirping of tiny green tree
frogs.

"A beautiful place," Josie murmured. Her mouth was

so close to his ear he could feel the warmth of her breath over the breeze "Already I am in love with it." She squeezed his hand harder. "I have a favorite place in this house, mine alone, where I sit and watch the water. Come with me, please, and I will show you."

He followed her away from the terrace to outside steps which they climbed to a gazebo-like structure set on the roof of the house. In the moonlight he saw the couch and low table that were its only furnishings. The view was magnificent, right across the broad dark waters of the sound to the bush-clad slopes opposite and then up into the sky where bright stars hung low. A hundred yards from them, the waters suddenly surged and a big, dark, flat shape came surging out, floated through the air and landed with a loud splash.

"What is that?" Josie asked, clutching his arm. "I saw one in daylight and it looked like a devil. A great big brown thing with a forked tail."

"It is nothing but a manta ray, my dear," Pike said. "A harmless creature, and still plentiful here because it is of no use for food and its skin cannot be tanned. So our people leave it alone. I have sailed close by rays when they leap from the water, and I can only surmise they do it out of exuberance, for the sheer joy of living."

"How wonderful! To do something for simple joy instead of for gain." She was holding herself against him and her face was turned up to him. "I try to be like your manta ray. To find joy for the sake of joy." She kissed him then and he was washed by the muskiness of her and the scents of the warm night; her full, firm breasts rose up to him and with one swift gesture she parted the bodice against which they had been straining all evening.

Pike gasped as her bosoms were exposed in the moonlight; he felt her arm come up around his head and gently bring it down toward them, and then his lips were on her rockhard nipples. The sensation was divine but he wanted to pull away: he had been so long resigned to the impotence of his age that he did not want to frustrate himself any more. And, he suddenly remembered, there was her husband downstairs, and her sisters and . . .

"What are you doing?" he gasped as her hand slid down inside his breeches and fastened on his poor limp organ. "Madame, I am old enough to be your . . ." But she was easing him back toward the couch, gently laying him down and skillfully undoing the buckles and buttons that bound him. He felt dizzy, slumped back on the silk cushions, the moon shining down on him and the tree frogs piping inches from his head. And then he felt something he had never felt before, a sensation steaming hot and slippery wet, as if his organ were gripped by some vital creature put there only for the purpose of pleasure, intensely stimulating. He thought of the manta ray and its joyous leap and he felt himself hard for the first time since . . . His orgasm made up for all the barren years, flooding out of him and into the loving receptacle, leaving him gasping and grateful.

"The French way." She giggled. "I think you English deprive yourselves of so much." And then she stood up and raised her voluminous skirts; he glimpsed the lush, dark bush as she straddled him, her white thighs riding over him and pushing him deeper into the couch. Amazingly, he was still erect and he felt himself enter her and be enveloped by her lushness. Her breasts danced in the moonlight just above him as she raised and lowered herself on him, almost pulling away then sinking down and immersing him in her again. He grasped her soft buttocks and strained against her as the flood came again. When at last he fell back, he was a man reborn; the sweat dried on his forehead but the moisture still clung to his groin; his weapon subsided but the memory of the pleasure and the joy remained.

"Josie, oh Josie," he gasped. "What have you done?" He answered himself. "You have revitalized me, restored my manhood for a moment. I can never thank you—"

"Hush," she whispered, a cool finger pressed against his lips. "Let me dress us again, and we shall go down for our coffee. Henri takes so much trouble over his coffee, he would be hurt if we delayed and it became cold."

Pike was nervous and flushed when they emerged into

the lamplit circle on the terrace, but neither the husband nor her sisters appeared to have missed them. Coffee was pressed on him, and liqueurs and little cakes. He tasted none of it, all his senses still occupied by the events in the room above.

A long, slow-rolling sea was working behind them and the Gulf Stream's steady breeze pushed them forward as Will Acton strode the bridge of the *Pride of Paget*, biggest and newest of his fleet. It was a beautiful, balmy day. He felt the clouds of last night's black rum passing from his brain. Tomorrow they would be in Port au Prince and his grand scheme would at last get under way; Acton patted the oilskin pouch on his hip where he carried the letters of introduction from Lapin to the men Acton would need to deal with in Haiti.

"We've made good time, Captain Jarvis," he said to the big man standing beside him. "I hope we can do as well on the return trip. Our cargo is perishable. We need to be at sea for the shortest possible amount of time."

"I'll clap on every sail coming back." Tom Jarvis nodded. "I make no secret of it, Mr. Acton, I'm nervous about getting into the slave trade. I've heard so many stories of black devils breaking loose and overcoming their ship. Quicker we get the bastards back to Bermuda the better."

"You need not worry about trouble from these fellows," Acton said. "A very special brand of black they've raised in Haiti, blacks who love to serve their white masters. At least, they love to serve the Froggies. They may find the solid British stock of Bermuda not fancy enough for them, but they'll adapt." He glanced across at his senior captain; it worried Acton to be in the hands of this big, stupid man. But he had no one else he could trust, no partners, no advisors. For a moment he wished he still had the stalwart Staley and Morris standing beside him, but of course, that would never be again. "This will be the most profitable cargo you've ever carried, Jarvis. If it works this time, you'll no longer have to fill the holds with stinking tobacco or wet salt. I will go to Lord Mar-

ley and get a long-term contract for both Bermuda and
the Americas, and we'll build ourselves a fleet of slavers,
properly fitted out to keep a couple of hundred of them
at a time locked and chained belowdecks."

"It's this trip I'm concerned about. The ship isn't
equipped to handle any uprising. They could swarm out
of the holds and kill us all. The leg irons don't look strong
enough to tether a child."

"I told you, Jarvis," Acton said patiently, "these are
a docile lot. The French have civilized them for us. And
in any case, we will keep a double watch at the hatch-
ways for the brief journey back to Bermuda. And we'll
never open the hatches fully. Just a crack and fling down
the corn to them. The water troughs will be filled before
we take them aboard, so there's no need for anyone to
venture into the holds."

"I doubt they're going to enjoy the voyage, then," Jarvis muttered. "Not if they've been having such a great
time under the Frogs. But what the hell." He shrugged.
"Everyone else is getting rich from slaving, so why
shouldn't we? But I tell you now, Mr. Acton, if one of
those darkies sticks his head out of a hatch, my men will
cut it off before he can blink an eye. I don't care what he
might have been worth on the auction block."

Acton retired early to the large owner's cabin below
the poop deck. He ate heartily of guinea fowl and rice,
washed down with a jug of claret, appreciative that on
this short voyage there would be no need to resort to the
crew's fare of salt beef and hardtack. He felt the roll of
the ship—his ship—beneath him and sighed in satisfaction. It was good to be at sea again, away from all the
land-bound difficulties, away from the constant disappointment his wife and child had become.

"I'm finished," he said to the young boy cringing in a
shadowed corner of the cabin. "Clear away and bring me
brandy from the captain's stock." He watched approvingly as Smutty sprang to his task. Quite a fetching lad,
he thought, for one who endured the total hell of being a
cabin boy in these waters. Working twenty hours a day,

living on scraps, buggered by every one of the crew . . .
and yet the twelve-year-old still had a brightness, a
freshness, about him. Sixpence a week for a life of so-
domy and the lash and still he could smile. Pity there
weren't more around like young Smutty, Acton thought.
There would be no need to import slaves if the damned
white trash all worked as hard as this lad.

The boy was back now with his brandy. He set it down
before him and waited, head bowed, for the next command. Acton looked at the dark head, the fluttering eyelashes. He felt a stirring in his loins and tried to laugh
at himself. It was all right for a sailor, months at sea, to
indulge himself that way—but not for someone like him!

Except that it had been months since Amanda had
consented to make love with him, and years since he'd
really cared, anyway. Since Prudence Odlum. He
drained a large goblet of brandy. Prudence Odlum. The
world had been so filled with promise then.

"Get on the bunk," he ordered the boy brusquely. Acton felt sweat break out on his forehead as the youth
swiftly dropped his canvas trousers and lay facedown on
the bed, his buttocks shining in the lamplight. Will Acton swayed a little as he rose out of his chair, undid himself and crossed to the bunk. All the frustration in him
rose to the surface; he didn't care what he did to himself
or anyone. His weapon felt huge and hard with an unquenchable appetite of its own. It homed in on the quivering boy.

Acton swung himself onto the bunk and parted the
lad's thighs. He entered him swiftly, brutally, pleased
by the gasp of pain. He plunged downward again and
again, grasping the frail shoulders of the cabin boy,
grinding him into the rough sheets. When he climaxed
it was like purging himself: evil water flowing out of him,
leaving him clean and free for the great task ahead of
him. Acton rolled over against the bulkhead and pushed
the boy away with his foot.

"You can go now," he said. "Leave the brandy."

"Yes sir," the boy whispered. He pulled his trousers
up from around his ankles. The pain was almost over-

whelming, as it always was. No matter how many times they did it to him, it was always as if they were tearing him apart. One day they would all pay for it, John Smutters swore. Particularly this beast, who wasn't even a sailor and therefore had no excuse for using a poor cabin boy so brutally. One day, he thought, as he bowed his way out of Acton's cabin, he would get his own back on a world that used him so cruelly. But for now he had to put up with it. He fingered the gold sovereign he had lifted from Acton's purse while the act was being committed on him.

They sighted the lush green of Haiti at noon, but the tide was against them and it was dusk when the *Pride of Paget* finally nosed into harbor and dropped anchor. From the shore they could hear sounds of revelry and see, dotted about the steep hillside running down to the water, the dancing flames of bonfires.

"Looks like we've arrived in the middle of a celebration," Acton grumbled to Jarvis. "I hear the Froggies are always having parties and drinking too much wine. I suppose we'll have to wait around for days until we're able to get any sense out of them."

"At least someone's coming out to welcome us," Jarvis said, peering through the dusk. A big open boat, a lantern in its bow, was being rowed through the gentle swell toward them. They watched as it drew near; the oarsmen were all big, black fellows and their commander was also black. But he was outfitted in a uniform that would have done an admiral proud.

"Godalmighty!" Jarvis said. "Look at that nigger dressed to the nines. There's no sign of a white man supervising the lot of them. Something's wrong here."

"Nonsense, Jarvis," Acton said. The man really was stupid. "I have been telling you how advanced these creatures are under French sponsorship; this is just more proof of it. Their slaves are good enough to be left to handle complicated tasks by themselves. I do think the uniform is overdoing it a bit, though."

The boat was nudging alongside them and the uniformed black saluted them.

"Permission to come aboard, sirs," he called, his teeth flashing white against his dark skin. "I am the Officer of the Port, and I would be pleased to place my seal on your papers." His English was excellent, Acton thought, and the French accent overlaying it gave the words a happy lilt.

"Permission granted," he called, ignoring the warning hand on his arm. He watched as the big man in the uniform grasped the rail and sprang up onto the deck.

"Welcome to Port au Prince," the black exclaimed as he strode toward Acton and Jarvis. He stopped before them and bowed. "This is a great honor for me. I do not usually enjoy the status of Officer of the Port, but tonight everyone else is celebrating and I have been asked to see you safely through the formalities." He looked toward shore and smiled. "We will be done with the formalities swiftly, for I was told to invite you to come and join the celebrations."

"We're not here to be entertained," Jarvis snapped. "We want to load up and get out of here as quickly as possible."

"And what is it you would be loading, sir?" the man inquired softly. "We have so little that others require, it's always a pleasure to see a fine merchantman like you arrive in our port."

"I have an introduction to M. Potger," Acton said. "From M. Lapin."

"Henri Lapin? Oh, sir, he and his lovely ladies are sorely missed here." He smiled broadly. "And you will be calling on John Potger? Then it is of course slaves you will be loading into your holds tomorrow."

"Yes," Acton said, feeling awkward in this situation, discussing slaves with one of them. "I want to buy some of your brethren and take them to Bermuda. They will be very happy there; Bermuda is a civilized place."

"Oh, yes, Potger's your man." The officer smiled. "Bring your papers with you and we'll go ashore and meet him now."

"I don't like this at all," Jarvis whispered. "Let's wait until morning."

"No," Acton said. "We both want to turn the ship around as fast as possible, don't we? So we'll go with this fellow and begin our transaction."

Room was made for them in the open boat, and the silent oarsmen sent their craft gliding away from the *Pride of Paget.* Acton could just make out the faces of his crew peering after them before the ship was swallowed up in the darkness. The fires on shore were brighter and bigger now, and by their light he could see the grand houses built on the hillside. The houses were all lit up and Acton could dimly make out figures moving in and out of them, all dressed as if for a grand ball.

"It must be some celebration," he said to Jarvis. "We should have decked ourselves out in something better than sea clothes."

The boat pulled up to wooden steps leading to a long, low wharf shed. The officer motioned for them to follow him. Inside the shed torches flared. Acton and Jarvis saw a handful of blacks lounging on hessian bales. They appeared drunk.

"You must excuse my people," the officer said, as if understanding their trepidation. "In Haiti, when the masters celebrate, we all celebrate. Haiti is such a happy place! I will take you to M. Potger now, gentlemen."

They went out onto a dark street and started up a rise. The first house they came to was a big, rambling wooden affair with lights at every window. Acton saw people inside, decked out in finery, laughing and talking, drinking and dancing. They were all black. This was indeed a strange place. The officer hurried them on, past several more festive houses, then led them up a stone drive to the biggest and most brightly lit house of all. They followed him up a flight of steps, through ornately carved doors, and then into a spacious entry hall. The place was thronged with men and women in ball dress, turbaned or helmeted, draped with jewels, their faces concealed by elaborate masks. Of course, Acton thought, a masked ball; the French loved dressing up in costumes.

"M. Potger is in here, gentlemen," their guide said,
opening a door off the hall. The room behind the door had
a flare burning in each corner. The room was thick with
smoke and a sickening stench.

"God save us!" Jarvis screamed. Acton followed his
gaze to the obscene object suspended from a butcher's
hook. The body was of a plump white man, hanging from
his heels. His throat had been cut and a pool of blood had
formed on the floor, inches from the slowly swaying head.

"May I present M. Potger," their guide intoned. "Your
host, gentlemen. Would you like to do business with him
now? Perhaps later. He appears to be under some strain
at this moment."

Acton looked around frantically. The room was crowding with revelers who had removed their masks. The
black faces beneath regarded him and Jarvis with
amusement.

"These fine gentlemen have come from Bermuda," the
officer called to them. "They are here to buy slaves to
take back to that fine island. Are there any volunteers
among you?"

The crowd laughed and jeered, and Acton began quivering with dread. The smoke and stench, the buzz of flies
around the gaping wound in Potger's throat, the menace
of the bizarrely dressed mob pressing against him . . . he
swayed and would have fainted had not the officer
reached out a huge hand and grabbed his shoulder.

"It appears my people do not fancy a journey to Bermuda," his voice boomed. "At least, not in the foul hold
of a slave ship. I'm afraid you picked the wrong time for
an expedition to Haiti. You see, my good sirs, you have
arrived for the greatest celebration of all. Last night we
captured the town! Our former masters are all dead or
fled into the hills, from where we will fetch them in good
time. But first we are enjoying ourselves." He clapped
his hands. "Bring food and drink for our guests," he
commanded. "Suitable food and drink."

Two goblets and a pair of gold-edged plates appeared.
"What have we here?" The officer chuckled. "Flesh

and blood, I think. But white flesh and blood—most suitable. Eat, drink," he ordered.

Acton felt his arms seized from behind; a grinning giant dressed in a vivid blue uniform glittering with silver buttons advanced on him and held a goblet to his lips. He gagged as the thick red blood touched his lips; he tried to shrug off the men holding him. From the corner of his eye he saw Jarvis break free and spring at the officer, smashing his fist into the black face. Then Jarvis was grabbed again and pinned to the floor.

"These are not pleasant guests," the officer said, wiping a bloody corner of his mouth with a white lace handkerchief. "Hold them down," he ordered, "and force our hospitality on them."

Acton choked, trying to scream as rough hands forced his mouth open and inserted some dreadful object there, something rubbery and foul. He heard the roar of the crowd and retched violently.

"A cock and testicles for both of them," the officer cried gleefully. "They who would rape us are themselves raped." He pulled the sword from its scabbard with a grand flourish. "Which of you shall die first, the big one or the thin one? The captain or the slave trader?" He touched the blade to Acton's throat and drew it gently across the taut skin, raising a little necklace of red. "It matters not. We have wasted too much time. There is their ship to be plundered still, and then a whole night of celebration."

Will Acton felt the dull blade sawing at his throat; the pain came in white sheets and then his own blood was coursing hotly down his chest. He felt cold air flowing in through an unfamiliar orifice, then hideous agony as the blade reached his spinal column. He died a second later, to the sounds of mocking laughter.

The crew of the *Pride of Paget* were restless and resentful. They could hear the mounting sounds of celebrating and wanted to go ashore and join in the fun. At first, when the open boat approached again, they thought it was their captain and owner returning. But when they saw the gang of cutlass-bearing blacks, they knew something was very wrong.

John Smutters was smarter than his shipmates; before the blacks could come over the side he had pulled himself up the mainmast to the tiny crow's nest high above the deck. He hid there, peering down at the carnage below, watched the deck run red and heard the dying cries of the outnumbered crew. He was still hidden when the officer came aboard and supervised the looting of the ship. Smutters heard whoops of joy when the chest of gold pieces, Acton's slave money, was dragged on deck. He lay still and sweating as the blacks drank and shouted and flung bodies into the harbor.

After the last of them had staggered off the ship, he waited two hours before creeping back down the mast and working his way to the pinnace tied down on the afterdeck. He found a barrel of water and some ship's biscuits. His hands shook as he fumbled with the knots and lowered the little boat into the water. He rowed it gently away from the lights and noise of Port au Prince, keeping the *Pride of Paget* between him and the shore. It was not until there were no more sounds on the wind that he raised the small sail and steered the pinnace away from Haiti and out toward the open sea.

"He got what he deserved! I'd kill him myself if that were possible." Sir Thomas Fleet was still furious at the news he'd received that day. "Your late son-in-law has cost us dearly, Sam. Set all our plans back by years."

"I'm sorry, Thomas," Cobcroft muttered. "As I've told you, I new nothing of his harebrained scheme or I'd have stopped it. Even poor Amanda didn't know where he was going on this voyage. He gave her only some drunken boasting about how he was going to 'show us all.' "

"He's shown us, all right!" Fleet slammed his fist down on the fine oak table in Nathaniel Pike's drawing room. "We have no chance now of bringing in a proper number of slaves. The people here are more terrified than ever—and justified, too, if even the best-trained blacks will perform such barbaric acts against their masters. Damn,

damn, damn . . . just when we had the Governor on our
side, Parliament at Home not caring, enough ships to
flood the place with slaves. . . . Now we must wait
again."

"There is plenty of time, Thomas," Pike said, passing
around the decanter. "The people will soon forget about
this incident. It has left a few widows and fatherless children here, but that's the risk taken by all men who go
down to the sea. I'm sure the climate will be right again
in a year or so, and we will make our move then."

"Time?" Fleet scoffed. "Nathaniel, you and I and Sam
are running out of time. We'll all be damned well dead
before we get any real action in this backward place."

"Don't complain about Bermuda's slow pace, Thomas," Pike counseled. "It's the very reason—that and the
gentle climate—why we are all enjoying longevity. Most
of our contemporaries at Home are long dead, yet we go
from strength to strength. You will see, there will be ample time for all our grand schemes to be completed." He
turned to Cobcroft. "Have you discussed with Amanda
the dispersal of Acton's ships? Even with the loss of the
Pride of Paget, she still inherits a considerable tonnage.
If she wishes to sell, I would be pleased to act as broker.
There's a great deal of interest in London right now in
the Atlantic trade. Our American cousins are finally
producing goods and becoming a market themselves.
And of course our Bermuda ships have a fine reputation.
So if Amanda would like help in the disposal of her sadly
acquired assets . . ."

Fleet shot Cobcroft a warning glance.

"I think, Nathaniel," Fleet said, "now is not the time
to bother the widow about her future. When there is an
occasion to speak with her, I am sure Sam will advise her
to pool her lot with us."

"Yes," Cobcroft said quickly. "We would keep it all in
the family. In fact," he confided, glancing at Fleet for approval, "Thomas and I are planning to marry her off to
Septimus. Really join the two families, as we should have
done long ago."

Pike shrugged. "It is of no matter to me," he said. "I

was only offering my assistance. I can see you two are
dead-afraid someone else might get into the Bermuda
shipping scene. Well, you have nothing to fear from me.
You can run the shipping so long as I and my people control the cargoes. There is plenty in it for all of us." He
poured more drinks. "Now, the Governor needs to decide
what to do about the cabin boy, Smutters. The Governor
feels his great feat of navigation should be rewarded, encouraged. It will do our reputation as bold seafarers no
harm." He shook his head at Cobcroft. "It did not help
our image, Sam, that your daughter seized the pinnace
from the lad and accused him of deserting his ship!"

"She's a tough one, all right," Cobcroft said. "I would
have let the boy keep the damned boat, but Amanda
reckoned the Haitian voyage had already cost her too
much."

"Give the young bastard nothing," Fleet said. "If he'd
been doing his duty he would have stayed with his captain, died with him."

"And we in Bermuda would never have known of the
dreadful events in Port au Prince," Pike said reason-
ably. "I think it is valuable to all of us to learn from the
experience. What I propose—rather, what the Governor
proposes—is that we reward the orphan Smutters with
twenty guineas and a medal. And a place in your fleet,
no longer a cabin boy but a midshipman."

"Why should we be stuck with him?" Fleet demanded.
"The men are going to think he's jinxed; he'll be nothing
but trouble. The Governor can give him gold if he wishes,
but—"

"I think you should remember, Thomas, the Governor
has been exceedingly kind to you and Sam. He has resisted all entreaties for new shipping charters, beat back
the demands of those in London who would take away
your protected trade. If you will not do such a minor favor for him, I cannot guarantee to continue to promote
your case with him."

"Another lad doesn't matter one way or the other,
Thomas," Cobcroft urged. "If it's what the Governor

wants, well . . . And I shall instruct Amanda to give him
the pinnace as her personal reward. That will look good."

"You're all getting soft," Fleet grumbled. "No good
will come of making a hero of a cabin boy who scuttled
away at the first sign of danger. Still, do what you like.
There's no need to remind me of our debt to the Governor, or to you, Nathaniel."

As they climbed into Fleet's carriage and nodded good-
bye to Pike, Cobcroft wiped his brow. He had always been
wary of Pike, had always felt out of his depth when faced
with the Agent General's sharp intelligence.

"We got off the hook then, Thomas," he said. "He obviously hasn't the slightest suspicion that Captain Jarvis was in our employ and would have pirated Acton's
cargo if the wild scheme had succeeded."

"Of course he suspects nothing." Fleet laughed.
"Really, Sam, you are an unobservant man. Nathaniel
Pike is currently without all his native cunning. He is,
the fool, besotted by the French whore. After all his years
as a bachelor, indulging in nothing more lustful than
lining his purse, he has fallen for Madame Lapin. Fallen
hard. I wait with interest to find out what that woman
and her smarmy husband want of Pike."

"I think you should tell the boy," Ewen Staley said.
"He is entitled to know who his father was, and how he
died. There is no need, though, for him to know what kind
of man he was."

"Will Acton ceased to exist long ago, so far as I am concerned," Prudence Odlum said. "I felt nothing when I
heard the news of his death, and I didn't notice the community mourning him greatly. I do not want to raise his
ghost with young Jonas."

"I have almost as much reason to hate his memory as
you, Prudence, but Jonas should be told about Acton. It
is not fair to start a young man off in life handicapped
with questions about who his parents were."

"Perhaps you're right, Ewen," she said. She smiled at
the shabby, nondescript man sitting across from her in
the little cottage. Even before old Sarah's death, Ewen

Staley had sought Prudence out and offered her friendship; after, he had been a steady visitor and a good influence on Jonas. She knew Staley would like to make his
relationship with her more than just friendship, but he
had easily accepted the none-too-gentle rebuff she
handed him. Now they were comfortable together and
she respected his advice. "I shall tell him everything
when he returns from his schooling tonight."

"The schooling," he said hesitantly. "You are sure
that is a good thing? I mean, it was all right your teaching him yourself, and very impressive too, but to send
him to the village school—it is supposed to be only for the
children of the merchants."

"I pay my money the same as they pay theirs," Prudence snapped. "My son is going to have every chance I
can buy for him with the sweat of my brow and the skill
of my fingers. Not that the school itself is so good: poor
stupid Pongrass teaching the Scriptures and little else.
But someday it will be important for a boy to be able to
say he went to a proper school. Good God, what else is
there for my Jonas? He will never be a farmer or a sailor
and he will never have capital. So he must be a scholar,
or a thief, or—"

"Or a nothing like me," Ewen said. "I am sure you're
right, Prudence, but this is such a small place, jealous
and suspicious, not wanting anyone to rise out of his
class. I do not want the boy to be hurt."

"Hurt? He and I can hardly be hurt any more than this
damned place already has hurt us. My father shot in the
town square, my mother killed from overwork, my
child's father cruelly denying his paternity. Bermuda
can't harm us any more than it already has."

When Jonas came home she sat him down and calmly
ran through his family's brief and violent history in Bermuda, concluding with the recent death of his father,
Will Acton. He listened without comment.

"Thank you, Mother," he said when she was finished.
"Of course, I had heard all the gossip, and much of what
you have told me is not news to me. But it is good to hear

it without embellishments and distortions and cruel lies.
You and Grandmother have had much to put up with in
this place. My own life has been so easy in comparison."
He came and stood beside her chair; he was taller than
the other boys his age and, although slim, had a well-
muscled body. I will need to be strong, Jonas thought as
he looked down on his mother's head, already gray and
bowed. So many passions, hatreds, between the various
families.

Of course he had seen Will Acton striding the streets
of St. George's and noted the resemblance between them:
it had been no comfort to know this man was his father.
And the weakling young boy, Richard Acton, who attended the tiny school with Jonas, was his half-brother.
But Jonas had no sense of kinship with him or anyone
else on the island, only with his mother and the dreadfully missed old Sarah.

"You must get to your studies," his mother said,
breaking the mood between them. "There is nothing to
be gained by standing here going over the past. And I
need more wood cut for the fire; it's going to be another
cool night."

Amanda Cobcroft did not grieve for her husband; even
if theirs had been the best of marriages she would have
been prepared for his death at sea, for such was a constant in a sailing colony where men set out to brave the
cruel, unpredictable Atlantic. She was well rid of Will,
anyway, and the child was unaffected, merely nodding
when she told him his father would not be coming back
from the sea. The two of them had always had a better
time together when Will was away. There was no reason
for Richard to miss his father's drunken ravings.

Amanda settled herself in the drawing room of the big
house. It was so quiet and peaceful now, Richard sleeping in his bed with his nanny beside him, the rest of the
servants in their quarters. Septimus Fleet had already
clumsily indicated his intention of paying court to her,
and her father had stressed what a good match it would
be for all their sakes. But for the moment she had fobbed

Septimus off: she would accept him, eventually, but now she wanted to enjoy a few months of peace and quiet and independence.

Marriage to Septimus made great good sense, of course, and her parents were pushing her. What Will had left her was only a small fortune, depleted by the loss of the *Pride of Paget* and a chest of gold, but the Acton ships put with the bigger Fleet-Cobcroft line would be significant. Her father and Fleet were quite old and would not much longer be able to run the enterprise; Septimus she could handle. The whole thing looked good to Amanda. She would bide her time, then take over the running of the enlarged shipping line, take it in new directions, attain new heights undreamed of by her father and Fleet. And then, when the time came and she had achieved all the things they didn't think a woman could achieve, then she would hand it all over to her son and he would be the most powerful man in Bermuda. So much to rest on the boy's frail shoulders, she thought, but she would protect him until he was adult, strong and wise. The boy would take his new father's name, she decided. She didn't care if she never heard the name Acton again. It had served its purpose. Richard Fleet. Yes, that would be a name to be reckoned with in the colony's great future.

Nathaniel Pike wiped her tears away and stroked her pale cheek; it broke his heart to see his little Josie so distressed, but it seemed there was nothing he could do to ease her grief. She had been obviously under strain when he collected her for their long-scheduled picnic, and she was quiet and withdrawn as the carriage passed through the pretty, winding lanes on the way to the little South Shore beach which was their favorite hideaway. It was not until the cloth was laid out on the sand, parasols erected, food and wine spread before them and the coachman had withdrawn that she spoke of her anguish.

"Henri knows all about us, Nathaniel," she announced, bottom lip quivering. "Last night I told him everything."

Pike started. All his life he had been a careful schemer,

a man who covered his tracks. And now, so late in that life, he had left himself open to grave damage. Lapin would sue him, or challenge him to a duel, or . . . but, strangely, he found he didn't care about the consequences. He was almost glad the cuckold knew. At last his love for Josie could come out into the open.

"I had to tell him," she continued. "Since I have known you, dear Nathaniel, I have refused him his rights in our bed. Last night he would have no more of it. He stormed into my boudoir and . . ."she blushed, determined to press on. " . . . He was going to take me by force, going to enter that sacred place that is now yours and yours alone, Nathaniel. And so I told him I loved another, you, and pleaded with him to let me go. He cried, poor man, he knelt and cried before me and begged me not to leave."

"There, there, my darling," Pike said, holding her head to his chest. "It is good he did not fly into a rage with you. I certainly would have done, had the roles been reversed."

"It was worse than a rage," she sobbed. "He said I must go with him, away from Bermuda and you. He said there was nothing here for us, no future, and nothing in Haiti, of course, so we are to return to France. Oh, Nathaniel, I am bereft!"

"But you cannot leave," Pike said. "I will go to your husband, pay him money to set up somewhere else and leave you with me."

"No. I love you but he is my husband and I must stay with him. If he leaves Bermuda, I must leave too."

"I could not stand it. I could not lose you after knowing such bliss."

Her tears eased then. She clung to him and began to speak in a near whisper.

"There is one way," she said."I'm sure it is impossible, but . . . Henri has always dreamed of opening a small hotel, a place of fine food and gracious service where both travelers and the local gentry could find pleasure and comfort. Lately he had been thinking Bermuda was the place to establish such a shelter."

"I don't see why that is impossible," Pike said. "In fact,

it's a damned good idea. We have no club here, no hotel, nothing but the vile taverns frequented by the peasants. I think a place where people like us could go would be most popular. I would be very pleased to invest in such a venture."

"Would you? Would you really?" Her eyes were dry now, and bright. She kissed him, darting her tongue into his mouth, instantly arousing him. "Oh, dear Nathaniel, you may have found a way out of my despair. It will all be wonderful. The house we have now, it needs some extension but would be most suitable. And I would be the hostess and preside over the most glamorous evenings, gatherings of the leading men in Bermuda where, in congenial company, they could for a few hours forget the rigors of running this colony. And my sisters . . ." Here she blushed again. "Oh, Nathaniel, I must tell you the truth. Angelique and Jeanne are not truly my sisters. They are two well-bred girls we met on the ship to Haiti. They had fallen on hard times and Henri took them under his protection. But with our new establishment they could play a part and repay his kindnesses. And perhaps, as our little salon expanded, we would bring some more young ladies out from Paris. Oh, it will be such a jolly establishment."

Pike was besotted by her but he was no fool. He looked at the gorgeous creature in his arms and began to laugh.

"You've set me up for this, by God! You and Henri. I doubt he's even your husband. You little vixen, getting me into your bed just so I would stump up with the money to buy you a knocking shop!"

"No, no," she said, tears threatening again. "It was not like that. And I am indeed married to Henri. No, this scheme seems the only way we can stay together. But you do not trust me and I shall speak no more of it. I shall just leave with Henri to a fate unknown, consoled only by my memories of our few, brief stolen moments in paradise."

He laughed again. The whole thing was so rich.

"Stop your denials, Josie. The truth appeals to me much more than any other version. So I am to be the

backer of our colony's first high-class whorehouse. I
think it's a capital idea! There's only one thing, though.
I don't give a damn who your various 'sisters' service—
they can take on every officer in the garrison, one after
the other, if they choose—but you will distribute your favors to no one but me. I want you and Henri to understand that, you hear. Because if you do anything to make
me look foolish, I'll have you and your red velvet drapes
and all your pretty harlots off the island before you can
pull your drawers up from around your ankles."

"There is no need to threaten me, Nathaniel," she
pouted. "I love you and want to be with you alone." She
kissed him again and sighed with content. "You won't
regret this. We will be together and at the same time we
will make a lot of money. And the community will look
up to us. Our establishment will be a place of good cheer,
of ambience, where men can come to discuss the great
issues of the day in a salon as fine as any in London or
Paris."

"You mean, where men can escape their wives and pay
for the pleasure of some lusty company," Pike said.

"That too." She giggled. "Oh, Nathaniel, it will be so
beautiful. The finest chandeliers, linen, silver. The most
beautiful young ladies. And our own loyal staff."

Pike frowned. "I think you'd better keep your darkies
out of sight awhile longer, Josie," he said. "The dreadful
events in Haiti have not yet been forgotten. And we must
be discreet. A facade of respectability must be maintained, no matter that many will really know what will
be going on behind your baize doors. We will need a suitable name for the place, something that conjures up its
raison d'être." He pulled at her bodice and watched the
marvelous breasts tumble out into the sunlight. He
glanced around to be sure the coachman was out of sight.
He threw her skirts up over her waist and, boots seeking
purchase in the coarse, pink sand, mounted her and rode
her to a lusty climax.

On the way home in the carriage, he leaned back
against the upholstery, watching her. If he had been
tricked—and of that he was certain—it was a capital joke

on him and one he would now happily profit from. Of course, sections of the community would be scandalized if they knew what went on in the Lapins' establishment. But only the patron-members would know, and they would keep it a secret among themselves.

"We shall call it, my dear, the Oceanic Debating Club," he said. "A true gentleman's club, with a membership fee high enough to keep out the riffraff and a policy of silence to conceal our activities."

And thus was established the colony's first and forever after most successful bordello.

> *Cliff Cottage,*
> *Paget,*
> *Bermuda.*
> *January 1650*

Dear Cousin Emma,
 Well, as you can see from the above, I am still here in the colony and as each year passes I become more attuned to it. I am quite the old timer and Hilda and I are accorded great respect for our dubious achievement in attaining such a fair age. We have become so close, my older sister and I, her in her widowhood and I in my confirmed spinster's role. I am truly glad what was to be a brief visit all those years ago turned into a residency. But still, like all of us, I dream of England.
 It could be England outside my window today, so chill and dark. The darkness is the result of the dense smoke which blankets the island; they are burning the whole place again, the third time they have taken such drastic measures to try and destroy the rats which plague us. Don't suggest we should import dogs and cats to put down the vermin; that was tried and the only result was a plague of feral dogs and cats to equal that of the rats! To my mind, the burning is a most short sighted policy. It does temporarily control the rats but at such a price. What will become of the vegetation? So far the cedar, a hardy tree, has survived. But for how

*long? And so much else has been destroyed. Bermuda
will never again be the lush place it must have been before we settlers brought civilization to it.*

*Hilda and I live in great comfort. When Amanda fi-
nally married the Fleets' son we thought she would
leave it to him—Sir Thomas is in his dotage—to run the
combined family shipping interests. But, over the years,
Amanda has taken complete charge and made a wonderful fist of it. She could be a man! Her husband is,
dare I say it, nothing but a fop who spends his time
drinking and gambling and who-knows-what at the
club to which most of the leading gentlemen repair each
day. And Amanda's son, by Acton, is as sickly as ever,
though he has reached the age of fourteen, which is
more than most of us expected. Septimus did manage
to get Amanda with child once, their daughter, Hilda,
but they desperately wanted a boy of their own to keep
the line going. They are now resigned to leaving the
Fleet name on the frail shoulders of Richard, not a reassuring prospect.*

*I have formed an Abolition Society here but I am
afraid our membership comprises little old ladies like
me, plus the handful of Quakers on the island. Not a
forceful group. These people are simply not interested
in the great moral issues of our time. The port is now
crowded with slavers, and their evil trade brings much
revenue to Bermuda, so that is all that matters. The
number of slaves on Bermuda is regulated but it is
common now to see them working in the fields and la-
boring in the shipyards. Worst of all is to see those being
transhipped, penned in a great cattle yard near the
wharves. These poor creatures, not knowing where they
are going. I rail against it but no one listens, except to
say that I live under a roof paid for by the great profits
of this human trade. Please, Emma, send me any tracts
your own group has prepared and any material that
will help our cause. Send them in volume, too; the man
who runs the only printery here is totally under the heel
of men like Pike and Fleet and would not print anything that might trouble his masters.*

*I suppose I should not rant against these people so—
they are not too different from those I knew in England.
They think about today, tomorrow, maybe next year,
and that is the reach of their horizons. I do not expect
everyone to have a sense of history but, surely, we are
making history here and it seems a shame the participants are so shortsighted. Just take one example: the
slaves. Forget for a moment the moral imperative
against this foul practice. The whole-scale introduction
of blacks to this tiny island, where at the start of this
century no person resided, will surely change the balance of the place forever. At present they see the blacks
as less than human, but surely the day will come when
they must be accorded freedom and the rights that go
with it. So, by their actions today—which are stirred by
greed and sloth—they are changing the future history
of their chosen country. It will be the same for America,
perhaps even more so when it is apparent the new settlers are not only introducing a new element with their
slaves but eradicating an existing one by driving away
the Red Indians.*

*I think, Emma, what I am trying to say is that people
who are making history should at least be conscious of
the fact, and therefore take note of their surroundings
before they alter them. That is what we have not done
here: a place that must have been so bountiful on settlement has been let slip to the point where almost
everything must be imported. Our new crops have
failed, the existing ones over-harvested, the fauna decimated—soon Bermuda will be solely a seafaring colony, but it might have been so much more, a place of
verdant fields and sturdy stock.*

*Or perhaps it will all work out. They argue about de-
veloping a major new town to take the place of St.
George's, of building new shipyards, of attracting a
Naval base here. I do hope they know what they are
doing. It would be a shame to damage these fair islands
any further.*

Next time I write I shall be more cheerful, because it

will be summer again and summer is a lovely time. My fondest regards to you, dear cousin. I am thinking of you.

Angela.

Chapter Seven
(1933–)

Rupert Marsden opened the *Royal Gazette* the house-maid had placed, carefully ironed, on the breakfast table. He scanned the columns for something to talk with his wife about; breakfast was the one time of the day when she would speak to him, and he tried to make the most of it. Today he was in luck.

"Your brother is in the headlines, my dear," he said. "He's going to establish a film industry in Bermuda."

"Which one?" Veronica asked. She didn't really care, but at least the subject would get her through one more session with Rupert. She tried not to let her boredom and impatience with him show, but sometimes it did. She glanced at her watch. Another five minutes and she could escape to her office.

"Robert, of course. The paper says Robert believes Bermuda is far better suited to filmmaking than Hollywood and he's going to bring a large number of writers, directors and actors here to work on projects. It sounds very exciting."

"Just another of his crazy schemes. It'll never get off the ground. He'll throw another million away, then move on to something else."

"He can afford it, my dear. Lapin was telling me the other day that Robert has trebled his capital in the last few years. He's perhaps the richest man in the colony, in cash terms."

"Lapin shouldn't go talk about his customer's affairs, Rupert. The man's become an awful gossip. I'm not sure I should keep him on the board of Fleets."

"He didn't mean to be indiscreet. It was just that we were talking about how lucky most of us have been in the past few years. Getting out of the U.S. market before the Crash; the Depression scarcely hurting us at all, thanks to our unique labor situation."

"That's the trouble with this damned place," she snapped. "It's too insulated from the real world and none of you men know what *work* is." She pushed back her chair. "Well, I've got a company to run."

He sighed as he watched her stride out of the room; she was always so abrupt with him and there was nothing he could do about it. The five-year point in their marriage had passed, and he lived in dread. If she wanted free of him she could be. And he loved her so desperately. If only she would agree to have children, he thought. Children might bring them together. He sighed again. He might as well wander down to the warehouses and sign papers. At least he was playing golf at eleven; that was something to look forward to.

"The movie business," Richard Billings said, putting down the paper. "He might be right. Going to the movies is all the people back home can afford now."

"And Kosmos products, darling," Primrose said. "It looks like another big year for us, despite the Depression. Thank God I took your advice and brought out the budget range."

"I wish a few more people would take my advice. But there aren't many here who feel the need to consult a stockbroker these days."

"It'll come back to normal soon," she said. She worried when he made remarks like that; Richard was normally cheerful, but sometimes he was haunted by the past, regrets about who he'd been and what he once counted for. It was a terrible comedown for him to be working as a broker in a quiet little market like Bermuda. She looked around the sunny breakfast room. Really, they had everything: wealth, position, the beautiful old mansion—and darling Jeff.

"Where is Jeff?" she asked. "He'll be late for school." She rang the silver bell on the table; and when the maid appeared, asked her to go and hurry their son along. He appeared a moment later, scrubbed and neat in his school uniform, mischief in his six-year-old eyes. She kissed him, marveling again at what a beautiful child he was. She was glad her mother had lived long enough to know him. Jeff was almost a mirror image of Julia Odlum.

"Good morning, son," Richard said, roughing the boy's brown hair. "Do you want to ride into town in our carriage or walk with the other kids?"

"I'll walk, thanks Daddy," Jeff said. "It'd be different if we had an automobile. Then I'd always ride with you. Why won't they let anyone have autos here?"

"We don't need the noise and pollution," his father explained. "The tourists come here because Bermuda is so tranquil, different from the cities of America. Cars would just spoil all that. And they'd scare the horses. Next year we'll get you a bicycle. That's better than a car any day."

"A two-wheeler? A real two-wheeler? You promise?"

They watched together as he gobbled his breakfast and dashed out of the room. They embraced.

"We're so lucky, Richard," she said. She kissed him. "And I love you so much."

"I love you, too." He patted her on the bottom. "Come on, get your hat. Off for another day's business in paradise."

"Just one paragraph about Adolf's triumph in the elections. What a provincial paper this is!" Lady Anne threw down the *Gazette* in disgust. "Really, Robert, you should speak to them. Here he's come out the majority party in all Germany—they'll have to make him Chancellor soon—and the *Gazette* gives twenty times as much space to your entry into the film business."

"They don't understand world affairs here," Robert Fleet said. "They'll be writing about our friend soon enough. Meantime, they write about me. It was a good article, wasn't it?"

"I really don't understand why you want to meddle with filmmaking," she said. "There are more important things to be done."

He poured another cup of coffee and went and stood by the window. His wife could be so dense. But she had other virtues, and by and large she made him happy. He remembered the day in London, at the anti-Zionist rally when after hand-to-hand battles with Reds, they'd met in the lobby of the Dorchester while waiting for the police to disperse the mob. Lord Hartley's eldest daughter, Lady Anne, the prettiest debutante of the previous season, now making headlines for her commitment to the Brownshirts.

"Wasn't it fun," she said, her brown eyes sparkling, and Robert Fleet fell in love. When he discovered, to their mutual delight, that she was a devotee of flagellation, his bliss was complete. Their marriage was reported at length in all the English newspapers. They honeymooned in Berlin, and were honored with a lunch in Hitler's own apartments. She settled a trifle unwillingly into Bermuda—a place she found too small for her particular interests—but they were happy in their way.

It was the closest he had come in years to leading a normal life. The headaches seldom occurred now, and when they did were eased by violent sadomasochistic encounters with his wife. She had even got him to abandon his night riders: the blacks would be taken care of by political means, said Lady Anne, when the time came. He should not risk injury and social stigma by thundering around on horseback flogging Negroes. What people like them, people with unlimited wealth and influence, should be doing, she said, was spreading the message of Hitler and the National Socialist German Workers Party.

He turned from the window, bored with the sight of ships on the picture-book harbor. The view also reminded him of how well his damned sister was doing with the family business, the one he should have been running.

"My dear Anne," he said, "I've explained it all to you. Films are the opiate of the people, the greatest weapon of propaganda in history. We will make films with a message, exposing subtly what Hitler rants against—the Jewish-Communist-black conspiracy to ruin the Western world. But our films must have the biggest stars, the finest writers, the greatest directors if the message is to be truly effective. I have never been more enthusiastic about anything."

"At least it will be a setback for those Hollywood Jews if you can shift the film industry here," she said. "Even in England they seem to be taking over." She pushed back her chair. "I must hurry. I've another session with the architects today. Really, Robert, they're so dense. They don't grasp what we are trying to build at St. David's—simply the finest mansion outside England. They keep cautioning me about the cost."

"I don't want any corners cut," Robert said. "It must be the perfect house. Hang the cost. I've always been prepared to pay anything for this dream of ours. Four million pounds, whatever, it doesn't matter."

Sam Fleet sat at the bar of the Royal Hamilton Tennis Club and pondered whether to have a third pink gin; it was only just past eleven A.M. and he had recently resolved not to do any serious drinking before noon. But there was damn all else to do. Crazy Robert had his titled wife, his mansion to build, his support of the Nazis and, now, his entry into the film business. Veronica had the family company. What, thought Sam, do I have? Nothing. A wife who was dropping her knickers for just about anyone who asked, an office in Fleets he seldom visited . . . Sam allowed himself a moment of self-pity. God, he'd be forty in a few years, and what had he to show for it except plenty of money and a good forehand? He nodded to the barman for another drink.

Sam was dressed in tennis flannels and would have liked to be on the court, but the professional—who was about the only person who could give Sam a decent game—was giving a lesson to some blasted tourist. He could see out over the shaded, flower-surrounded courts where all the happy, wealthy, tanned young people were playing. Was this going to be his life, another of the idle Forty Thieves going to seed at the club bar?

"Cheer up, Sam," Heather Baseheart said as she passed through from the women's lockers. "You can't be gloomy on a glorious day like this." She reached across him and took a sip of his drink, then put it down, making a face. "Gin and bitters! I don't know how you men can drink such muck. I was introduced to daiquiris last night. Lovely taste. You should try one."

He smiled at cousin Jamie's daughter, so fresh and pretty and young with her tanned legs shining under the daringly short tennis dress. He'd been her age once, but had forgotten what it felt like to be sure the world was a charming place.

"If you're looking for a game," Heather said, "my partner hasn't turned up. We're supposed to be playing this American couple Daddy knows. I don't know what standard they'll be, but if you're willing to put up with my lousy backhand . . ."

He shrugged, drained his drink and walked out of the bar with her. The American couple was already on the court but stopped their warm-up to meet Sam. Tom Bellowes was one of those big, bluff, successful Americans with a steely grip who turned a simple handshake into a test of strength. His wife, Jane, was small and soft, younger than her husband, with a halo of fair hair around a pale, lively face in the center of which was a retroussé nose and bright almond eyes. She had a coltish look about her, as if she could be scared into flight or gentled into loyal service. He liked her at once.

They started to play. It was apparent that Tom Bellowes was there to win. His wife, Sam thought, probably would have been all right if she had been left alone to get on with the game. But Bellowes was all over the court, shoving her aside, swearing when she did make a stroke,

groaning even before she served. Sam and Heather took
the first set, six–three.

"Why don't we change partners?" Sam suggested as
they took drinks. "Heather and I have played together
too much. It gets dull."

"You mean, Mr. Fleet, let's even things up a bit," Bellowes snapped. "I'm all for it, if you can stand playing
with my ninny of a wife. A thousand dollars worth of
coaching I've paid for, and she still has no idea of playing
doubles."

Sam let her relax in the second set, never crowding her
or hogging the play, encouraging her all the time and
making sure he put his own best effort into every shot to
ensure the returns to her were playable. They won
seven–five and Bellowes was red, sweating, angry.

"You carried her," he snarled. "I'm damned if I will.
She's useless." He slammed his racquet into its press and
stalked from the court.

"I'm sorry," Jane Bellowes told them. "Tom takes it
all so seriously." She looked as if she was about to cry.
"I guess I'm not good enough to partner him, but I try
my best."

"You're very good," Sam said. "Frankly, I don't think
Helen Wills would win a point partnering your husband.
He does take it all very seriously."

"Tom takes everything very seriously," she said as the
three of them walked back up to the clubhouse. "I still
can't quite figure out why he married someone as unser-
ious as I am."

"Fell in love with that upturned nose," Sam said. He
suddenly felt protective of this girl. She blushed and he
liked her all the more. "Come on, I'll buy you two a
drink."

Heather begged off because of a lunch date at the Tropicana, but Jane, after a moment's hesitation, joined him
at the bar.

"You mustn't mind Tom," she said. "He's just so anxious to succeed in everything that he does. His family and
mine own a bank in Philadelphia. Someday it will all be
Tom's. But for now he's been sent down here to drum up

business." She laughed for the first time since they'd met. "I know you are all very protected down here, Mr. Fleet, but the way things are in America, with this dreadful Depression, bankers have to go out and find new clients. Tom's trying to win over the cosmetics people, the Odlums, and it looks as if it's going to be a long campaign. If it were just me, I'd love the idea of being forced to stay here for weeks or months, but Tom's not like that."

"He'll not have an easy time with Primmy Odlum." Sam laughed. "She's as tough as all her family, and smarter than most of them. The only harder task I can think of would be trying to win over *my* family."

"Of course," she said and blushed again. "I'd forgotten for a second who the Fleets are. You're one of them. It must be wonderful to be a member of the first family in a beautiful, traditional place like this. What do you do?"

"Nothing." He scowled, nodding to the barman for more drinks. "It is not wonderful, my dear young woman, to be the middle child in an illustrious Bermuda family. There is no need to work and no chance of making your own mark if you do work. So I am concentrating on becoming a lush. My father used to say I was in training to be a playboy, but I fear he was over-ambitious for me."

"Don't talk like that." She was still shy and demure, but her words were firm. "You don't have to be a prisoner of your family. You're a man. You can be anything you choose. It's only women who are forced into positions by their families." She stopped talking suddenly and fiddled with her glass, embarrassed.

"You're that unhappy, are you?" Sam said. "It shows. Why don't you just leave the fellow? I already suspect he doesn't deserve you."

"You don't understand the way families work. Our union was perfect from the point of view of both families. The dynasty goes on with no dilution of capital. To leave him . . ." She stopped again.

"I'm sorry," Sam said. "I didn't mean to intrude. I guess I was talking from a male point of view. If there

were anything I wanted desperately, I'd let the family go
to hell. Nothing's worth being unhappy." He listened to
himself say it and wondered what he meant: at this same
bar an hour ago he had been feeling deathly sorry for
himself.

"How about having lunch with me?" he asked. "If I
promise not to intrude on you like that again."

They lunched at a little pub by the water in Riddell's
Bay, tossing crumbs to the white herons which stalked
around their table. It was a typically beautiful Bermuda
day, the temperature around eighty degrees and kept
pleasant by a gentle, flower-scented breeze, the sun
beaming down from a deep blue sky flecked with fluffy
clouds. Sam was enjoying himself very much and, he
noted with surprise, he was hardly drinking now.

"Why don't we continue on after lunch and I'll show
you the South Shore, the lighthouse, all the tourist bit,"
he suggested. "It's a long time since I've seen my country through fresh eyes."

"Oh, I can't take up any more of your time, Sam," she
said. "You must have lots of things you have to do."

"No. I told you. I do nothing." And the truth of it made
him ashamed.

"We've got to face facts, Tom. The aeroplane is not a
passing fad. It's only a matter of time before they're
flying here from New York. Five hours instead of five
days by ship." Veronica watched Tom Winders carefully. He was not a stupid man, and of all her fellow directors it was his support she needed. "Now that they've
developed the flying boats, people will lose their fear of
crossing the ocean in a plane. So what's that going to do
to the Fleets passenger business? Eventually, it will hurt
us badly."

"Perhaps we could shift more into cargo," he suggested. Tom Winders knew why Veronica had got him
into her office for this cozy little chat. She needed fresh
capital; there was no other reason for her to be so nice to
him. A shame about Veronica; for a while she had been
the most approachable of the Fleets. Now she was turn-

ing into a hard replica of that old bastard Horatio. They reckoned she had balls, probably stolen from her poor wretch of a husband. Tom jerked his attention back to the formidable woman sitting across from him.

"The Smoot-Hawley Act has pretty well closed the door on our exports to America," she said. "The only Bermuda onions the Yanks will get from now on will be from Bermuda, Texas. No, Tom, there's no way we can switch to cargo carrying. What I plan to do is get involved in aircraft now. Set up our own airline so when the tourists want to fly here we'll still be getting their dollars. It'll take a lot of money. I propose we make a share issue, and I want you to take up the bulk of the new scrip."

"What about your brother? He's the most cashed-up chap in the colony. I see he's going to start a film industry here." Winders laughed.

"I wouldn't take money from Robert if he were the last man on earth," she said. "You know what he did to me, and almost did to Fleets. If he'd got his way we'd all be working for some crowd of accountants in London. As it is, we all do very well from Fleets. I can't put any more capital in. Every penny I have is invested in this company already. I need you, Tom. And I trust you. We're family, through Ginny and Sam."

He frowned. "I'm not so sure how well that marriage is going. I hear . . . gossip." He frowned again. "Young people, I don't know, they never seem satisfied these days. When I was young we just did our duty, made our bed and lay in it." He stood up and stretched. He was due at the club for a hand of cards. "Let me look at the figures and think about it for a while, Veronica. I'm loath to put any more of my capital into the one area, but I must say you have got the company into fine shape. I'll think about it."

"There's no urgency," she said. "But I hope you'll go along with me. You'll not regret it."

"All right. And we'll see you at Gov House tonight. Marcia is so excited. You'd think it was her debutante ball. Poor old girl can hardly get around anymore, but she wouldn't miss this one for quids. You are going, aren't you?"

"I can't get out of it. We've turned down the Governor's last three invitations but this one's almost compulsory."

"Yes. Everyone will be there."

"That's the worst of it."

The grand ballroom of His Excellency's residence was jammed with Bermuda's finest; diamonds sparkled at the throats of the women while the men sweated in stiff shirts, white ties and tails. All the leading households had lent their best staff for the big night, so there was a small army of white-jacketed waiters to dispense the food and wine.

"Sir Norman's not stinted this year, I'm pleased to see," Dimity Lapin said to Roy Benbridge seated on her left. "I mean, all the dreadful news from Home—the riots and the suffering—one thought the Governor might tone things down for his annual bash."

"Never," the old lawyer replied, quaffing a large glass of burgundy. "He's the Governor of Bermuda, not one of the poorer colonies. There's no need for us to worry about what's happening in other parts of the world. Be no point in having a Governor if he has to do things on the cheap."

"Faith is looking lovely tonight," Dimity said, glancing across the table. "Green really suits your wife, Roy. She seems younger and more radiant every year. But of course she's just come back from one of her little trips. That must explain it."

Benbridge didn't rise to the bait; he knew they all gossiped about each other in the incestuous community. He could see Henrietta Baseheart now, whispering to Steven Lapin, no doubt spreading the latest rumor. Dreadful woman, that; it had taken years for the guffaws to stop after she regaled her friends with a graphic account of Faith and the Odlum lad in his surgery. Roy squirmed at the memory. Thank God Faith was a little more discreet now that she had passed into her fifties. She was a damned attractive woman, he thought, glancing at his

wife. He wondered if there were still lovers when she was
away from Bermuda. Probably not; she would surely be
past it now. He certainly had been past it at her age. He
turned his attention back to Dimity.

"Steven's promised me we can make our long-post-
poned trip to London next year," she was saying. "Little
Edward is nine, now, old enough to appreciate it."

The chance for a shaft of his own. "You might even be
there for the Prince of Wales's wedding," he said and was
rewarded with a flash of jealousy in her eyes. "I'm told
his parents are becoming quite concerned with his liaisons with unsuitable women. They want him married off
to the right girl. I mean, he's been carrying on with Lady
What's-Her-Name, the American woman, for a couple of
years now and there's no future for that."

Ginny Fleet chatted with her sister-in-law, Lady
Anne, at the main table.

"I really admire the way you've settled into our little
society," Ginny said. "It must be awfully boring after
London and being deb of the year and all that kind of
thing."

"Not at all," Anne Fleet replied. "The deb season, the
Bright Young Things, all that nonsense I don't miss at
all." She frowned. "Of course, one would welcome some
decent newspapers and the chance for more contemporary conversation."

"You must come to tea with me, then," Ginny said.
"While I've got Terrence Howard staying. Plenty of
'contemporary' conversation from him. You know his
plays, of course. He would have been the toast of the West
End while you were still in London. And he is even wit-
tier in the flesh. I'm so thrilled he's coming out here for
a visit."

"Yes. Quite a coup for you, Ginny, getting the Great
Man as your guest." Anne wasn't really impressed; Terrence Howard was a lost cause as far as she was concerned. She had tried once to recruit him to the Fascist
banner, but he had just laughed at her and said he was
too busy writing froth for the masses. "I wonder how your

husband will take to him, though. Howard is rather ris-
que for Bermuda."

"Oh, Sam doesn't matter." She shrugged. "I don't
think he's read a book in his life, much less seen a play.
He wouldn't know that Terrence is considered fast. Anyway, Sam's got other interests right now. He's gone all
moony over that little American mouse, the banker's
wife, Bellowes. He's like a schoolboy, poor lamb. And Mr.
Howard will be well out of the way. He wants to work on
his new play, so I'm going to put him in the gatehouse
where he won't be disturbed. But I'm sure I'll be able to
have lots of little functions for him. You must come,
Anne, and perhaps Robert as well. Maybe Mr. Howard
will write a film for Robert."

"I don't think his kind of material is quite what Robert has in mind to produce," Anne said. "He's looking for
more serious, socially uplifting things."

Richard Billings enjoyed the feel of his wife soft in his
arms as they moved smoothly around the dance floor.
The orchestra was making a hash of playing American
dance music, but Richard didn't mind. He realized he had
come to love Bermuda, even her drawbacks of isolation
and size. He felt he belonged here at last.

"You look lovely, as always, Primrose," he whispered
as she nestled her head into his shoulder. "And so happy.
No one would ever guess how hard you work, how much
you do." He squeezed her and she looked up into his eyes
and smiled.

"I am happy, Richard. I've got you and the boy and we
live in the most beautiful place in the world. There's
nothing more anyone could need for happiness." She
glanced over his shoulder to the Governor's table. "I'm
so happy, I can even find it in my heart to feel sorry for
the Fleets. What a dismal-looking lot they are. I nodded
to Veronica when we came in and she cut me dead. It's
funny, we are almost pals when we were girls. But now
she's as hard as the rest of her family. And her poor husband—well, anyone can see how she treats the man. He
looks so miserable, sitting up there with the Fleets at last
and being ignored by all of them." She chuckled. "Aren't

I lucky I didn't have to make a 'suitable' marriage? I ended up with naughty old you."

Dale watched the dancers and hummed along with the music; it was so good to be a part of this rich, secure world. He did not at all resent being relegated to the worst table in the ballroom, along with the other heads of government departments. As the newly appointed Commissioner of Police, Dale was thrilled to be in the exalted company of the Forty Thieves. The only pity was that his wife hadn't lived to share in his success. The promotion had come as a surprise; he had really given up any hope of getting the top job. But Johnson had "gone troppo" and started defending the blacks. So the old Commissioner was suddenly gone and Dale had his job. Dale had instantly curbed any tolerance he himself had ever had for the blacks; he knew what his masters required of the Commissioner and he would deliver. The job was everything. Indeed, now that he was on the edge of the charmed circle in Bermuda, Dale found himself thinking like them. The black newspaper, the *Bugle,* for example. It would have to be closed down quickly. For a while, the *Bugle* had been tolerated, even encouraged. Set up with funds from the American radical, Marcus Garvey, it had at first followed Garvey's line that all blacks should work toward returning home to Africa—a theory that sat well with Bermuda's whites. But these days, since John Clay and his cohorts had taken over the newspaper, it advocated staying in Bermuda and demanded a share of prosperity for blacks. The *Bugle* was for trade unionism and even hinted at blacks being given the vote someday. It was all nonsense, but it was dangerous nonsense and would have to be stopped.

Robert Fleet was still trying to explain it all to his obtuse cousin; Jamie Baseheart seemed incapable of understanding anything not laid out in the neat columns of a bookkeeper's ledger.

"You can't fail in the film business, Jamie," he said, his blue eyes animated for once. "America is crying out for more product. The dross now being turned out from Hollywood packs them in, so imagine how people would respond to films with a real message. We'll make a fortune, put Bermuda on the map, and spread the gospel of Fascism at the same time."

"You know I am totally ignorant of politics, Robert," Jamie said. "All these 'isms'—I can't tell one from the other. Fascism: is that the dago chap, Musso—?"

"Mussolini. No. The rising star is Adolf Hitler, in Germany. All the best British families support Hitler."

"Still, that doesn't sound like the kind of thing one would go to the cinema to see. *The Thirty-Nine Steps,* now, there's a jolly good plot for a film. I'd certainly pay my shilling to see that at The Palace."

Robert would have given up on the old fool, but he was eager to involve as many of them as possible in his film venture. Not that he needed their financial backing, but it would be better if all the Bermuda Establishment were seen to be behind him.

"The films I'm intending to make will not have an overt propaganda purpose," he said patiently. "They'll be rattling good yarns as well. And fun to take part in. Because," and here he played his trump card, "every investor who puts up a thousand pounds will get to play a part in the film."

"Now you're talking," Jamie said. He called across the table to his wife. "Henrietta! Robert can make you a movie star. How would you like that?"

Sam Fleet watched the flushed face and listened to the loud voice of Tom Bellowes; it was impossible that anyone as sweet and gentle as Jane could be tied to that American oaf. God, she was beautiful. And different from other women he'd known. He glanced across at Ginny and felt revulsion at the things they had done to each other in their marriage, the bed-hopping, the kinky sex. It would never be like that with a girl like Jane. He felt so pure, remembering the shiver her casual touch sent through his body, the glow she caused in him when their eyes met. Bellowes was engrossed in conversation with Richard Billings; their American accents grated on Sam. They were discussing business, which was not the done thing at Government House.

The moment was right. Sam felt as if he were floating as he crossed the floor and invited her to dance. Bellowes didn't even look up.

"I hope you didn't mind my snatching you away from such a fascinating table," he said when she was in his arms. "I was watching you and I couldn't resist."

She blushed. "Please, Sam, don't hold me so close. People will see."

"But I want to hold you close," he said. The champagne rushed to his head. "We've only known each other a moment, but you must be able to see how I feel about you."

"I'm going to go and sit back down if you don't stop all this," she said. She was truly embarrassed. No one had ever flattered her, fussed over her, like this. Of course, everyone was afraid of Tom's temper. She could feel Sam's hand firm on her back. She would have to be careful because she was attracted to him. He was so unlike her husband: gentle, relaxed, funny. Poor Tom, he was so driven. It had been all right when they were first married, she remembered, but lately it was as if she had let him down. He was always so brooding and angry, brushing her off when she tried to reach him.

The music stopped and they stood in the center of the floor, Sam holding her hands. She looked up into his pale blue eyes and saw love. It was so long since anyone had looked at her like that.

"Come on," she said at last. "We must look like fools standing out here all alone." She freed her hands from his. "Thank you for the dance."

"Is tomorrow still okay?" he asked. "The boat's all ready to go and the weather will be marvelous. You will come, won't you?"

"Yes," she said over her shoulder as they moved back to her table. She should stop it now, before things got out of hand. But Tom was still deep in conversation and didn't notice she had been away. So he wouldn't notice if she went sailing with Sam Fleet for the day. But after their outing, that would be it.

The Governor looked out over the crowded room, at all

the contented, prosperous, stable citizens who made
Bermuda such a tranquil colony. What a shame the Empire didn't have more places like this one. Small but
strategic and forever loyal to the Crown. Insular, true,
but if insularity was the price of stability, Sir Norman
thought it a fair price.

"I think the evening has gone very well, my dear," he
murmured to his wife. "I'm quite looking forward to the
next one."

The evening had gone well in Court Street, too. Court
Street had lately become a town within a town, the black
quarter of Hamilton where black churches nestled
alongside black bars and cafes, where a dozen mixed
stores extended almost unlimited credit to their pitifully
poor customers. Court Street policed itself; as long as no
disturbance spilled over into the white community,
Commissioner Dale and his constabulary would leave it
well enough alone.

"We're wasting our time," John Clay said as he
downed another rum. "The *Bugle* is nothing more than
a collection of church and lodge notes, plus the births,
deaths and marriages the white papers won't run. We
need to put some guts into it."

"Relax, John," Derry Smith, the *Bugle*'s printer, said.
Publication night at the *Bugle* was supposed to be a
happy time when the staff could get together over a few
drinks after putting the slim tabloid to bed. "We've got
to go quietly until we get some respectability. We need
to do it step-by-step. You see how many advertisements
we got from the white shops this week? It keeps up like
this, we'll be able to draw a wage one of these days. But
don't frighten them all off before we've got the means to
stand on our own."

The crowd around them in the bar was moving to the
jazz rhythms coming through the phonograph; Friday
night and all in their best clothes, drinking and flirting
and dancing, forgetting the drudgery of the rest of their
week.

"We'll never stand on our own—no black business ever

will in Bermuda because we don't have any capital,"
Clay said. "And we'll never have any capital because
none of us will ever earn a decent wage. As long as they
keep us as domestics and waiters and pay us shit, they
have us under their thumb."

"Sure," Derry soothed, "and didn't you say all that in
tonight's editorial. I'm just arguing we have to go forward slowly, don't make too many waves right off." He
leaned over the bar and pinched the girl on her bottom.
"Two more rums, Maizie, and put 'em on the slate." He
looked around the bar and slapped his friend on the
shoulder. "Hell, John, I bet we're having a better time
than all those white folks up at Government House tonight."

"I'd like to burn the bloody place down with all the
Forty Thieves in it."

Jake Beam slapped his bald head in exasperation; he
was tired of this argument, tired of trying to convince
Mark Rider that his agent, Beam, knew what was best
for him. The afternoon sun was streaming into the Hollywood office, and Beam thought longingly of the pool
waiting for him at home.

"The studio would like you out of the way until this
drug thing blows over," he explained again. "They're
certainly not going to put you in another picture until
they're sure you're in the clear. And then there's your
affair with Mary. Hell, Mark, if that comes out you're
finished with the American public. So listen to what I'm
telling you. Go off to Bermuda and make this cockama-
mie picture, get yourself out of the limelight. Take
America's Sweetheart with you and fuck her brains out
on a pink beach and get her out of your system. You can
do anything you like in Bermuda, then come back here
with a clean slate and I'll have a major pic lined up for
you. The money's good; this Fleet guy's rolling in it. So
the script is shit and the director's a drunk. So what's
new? Take my advice, Mark. Get out of town for a while."

Mark Rider was getting tired of the argument, too. The
cocaine he'd had instead of lunch had worn off and he

couldn't take another toot in front of Jake. He'd had to
swear that he'd kicked the habit before Jake and the studio would fix the charge with the police. Maybe three
months on this island would be okay, particularly if he
had Mary along. Jake was probably right; by the end of
the shoot he'd be through with her.

"So what's the picture about, again?"

Jake Beam sighed. Actors were so goddamned dumb.
He was really looking forward to when it would be his
turn to be a studio head and he wouldn't have to deal directly with actors anymore.

"It's your basic oater. Instead of redskins, though, it's
coons. You play the brave white settler in an island paradise; Mary's your plucky wife. Everything's rosy until
a Jew agitates the coons to try and reclaim the land you
and the other settlers stole. There's a lot of stuff about
the niggers lusting after Mary and planning to carry her
off, and then you ride up and give 'em hot lead up the ass
and save the day. The difference is, after you've beaten
them you put them all on a ship and send 'em back to
Africa instead of banishing them to a reservation." He
spread his hands in a helpless gesture. "A piece of cra-
pola, but it might just play here. And you'll do it standing on your head."

"Okay. And you think you can get me fifty thousand
dollars?"

"Sure. This Fleet guy is a hick, a know-nothing Limey
with lots of money who wants to get into pictures. We get
one shot at him before he finds out what the business is
all about."

"Cut out the Limey shit. I'm an Australian and no one
calls me a Limey. Those guys in Bermuda probably feel
the same way."

"Okay. Mark, call yourself anything you like. Just
don't call me again unless it's from Bermuda."

"I love you," he said.

Jane shivered in the hot sun and kept her eyes downcast, studying the patterns her bare toes made in the
pink sand. She didn't want to hear those words and yet

her heart cried out to hear more. She should have put a stop to it all ages ago, but his courtship of her had been so fast—and so gladly received.

"Please, Sam," she said, "don't make it any harder on me. I belong to Tom. There's no way around that."

"Just admit you love me, too. Then we'll worry about the future."

"All right," she said wretchedly. "Yes, I love you."

He moved closer to her and put his arm around her shoulder; she did not resist. She needed love and Tom would not give it to her. But this thing with Sam Fleet terrified her. If she were one of those women who could have a shipboard romance or a holiday fling, it would be all right. But Jane proudly thought of herself as old-fashioned, and regarded adultery as a sin.

She was crying in the bright summer day. Sam's heart lurched as he saw the tears, and he strengthened his hold on her and moved his lips to hers. For the first time, they kissed. For Sam it was the most intimate moment he had ever known. He swore then that there would be a lifetime of such moments with Jane.

"Sam," she whispered, trying to turn her head away, "Sam, we're both married. We must stop this now."

He kissed her again and felt her respond.

"Both our marriages are shams," he said. "I've told you how it is between Ginny and me, and the world can see how badly your husband treats you. Why should we spend our lives in misery when we can have bliss together?"

She could feel herself slipping past the point of no return, almost beyond caring about consequences. His lips were at her throat, and his thin, pale hand was caressing her bare arm. When he touched her breast through the cotton blouse, she trembled. She made no move to stop him.

And then he was exploring all of her, gentle but demanding. Their yearning bodies came together on the deserted beach, and all their frustrations and desires were released in one great wave of passion.

For minutes afterward they did not speak. They only held each other.

"I'm glad," she whispered at last, "glad. It doesn't matter where it leads us, or what price we have to pay."

"There will be no price," he said. "You will never regret that we met. I promise you."

He was even more romantic than she remembered from London. Ginny Fleet watched the playwright stride down the gangway resplendent in white suit and Panama. Terrence Howard doffed the hat to the cameraman from the *Royal Gazette* and looked around the dock for his hostess. A smart move, coming to Bermuda for a few months, he thought. By the time he went on to New York for the fall opening of his new show on Broadway, he'd have been away for six months; surely by then the scandal would have died down. Ah, there she was, the leggy brunette in the big picture hat. Terrence put on his best Mayfair smile.

"Mr. Howard," she said, running to his side, "I hope your voyage was a good one. I issued orders that you were to have the best of everything, but of course our ships don't compare with the Cunarders for size and luxury."

"It was most pleasant, my dear," he said. "I'll never be able to thank you enough. I feel totally refreshed and ready to start churning out hundreds of words." He looked across the busy dock to the orderly old buildings of Front Street and the ranks of waiting horse cabs. "I'm in love with the place already. Such a bright change from gray old London."

"The servants will bring your luggage after us," she said. "Oh, I hope you'll like the arrangements I've made for you. I set aside the gatehouse for your sole use, through of course if you'd rather have a suite in the main house—"

"My dear, it sounds wonderful," he said. "Whatever you have arranged for me will be delightful." He was not only the hottest playwright on both sides of the Atlantic, he also knew how to charm a hostess. He liked to main-tain a string of big houses in which he was a cherished guest.

He listened to her chatter as the carriage took them out of the town and through the winding lanes, past the massive gates and groomed grounds of a succession of great houses that would not have looked out of place in England. She was so eager to please him, to have him like her homeland; Howard suppressed a smile. It was always like this in the colonies and America. The leading citizens were very sure of their place and position until it came to dealing with a distinguished visitor from England; then they were afraid their provincialism showed.

The gatehouse, he noted with pleasant surprise, was absolutely charming. Downstairs a long, beamed sitting room opening onto a flower-covered terrace; a kitchen, dining room and bathroom. Upstairs a master bedroom, dressing room and bath, and a little second bedroom that would serve admirably as his study. And to take care of all his needs a plump, smiling black woman. He noted the fine liquors in the cabinet and the champagne in the icebox. Yes, the ideal place to lie low for the summer.

"Ginny, you've done me proud," he said as she hovered nervously, waiting for his verdict. "I shall dedicate the play I write here to you."

She almost swooned with delight, and as they strolled back up the drive to the mansion, she felt secure enough to take his arm. The staff had been busy for a week grooming the gardens and everything was at its tropical peak; vivid flowers against brilliant greens, and here and there a flash of color from the preening peacocks she had imported from Ireland.

Ginny sat across from him in the sunny front living room, studying him while the butler served iced white wine. He was just a little plumper than she remembered and his fair hair was thinning, but looks didn't matter: it was the man's skill, his brilliance with words that made him the catch of this or any other season. And he was all hers.

"And your husband?" he was asking. "When shall I meet him?"

"Oh, Sam," she said vaguely. "Probably at dinner this evening. You can never tell with Sam. He's so involved with all his sports, and messing around in boats. You see, Mr. Howard, like so many of the wealthy men in the colony, he doesn't actually do anything, so he's hard to nail down. If only he had a talent like yours—"

"Terrence, Ginny, please. And don't disparage the idle rich. Without them I'd have no one to write about."

The Twentieth Century pulled out of Chicago on time and Cable Odlum only just made it; the conference of surgeons had run late on the last day, and the rest of the New York delegation had decided to stay an extra night, but Cable wanted to get home to Muriel and the children. He sank back into his seat and watched the lights flashing and falling behind them as the glamorous train gathered speed. Cable was very tired, and the print of the *Tribune* was too small for him to read. He put the paper down and went through to the bar car instead. He was nursing his second Scotch and water when the porter came through announcing dinner. The porter was a tall, light-skinned black, and there was a familiar lilt in his voice.

"Excuse me," Cable said as the man passed him. "Aren't you from Bermuda?"

"Yes, sir," the porter said and flashed a wide smile. "And I know who you are, from your accent if nothing else. We never lose it."

"What's your name?"

"Youngblood, sir. Billy Youngblood."

"Of course. I used to watch you play in Cup matches. You were a great cricketer, Billy."

"Not much chance to play cricket here, Dr. Odlum."

"You know my name?"

"A small place, Bermuda; and a big name, the Odlums. I hope your family is all well, sir. Fine people, the Odlums."

The eyes of the two men held for a moment while each

realized the other knew all about him. It didn't bother Billy too much; he didn't figure Robert Fleet would still have a contract out on him. But it did bother Cable; this chap would be able to recall the scandal of Cable's sudden departure from the colony. Oh, what the hell, he thought, and laughed.

"Well, Billy, we've ended up in a much bigger place here, haven't we? But you know, I still miss home every day. I guess it's changed a lot."

"I miss it too, sir, and I hope it hasn't changed. I want it to be there for my children to return to someday."

"So do I, Billy. So do I."

Farther along the train in his private compartment, Mark Rider poured highballs for the two of them and looked out into the dark. Lake Michigan was behind them; he figured the next water they saw would be the Hudson River.

"I hope you're a good sailor, toots," he said. "It could be a rough passage down to Bermuda. We're approaching the tempest season, I'm told."

"I don't give a damn about any storm at sea," Mary Daintry said, swinging her silk-stockinged legs up onto the double berth. "I'm just glad to get out of Hollywood and the storm that was gathering there. If that cheap husband of mine had been able to prove there was anything going on between you and me, he'd have taken me for every cent I ever earned. And blabbed to the gossip columns and seen to it I never worked again. Jesus, Mark, the risks I'm taking to be with you."

"I'm worth it," he teased. "And when we get to Bermuda there'll be no need to hide. The fellow we're making this picture for runs the whole island. He won't let anything nasty be written about his stars."

"It sounds boring," she said. "You sure you brought plenty of stuff?"

"A solid pound of a hundred percent pure," he said. "And if we run through that, I'm sure our host will fix us up with more."

"Give me a line now, then. I hate train travel. Jesus, it's boring."

* * *

Henry Smutters watched the flurry of pressmen around the gangway as the stars prepared to board his ship. He studied the pair through his glasses: she was better looking than her screen image. No wonder she was America's Sweetheart. The fellow was young and ruggedly handsome, and Smutters could see how he'd become a star on the strength of only two pictures. They would make a change from the usual dull rich people who dined at the captain's table on the *Pride of Pembroke.*

Except, as he discovered when the voyage was under way, they never left their staterooms. Or, rather, never left her stateroom, the purser reported to him.

"I don't know why they bothered to book two," the purser said. "A waste of money. Still, I guess they've got plenty to waste." He dropped his voice. "The steward says they're doing a lot of drugs, sir."

"None of our business," Smutters said. "So long as they don't bother the other passengers, they can do what they like."

"Come on, Billings," Tom Bellowes said, "we're both Americans. Surely we can talk about how this goddamned place works." He drained his beer and called for two more. They were sitting in the Yacht Club bar, otherwise deserted in mid-afternoon. "Christ, I feel I've wasted all the weeks I've spent in Bermuda. I've been getting the runaround—a very genteel runaround, for sure, but that's all it is. How in hell do you do business with these people?"

"It's not easy, Tom." Richard Billings grinned. "They come on like hicks but they're very smart operators. They don't like to make quick decisions. I'm still learning. When I came down here, I thought a bit of the old New York get-up-and-go was all this place needed. But that's not the way it's done. They have this sense of tradition or something, and it protects them from doing anything rash. But, hell, you've got to admire what they achieve. Their companies may still be tightly family-controlled and they look undercapitalized, but they make the kind of profits anyone on the Big Board would die for."

"Your wife," Bellowes said, his lips curling. "Your wife is so damned polite to me, but she won't consider seriously what I'm putting to her. She just smiles and says she's perfectly happy with the bank that's handled her family's affairs for generations."

"That's the point. These people like the idea of dealing with each other. You've heard of the Forty Thieves?" Bellowed nodded. "Well, in the beginning it was what they called the first forty or so families who settled here, grabbed the best land and established the businesses. Over the centuries it's expanded a little to include a few latecomers—like the people who didn't come here until 1850, even. But the Forty Thieves is a closed shop to people like us. They've been running this place successfully for so long they don't see why they should let outsiders get a piece of the action. The Forty Thieves are really one big family, looking out for each other."

"Even when they hate each other, like the Odlums and the Fleets do? Hell, Billings, I've heard about the feud. I'd have thought your wife would love the chance to get one up on the Fleets."

"What do you mean?" Richard asked.

"She hasn't told you about the proposition I've made to her?" Bellowes was incredulous. This Billings was an even bigger wimp than he'd thought.

"I guess you don't understand the situation," Richard said. "My wife owns and runs her business with no help from me. I can't take any credit for the fact that she's built one of the most successful cosmetics firms in the world. I'm just a semi-retired stockbroker."

"But it was you who took her public in the States," Bellowes said shrewdly. "Surely that success gives you some say in the running of Kosmos?"

"Primmy listens to my advice if I offer it, which I don't, or not often, anyway," he said. Richard didn't really like this man. He was too like the drummers he'd had to deal with in the early days on Wall Street, all grand schemes

and fast bucks. "So what is the proposition my wife is not
too impressed with?"

"The airline business. I've told you how much my bank
wants to get the Kosmos account. Well, I've been trying
to convince her it's time to diversify her company and
airplanes are the way to go. Bermuda's going to be dependent on air travel one of these days. I see a tourist
airline covering Bermuda and the Caribbean, a fleet of
flying boats with a locked-in market." He watched Billings over the rim of his glass. The hook was baited. "You
were a flier—Lafayette Escadrille, if I remember *Who's
Who* right. So you must see the commercial potential of
aviation. Now, my bank, as a demonstration of how big
we are and how sincere, would be willing to set up the
funding for your wife's company and a couple of others
to form a Caribbean airline. And she just smiles at me
and says 'I only know about the cosmetics business, Mr.
Bellowes.' "

Richard tried to conceal his interest. It was a grand
and daring scheme, but he believed it would work. He'd
helped handle the paper for Pan American back in '26
when everyone else thought Juan Trippe was mad. And
now he was being offered again the chance to do something in a field he knew about. He wanted it, badly, because in his heart of hearts, Richard felt like a kept man.
He loved Primrose and Jeff to distraction, but he was too
young to be a failure.

"The bonus points," Bellowes said, dropping his voice
despite their aloneness, "are that I know the Fleets are
trying to set up a similar scheme. Veronica Fleet's convinced it's the way to go and she's running around now
trying to raise the capital. I thought the idea of getting
the jump on her would appeal to your wife, but so far
she's just not interested."

Richard licked his lips; the desire in him made him feel
parched. An airline division for Kosmos, something he
could run and succeed at. It would show Primrose she
hadn't been wrong in enduring so much for their love.
And it would compensate him for his loss of career.

"Your bank would finance the whole thing?" he asked casually. "It's a high-risk scheme you're looking at."

Bellowes nodded. The bait was taken. He ought to've worked through Billings from the start. With Kosmos stock as collateral, the money would be raised at no risk to the Bellowes Bank. They would also get the Kosmos business, and he could get the hell out of this godforsaken colony.

"I'll talk to my wife, Tom," Richard said. "If she does do it, though, it won't be to score points off the Fleets. Primmy's not like that."

He talked to her that night, after they had put Jeff to bed. He had earlier told the boy stories of his flying exploits, a part of his life he had until today almost forgotten, and been rewarded with Jeff's undivided attention. Planes, Jeff declared, were even more exciting than automobiles.

"So you really think it's a sound scheme?" Primrose said when he had finished his argument. She didn't care whether it was or not. She was just pleased to see Richard totally enthused about something. He never complained, but she knew how hard it was for him stuck here dabbling in odd-lot orders when he had been a champion on the Street. She would have set him up in anything, but had never offered because she knew his pride could not have borne it. Now, out of the blue, was the opportunity to put him back on his feet. "I'd have to be guided by you, totally, Richard. If we got into this, you'd have to run the whole thing. It's out of my field."

"I think I could find the time to handle it," he said wryly. "And I swear it's no risk to Kosmos. All you have to do is let the Bellowes people have Kosmos's U.S. business. Hell, it's going to take several years to set it all up, but I think it could be something you'll be very pleased with, one day."

"Lapin's not going to like it, losing the U.S. end of our business," she said. "And I'm not keen to upset Veronica Fleet any more than I need to."

"You don't owe any of them any consideration," he said. He crossed to her and stroked her head. "Sometimes, Primmy, I think you're too damned nice to have come out of this place, with all its bloody history." He hugged her. "I love you so much."

The cast and crew were quartered in the St. George's Hotel; Robert wouldn't have them in the Tropicana because he wanted nothing to do with his sister or any of her enterprises. He was fairly well pleased with what he had assembled for his first film: Rider and Daintry were all he could have wished for, and the English director, Gary Powell, was supposed to be good if unreliable. The scriptwriter had already quit but it didn't matter: Robert had his semifinal draft and he and Anne had worked on it to make it more ideologically suitable. Robert was finding he liked the movie business, not least for the new status it gave him in the community. A lot of them had come aboard with money, attracted by the chance to play cameo roles in the picture, but there was no question about Robert's being firmly in control of the whole project. He was about to move down to the set when Powell entered his office.

"Good morning, chief," the director said. "Everything's set to roll, the weather's perfect and the omens are good. But the cameraman just asked me what we're going to do about copies. He reckons there isn't a film lab anywhere in Bermuda."

"Copies? What do you need copies of?"

"The film, chief." He tried to be patient. This Fleet fellow was paying a handsome salary. "You always have to have copies made after each day's shoot. It's too dangerous to just have the one master film in the can. It gets lost or damaged, you've lost everything."

"Well, you'll just have to be careful with it. If it can't be copied here, it'll have to go to New York, and that could take forever." Really, the petty details they bothered him with.

"And we need more copies of the script," Powell said. "All the cameos are insisting on having their own. A souvenir, I guess. None of them gets to speak more than a couple of words."

"Tell the production assistant to have copies printed over at the *Gazette*," Robert said. "Come on, let's get on the set. I want to see how my money's being spent."

"I'm afraid you're not going to be able to see until the whole thing's finished," Powell complained. "With no lab, I can't even get the dailies printed. I'm going to have to shoot everything over and over again to be sure we've got it right." It was a hell of a way to make a movie, he thought, but he'd had worse jobs.

It was an establishing shot today, to get everyone settled, the director explained. As he walked with Fleet down to the sandy cove, they could see the organized chaos on the beach. Equipment was strewn around the edges and about a hundred extras milled about in costume. Mark Rider and Mary Daintry were at the center of the throng.

"Hi there, Robert," Rider greeted him. "That was some night last night. I hope the bags under my eyes don't show."

Robert smiled. It had been quite a night up at his house. Just him and Anne, Mark and Mary. His wife at first hadn't liked the idea of entertaining the actors, but Robert had insisted. Good wines with dinner and then the drugs had come out. Robert had found the cocaine most satisfying; even Anne had indulged, casting aside her usual reserve, forgetting for once that she was a titled woman.

"And you, my dear," he said to Mary. "I trust you had a good time."

"Oh sure, Bobby," she said. Her dress was cut very low and she made a mock curtsy, giving him a good look at her boobs. "It was fun. We must do it again soon, just as long as you don't work us too hard on this picture."

He would like that very much, Robert thought. There had been a moment there late last night when he thought they might have got a scene going. Anne had been obviously attracted to Rider and Robert would not at all have minded a tumble with Mary. He wondered if they might be into whips . . .

"Well, let's get down to business," Powell said. "They

all know their places, and they better know their lines
by now." He set himself up behind the cameraman and
studied the tableau. Mark and Mary were playing a
young couple leading a band of settlers and freed slaves
who wanted to establish Utopia on a deserted Caribbean
island. Apart from the principals, the shot included
about forty white extras and the same number of blacks.
"Okay, Max," he told the cameraman, "start shooting.
Get plenty of her tits and lots of palm trees in the background."

Derry Smith, the *Bugle*'s printer, tossed the still-wet
papers onto the bench that served as John Clay's desk.
"Have a read of that piece of garbage," he said. "It's
the script for Fleet's movie. They wanted the *Gazette* to
print up another forty copies, but the *Gazette* couldn't
handle it so they slipped the job to us. Fleet would have
a fit if he knew the nigger press was involved in his epic."
"I haven't got time to wade through it," John said.
"Anyway, it'll be just another bit of Hollywood junk."
"I think you should read it," Smith said. "There's a lot
of stuff in there about our people I don't like. Maybe we
should do something about it. You've been looking for an
issue to campaign on."
Clay sorted the pages in order and began to read. At
first it was just another movie glorifying brave white
settlers. But as he read on, his anger grew.
"Jesus! This makes us out to be savages, hardly out of
the trees, not to be trusted. It's like those tracts Fleet was
putting around when he still had his night riders."
"Yeah," Smith nodded. "And the bit where the Jew-
ish agitator comes in and stirs our people up to rape and
murder . . . it's pretty well an incitement to string us all
up."
"I'll write a piece about it for next week," John said.
"Expose the whole thing and tell our people no self-
respecting black can work on their damned movie. That'll
fix 'em, when all their Uncle Toms walk off the picture."
He glanced through the pages again. "It really is shit,

Derry, but dangerous shit. We've got to do something about it."

It was the following Saturday morning when the *Bugle* appeared with its angry attack on Robert's film. Robert laughed it off, but when a quarter of the black cast members quit on him he became very angry. "We've got to teach these bastards a lesson," he told his director. "For the moment we've still got as many niggers as we need, but I know these people. If nothing's done they'll all slowly drift away and we'll be left without any of them."

That afternoon he called on Commissioner Dale.

"It's libelous, of course," he told the policeman, throwing a copy of the *Bugle* on the floor. "I could sue but the bastards haven't got a penny and I've no desire to end up owning their clapped-out press. So I want you to handle it."

"I'm not sure what I can do, Mr. Fleet," Dale said nervously. "Perhaps if I had a word to Clay, gave him a warning—"

"Jesus Christ! Do I have to teach everyone his job in this place? Look, man, that newspaper story is a clear incitement to strike. They've told the blacks working for me to strike. That is an offense under our law. If you don't step in now, Dale, with the full majesty of the law, they'll think they've got away with this and they'll start agitating for a union again." He glowered at the officer. "Will you act, or shall I get a few men together and do what has to be done?"

"I suppose, under the Sedition Bill, I could move in."

"You bet you can. Go in there now and smash their presses. You've got the law on your side. And there'll be no one in the place today. They'll all be sleeping off last night's drinking."

When John Clay finally got the message about what was happening in the *Bugle* office, it was too late. The police had done a thorough job on his fledgling newspaper; the flatbed press had been destroyed by a sledgehammer and the two linotypes reduced to rubble. Tears of anger formed as he surveyed the wreckage. The *Bugle* had been his dream and the dream of others, the means through which they were going to get a fair deal for their people.

"Come away, John," Derry Smith said. He picked up a slug of type and dropped it in his pocket as a souvenir. "It's over. We can stop pretending to be newspapermen. The Forty Thieves were always going to beat us."

Tom Bellowes peered out at the dark harbor; he could just make out the whitecaps on the normally placid surface. The storm warning had been posted in late afternoon and it suited him fine. Summer was over. He'd finally gotten Primrose Odlum to accept his deal, and tomorrow he and Jane would be on the boat heading back to the real world. He glanced around the handsome old Bermuda house they had rented for their season in the colony: he wouldn't miss it at all. This damned place had been so stifling, so unlike the world he was used to. But the deal had been worth all the months spent here.

He heard Jane come into the drawing room and turned to greet her, determined to be pleasant.

"Good evening, dear," he said. "Will you join me in a cocktail?"

She looked pale under her tan, he thought, pale and scared. He had paid so little attention to her these past months. When they got home he would do something about it, try and spend more time with her. Maybe they should have the child he had been postponing.

"No thank you, Tom," she said. She fumbled with the little beaded purse she carried, looked inside and found the check she had written a few hours earlier. "Here," she said, thrusting it at him. "It's what I calculated I owe you for the passage I won't be taking on the boat tomorrow."

He glanced at the slip of paper and looked at her in puzzlement.

"I'm not coming back with you," she said. "I'm sorry, Tom, but everything has changed. I don't love you anymore."

"Hey, come on," he said, forcing a laugh. "You're up-

set. It must be the weather, the storm coming." He
drained his martini and moved across the room to fix another and give himself time to think. "Look, Jane, I'm
sorry I've been such a bastard lately. But it was so important we tie up the Kosmos thing. You know how
tough it's been for the bank. But tomorrow we sail home
and everything will be fine again. I'll make it all up to
you."

"There's someone else, Tom. There is a man I truly
love. I am going to stay here with him. I feel dreadful
about what I'm doing, and ashamed. But I am determined to grab this one chance to be happy."

He felt the blood rushing to his head, and only by supreme effort did he keep his temper from flaring or his
anguish from showing.

"Don't talk nonsense, Jane," he said. "We belong together. I told you I'm sorry I haven't been the best husband lately, but I'm going to try harder." And then he
reviewed what she had just said. "Another man? What's
this shit?" The anger began to take over. "You don't
mean that hopeless, weak Fleet bastard who's been
hanging around like you were a bitch in heat? Jesus,
Jane, I know you're not very smart, but this is a joke!"

"Sam Fleet has been kinder to me, and nicer, than
anyone in my whole life," she said. "I am truly sorry,
Tom, but I am going to stay here with him. I can't lose
what I've found here. I want a divorce."

"No," he said. "No." His voice was cracking and he
could see red through his eyes. Goddamn it, couldn't she
understand that he loved her? A holiday flirtation, that
was all this was. Poor little Jane, so unworldly; she let a
chap hold her hand and thought she was in love. "You'll
see this differently in the morning," he said. "Don't
worry. Nothing has happened. We'll go home and everything will be as it was before. Except I'll try harder to be
a better husband."

"Tom," she said gently, "nothing can ever be the same
again between you and me. I'm in love with Sam Fleet."

The dam in him broke then; the fragile barrier holding back all his emotions collapsed and he surrendered

to total, frustrated savagery. He would never remember
how many times he hit her, only that as she sank to the
floor he went down too, crying and confused.

There was no one to farewell him in the morning as he
boarded the *Pride of Pembroke,* and he stayed in his cabin
as the ship sailed out through the Great Sound and into
the rising waves. Jane saw the ship leave from the balcony of her room in the Hotel Princess. The guilt almost
overwhelmed her; the realization of what she had done
made her nauseated. She swayed back into the bathroom and looked at herself in the mirror. Her face was a
mass of purple bruises, but the damage was inside her.
None of it mattered, though, not as long as Sam was
there. She ran cold water on a towel and put it to her face.
In the end, it would all be worth it. But she shivered as
she heard the storm strike the window; she had no idea
what winter might be like in this summer place.

Gary Powell stood in the courtyard of the St. George's
Hotel and cursed the rain. Only two more days of shooting and they could be finished, if the storm didn't change
everything.

"I can't delay," he told Robert Fleet. "All their contracts run out this week, and you'll be up for horrendous
penalty clauses if we go overtime. I guess we'll just have
to shoot the attack scene in the rain and pray the sun
comes out for the closing shots."

"Okay," Robert told his director. "Do it that way.
Maybe the storm won't look too bad on film. Thunder and
lightning to accentuate the gunfire."

Neither man paid any attention to the tall black man
sheltering under a palmetto tree at the side of the courtyard. John Clay had hung around the hotel and the film
set almost every day since the police closed down his
newspaper; he'd become a fixture, and now went unnot-
iced. But he had kept his ears open and he knew as much
about the film's schedule as Fleet and Powell did. He
watched them walk through the rain to their waiting
coach. Then he started around to the staff entrance at the
back of the hotel.

Robert sat back in a corner of the carriage as it made the short journey down to the cove for the day's shoot. He was sad the picture was almost at an end; it had been about the most enjoyable period of his life. He still hadn't made it into bed with Mary Daintry, although he'd been within a grope of it on several occasions, and Mark Rider hadn't risen to Anne's innumerable baits. At least, she said he hadn't. But they had all had a lot of fun together, and he and Anne had just about converted Rider to their Fascist cause. It would be invaluable, having one of Hollywood's biggest stars a fervent supporter of Hitler.

"At least they've all turned up despite the storm," Powell said, looking out the window. "I must say, Robert, all your locals have been bloody good. I thought they'd get over the novelty of it the first week and never show up again."

"Not these people," Robert said. "They all paid for the privilege of being in my film and they're determined to get their money's worth. I should have charged Baseheart more, the amount of time you're giving his wife on film. Old Henrietta's beginning to think she's a real star."

"Well, she gets her big moment today. The grand death scene."

John Clay moved along a back corridor of the hotel and took up his station where he could see the door of the suite which served as the film's production office.

"Hurry it up," the property man snapped at the score of blacks milling around his umbrella. He rationed out the blank cartridges to each of them. "Just remember to keep out of each other's way," he said. "You could still get a nasty burn if you get too close to the end of a barrel."

Henrietta Baseheart studied her appearance in the hand mirror the makeup woman held for her. She would have liked it better if they let her color her cheeks a little, but the director wouldn't listen to her suggestions. She felt an exhilarating nervousness about today's filming, the culmination of all the little scenes she'd been featured in over the past weeks. Now she would be center stage when the mob of blacks came storming up the beach firing at her. And she would get to die in the arms of the settlers' leader, Mark Rider. What a handsome devil he was. Henrietta had heard rumors of the goings-on up at Robert's house. Lady Anne might have a title, but it seemed she was as likely as any other woman to have her head turned by a handsome man, even if he was a mere actor.

"Places everybody," Powell called through his megaphone, and they all positioned themselves around the cove. Henrietta found her spot in the center of the beach and, as directed, stood stock-still with hand upraised to halt the oncoming blacks.

"Okay, action," she heard Powell say, and then they were running toward her, firing their weapons. At first she thought she had been hit by a handful of gravel; then a terrible thump in her chest and she was reeling backward, falling into the sand. When she put her hand to the bodice of her dress, it came away covered in blood. She heard her own scream lost in the screams of the crew and cast. Something had gone dreadfully wrong, Henrietta thought as she felt the pain sweeping over her. She hoped Powell had captured it all on film; she was proud of her performance.

When he heard the shots and screaming, John Clay ran down the corridor and into the production office. There were just the two secretaries working there.

"Mr. Powell wants you down at the cove in a hurry," he shouted. "There's been a terrible accident."

The women could hear the screaming too; they left their desks and ran from the office.

Clay moved swiftly, gathering all the loose paper he could find in the office and stacking it around the cans of film in the open safe. He found a match and threw it into the pile and waited until it was well aflame. Then he slipped out of the office and walked casually back down the corridor and out into the driving rain.

* * *

"My poor baby," Sam Fleet said as he touched her swollen cheek. "I'd kill the bastard if he were still here. How could anyone be so brutal?"

"The wounds will heal, Sam," Jane said. "I don't blame Tom. He loves me, in his way. Or did love me. This has shattered him." She gazed out at the rain. "Oh, God, I've done the right thing. I feel like such a sinner."

He held her tightly, stroking her hair.

"You have done the right thing, darling," he said. "And now I will carry out my part. I'm going to tell Ginny about us tonight and ask her for a divorce. I suspect it'll be an easier scene than yours with Tom. Ginny doesn't give a damn about our marriage."

"I hope you're right, Tom. We are hurting so many other people with this love of ours."

"After this evening it will all be fine," he said.

And it seemed right. He sat down with Ginny before dinner and told her, quickly and unemotionally, that he was in love with Jane and wanted to marry her.

"I can't say it's a shock," his wife said when he had finished. "We always played fast and loose with our marriage, Sam, didn't we? Actually, I'll quite miss you." She studied him across the table, the long, pale face and faded blue eyes. They'd been a long time together. But his decision helped with the one she had to make for herself. Terrence Howard would be leaving soon and she wanted to go with him. New York, then London; they would travel the world. With his fame and her money they would be an unstoppable couple. He hadn't asked her to run away with him, of course. He hadn't even tried to take her to bed in all the time they had been together. But Ginny was confident he longed for her as she did for him. The way he touched her hand, kissed her cheek, made her laugh . . . she would be a little bit sorry to leave Sam, but Terrence would more than replace him. She looked at her watch, thinking she might run down to the gatehouse now and tell him the news. But he was dining at the club this evening as the Drama League's guest of honor, then spending the night at the Lapins' place in

Southampton. She would just have to keep her news for
a couple of days.

"I can't believe it," Tom Winders said. "Poor Henrietta maimed. It's like some kind of joke gone wrong. Your
brother must be feeling tragic."

"Robert's only upset that his blasted film went up in
flames," Veronica said. "The whole thing's very suspicious. Accidents just don't happen like that. Still, they
were playing around with guns and that's always a risky
business." She waved her hand in dismissal of the incident; it was Henrietta's own damn fault, gallivanting
around in a film at her age. "Anyway, Tom, what have
you decided about our airline?"

God, she was a tough woman, he thought. Her cousin's
wife wounded, her brother's film destroyed, and all she
wanted to talk was business—her own business.

"I'll come in with you," he said, "but on one condition.
You know Sam and Ginny have been acting up these past
few years. I want to bring them to their senses. We don't
need a divorce in the family. I suggest Sam and Ginny
set up and run the airline. You'll be the real boss, of
course, and you'll employ experts to see they keep on the
right track, but I believe if they've got something to keep
them busy, if they're working together, they can iron out
all their domestic problems."

"That's not a bad idea, Tom," she said. "Sam hasn't
done a speck of real work since he came home from the
war, and it doesn't look like Ginny's ever going to have
a child. Yes, it might just bring them together and, as
you say, I'll keep an eye on them."

"We'll have to move quickly," he said. "I hear Primrose Odlum has come up with a similar idea. That husband of hers was a flier in the war, so he's probably
behind it. They'll not be able to match the Fleet ex-
pertise or your connections in the travel business, but
still—"

"But still it'll be important to be first in the air, Tom.
Yes, I'll get moving on it tomorrow."

                         * * *

Ginny fixed cocktails and came and sat beside the playwright on the swinging seat in the garden of the gatehouse. The sun was just going down and the clouds were building again on the horizon. A shiver of nervousness went through her.

"The Lapins are such awful name-droppers," Terrence Howard said. "And the way they parade that boy of theirs. You'd think he was the only Royal by-blow in the Empire. I'll never be able to thank you enough, dear Ginny, for lending me this haven and allowing me to avoid most of the locals." He sighed. "It is a most beautiful colony, but so remote. I don't know how a beautiful, cultivated woman like you can exist here so far from the great cities of the world."

"It's stifling," she said. "Your visit has been like a window opening onto the real world. I can't stand to think of you leaving." She moved a little closer to him and impulsively rested her hand on his knee. "Come inside now, Terrence. It's getting quite cold out here."

They moved into the living room; she felt an awkwardness between them and wondered what to do to dispel it. She would just have to be direct with him.

"Terrence," she said, standing close, "my husband and I are going to split up. I want to go with you, take care of you. Please, will you have me?" Her lips were only inches from his; if he would kiss her now it would all work out. But he was taking a step backward and he looked confused.

"I'm afraid I've misled you terribly, Ginny," he said. "I must be a better actor than I suspected. You can't come with me."

"There is someone else," she said sadly. "I should have known, a man as brilliant as you are."

"No, my dear," he said. "I'm homosexual. A fruit, faggot, pansy, pooftah, shirt-lifter, queer, sodomite, Nancyboy . . ." He watched her clap her hands over her ears to shut out the stream of ugliness. Poor, silly woman, he thought, not to have understood him right from the start. Most others did.

"I'm sorry," Ginny said. She didn't know what she was

apologizing for. For being a fool and an idiot, she supposed. She was humiliated and angry . . . and desperate.
God, she couldn't let Sam just walk out of their marriage. She'd be left high and dry. "I hope I haven't embarrassed you, Terrence," she said. She started for the
door. "I must get back to the house." She let herself out
and ran across the wide lawns in the gathering dark; the
storm clouds were overhead now and she could hear the
growling thunder.

"Don't be so damned stupid, Sam!" Veronica glowered
at her brother from behind her desk. It seemed she'd got
him in for this dressing-down just in time. A divorce
would wreck everything. Damn it, why was she the only
one in this family with a sense of responsibility? "You
and Ginny are not going to split up. Quite the opposite.
Her father and I have decided you two had better pull
your weight around here. The pair of you are going to
run an airline for Fleets. It will be a great challenge and
you'll be well paid if you succeed."

"I don't want to."

"I'll tell you what you want, Sam. Because otherwise
I'll make life very unpleasant for you. I'll kick you off the
board, for starters, and you'll have to get along without
your director's fees. And Tom will cancel Ginny's trust
fund if the two of you don't come to your senses." She
stood up and advanced on him. "You have no choice,
Sam. I've arranged with the *Gazette* to announce our big
scheme on Friday. We'll have a nice, loving picture of you
and Ginny on Page One with a story about how you're
banding together to bring this exciting new development to Bermuda."

Sam would have fought back, but as always, Veronica
had him intimidated. All he wanted was to get out of her
immediate presence. He had just left Jane at the hotel,
and he longed to be back with her. But he had to talk this
new development over with his wife.

She was in the drawing room when he reached home
and she poured him a drink as he pulled off his dripping

rain cape. She looked pale and drawn but there was a determined glint in her eye.

"Sit down, Sam," she said. "Things have changed since our talk. I'm not going to let you have your divorce. I think we should try again, try a bit harder."

"Your father's got to you already, has he?" Sam said. "Jesus! Our families."

"No," she said, puzzled. "I've not spoken to anyone about this. It's just something I've decided for myself."

He told her of Veronica's ultimatum. When he had finished she nodded.

"All the better," she said, "in light of what I had already decided. We'll plunge into this thing, Sam, give it our best shot. I'm sure a lot of our problems have been caused by boredom. Now, what am I going to wear for this photograph? Something really stunning."

He drank his whiskey and watched her. It was a temporary setback to his plans. Jane would have to understand that this reunion was only a business ploy. They could still be together a lot of the time. Maybe she should go back to New York. He would visit her there, often. Anyway, he had no say in the matter. With both his sister and his wife against him, Sam Fleet would do as he was told.

"I'm not so sure now the film business is the right way to spread our message," Robert Fleet said. "Maybe more direct action is needed."

"I agree," Anne said. "Perhaps if we persuaded Adolf to visit us here and speak directly to the people."

"Do you think he'd come?" Robert was excited. Hitler visiting them! That would stir things along. He wasn't really sorry, now, about his film being destroyed in the fire. The message he'd wanted to put across had become confused in having to go through so many other hands. Besides, the picture had been fully insured, so he hadn't lost anything.

"Not yet," Anne said. "But once he has Germany running properly I'm sure we can persuade him."

"Did you arrange flowers for Henrietta?"

"The best they had. Poor old Jamie is quite cut up about it all."

"That bloody fool Dale isn't getting anywhere with the investigation. I know the niggers were behind everything. Dale ought to pull a few of them in and beat the truth out of them. Thank God it wasn't one of the stars who were wounded. They'd have sued us for a fortune."

"Perhaps it's best if no arrests are made," Anne said. "This way the whole black community is under suspicion."

"I was getting bored with all those film people," Robert said. "They were really quite shallow. Mark Rider didn't have a brain in his head. But you seemed to quite like him, at least in the beginning."

"You're right. Just a good-looking, empty-headed Australian." Who couldn't perform in bed, she added to herself. All those drugs, she supposed. It had been a bitter disappointment. "At least we indoctrinated him well. I think he'll work for us when the time comes."

"I hope we don't need people like him. It's the ruling classes we must win."

"It's happening. Daddy had more than a thousand at his last rally in London. And the Americans are climbing aboard. They're already quite keen on Mussolini; they just need to be exposed to Adolf and he'll be a hero to them too. At least, outside New York."

Jane waited all through Thursday and Thursday night, but no message came from Sam. She feared he was having trouble with his wife, and her heart went out to him—all the upsets he was willing to suffer so they could be together. She tried not to think of her own position—pregnant, disgraced before her family, all alone in Bermuda apart from Sam. It would all be worthwhile in the end, though. Friday dawned gray and wet, the wind howling across the ocean and lashing Hamilton, and still there was no word from Sam. She sat by the window in her hotel room and watched the deserted harbor as the realization grew that something was wrong. She ran to

answer the knock on the door but it was only the waiter
with her breakfast.

Jane took her coffee by the window and idly picked up
the *Royal Gazette* that had come with the tray. She saw
the photograph at once, three smiling columns of Sam
and his wife above a story about their bold new venture
into air transport. She checked the story and photo cap-
tion: each referred to "yesterday." It was not a picture
from the newspaper files.

She stayed at the window awhile longer, feeling numb
and heavy. Then she bathed and dressed and went to the
lobby of the hotel to make one last check. No, there was
no message.

The little sailing dinghies for the use of guests were
tied up to the dock, their masts swaying in the wind. The
old black man who had charge of them was nowhere to
be seen; it was not a day on which anyone would be ven-
turing out onto the Great Sound in a twelve-foot sail-
boat. Jane clambered into the nearest boat, undid its
mooring line and hauled up the sail. The wind grabbed
it at once and set the boat racing around the breakwater
and into the full force of the storm. No one from the hotel
saw her go, no cry sounded from the shore for her to return. Soon she was out of sight of land, the dinghy always threatening to nose under the heavy chop, the wind
attempting to lay it flat on the water. She was drenched
and shivering but she sailed on, the rain and spray mixing with the tears flowing down her cheeks.

Primrose draped another blanket around Jeff's shoulders; his croup was almost gone now but she was glad
she had decided to take another day away from the business to take care of him. He was bored with bed and
wanted her company and she enjoyed being with him.

"I can hardly see anything through your telescope,
Mummy," he complained. "The rain blots everything
out."

"You just keep covered up or you'll be right back in
your bed," she said.

"Ooh, look," he said, "there's a little boat out there."

He chuckled. "It's going to tip over any minute. What a silly person, to go sailing in a storm."

"Let me see," Primrose said. She focused the telescope on the figure. The boat was a good way from shore and out of control. As she watched, the boom was swinging wildly from side to side and the dinghy appeared to be settling lower and lower in the water. There was a small, huddled figure in the stern making no attempt to bring the boat under control. Primrose tugged the bellrope to summon the maid.

"Is the boatman here, Lucy?" she asked when the girl arrived. "There's someone in trouble out on the Sound. We'd better go take a look and see if they want towing in."

"No, ma'am. John figured you wouldn't be using any of the boats today so he went into Hamilton to buy some things."

Primrose gazed through the telescope again. The wind was mounting, and as she watched, a fresh squall hit the boat. It gave up the long struggle and heeled over, the sail dipping into the water and being pulled under. The figure in the boat was flung out, and now only the upside-down hull could be seen.

"I'll have to go out there," Primrose said. She ran into the hall and grabbed a heavy rain cape. "Keep an eye on me through the glass, Lucy, and see I don't get into trouble. And keep Jeff covered up."

She hurried down the lawn to the boathouse. It was quiet and calm inside, their various craft riding gently in the enclosed water. But when she raised the rolling door at the water end of the shed, she felt the full force of the storm. The boat she selected was a heavy cedar captain's gig, powered by a slow but reliable diesel. It fired on the first turn, and Primrose steered the craft out into the surging water.

It took her several minutes to locate the hull of the dinghy, and she circled it a couple of times looking for the occupant. She pulled alongside and thumped her fist against the hull but there was no answer. Her own boat crashed against the dinghy and she had to pull away, which was when she spotted the figure about thirty yards away, drifting off into the center of the Sound. Primrose chugged after the sodden mass and brought the gig up-wind of it, giving some shelter from the storm.

"Grab on to this line," she screamed, but there was no response. Good God, she thought, it was a woman. She could see the long hair trailing in the water, and the billowing skirt which seemed to be keeping the wearer afloat. She grabbed a boat hook and lunged out, trying to avoid the woman's head. The hook finally took hold of her jacket and Primrose started pulling in. God, she was a dead weight. It took a supreme effort and almost capsized the gig, but at last Primrose had the woman draped over the side. She was facedown, water streaming from her mouth and nose; with one last effort Primrose pulled her the rest of the way into the boat and turned her on her back. "Jane Bellowes!" she gasped. She put her ear to the woman's white lips to check her breathing.

"Leave me. Please leave me," she heard Jane whisper.

The doctor was waiting when she got back to shore and they carried Jane up to the house. Her breath was coming in gulps, rattling and rasping, but there were spots of color in her cheeks. Dr. Inglis was with her a half-hour in the guest room and emerged looking puzzled.

"She'll be all right," he told Primrose. "The worst she's suffering is mild exposure and a little hysteria." He dropped his voice. "But she's pregnant; and when I told her she hadn't lost the baby, she started to cry. I'm worried about her mental state. To go out there on a day like this . . . I think she meant to do herself harm."

"Surely not, doctor," Primrose said firmly. "So many of the tourists get into trouble in boats. Look, I know her quite well and I can take care of her here better than the hospital. Don't worry about her attitude. She's had a terrible fright. I'll call you if there's anything to worry about. Thanks for coming." She had him out of the house before he could protest.

She sat with Jane most of the day. The girl was distraught and wept a lot of the time; she did not speak and

Primrose did not try to draw her out. When she heard
Richard come home, she tiptoed from the room and met
him in the hallway. She filled him in on the day's events
and saw him frown.

"I wish we hadn't gotten involved in all this," he said.
"I don't want to upset Tom Bellowes."

"Really, Richard," she said. She was quite annoyed
with him but, after all, he hadn't yet seen the pitiful little figure in the guest room. "I know how much the airline scheme means to you, but Jane needs our help badly.
You don't think I'm going to cast her out into the street?"

"I'm sorry. I wasn't thinking." He grinned suddenly.
"I, of all people, should show compassion for adulterers." He guided his wife away from the sickroom and
down to the study. "It is going to be bloody awkward,
though. Shouldn't we tell Sam Fleet she's here?"

"Sam Fleet? Why?"

"Darling, you're too good to be true. I forgot you never
listen to gossip. Little Jane's been on with Fleet for most
of the time the Bellowes were in Bermuda. Bellowes
thought she'd get over it, but I saw him just before he
sailed off without her and he was mad as hell."

"He was such an angry, brutal man," Primrose said.
"I'm amazed Jane found the courage to go against him.
Sam too, for that matter. Still, Bellowes is a business
partner now and he'll have to be told what's happened.
I think you'd better call him at sea and I'll get in touch
with Sam." She decided there was no need at this time
to tell her husband Jane was pregnant.

Richard finally got Tom Bellowes on the ship-to-shore
radiophone. They talked briefly; he put down the phone
and rejoined Primrose.

"He's tough, all right," Richard said. "Wasn't interested in Jane at all. Said divorce proceedings would be
under way immediately and she had better find herself
a lawyer. Then he started talking about the airline as if
nothing had happened."

Primrose got an even more brusque response from
Sam Fleet.

"I can't talk," he said. "I'm glad she's all right, but it's best I have no contact with her for a while." And he hung up.

"I guess we've got a waif on our hands," Richard said. They had sat with Jane a half-hour, encouraging her to take a little chicken broth. She shyly thanked them for caring for her, but—Primrose noted worriedly—not for pulling her from the waters and certain death.

"We'll just let her rest and recover and see what happens," Primrose said. "There's no hurry."

"One thing that is urgent," Richard said, glad to put the domestic drama aside for a moment, "is the airplane business." He waved a copy of that morning's *Gazette* at her. "You see the Fleets are plunging right into it. If they beat us to the punch—"

"Does it really matter so much?" she asked. But she saw it in his eyes; the airline was Richard's one chance to build a new career for himself. She owed him support to make the attempt. "Well," she laughed, "here we go again. Head to head with the Fleets. Nothing ever changes in Bermuda."

Somehow, Jane Bellowes was just absorbed into Primrose's household. She scarcely spoke in the first weeks, moving pale and ghostlike among the upstairs rooms; but gradually she began to confide in Primrose. The two women became close. Jane felt totally dependent on Primrose: no one else wanted to take responsibility for her and she felt she could not be responsible for herself.

"My parents have disowned me," Jane said, carefully folding the letter that had arrived in the morning post. It was a cold day in December and she and Primrose were sitting before a fire in the library. Young Jeff had gone off with the gardener to select a Christmas tree; Richard was still stumping around the West Coast of the U.S., selecting a suitable flying boat. "They're terribly worried the divorce will upset their partnership with the Belloweses. And the scandal threatens their position in society. They don't want me anywhere near until the worst of it has blown over." She looked into the fire. "But

I must do something, Primrose. I've imposed on you and Richard far too long."

"We love having you," Primrose said. And it was true. Since Jane had been in the house, Primrose had come to realize how few friends she had outside her husband and son. The business took most of her time, but on weekends and evenings she enjoyed being with a woman friend for a change. "And with Richard off on his airplane search, you've been wonderful company for me. Don't think about leaving yet."

"I don't suppose I can until this," she said, patting her stomach, "has arrived. Oh, damn, I wish I hadn't gotten pregnant. It was all such a mess, anyway, without a bastard child to complicate things even more."

"Sam still doesn't know about the baby?" Primrose found Jane's attitude to the forthcoming child hard to understand. She had no feeling for it; she just wanted to have it and then set about rebuilding some kind of life for herself.

"Sam doesn't know anything, nor want to know," Jane said. "He wrote me one note in all the time I've been with you, saying how sorry he was things 'didn't work out' for us." She forced a smile. "Women in love; we're all blind. I should have been able to see how weak Sam was from the first, but I mistook it for gentleness. He seemed so kind and loving after Tom. So I end up with no one. Except you, and I'll never be able to repay you. After the baby I'll go back to the States and start again. Get a job, though God knows what I'm trained for. And there's a small trust fund, so I won't starve." She frowned. "I've decided to put the baby up for adoption, Primrose. It's the only way. It's not the child's fault, but I shall never be able to love Sam Fleet's baby."

"It will be different after the event," Primrose said. "You'll see. Lots of mothers think they're not going to love their babies."

Jane shook her head. "No," she said, "I won't feel any different later. I want to put every trace of my shame behind me. I've been a fool. If I'm to have a second chance it must be a clean break."

"Let's wait and see. You will have the baby here in the house and no one need know about it, just Dr. Inglis and Richard and me. The walls are high and the staff is loyal. Bermuda may be tiny but we can keep our secrets if we really want to. We'll just see what happens."

Robert Fleet looked at the mousy, bespectacled doctor hunched over the desk in the Berlin consulting room. He'd come to this fellow because he had a marvelous reputation in treating headaches. Instead, all Robert was getting was a lecture about sexual hygiene. He was about ready to walk out; didn't this stupid doctor realize who he was? That in one hour he and Anne would be lunching with Air Minister Goering?

"I am sorry, Herr Fleet," the doctor said. "It is not good news and it is delivered too late to have anything done about it. Your disease, your syphilis, was contracted at least twenty years ago; and although the physical symptoms have vanished, the treponema pallidum has continued to attack your system down through the years. The blinding headaches you complain of, the fits of rage followed by depression, these are clear signs. Our own Ehrlich pioneered the 'cure' for this disease, but even he admits defeat once it has taken hold. I will be blunt with you, Herr Fleet. You will go on deteriorating and eventually be reduced to insanity. It is possible, though, that the mental condition will be controllable with drugs. That is why I am being so frank now, to prepare you for what is going to happen and to ensure that your own doctors will know what to do." He again studied the form Fleet had been obliged to fill in. "That is good, you have no children. Because your disease is hereditary, passed on through the mother to the child, and the child born with it will have no chance of being cured."

Robert wasn't going to tell this old quack they already had a child, Colin, who was healthy as a Fleet could be. It was only the bloody headaches that bothered Robert. He stood up abruptly and towered over the little German.

"You don't know what you're talking about," he

snapped. "I should report you to the local medical association." He found his wallet and flung down a ten-pound
note. "I don't know what your regular fees are, doctor,
but I would suggest this is a damn sight more than you're
worth. Good day, sir."

He stormed out of the consulting room. The quack had
actually brought on another headache; he was a fool to
have gone to him. Robert, tall and blond and indistin-
guishable from the new ruling class of Germany, strode
through the chill February streets of Berlin, trying to
calm his temper and his headache before the luncheon
appointment.

Hermann Goering was a charming host and obviously
enchanted by Anne. English gentlewomen were quite
the fashion in the new Nazi hierarchy, Robert had noted,
and his wife's title put her ahead of Unity Mitford. It was
a jolly lunch, filled with toasts to German-British cooperation, and Anne sparkled.

"So sad Adolf couldn't make it," Anne said as the limousine took them back to their hotel. "But there is so
much he has to do for this country and for Europe. It must
be daunting, even for a man of his talents."

"You mentioned the idea of coming out to Bermuda?"
he asked. "Goering would be perfectly suitable if the
Chancellor himself can't make it."

"I did more than mention it." Anne laughed. "I said
one of them had to come out to Bermuda to open the 'Pink
Palace' when it's finally completed. And he promised
they would do their best to attend. Oh, I do wish the
workmen would hurry up, Robert. The place seems to be
taking forever to build."

"You wanted a great house, my dear, and that's what
you're going to get. Greatness takes a little longer to
achieve than ordinariness."

"It's so damned expensive to build something really
special in Bermuda," she said. "The price of shipping
Italian marble—no wonder your family makes a fortune." She was happy that day, happy to be in Berlin,
with the new leaders, to be present at the dawning of the
New Europe. She felt positively loving toward her hus-

band for helping her to attain all this. She snuggled up
to him. "I know what we'll do this afternoon," she whispered. "We'll stay in the suite and you can put on your
Nazi uniform and give me what I deserve, a sound whipping." She giggled again as her hand, resting in his lap,
felt his erection.

Ginny watched Sam across the breakfast table; she
had been more attentive to his moods since their recon-
ciliation. She figured since it looked as though they
would have to spend the rest of their lives together, she
might as well make an effort to get along with him. Today, she could see, he was not in a good temper.

"What's wrong?" she finally asked. "You've been
glowering at the paper for twenty minutes. Surely
there's nothing in the *Gazette* to upset you."

"It's bloody Veronica," he snapped, slamming down
the newspaper. "We had a dreadful fight last night. She
thinks I'm not moving fast enough on her blasted airline. My sister is driving me up the wall." He sipped his
coffee and gestured to the maid to bring more. "Her spies
tell her Richard Billings has already found a suitable
plane and plans to fly it down here within a few weeks
and get all the publicity for being first. Hell, Billings
knows all about aviation, so of course he's likely to be
first. So what? We'll win in the end. But try telling that
to Veronica. Jesus, she's a worse dragon than our father
ever was."

"Poor Sam," Ginny smoothed. "She does make life
miserable for you. It's not right, either, for her to be running the family company. You'd make a much better fist
of it."

"Of course I would. But she's got the board in the palm
of her hand. So long as she keeps increasing the dividend
every year I'll never wrest control from her."

"Well, my father isn't getting any younger. Maybe
when he dies and I inherit we can do something about
changing the balance of power. In the meantime, I suppose we'd better see what we can do about this airline. I

haven't been much of a help to you, but I'll try harder. What does Veronica think we should be doing?"

"Winning the race against the Odlums," he said. "I've already hired a couple of pilots and they're out looking for a suitable plane. But it's not the kind of purchase you make on a whim."

"A race," Ginny said. "That might be the way to do it. Lots of publicity as well." She clapped her hands. "What we'll do, Sam, is find a plane at once and issue a public challenge to Billings to race us from the U.S. to Bermuda on an agreed date."

"But what if we don't win?"

"We can take out some insurance against that," she said. "Hire someone to spike his fuel or whatever it is you have to do to stop an airplane from flying. And make sure you've got a better plane than his to begin with." She got up and paced the room. "What about those people on Long Island who came down to see us? Grumman. Didn't they say they could deliver quickly?"

"Their flying boat wasn't big enough for what we need," he said. "But there's another outfit in Hartford I've been talking to who may have come up with the goods." He frowned again. "That's why I hate rushing this, Ginny. It's a big decision."

"But it can't wait, not with the Wicked Sister throwing her weight around. I think we better get up to Hartford, buy ourselves a flying boat and throw out the challenge. Trust me, Sam, and we'll come out winners in this."

She felt the baby move as she strolled the lush grounds of the Odlum mansion on a bright spring day. She felt regret; after it was born she would have no excuse to stay on here. She would have to return to America and start a whole new life. The months with Primrose had been calm and sustaining, despite the unwanted life growing inside her. Primrose had shown her strength and compassion and guided her through the worst of the despair. Most astonishing, she had said that if Jane didn't love the child after it was born, Primrose and Richard would adopt it.

"We wanted another child," Primrose explained, "But since Jeff was born we've been trying without success. Your child would be loved by us and have a happy and secure home here in Bermuda."

It had all made sense. Now, though, now the time was near, she felt the regret of being parted from Bermuda, from Primrose, and, she admitted to herself, from the baby. But it was the best thing she could do for all of them. At least the child would be loved. No one need ever know its parentage; as Primrose had promised, Jane had been totally protected behind the walls of the great house. It was a happy prison for her; she had not been out into the world—had not wanted to go—since the day Primrose plucked her from the sea.

"There you are," she heard Primrose call. She looked up at her friend striding through the garden toward her. Yes, this was the right place for the child. "You're looking so well today," Primrose said. "It must be the weather. I always feel good when winter has passed." She handed Jane a small glass vial. "See what you think of that. It's the new summer fragrance we've been working on, Bermuda Blue."

Jane took the stopper from the bottle. The delicious scent of sun and flowers rose to greet her; for a giddy second she was transported back to the previous summer in the colony, when every day sparkled and love seemed never-ending. She started to cry and was grateful to Primrose for taking her in her arms and trying to shield her from the sadness.

Richard Billings was nervous but elated. He didn't like all the hoopla surrounding the great race from Miami to Bermuda—the Miami *Herald* was full of it in the days before the flying boats were to set out—but he was confident of his airplane. He and his copilot had taken delivery in Seattle and flown it down the coast and via the Panama Canal to Miami; it had performed perfectly and Richard was confident he could beat Sam Fleet's crew.

He had kept well away from the Fleet contingent in Miami. Anyway, Sam and Ginny seemed more interested in throwing promotional parties than in getting ready for the grueling trip ahead. Richard supposed all publicity was a help to both airlines, but he preferred to do his boasting after the race was over. Which wouldn't be long now, Richard thought as he listened to the mayor's enthusiastic farewell speech. There were several thousand people gathered on the shores of Biscayne Bay on this bright sunny morning and hundreds more in boats on the bay itself. Some five hours away, across the Gulf Stream, the crowd would already be gathering around Hamilton Harbor to welcome the flying boats.

"It's going to be the devil of a job taking off through all the spectator craft," Josh Reid, his copilot, muttered. He was a lean, taciturn Oregonian and he hated the pre-race fuss even more than Richard did. "I was down here at dawn and I felt like taking off then. Not a soul in the way—except one of the Fleet mechanics who was giving our plane a good looking-over. I had to chase him off. I guess they'd like to learn our secrets. I figure we're certain to outfly them today."

"I hope you're right, Josh. I don't want to lose this race after all the crap we've had to put up with in the past week." They climbed into the waiting speedboat and started out for their craft, bobbing gently at its mooring buoy. A round of cheers followed them from the shore. "Anyway, we're almost gone. And before the sun goes down I'll be home in Bermuda with my wife and son. God, how I've missed the place! You don't know what treat's in store for you, Josh."

"I'll appreciate it when I see it coming up under the port wing," Josh said. "We miss that pile of rocks you call home and there's nothing but water until we hit England."

The breeze had stiffened when they stepped onto the flying boat's pontoon and whitecaps nipped at their leather boots. A hundred yards away they could see Fleet's fliers clambering up into their cabin; Richard threw them a salute, then went up the ladder and into the cockpit. They warmed up for five minutes then; when the mayor dropped a red flag from his patrol boat, they gunned the motors and bumped across the water and up into the sky. Richard had set a course that would take him in a high, north-pointing arc; glancing down and behind, he saw the Fleet craft had opted to go low and straight. He hoped he was right in gambling on finding lighter headwinds higher up. Already it was very cold in the cockpit; the brightness of the day was misleading. Far below he could see the Atlantic with a surface wind pushing up waves that looked to be eight feet and rising.

Two hours out of Miami, they drank hot coffee and shouted to each other over the engines' roar; according to Josh's navigation they were right on course and timetable. An hour later, though, both men knew they were falling behind schedule. The wind was dead against them and precious fuel was being used up as the big plane lumbered on.

"We'll need the auxiliary tank in a minute," Josh shouted. "I'd have hoped for another hour on the main tank. Still, we've got plenty of gas." Except that when he made the switch nothing happened. The gauge to the auxiliary showed it was full, but no fuel seemed to be coming through. The port engine coughed first, then died. A minute later, the starboard fell silent.

"Christ," Josh said. It was now silent in the cockpit except for the scream of the wind outside.

Christ, Richard prayed as the flying boat's nose dipped down toward the angry sea, Christ save us. It was hurtling up at them now, the waves high and solid as brick walls. The flying boat had little gliding capacity; its unwieldy pontoons were dragging it down from the sky too fast to hope for a cushioned touchdown. He managed to pull the plane over the crest of one wave, but the next was racing toward them. Good-bye Primrose, he whispered in his head. Good-bye Jeff. They hit the wave full on. The force ripped the wings off; the nose and cockpit went under the surging waters, and the hull cartwheeled. The last sound they heard was water pounding down on them as the frail shell around them collapsed.

* * *

Young Jeff had been jumping up and down all afternoon waiting for the flying boats to arrive; he wanted to be out in the boat, but Primrose restrained him. There would be plenty of time to leave the house and take to the water when his father actually flew into view, she explained. So they sat on the terrace of the house in the shade and sipped cool drinks and felt their excitement mount. Jane was with them and Primrose kept a close eye on her; the baby would arrive anytime now, Dr. Inglis said.

"Here he comes, Mummy!" Jeff yelled. There had been false alarms earlier in the afternoon, but this time all of them heard the unfamiliar roar of airplane engines and, soon, saw the dark shape in the eastern sky. It was several minutes, though, before they realized the flying boat sweeping toward them was decorated in Fleet livery.

"He's lost the race," Jeff said, close to tears. "How could they have beaten Daddy? I was sure he'd be here hours before them."

"It's no great matter, darling," she said. But she felt sorry for Richard. She knew how much he wanted this venture to succeed; winning the great race would have been a good start. She settled back to wait some more, and watched the small boats on the harbor flocking around the flying boat, throwing streamers at it and waving huge Union Jacks. The boat was a big, ungainly creature, she thought as it lumbered through the water to its docking pen. But solid enough to brave the long journey over open water.

An hour passed, and another; only the most enthusiastic of the spectators were still waiting around the shores in the gathering dusk. Jeff was cross, and then silent. He knew something was very wrong but would not say so for fear he would make the worst come true.

"I think we should switch on every light in the house and the gardens," Primrose said as the darkness came down. "They will need something to guide them in." She gave orders to the servants, and at once the mansion glittered with light, as if some spectacular party were

going on inside. Their neighbors around the waterfront
saw what was happening and followed suit until the
whole vast harbor was a circle of brightness, tiny cottages and grand halls alike doing their best to create a
homing beacon for the missing adventurers. It looked so
festive, but for Primrose it seemed the gesture of a primitive tribe attempting to defend itself against the forces
of darkness.

Commissioner Dale arrived at ten P.M. to tell her there
was no signal or communication of any kind from the
flying boat; search boats would go out from Miami in the
morning, and all shipping in the area had been alerted.

"They're probably bobbing around out in the Gulf
Stream, safe and bored to death," the old police commissioner said. He wished he could believe it, but the Fleet
pilot had told him about the big seas out there.

Dr. Inglis came to the house just before midnight to
check on Jane and administer a sedative to Primrose. He
thought the baby would arrive the next day, and promised to return at dawn.

"There's no point you sitting up here gazing out to sea
all night," he chided Primrose. "Drink this and get some
rest. It's going to be an eventful day tomorrow."

But she couldn't sleep, even with the draught the doctor left her. She sat at her bedroom window, a light shawl
around her shoulders against the cool of the night. She
listened to the sounds of her island and waited, as generations of Bermuda women had waited for news of their
men missing at sea.

She was still there when dawn came up, a red sky
traced with low gray clouds and a rising wind snapping
at the palms. She knew Richard was gone. The knowledge was like a lead weight around her heart. She was
only thirty-three, but the romantic part of her life was
over; the only man she had ever loved or would ever love
was dead. Primrose got up from the window and quietly
went to check on her son. He was scrunched up in his bed,
his little fists clenched, the tangled sheets evidence of a
night of bad dreams. She touched his forehead and his
eyes flickered open.

"Daddy," he murmured. "Has Daddy arrived?"

"No, dear," she said. "Just go back to sleep." She tucked him in and stood awhile longer looking down at him. He was her future now and she would fiercely defend him until he was grown and strong enough to fend for himself.

She went down the hall of the old house, listening to echoes from generations of Odlums, feeling their presences all around her. She slipped into Jane's room and found her friend sitting up in the pale early light.

"Nothing?" Jane asked. She did not need an answer. She opened her arms to Primrose and the two women held each other in shared grief. "I'm sorry," Jane said. "It's not an appropriate time, but the baby is coming. Could you call Dr. Inglis?"

Sam and Ginny were already on a Fleet liner sailing from Miami to Bermuda when the news of their victory in the air race was radioed to them. A few hours later they got the news that Richard Billings and Josh Reid were missing. They said nothing to each other, but that night, celebrating with champagne, Sam got quite drunk.

When they berthed in Hamilton four days later, there was no welcoming party and no sense of celebration about the momentous arrival in Bermuda of the air age.

"You seem to attract bad luck, Sam," Veronica said when he finally stopped by her office. "Sure, we won the air race but damn all good it's going to do us. The American papers have been playing up the story of Billings's death instead of our victory. They've dredged up every story of ships lost in the Gulf over the past hundred years and have started that stupid Devil's Triangle stuff again. No one is going to risk his life flying to Bermuda, not for years, anyway. The Odlums' loss is going to cost us, as well as them. Christ, will we always be linked to that family?"

Ginny was disappointed at the reaction from their family and friends. She and Sam were supposed to be heroes, the pair who'd put together a mighty victory in the greatest challenge Bermuda had ever witnessed. Instead they were being treated like an embarrassment; everyone seemed to be grieving for Primrose Odlum.

"How the hell was I to know there'd be a big wind in the Gulf that day?" she demanded of Sam. "All I had the mechanic do was crimp his fuel line; it should have slowed him down or, at worst, forced him to make a soft landing in the sea. Sam, we didn't mean to kill him." He slapped her, hard, then grabbed her wrists and pulled her close to him.

"Don't ever speak of it again," he hissed. "Just be glad the plane is deep beneath the sea and no one will ever know what happened. No one but you and me; we will have to live with what we know."

Chapter Eight
(1650–)

Prudence Odlum was weary, but she tried to pay attention to her guests; Ewen Staley and his young wife, Brigid, were her only friends. Ewen and Jonas were deep in debate about politics, particularly the colony's increasingly strained relationship with England. Prudence felt pride for her son, who was better than holding his own with the well-read Staley.

"They were wrong to increase taxes," Jonas was saying. "The very fact that our crops have proved a disappointment to the Company means we need more help, not more hindrances."

"But they must get a return on their capital," Staley argued. "They are businessmen first and statesmen second. We cannot expect them to just go on paying for this place when the chance of a return gets less each year."

"No one will get anything if these imposts continue to weight us down. This is a young colony, still, and like any young thing, needs nurturing if it is to grow up strong."

Dear Jonas, Prudence thought. So idealistic, despite all that had happened in his life. She would not have blamed him if he'd hated this place the way she hated it. But instead he had immersed himself in books and learning; first under her guidance, then, in the past few years, sharing the thrill of knowledge with Ewen Staley. The older man was self-taught, but Prudence recognized

in him one of the keenest minds in Bermuda. Both he and
Jonas had an amazingly wide field of interest: botany,
medicine, theology, navigation . . . whatever was in the
books they had studied.

Prudence glanced across to where Ewen's wife was
nursing their infant daughter, Rose. Brigid smiled back
at her shyly. A real catch for Ewen, Brigid had been. The
Fleets had brought her out from Ireland as a serving girl,
found fault with her and left her stranded. Ewen took her
under his wing and, after checking one more time with
Prudence that there was no point in his further pressing
his suit with her, married the girl. A year later Prudence
had been pleased to deliver little Rose.

Now her son and Staley had switched to a topic of even
greater interest to them, their next walk around the islands. So far they had covered most of the distance, wad-
ing from island to island at low tide, hacking through
dense bush and scaling sheer cliffs, to places where no
other settlers went. Others who went exploring Bermuda's coastline did so in the hope of finding riches cast up
from the galleons that came to grief on the far-out reefs;
these two, she thought wryly, made their expeditions
just for the sake of knowing what was there. They would
be away at least a week this time, and she would look
after Brigid and the little girl. She did not begrudge her
time because she liked Jonas to be off with Ewen Staley,
who was all the father he had known. It was ironic, Ewen
caring so much for the son of Will Acton, the man who
had cheated him. Rose began to cry, the sound shatter-
ing the peace in the warm, smoky room. Prudence opened
her arms and Brigid brought the baby to her; she cradled
it to her breast and slowly the sobs ebbed away. Poor little mite, Prudence thought as she stroked the small,
damp forehead. She would have been beautiful but for
the hideously disfiguring split in her lip. The baby teeth
even now gleamed through the gap as the child smiled
up at her. Everyone had some handicap to carry in this
world, Prudence acknowledged, but to scar a child at
birth like this, to condemn her to a life of taunts and vicious whispers about a "Devil's mark" was too cruel.

Prudence rocked the baby in her arms until it slept. "Poor little Rose," she murmured, "you are as badly marked as we Odlums are."

Staley stood up and stretched; Jonas rose with him. They would be on their way at first light and would be sleeping rough around the islands, so tonight they needed all the comfort they could get. Jonas put his hand on the older man's shoulder.

"I am greatly looking forward to our journey, Ewen," he said. He wanted to say more, something about the way in which Staley had over the years given him confidence and pride and love. But Staley, he knew, was as shy as he was. Instead he squeezed Staley's shoulder and was given a quick smile in return.

The old doctor wiped his brow and thought of the supper waiting for him at home; if it had not been the Fleets, he would have been long gone by now. But the family, and particularly the wretched youth tossing and sweating in the narrow bed, had been his mainstay for years. Simon Brothers was at a loss as to what to do next for the boy. Brothers' medical skills were rudimentary—he knew how to cut, how to purge and how to bleed—but even with the finest modern London schooling he would have been helpless, he knew, in treating Richard Fleet. The boy, Brothers thought gloomily, did seem to be under some kind of spell. Oh, this time it was just another of the severe fevers that regularly swept the colony. Either he would recover or he wouldn't. But the difference with Richard was that he caught everything, never developed any resistance, never built any strength to combat the next attack. He heard the mother enter the room behind him.

"Well?" Amanda demanded. "Have you cured him?" She pushed Brothers aside. "Oh, God, he looks worse than ever. What are you doing for him? Seven days he has lain like this and I see his strength slipping away." She fell on her knees and put her arms around her son's bony shoulders.

"I am sorry, madam," the old doctor mumbled. "We

both know he has always been a most unfortunate lad, contracting everything that comes along." He caught the brandy on her breath as she turned to him. You'll be needing the doctor yourself soon, he thought, seeing the strain in her face. Two bad men you've married and now you are slipping into trouble yourself, filled with hatreds and strong liquor. "But I'm sure Richard will come through this latest trial," he said. "He needs rest and sponging down to cool him, lots of liquids, patience."

Amanda wanted to yell at the doctor, to send him away, but he was all she had to take care of her boy. Her mother and Aunt Angela were no help at all. Whenever Richard was sick, they could only suggest he be sent home to England for better treatment and a change of climate. And Septimus! He'd never been a father to the boy and hardly a husband to her. No, she had to be patient with Brothers. He was a stupid man, but for now it appeared he had the power of life or death over the only person who mattered to her in this world. Her head was spinning and she wished she was not drinking so much. But she needed the drink to get her through the days, days filled with making the decisions no one else could make about the shipping line, of fighting for a fair deal, of building an empire to leave to Richard. And the nights; playing the attentive hostess, so none could accuse her of being unwomanly; sitting hour after hour over tea and embroidery with her mother and aunt, when she would rather have been doing the line's books; putting up with Septimus's fatuous blabbering whenever he decided to stay in instead of cavorting with his cronies at the Oceanic Club. She could weep for herself, so little had the glittering promise of her own youth been realized. And she did weep for Richard, beset with illness, too weak to claim his heritage. For a moment she saw the Odlum boy in her mind, Will's other son. Big and strong, handsome even—it wasn't fair that Will Acton's seed could produce two such different children. She would even things up, she swore; anything money and her own fierce devotion could purchase, Richard would have.

She raised a weak smile for the ineffectual doctor, wiped her son's hot forehead and rose from her knees.

"I am sure you are right and the boy will soon be well," she said, leading him from the room. "You will call again first thing tomorrow? Good. My husband will be home and will want to hear your prognosis. We put great stock in your ability, Dr. Brothers." She closed the big main door behind him and leaned against it for a moment, her head pressed to the polished cedar, enjoying the welcome cool of the fine wood. Amanda felt the tug at her skirt and glanced down; the little golden head picked up the last rays of sun in the hallway.

"Nurse Greaves!" she shouted into the rear of the house. "Nurse Greaves, come here at once. The baby is out of her room and crawling around in the hall."

"Mama, mama," the child whimpered, clutching tighter to Amanda's skirt, knowing she would be dragged away at any moment. "Mama," she called again as Greaves scurried down the hall, whisked her up and hurried her off to the nursery.

Poor little Hilda, Amanda thought as she watched the child's imploring face vanish into the shadows. I should love her but it is not in me. I care only about the boy. Amanda pushed herself away from the door and started back down to Richard's room, stopping in the library first to fix another brandy. It would be one more long night in her life, maintaining the vigil by his bed. It seemed as though she had been doing this forever.

Nathaniel Pike banged his silver-tipped cane on the polished floor. As the noisy conversations died, he let his gaze wander over them, the cream of Bermudian male society. They were all jolly, claret-flushed, finery in slight disarray, sure of themselves and their place in the colony. Quite a contrast to their daylight faces, set firm on a course of commerce and Christianity. Pike was well pleased with the way his club had developed. All the menfolk of the Forty Thieves families belonged, as did the garrison officers, the more reputable of the ships' captains based in Bermuda and the small professional

class which eked out a living in the sluggish economy.
Pike smiled approvingly at Sikes, the fat, crafty vicar
who on Sunday would sermonize against lust but tonight
—after quaffing more tankards of good red wine—would
go upstairs to sport with the Lapins' latest import, a
spirited half-caste beauty from Jamaica. Sikes had won
the raffle the club always ran to determine who got first
crack at a new girl. Tonight's raffle had realized twenty
guineas each for Pike and the Lapin family.

"The meeting of the Oceanic Club will come to order,"
Pike rasped, rising painfully to his feet. The gout had
him these days and any movement was agony. But he
was having such a good time of it—and making a handy
income on the side—he never complained. Dear Josie.
When he tumbled with her he could forget all his infirm-
ities. "There's little enough business for consideration
this month," he said, acknowledging the raucous cheers.
"New membership applications are posted on the board
and you have another week to vote on them. The wine
committee has noted your objections to our last shipment and action has been taken to secure new stock from
Portugal. The catering committee has arranged the importation of several more pair of deer and we may yet
have fresh venison on the menu. I must remind you annual membership fees are now due and there's been a
small increase to cover our rapidly rising overheads. The
new fees are a hundred guineas a year." He raised a hand
to stop the boos. "It's either that or widen our membership," he said. "I know I'd rather pay a little more than
be forced to open our doors to the tradesmen and small
farmers. We have a place here we can all be proud of, the
best gentlemen's club outside of London. The meeting is
closed." He sat down to loud applause.

The members pushed back their dining chairs and began to mingle. Some made a beeline for the *chemin de
fer* game presided over by the lovely Josie; a few settled
at the backgammon tables; others sidled off to the parlor
where the whores were demurely assembled. Pike
watched keenly: the club enabled him to keep a check on
all that mattered in Bermuda. He could tell which prom-

inent men were drinking too much, or gambling beyond their means, or—after consulting with the girls—were in failing health. Now he saw young Fleet settling in to guinea-a-point backgammon with John Connell, the club champion. He hobbled over to the board.

"Good evening, Sep," Pike said. "I'm surprised you could make it. Your boy is sick, I hear."

"The Fleets must be represented here!" Septimus said loudly, a trickle of red wine flowing down his chin and onto his cream doublet. "My poor old father is confined to bed for the last time, I fear, so I must show the flag of the colony's first family." He was very drunk. "There would not be an Oceanic Club without our patronage."

"Without your losses," Connell said under his breath as he offered a double. He was six hundred guineas ahead this year in his games with Fleet, and it was the easiest money he had ever made, much easier than practicing as a notary for these pinch-penny merchants. Fleet doubled him back and Connell had to hold a handkerchief to his lips to hide his glee.

"I shall call again on your father soon," Pike said. "I miss his wise counsel very much. And please give my best wishes to Amanda for Richard's speedy recovery."

"The boy will never be any damn good," Fleet said. "Bad blood, you know. The doctor's been with him seven nights straight and can't do anything for him." He threw his dice and cried out in triumph as double sixes spilled out. Except that he couldn't play sixes. "Goddamn you, Connell!" he cursed. "You have all the luck."

Pike walked on to the *chemin de fer* game and stood beside Josie. He let his hand brush her arm and felt a thrill at the touch of fine silk. He bent his head to her ear.

"Finish this quickly, my dear," he whispered. "I want to be with you." While he waited for her to pass the game over to one of the girls, Pike reflected on his happiness. There was the reawakened passion, of course. Every time with Josie was like the first time. But since she had told him she was with child—his child, their child—a new dimension had come into Nathaniel Pike's life. He had

never married, never felt the need for a son to carry on
his name, but now that there was to be a child, he was
elated. The boy—he was sure it would be a boy—would
be given his name and would inherit his vast estates. It
did not bother Pike in the least the child would be by another man's wife, a Frog at that. And he did not need Josie's assurances the child was his: her passion for him
had long ago convinced him she had no other lovers.

Now she was free of the table and coming to him across
the big room, nodding and smiling and exchanging jokes
with the members. They are all besotted by her, Pike
thought proudly, but she is mine. He took her hand and
raised it to his lips.

"You look ravishing, as always," he said. "And the
dress! It is beautiful."

"It is one you had made for me in Paris, dear Nathaniel," she said, rewarding him with a flashing smile. "You
are so generous to me, you forget your own gifts." She
pouted then. "Soon I will not be able to wear such beautiful gowns. The baby will begin to show."

"It will only make you more desirable to me," he said,
still holding her hand and not caring who observed them.
He supposed they made an odd pair, this elegant young
woman and a wizened old man. But it didn't matter to
Josie, so it didn't matter at all. "Shall we go upstairs?"
he asked and led her through the velvet curtains to the
steps leading to her private chambers.

He was disappointed and annoyed to find Henri Lapin
lounging there in her boudoir as if he belonged. Lately
Pike had been able to put M. Lapin right out of his mind,
as if he were only the business manager of the club and
nothing to do with Josie.

"My dear Nathaniel," Lapin said, rising to greet him.
"You do not look at all well, poor chap. The gout again?
I think it may be the red wine. There is a new theory in
Paris linking strong drink and a variety of illnesses.
Still, life would not be worth living without our pleas-
ures, would it?"

The man's familiarity annoyed Pike, but he supposed

he had to put up with it. After all, he was cuckolding the
little Frog and did have his lovely wife with child.

"There's plenty of life left in me, Lapin," he said. "And
in the club. There's a full house downstairs. Don't you
think you should be keeping an eye on things?"

"In time, dear chap." Lapin smiled. "First, though,
Josie and I have something to talk to you about." He lit
a thin, brown cheroot and grinned at Pike. "This situation with you and Josie and the child coming. We feel it
should be . . . normalized."

"What's going on?" Pike demanded of Josie. "I've said
I will give the child my name. What scheme is Lapin
cooking up? I'll not be used by him, not threatened, not
blackmailed."

She put a cool hand to his cheek and her eyes sparkled.

"Silly Nathaniel. Henri is not threatening you. He is
offering you a gift. Me. If you want me."

"Yes, Nathaniel," Lapin said. "Josie and I have talked
it over and I realize I should not stand in the way of the
happiness of each of you. So I propose you marry each
other."

"Marry? How can we marry? You and Josie—"

"Ours was only a form of marriage, not recognized by
the church," Lapin said easily. "As long as I do not object, there is no barrier to you and Josie being wed. The
good Vicar Sikes can perform the ceremony knowing
there is no impediment, legal or religious, to it."

"Dear Nathaniel," Josie said. "You look stunned. Is it
that you do not want to marry a poor little French girl
with no background, no family, no breeding? I can understand that." She lowered her head and he saw her
eyelashes blinking.

"There is nothing I would want more," Pike said. "But
I thought it impossible."

"Good," Lapin said. "I shall release Josie to you then,
and I hope you will both be happy ever after. For me, I
will try and live with the hurt. Josie's happiness is more
important than my own. After you are wed I shall send
home to Paris for some poor but well-bred girl to come
out here and be my wife and give me many children. I

want to establish my own family here, Nathaniel, just as
you will be establishing yours. I trust I will have no difficulties in getting all the necessary permissions from
your friends in government."

"Of course not," Pike stuttered. He was overcome with
elation at this new turn. "Anything you want. I'll see to
it."

"There is one other thing," Lapin said. "When Josie
is the wife—as opposed to the mistress—of someone as
prominent as you, I do not think it would be good for her
to be involved in an establishment like this. I propose
taking over both your shares in the club and paying you
an annual dividend from the profits. Does that suit?"

"Absolutely!" He would have agreed to anything. "Josie would have had to have given up the club, anyway.
And I think it best I remove myself from the operation
for the sake of our child. I mean, while it was just me,
standing alone, no one in this community could harm
me with their gossip and lies. But with a child to think
of . . ."

"Quite right," Lapin said. "I have drawn up all the papers and will leave them with you." He bowed to them
both as he left the room. "I know you are going to be very
happy."

They made camp just before dusk in a secluded cove at
the very tip of Sandys Parish; through the day's walking
they had seen no one and they could be fairly sure they
were the first men to walk on this sheltered beach. Even
the ravages of the last great burning-off had not reached
this far, and the hills behind them were thick with lan-
tana and cedar. They ate gulls' eggs and salt pork for
their supper and huddled close to the fire as the sun went
down and the cool night air surrounded them. The only
sound was the gushing of the sea as it was sucked into
and out of the narrow, rocky opening to the cove. Jonas
pushed himself up on an elbow and peered out into the
night.

"What is the future of this place, Bermuda, Ewen?" he
finally asked. "It's blessed with a wild beauty and a

gentle climate, there are no natives to contest ownership, no predators to challenge man. It should be paradise and yet I fear for it. The people who are here have
no feeling for the place; most are looking for a fortune
before moving on to somewhere bigger and more important, like America. It seems a sin to treat this as nothing
more than a place to be plundered before leaving."

"No one thinks of the future," Ewen said. "It is not in
the nature of people to wonder what they are doing and
where they are going. For most it is struggle enough to
just get through each day. A man of vision will be mocked
or, worse, ignored." He fished an old pipe from his pocket
and carefully spilled a pinch of tobacco into its bowl. "But
you are right about our new land. Its future is worth
thinking about. When the exploiters have moved on,
Bermuda will still be here, rich with promise. I don't
know what its destiny is, but it must lie with the natural
charms of the colony. Let the Fleets and the Pikes and
their ilk get rich from commerce and connivance: young
men like you, Jonas, will find happiness here living in
harmony with the land and the sea."

"There's been little harmony for Odlums in Bermuda," Jonas laughed.

"All that will pass," Ewen said. "And the hardships
of the past can only make you stronger and better prepared for the future. Who better than you to develop a
vision for this place? Your grandfather must have known
these islands better than any man today. Those years in
which he roamed here alone . . . it was not only Jonas
Odlum's life Thomas Fleet took when he shot your
grandfather down. He also robbed us all of that accu-
mulated knowledge. I think we would not have made so
many assaults on nature had we had the benefit of your
grandfather's experience from his years of solitude."

"It would seem my father was more in step with Bermuda as it has become," Jonas said without bitterness.
"He thought nothing of abandoning my mother, cheat-
ing you out of a partnership. He would have been a worthy member of the Forty Thieves."

"I stopped hating him long ago," Ewen said. "He was,

like so many of our people, driven by ambition. It did nothing for him in the end but bring a horrible death in Haiti. And he was a desperately unhappy man for years before that. Your mother has not had an easy life, but it is a more satisfactory one than Will Acton enjoyed."

That night the young man dreamed of the first Jonas Odlum, totally alone in the splendid islands, tramping through bush and over sand, discovering new wonders every day, happy in his solitude yet always yearning for the return of the party he had deserted.

Jonas awoke shivering in the heavy dew that had crept under his blanket. He glanced across the ashes of the fire to Ewen, still sleeping soundly. Silently Jonas rolled out of his coverings and moved away from the beach up to the overhanging cliffs. At the crest the first rays of the rising sun warmed him; a flock of seabirds rose out of the next bay and flew close by him, heading out to sea and the plentiful fish awaiting them. Jonas continued to walk along the cliff top until, pushing through thick growth, he was standing in a clearing looking down on a vast, broad beach stretching at least half a mile. At first his eyes could not adjust to the bright morning light on the pink sands. The white skeletons were surely a mirage. But when he had plunged back into the bush and made his way down to the beach and stood among the great, bare bones, he knew he had not been seeing things.

"There must be hundreds of them," Ewen said after he had been led, blinking sleep from his eyes, to the hidden beach. "The graveyard of the sperm whales. I've heard old sailors talk of places like this where the whales cast themselves ashore to die. But never have I heard of numbers like this." They were picking their way between the skeletons, some towering twice Ewen's height, others small and delicately formed. "You see, Jonas, it was not just sick, old whales which came ashore. The whole mighty herd—females, children, thrashing up this beach to certain death."

"How long have they been here?" Jonas wondered. "The bones are so white and bare."

"Not so long as it would appear," Ewen said. He was

digging with his hand in the sand around the bones of
one of the biggest specimens. "See, the sand has only
covered them to a depth of a foot or so. It may be only a
year or two since they made their suicide pact. The crabs
and the birds, plus the sun and wind, would bleach their
bones very quickly." He continued to scrabble around
inside one skeleton. "Yes," he said, holding a lump of
solid, yellow-colored material out to Jonas. "I think they
may have been here only since last summer. This is ambergris, a substance the whales generate in their intes-
tines. If they had been here for too many years, it might
have eroded by now."

Jonas hefted the lump in his hand; it was heavy and
solid, and yet somehow it felt as if life still pulsed
through it. He rubbed the object on his sleeve and the
color heightened, almost glowing. He passed it under his
nose and smelled a rich musk. Ewen had moved onto the
next skeleton and was digging out another, similar
lump.

"There'll be one of these in each of the remains," he
said. "I understand this substance is of great value. They
use it in the manufacture of perfumes, as a stabilizer or
something." He came and stood beside Jonas. "And the
whalebone itself has a variety of uses. I suppose the next
people to find this graveyard will turn it to good profit.
For now, I would like to leave it as we have found it. Just
take our two souvenirs."

Jonas readily agreed. Back up on the cliff he took a last
look at the bizarre beach; so sad and noble it seemed, the
great herd swimming majestically through the seas and
homing in on this beach, the place they had chosen to die.

"Are you sure you know what you're doing?" Amanda
demanded. She was sick with apprehension about calling Prudence Odlum in on the case. But the old doctor
had been making no progress; Richard had been sinking
before her eyes.

Now she watched the gaunt, silent woman bent over
her son's bed. It was hard to realize Prudence Odlum was
about her own age; the Odlum woman's every trial

showed in the lines deep-etched in her face. Amanda,
when she examined herself in the mirror, thought she
had not changed since girlhood. Even her drinking,
about which she felt less and less guilty, had hardly rav-
aged her features. So life had been unfair to Prudence
Odlum—that was the way it went, Amanda thought. Her
only real concern was that the woman might harbor
some great grudge against her, the house of Fleet in general and poor young Richard in particular. And, she supposed, there was good reason for such a grudge. But she
had to take the risk now; Richard was very ill, sicker
than he had ever before been.

"I'd work easier if you were not hovering over me,"
Prudence said, not looking up. She was applying steaming cloths to the boy's chest. Spread out beside her on the
floor were a range of powders and potions. "There is
nothing you can do for him." She spoke rudely, not caring if she offended this woman. She had felt no sense of
triumph when they sent for her; it was her duty to go and
do what she could for the sick boy. Now that she was here,
she was professional and uninvolved. It was only when
she looked into his fluttering eyes and saw the ghost of
Will Acton that she felt nonplussed.

Amanda withdrew from the room reluctantly. She had
formed a tight bond with Richard in the long nights of
his latest sickness and she felt that if she was not close
at hand, his soul might slip away from both of them. But
Mistress Odlum's hostility overpowered her. Amanda
wandered around her great, dark house, touching familiar objects, seeking some useful task to take her mind
away from the sickroom. Finally she gravitated to her
own sitting room and the decanter, and there, in a
straight-backed chair before a window open to the night,
she sat and drank and waited.

She heard Sep's coach come up the drive very late, a
muffled curse as he stepped down, the crunch of gravel
as he lurched toward the house. Goddamn him! Carousing as if there were nothing wrong. If he disturbed the
boy . . . well, the Odlum woman would give him a great

piece of her sharp tongue. At last the brandy was taking
her down into a kind of sleep.

The maid was shaking her. Outside the window it was
half-light.

"The Odlum woman wants you, ma'am," the girl said.
She seemed close to tears. "I just saw young Master
Richard, ma'am. He looks awful poorly. I think you
should get the doctor back, the proper doctor. That
woman . . . you know what they say about her in the village. Her mother was a witch. She's probably one, too."

"Be quiet, you stupid girl," Amanda said, trying to
gather her wits. The cognac was swirling in her head,
mixing with the panic. If something had gone wrong, she
would never forgive herself. If Odlum had harmed her
son, she would strike back. Amanda hurried down the
long hall, clutching a wall for support, and burst into the
sickroom. She saw Prudence, slumped exhausted in a
chair, and ran to the bedside where Richard lay white
and unmoving. She put her lips to his and recoiled. He
was not breathing; his skin was cold and waxy.

She heard her own scream echoing in the room,
watched herself fall on the Odlum woman and tear at her
face.

"You've killed him, killed him," she shrieked. "My
son, my own precious son. You've wanted him dead since
the day he was born. Your mother cast a spell on him and
you have seen to it the curse has now been realized." She
was still slashing with her long nails, seeing rivers of
blood before her.

Prudence was almost too tired to defend herself, but
she made a last effort, grabbed Amanda's hands and
forced her back. There was no point in talking to this
madwoman. She stood up and gathered her things, ignoring Amanda who now lay sobbing across her son's
body.

"The next few hours will tell," Prudence said as she
prepared to depart. "I have dosed him with horehound
and elder and he is in a deep trance, resting. By noon he
should come out of it and we will know if the sickness has
gone from him."

Amanda did not hear her, did not notice her go. She
lay there, her ear on her boy's chest, straining to hear a
heartbeat. But there was nothing. She remained there
for another hour; Septimus, roused by the servants,
shambled into the room and tried to pull her away. But
then her grief was transmitted to him and he fell on his
knees beside her and wept for poor Richard.

It was full light, and the village was up and about
when the disheveled figure of Amanda Fleet came running into the square. At first they looked away in embarrassment; it was not right for them to observe one of
the colony's leading ladies in such a state. But her shrill
cries demanded their attention, and slowly, keeping a
watchful distance, a crowd formed around Amanda.

"The Odlum woman has killed my son," Amanda
shouted. "She made her witch's brew and forced it between his innocent lips and now he lies dead. She must
pay for this sin against Christ! Punish her. Punish her!"
The crowd was unmoving, stolid. These stupid peasants,
Amanda raged to herself. She was totally out of control
but she knew she had to make them act, to avenge her
son. "You know what to do with witches," she cried. "Go
and take her from her evil house and place her in the
ducking stool!"

There was a murmur from the crowd, the shared thrill
of good sport. It had been months since the ducking stool
had been employed, and now there was the prospect of
some real excitement in their drab lives. The old wives
muttered among themselves, recalling past examples of
Prudence Odlum's behavior. Wasn't it true she never
talked to any of them, that she wandered the shores and
the hills gathering strange materials, that her mother
had cast a spell on all the sons of Will Acton? "Drown the
witch!" someone called, and they all took up the chant.

Amanda stood, hands on hips, watching them form a
ragged parade and swarm out of the square heading for
the Odlum cottage. She could hear their excitement; it
matched the buzzing in her own head. She was seeing it
all through a haze of bright red.

Prudence heard them coming up the narrow alley,

their numbers swelling and the noise rising. It was an ugly, primitive sound, a mob crying for blood, and the baby, Rose, began to wail. Brigid scooped up the child and retreated to a dark corner of the cottage where she huddled, the whites of her eyes gleaming.

"Please, Prudence," Brigid whispered, "you must flee. Hide in the hills until the madness has left them. I fear they are going to do you an injury. Hide until Ewen and Jonas return to protect you."

"I shall not run from them," Prudence said calmly. "They need us Odlums, these poor, primitive fools. We are their shibboleths. If I flee I will be just like them and they will believe they were in the right." She stood in the center of the little room, arms folded across her chest, as the door burst open and the vanguard of the mob came flooding in.

At first no one would lay a hand on her. They tried to push themselves back from the forbidding presence, the big woman who fixed them with such a defiant stare. But the crowd at the rear had those in front to protect them and pressed on until the room was jammed with shouting people and Prudence was being jostled and punched. When she was finally forced to her knees, the mob roared and many hands reached out to clutch her, dragging her by the heels out of the cottage and into the bright sunshine. Her head banged on the hard ground as the procession started toward the harborfront; the braver urchins dashed out of the following crowd and spat on her or kicked at her. Her eyes were open and she saw all the familiar faces jeering down at her, their eyes wide and wild with excitement, their mouths drooling at the sport to come. She shifted her gaze so she was looking straight up into the flat blue sky.

Fred Pipe, that year's ducking master, waited by his equipment as the mob swirled about him. He was nervous, anxious that the ceremony be properly conducted.

"Keep back, there!" he shouted, fearful his stool would be damaged in the excitement. He looked around for someone in authority, someone to take responsibility.

But there was only the mob. "There should be a trial first," he insisted. "What is she accused of?"

"She murdered the Fleet boy," someone cried. "Killed him with her witch's poisons. There's no need of a trial. The stool will return its verdict." The crowd shouted its agreement.

Pipe shrugged. It was not for him to defy their wishes. He beckoned for the men holding Prudence to bring her forward. As he unbuckled the straps on the stool he stole a glance at the Odlum woman and shivered: her gaze was cold, defiant and there was no fear there. They were probably right: only a witch could have an eye as evil as this one.

"Do you want to say anything?" he mumbled as they forced her down into the stool. He carefully avoided meeting her eyes. "Speak up now, before you're under the water."

"You are all fools." Her voice carried over them and they fell silent. "The boy is not dead. He is resting, in a deep sleep which will allow the sickness to flow out of him." She swept the mob with her gaze and they looked away. "But none of you want to know the truth. You want your sport. To hell with all of you!"

Fred Pipe fussed around the stool, making sure she was secured, then swung it out at the end of its long pole, over the blue waters of the harbor. The pole bent under the weight until Prudence's feet were just immersed. Then Pipe moved to the wooden ratchet at the base of the machine and let off the ropes; there was a great creaking sound as the stool and its contents slowly sank beneath the surface.

Prudence concentrated on a spot between her eyes but far away; it was a warm green spot, promising peace and comfort. Perhaps it was heaven, she thought, or Home. It was silent now, below the water, and almost pleasant. Warm. But the pressure was building in her lungs and behind her closed eyes.

Around the stool they were counting aloud, shouting the numbers. When they reached fifty Fred Pipe made to wind in the ropes, but an angry cry from the mob

stopped him. When the count reached one hundred, he
looked around but all their thumbs were pointed to the
ground. The count went back to one again, reached fifty.
This time he was not opposed as he slowly raised the stool
out of the water. They cheered as her head emerged and
then the rest of her, arms still folded across her chest.
The stool was swung in to shore and many hands reached
out to fumble with the bindings. When it was released,
the body of Prudence Odlum slumped forward and lay on
the dry, dusty ground.

They cheered at first, then fell silent. Those at the rear
of the crowd quietly withdrew, suddenly anxious to be
about their daily business. Soon there was only a handful of people left to regard the crumpled shape on the
ground.

"Go fetch the undertaker," Pipe told one of the re-
mainder. "She can be buried in the village plot now. She
has passed the test."

In the early afternoon Richard Fleet came out of his
coma; soon the color flooded back into his cheeks and his
forehead was cool and dry. He was hungry and the staff
delighted in placing the most tempting foods before him.
That evening Amanda knelt and said a prayer of thanks
for the return of her son.

Ewen noticed it at once, the way the townspeople could
not meet their gaze as they wearily trudged up from the
shore and through the streets of St. George's. Faces normally civil were turned from them; the people seemed to
shrink away. Jonas did not take note of their reception:
he was, by nature, a solitary young man and he expected
others to be the same. It was not until he reached his
mother's cottage that he realized something might be
wrong. The one small door and two little windows were
all firmly closed in the day's heat; on the door itself
someone had tacked a posy of wildflowers. Jonas dropped
his bedroll in the dust and fumbled with the latch of the
door. Inside the cottage the air was hot and still and a
chair lay on its side in his path.

Outside, Ewen spotted Brigid running toward him

down the rise from their own cottage. He saw the tears flowing from grief-stricken eyes, noted her deathly pallor, her long red hair flying free and unbrushed. She flung herself into his arms and clung to him, sobs racking her body.

"It's Prudence," she gasped out. "Prudence. They said she was a witch and put her in the ducking stool. They came and dragged her from her house, then drowned her. That good woman . . . Oh, Ewen, I hate these people. They are all savages. Poor Prudence. She was so good to them, curing their ills, and this was the way they repaid her."

"Where is she now?" Ewen asked, holding Brigid to him. He looked over her shoulder and saw Jonas had reemerged in the street, concern in his eyes. "Is she recovering from her ordeal?"

"You don't understand," Brigid said. "They let her drown in that dreadful contraption. We buried her yesterday. We could not wait. No one knew when you and Jonas would return."

Jonas heard the words and they were like sharp blows falling on him. His mother could not be dead, she who had always seemed so indestructible. Brigid had to be mad, or playing some cruel jest. But as he saw her desperate face, Jonas knew the truth. He fell down on his knees then and cried out—a long, anguished note that rose up from the dust and through the air into the hot, blue sky. The gawking townspeople withdrew farther into the shadows; their collective guilt hung in the air, almost tangible.

"You scum! You cowardly scum!" Ewen was shouting at them, his voice cracking with grief and rage. "Prudence Odlum was the finest woman in this godforsaken village and you have killed her to satisfy your stupid beliefs. Oh, you will pay for this, you will pay." He gently put Brigid aside and moved to where Jonas still knelt in the street. He put his hand on the young man's shoulder. "Come, Jonas," he said softly. "Come away from the stares of these peasants. We will grieve together, in private." He squeezed the strong shoulder beneath his hand

and drew Jonas up beside him. Brigid stood at his other side, and they shepherded Jonas into the chillingly empty little house.

Jonas lay in his bed for two days. He still could not accept she was gone; and the manner of her going, the sheer barbaric horror of it, brought him screaming awake from his fitful sleep. Brigid brought him gruel and hot tea and sponged his fevered brow. Ewen stayed close by the bed, reading the Bible and waiting patiently for Jonas to recover from the initial shock. No one else in the village came near them.

On the third day Jonas roused himself. He felt a great emptiness inside him, but he knew he had to face the world again; Prudence, and old Sarah in her time, had raised him to recognize the harsh facts of life and death in a rugged colony like Bermuda. You had to go on living until death called. Death, he thought, would be a blessed relief for him right now, but he was strong and young and the relief would be withheld.

"What am I to do, Ewen?" he asked his friend. "Is there any message for me in your Bible? Does the Good Book advise me to turn the other cheek? Because that is no comfort for me. I can never forgive them for what they did to my mother."

"No, Jonas, I have no forgiveness in me, either. But you must not be consumed with hatred at this time. It is their savage ignorance that has produced this tragic event. At least understand the demons that drive them, because with understanding will come acceptance of what has happened, if not forgiveness."

"I don't want to understand them! What is there to understand about someone like the Fleet woman, highborn and educated. It was she who incited the mob to murder my mother."

"Amanda Fleet is just another woman, like all the men and women here, pursued by her private devils," Ewen said. "Only knowledge will save them, and there is precious little demand for knowledge here." He filled his pipe carefully and regarded Jonas. "You have a fine brain and have already learned much from books. I think the only place you will find solace from this tragedy is in the halls of learning. I have been thinking about your situation while you lay grieving and I believe it would be best for you, Jonas, if you went away from here for a while. I have in mind your going to London, and perhaps Paris, to study. You have learned all you can from books. Now it is time to sit at the feet of great teachers. You have a natural bent for the sciences, just as your grandmother and mother did. Go, Jonas, and learn surgery and the healing arts, astronomy and navigation, chemistry and botany. Then come back here and with your knowledge help lift the terrible cloud of ignorance which hangs over these islands."

"It would be good to get away from here," Jonas admitted. "It is the only home I know, but it repels me now. But London, Paris . . . out of the question, Ewen. I cannot afford such grand travel plans, and anyway, they would take one look at me and know me for a bumpkin."

"There is your mother's estate, this cottage and other funds she was putting aside for you. It was, in fact, her dream for you to study in Europe and become a learned man. She discussed it with me often. And if the funds are not quite sufficient, I have money put by myself. That is what Prudence wanted for you, Jonas, and you must do it for her so her death will not have been futile."

"I will try to consider it, Ewen. But it is hard to make plans when grief is all I can think about. I would prefer to just lie here in the dark like a wounded animal."

"Rest awhile longer, then, but think about what I have said. There is nothing for you here and everything waiting for you in the great colleges of Europe."

In the days that followed Jonas came to see sense in the plan his mother and Ewen had mapped out for him. He was not afraid of the challenge of scholarship—he welcomed it, knowing study would help erase the dreadful loss he had suffered. He left the arrangements to Ewen, right down to the purchase of the clothes he would need for the voyage. Jonas was willing to go along with the plan but, as yet, he could arouse no enthusiasm for it.

He had one unexpected caller on the evening before his ship sailed. His half-brother, Richard Fleet, came furtively to the cottage door and waited there, head bowed, expecting to be rebuffed. The young Fleet at fifteen and only just recovered from his latest long illness was not an impressive sight. He was deathly pale, his hair lank and white, his dull blue eyes in a permanent squint against the bright sunlight of his homeland. Jonas would have sent him away; the very name Fleet had never meant anything but trouble for an Odlum. But for all the young man would inherit, for all the power and fame that went with his name, he was a pitiful creature standing trembling there in the doorway.

"There is no reason, no reason in the world, for you to speak with me, Jonas," Richard Fleet began. "I was the unwitting cause of your mother's death, while it was she who restored me to life and comparative health. There is no justice in it and I would understand if you struck me down, or at least turned your back on me. All I want to say is I shall forever bear the burden of what happened. My mother knows no guilt—she is deranged when it comes to the matter of the Odlums and tries to poison poor little Hilda and me against you all." He stopped, realizing his error. "It is no longer 'you all' is it? Just you now, Jonas. If it is any consolation, the Fleet line is scarcely more abundant. My own prospects of ever attaining healthy manhood would appear to be bleak."

"I have no hatred for you, Richard," Jonas said. "There is enough of that evil in this community without my adding to it. I have grief, but that is not the same thing. Your mother must live with what she has done, but you need not carry her burden. When I return here, many years from now, I would want to have forgotten our bloody past. I will have no use for old feuds. I want now, and will always want, to be left in peace. Your destiny is to take your family's fortune and make it ever larger; mine is to try and play a worthwhile part in the future of our little colony."

"Can I help you with money?" Fleet asked hesitantly. He pulled a leather purse from his jacket. "I have a hundred guineas here." He shrugged. "In our family, such a sum is nothing. But I would hope it might be of some help to you in the long voyages that lie ahead of you."

"Keep your money, Richard," Jonas said. "I have been well provided for. And I think I have already inherited more riches than you will ever know. I am sorry for you."

"I am sorry, too. I can see already what my life is to be. It does not inspire any joy in me."

London,
May 1661

Dear Ewen and Rose,
    I was deeply saddened to hear of Brigid's death. She was a fine wife and mother, and I know she has gone to the peace and happiness she deserved. My thoughts are with you both. That she should be taken by the plague when you were finally enjoying prosperity after the strenuous years in that harsh but beautiful place! Rose, you must be a big girl now and look after your father just as he looked after me.
    Death is all around me. The great city is only just recovering from another of its regular fires; when it rains, as it has incessantly this spring, a stench arises from the streets as if the houses are still smoldering. It is a wonder the city was not destroyed, built as it is of crude wooden shelters placed against each other for support. Astonishing though it is, the fools are building the city again in the same manner—hovels with fragile common walls of the lightest timber. It is an invitation for another fire. And the sanitary conditions are appalling. Bermuda is a model of modernity in comparison. These conditions encourage every disease to breed here. The rats were the real survivors of the great fire, and are bigger and more aggressive than ever. Daily I am called on to treat little babies with the most appalling wounds: ears and noses chewed off. There is so little we of the medical profession can do for the people. For all my training in Paris I still have to resort to the saw to

*remove diseased limbs, the needle and thread to patch
up scarred faces. It is little wonder the entire poor population of London find solace in the gin bottle.*

*I feel guilty to be prospering in the midst of this suf-
fering. But the apothecary shop is a great success. You
would not believe the demand for the scents and perfumes I concoct. Londoners have at last realized they
smell most offensive and, like the French, have taken to
splashing themselves with anything that promises to
inhibit odors. I do have some sense of purpose when
ministering to the sick, woeful as my patients usually
are.*

*Speaking of death, a funeral, a grand one, passed by
my shop the other week. I inquired as to who inspired
such tribute—I counted forty carriages before tiring of
it—and was told the sainted corpse was that of old Lord
Marley. And there, in one of the foremost carriages, fat
and red and looking ready for the grave himself, was
Septimus Fleet. He would, of course, be one of the chief
mourners. He and his Bermuda cohorts have, it is said,
made hundreds of thousands of pounds from the slaving they engaged in with Marley.*

*Seeing Fleet, it was as if nothing had changed in
Bermuda, that I could return there tomorrow and find
the same forces in control. But even if that is so, I sorely
miss my home. Ten years away and it is as if we roamed
the hills and shores yesterday, Ewen. I still have my
chunk of ambergris taken from the whales' beach in
Sandys Parish; it rests now as a paperweight on my
desk, and when I hold it to my nose the heady musk it
releases takes me back to that time.*

*In any event, I think the time for me to return to our
island is not far off. I have had enough of cold, gray
skies and sullen water. And I so want to sit with you,
Ewen, while there is still time, and take more wisdom
from your generous store.*

*I think I will be able to survive there with a shop sim-
ilar to the one I have established in London. My needs
are simple—no wife or children to support—and I have*

*a most pleasant vision of the quiet and good life with
both of you.*

*I have not booked a passage yet, but ships are de-
parting here almost weekly, so great has the trade become between here and the Americas. Bermuda must
be prosperous indeed with so many vessels stopping
there for provisions. I shall write one more time to advise you of my sailing.*

    Again my love and sympathy to you both,
               Sincerely,
               Jonas Odlum.

Chapter Nine
(1939–)

Another war. It couldn't be, Primrose thought, sitting silent before the radio. Of course she had listened to all the lead-up to it, but she had never believed it would reach the stage of no-turning-back madness. She had been through The Great War, the war to end all wars. Surely that same generation was not to embark on another bout of death and destruction.

She looked up as Jeff entered the room; she opened her arms to him. He allowed her to hug him briefly, then slipped from her grasp and flung himself into the window seat.

"I suppose this means we'll have to delay my going away to school," he said, gesturing to the radio. "Blast it, Mother, sometimes I think the whole world is conspiring against me!"

She concealed her smile. The thought had immediately crossed her mind, too. With England at war, she could hardly be expected to commit her only child to the dangers of an Atlantic crossing when Germany would clearly—for a while at least—rule the seaways. So. Eton could wait until it was all over and Primrose would have the pleasure of his thirteen-year-old company a while longer. She had known she would have to let him go off to England to school. It was no life for Jeff, growing up with a busy, lonely mother. But now the break would be postponed. He could stay at the local school, and when

the war was over, they would both be that much older,
better prepared for the parting. Of course the war would
be over before he was of age; only the defeatists were
suggesting a conflict of more than a year or two. She
could not countenance the thought of his going off to a
war: she knew what war had done to her brothers, leaving one maimed and both changed.

"The war will be over before I can get into it," Jeff
grumbled from across the room. "Daddy would have
wanted me to do my bit. He was a hero even before his
own country joined in the last one. I want to be like him.
A brave man."

She got up and crossed the room to him and held him
again.

"You are like him, just like him, my darling. But neither of you had any need of a war to make you great.
Richard loved us and loved Bermuda. He would never
have wanted you to risk our happiness here to go off and
fight." She switched on the light; it got dark so early
these days. She found the envelope that had arrived that
day. The mail from the U.S. was so fast now, thanks to
the Fleets' triweekly flying boat service. Sometimes she
had to hold back tears when she received an airmail-
franked letter, but she always told herself she was being
stupidly sentimental. "Aunt Jane has written to us," she
told the boy. "She thinks it is finally time she returned
to Bermuda with Carol for a holiday. She wants some
sunshine before that dreadful winter comes in New
York; the little girl isn't very strong."

Jeff shrugged. He wasn't interested in his mother's
friend and her baby daughter. They were just part of the
world outside Bermuda, a world he knew only from mag-
azines and radio and the antics of tourists. A world that
was going to be denied him because of this blasted war.

"Heavens," Primrose said, reading the long letter
again, "Carol's just had her fifth birthday. It only seems
a couple of months since she was born in this very
house." How well she remembered. "She was almost
going to be a sister to you, Jeff. Jane was going to leave
her here with us. But then when she saw what a beau-

tiful, tiny blond thing she was . . ." She saw Jeff scowl
and again hid her smile. She couldn't expect the lad to
be interested in the doings of a lot of women and girls.

"Anyway," she continued, "at least America won't be
getting involved in this dreadful war, so it will be safe
for them to travel. And Jane can take two whole months
away from her job. That's how successful she is. Imagine! The first lady vice-president of a bank, and a bank
a blessed sight bigger than her own family's." She ruffled the boy's long, dark hair. He needed a cut. He was
getting to look like her. "So when they come, Jeff, you
will be the man of the house and see they're well looked
after." She was rewarded with a grin; he was really a
sweet boy, and she understood his disappointment at
having to delay his entry to Eton.

"Okay, Mother," he said, offering her his arm. "Come
on. I'll take you down to dinner."

"They'll intern my father, of course," Lady Anne said
with some satisfaction. "He's been telling them for years
to join with the Germans; and now it's too late, so they'll
try and silence him."

"Lord Colin in prison?" Robert asked. "I say, that's a
bit rough. The old boy has only been speaking the truth.
If he goes inside, a lot of our friends will go, too. Why,
even the Yank Ambassador is on our side. I just don't understand what's going on anymore, Anne. The world's
gone mad. Adolf would have put things right if only
they'd listened. Now we're going to have to punish them
all with a war, when all we wanted was to punish the
real enemy."

"At least we shall be all right out here," she said. She
looked at her husband over her brandy glass. He was
really quite dotty these days. The pressure of international events, she supposed. "And I shouldn't think Ambassador Kennedy would be in any bother, either.
Roosevelt's the only leading American who's stupid
enough to want to wage war on Hitler—and he'll be dis-
credited soon enough." She laughed. "Daddy won't mind
being a martyr to the cause; he'll organize the other pris-

oners. And it will be over with quickly, too soon for any
of us to play an active role. I just feel sorry Colin's not
going to have the chance to march for the Fatherland. I
dressed him in his uniform today and, Robert, you would
have sworn he was a German. That's one thing I'll never
regret about getting involved with you Fleets—perfect
Aryans, all of you."

"I wonder if it would be appropriate for us to throw a
party to celebrate?" Robert asked. "I mean, this wonderful house has hardly been used since we opened it, and
I'd dearly love to see the gardens and terraces filled with
true believers, all raising a glass to the Fuehrer."

"I don't think that would be wise, dear, not with Bermuda being a British colony." Yes, he was quite dotty.
But she almost loved him for it. At least he had more real
faith in the cause than most of the bright young things
they had attracted to their London rallies. "You just
keep on with the Blackshirt meetings, but a little more
discreetly. Having my father behind bars is quite
enough. I don't need my husband there, too."

"Well, there's nothing to stop you and me opening a
bottle of Krug and toasting the glorious future," he said.
He pressed a button which buzzed in a far corner of the
vast, spreading, pink mansion. All electric, the place
was, and grander than anyone had ever conceived in
these islands. He only had to sit in his boat on the water
and look up to its bulk—spilling down the hillside on
three levels—to feel a rush of proud ownership: he'd finally given Bermuda a real and fitting monument to its
founding family.

The butler appeared with the champagne, bowed and
poured their drinks. While he was in the room, they were
silent. Robert had lately begun to suspect the servants
were spying on them. The butler was white—only the
Governor could match them in this—but the rest of the
household were blacks, and Robert wouldn't trust any of
them.

Henry Smutters blotted the latest entry in the log-
book, sat back and lit his pipe. There would be a few more

voyages back and forth to the States, he guessed, before
his ships were again conscripted into carrying troops. He
thought he might stay ashore through this one. It was
one thing ferrying tourists back and forth in safe waters,
and quite another dodging U-boats when you were up to
the gunwales with scared soldiers. But if he stayed
ashore in Bermuda for the duration of the war, there
would be no escaping Veronica Fleet. He sighed; if she
weren't a Fleet she would have been quite a catch. But in
their rough physical encounters, particularly since her
poor weed of a husband had passed on, Veronica had become increasingly demanding, the lady of the manor dis-
pensing favors to the gamekeeper. Smutters didn't mind;
it was about what he expected of the Forty Thieves. But
too much of it—which is what it would be if he stayed
ashore—would result in his speaking out and jeopardize-
ing his generally satisfying position. He poured himself a
stiff glass of rum and peered out through the porthole: a
quiet, calm night. There wouldn't be many more like this,
not with Europe at war again. Bloody Bermuda didn't realize it was part of the modern world. Still, it would be nice
to be home tomorrow.

Muriel Odlum was sorry they had guests coming to the
Beekman Place house tonight: two months after the real
war had begun, and her fellow Americans were beginning to annoy her with their smugness about the world
situation. They couldn't seem to realize that where Europe went they were surely going to follow. She heard
Cable come clattering into the entry hall and hurried
down to greet him: poor man, he'd been at the hospital
since dawn and he looked so tired. She watched him
stamping the early snow from his boots, undraping the
layers of protective clothing and handing the pieces on
to the uncomplaining Irish maid.

"Hello, darling," she said, reaching up to kiss his
flushed cheek. "It must have been awful for you today. I
heard on the radio your hospital got the victims from the
subway smash."

"There was no time to disperse them around the other

hospitals," he said. "It was like a battlefield. Cutting and sawing and patching—not surgery at all." He scowled. "Still, good practice for what's coming. We shall have to learn to deal with barbarism."

"Come up to my sitting room and I'll fix you a good strong Scotch," Muriel said. She chattered on as he followed her up the curving stairs. "I've been listening to nothing but war news all day—apart from your disaster. I'm so upset. Will Tom get involved? I'm sorry, but that's the first thing I thought about when I heard of the huge mobilization."

"He's only seventeen. There's time for the world to come to its senses before he has to go," Cable said. "And he doesn't have to enlist for England, anyway, because of his dual citizenship. But if it goes on and if America gets involved—"

"Surely we won't!" Muriel said. "We will support England, and with that support she will defeat Germany. But for America to join in . . . surely not."

"Ask cousin Spencer tonight," Cable said. "He's the Odlum who knows what you Americans will or will not do. I'm sure Spencer will tell us what the State Department plans and what the President thinks."

"Don't be such a tease about your cousin," she said. "He really is a big wheel at State. His name's now sufficient to make my father forget how opposed he was to my marrying a struggling colonial doctor like you."

He laughed and hugged her. "You Bostonians! No one's good enough for you. The American branch of my family beat yours here by fifty years." He drained his Scotch and poured another. "I think we'll have forgotten that kind of nonsense by the time this affair is over. And maybe some of our racism will vanish, too. It came home to me today, Muriel, just how blinders we are about the color of other people's skin. When you see injured and dying people scattered around the bloody floors of an emergency room you don't notice whether they're black or white.

"Actually," he told her, excited, "the hero of today's wreck was someone I know from Bermuda—Billy

Youngblood. He was badly hurt, but he crawled through
the train getting people out. He should get a medal.

"His wife and children came to the hospital—the boy
Matthew is one hell of a young man. Tall, good-looking,
intelligent. He told me he's starting law school next year.
Just the kind of young man Bermuda needs, but the family was driven out by prejudice and I doubt they'll ever
return."

"You still miss Bermuda, don't you? Yet you never go
back there."

"I could return now," he said absently. "The reasons
I had to leave have been removed." He glanced across at
her and shut up.

"The husband of the *femme fatale* is dead, you mean?"
Muriel said. She laughed at his confusion. "Poor Cable,
hiding your shame all these years. I got a nasty anonymous letter ages ago telling me about it. You were quite
a wicked young man, weren't you?" She laughed at his
look of amazement. "It's all right, darling. In the years
since, you've more than made up for the indiscretions of
your youth."

"It was quite sordid," Cable said, glad his wife knew
the truth. "It caused my family the most awful grief. Yes,
I'd love to go back to Bermuda, but I shall stay on here,
where I can do some good."

Over dinner, there was more talk of Bermuda. His
American cousin, Spencer Odlum, was full of high-level
gossip from the White House and the State Department,
gossip that included Bermuda.

"The President isn't waiting until popular opinion
swings behind him and we officially enter the war,"
Spencer told them. "He's already working closely with
the British, helping them any way he can. Bermuda's
important, Cable. She's vital to the defense of the western Atlantic. So the British have offered us air and naval
bases there on ninety-nine years' lease. The President is
very excited about the whole scheme and he's asked me
to go down there and select the site for the bases. 'If we
must pollute paradise for the sake of peace,' he told me,
'I would rather it was a Bermudian who made the hard

decision.' " Spencer chuckled. "And it will be a hard decision. You can bet the Forty Thieves will be in favor of the bases—so long as they're adjoining someone else's ancestral seat."

"I'm glad it's you, not me," Cable agreed. He clapped a hand to his head. "And I suppose this means the damned automobile will finally be admitted to Bermuda. Uncle Sam won't travel the place on horseback. My God, Spencer, you're going to be a thoroughly unpopular man in Bermuda. The poor old name of Odlum will be dragged through the gutter again."

"We all have to make sacrifices," Spencer said.

"I am sick of our life," Sam said. "I despise both of us."

"Don't make one of your speeches," Ginny said. "I'm not in the mood for it." She looked at him anxiously. "And you should be dressed. You're going to the club for dinner, aren't you? You promised."

"I'll be out of the house before your strange friends arrive," he snapped. "It's bad enough my wife is what the Americans call a fag hag. I certainly don't want to spend an evening with your latest visiting homosexuals."

"They're a damn sight more interesting than you are," she said. "And I don't care what the locals call me. Silly little provincial people don't understand culture. Now do hurry along, Sam."

He sat in the club, moodily drinking, shunning company. Not that there was anyone he really wanted to talk to these days. All the young chaps had already gone off to the war; the remaining members were mostly old bores. The obvious thing to do, he thought, was to join up, fight for His Majesty again. He had made quiet inquiries and been told he was too old for active service. They could find him a desk job if he insisted, but Sam didn't want that; too much like the last show. No, he wanted action of the kind that would purge him of his wasted, careless life. If only there had been a child. If only he hadn't married a tramp like Ginny. Or since he had, if only they had tried a bit harder. He wondered what it would have been like if he'd had the guts to stand up to his sister and stick with Jane Bellowes; surely it would have been better than the hell he had descended into.

"Hello, Sam, can I get you a drink?"

He looked up in annoyance. Insolent young pup, Edward Lapin. Just because he was wearing his Royal Air Force officer's uniform—the commission obtained for him entirely by his parents pulling strings in London—the little bugger thought he could address Sam as an equal. Those flapping ears and the big nose and the weak chin: it was probably true what they whispered about his parentage. Well, bloody Dimity Lapin had come down a peg or two when the King abdicated for an American divorcée. Dimity probably believed she should have been the one to plunge the Royal family into a constitutional crisis.

"No," Sam said. "I'm about to leave."

"Just one," the young man insisted. "It's my second-to-last night. Then I'm off for training in England. I want to be a fighter pilot," he confided, sitting down beside Sam and signaling a steward. "What I'd really like is to be posted back here when the new air base is completed. But I guess it'll be just for the damned Yanks." The drink Sam hadn't ordered arrived, and he accepted it with a sigh of resignation. He couldn't go home anyway, not with the house full of Ginny's bloody queers. "Where do you think they'll put the base?" Lapin asked. "Everyone's tipping Riddell's Bay."

"There's not enough room there for an airstrip," Sam said. "I've looked at the problem myself, trying to find a base for our airline. We don't want to depend on flying boats forever. No, Riddell's Bay would cut the colony in two because they'd have to build such a long strip. I figure it will have to go somewhere out near St. George's, where they can reclaim a lot of land from the water."

"Well, I'm jolly pleased our house is out at Southampton then." Lapin grinned. "Much as I love flying, I wouldn't want to live with a whole lot of thundering great planes skimming our rooftop."

He listened to the young man's chatter, trying to remember when he had been that age: during the war and just after. There had still been hope then and a sense of adventure. When had things begun to fall to pieces? The shameful night he'd abandoned Jeff Odlum on the beach at Shelter Island, he supposed. It had been downhill from then. He nodded for another drink; feeling the way he did, he might as well be drunk.

"I wonder what you'll be like when you come home from the war," he said. He was looking past the young man, not thinking particularly of him, but of all of them. Children of the Forty Thieves, rich and pampered, secure in their positions ... For most it had turned to ashes. "Better than we were, I trust," he said. He stood up, staggering slightly. "Good luck, anyway," he said and walked out into the soft night.

The horse cab took him home; when it turned into his driveway, he felt blind rage to see that Ginny's guests were still there, their carriages parked on his gravel, the horses chomping on his fine lawn. He lumbered up the steps and into the drawing room where she was holding court. There were five of them surrounding Ginny. The local drama teacher, who everyone knew was a lesbian; the artist Hansen; his young male lover; and two writers visiting from London. Sam stood swaying in the doorway, surveying them. There was marijuana in the air, a white powder on the glass coffee table, and many empty bottles of what had been Sam's finest burgundy.

"A fine lot you've gathered tonight," he shouted, "a dyke and four queens. There's no fucking in it for you, Ginny, not unless you've gone queer yourself."

"Good Lord!" exclaimed one of the English visitors, a florid young man in silk jacket and cravat. "Don't tell me this is the master of the house. Poor Virginia, how hard it must be for you."

Sam lurched across the room and tried to clutch the man by his cravat; his boot caught in the Persian rug and he went crashing to the floor, taking with him a sideboard laden with fine porcelain. He lay stunned in the debris.

"Beautiful!" his tormentor shouted. "Encore! Encore!"

Sam crawled across the floor and grabbed the man by his ankles, tipping him off–balance. He had him by the throat when two of the others fell on him. They were, he thought as they restrained him, surprisingly strong for queens. He felt himself pulled to his feet, held firmly.

"Sam, you are disgusting," said his wife. "Apologize to my friends and then get to your room."

Sam turned his head toward the man holding his left arm and spat in his face. His arm was released and he swung around and punched the man on his right. All four men set on him then, pummeling him to the floor. As he went down he caught a glimpse of Ginny's face; she was loving the scene.

"What shall we do with him, Virginia?" an Englishman asked. "Too dangerous to release him. He might do you a mischief."

Ginny licked her lips. She would show Sam what a drunken oaf he was.

"He's behaving like a jealous schoolboy," she said. "We should treat him like one. A sound caning, I think."

He struggled mightily, but their hands were all over him, pinning him across a chair. He felt his pants pulled down and heard their cheers. He clenched his eyes shut to try and close out the spectacle of himself, in his own house, being treated like this. The cane, when they laid it across his bare buttocks, only stung. What cut him to the quick were their catcalls and jeers. Finally they released him, the two Englishmen standing close.

"I think you should take a walk and cool off," said the one in the cravat. "Otherwise we'll have to give you another thrashing."

"I'll kill you for this, you bitch," Sam said as he blindly tugged up his trousers and staggered to the door.

"No, you won't, Sam," his wife replied. "You've never had the courage to do your own dirty work."

Then he was running through the night air to escape the laughter behind him. Tears of frustration ran down his cheeks. It had come to this, a Fleet set upon and chas-

tised by a bunch of deviates. Tomorrow he would be the
laughingstock of the colony.

He doubled back along the stone wall of his property
toward the stables. There was a bottle of brandy secreted
there and he desperately needed a drink. The horses
snorted and stamped as he blundered around in the dark,
then fell silent as he found his brandy and flung himself
down in the straw. He could, he thought, sneak back to
the house and set fire to the place and all the bastards in
it. But that would only cause him more trouble. He was
now completely befuddled by the long night's drinking
and the terrible humiliation he had suffered. He had to
get out of the bloody place, that was it. And get out
quickly. The flying boat, lying down in the bay, was
fueled for tomorrow's run. He could handle it alone. That
was it, get away to New York in the dead of night and
not be tormented by their laughter.

The young soldier guarding the dock at Riddell's Bay
was nervous. He knew he was lucky to have been gar-
risoned in Bermuda instead of somewhere near the real
war, and he wanted everything to be perfect. He couldn't
believe any German would actually try to steal the flying
boat, but that was what they'd told him to watch for. He
peered out over the dark water at the big shape resting
at its mooring. He shook his head, then looked again.
Someone was emerging from the water and climbing up
onto the flying boat's pontoon.

"Stop!" he shouted. "Who are you?" Then he remembered what he'd been taught: "Halt! Who goes there?"

The figure on the pontoon took no notice. He reached
up for the cockpit door.

"Stop that or I'll shoot," the guard cried, his voice
echoing out over the bay. The figure had the door open
and was about to pull himself inside. The young soldier
raised his .303 and sighted through the dark; the figure
on the pontoon was long and pale and stood out against
the hull. White hair, white skin—a German for sure. He
squeezed the trigger once.

Sam felt the bullet like a hammer blow between his

shoulder blades. No pain at first, just a sense of release as his hands relaxed their grip on the doorjamb. He slipped easily into the warm water, sinking down through it, glad to feel the last of his carelessly spent life flowing out of him.

"I stopped hating him right after Carol was born," Jane Bellowes said. "She made up for the heartache he caused me. And now that he's dead, I feel nothing at all." She looked across the lawn to where the little blond girl was laughing in a swing as Jeff pushed her higher and higher. "I haven't told Carol who her father was; I suppose she thinks it's my ex-husband. Now, if she asks, I'll be able to truthfully say he's dead." She turned to Primrose. "Am I being callous?"

"No," her friend said. "Sam Fleet was the callous one. He went through life not caring whom he harmed. I don't think he even cared much about himself, judging from the way he died. Blind drunk, trying to steal his own flying boat. It wasn't fair, court-martialing the poor guard. He was only doing his duty and it got him five years in prison. But there's always a price when anyone crosses a Fleet."

"I wonder if the Fleet blood will show up in Carol," Jane said. "She certainly looks like them. From all I've heard, I wouldn't want her to act like one."

"The Fleet women have generally been the strong side of the family," Primrose said. "Most of the excesses were committed by the men, and most of the tragedy struck the male line. I don't think you need worry. She's a darling child."

"It's good of Jeff to be so kind to her," Jane said. "Most boys his age wouldn't be so patient. Already she's trying to twist him around her little finger. I'm going to have to keep an eye on her when she's a little older."

"It's hard, isn't it," Primrose sighed, "raising them without a father. You try to make up for the loss and then you worry about spoiling them. What about you, Jane? You're still so young and pretty. Is there a man in your life?"

"No. Work and Carol take up all my life and that's the way I want it. You're the same, Primrose."

"You can't compare our work. You're really achieving something on your own; I merely took over the family company. And more and more it runs along without me. It's so big now, with so many staff all over the place. I don't even know all our managers anymore. When Jeff finally does go away to school I'm going to have to find something useful to do. I've been thinking about getting myself into the House of Assembly. There's been an Odlum there for quite a few generations and it's one way to serve Bermuda. I know the Assembly hasn't got much power, but this place can't remain a British colony forever. When this war is over, we are going to have to start moving toward being a true democracy, and the Assembly is where we'll have to begin. We must get the blacks involved as a matter of urgency."

"You'll make quite a politician, Primrose. I wouldn't like to be opposed to you. You may look gentle, but beneath it you're tough as nails."

Primrose laughed. "You've got to be tough when you spend most of your time up against the Forty Thieves. Bermuda may be paradise, but the people who live here are as shrewd as any New Yorker. We're all descended from pirates, one way or the other." She stood up and called to the children to come inside for lunch. "I love Bermuda, but you always have to remember, the most extreme passions are simmering just beneath the surface."

"I'm glad you picked the site," the President chuckled. "As it is they'll say I put the airfield there just because I abhor Fleet's Fascist stand. Which I do."

"It is simply the only place suitable, Mr. President," Spencer Odlum said. "I was scrupulously fair about it. God knows there's been enough trouble between our families down through the ages. I'd do anything to avoid exacerbating the situation. But St. George's is where the airfield has to go."

"And the flight path will be right over their pink pal-

ace? I couldn't be happier, Mr. Odlum." He chuckled
again. "You have served me—and your ancestral home—
very well."

"Well, after the war the airstrip will certainly be a
great benefit to Bermuda's tourist trade," Spencer said.
And then he laughed. "My God, I just realized! It will also
mean the Fleets' own airline will be obsolete. Their lumbering old flying boats will be out of business once there's
an airstrip on the island."

The headaches were blinding. They got worse when
the bulldozers began ripping up the coral in front of his
house, and increased as construction moved feverishly
ahead. And now the planes had arrived—huge, roaring
beasts almost brushing his soaring rooftops, never stopping day or night, leaking stinking petrol fumes down
on him. Robert Fleet felt his bed shake in the dawn as
yet another monster passed overheard. The boy, Colin,
stuck his fair head around the bedroom door, terror in
his pale blue eyes. He made a sudden dash across the
room and flung himself under his father's bed.

In her own bedroom Lady Anne cursed the din. It was
time for her to get out of Bermuda. Roosevelt had done
this to her on purpose. He had won, for the moment, by
making her home uninhabitable. But she would have the
last laugh. When the inevitable happened and the
American people rejected him and fell in behind Hitler,
she would be at the White House gates to jeer Roosevelt
on his way.

For now she needed a tranquil place. Perhaps Rio was
far enough from the front. Certainly the Brazilians were
more sympathetic to her political views. She climbed out
of bed and angrily jerked open the draperies to gaze down
on her beautiful garden, now befouled by the noisy ma-
chines of her enemy. She saw her husband standing on
the dewy lawn in a dressing gown, his Purdy shotgun
cradled in his arm. He must have lost his mind, she
thought. There was nothing left to shoot at now—the airplanes had frightened all the wildfowl away. And then
she saw him raise the gun and blast both barrels at a

DC-3 as it passed slowly overhead toward the white runway. He broke the gun open, reloaded from the box of shells at his feet and waited for his next target. She sighed.

"Take that, you bastard!" Robert yelled as he blasted another load of shot into the underbelly of the big transport. The plane was so close he could see the whites of the pilot's eyes gazing down at him in amazement.

He was still firing when they came to take him away.

"No," Veronica said, "you will not take the child with you. I don't give a damn where you go—the farther from Bermuda the better—but Colin will stay with me. He is the last Fleet now. You have driven his father into the lunatic asylum with your crazed ideas and you will not corrupt the boy."

Anne studied her sister-in-law impassively. She didn't much care for the child, anyway.

"As you wish," she said. "But if I leave him with you, will you in return arrange a passage to Rio for me? I have many enemies in the governments of Britain and America, and they would do anything to hinder me. I want one of your ships to take me away from this damned place."

Veronica nodded. "I'll arrange it. It will take a few weeks. You'll need time to close up the house, anyway."

Anne laughed bitterly. "No," she said, "the house is off my hands. Yesterday the Americans requisitioned it. It's going to house their troops. I hope they never get a single night's sleep in the cursed place."

In the months and years that followed, Veronica came to dote on the pale and sickly Colin. His frequent temper tantrums did not worry her; he was, after all, a Fleet. In him she found the answer to her suppressed maternal instincts and her fierce desire to preserve the Fleet name in Bermuda. When his father died in the asylum, believing Hitler's armies were on the verge of victory, she was glad; an embarrassment to her and a threat to her possession of Colin were thus removed. There was one brief, formal note from Lady Anne, which said she had become prominent in Rio society, had married again, and trusted the boy was in good hands.

On a bright August day in 1945, Veronica sat in her office on Front Street talking with her senior captain, preparing to pick up the company from where it had been left at the outbreak of war.

"The government promises all the ships they requisitioned from us will be returned within a month of the peace being signed, Mr. Smutters," she said. "Then, perhaps, six months to refit them. We should be able to service next year's tourist season."

"You think the tourists will return that quickly, ma'am?"

"Of course. The war has created a lot of new wealth in America. People will want to spend their money. I plan a massive advertising campaign in the Eastern states, playing up the luxury of the Fleet ships and showing that the trip to Bermuda in a Fleet ship is a vital part of a magical Bermuda holiday.

"I've decided we're not going to get back into the airline business. Lets others fly people here, if anyone's in such a hurry. We'll offer a luxurious cruise before and after a Bermuda vacation."

"I'll be glad to get back on the bridge," Smutters admitted. "It's been boring, sitting out the war in an office. But not as boring as captaining a troop transport would have been."

She looked at him sharply. Bored, was he? There had been nights when she would have erased his boredom, when her body cried out for someone to share her lonely bed. But Smutters had signaled her early in the piece that he didn't want to continue their intimate relationship. He had done it in such a subtle way, she had not taken offense; indeed, she needed him much more as a loyal and wise manager than as a lover. But the rejection had hurt her until she had Colin to take care of.

"The boy, Mr. Smutters, my Colin. When he is a little older, I shall ask you to take him along on a few of your voyages. I want him to learn about the sea. It's in his blood, for one thing. And for another, someday this whole operation will be his."

Smutters nodded. He had decided to keep as far away from the little monster as possible. Colin was already displaying the worst characteristics of the Fleets; old Horatio's stubbornness, Robert's crazed ruthlessness and Sam's weakness. He almost felt sorry for Veronica Fleet, blind to the boy's faults because of her love for him. It was funny, he thought, but for all the power and wealth she'd won, Veronica didn't really have much.

"It's lucky I'm starting at Princeton this fall," Jeff said. "By next year the war will be well and truly over and the college places will be taken up by returned soldiers. As it is, I'm still not sure they won't kick me out to make room for an American. That'd be rich! I missed out on school because of the war, then I'd miss out on university because of the peace."

"Don't forget to thank Spencer Odlum for getting you into Princeton," Primrose said. "He says it's the best law school in the country."

"You really are happy that I'm doing law and going to an American college instead of Oxford?" he asked. They both knew his decision meant it was unlikely he would ever take over the running of Kosmos. But his mother hadn't demurred.

"I want you to do what you want to do, Jeff." It was true. She intended to go on running the business for many years yet, and it was right for her son to make his own way in the world. She felt no need to establish a dynasty. "As for going to the U.S. instead of England—we have more family and friends in America, anyway. Your uncle Cable and his family, and Jane and Carol. You'll have plenty of people to take care of you when you visit New York."

"Oh, Mother," he laughed. "I'm nineteen years old. I don't need taking care of."

"And neither do I, young man. So don't worry about me down here on my own. With the business and the Assembly, I'm kept fully occupied."

"Do you think you'll remain in the House of Assembly when the men come home from the war? Won't they expect you to make room for them?"

"Sometimes, Jeff, I think I've failed to bring you up right." She laughed. "What a stodgy male thing to say! I'm there on my merits, not because there was a shortage of men to fill the Assembly. And I intend to stay there. Now that women have the vote, I'm going to run for an elected seat instead of an appointed one."

He leaned down and kissed her cheek. "Well, you usually get what you intend, so I guess some worthy veteran is going to miss out on his rightful place."

"There are no 'rightful places,' " she said. "Places have to be earned. You're an Odlum. Odlums, of all people, should know that."

"I'm only kidding you, Mother," he said. "You go on giving them hell in the Assembly. Someone has to drag this colony into the twentieth century."

"Sometimes I think I'd settle for the nineteenth," she sighed. "Or even earlier. They were tough times, the founding years of Bermuda, but at least people had a sense of shared purpose. The way we're going now . . ." She broke off. "I'm sorry, Jeff. I don't want to get serious in your last time at home. And I don't want you to, either. Enjoy yourself while you're here." She glanced at her watch. "Heavens! I'm due at the Finance Committee meeting. I've got to run. Will you be dining in tonight?"

"Yes, Mother. But after dinner it's the tennis club dance. You don't mind my leaving you alone?"

"I'd better get used to it, hadn't I?" She laughed and hurried from the room.

He remained by the window, enjoying the sun on him. Down below in the harbor there were three British warships, already looking out of place. The war would soon be over and Bermuda and her harbors would be able to get back to what they did best: trade and tourism. Jeff wondered if he would be a part of the colony's future. He loved the place; it was his home. But as he had advanced into young manhood, he'd thought more and more about what seemed to be the real world. Bermuda was so safe

and secure, his own position in it assured. His mother
had almost encouraged this thinking with her lectures
about being independent and bold, and with her personal example of self-sufficiency. Sometimes he had
heard her in the night, sobbing for the husband she'd
lost, the father who was to Jeff only a dim, happy memory. The next morning, she would be all good cheer and
optimism. He desperately wanted to be as good as she
was, for his own sake as well as hers. His instincts told
him he would have to go away to test himself.

From the window he watched he chauffeur helping his
mother into their car. He grinned. She had fought so hard
against the automobile. But now she accepted its advan-
tages. She was like a tree, like one of Bermuda's cedars,
knowing when to bend before the wind but always conscious of the need to reach for the sky.

Chapter Ten
(1663–)

"It's time that boy of yours was married, Sep. Or else you won't be around to see it. You've looked half dead ever since your trip to London. It's only the brandy in your veins keeps you going now." Nathaniel Pike, old enough to be Septimus's father, looked around for a steward to order more of the spirit they both relied on to get them through their days. The Oceanic Club still had the best cellars in the colony and, as the members were quick to remind themselves, decent white stewards to serve them. Slaves were all well and good in the kitchens and the gardens, but it took a London club–trained man to handle vintage wines.

"Richard shows no inclination, Nathaniel," Fleet replied. "His bloody mother has him cowed. You mark my words, Amanda just wants me dead and out of the way so she can take over. And she doesn't want the boy intruding."

"Come on now, Sep. We all know Amanda has been running Fleet and Son for years. But that's no bar to Richard marrying. Good Lord, he must be twenty-six or twenty-seven now. You have to think of ensuring a line of succession, Sep."

"Not through blasted Richard, I won't. The fellow has no spunk. Weak! He catches everything—except good common sense. I tell you, Nathaniel, if only young Hilda had been a boy there would be no worry about our name being preserved in Bermuda. What a shame she's just a girl."

"You have been unlucky," Pike agreed. "There was that fine strapping lad you fathered by the nigger woman. Youngblood. From what I've seen of him around the docks, he would be a worthy successor. Maybe you should have acknowledged him."

"Don't be ridiculous, Nathaniel. It was enough I sent him off to sea in my ships. There's no way I could give him my name. No, I'm afraid all my hopes have to rest with Richard. I'm almost reconciled to the name dying out."

"Marry him off before it's too late. You might be lucky. Married to a spirited woman, he might get you a strong grandson."

"I suppose you've got someone in mind."

"Of course, Sep. My own little Anne is fifteen next birthday, and it's time I made a suitable match for her. Compared to you, I really am old. Just what you Fleets need, some new blood instead of the same tired old English stock."

"But her mother, Nathaniel. She was next thing to a whore when you married her and made her respectable. You always did cock a snoot at the Establishment, and you could get away with marrying your little Frog. Damned attractive she was then and still is. But we're talking about the Fleet lineage here. Why, if your Anne married my Richard, that poncey Lapin himself would be claiming some kind of relationship to us. And no matter that Monsieur Lapin owns our club and charges us outrageously for the privilege of belonging, he is still a tradesman."

Pike laughed uproariously, and some of the nearby members glanced across to see what it was their most senior colleague found so funny. Pike reflected that it was one of the great joys of a long and enduring friendship that he and Sep could, these days, say to each other exactly what they thought.

"Lapin won't bother you, Sep. He may be no gentleman, but I swear from the day I . . . I bought Josie from him, he has respected our agreement. And now he's rich in his own right and has established a strong line of his own. The Lapins are breeding like rabbits." He chuckled at his joke, but it went by Sep who had never bothered to learn any French. "I want you to think about Anne for Richard. She's a rare beauty, strong as a horse, and if she makes love like her mother, will get a horde of children, even by Richard. I'd send her to him with a most handsome dowry, too. Even throw in that new coachman you've been trying to steal away from me. Best man with horses in these islands, and strong enough to carry you everywhere when your legs finally collapse. Which won't be long, judging from the way you hobbled in here today."

"I don't know, Nathaniel. I think your daughter might be too much of a handful for him. Poor bastard already has a mother who rides roughshod over him. A willful wife would be the last thing he needs."

"Maybe it's Amanda I should be talking to, then, since she wears the pants in your family."

"Keep Amanda out of this. She controls every other aspect of my life and fortune. If my boy is to be married off, then I'm going to make the decision." It was his turn to call for brandy. "I'll think about it, Nathaniel. An unlikely match, but I'll think about it."

Angela Jenkins heard a noise from the back of the house and started forward in her rocking chair.

"Hilda!" she called. "Is that you Hilda?" But then she came fully out of her doze and remembered her sister was long dead and she was alone in the house. She sighed. She had outlived her usefulness—if she ever had been useful, she thought glumly—and she was just a burden to Amanda. Her niece made it very clear she couldn't wait for Angela to die and vacate the old family cottage.

She stiffened. Yes, there was a noise back there.

Angela moved slowly, supported by a walking stick in each hand, down the corridor to the kitchen block. She saw a flickering light under the scullery door and quietly opened it, not the least afraid of what might be lurk-

ing there. At seventy, there was nothing to scare her. She
was staring at a young black man stuffing a sack with
the contents of her larder.

"If you are hungry, you only need to ask," she said.
She spoke quietly, but the sound of her voice made him
leap back, dropping the sack and falling into a crouch in
the far corner, from where he regarded her with huge
white eyes. Angela moved into the small room and began to gather up the spilled provisions. "Come now,
young man, stand up and help so we can prepare you a
fine supper." She glanced at him. He was trembling in
fear of her. "Have you run away from one of the big
houses?" she asked.

"No, ma'am," he said haltingly. "I live in the general
quarters. No one misses me if I go out at night. Except,
if they see me, then I'm in trouble."

"Well, I've seen you." She laughed. "Do you think
you're in trouble?"

"No, ma'am. All the slaves know about you. You say
we should be free. So I came here to get food for my brothers in the barracoon. I thought you would be pleased to
help feed the poor people down there in that awful stock-
ade."

"I haven't been down to the barracoon for weeks," Angela said. "It's my legs, you know. Walk a hundred yards
and they go so tired. But if you are taking food to a new
shipment of slaves, then you are more than welcome to
it. Take all you can carry. I think it disgraceful the way
they pen those poor people up like cattle, then ship them
on to America." She found another sack and began loading more food into it. "I'll come along with you, young
man, and we'll deliver our offerings over the wall. At
least a little fresh food will alleviate their suffering for
one night."

The slave was nervous and silent as they set out in the
little pony trap, but Angela was enjoying herself. She
geed up the horse and chattered away to her partner as
they bounced through the night and down the narrow
dark streets to the barracoon in St. George's. It was only
when they were near the forbidding structure that An-

gela's enjoyment of the outing left her. The barracoon was nothing more than a dirt compound fenced with twelve-foot-high stakes, pointed at the tops and lashed tightly together. Inside, a lean-to roof three feet wide provided the only shelter from the elements. Even now, in the dead of night, Angela could hear a continual low moaning from the wretched inhabitants.

She reined in at the rough gate to the construction and clambered down from the trap. Her companion saw the guard approaching before she did and jumped from the other side of the trap, melting into the night.

"What are you doing here, old woman?" the guard demanded. "Nobody's allowed near this place at night. It's dangerous." He was just a youth, she saw, and as nervous as Angela's erstwhile companion. He took a step closer, hefting his musket. "Oh," he said, "it's Miss Jenkins. I'm sorry, ma'am. I didn't mean to shout at you. But you shouldn't be here."

"I've come to deliver some sustenance to those poor creatures behind that wall," Angela snapped. "Listen to them crying. Tomorrow, or the next day, they'll be bound for the next port to be paraded on the auction block. You put down that stupid gun and help me pass these sacks of food over the wall to them. I want them to have one happy memory of Bermuda."

"I can't do that, ma'am." He was in a nervous sweat. The old woman was obviously crazy, but she was a Fleet relation and to some extent the slaves were her property. "Look, you just wait here and I'll go fetch my sergeant. He'll know what to do."

Angela waited in the dark, tapping her foot. She was annoyed with herself for not having done something practical for the slaves before. So far her years of effort against the slave trade had gone for nothing, and now the poor creatures were flowing through the colony like a sad brown river, bound for God knew where. At least by tonight's action she would give a few of them a moment's pleasure. She took a good look at the door of the pen; it was a crude affair, just a log set in two brackets. She stepped forward and tried lifting the barrier. It

moved a little and she summoned up all her strength,
raising it until one end fell out of its bracket. She
watched in delight as the gate swung outward.

Angela found herself staring into the scared faces of
about fifty Negroes. She suppressed a giggle when she
realized what they were seeing—a little old lady standing in the night wearing a sleeping robe and carrying two
lumpy sacks.

"Come out, all of you," she shouted. "Head for the
hills. There's food here and more to be found in the land
out there. Come on! You've nothing to lose."

Some understood. They didn't know English, but they
caught the spirit of it. First a couple, then a half dozen
slipped through the gate to stand outside their prison.
Angela nudged the sacks toward them and two of the
bigger slaves gingerly picked them up and threw them
over their shoulders. Those still in the compound were
pressing forward now, whispering among themselves,
poised either to run or to retreat. Probably many would
have stayed, numbly accepting the fate that had befallen them when the Arab traders snatched them from
their African villages. But at just the moment of decision, the sergeant arrived. He took one glance at the situation and fired a round at them.

The stinging buckshot turned the slaves from timid
captives into a cohesive mob; as one they rushed the sergeant and his young assistant and pummeled them to the
ground before streaming away up the silent streets to
the surrounding countryside.

"That's the way to do it," Angela shouted to their retreating forms. "Run and don't stop. You'll be all right."
She glanced over as the two guards slowly got up off the
ground. "And good night to you, gentlemen," she said
sweetly, before painfully climbing back up into her trap
and driving sedately home.

It was Amanda who awoke her the next day. A very
angry Amanda.

"You are a madwoman!" her niece shouted at Angela.
"Do you know what you have done? Fifty-odd slaves set

free to pillage the islands. The colony is in turmoil, no one able to leave their houses until these creatures are caught. If you were anyone else, you'd be arrested. I myself would like to see you in the stocks." She started crying then, but Angela surmised they were tears of anger and frustration, so did not feel she need show any sympathy.

"I'm sure I don't know what got into me, dear," she said. "I'm what you say, just a crazy old lady who shouldn't be allowed out without her keeper." She sneezed. "And look at me! I've surely caught a cold by being out in the night air. It must be God's punishment for what I did. I wonder, dear Amanda, if you would fetch me brandy and hot lemon before you leave. I don't think my tired old legs will carry me to the kitchen."

In the following days Angela got reports of the slaves' exploits. They had scattered to every corner of the islands, and all able-bodied men were asked to hunt for them. Hysteria was rampant, even though none of the colonies had yet had any contact with the escapees. It was a week before they were all rounded up and placed back in the barracoon, and even then no one could be certain there were not a few missing. The barracoon's records were sketchy.

"You have caused my family a dreadful harm," Amanda said on her latest visit to her aunt. "Because of your action the Governor has made a new order-in-Council. He was always ambivalent about the trade, anyway. Now he's decreed there will be no more actual trading here. The barracoon is to be torn down. We may purchase slaves only for our own use, not for transshipment. Worst of all, the slaves you set free are no longer resalable to Virginia. They have the reputation of being troublemakers now, so they will have to be absorbed into our community. At a huge loss to my family."

"I'm so sorry, my dear," Angela said, trying not to smile. "But look on the bright side. I've been so happy in Bermuda, and I'm sure those poor creatures will be, too." She did laugh, long and silently, as her niece's heels clattered angrily down the hall.

* * *

The surgery above the apothecary shop was large, bright and airy. It was kept scrupulously clean, Jonas's housekeeping scrubbing every corner of it twice a day with lye and boiling water. Jonas had learned in Europe that cleanliness reduced the risk of postoperative infections; he had too often seen the grim results of operations carried out amid squalor. Today he had instructed Mrs. Hoskins to lay on her best effort because he had a special patient and was going to attempt an untried operation. Jonas bent to remove a crease in the fresh-starched sheet covering his operating table, and in that moment he heard the timid footsteps on the stairs.

"Come in, Rose," he called. "Everything is ready."

Rose Staley was only twelve but she was tall like her father and she had to duck to come through the surgery door. Actually, he thought, watching her, Rose always kept her head averted. She was so ashamed of her marking she tried never to let the world look her full in the face. The harelip had already badly scarred her personality, and it was for this reason he had decided to do the risky operation. He had explained to both Rose and her father that the chances were great she would be scarred worse after he attempted the procedure. Ewen had answered for the girl.

"We have complete faith in your skills, Jonas. We want you to attempt to undo the cruelty fate played upon Rose at birth. She has no hope of a normal life as it is."

Now his mentor's daughter stood before him, eyes fixed firmly on the scrubbed floor. He sensed her desperate yearning to be a normal girl instead of the object of pity and revulsion. He was afraid of the responsibility resting in his hands and felt inadequate for the task ahead.

"Come forward into the full light, dear Rose," he said. "Lift up your face for me. I must be sure my calculations are correct." He touched her cheeks, so soft and fair, and felt her flinch. The poor child. What she had suffered from her disfigurement. And what she was risking now! The split in her lip was almost a quarter-inch at its widest point and was made even more horrible by the fact of its marring what were otherwise classically beautiful features.

"Come lie down," he said. "Be as comfortable as you can. This will be a tiresome and sometimes painful affair. Clutch this," he said, pressing his treasured ambergris rock into her hand, "and when the pain is severe, squeeze it with all your might."

She met his eyes as she lay back on the operating table. She smiled, timid and afraid but trusting him.

"Thank you for doing this for me, Jonas," she whispered. "No matter the outcome, I will know we tried to correct this scar. That is better than to go through life wondering what might have been."

He checked his instruments again, running his thumb along the blades of the set of tiny scalpels made for him in Paris. They were the finest available and gave him some reassurance. He lit a candle and carefully heated the scalpels and the fine, thin bronze needle.

"See," he said, holding a length of thread before her eyes. "No crude catgut for you, Rose. This is silk, woven thin but strong. It will not withstand the strain you could put on gut, but it will leave no visible marks when we remove it after your lip is healed." He had decided it was better to keep her informed of what he was doing; she had a keen intelligence and would not, he thought, appreciate being ignored while he worked. He showed her a bottle. "Whiskey, Rose, the purest spirit. We will swab it inside your lip to deaden the nerves, and outside to remove the risk of infection." He dipped his finger in the bottle and rubbed some of the spirit on her gums. "Do you feel it numbing you?"

She nodded, grimaced and then laughed.

"It tastes foul! I do not understand how men can so prize such a concoction. But, yes, it does take away feeling."

"Right. Now I'll place this swab soaked with the spirit inside your lip and in a few minutes we will begin."

They waited in silence as the alcohol worked. When he gently pricked her lip with his needle she did not flinch;

it was time to begin. He took his smallest scalpel and delicately parted her lip with his fingers until it was stretched taut. Then, cutting up toward her nose, he severed the membrane at the crest of the lip. A trace of blood appeared and he swabbed whiskey there. The two edges of her lip were now parted and open to his tools. Slowly, making each incision as cleanly as he could, Jonas began to cut diagonal slits down each flap, aiming to make them match each other when he eventually sewed the two surfaces together. There was a great deal of blood now, but her eyes showed no fear. He swabbed again before taking up the needle.

His hands felt too big and clumsy for the delicate task, but pinching the flesh beneath her nose together, he pushed the needle through and gently pulled the silk thread after it. She winced under his hand but he had to press on now, restraining her while he sewed tiny stitches close together to pull the lip tight and force the skin to stretch and cover the gap.

It was almost an hour before he was finished and satisfied he had done the best he could. Rose's forehead was clammy with perspiration and her eyes bright with pain, but she lay absolutely still, willing herself not to impede his work. He wiped her brow and his own, and sat back.

"That's it, Rose. It's finished now. You were very brave." He felt drained by the operation and made a silent prayer that it would prove worth the pain and suffering he had put her through. He was not a drinking man, but he reached for his anaesthetic and poured himself a measure. She watched him toss the glass off and smiled, except the lip movement hurt viciously.

"No," he said, "you must try not to smile, or laugh, or shout. Your poor lip is stretched cruelly and must have time to grow together." He stood up and reached for a mirror. "I'll show you what it looks like now. Don't be distressed at the stitches and the swelling. They will go in time." He was nervous as he held the glass for her; he could only look at his work from a surgeon's point of view.

She studied herself for several minutes, imagining

away the fine stitching and the raw wound. Then she
slowly nodded. The gaping split that had made all her
young life a misery was gone. She lay back and spoke
carefully, slowly, trying not to dislodge the threads that
gave her hope.

"Thank you, Jonas. You have made me a new person."

"Don't stop," she gasped. "More! Give me more. Jesus, God, keep doing it to me. Harder, harder." Amanda
Fleet's naked legs were locked around his hips and she
ground herself against him, striving to squeeze more
pleasure out of his huge member. Her riding habit was
up around her waist and she felt the straw scratching her
buttocks. She frantically squeezed her own bare breasts
as, standing on the hayloft floor, he thrust into her again.
Her head banged back against the edge of the shelf on
which she lay, but she felt no pain, only the exquisite
searing rod probing high inside her; she was on the verge
now, panting in anticipation of the flow about to be released. "No. Please no," she begged as yet again he
pulled back and denied her the ultimate pleasure. She
looked down, and there it was between her thighs, rock-
hard, gleaming wetly, the big red hood just emerging
from her. "Why do you do this to me?" she whimpered.
"Pleasure me fully, please, I beg you." She looked up into
his face, hated him for the mockery she saw in his dark
eyes, the insolence in his grin. She reached down and
clutched him, forcing him back inside her, frantically
moving her hips to bring on her climax before he could
again pull away from her. At last the pulsing began, the
pounding, throbbing surge that wracked her body and
burned her brain. She heard herself screaming crude ob-
scenities as still the hot tide raced inside her; she did not
care how much he humiliated her. Anything was worth
this savage release. He took a pace back as her hand released him and her legs, trembling with exhaustion, fell
from his body. He stood there—a shaft of sunlight striking his long, black hair, his great weapon still standing
stiff as a flagstaff—grinning contemptuously. And yet
she wanted more of him.

Amanda raised her hands again to her breasts, squeezing them together, erect nipples touching each other. She would never get enough of this. She dropped her left hand into her mound, fingers splayed out, one searching inside her forest and finding the wet core. She brought herself to another climax, not caring—even perversely enjoying—that he continued to regard her with amused contempt. For the moment she was finished and she slumped back in the straw, not bothering to cover herself.

"You really are a bastard," she said at last. "Why do you come riding out with me, tumble me in haylofts and hedgerows, then deliberately withhold yourself and deny me pleasure? Does it please you to hear me beg? Does it amuse you that a woman of fifty still exhibits the lusts of a young girl? Or is your satisfaction in humiliating the wife of your nominal master? Whatever, I don't care. Because, John Smutters, I am at least as perverse as you. Your treatment of me actually brings me to greater heights." She smiled then, feeling she was back in command. "I do not need to put up with your conduct, you know. There are plenty of lovers I could take. There may be other younger and more beautiful women in Bermuda, but none has my power. You are our senior captain because I engineered it. You have become moderately prosperous only because old Tom Fleet gave you a job. And I gave you a pinnace, remember, when you were my late husband's cabin boy on that disastrous voyage."

"You didn't want to give me the wretched pinnace," he said dryly. "You accused me of deserting the ship. It was only because it suited them to pretend I was a hero that I got on the road to becoming Bermuda's most exalted captain."

"But that is the point," she snapped. "We Fleets made you and we can unmake you. So why do you risk my wrath? I watch you and see what is in your eyes. Contempt, loathing, hatred. If I were not so twisted myself, I would not stand for it."

"You really want to know?" He was not smiling any more. "Would you like me to tell you why I have always

hungered to humiliate the wife of damned Will Acton,
why it gives me so much pleasure to see you lying before
me, legs spread like a trollop, to hear you begging me to
fuck you? All right. The night before we reached Port au
Prince your then husband used me, cruelly and foully."
He was watching her carefully. She did not understand.
"Your husband, madam, buggered me."

She felt the flush come to her cheeks; she licked her
suddenly dry lips and tried to swallow.

"You were so young, I remember, such a pretty boy,"
she said. Her voice was trembling. "He must have been
attracted to you." She licked her lips again. "Why don't
you complete your revenge on Will Acton, then? Do to
me what he did to you."

She lunged forward and fastened her lips to his member, feeling it grow rigid again. She heard him laugh, a
harsh, triumphant sound, and she shivered in frightened anticipation. Then she lifted her mouth from him
and lay back, turning on her stomach, her face pressed
into the sweet-smelling hay. She shivered again as she
felt his body move between her legs. She momentarily
drew away as his weapon nudged at her, searching for
the entry, but his big hands grabbed her hips and pulled
her against him. It hurt, a burning, searing pain as he
forced himself inside her. She bit her lip to contain the
scream and then it was past and she had taken all of him,
nothing held back this time, no withdrawal, deeper and
deeper, feeling him grow ever larger, filling her inside
and then exploding, gushing, flooding her. And, face still
buried deep in the hay, she shared his passion, gained
complete release for herself. And gained the satisfaction
that somehow or other she had broken his hold over her.
Now she could use him as she pleased. Which meant, she
thought, that she probably wouldn't bother.

"No, I don't want to marry Richard Fleet. For all his
money he is no catch. Sickly, ugly, under the thumb of
his mother. What kind of life would it be for me?" Anne
Pike put all the passion of her fifteen years into her
pleading, but she could see she was not going to get

through to her mother. Yes, she thought, you French
bitch, this will be your crowning glory, to deliver your
daughter into the Fleet family. Not bad for someone who
would have ended up a streetwalker if she hadn't left
France.

"Don't be tiresome, Anne. It is all decided." Josie regarded her daughter with amusement. "You will be the
loveliest bride Bermuda has ever seen and the wedding
will be the grandest. The Fleets and the Pikes united at
last. Your father is as happy as I am."

"You treat me like a chattel, just some piece of furni-
ture to be sold or given away," Anne shouted. She tossed
her head, sending the long black curls flying from her
shoulders. "You can't force me into this union. I shall . . .
I shall run away!"

Josie laughed. "Do be quiet, darling. You love luxury
and position even more than I do. And there's nowhere
for you to run to. You'll see. It will all be perfect for you.
And Richard won't be any bother."

"Of course he won't! That's the problem, Mother. You
think of me as a child still, but I have the passions of a
woman. Would you condemn me to a loveless life with a
weak man who appears incapable of ardor?"

"We all have to make sacrifices, dear. And perhaps
he'll surprise you in bed. Anyway, it's not nearly so important as you think. What really matters is to marry
wealth and position."

"As you did."

"Yes, as I did," Josie said. "In your case, though, you'll
be starting with the advantage of all your father's money
and power. You will be acknowledged as the leader of
Bermuda society."

"Is that to be my lifetime achievement? Leader of Bermuda society? Heavens, Mother, I aspire to be something more than that. This dreary little colony isn't
worth presiding over. I want to be the toast of Paris and
London."

"And so you shall be. After the wedding you and Richard will go to London for the season, then travel on to
Europe. There will be no hurry to return; Amanda

doesn't want her son interfering in the way she runs the family business."

"That at least sounds promising," Anne said. "And the wedding could be quite fun. I know just the dress I want to wear. You won't approve, I'm sure."

"Don't be so glum, Richard. Everyone has to get married sometime." Hilda was determined to cheer her brother. His gloom had deepened each day since the formalities had begun; now the wedding itself loomed and Richard was sunk in melancholy. "All our parents want is for you to produce a male heir. After you've done your duty in that direction, you can lead a life just like father's—drinking, gambling, hunting and watching the money pile up." She continued to vigorously brush her long, dark hair while studying her countenance in her boudoir mirror. "It's not as if you even have to work at anything. Mother seems set to go on controlling the business for years to come." The shoulder strap of her silk shift slipped, but she did not bother to cover the pert breast thus revealed; she and her half-brother had always enjoyed a certain intimacy. When Hilda was growing up, ignored by her mother and scarcely noticed by her father, it had been Richard—poor lonely, sickly Richard—who was her closest companion. Seven years her senior, he had always sought her advice and approval, always found sanctuary in her cozy bedroom high up and at the rear of the grand house. She liked his dependence on her and played on it, flirting with him, teasing him, able to twist him around her slender fingers. She watched him via the mirror now and saw his eyes fixed on her bare breast. How often they had played out similar scenes, Hilda experimenting with her budding sexuality to see just how easily she could arouse him, then leaving him in flushed confusion. She put down the brush, stood up and crossed to him sitting on her bed.

"It is funny to think of you married, though," she said. "I shall quite miss you when you have gone off to live with little Anne." She reached out and touched his hair. "I wonder if you'll have as much fun together as we did.

Perhaps you can teach her to wrestle." She leaned on him, forcing him back on the bed. "Let's see if I can still beat you." She fell on his chest, trying to pin his arms, and then they were romping all over the bed, playful as two puppies, giggling like children. He flipped her on her back and she struggled out from under him, kicking her legs in the air and pummeling him with her two small fists. They were both flushed and breathing hard, immersed in their game, conscious of the need not to make too much noise. He threw her again and pressed down on her; Hilda felt her shift ride up around her waist and his weight and sudden hardness pushing against her. His face was within inches of hers and she saw the beads of sweat forming on his forehead, the imploring look in his eyes. She let the game continue a moment more, enjoying the sensation of his blouse brushing her breasts and his maleness against her belly. And then she slipped out from under him, pulled down her shift and sprang from the bed.

"See," she teased. "I'm much too quick for you, dear brother. You'll have to move faster than that if you're going to have your way with your new bride."

Richard clasped his hands together to control the tremor there; he was hot and nervous, flustered. It was always like this when he and Hilda played their boisterous games. He placed his hands in his lap to cover his erection; she would laugh at him, tease him even more, if she saw it. It was all just innocent, he was sure, but he felt guilty at the way their games aroused him. He didn't want Hilda to realize the effect she had on him. Little Hilda, just a loving sister and innocent girl. And yet, sometimes, he wondered if she didn't get the same sensations as he. But of course not, it was just his own maleness that put such constructions on her girlish play.

"I shall miss you very much, Hilda," he finally said, getting himself under control. "I used to think we could go on like this forever, together. We have such fun."

"It's not as if you're going off to a foreign land, Richard. You'll be living not a mile from here and we shall

see each other daily. Unless your little Anne is jealous
of me."

"Don't call her 'my' Anne. You know I am only doing
this because Mother ordered. I don't have any feelings
for the girl. I scarcely know her. Good God, I'm twelve
years her senior. I doubt we will have anything in common."

She studied him for a moment, so awkward and shy.
He would be no match for the Pike hussy. Poor Richard,
she thought, suffering the bad blood of his natural father
and the weak example of his adoptive one.

"Goodness," she said, "my bath was drawn ages ago
and will be cold. And you should be dressing for dinner."
She crossed the room and stepped behind the screen
where a hip bath filled with tepid water stood. She
shrugged off the shift and stood naked. The screen was
between them, but the angle of the mirror allowed him
an unrestricted view of her. Their eyes met in the mirror
and held. Then she blew him a kiss and stepped into the
bath.

Jonas grasped the last strand of silk and gently drew
it out of the lip, then closely surveyed the results of his
surgery. There was scarcely a trace of what he had done;
the scar had healed and the skin was smooth and un-
blemished.

"You've been a very good patient, Rose," he said. "I
hope you will decide the result of my clumsy efforts is
worth the pain I have put you through." He ran his
thumb over the lip; there was a slight ridge of scar tissue
beneath the surface but that would disperse in time. Not
a bad job at all, he thought. "Would you like to see yourself in the glass?"

Her hands shook as she picked up the looking glass.
She feared what she would see. All the weeks of waiting
for the wound to heal, time in which she had cursed herself for her vanity in seeking to have corrected Nature's
mark, the daily examination of the ugly stitches joining
the bloody tissue. She never should have hoped to be
normal-looking. Pride was a sin. At last she raised the

glass and gazed into it. She gasped and cried out and the mirror fell from her hand.

"Jonas! Jonas!" she cried. "What have you done to me? Look, look at me. I am normal at last. I look like any other girl." The tears came then, flooding from her. After twelve years of shame, the ordeal was over.

"There is nothing to cry about," he said, trying to conceal his own pleasure. "And, dear child, you are more than 'normal-looking.' You are indeed beautiful and the young men of the village will be beating a path to your door."

She put her fingers to her lip, an expression of wonderment in her eyes.

"I am a new person," she said. "And it is you who have made me so. I will be forever in your debt." She stood up shakily, half laughing, half crying, and kissed his cheek. "I shall be your servant, your nurse—whatever you want of me."

"Don't say such things." He was blushing in embarrassment. "I owe your father so much. He has been everything to me." He bustled around the surgery, putting away his instruments. "And, speaking of Ewen, don't you think we should go to him and show him his new and beautiful daughter."

There were more tears when Ewen looked upon Rose's now perfect features. He held her hands in his, their faces close as he strained with fading eyesight to behold the wonder before him.

"You will never understand what you have done for me, Jonas," he said finally. "For all these years I have silently wept for Rose and for myself. For Rose because she had to bear a stigma no one, least of all a young girl, should be branded with. For myself because I secretly believed the mark had been put on her as the result of some sin I committed. And now you have lifted the burden from both of us."

Later in the evening, the two old friends sat over glasses of sherry and listened to Rose singing in the kitchen as she did the washing up. Ewen was reflective, pleasure still showing in his eyes, but concern too.

"I think, Jonas, you have achieved your miracle just in time for me. I can die happy, knowing Rose will have no greater burden to bear than any other young person growing up in our colony." He raised his hand to stop Jonas's protest. "No, it would be silly to pretend my days are not numbered. I am very old, and even on the warmest days I feel the chill of death in my bones. My only concern is to hold on long enough to see Rose taken care of. She is of marriageable age, and now she is of such pleasing features it should not be long before some young man comes courting her. I have never worried much about worldly goods, but I do wish I had been able to leave her with a respectable dowry. As it is, there will only be this cottage."

"I don't like this talk of death, Ewen; but since you insist on raising the matter, I must say I have been giving some thought to all our futures. Like you, I have not much cared about the accumulation of worldly goods, but slowly I have come to realize there is nothing inherently wrong with making a little money." He laughed. "I don't mean pursuing wealth with the single-mindedness and ruthlessness of our contemporaries in Bermuda. Just getting enough so as not to have to worry constantly about the future." He paused, filling his pipe and staring out into the dark. "You remember, of course, the beach of whales we found so long ago. And the substance buried there, ambergris?"

"Surely I do. I still have my own sample on my desk. I went once more to the beach during your long absence and—as we both feared—others had been there. The bones had been desecrated, almost none of them left."

"Oh, that is bad news." Jonas saw the scheme he had been hatching vanish. "Because when I was in Paris I talked with a family of perfumers and they explained the tremendous importance of ambergris. The Paris market pays quite incredible prices for the substance and can never get enough of it. Lately I had been thinking, if you were agreeable, we might return to the beach and gather ambergris, export some of it and raise the funds to start our own perfume factory here in Bermuda. I thought it would be a worthy industry, offering some employment to the locals and producing an export product which these islands sorely need. But now you tell me our treasure trove has gone." He laughed again. "It serves me right, always procrastinating."

"I said the whalebone had all gone. I scratched around in the sand, and the ambergris remains, as good as the day we found it, protected from the elements. The vandals who took away the skeletons did not know to look beneath the surface."

Jonas was on his feet, excited. "Good Lord! Then my scheme is still alive. Ewen, Rose will have as grand a dowry as you desire. I know enough about the perfume business to produce desirable products, and we have access to the most expensive ingredient. We could be rich by merely selling all the ambergris to the French, but the whales chose these islands as their last resting place and I would think it better if, apart from exporting enough to get us into business, we manufactured here, using Bermuda's own flowers."

"But what of your work as a surgeon, if you are to become a business magnate? Will you no longer heal the sick and mend the broken?" Ewen was teasing him, but in his excitement Jonas did not realize this.

"Once the factory is established I will be able to perform far better surgery," he said. "I can bring a trained assistant here from Europe, import the latest equipment, teach others what I've learned. I swear to you, Ewen, the money we make will be put to good and noble purposes."

"I believe you, Jonas. Go harvest the riches cast up by the sea and set your scheme in motion. Rose will help you in the venture; she has learned much of botany and, now she is suddenly a beautiful girl, I think she will display great interest in perfumes and powders. And of course she will be loyal to you until the day she dies."

The Virginian was already a fixture in the Seahorse Tavern; night after night he would sit in a corner, mumbling incoherently to himself until someone would throw

a copper at his feet. Then the tall, shambling, graceless
figure would leap into the center of the tavern and dance
until he dropped—executing, to the sawing notes of Old
Jamie's fiddle, the most intricate jigs and reels and
hornpipes on feet that seemed as light as swansdown.
And then, cup of rum clasped firmly in his horny hand,
he would relapse into his stupor. No one knew, or much
cared, what his name was. He had literally washed up
on the shores of Bermuda, swept in by the tide, riding a
rough raft made from the wrecked timbers of a ship. He
was quite mad from his long exposure at sea and would
have been left to die on the beach had not the Rev. Sikes
taken pity on him. Sikes made a bed for the shipwrecked
sailor in the stables behind the rectory and instructed
his housekeeper to feed him scraps from the table. The
good vicar, who was in his dotage, would some evenings
allow the wretch inside the house, read him old sermons
and favorite passages from the Bible. He at first assumed the man was a mute, but one night did hear him
croak the word *Virginia*. And so he was known as "The
Virginian," and slipped into the shifting populace of the
busy seaport. He lost the shelter of the vicar's stable
when the Rev. Sikes caught him at the brandy bottle;
cast into the street, The Virginian shambled into the
Seahorse Tavern, picked up a straw broom and began to
sweep the dirt floor. He made himself a bed of sacks in a
lean-to at the back of the tavern and stayed on there, a
hollow-eyed ghost existing on scraps and the coins his
evening dancing earned. If he did venture out into the
lanes of St. George's, small boys followed him, jeering
and throwing rocks. It was only when he danced that
anyone took notice of The Virginian.

On this hot September night he had had to work particularly hard for his pennies; it was a sullen crowd in
the Seahorse, cranky after unending days of century-
plus temperatures, even more tight-pursed than usual
because of the lack of work caused by the seasonal falloff
in shipping. A tempest was building out in the Gulf; and
until it swept through, all sane captains would remain
in port.

"Damn and blast the weather," Young Tom Winders muttered, staring gloomily down into his half-empty tankard of porter. "I can't afford to be standing here frittering away my last coppers. My landlady will throw me into the street if I don't stump up with the rent this week. And Melony refuses to let me call on her until I've got a job."

"We're all in the same boat," Joshua Crooke said. "The Forty Thieves get richer come rain or shine, but we landless ones eat or starve depending on the vagaries of the weather and who has a cargo to be unloaded. If we had a trade, or capital to buy a boat . . ."

"Face it, we're just peasants, only the color of our skin to distinguish us from nigger slaves," Ben Tropp said. He fished a jumble of small coins from his pocket. "To hell with it. There's just enough here to buy us another round. Three porters, Eliza," he ordered. They watched the sour-faced barmaid place the drinks on the scarred wooden surface. Tropp gulped at his and made a face. "Did you pull this from the slop tray?" he demanded. "It tastes like weasel's piss."

"Go drink somewhere else if you don't like it," the barmaid snapped. "The loss of your custom certainly wouldn't send the Seahorse broke."

The three young men sank back into morose silence. Behind them a section of the crowd cheered on the two growling Staffordshires being pitted. One of the dogs yowled in agony as his adversary locked his teeth into the soft flesh of his nose; the unfortunate animal's backers also yelped as their fancy, now bleeding from a slashed throat, died in the dirt.

"There is no justice," Tropp said. "All her life my mother slaved over a tub of hot water, washing the gentry's clothes. When she died her arms were the color of raw beef and her estate totaled ninepence. And your father, Tom, beaten to death by footpads for the coppers in his pocket. Was that a fitting end for One-Armed Winders, the only man who stood up to Monserat's pirates? No justice at all."

"I don't want justice," Young Tom replied. "I just want

a job." He was a solidly built man, with broad shoulders and arms thick as tree trunks. Whenever there was a job of heavy lifting to be done, they sent for Winders. But lately, just when he so badly needed money to press his suit with Melony Stannard, there was no one who required his services. He was normally bright and amiable, but his circumstance—and his frustrated love for Melony—were beginning to weigh him down.

The dead pit bull had been dragged away and the victor given a bowl of ale. Now The Virginian was being pushed forward to do his stuff. He looked scarcely able to walk, let alone dance. But when Old Jamie pulled his bow across his strings, the feet responded and The Virginian was moving, smooth as ever, leaping and twirling and bringing with his performance a touch of magic into the dingy tavern. Except that, as he made one last soaring leap, his foot slipped in a pool of dog's blood and he spun into a table laden with drinks.

One of the drinkers who lost his glass cuffed the dancer and sent him sprawling backward; another rose and gave The Virginian a solid kicking. The dancer lay still, wild eyes staring at the low ceiling, his body used to absorbing blows. It would have been just one more night in the tavern had not one of the dancer's tormentors picked up an oil lamp and poured its contents over the scraggy figure. The flame followed the oil and suddenly The Virginian was ablaze.

Tom Winders acted without thinking. He pushed through the jeering crush and flung himself on The Virginian, seeking to smother the flames. His own eyebrows were singed as he rolled the man in the dust and used his cap to beat out the flames scorching the dancer's beard. And then someone delivered a heavy boot in Tom's backside, lifting him up off the floor and throwing him against the wall.

"Mind your own business, you interfering young bastard," his attacker yelled. He was a huge, dark man, one of the contingent from a British ship that had been tied up at the docks for two weeks waiting out the tempest. "This old turd needs burning; it's the only way we'll rid

him of his vermin." As Tom struggled to his feet the seaman picked up another oil lamp and made to douse The
Virginian.

Tom sprang at him and got his hands to his throat; the
same mad obstinacy that had led his father to challenge
the pirates burned in him now. The giant seaman was
trying to shake him off and Tom shifted his grip, plunging a thumb deep into the man's eye. The seaman
dropped to one knee and fumbled in his boot; a long knife
now glinted in his hand and three of his companions
ranged up beside him, similarly armed. Then Crooke and
Tropp were beside him, bearing long clubs grabbed from
behind the bar; there was one for him too. The three
young Bermudians stood back to back as their foreign
foes circled them.

"Bugger this!" Ben Tropp shouted. "Lay into the bastards. I'll not be pushed around in my own port by a
bunch of Liverpool thugs." He lashed out with his club
and the sound of an arm breaking rang through the now
silent tavern.

Tom and Joshua responded to his leadership and began thrashing about with their weapons, ignoring the
slashing knives and wreaking havoc on their opponents.
One of the sailors went down, his forehead split open by
a blow from Tom; another collapsed as Joshua slammed
him in the ribs; the last, unwounded, scrabbled backward and ran from the tavern.

Now there was much cheering in the bar and drinks
were pressed on the conquering trio; it was several minutes before Tom paid any attention to The Virginian,
still lying burned and bruised on the floor.

"I'll take him into his shelter out the back," he said.
"If he's going to die it might as well be in his own bed."
He lifted the man off the floor and draped him around his
shoulders. "Mind my drink for me." The Virginian
smelled bad and was a dead weight, and Tom was glad
to dump him on the grubby sacks that served as his bed.
He was almost out of the lean-to on his way back to the
bar when he heard the man speak.

"You saved my life tonight. I am most grateful."

"We thought you were a mute," Tom said, returning to the sorry bedside. "All these months and only one word out of you."

"I have nothing to say to people anymore, except when they do me a service such as you did tonight. Here," he said, rummaging among the sacks. "Take this as a gesture of my thanks." It was a small leather purse and surprisingly heavy in Tom's hand. He opened the drawstring and saw the dull gleam of gold.

"Good God!" he said. "These are pieces of eight." There were a dozen of the coins in the bag. "I can't take this." But even as he made to hand the purse back, he thought of Melony; there was enough money here to buy him several cattle, or a small boat. If he was a man who owned something, she would marry him.

"Keep them," the man said gruffly. "There's plenty more where they came from. I only hope they bring you better luck than they did me." He eyed the younger man. "I suppose I should tell you about it. A year ago we sailed from Jamestown down into the Caribbean, looking for cargoes. Our ship struck a reef off a place called The Turks and most of the company perished. Six of us got ashore onto those dreadful islands—nothing but sand and salt, no water, no food. There was another wreck already there, a great Spanish galleon, and thousands of coins like these in her. And gold and silver. I guess she had come from raiding the treasures of the southern Indians. In any event, there were the six of us surrounded by the greatest wealth we had ever dreamed of, and we would have exchanged all of it for bread and water." He sank back on the bed and sighed. "We were starving and near mad with thirst. On the fifth day we drew straws and young Jefferson was the loser. We killed him, ate him and drank his blood. A week later we drew again and Walters was the loser. While the other three slept after their 'feast' I lashed together a couple of spars and let the tide take me away from that terrible place. I preferred to die alone at sea rather than dine again on a shipmate—or be the next course myself. I don't know how long I drifted, but eventually I was cast up here in Bermuda. It is painful for me to recall those terrible events, so I hid myself in silence. Better to dance for coppers and drink myself into oblivion than face what happened to me." He sighed again. "So do not thank me for those coins. They brought me no good fortune."

Tom had listened to his story with horror at first, then with mounting excitement. All that treasure lying there to be collected. He could set himself up for life, be as rich as any of the nobs, marry Melony, be respected.

"Where in The Turks does the wreck lie? Could I find it?"

"It is about seventy-five yards off a long, low spit at the northeast corner of the northernmost island. When the tide is low the spars of the galleon are revealed. Yes, you could find it easily." He studied Tom in the dim light. "I suppose someone should get benefit from the treasure. I want nothing to do with it but you are welcome to try and recover it."

"If I succeed I shall be forever indebted to you. Anything you ask of me . . . surely you want to go home to Virginia. I will see you get there."

"No, I do not want to go home. I ate the flesh of a shipmate and deserted the other survivors. I must live with that for the rest of my days. So I wish to be seen as a drunken, insane mute. That is my penance. If you wish to do anything for me, you will merely keep my secret. Tell no one what I have told you and leave me in peace. Plunder the treasure if you wish but don't blame me if it brings you unhappiness."

Anne flung herself on her mother's bed, kicking her heels in frustration. She glared at Josie when she saw her smile.

"There's nothing funny about it, Mother," she snapped. "Two months married to that milksop and already I am going out of my mind. He floats about the house like some pale ghost, scared of his own shadow. All he worries about is his health. I swear he reads all the tracts from England, and everything in his medical library, looking for some new disease to catch."

"But look at who you have become, my dear. The grandest young lady in Bermuda. They are still talking about the wedding. And the house you live in; that should give you pleasure every day."

"I would sooner live in a hovel with a full-blooded man than in a palace with such a puny creature. His mother dominates him, just as she does her stupid husband, Septimus. And that sister—I think Richard would be happier married to her. They are a peculiar family."

"But they are our most successful family, and now, through you, we Pikes have joined them," Josie said. "That's all that matters—strengthening our position in the community. You have money and power, Anne, and that is all you need in life. Look at Amanda Fleet herself—how she runs her family—and emulate her."

"I could perhaps stand it if Richard were just a little more manly," Anne replied. "But the wedding night! Mother, all those things you told me didn't prepare me at all. It was a disaster. He tried and tried but nothing happened, pushing away at me with his limp little thing and all the time one hand on his chest to feel his heartbeat. I had to coax him along for hours before he got it where it was supposed to go. And then he gasped, jerked and thrashed around a moment and fell away from me. Well, you told me not to expect stars falling from the sky, or whatever, but it was such an anticlimax! He's only tried a couple more times with not much greater success." She laughed suddenly. "But I am pregnant, so he must have done something right."

"Pregnant? Are you sure? Oh, Anne, then there's nothing else to worry about. All the Fleets want is an heir. If it's a boy you can stop concerning yourself with Richard in bed. Take a lover, or forget the whole business of lovemaking. This is perfect, my dear, I could not be happier."

"Well, bully for you, Mother. I feel like I'm going to achieve virgin birth. If I have to be married, couldn't I get some passion from it? Over the years I have heard you and Father through the wall, and it certainly sounded as if you were enjoying the heights of passion. I'd like to have that, too."

"Later, dear, later. This is more important. The child is all that matters for now. After you've borne him a son you can do what you like with Richard Fleet." She counted on her fingers. "Let's see, then. The happy event will occur while you are overseas. That's good. You can have the child in Paris or London, where there are much better hospitals. And the birth will extend your trip, which is what you wanted."

"But I won't have any fun with a mewling child along. I wanted to be belle of all the balls; instead I'm to be a matron with ruined figure and squalling brat."

"Don't be tiresome, Anne. You will have wet nurses and nannies and maids, anyone you require. You won't need to spend a moment of your precious time with the child."

"I hope you're right," Anne sighed. She sat up. "I'll tell the Fleets the glad news tonight. That should put me in their good books. And, Mother, I want you to come to the house tomorrow to help me pack for the voyage. Only a week until we sail and I haven't done a speck of planning for my wardrobe. The carpenter has delivered the six cabin trunks I ordered, but I don't know if they will hold everything."

"No, six trunks will not be enough," Josie said. "But you can have some of mine. We must have you looking your most beautiful in Europe. I'm sure Europeans think we're just farmers in these faraway islands."

"It's her laugh that makes me grit my teeth," Richard scowled. "I hear it everywhere in the house, as if she is mocking me. And she's such an ignorant girl, Hilda. We have nothing to talk about."

"Poor Richard," his sister said. "You will just have to immerse yourself in other things. Your books, men friends. Be like Father and spend all your time at the Oceanic Club."

"What am I going to do with her on this extended jaunt through Europe? Every day the trip assumes new proportions. Now she talks of a year or more away from Bermuda."

"You can afford the time, Richard. After all, while Mother controls the company there's little enough for you to do here. Anyway, there's no use complaining about her just now. Little Anne is quite our mother's darling after last night's news. Good Lord! Do you realize this will make me an aunt! I feel positively old."

"Yes, at least I've done my duty by the family in that direction. I pray it will be a boy. The blessed Fleet name will be preserved and I will be left in peace."

"I don't know that this family is destined for peace. Prosperity, certainly, but peace, well, you must just make the best of it, Richard. Enjoy what you can." She kissed him lightly on the cheek. "It's time you were back to your own house, dear brother. You must have lots of packing to do and many farewells to make. Allow time to pay a formal call on the Governor. His daughter tells me he is sending the Marine Band to farewell you and Anne from the quayside. Quite an honor."

The owner's suite in the *Devonshire Queen* had been fitted out to Sep and Amanda's specifications. It was as sumptuous as befitted the flagship of the Fleet line, two bedrooms below the poop deck, a large sitting room with generous ports, and even a bathing tub and privy. Richard took his meals with the officers but Anne preferred to stay in the suite, pleading illness. She went on deck only once in the first seven days at sea.

The arrangement suited Richard. He enjoyed the company of the officers as much as he had come to despise the company of his wife. He found Captain Smutters's manner a little too familiar, but the captain was busy about the ship's tasks and dined alone, so Richard was not often exposed to him. The evenings passed pleasantly with a few tots of rum to accompany the game of whist in which, partnering the first mate, Richard was showing a handy profit.

This night he had forgotten to bring up the cards from his cabin; while the others waited patiently around the table he hurried below and stepped into the suite. It was the laugh that stopped him—her laugh, so distinctive and grating. But it was not mocking now. He stepped silently across the sitting room to the closed door of his wife's bedroom. The sounds were distinct: the laugh was a throaty chuckle and he heard her moaning as well, pleading. Richard listened with a sick fascination as the couple behind the door thrashed about and came to a noisy climax.

"Take it in your mouth," he heard Captain Smutters order her. "That's right, deeper, deeper. See how it grows. Now spread your legs again and I will ride you to another peak. Like this." Richard could hear her breath coming in gasps, then a quick, sharp cry.

He silently crossed to his own sleeping quarters, found the playing cards and returned to the whist table. The first mate said he looked pale and wondered if seasickness wasn't finally affecting him. Richard played very badly that night.

The secret would have been revealed sooner or later; Bermuda was too small a place to conceal anything important. Tom Winders felt he had to tell Crooke and Tropp about his good fortune. They had stood by him in the brawl and they would share with him the wealth to be plundered from the Spanish galleon. He swore them to silence about the source of his information, but within a week Ben Tropp had drunkenly blurted it all out to the mob in the Seahorse. Suddenly, treasure fever seized the colony. Tradesmen downed tools, farmers left their cattle, laborers walked off their jobs. Every man who had a shilling to his name decided to grab for the golden chance. In the end, sixty hopeful treasure seekers pooled their funds, chartered a leaky old schooner and set sail for The Turks.

"Let them go," Tom Winders said disgustedly as the hastily provisioned ship cast off from St. George's wharf. He was standing with Ben and Joshua among a throng of fearful, weeping wives and children. The three young men had, in the end, decided not to go on the voyage. It was too hastily conceived. There were too many desperate people going along; the whole endeavour had a pall of tragedy over it. "They are like a pack of dogs attacking one small beast; there will not be enough to go around and they will fall on each other," Tom said.

"If only I had kept my mouth shut," Ben muttered, deeply ashamed of letting Tom down and of the atrocities committed on the pitiful Virginian. The man had been tortured by a mob seeking more explicit information about the treasure; he had died of shock when the redhot fire-iron was applied to his eyes.

"Too late now," Tom said. "Just hope those desperate fools do not come to too much harm." He pushed his way through the crowd, leaving his companions. A new scheme was hatching in his brain now that his brief days of believing a Spanish treasure could make him rich were over. Now he hurried to Melony Stannard's house to tell her of the undertaking that would bring him more than enough fortune to marry her.

He found her in the blacksmith's shop at the back of the house, serving tea to her father and his assistant. Stannard the smithy nodded approvingly when he saw Tom.

"I thought you might have joined the other fools on their treasure quest," he said. "It was all I could do to stop the lad here downing tools and going with them. No good will come of it. Hard work is the only way to prosperity."

Tom accepted a cup of tea, thrilling to the touch of Melony's hand. She was so beautiful and delicate, unlike her mountain of a father who, for all his gentle nature, was the strongest man in the colony. And Melony's late grandfather: Tom could not believe she was from the same stock as the legendary figure who had chewed off Will Acton's ear in a tavern brawl.

"I think, Mr. Stannard, there is still money to be made in The Turks," Tom said. "But I agree with you hard work is the vital ingredient. The Virginian told me, in passing, there are vast deposits of salt in those islands. Both this colony and the Americas have an unquenchable appetite for salt. Without it they cannot preserve or ship their food. But the nearest deposits are at least a thousand miles south of The Turks. It seems to me a man could ship salt from those islands and undercut the market price by a few pennies a pound."

"You make good sense, Tom," Stannard said. "But how do you propose getting to the islands and mining the stuff?"

"The money the fellow gave me will suffice as a deposit on the charter of a slow but sturdy ship. And I shall hire some of the local slaves to do the digging and loading. Their masters will be pleased to turn a profit from them for a change. I can obtain provisions on credit, against an allocation of salt from the first shipment at a discounted rate."

"I like it," the smithy said. "I might invest a few pounds in your scheme myself if you can put it all together."

It was eight weeks before the handful of survivors of The Turks expedition steered their longboat into safe harbor. They brought with them a tale of horror, of friend battling friend at the site of the wreck, murders done in the night as each member of the party sought to increase his share of the plunder. A quarter of their number died before some sanity took over and all the treasure was loaded in the holds. The ship was resting dangerously low in the water when they finally set sail for home; supplies were almost exhausted and morale was low. And then a tempest that had been lurking in the area struck them. The ill-fitted ship had no chance and went down in the Gulf Stream with most of its complement and all the treasure. The expedition brought no wealth to Bermuda: it created forty-three new widows and their children, plunged into the most desperate poverty.

Westminster,
September 1664

My dear Hilda,

Greetings from the capital of the Civilized World! At least, now we have restored the monarchy, London can again make that claim. Really, the change since my last visit is incredible. That dreadful man Cromwell has gone from the scene, fled to France, I believe. He was never a patch on his father and is not at all missed here. Charles II is a most popular King and looks set for a long reign. The worst excesses of the Puritan times have been eliminated. Even the theaters are open again.

I have talked with our agents here and attended Parliament at their suggestion to lobby support for Bermuda. I was not awfully successful. They are content to leave our affairs in the hands of The Bermuda Company, and you and I well know how that once-great organization is failing us. I think it will soon be time for us to petition the King directly for some form of Home Rule. You might pass these thoughts on to our mother and present them as your own: I know she would pay no heed to anything I suggested.

The season is uncommonly mild and I have been walking great distances around the City. It is more crowded than ever and the conditions under which the poor live are deplorable. Rats, fleas, rabid dogs and cats—all the conditions are right for a really severe Plague and I intend to bring little Benbow home to Bermuda within the next few months. He is my son, all right! Pale, and susceptible to every illness. Poor child, cursed to be a weakling like me. His mother treats the little chap with contempt; she is most days too busy on her social rounds to see him at all. His first words were spoken to the wet nurse. Just between you and me, our marriage is a sham. She is a stupid, selfish girl and I fear she will blacken our good name. Oh, Hilda, I feel so sad when I think what might have been. I could have been a useful member of the family, I am sure, if our mother had allowed me some responsibility. But she

*has emasculated me as surely as she did our father.
And now I am saddled with another as bad as she.
There is no justice. The only bright speck on my hori-
zon is that I will see you by Christmas at the latest.*
                    All my love,
                    Richard.

Jonas Odlum stood bareheaded, the rain mingling
with the tears coursing down his cheeks, as the damp
earth was shoveled onto the coffin of Ewen Staley. His
loss was immense, for Ewen had been everything to
him—father, mentor, friend.

"Do not weep for him, Jonas," Rose said, her hand on
his arm. "He had a long and mostly happy life, and he
lived to see you successful and me married to you. It was
all he wanted."

Together they turned away from the grave and walked
out of the little churchyard. Jonas held her hand tightly.
The worst of his grief lifted. He again felt a sense of wonderment that this beautiful young creature was his wife.
They had married a year ago, on her fifteenth birthday.
At first Jonas approached the marriage as one of convenience: Ewen had not long to live and Jonas would be
his daughter's protector. But Rose would have none of it.
She loved him fiercely and brought that love to their bed
and into their daily lives.

Rose was a born businesswoman. Under her management the perfume factory expanded over and over again.
They now employed twenty workers and their product
was in great demand throughout Europe and even in
such unlikely places as New Amsterdam.

"He gave me so much," Jonas said. "And the greatest
gift of all, dear Rose, was you. I do not care about our
newfound wealth or even my surgeon's trade. All that
matters is being with you."

Their carriage took them back through the winding
lanes of Devonshire Parish to the big house Jonas had
built for them. Their four house servants were standing
at the foot of the entranceway, black faces sad with
mourning.

"He loved this house, Jonas," Rose said as she stepped down from the coach. "A week ago, as he was sinking, I sat with him in his room and told him a little white lie. That we would have to move him because his room would make a perfect nursery. I wasn't sure then, but it gave him so much pleasure to think a grandchild was on the way. And now, a week and many prayers later, it is no longer a fabrication. I'm pregnant, Jonas."

He held her to him; his joy, even on this day of awful sadness, was great.

"We must hurry and prepare for the people who are coming to pay their condolences," she said. They stepped into the front parlor dominated by a long table laden with food. "It looks fine, Mary," Rose told her cook. "Thank you."

They could hear the first carriages on the coral driveway; much of Bermuda could be expected to call and pay their last respects to the well-loved old man.

"There will be no Fleets here today, though," Rose said. "I personally called on Amanda Fleet to say she would be most welcome. I wanted those old hatreds dispelled at last. She was cool to me and said none of the family would be in attendance. I almost felt sorry for her, consumed by jealousy and suspicion."

"It will not matter for long, my dear," he said. "Future generations will forget about the bloody beginnings of our colony. And Amanda Fleet has much to·regret. Poor Richard has sunken into drunkenness and debauchery. He seems to feel the world has dealt him a bad hand and blames everyone around for it. And I hear the child, Benbow, is as sickly as Richard ever was."

That night, when the last of the mourners had gone, Jonas held her close to him in their bed. He gently touched her all over, thrilling at the life growing inside her.

"You do not need to treat me like glass," she teased. She kissed him firmly. "The baby will not come between us in any way. Make love to me now, Jonas."

Chapter Eleven
(1675–)

"I nominated Odlum for membership, Richard. I think
the least you could have done was talk to me before you
blackballed him." Tom Amberley was flushed with anger and wine. He waved a hand at the small number of
men in the Oceanic Club's bar. "God knows we're short
of members. And Jonas Odlum seems a perfectly suitable candidate. He's made a fortune in a very few years."

"This is a club for gentlemen, Amberley," Richard
Fleet snapped. "Just having money isn't enough to qual-
ify a man as a gentleman." He was drunk and surly. His
harlot of a wife had given him a hard time throughout
dinner and he had finally tossed a glass of claret in her
mocking face, stormed out of the house and made for the
sanctuary of the club. God knew he spent little enough
time in his own house anymore. His mother's death had
given him the excuse to occupy himself with the business of the shipping line. But there was little satisfaction in that. Richard always thought he was being
compared, poorly, with old Amanda and her skill.

"Why, having money is about the only qualification
any of us possess," Amberley said. "There's certainly not
a damn lot of breeding involved here."

"Speak for yourself," Richard snapped. "You're just a
damned lawyer and only in the colony a few years. Some
of us go right back to the founding fathers."

"Well, Odlum qualifies on that score," Amberley

taunted. "You and he have a father in common, the unfortunate Mr. Acton."

"I am a Fleet, sir. I bear the name proudly and warn you not to take it lightly."

"Of course. Of course," Amberley soothed. He had just remembered through the wine haze what important clients the Fleets were to his firm. And Richard was so unpredictable these days, the littlest thing could upset him. "Here, old chap, let me pour you another brandy."

Richard nodded grudgingly. No point in quarreling. There were few enough gentlemen to associate with in Bermuda that he had better not fight with any of them. He wondered if it wasn't time to take himself off on another trip; he could justify a little time in Boston, where the company's interests were large, or even London again. But his father was quite senile, sister Hilda showed no interest in the business, and Richard certainly was not going to let his wife anywhere near the office. He still believed his mother had schemed with Anne to cut him out of the running of the firm, just as his mother had brushed Septimus aside.

"Have you tried the new girl yet?" Amberley murmured. "The little dark English one. Does incredible things with her hips. Left me exhausted." He raised his glass solemnly. "A toast to your late father-in-law, Richard. Mr. Pike did us all a great service when he established this club."

Richard scowled. He did not like to be reminded of Nathaniel Pike's scandalous association with the Lapins; that was where his bitch of a wife had come from.

"No," he said. "I have not been with her. I'm getting to an age when whores offer little pleasure to me. Actually, I don't know that having a fancy bordello attached to our club is the right thing to do. It lowers the tone of the place. We're not some insignificant colony. I don't think our leading club should be part bawdy house."

"You'll find a lot of resistance to doing away with the girls," Amberley laughed. "For most of us it's the only sexual fun we get. Our wives are too busy competing in

the fashion stakes and gossiping about each other to give
a man a hearty tumble."

Fleet nodded. Sometimes the desire to go through the
baize door and up the stairs to the young women's apartments was overwhelming. But he mostly resisted,
through fear of being laughed at. Anne had certainly
done a job on him, aided by his mother. An image of Hilda flashed through his mind. Dear sister Hilda. If only
it could have been between them. Everything would
have been perfect. Sometimes he had to blink back tears
when he saw Hilda in her house, so happy with her children and her stolid farmer husband, Henry Baseheart.
Everyone seemed happy except him. Hilda with her fine,
healthy brood; Odlum with three strapping sons and a
lovely daughter. And all Richard had for his long and
miserable marriage was young Benbow, pale and weak
and timorous, twelve years old thanks only to the constant attentions of a nurse and the regular consultation
of doctors.

Tom Winders entered the club, brushing dust from his
cloak, and joined them at the bar.

"You would think, the scale of fees our host charges
us, he could at least put a new surface on the road," Winders complained. "I damn near choke when it's dry and
my carriage slips and slides all over the place when it's
wet. Really, Richard, the standards of the Oceanic are
slipping."

They certainly were, Fleet thought. A few years ago a
man like Winders would have been working in the cellars instead of expounding at the bar. But he held his
tongue; Tom Winders and his salt shipping were big revenue earners for the Fleets. It was all just commerce, he
reflected bitterly, everything that guided them. A man
might as well be living in London for all the romance and
adventure there was in Bermuda.

"Richard wants to get rid of the club's whores," Amberley said. "He thinks that would raise the tone of the
place."

"We may be forced to before long," Winders said. "It
was all very well getting rid of the Bermuda Company,

but now our own Assembly is making most peculiar noises. The Whig element campaigns for all kinds of moral reforms. I fear we have created a monster there."

"The Assembly can be safely ignored," Fleet said. "The real power will always rest with the Governor and the leading families. But this time I agree with the do-gooders. Prostitution should not be condoned by our leading citizens."

"That's nonsense, Richard." Young Guy Lapin had come up behind them unseen. "What harm can there be in the club's keeping an assortment of delightful young women for the members' enjoyment? It's in the finest traditions of the Oceanic." He signaled for a fresh round of drinks and slapped Fleet on the back. "Just because you're getting past it . . ."

Richard looked at him with loathing. So young, hand-some, sure of himself, growing rich from this club and clever investments instead of working hard for the colony as the rest of them did. Well, here was one chap he didn't need to be polite to.

"If you don't mind being known as a pimp, just as your father was a pimp, Lapin, that is your affair," Richard sneered. "But I value my good name and I think it is time we cleaned up this club. If need be, I and members of like mind will form a new one and leave this place to the Johnny-come-latelies."

Lapin flushed with anger.

"If you did that you'd be severely reducing your own wife's income," he said. "She still receives the dividend from the club she inherited from her parents."

"You will not mention my wife's name or affairs in this place, you insolent young cur!" He was shaking with rage and all the frustrations inside him. He forgot his puny stature and weak chest and took strength from the anger. He lashed out an arm and was lucky enough to catch the young man unbalanced: Lapin fell back against the oak bar and into the arms of Amberley.

"You have gone too far, sir," Lapin muttered as he re-gained his balance. "You Fleets may own every damn thing in these islands, but I am a free man and you have assaulted me. I will have satisfaction."

"Come now, Guy," Amberley said hurriedly. "It is only a drunken quarrel. No need to duel over it. Fleet will apologize to you; we'll all have a drink and be friends again."

"I shall certainly not apologize," Fleet snapped.

"Then choose the time and place and weapons," Lapin said. "I do not fancy handing a poor creature like you a lesson, but honor must be satisfied."

Suddenly Richard Fleet felt the courage drain out of him. All his life had been spent avoiding illness and danger, and here he was being cornered into a duel with this upstart young Frenchman. How he wished he was a strapping young man just for long enough to settle this fellow's impudence. But he knew he would have no chance against him on the dueling field. He looked around the bar: everyone was staring at him, waiting for him to accept the challenge.

"There is no honor involved," he finally said. He turned his back on Lapin and hurried toward the exit. He heard the mocking laughter all the way into his carriage and down the dusty drive.

"Leader of the Assembly," Rose teased. "How grand it sounds, Jonas. Should I sew you some fancy robes of office, or have the boys make you a mace to thump on the floor and bring them all to order?"

"Don't jest, my dear. I did not seek the office, but now they have elected me I must do my best. The Assembly has little enough power, but it is a gesture toward more democratic rule." Jonas smiled at his wife, knowing she was very proud of him.

"The children are certainly impressed," she said. "And the servants. And, dear Jonas, so am I. No one has worked harder for our community than you. You truly deserve the honor."

He put his hand on hers and lifted it to his lips. All the years of marriage and childbirth, of struggling to achieve success and dignity, had not changed her at all. She was still the beautiful creature he had so reluctantly taken under his wing. And now, in truth, it was she who looked after him.

"If there is any honor in this, the honor is yours," he said softly.

The grand offices of the Fleet Company were now the only refuge Richard had; his own home was a constant torment to him, with Anne jeering at him about his being shamed by young Lapin and even Benbow looking at him askance. He supposed the boy was suffering the taunts of his schoolmates—the story of the declined duel was all over the islands—but he wondered what the lad would have done in the same circumstances. Neither of them was adept with pistol or sword. Richard moodily listened to his chief clerk read the lists of ships and cargoes for the next month, gave his orders and dismissed the man. He gazed out into the dusty town square. He couldn't even walk out there without suspecting he heard laughter. He was Bermuda's favorite jest and all because of that smarmy son of a brothel-keeper.

He watched a pair of sailors from the French merchantman cross the square and stand before the Seahorse, apparently debating whether they had the price of a drink. Then, with exaggerated Gallic gestures, they turned away from the welcoming tavern and started back across the square. Blasted French, he thought, always making trouble but never there to pay the price when their fun was over. The current treaty with Paris wasn't worth the paper it was written on. The Frogs would abrogate it any moment now. He continued to watch the disgruntled matelots and the idea began to form.

It was all so simple. In the current climate of distrust of the French, the flimsiest of "evidence" would suffice. And Lapin's establishment was already unpopular with the Puritanical elements in the colony. Richard was so excited by his scheme, so pleased at the prospect of retaliating at his tormentor, he broke one of his few rules

and poured himself a large brandy even though the sun
was not quite over the yardarm.

Two weeks later, acting on the tip of an anonymous
informer, a platoon of His Majesty's Bermuda Regiment
smashed their way into the cellars of the Oceanic Club
and found, behind the wine barrels, three kegs of gunpowder and a letter to Guy Lapin from someone pur-
porting to be the French Government's agent in
Louisiana, exhorting him to move against the British in
Bermuda.

"Your Excellency, the trial must be stopped," Jonas
Odlum said. "It is a travesty of justice and will do Bermuda no credit, no matter how high the level of suspicion of France."

The Governor looked across his desk and sighed. He
was enjoying having their very own Gunpowder Plot; it
diverted attention from the real problems the colony
faced. And Lapin was the perfect scapegoat. He should
be in gaol, anyway, for the scandalous conduct he allowed at his club. But now Assembly Leader Odlum was
upsetting the applecart.

"Privately, Mr. Odlum, I may agree with you that this
Lapin fellow is just a dupe," the Governor said. "But he
is French. The gunpowder and the letter were found on
his premises. I think it will be as well that we hang him.
Swiftly. That action will discourage more efficient plot-
ters from trying to overthrow us. Do you see?"

"He has been set up," Jonas said. "We all know that,
and by whom. I urge you, sir, to abort this trial and we
can forget the whole sorry incident. I carry no grief for
Lapin—I was blackballed from his damned club—but I
cannot see injustice done, particularly when the action
will kill an innocent man and harm Bermuda in the eyes
of all fair men."

"It's gone too far," the Governor said. "And there are
powerful people interested in this prosecution. I couldn't
stop it without the most devilish difficulty."

"Sir, I have examined both the gunpowder and the letter. I know a little about the manufacture of various products and would be prepared to swear both paper and powder were made in England. And the language of the letter . . . no Frenchman wrote that!"

"Really, Odlum, this is getting us nowhere." The Governor was quite exasperated now. "The decision has been taken and this fellow will swing for his actions just as soon as the court reaches its verdict."

"I am sorry, sir. I must then warn you that I will raise this matter in tomorrow's session of the Assembly."

"The Assembly! It is just a sop to the people. I could abolish it like that." He snapped his fingers. "Don't threaten me with the Assembly, sir. I won't stand for it."

"I am not threatening you, Excellency, just seeking to avoid an injustice." He stood. "What can I tell my concerned fellow members?"

"Tell them to go to hell. The trial will proceed."

Jonas Odlum had no great gift for public speaking—and no love of hearing his own voice—so he relied on clarity to get his message across to the members of the Bermuda House of Assembly. He told them of the events surrounding the arrest and trial of M. Lapin, of his own deductions about the source of the evidence against Lapin, of the fact that Lapin was a Bermuda-born citizen and should not be condemned as a Frenchman. He stared back into the spectator pews as he mentioned that other citizens might well have motives for destroying Lapin; for a second his eyes met those of Richard Fleet, sitting with the boy, Benbow, beside him. Jonas was forced to look away, so intense was the hatred in Fleet's stare.

Jonas reminded the Assembly its charter was tenuous, that it served at the English government's pleasure. "But," he finished, "I would rather we were destroyed at birth than functioned impotently to a ripe old age." When he finished speaking, the Assembly voted unanimously to send a message to the Governor seeking the dropping of all charges against Lapin.

The Governor spent two days considering the message: on the one hand he would gravely offend the Fleet family if he set Lapin free; on the other, he would annoy the reform element in the English Parliament if he ignored the Assembly vote and disbanded the body. In the end he ordered Lapin freed and issued a proclamation to all citizens forbidding them from indulging in slanderous gossip about the events.

Richard Fleet was socially ruined by the affair. He heard the laughter of his fellow citizens, felt the lash of his wife's tongue, saw the pity and contempt in his son's eyes. It all forced him over the brink from deep melancholia into madness. If the Fleet companies had not been so well-established and prosperous and if Anne Fleet had not suddenly developed a business acumen as acute as her late mother-in-law, the family fortunes might have suffered severely.

But Anne, and later Benbow, kept the shipping line sailing ahead, and profits grew enormously. It was only when they gazed across the sound, to the large and happy home blessed with strong young sons to carry on the name of Odlum, that the Fleets felt impoverished.

Chapter Twelve
(1773–)

Staley Odlum twisted and turned, trying to get comfortable, but the hard wood of the family pew was not designed for comfort; church attendance was meant to be something of an ordeal. He listened to the Rev. Gilbert Bottom droning on, the recycled sermon already so familiar to Staley. Three months since his return from medical studies at Cambridge, and they seemed like months of Sundays all spent in the hot, dank little church with the droning of flies competing against Bottom's nasal sermonizing. Still, church attendance was about the only thing his mother demanded of him, so he would continue for her sake. He glanced at her beside him; she appeared to be immersed in Bottom's outpourings. The brim of her broad white hat bobbed as she nodded agreement. Staley smiled to himself. Constance was a paradox: so tough and brave within the family, so capable in business and yet so pious when exposed to a ranting little hypocrite like Bottom. Staley had heard about Bottom's scandalous conduct with the rectory maids, his drinking and the gambling debts he had incurred at the Oceanic Club. Yet every Sunday he was up in his pulpit haranguing them about what a sinful place Bermuda had become. Staley's father, Jason, had no time for hypocrisy. He simply refused to attend any of Bottom's services, so it had become Staley's task to escort his mother, little brothers and sister to church. There was one compensation, though. If he craned his neck he could just see the back of Mary Fleet's blond head, bowed and reverential as she sat in the Fleets' front pew. He concentrated his thoughts on her, willing her to glance around, and was rewarded a moment later when she did risk a glance in his direction. Staley winked, she blushed, and her brother Grantham glared at him.

"To convert the Chinese heathens, or the Hottentot, or the headhunters of the East Indies," the Rev. Bottom declaimed, "would be more easily accomplished than bringing real Christianity to Bermuda. This community owes allegiance only to Mammon. You leading citizens could do so much by example to lift up the lesser orders. But all of you are interested only in material things."

Constance Odlum's hat bobbed vigorously; Staley sighed. Bottom was half right, of course. The Forty Thieves, epitomized by the Fleet clan, were a puffed-up, self-satisfied lot, convinced God had put them down in Bermuda for the sole object of getting fat and rich. And what an uncultured crowd they were. He despised them as only a twenty-two-year-old fresh from the heady delights of sophisticated Cambridge could despise the bourgeoisie. Thank God his own family was humble about their success and realized Bermuda was just a very minor place in the scheme of world things. And thank God that Mary Fleet wasn't like the rest of her family. He ached for her touch, to taste again her cool lips, to laugh with her and share her joy with everything in her world. Bloody Grantham was glowering at him again. Stupid family feuds. It had all happened one hundred fifty years ago and surely ought to be forgotten now. But he was forbidden to call on Mary at the Fleet house, and when they could steal away to be together in the fields and woods, she was in constant fear of discovery.

"A new challenge faces us," Bottom said. Staley pricked up his ears. Anything new the minister had to say would be a welcome relief. "The American colonies," Bottom continued, "are becoming more fractious every day. An attempt at independence from Britain, while unlikely, is becoming a possibility. There has, from time to time, been similar seditious talk here. But we are English and will always remain English. That is our heritage. We must never give aid and comfort to misguided Americans. Should revolution come, it will be swiftly and savagely put down. But I caution each and every one of you against aiding the American rebels, if rebellion comes.''

Staley grinned to himself again. Any trouble in America would only work to Bermuda's benefit. These merchants and shippers had already grown rich on other people's conflicts. If the Brits went to war with the Americans, Bermuda would see to it that it supplied both sides. Ah, Bottom was running down at last and soon they would all be released into the summer sunshine. He hoped Mary would be able to disengage herself from the family circle and linger behind to walk with him awhile.

"I'm not sure I agree with Rev. Bottom about America,'' Constance Odlum said as she held Staley's arm and they walked from the church. "Here in the New World, England seems somehow irrelevant. And the taxes they impose on us to help pay for their constant wars! It would be better if we could leave all the old European feuds behind and get on with creating a new and just society here.''

"Leave old feuds behind!'' Staley laughed. "We've got enough feuds going in Bermuda to keep everyone happy. The ridiculous thing with the Fleets, for example.''

"Hush,'' she said, glancing around. "Poor Staley. Falling in love with a Fleet girl. If I had my way there would be no hurdles in your path. I'm only too happy to forget the feud which, God knows, has cost both our families so dearly. But you know it's Mary's family, not us, who keep it going. They hate us; they really believe the curse of Sarah Odlum is still on them.''

"A curse. How quaint.'' He waved his arm around, indicating the trim little church and its Sunday-suited worshipers. "How can people who profess to be Christians believe in curses?''

"My, you've become an intolerant young man since you went to university,'' she chided him. "We're really very simple people here in Bermuda. You'll have to bear with us."

He squeezed her arm affectionately. Dear Constance; she could see good in anyone.

Hiram Fleet was still congratulating Bottom, whose plump pale face glowed with pleasure at being spoken to by the colony's leading citizen.

"Quite right," the Fleet patriarch said again. "Got to strengthen our ties with England. Some of those Americans are mad. Had to be, didn't they, to sail on past Bermuda and settle in a hellhole like Virginia? Still, it will all come to nothing and they'll buckle under and do what London tells them to." Which was not quite what Hiram Fleet's agents in New York reported to him. They were sure there would be war, and he was well geared for it. If a Continental Army were raised, there would be an incredible demand for food and supplies; Fleet would be ready to supply that demand while at the same time replenishing the English forces. The prospect pleased him greatly, and he smiled and nodded when little Mary asked him if she might walk down into the village to sit with her friends.

Staley found her there after he had deposited his mother and the boys at home. His sister, Martha, accompanied him down to the St. George's waterfront and there, as he had hoped, was Mary sitting with a group of girls.

The waterfront was the one place where the young people of Bermuda—at least those of the prominent families—could meet and talk away from parental supervision. Soon Mary disentangled herself from her group and Martha wandered off to friends of her own.

"You looked so beautiful in church," Staley said as they strolled along the dock keeping a discreet distance between them. "The back of your neck was something to die for."

"Don't be silly, Staley." She blushed.

"And brother Grantham looked at me as if he'd gladly kill me," he said. "When will your family realize what a fine chap I am, what great prospects I have? It's time we were married, Mary."

"Be patient, please. You know how they feel about your family. I will work on them slowly."

"Can you sneak away on Wednesday afternoon? I'll be free of surgery until the evening. We could ride down to the South Shore."

"I'll try. It is very difficult. They watch me all the time. If I can get away, I'll meet you at the junction. Now I must go." She let her hand brush his for an instant, then hurried back down the dock to where her friends waited.

Tom Hogan left his attic above the Oceanic Club and made his way down the stairs to the main bar where the sounds of Sunday afternoon revelry were rising. If he spouted a few of his poems, someone would stand him drinks and for a while he would be able to banish the boredom and loneliness of his Bermuda exile. Three months now, and he'd just about worn out his welcome. At first, as the Irish poet down from America, he'd been lionized, invited to stay in the best houses, an honored guest at the great tables. But now, like all the Irish poets before him, he was wearing thin on the Forty Thieves. A little bit of culture was all right, but they couldn't be expected to subsidize it for more than a month or so. And now Hogan was reduced to the servants' quarters in the club.

"Ah, Hogan," Maurice Lapin called as he entered the bar. "A minute of your time, please." The club's proprietor was sitting at his baize-topped desk, a stack of chits in front of him. "There's the matter of your accounts, Hogan," Lapin said. "Over twenty-five pounds here. I'd like it settled."

Hogan would have liked to smash his greasy French face, but the Oceanic Club really was the end of the line for him and he needed to spin it out for a few more days; then the ship would be here for him and he could forget about Bermuda and all he'd been forced to endure. So he grinned the grin that had charmed all the ladies of the colony and clapped Lapin on the shoulder.

"I'll settle this week, my dear Maurice," he said. "Funds are coming from America at last. You've been most patient and I appreciate it. I shall write a new poem in celebration of your wonderful establishment." He leaned across the desk so his mouth was close to the proprietor's ear. "And what about the talks we've had, eh? When the war comes you'll get the chance to be most helpful to our cause. All the French will be on the side of the Americans against the British and you will be our man in Bermuda."

"For God's sake, shut up," Lapin said. He was pale suddenly. "Don't mention revolution here or you'll have us both hanged. It's hard enough being French in these times—it almost got my grandfather executed. I want nothing to do with your wild schemes. Just pay your bill and leave me in peace."

"You'll regret it," Hogan whispered. "Losing the chance to be a true friend of America. And men like Hiram Fleet will get rich out of the conflict, anyway, by shipping to both sides." He clapped Lapin on the shoulder again. "Just think. Bermuda could go independent too, in an alliance with America. You suffer just as badly as we do at the hands of London's tax collectors. I'm offering you the chance to get in on the ground floor, Maurice."

Lapin shrugged off his hand. He wanted nothing to do with revolutionaries and dreamers; he was very happy running his club and offending no one. He would have reported Hogan to the authorities, but he was not sure what kind of reception he would get. Anti-British feeling was running quite high in the colony, fanned by the stirring reports of the Virginians' refusal to knuckle under.

Hogan moved farther into the barroom. He'd never held out much hope for enlisting Lapin to the cause, but at least mentioning it had diverted his attention from the bill. Now he spied young Odlum sitting alone and looking gloomy at a table by the window.

"Dr. Odlum," he shouted. "Lost a patient? You look so unhappy, man. Let me sit with you and cheer you up. You're not even drinking. No wonder you are so down."

He called for two pints of porter and sat. He liked Staley Odlum; while both admired Bermuda's beauty, they shared the knowledge that it wasn't, as the Forty Thieves thought, the only place in the world. "What is it, Staley?" he asked more quietly. "The Fleet girl?"

Staley nodded miserably.

"The situation just gets worse, Tom," he said. "She cannot even speak to her family about us. They are implacable. All we can have are a few stolen moments, and never be too sure when they are going to be. I'm desperate."

"You should elope with the girl," Hogan said.

"Elope! In Bermuda? There's nowhere to elope to. You forget what a tiny place this is."

"No, elope to America. Start a new life in a big country. There's a great shortage of trained doctors. You would make a fine living. And think of the exciting events that lie ahead."

"Your revolution." Staley forced a smile. "Ah, Tom, I don't see me, a loyal colonist, coming to help fight your wars with Mother England. Though I'll concede you've got a good cause. But the thing is, for all my complaining about its provincialism, I love Bermuda. No, I could not run to America even if it meant Mary could be with me. I doubt she would leave Bermuda. Remember, she is a Fleet and that's about as important as you can be here."

"But she's only a woman, Fleet or not. She'd be better off with you than living forever in the shadow of her brothers."

"You'd be surprised just how much power the Fleet women have wielded," Staley said. "For all old Hiram's bluster, it's his wife who wears the pants in that family. And Mary's like her mother—clever and strong, streets ahead of her brothers."

"Spoken like a man in love! I'm afraid you too are a lost cause to me. My mission here has been an almost total failure." He signaled for two more pints. "George Mason and the rest of the Virginians will not be pleased." He dropped his voice. "They have arranged for me to sail from here on Thursday's tide and I'll be leaving most discreetly. If you change your mind between now and then, I'll be able to arrange a berth."

Staley let his gaze wander around the handsome, teak-lined room. At the big table in front of the windows overlooking the sound, a rowdy group was ensconced. Grantham Fleet was there, deferred to by the others. And his teenaged brother, Dorian, even more pale and frail than Grantham. Staley marveled at the bloodline which could produce sickly individuals like those two as well as a magnificent creature like Mary. He felt pity for them, despite their antagonism toward him. Staley was blessed with a strong body and robust health, and he always felt a little guilty when exposed to those less fortunate.

"You have to admire them," Hogan said, following his gaze. "A mean, untrustworthy pack of bastards, but my how they know the way to make fortunes build on fortunes. We shall have to deal with Hiram Fleet in the end and it will cost us a pretty penny. But he has the warehouses stuffed with the supplies we'll need and has the ships to deliver them to us."

"I wish you weren't so determined that there will be a war," Staley said. "I saw so many glimpses of war in Europe. It has become almost a sport there, a sport no one ever wins. I'd have hoped we could leave that stuff behind in the New World."

"It's not in man's nature to avoid war, Staley. Either the huge conflicts, which this one will surely be, or the small, personal ones that we all face. Else you would never consider courting Mary Fleet."

He thought of Hogan's remark as he waited for her at the junction of the South Shore road; the day was beautiful, with birds swooping and singing in the blue skies and a gentle wind bringing cooling relief from the ocean. He wished he did love someone else, so there would not be this need to skulk around, so he could shout his love aloud, celebrate it in public and consummate it in marriage. But as it was, he did not know from week to week when he would see her, when they could steal a few min-

utes together. He worried now that she would not be able
to come to him; it was long past noon. And then he heard
the clatter of hooves on the coral road and she came into
view, superbly mounted on her big gray hunter.

He sprang forward and grabbed the reins of the horse
and she bent down and offered her cheek to him. Then
she slipped down from the saddle and into his arms. For
a few moments they stood there embracing against the
wild and lovely background, ignoring their exposure.

"I'm sorry I was so long," she said, breaking away from
him. "Father was at home for luncheon and insisted on
my staying at table with him. He was talking about the
rumors that I have been seeing you. He was most unhappy."

"Let me talk to him," Staley said. He held her hands
in his. She was so lovely, and they were so suited to each
other. Surely her family would see that, understand, and
forget the old feuds.

"There is no talking to my family," she said, her pale
blue eyes clouded. "Not yet, at least. I think I shall be
able to win my mother over in the end." She glanced
around. "But not if we stand here in broad daylight
where any passing rider will see us. Come, Staley, tie the
horses in the trees and we'll walk down to the shore."

They moved down through the light timber, hand in
hand, and reached the ocean. The wide pink sands
stretched away from them in either direction; in the far
distance the hard white bones of a long-dead whale
framed the curve in the beach. They walked to a sheltered cove and dropped to the warm sand, immediately
embracing, their lips meeting hungrily. He felt her slim
young body against his and shivered in the heat; Staley
had no lust for her, only love, but when they were together like this he wondered if he could control himself.

"Don't pull away from me," she said softly. Her eyes
were open and staring into his. There was a look there,
something that made him tremble. "Stay close to me,
Staley. They give us so little time together. We must
make the most of it."

He trembled again when she raised his hand to her

breast; he would have stopped if he could but she was moving against him and his own body was responding. Her desperation and frustration were conveyed to him, and suddenly they were over the brink, going further than he had dreamed of.

"Take me," she whispered, "please take me. They will never let us be together, I know. Take me now and give me something to cherish for the rest of my days."

Her firm young breasts were somehow bared and he gazed upon them in wonderment. His lips descended to her nipples and at once the world was banished, the world that opposed their love. The sound of sea and wind and birds was stilled; only their breathing remained. Her riding skirt was pushed aside and his breeches unfastened as they joined together, defiantly, desperately, lovingly. It was out of their hands. Forbidden to love, they would take whatever they could get. Staley felt the climax rushing upon him; he opened his eyes and saw her wondrous face so close, a damp glow of desire bathing her forehead, the tiny pink tip of her tongue edging from her full lips. He felt himself coming, and the blood was thundering in his head, like hoofbeats pounding on firm sand. And as he released himself inside the girl he loved, he heard a whooping, hooting laughter.

The pack of horsemen were yelling and jeering, crowding each other for a better view of the lovers exposed in the cove. There were half a dozen of them, he thought, but it was hard to tell. His brain was swirling. Staley tugged down Mary's skirt and kept himself across her to give protection from the leering riders. And then the hullabaloo stopped, sinking to an embarrassed murmur as the invaders saw who it was they had disturbed.

"Mary!" Grantham Fleet shouted. "Get away from him! You flagrant whore!" His voice was cracking with rage and shame. He watched as Odlum stumbled from his sister, scrabbling to correct his dress. Grantham gave way to the fury in him and swung his riding whip across the young doctor's face, seeing the leather thong split the cheek. Blood began to bead along the raw edges of the wound.

He swung again and Staley threw an arm up to protect himself; the whip twined around it and he fell back, pulling Grantham from the saddle. And then the two young men were facing each other on the sand.

"I'll kill you," Grantham shouted, advancing. He was as tall as Staley but had none of his strength. When he tried to punch Staley the young doctor easily evaded the blow and pinned his arms to his side.

"I'm sorry, Grantham," he said. He was ashamed, embarrassed, horrified. "I want to marry your sister. Don't you see?" The other man seemed to relax so he released his grip. Grantham spun away from him and reached into his belt, withdrawing his pistol.

"She'll be a widow, then," he said, leveling the pistol at Staley's head.

"Hold on, Grantham," one of his companions called. "He's not carrying a gun. You'd better not shoot him."

"Someone give him one, then. We will duel like gentlemen, though I doubt an Odlum would understand the Code."

Another of the riders got down and thrust a pistol into Staley's hand; he let it hang down while he continued to stare into the long barrel of Grantham's weapon.

"Prepare to fight, damn you," Grantham said, "or I'll shoot you down right now."

"You'd better defend yourself," said the man who'd handed him the pistol. "I'll be your second." He laughed suddenly. "Though it'll not do you any good. Grantham's a crack shot, even in a blind rage."

Staley allowed himself to be led twenty paces down the beach. There was a buzzing in his ears, a film over his eyes. It was a dreadful nightmare being played out under the hot sun and clear blue sky. His second turned him around to face Grantham, and for an instant the tableau before him froze. The riders off to one side, Mary white-faced, in shock, huddled against a boulder, Grantham with feet apart, hate in his eyes and the pistol aimed.

The ball hit Staley in the left eye like the kick of a mule; he felt the flesh and bone expand and shatter. He staggered backward and involuntarily raised his own

pistol. He thought he would just discharge it in the air
and the whole thing would be over, except that, half
blinded and swaying from pain and shock, he had no control over the shot. It struck Grantham in the heart and
he pitched forward, his blood darkening the pink sand.

The scream seemed to be coming from far away, like
the call of a gull at sea. Staley shook his head and put a
hand to the gory mass where his eye had been. He could
just barely see Mary standing between him and the body
of her brother, her mouth open, desperate hands
stretched toward both of them. And then she turned from
him and fell, weeping, on Grantham's body. He had lost
her.

Constance held her son's head in her lap while Jason
Odlum heated the iron in the fire. Martha knelt on the
other side of the couch, dabbing cold cloths on her brother's wound. The two women closed their eyes as Jason
advanced on his son with the white-hot iron, but they
could not shut out the hissing sound as he cauterized the
wound, or the sound of Staley's gasp as the agony swept
through him just before he fainted.

They bandaged his head, trying not to look at the ugly
empty socket where an hour earlier a bright brown eye
had sparkled.

"I'm afraid, Father, deathly afraid," Martha said. She
saw her brother stir, and she clutched his hand. "He has
killed a Fleet. They will make him pay for it."

"Don't worry about that just now," Jason said. "It was
a duel and not illegal. But it is a terrible tragedy for both
families. Tomorrow, after the worst shock has passed, I
shall call on Hiram Fleet and offer my sympathy."

But that night the poet Tom Hogan rode up to their
house bringing bad and urgent news.

"Tomorrow the Fleets will swear out a warrant for
Staley's arrest," he told them. "Witnesses will say it was
not a duel, that Staley fired first and Grantham got off
a dying shot in self-defense. Hiram is determined Staley
will hang for this."

"What does Mary say?" Staley called. He was just

coming out of a drugged sleep. He pushed himself up from the couch and moved toward where they were huddled in the parlor. "She was there. She knows what happened."

Tom assisted Staley into a chair.

"She's in shock," he said gently. "But even when she comes to her senses, I do not think she will be able to speak for you, Staley. Her brother is dead and she has plunged back into the bosom of her family. Things are very grim."

"I don't care, anyway," Staley said. "Everything is ruined now. I have lost the one I loved. I have killed a man. And am myself hideously maimed. I may as well be hanged for all the grief I have caused."

"Nonsense," Tom Hogan said. "This is only a tragic setback, not the end of the world. But you have to get out of here, Staley. No jury will go against the wishes of the Fleets." He clapped the younger man's shoulder. "I sail for home on the morning tide, to Baltimore. It is a secret passage. You can come with me, at least until the situation here has resolved itself. And you might just prove useful to us. The way events are moving at home, I fear we are going to need the services of many doctors, even one-eyed ones."

Mary Fleet stood at the foot of her brother's grave and watched the sandy soil being piled on the coffin. It was no day for a burial, the wind warm and gentle, the sun high over the little graveyard, birds singing joyously. Mary felt herself in a trance and imagined it was she in the gleaming coffin unable to see the glories of a Bermuda day. It should be her body there, she thought. She had brought on all these dreadful events. She could not bear to look at her mother and father or her younger brother. Neither she nor they had been able to face the shame she had brought on the family. But when the grief was gone the shame would still be there. Mary knew that, at seventeen, her life as a respectable woman was over.

As the funeral ended she walked away from the mourners, slowly climbing through the narrow lanes and heading for the fields beyond the town. No one moved to stop her going and no one saw her continue to the edge of the cliffs. She stood there some minutes, looking back at the island she loved so, then out to sea, to where the man she had loved had escaped. She whispered Godspeed to him and Godspeed to her brother and then flung herself out and over the cliff edge, flying through the warm air toward the blue sea, crashing on the rocks far below.

"You must be strong, Father," Martha Odlum said. "We have suffered, but not so grievously as the poor Fleets. Staley is all right in his new life in America, though I wish he hadn't embraced the cause of independence so vigorously. But look at the Fleets! Two of their three children taken from them."

"I know, my dear," Jason said. "I should be grateful our loss was not greater. We still have you and the little ones. But somehow, Staley being the firstborn and a surgeon . . . you know I don't love any of you the less. It's just that I wanted to see him practicing medicine here, for the good of all Bermudians. I suppose the great success of our factory is fine, but that's more the doing of your mother. And you will take after her. The medicine was something I could share with the boy."

"Perhaps Justin or Corin will become doctors," his wife said. Constance had put aside her own grief; she knew how deeply the tragic events had hurt her husband. "And perhaps, in time, Staley can come home."

"No. I am resigned to that. It will never be safe for him here again." The sadness in his voice brought tears to the eyes of mother and daughter. Later, when he had wandered off into the garden to sit gazing out over the water, they talked.

"You mustn't think of him as a weak man," Constance said. "Rather, he is gentle. Tragedy and violence bewilder him. The Odlum menfolk have all been like that, which has put them at odds with the tempestuous nature of Bermuda. It seems the women of the family have been able to cope better here."

"I agree," Martha said. "I have always admired the way you have handled things—the family, the business, the politics of life here. I fear, though, I'll never be able to do as well."

"God knows, I hope you won't have to. Surely, one of these days, things will settle down." Her mother looked suddenly old and tired, at last letting the shocks of the past week wash over her. Martha stood by her and held her hand. They would need to pool their strength if the family was to be kept going.

Hiram Fleet had been drinking heavily for many years; he now increased his consumption to cushion his anguish. His wife, Jane, and the boy, Dorian, became almost used to the nightly stream of incoherent abuse he poured on them. The Fleet women had always been whores, he said. If Mary hadn't been a whore, Grantham would still be alive. If Jane had been a respectable wife and mother, instead of scandalizing Bermuda with her conduct, maybe Dorian would be growing up into something a father could be proud of. If the cursed Odlums had never arrived in the islands . . . it was a relief when he would finally pass out and be carried to bed by his servants.

"Don't ever become like him," Jane Fleet warned her surviving child. "He has always blamed his misfortunes on others. There is a bad streak in this line, but some of the Fleets have gone out of their way to make it worse. The Fleets have always been blessed with wealth and influence but have not often put them to good use."

"Yes, Mother," Dorian said. He tried to be a dutiful son, but it was hard. His father had been cold and unloving to him from birth; during Hiram's long trips overseas there had been other men, like Mr. Amberley, the lawyer, who came to dinner and, after the children were in bed, could be heard laughing in Jane's boudoir. Dorian hadn't liked Grantham much, either. His big brother had been too much a model of their father. Only Mary had been good to him and he missed her dreadfully. It was the fault of the Odlums that she was taken from him, and he hated the Odlums for it, hated in the way that only a lonely, confused fifteen-year-old could.

Jim Youngblood was never prouder of his reading ability than on the occasions when the *Clarion* contained real news and his neighbors gathered outside his cottage to hear it from him. On this night there were more than a dozen standing in the dusty street, a few freed slaves, and others of mixed race like Youngblood.

They listened quietly as he read them the news of the first months of the War of Revolution, repeating silently to themselves the strange place-names where the battles were being fought. The questions started when Jim had finished the three pages the *Clarion* had devoted to the stirring events.

"It doesn't say who will win," a freed slave said. "Surely the British will triumph? Their army is so big and well equipped. And their navy rules the seas."

"General Washington is outnumbered, yes," Jim replied. "But, as the reports say, he plays hit and run with the enemy. And the British troops move very slowly."

"If the Revolution does succeed, what would it mean for us black people?" another who had achieved manumission asked. "Would this General Washington abolish slavery in the Americas?"

"I'm afraid this war is about freedom for whites only," Jim said. "It will be a long time before an army will march to defend the rights of the black man." The listeners nodded; they all respected Youngblood's opinions. He had, like his family before him, sailed the world's oceans in the service of the Fleets but had not been content to remain a mere seaman. With his savings and his knowledge, he was now the owner of a waterfront stall catering to visiting sailors. And of course the white blood in his veins was from a Fleet.

"At least the war is bringing prosperity to Bermuda," Jim said. "The port is constantly filled with provisioning warships; the warehouses are overflowing with American produce waiting to be transshipped. Even our slave brothers benefit when times are good here."

* * *

Times were not good for Staley Odlum. He was a Sur-
geon-Captain with General Arnold, and the winter siege
of Quebec was producing terrible injuries in the American ranks. Staley cursed his missing eye for the way it
hampered his surgery, cursed the stupidity of the American leaders who had ordered this futile Canadian campaign, cursed the snow and biting gales. But he worked
tirelessly and skillfully, and among the lives he saved on
the operating table there were many who would forever
sing his praises.

After the Quebec campaign was abandoned, Staley
found himself transferred to Washington's staff where
things were marginally better. At least it wasn't cold all
the time, although supplies remained woefully inadequate. He had no time to mourn his lot, could only dream
of Bermuda and sunshine and the loved ones he had left
behind. But somehow the war was purging him of grief
and guilt; during the disaster of Long Island he and his
fellow surgeons ministered to hundreds of American
casualties. Amid the blood and gore he found a kind of
peace in his work and a real commitment to Washington
and the American cause. Washington had already recognized the eye-patched young doctor as a man of great
skill and bravery; Staley was twice promoted by the
General himself.

The sad news reached Staley just after the successes
at Trenton and Princeton. The letter had been following
him for three months. His sister wrote that their mother
was dying and could Staley possibly make contact with
her. Just a letter to tell Constance of his doings, Martha
wrote, would cheer her tremendously.

Staley's General arranged more than that. There was
a lull in the fighting, and the Americans again had some
access to the sea-lanes. He suggested Staley accompany
an American frigate to Bermuda in an attempt to raise
supplies and support in the colony.

Maurice Lapin was nervous but he was also ambitious
for his scheme. Since the French had joined the Ameri-

cans against the British, Lapin had gone to great pains
to remind the community he was a fourth-generation
Bermudian; still, he knew they were suspicious of him.
Now he sat in Hiram Fleet's outer office twisting his hat
in his hand and waiting for the old man's summons.
When it came, Lapin stood awkwardly before Fleet's
desk, unsure of how to proceed. The two men had never
met except in the confines of the Oceanic Club.

"You might as well sit down," Fleet said. His head
ached, his gout was raging and the last thing he wanted
to be doing was meeting with this Frog. "Get on with it,
man. What's this scheme you have to put to me?"

Lapin began haltingly but his confidence grew as he
explained his desire—to start a new bank in Bermuda,
with men like Fleet and Amberley on its board, a bank
to do real business, not like the existing ones, which were
only countinghouses.

"And it would have connections in New York and
Paris," he said. "We would break away from the financial domination of London and find new sources of funds
to advance our various schemes." He dropped his voice.
"It now seems inevitable the British will be defeated in
the Revolutionary War. When that happens, a tremendous new area of trade will open between Europe and
America. We in Bermuda will be in the box seat to service it. No one has yet realized the vast profits a modern,
well-connected and well-financed bank could attain."

Fleet nodded. He had long found dealing with the London banks irksome. They took so long to make decisions
and charged such usurious rates when they did decide to
make a loan. But Lapin was hardly the man to start such
a venture.

"You couldn't afford it," Fleet said. "It would cost
thousands of pounds."

"I'm prepared to put up ten thousand pounds," Lapin
replied. "I would expect each of the directors to put up a
thousand each. And I have a line of credit in Paris for
fifty thousand francs. There would be more than sufficient working capital."

Fleet whistled under his breath. The Oceanic Club

must be a bigger gold mine than any of them had estimated. He wondered how much of his own family's vast fortune had been squandered there.

"The money sounds right," he allowed. "But why you? Why should we do business with you, earning you instant respectability?"

"For the reason all good business decisions are made. Profit." Lapin was not at all afraid now. He could see the greed in Hiram Fleet's bloodshot blue eyes. "I have the connections in America and Europe. The Americans, in particular, would deal with no one else but me. I have been working with them as their secret agent here. When victory comes, I will be rewarded." He stood up. "Perhaps this will convince you to join in my scheme. There is a party of Americans here now, moored off Sandys Parish. They are taking on some vital supplies I have arranged for them."

Fleet shrugged. "So what? As long as the Americans have been discreet, we haven't minded their calling here. It's the British Navy they've got to worry about, not businessmen like me."

"It is not what they are taking on that should interest you," Lapin said. "It is the cargo they brought here. Staley Odlum arrived last night, heavily disguised, to visit his dying mother. I believe he is even now at her bedside and will be until the frigate sails tomorrow."

Fleet shoved back his chair and started for the door, brushing Lapin aside.

"If what you say is right," he said, "I shall be in your debt. I will support your bank."

"She still looks so strong," Staley said. "It's hard to believe the disease will take her soon. The only thing I'm glad of is that she is still herself, still brave old Constance, right to the end."

"Your visit has lifted her tremendously," his father said. "She had given up hope of ever seeing you again. Now she will die happy."

"It seems so unfair," Martha said.

"No," Jason Odlum told his daughter. "Your mother

and I have each enjoyed full and satisfying lives. My time will come soon and, like Constance, I shall have no regrets. It's your turn now."

"Tell us about the war, Staley," Justin demanded. "Are the Americans going to win?"

"Everyone here reckons the British will be unbeatable in the long run," Corin said.

Staley smiled at his young brothers, so enthused by the historic events taking place eight hundred miles from their tranquil island. He fervently hoped they would never see what he had.

"The Americans will win," he said. "Washington is a genius and has the people of the colonies behind him. He is, really, the only thing holding the revolutionaries together. As for the British, they outnumber us but we are more mobile. And now that the French have the English Navy tied up, it is only a matter of time."

"I wish it would end and you could come home," Martha said. "We all miss you so."

"Even if I could come home to Bermuda a free man, I doubt that I would," Staley said. "My future is in America now. I shall just have to start a new branch of the family there. The opportunities are so great, the challenge so worthwhile, in America."

There was a banging on the door; the lamp on the table before them flickered and they all looked up in alarm. Then Jubilee, their manservant, was being pushed into the room by three soldiers carrying flintlocks. From the corner of his eye Staley saw his brothers rising to oppose them. He waved them back down.

"Do nothing," he ordered. "We must not disturb Mother." He stood up and crossed to the soldiers. "You've come for me, gentlemen, and here I am. Let us depart."

The charges were murder and treason, Martha was told when she called on the magistrate at St. George's first thing the next morning. The magistrate was almost apologetic; it was a damned shame Staley had taken the risk of coming home, he said. Now he would certainly hang. Martha wept and begged to see her brother. There would be no difficulty about that, the magistrate said. He would issue her with a laissez passer.

Just before noon, with the sun hot overhead and no one stirring in the town square, Martha entered the jail accompanied by Jubilee, who carried a parasol to shade her and a basket of food for Staley. The guard admitted them to the cell, then withdrew.

"We've got to hurry," Martha said before Staley could speak. "Change clothes with Jubilee, quickly." She turned her back as the two men stripped and redressed. From the basket she took creams and powders and went to work on Staley's face with a blend of soot and soft soap. Within minutes he was as black as Jubilee. Then she reversed the process, using powdered chalk to lighten Jubilee's features.

"A nice try, Martha," Staley said. "But it won't work. You forget about my eye." He touched the black eye patch.

"Trust me," she said. "The guard didn't bother to observe Jubilee as we came in. He was indifferent to him. But we will give him something to look at as we leave. You, as Jubilee, will give him 'the evil eye.' He'll be so disturbed we will be able to stroll away from here. A horse is waiting for you and you'll just have time to make your ship."

He looked puzzled, but allowed her to remove his eye patch and put it on Jubilee. Then she produced the last item from her basket, a glowing, bright amber orb.

"I trust it will fit in your socket," she said. "Father and I spent all night cutting and polishing it to what we guessed were the right dimensions. Try it." She passed it into his hand and watched as he squeezed it into his eye socket. "It's ambergris, Staley, carved from the lump Jonas Odlum found one hundred fifty years ago." She studied him. "Oh, yes! That is most effective. You look quite terrifying. Now we must go. Jubilee, my family will never be able to reward you enough for what you have done. But we will try. Staley, you must knock Jubilee unconscious, or at least produce a promising bruise on his chin."

Staley shrugged; he was bemused by all this. It would never work. But he did as she told him and gave Jubilee a smart tap on the jaw and the tall black man sprawled on the cot against the cell wall.

When the guard answered Martha's call, he glanced into the cell and saw the prisoner slumped on his bed, the eye patch black against the white skin. And he looked at Martha's servant and recoiled: the nigger had a blazing yellow eye, the look of the devil for sure. The guard waved them out of the jail, keeping his distance from the slave with the ferocious countenance.

There was talk of charging Martha and lynching Jubilee; but she stuck to her story that her brother had overcome the slave, then threatened her with death if she did not do his bidding. No one really believed it, but it was easier to let the matter rest. And it was putting one over on the Fleets, an enjoyment the community did not often get.

From the Bermuda Clarion,
August 30, 1789

His Excellency the Governor reports receiving several petitions seeking to make the new town of Hamilton an official port of entry for the colony. Already many colonists have taken up land around the new town. Mr. Maurice Lapin, of the Bank of Oceania, informs us he will shortly open a branch office in Hamilton to serve the bank's customers residing there.

News of interest to the colony from New York concerns a former resident of Bermuda, Dr. Staley Odlum. After his recent inauguration, President George Washington was pleased to grant Dr. Odlum an estate of some seven thousand acres on the Hudson River, which flows past New York. Dr. Odlum is currently chief surgeon at the American Hospital on Broadway, New York. He was Surgeon General under Pres. Washington in the Revolutionary War and was known to all as

"Dr. Yellow-Eye" for the distinguishing glass eye he wears.

Dorian Fleet, Esq., announces a new monthly passenger and cargo service between Bermuda and New York. One innovative feature of the new service will be that small items, viz. letters, packages, will be accepted at a rate of one shilling per ounce. The service will also attempt to land, fresh, in the New York markets the Bermuda Onion, which delicacy has the potential to earn great profits for our farmers.

The Odlum Perfumery advises it has vacancies for one dozen more Willing Workers due to the rapid expansion of its output. The Perfumery has just secured its first major order from Paris, which may be described as shipping coals to Newcastle successfully. The proprietor, Miss Martha Odlum, assures all that their renowned range of patent medicines will continue to be manufactured for the health of the Colony despite the rapid expansion of production in other lines.

Chapter Thirteen
(1950–)

Matthew Youngblood was shown into the office in the Assembly building. He waited, hat in hand, until Primrose Odlum Billings arrived from the debating chamber. He was nervous but determined not to show it. He had caught the glances as he'd strolled to the building in the morning sun; his well-cut New York suit was not the garb of a normal young black Bermudian. But he had walked tall and proud, trusting his education and experience would carry him through in the land of his birth, a land he scarcely knew.

"I'm sorry to have kept you waiting, Mr. Youngblood," she said. "Please sit down." She studied him with interest; Billy Youngblood's boy come home at last. She saw a tall, light-skinned young man, perhaps thirty years old, leanly handsome. She had responded at once to his written request for an interview; like everyone else in the colony she was keen to know just how the first black Bermudian to gain professional qualifications had turned out.

"It's good of you to see me," he said. "My father suggested you would be one of the first people I needed to speak with. Since father's death, your brother, Dr. Cable, has kept an eye on our family." He could see the family resemblance. Primrose Odlum Billings was tall and strong, almost rawboned, maturely handsome, her steady brown eyes meeting his.

"So what can I do for you, Mr. Youngblood?" she asked. "You said in your note you are returning to live in Bermuda."

"Yes. It's time to make that decision. I have a young wife, and when we start our family I want it to be here, in my own birthplace." He grinned suddenly and his whole face lit up. "My father was very much against the idea, based on his own experience. He said if I was crazy enough to come back to Bermuda, to make darned sure I had nothing to do with the Fleets."

"Good advice," she said, smiling, too. "But, really, there aren't many Fleets left. Just Veronica and her nephew. Time hasn't been kind to their clan, unless you count all the new ships and hotels they've acquired since the end of the war."

"The help I'm going to need, ma'am, is in being allowed to practice here as a lawyer. I understand there's never been a black one before and I figure I'm going to need all the guidance I can get. I don't want to make any waves, so I thought if someone like you would be prepared to explain to the Admissions Board and to the Assemblymen that I only want to work among my own people—"

"We could use a few wave-makers around here," she said, "but I guess you're right to start quietly. Don't upset the Forty Thieves, right? Anyway, I'll be glad to sponsor you before the various committees." She laughed. "Some of them aren't going to like it at all."

"Thanks. Your own son's a lawyer, I understand. Is he going to practice in Bermuda?"

"No, I don't think so," she said. He saw the sadness in her eyes. "After Jeff finished Princeton he took a job in Boston and I don't think we'll ever get him home again. He's not even working with our family company. But we can't dictate to young people, and I understand how confining Bermuda must seem to them once they've been in the outside world. We should all welcome you back, Mr. Youngblood. You are reversing the drift."

"I don't think too many other whites will look at it that way," he said. Their eyes met again and they understood each other. "But I give you my word, I'll do nothing to embarrass you in sponsoring me."

"It's 1950, Mr. Youngblood. Modern times. We don't have to worry about embarrassments, we have to do something about making this a unified community. You could play an important role."

He waited until the evening to call on Captain Smutters, not wanting to visit the Fleet offices. The housekeeper at the Smutters cottage looked at him curiously: his dress entitled him to be there at the front door but his color did not. She was deciding whether to send him around the back when Smutters appeared in the hallway.

"Come in, come in," Henry Smutters boomed. "You're Billy Youngblood's boy. I'd recognize you anywhere, even if I hadn't already heard you were back in town." He led the younger man down the hall and into a cozy study. "I was sorry to hear about your father," he said, waving Matthew to a seat. "He was a good man. And I'm very pleased with the way you turned out."

"All thanks to you, sir. My father told us, over and over, what you did for him. The money—"

"Nothing more than he deserved. He was badly treated. And the money came from a place it would never be missed. You don't owe me any thanks. So what have you come back for?"

"It's where I belong. And I want to help my people. I saw what being able to afford an education did for me; I want more of our young people to have the same chance, to prove we don't have to remain domestic servants and taxi drivers."

"You'll find lean pickings from your own people," Smutters said. "They have so little money. And you know none of the whites will ever employ you as a lawyer. But good luck to you, anyway. If there's anything I can do to help, just call."

They found a cottage to rent in the black section of St. George's. It was much humbler than the Harlem apartment, but as each day passed Matthew found himself falling more in love with his island. Instead of the rush of New York there was peace and warmth, soft evenings with the sea lapping the sand, and shared laughter and talk.

"It's going to be all right for you, Allie, isn't it?" he asked his wife as they lay in their bed. It was his one big worry, that Allie—New York born and bred—would not be able to settle here.

"I'll adjust," she said, snuggling against him. "The women think my clothes are too smart and my skin's too light, but they'll come around. And as long as I've got you, nothing else matters." She pressed her long thin body against his, felt the hardness and brought him into her. They made love long into the night and then he slept with his head between her breasts. She cradled him there and lay listening to the night sounds of tree frogs, the sea and a lonely bird. "There was never any choice, Matthew Youngblood," she murmured. "From the day I met you, I knew you had to come home to Bermuda; and if I wanted to be with you, I had to come too. We'll make it work."

The meeting of the Bermuda Hotels Association was dominated, as usual, by Veronica Fleet and her various managers. Most of the members operated guest houses or small cottage colonies and had little say in the association's affairs; policy was set by the Fleets. Today Veronica was determined to have her way.

"Last year," she reminded them, "against all good sense, to avoid a confrontation with the so-called 'union,' we granted the hotel workers a ten percent pay rise. We were assured we would get better productivity and a higher standard of work from them in return for that." She swept her ice-blue gaze around the table; no one was willing to meet it. Veronica Fleet in full cry was not a person to be opposed. "Well, I've just done my figures for the period since that rise and it has cost me dearly. Of course productivity hasn't improved; of course standards are no better. Will we never learn about these people?" There was no reply.

"All right. I propose we fix this situation once and for all. We do not need all our workers during the off-season. Probably three in four can be laid off for the winter months. So all employment contracts will be written for only eight months of the year."

More silence. The simplicity of the plan—and its ramifications—sank in.

"I say, Mrs. Marsden," Harry Groth, who ran the Placid Beach Cottages, began tentatively. He caught the full force of her glare. "I'm sorry . . . Miss Fleet. What I wanted to say was that surely this would cause terrible hardship to our workers. The layabouts among them might like the idea of a four-month holiday, but the best and most conscientious would be hurt badly. How would they support their families in the off-season?"

"I've thought of that," she snapped. "During the period they are working, we deduct and hold in trust for them twenty percent of their wages. Then we return the money at the beginning of the layoff season. Apart from anything else, it will teach the blacks the value of saving."

"And it will more than make up for last year's raise," the proprietor of the Blue Grotto Guest House said, beaming.

"Precisely, Mr. Thomas," she said, favoring him with a smile.

"They won't stand for it," Harry Groth said. "No white worker would. And I doubt it's legal."

"Nonsense," Veronica said. "We are the employers and can do as we damn well please. And if they want to strike, let 'em. We'll be retaining our best workers—say about a quarter of the total force—all year round, anyway, so they won't go out on strike, and we'll be able to keep operating until the others are starved back to their jobs. And there'll be no nasty picket lines to disturb our guests—the police will see to that."

They filed out of the meeting in silence, impressed yet again by Veronica Fleet's ruthlessness.

"She could be a man, that one," Thomas said when they were safely out in Front Street. "She's as tough as her old father ever was."

The years of frustrated drinking had taken a heavy toll on John Clay's body, but this night he was almost as strong and pure as the youth who, three decades earlier, had enthralled them with his feats on the cricket field. He stood at the lectern in the Good Hope Bible Society Hall and looked out into the sea of black faces. It was the biggest industrial meeting ever held, bigger even than the one where they had finally formed their hotel workers' union.

"Brothers and sisters!" Clay roared, raising his massive hands above his head to silence them. "Brothers and sisters, and the few of you in this hall who are police spies, we are gathered here to protest this latest evil act committed on the honest workers of Bermuda. They cannot do this to us and they will not!" He waited for the cheers to subside. "It is more than a hundred years since slavery was officially abolished here. But we know the cursed thing has never ended. As long as a group of privileged whites can do to honest workers what these people are trying to do, we will never be free. So what we must do, tonight, is send them a resounding No to their cruel scheme." More cheers. "It will not be easy," Clay said. "They will try to divide us, to offer some of us jobs while the rest of us stand in the streets. We must stick together to the end, to the point where they know we can never again be taken for granted. If we stick together, if we share all we have, if we join in to harvest our fields and fish our ocean, we can hold out longer than the oppressors in the Hotel Association."

They held for a week, and by the end of that time the hotels were desperate. It was the height of the season and the white managements could not cope with the demanding tourists who packed their hotels. Worse, a report of the strike appeared in the New York *Times* and cancellations began to flow in. Even those non-members of the Forty Thieves who were secretly pleased to see Veronica Fleet fall flat on her stuck-up face knew the strike had to be ended quickly: every business was beginning to suffer.

"Sure, they're hurting," Matthew Youngblood said. "But so are we all. And if Bermuda's economy was to suffer long-term from this dispute, John, we would all be equally to blame. I think the time is fast approaching for negotiations."

"Bullshit, man. No negotiations, only capitulation on the bosses' part." John Clay was feeling jubilant and defiant and he didn't need some kid lawyer from New York to tell him what to do. "You've done your job for us, drawing up the union's constitution, but it's me who has to put steel in the workers' spines."

"I'd rather be putting food in their bellies by finding a way to end this," Matthew said.

"God, you're just like your daddy. I always told Billy he was an Uncle Tom. We're going to make this strike bigger and more painful before we end it. I reckon I might bring all the shop workers out, as well."

"And what will that achieve? The few households who do have someone bringing in a wage will be reduced to nothing and there'll be even less for everyone to share."

"You don't know about industrial relations, sonny, for all your fancy schooling. You just leave this to old John Clay. I'll have those bastards begging for mercy."

The Governor, under extreme pressure from the hotel owners, declared a State of Emergency in the second week of the strike. The declaration ordered the strikers back to work under threat of jail. Primrose was the only member of the Assembly to speak against it; she called for negotiations but was howled down.

Baton-wielding police were sent into the black ghetto to round up John Clay and his key followers; in the pitched battle that followed, three constables suffered severe injuries, the unionists were beaten into insensibility and Clay himself was charged with inciting to riot, assault causing grievous bodily harm and resisting arrest. He refused Matthew's legal help and defended himself, his address to the all-white jury comprising a bitter attack on the oppression of his people and the promise that blood would flow in the streets. He was jailed for two years.

Matthew Youngblood was eventually able to have this reduced to a suspended sentence, although he could not get the lifetime ban against Clay's holding any union office lifted. Matthew also negotiated a new deal with the hotel association guaranteeing ten months' work per year and removing the forced savings scheme. The more moderate blacks thought he had done well by them; Clay's faction was outraged and, forced underground, began what would be years of plotting against the entrenched whites and what they saw as their black lackeys.

But tourism again boomed and Bermuda was, on the surface, happy, prosperous and secure. When Matthew and Allie Youngblood's son, Stephen, was born in 1955, the proud parents had some reason to believe he would grow up in peace and plenty on the island of his people.

Primrose attended the christening ceremony along with a handful of other whites who were quietly working for change and a better deal for the blacks.

"Thank you for coming, ma'am," Matthew said. "I just hope I've kept my first promise to you, that I wouldn't embarrass you."

"Oh, no, Mr. Youngblood," Primrose said. "There's been no embarrassment. But let's see what the future brings." She patted the head of the baby. "This little fellow will be in for quite a tempestuous time."

"I don't see why you needed me here, Mother," Jeff Billings grumbled. "It's only a publicity stunt, the revealing of the Kosmos Girl." He looked around the Manhattan boardroom, the tables laden with food and drink for the media. "My Boston partners wouldn't approve of a show like this."

"Don't be so stuffy, Jeff," Primrose laughed. "Not yet thirty and turning into a prim and proper Boston lawyer. You need a little fun in your life. And you are a member of the Kosmos board, and the Kosmos Girl is winning a hundred-thousand-a-year contract to be our 'image.' It's all quite serious business, really."

"You never cease to amaze me," he said fondly. "In your own quiet way you've taken the company so far, and now this—I've got to admit you've had a hell of a lot of exposure with the search for the Kosmos Girl. The shares are booming again. I see the *Wall Street Journal* nominates Kosmos as one of the ten most desirable takeover targets this year."

"No one's going to be taking us over," she said. "Always keep more than fifty percent of the stock in family hands. You remember that after I'm gone. The company isn't something for a bunch of speculators to own. It goes back three hundred years, to a whales' graveyard."

"I know the story, Mother, and when it's time for me to run things I'll see to it we never lose control." He kissed her cheek. "But you're going to be around a long time yet, which is just one reason I'm glad I've got my own career. The Odlum women never did believe in early retirement."

The publicity director peeked in the door, and Primrose nodded to him to bring in the journalists. In an instant the boardroom was crammed with reporters and photographers jostling for position, drinks and sandwiches. She gave them ten minutes before stepping forward and calling for their attention.

"Thank you for coming today," Primrose said. "As you know, the search for the Kosmos Girl has gone on for many months and featured several thousand beautiful young women. It's been very important to us to find the right person—a girl who will symbolize to the world what our products are. Fresh and sunny and relaxed like Bermuda itself, where all this began." She turned to the publicity man. "Ron, would you bring our winner out to meet the people, please."

Flashbulbs popped and heads nodded approvingly when she was escorted into the room; tall and reed-slim, shining blond hair and the bluest eyes, a perfect, fine-

boned face. She was the epitome of what the huge and
costly promotion had been about: a wonderful, fresh new
face.

"Ladies and gentlemen," Primrose said, "I'd like you
to meet the Kosmos Girl, Carol Bellowes."

"Jesus!" Jeff said. "I don't believe it, Mother. You
could have warned me."

"Just my little secret, Jeff." She laughed. "And if I'd
told you in advance, you might have accused me of nep-
otism. But look at her! Isn't she beautiful? To think we
searched America and all the time Jane's daughter was
right here, waiting to be discovered."

"I don't believe it," he said again. "Hell, last time I
saw Carol she was just a skinny kid, all legs and arms."

"Look at the difference five years make," Primrose
said. "She's perfect."

Jeff fell silent, watching the press besiege Carol, posing her, questioning her. No, she'd never modeled before. Yes, she was interrupting college for this marvelous
chance. He felt a surge of protectiveness for the kid he'd
known, but she was obviously able to handle herself. And
when she caught his eye over the crowd, she winked and
he saw the kid was still there. Finally, when the press
had what it wanted and returned to the refreshments, he
reached her side.

"Look at you," he laughed. "The ugly duckling."

"And look at you," she replied. "Mister Success in a
three-piece suit."

Their eyes held, laughing, and he felt a new emotion.
Regret that he'd gone off to Boston and missed the years
of her transformation.

"You're lovely," he said quietly. "Kosmos is very
lucky."

"I'm the lucky one," she said. "It's a dream job. I only
hope I can live up to all the faith your mother's invested
in me." She touched his hand. "I'm scared, Jeff, but I'll
do my best."

"If there's anything I can do to help—"

"Thanks. But I'm working for you too now, so I suppose we'd best keep a professional distance."

"Like hell!" he said, then relaxed when he saw she was kidding him. "Can we have dinner tonight and talk about your new career?"

"Ask your mother. My mother and I are dining with her and I'm sure she won't mind if you come along too."

They went to 21, and the glances Carol attracted were as much for her own bright beauty as for the front-page treatment she'd had in the evening papers. Jeff couldn't take his eyes off her. He toyed with his food and hardly heard what Primrose and Jane were talking about. His mother noticed his entrancement and smiled to herself. Jane saw it, too, and wondered if she should be concerned. After dinner they all strolled over to Jane's Park Avenue apartment and stood talking on the sidewalk.

"It's still early," Jeff said as they were about to part. "Maybe Carol would like to come over to Elmer's for a drink and a dance."

Jane frowned. "There's going to be a lot more promotional work tomorrow and you haven't finished packing for the national tour . . . Oh, all right, but don't bring her home late, Jeff."

The mothers watched the handsome young couple climb into a cab.

"They look good together," Primrose said. "I'm glad they've met again."

"Yes," Jane said, kissing her friend good night. "I hope everything is going to be all right."

A couple of society photographers were waiting by the zebra-striped entrance to El Morocco and they snapped Carol getting out of the cab. Jeff felt a tinge of annoyance; was she public property already? But inside the club he relaxed and managed not to be overawed when Earl Wilson stopped by their table and produced his notebook. It was all good publicity for Kosmos.

"It's funny," he said when they were at last left in peace. "I feel I've known you forever and yet I don't know you at all. I pushed you on a swing when you were five years old and visited with us in Bermuda. Do you remember? And the years when I was at Princeton, visit-

ing with you and your mother all the time. I thought you
were a brat."

"I was," she said. "And the more I idolized you, the
brattier I got. Trying to attract your attention. But you
never gave me a second glance. Stuck-up college man,
you were."

"I must have been blind," he said, meaning it.

"Your visits were agony for me," she laughed. "I
wasn't pretty and I was far too young for you to notice
me, anyway. I used to cry after your weekends at our
place." She laughed, an easy, unaffected sound among
the sophisticated conversations going on around them.
"The past three years in college I refused to date Princeton boys because of you. I convinced myself Harvards
were better."

It was silly, juvenile, but he felt pure jealousy.

"Are you . . . going steady?" he asked.

"Not now," she said. She teased him some more. "I'm
playing the field these days. Dozens of men. Any Ivy
League except Princeton." She wouldn't tell him that
none of the dates had measured up to the standard she'd
set, that none of them could erase her teenage memories
of him.

"It won't be college boys after this," he said, waving
his hand around the club. "You'll have every dirty rich
old man in the country pursuing you. You're going to be
famous."

"I wonder if I'll like that. Still, it's all for the Kosmos
cause, so if I'm to be lusted after, you'll be happy."

"Cut it out, Carol," he said. "I deserve it, but you've
made me jealous enough. Let's start off again, with you
forgetting what a prig I was. Will you have dinner with
me tomorrow?"

"I can't. The rest of the week is all blocked out and then
I have to travel for a couple of months, promoting your
family's products." She let her hand rest on his; the touch
thrilled him. "But I'm going to be in Boston for a week
at the end of this month. If you can drag yourself away
from your clients, maybe we could get together then."

"I'll clear the decks and we can do the town together. Maybe run down to Newport—"

"Hey," she laughed. "I'll be there to work. But I figure I'll have some free time to go out with you. Or one of those dirty rich old clients of yours."

Colin Fleet's twenty-first birthday celebration was the party of the year in Bermuda: Veronica saw to that. The Tropicana refused all bookings for the two weeks surrounding the big date and the hotel was filled with Colin's friends from Oxford plus the brightest of the young society crowd from Europe, New York and London. Veronica would have done anything for the boy. He was the light of her life, and all her ruthless ambition was now chaneled into him. He would be the best of the Fleet men and would, someday, take over the dynasty. For now, she just wanted him to be happy. If money could buy him that, then price was no object. She thought he might have been a little more excited over his main birthday present, a sixty-five-foot cruiser hand-built in Italy and freighted to Bermuda under wraps in a Fleet ship to be unveiled that morning. He kissed her in thanks, but then went off to play tennis at the club without even inspecting his very expensive new toy.

At least tonight he seemed to be enjoying himself in the ballroom, surrounded by his rich, famous and pretty friends. Veronica sat at her table acknowledging the compliments and watched her nephew. He was very tall and painfully thin, but his health seemed sound enough. And now that he was home to stay in Bermuda, she would see to it that he ate properly. The hair, so long and fair, needed cutting. He'd slipped into slovenly habits at Oxford. But there was no mistaking he was a Fleet: the cold, blue eyes established it, and she was sure when the time came he would prove as tough as the most illustrious men of the Fleet line. It was the bloodline that counted, of course. Just because his father had been crazy and his mother a bitch didn't mean Colin would turn out that way.

Colin was dancing with his aunt, Ginny Fleet. She had

lately dyed her hair bright red, most unsuitable for a woman of her age, and Colin didn't like the way she pressed herself against him. He'd already heard the stories about her conduct, the bohemian parties at her house. But she might be a good connection when he needed to score drugs. He just wished Sam's widow wouldn't thrust her groin at him as they danced. He actually had his eye on Jennifer Baseheart, his second cousin. She was a beautiful little thing, seventeen, and, Colin figured, ready for anything. He would dance with her soon and, if she was lucky, make a date for tennis or sailing.

"I'll bet you're glad to be home and finished with the university," Ginny said, bumping him again. God, he looked like Sam. For a moment she thought of their strange and sometimes passionate marriage and wondered what it might have been like if they both hadn't been so spoiled and selfish.

"I don't know," he muttered. "The place seems smaller than ever." Over her shoulder he could see Max Dalrymple dancing with Jennifer Baseheart; Max was one of his Oxford pals, a Rugby player and notorious womanizer. Young Jennifer had better watch out or Max would be up her like a rat up a drainpipe before he, Colin, had a crack at her.

"But look around you," Ginny said. "All the old families of Bermuda, all the money and power and tradition—and it's all yours. The Last Fleet. You're the uncrowned king of the colony."

"Not until Veronica's out of the way," he said sourly. "My aunt may dote on me, but she's not going to abdicate in a hurry. All I have to look forward to are years of depending on her goodwill."

"Then have fun while you're waiting to take over. This place may look quiet on the surface, but underneath, we have ways of enjoying ourselves. Anytime you get really bored, come and see me. We'll have fun."

He steered her back to her table and went to join his friends at the bar. Sandy Closter, another Rugby Blue, was quaffing champagne with Max Dalrymple.

"Jolly good party, old man," Closter said. "I never thought a little place like Bermuda could bung on such a turn. I'm quite envious of you now, inheriting all this."

"And the women—some of them are damned attractive," Dalrymple said. "Your little cousin, Fleet. I think there's the chance of some action there." He dropped his voice. "I asked her if she'd like to try something better than champagne later in the evening."

"Be careful with the cocaine around here," Colin said nervously. "They're a bit old-fashioned about drugs in Bermuda. We can do as we please but we must be discreet. What did she say?"

"Said she'd love to have a blow with us. The girl is ready to try anything. Maybe we should all slip away and have a look at that new boat of yours."

"Sure," Colin said. "Later in the night when the oldies have packed it in."

Supper was at midnight, a buffet of Bermuda lobsters, Canadian ham, Scottish salmon, English beef. The tables sagged under the feast, and a hundred waiters rushed around the room with fresh magnums of champagne. There was a string of toasts from people with names like Lapin and Benbridge and Winders, who talked about the colony's proud traditions and the preeminent position of the Fleets in preserving them. Shortly after one A.M. Veronica rose from her table, kissed her nephew good night and gave the signal for the older generation to depart. The band flown in from New York switched from slow to swing and the party suddenly took on a whole new life. Colin at last got to dance with Jennifer.

"Do you want to slip away and have a look at my new boat?" he asked as they locked together on the dance floor. "The car's outside and no one will miss us."

"I'd love to," she said. She was in awe of Colin Fleet and his friends from Oxford; they seemed so adult, so sophisticated after the local boys at the tennis club. "I won't need a wrap. It's such a lovely warm night." She didn't want to cover her shoulders or conceal the quite daring strapless ball gown.

She didn't seem surprised to find Max and Sandy already in the car, fresh bottles of champagne clutched in their hands. The four of them jammed up tight in the little open sports car and swept down the road to the docks. Jennifer was supremely happy; she had snared the three best catches at the party.

"Not bad at all," Max declared when they were in the main cabin of Colin's new boat. It was all gleaming mahogany under the soft lights; broad divans covered in soft leather were along the walls; Persian rugs were scattered over the Italian-tiled floor. Colin searched in the gleaming galley and found crystal goblets for their champagne.

They sat around the table drinking and listening to the music from the built-in record player. Then Max produced a small bottle from the pocket of his dinner jacket and spilled some of its contents out before them.

"I've heard so much about this stuff," Jennifer said. "What will it do to me?"

"It'll make you feel like you're over the moon," Max said. "Higher than you've ever been before." He formed the cocaine into lines and passed her a silver straw. "Just snort it up, my dear."

She did as she was told, and within seconds felt an exciting rush that started at the base of her neck then ran to her brain. The others did their lines and then there was more champagne and the whole process began again. Jennifer felt wonderful, confident, sophisticated. When they took turns dancing with her in the confined space, she was on top of the world.

It was Max who started tugging at the front of her dress. At first she giggled and pushed his big hand away. But then the other two got up and joined him, holding her from behind. She felt the wide skirts of her gown hiked up and she struggled when the hands reached inside her panties. Suddenly it wasn't fun anymore and she was coming down fast from her high.

"Cut it out, fellows," she begged, but one of them had undone the back of her gown and she was standing there in just her bra, panties and gartered stockings. "Let's go back to the party." But they were forcing her back on the divan; Max pulled her bra down and they were all pawing her breasts. They pinned her arms while her panties were tugged down around her ankles. She desperately tried to cover her nakedness but could not fight free. But surely they would stop now, she thought desperately. They'd had their fun, had stripped her. If they would just stop, it would be all right.

Max stepped back from her and she wanted to sob with relief. Except that he was unbuttoning himself, and when his huge red thing sprang into view, she had to clench her teeth to keep from crying out. It came closer to her, menacing, growing even bigger, and when he did plunge it between her thighs there was nothing she could do to stop the scream. It hurt so terribly; she felt she was being split in two.

"For Christ's sake, shut her up!" Colin said. "They'll hear her all over town."

Sandy grabbed her panties from the cabin floor and stuffed them in her mouth; she gagged as Max plunged into her again. She wished she could faint before having to feel any more pain and humiliation.

Captain Henry Smutters was at the far end of the docks when he heard the scream. He often strolled there late at night and was used to the drunken shouts and laughter from sailors and their tarts on the waterfront. But this sound was different, urgent and piercing, the sound of someone in pain. He hurried toward the source of it and stopped when he reached the gleaming new cruiser. From aboard came muffled noises and the sound of flesh against flesh. Silent in his deck shoes, Smutters swung over the rail of the cruiser and moved toward the main cabin. One of the draperies was slightly parted, and through the gap he saw the three young men pinning down the naked girl.

Smutters put his shoulder to the cabin door and the catch parted at once, plunging him into the dimly lit interior. At first the trio inside were struck dumb as they gazed at the intruder. Then they drew back from the naked, sobbing girl. She scrabbled around and found her dress and covered herself with it.

"And who in the hell is this?" Max drawled at last. "'A trespasser on your boat, Colin. A thief, or a pirate. We'd better teach him a lesson he'll not forget, then turn him over to the police."

"What the devil do you think you're doing here, Smutters," Colin demanded. After his first shock he was now only annoyed at the old captain for bursting in like this. "Get off my boat at once."

"Are you all right, miss?" Smutters asked, ignoring the others. "Do you want me to see you safely ashore?"

She nodded, still trying to cover herself.

"Bugger this," Sandy said. "Let's give the old man a thrashing. He's had his chance to clear off."

Colin hung back, but the two big football players advanced on Smutters, bumping each other in the narrow space. Perhaps if there had been more room they would have overcome him; perhaps if Henry Smutters had not had a lifetime in the back streets of the toughest seaports they would have triumphed. But Smutters fought dirty, not at all like the Rugby oafs who thought they were gentlemen. He moved forward on the balls of his feet and smashed the side of his hand into Max's throat; even as the big man was choking, he struck again, a chopping blow across the bridge of his nose. In one movement he spun on Sandy and jabbed a thumb into his eye. His knee came up and caught Sandy in the groin. Sandy moaned in pain and fell to the floor.

"Get dressed, miss," Smutters said. "Hurry it up." He saw Colin take a step forward. "I wouldn't try if I were you, Mr. Fleet," he said. "Why don't you just tend to your mates?"

"You wouldn't dare hit me, Smutters." Colin snarled. "I'm a Fleet. You work for me. At least, you did. You're fired, of course."

"We'll see about that. In the meantime, don't try your luck about whether I'd hit you. Just step aside so I can see the girl away from here."

* * *

"I want you out of this office immediately," Veronica Fleet said. "Your conduct last night was disgraceful. You're lucky charges aren't being pressed against you."

"As you wish." Henry Smutters couldn't be bothered arguing with the woman; he knew her too well to be surprised that a lifetime of service to her and her family could be ended so capriciously. It was unfair, but no one had ever accused the Fleets of being fair.

"One of the young men is severely injured," she said. "Colin wanted to have you arrested for assault but the others persuaded him not to, so's to avoid any more scandal. The poor girl, Jennifer, was so upset by the incident that she's in the care of a doctor. You amaze me, Mr. Smutters. All the years I thought you a responsible captain—"

"Just cut the bullshit, ma'am," he said. He was only now realizing what the incident last night had cost him. He had only a little money laid aside; most of his earnings had gone into the house and his books. He wondered if he could find another job. Not likely for a skipper fast approaching sixty and living in a place controlled by the Fleets. "If you're interested in a little advice," he said, "I'd put a curb on your nephew. Next time he might pull a stunt like last night's somewhere else—somewhere his name won't mean a damn thing."

"Just get out. You're finished with me," she said. She watched him shrug and start out the door. Damn, he was going to be hard to replace but it would have happened sooner or later. The man was getting old. So was she. Twenty years since that night on her honeymoon cruise, the night in Smutters's cabin . . . even now, in all her anger with him, the memory still brought a flush to her cheeks and a stirring in her loins. It was a shame it had to end this way. But she'd had to do it, for Colin's sake.

She rang for a cup of tea, left her desk and settled on the leather couch in the sun-filled window alcove of her office. That day's *Gazette,* unopened, lay on the table by the couch and she glanced at it with little interest. The report of Colin's party would not appear until tomorrow. On Page Three there was a picture of some girl selected in America to represent Primrose Odlum's company. She frowned. She must speak to the editor of the *Gazette*. Primrose was getting far too much publicity, with all her carrying on in the Assembly and gimmicks like this for her blasted company. Veronica studied the girl's picture again. There was something about her, something that shone through the black and white of the photograph. She looked so familiar. Veronica read the description; blond, blue-eyed. But they all were, those American models. She looked at the face. The tip-tilted nose was different, different from whatever it was she thought she had seen. She tossed the paper away and settled down to her bookkeeping.

They kissed again and he felt the sense of wonderment at being with her. She transformed his dreary little apartment, just as she had transformed the gloomy Boston days as they roamed the city together. He gently stroked her long, soft, blond hair and knew what he had decided on the first day was right. He had almost lost her once; he must never take such a terrible risk again.

"I love you, Carol," he whispered. "Will you marry me?"

She snuggled closer. She wasn't surprised by the proposal. But things were moving too quickly and she needed time. Time to be sure her own love was not really just a carryover from her teenage infatuation with Jeff.

"Maybe," she whispered.

"Maybe!" he said, sitting up suddenly. "Maybe? What kind of an answer is that? You can't—"

"It doesn't suit your orderly lawyer's mind, does it?" She laughed. Then she kissed him. "I guess I mean yes, but not right away. I love you too, Jeff. But we've only known each other as adults for a moment. There's no rush."

"There is for me." He felt suddenly miserable and threatened. "I'm scared about you traveling the world, being fêted by everyone, meeting new people. You'll forget about me as soon as you climb on that plane tomorrow."

"I won't," she said. "I promise." She looked into his brown eyes and almost surrendered then. She loved him and it would be so easy to just dump everything else and live happily ever after with him. "But I've got a year's contract to fulfill for your company. You of all people shouldn't be trying to get me to break it."

"Damn the contract. Marry me. We never know what's going to happen tomorrow. We have to grab today."

"I'll marry you when the year's up, if you still want to. You'll probably have met someone else by then, anyway."

"Never. It's you who'll be under siege this year." He held her hand tightly and pulled her against his chest. "Please, Carol, please be careful. I can't stand the thought of you leaving tomorrow."

"I can't either." They kissed again, and if he had wanted to go further she would have let him. But it was a time to be sensible. Regretfully, they disentangled, and left the apartment.

"I've got a great idea," he said as he helped her into his Mercedes. "You're going to be in Los Angeles for ten days next month. Why don't I fly out and join you there? It'll make tomorrow a bit more bearable."

"I'd love you to do that," she said.

It was late when she was back in her room, but she called her mother in New York. She wanted to share the joy she was feeling.

"Mom? I hope I didn't wake you. No, I'm all right. Wonderful, in fact. I just wanted to tell you what's been happening. I've been seeing Jeff and he wants to marry me."

Jane Bellowes almost dropped the phone. She should have seen it coming. Maybe she had, and had just shoved it into the too-hard file. But now it had to be faced.

"Have you accepted?" she asked. "Carol, you're so young and there's so much ahead of you."

"I put him off," Carol said, and giggled. "But not for too long. Mom, I love him. I do. I have since I was a kid. You're happy about it, aren't you? He is the son of your best friend and he's successful in his own right, and handsome, and he loves me. What more could a girl ask?''

"There are some things you don't know, things I should have told you long ago. They might affect the way you both feel about each other." Jane was confused and worried, treading on dangerous ground. "Look, you're coming through New York again in a couple of days. Just don't do anything until we've had a talk, will you, please?"

"Oh, Mom, you're so funny. I'm not going to do anything silly. I'm going to finish this wonderful assignment, and then I'm going back to college and get my degree. But I am going to marry Jeff Billings."

After she put down the phone Carol fell into bed and hugged herself with joy; she was not worried about her mother's remarks. Mothers were always concerned that their daughters were diving into strange waters. But she and Jeff would be wonderful together. Look how mature she'd been in saying they had to wait a year. As soon as her mother saw how happy she was, all her doubts would vanish.

But when they did sit down together three nights later in the Park Avenue apartment, Carol realized her mother was gravely worried about something, more worried than just whether she was in love with the right man.

"You never wanted to know about your father, about what happened to us," Jane said. "I should have told you anyway, but I guess I wanted to hide it from myself. It doesn't bring back any pleasant memories.

"Now I've got to tell you. Jeff makes all the difference." She looked out at the Manhattan skyline. It seemed so far away in time and distance, that summer of forbidden love with Sam Fleet. But every day since, she had been reminded of it, just by looking at her daughter. "Twenty-one years ago I went to Bermuda with my husband, Tom, for several months. Tom Bellowes wasn't a bad fellow, I suppose, but he was terribly moody and short-tempered and inclined to violence. Maybe if I'd had more experience I could have handled him better. I don't know. Whatever, I had a lot of time on my hands that Bermuda summer and I met a man who was kind and thoughtful and gentle—and who said he loved me. He gave me all the things I didn't get from my husband." And Sam had been in love with her; of that she was still sure. What she hadn't known was how weak he was.

"Anyway," she continued, "we had a wild fling together, and out of it you were conceived. Tom stormed out, of course, and I waited for my lover to come to me. We were going to be married and everything. But he didn't come. In the end he couldn't leave his wife.

"I was left there desperate and alone. I tried to drown myself, but Primrose rescued me and nursed me back to health and sanity. You were born under Primrose Odlum's roof."

"Oh, Mother," Carol said, crossing to her and kneeling beside her, "you poor thing. What a terrible story." She held her mother's hands and looked into her eyes. "But I still don't see—How does being born in the Odlum house affect Jeff and me?"

"Your father was Sam Fleet." It didn't register. "Of course, that won't mean anything to you, but in Bermuda it means everything. The Fleets are the most powerful family in the colony and they hate the Odlums. More than hate. On their side it's been a blood feud down through the centuries. For a Fleet to marry an Odlum . . ."

"Do the Fleets know I exist?"

"I believe not. Sam was killed more than fifteen years ago and he didn't know what happened to me after he . . . after he jilted me. But Primrose knows."

"And you don't think she'd want her only son marrying a Fleet?"

"How could she, given the history of the two families? You've got to understand, Carol, Bermuda isn't like here. It's a tiny, tempestuous island where old hatreds never die."

"What do I do? Should I tell Jeff?"

"I don't know, darling. All I am sure of is, we must do

nothing that could ever hurt Primrose. She saved my life—and yours, for that matter. We owe her everything."

Carol spent two days trying to decide. Finally she convinced herself it was best to end the affair before they both got even more deeply involved. She called him in his Boston office.

"Jeff," she said, "I'm sorry, but I don't want you to come to Los Angeles. I'm just going to be too busy to see you and the trip would be a waste of your time and money."

"Don't worry about it," he said. "I'll understand if I only get to see you fleetingly. A minute here, a minute there—that's all I ask of you, darling. Just to be in the same city as you . . . you don't know what a bleak old place Boston has become since you left." He laughed. "I feel better just thinking about seeing you again. Please, I do understand the demands of your assignment. I won't get in the way."

"I guess I didn't explain properly, Jeff." Her heart was breaking. "I don't want you to come at all. I'm not ready to get tied up with someone. I need to be free for a while."

"I see." He slumped back in his leather chair, his lawyer's brain searching for some point of advocacy that would change her mind. It was what he had feared all along. A beautiful young girl out in the glamorous world . . . Why would she want to be tied down to a dull, respectable man like him? "I see," he said again. "Well, I'm . . . I'm sorry you feel this way, Carol. Maybe I'll see you in New York or Bermuda or somewhere." His voice was cracking. "Do a good job for Kosmos, you hear? Goodbye." He put down the phone and rested his head in his hands, more miserable than he had ever been in his life.

"Banking. International banking." Edward Lapin thumped the board table and looked around, daring anyone to contradict him. "We can change the whole economy of Bermuda by becoming an international finance center. The higher they tax companies in the U.S., Canada and Britain, the more there will be a demand for a safe offshore tax haven. And our bank will be the first into the field."

There was a respectful silence. Edward Lapin might have looked a fool, with his large flapping ears and receding chin, but he had been well taught by his parents. His bank wasn't the biggest in Bermuda, but it was the most profitable because first Steven Lapin and now Edward were always willing to cut corners, ignore red tape and sail very close to the fiscal wind. And like all the Lapins before him, Edward made it his business to know everyone else's. There was always a favor that could be called in, a veiled threat to be made.

"The re-insurance industry is looking for a permanent, untaxed home as well. There's billions in it," he continued. "Now, obviously, we don't want to become a flag-of-convenience type country or just another banana republic." He laughed. "Of course, we will never be a republic of any kind. The links with England will always remain, for England's good and ours. The very thing that makes us attractive to the international financiers is our stability, our Britishness. Anyway, I've had a study made, and the demand is there. All we have to convince the international institutions of is that there is committed government backing for the scheme and that the support services exist."

"The Government will do as it's told—do as we tell it, that is," Duncan Baseheart said. "And I like your scheme, Edward. My father always felt there was an international role for Bermuda banking. But the support side of it worries me. In New York now they're moving into computers in a big way. The banks of the future aren't going to be places where little old tellers sit at high desks and add handwritten columns of figures. The kind of thing you're talking about will need an army of professionals to staff it."

Colin Fleet began to take an interest in the debate. He hadn't particularly wanted the Fleet seat on the Lapin board, but his aunt had insisted. So far the meetings and the business had been dull. But Edward's scheme of-

fered some interesting possibilities. Like the excuse to
go on a grand tour of the world's financial capitals recruiting the senior staff they would need. And if they had
a full international setup, including Swiss bank–style
secrecy, they could get into the money-laundering
racket. A fellow could make millions on the side there.

"I like the scheme, too," Colin said. "It's time we extended Bermuda's economic base. If it weren't for tourism, this place would be worthless. I'm sure if we used
our overseas connections, we could round up all the staff
we need."

Duncan Baseheart stared out the boardroom windows. He did not want to look at the obnoxious young
Fleet. He had eventually wrung from his daughter the
story of what had really happened the night of Colin's
twenty-first; if Colin's name had not been Fleet and this
had not been Bermuda, Duncan would have horse-
whipped the young cad and then had him thrown in
prison. But business, and the need for the leading families to hang together, meant that nothing could be done
about the outrage perpetrated on little Jennifer. Sometimes, Duncan thought, he despised all of them and himself.

"Be no trouble at all," said Eric Amberley, the lawyer.
He and Edward Lapin had worked on this scenario before the meeting. If they had the Fleet vote, the scheme
would sail through any objections. "A young chap like
you, Colin, fresh from Oxford, must be in contact with
the best and brightest of the men we'll want. What we
need is a framework, some kind of overriding body so it
wouldn't look as if this was only a scheme to make our
bank richer. I had in mind setting up a Development
Council of some kind, involving the other banks, the
government and so on. I think Colin would make an excellent chairman of the new body. Show the world we're
not a lot of old fuddy-duddies, eh, by having a bright
young chap in charge."

There was a rumble of agreement around the table and
Colin beamed.

"What kind of numbers are we talking about?" Baseheart asked. "It seems to me you couldn't work something as big as this with just a handful of managers."

"No," Lapin said. "The projections I've made would eventually see perhaps two thousand professionals of varying grades living here."

"Two thousand! Good Lord, you'd upset the whole structure of society as we know it," Baseheart protested. Some of the other board members nodded; they had envisaged a much smaller scale operation. "I don't think the community would stand for it," Baseheart added. "You know what pressures there are already on housing, schooling and the health services."

"I've thought of that, too," Lapin said. "We point out to the community how delicately the budget is balanced. Float a rumor that the government is finally going to be forced to introduce some form of income tax. That'll terrify them all, even the blacks. Then we step forward with our scheme, demonstrating that the fees the international companies will pay would alleviate the need for an income tax. As for housing, we can buy and upgrade some of the existing places and make a profit in the process. If we have to resettle a few people in some kind of public housing, so be it."

"Having a couple of thousand new whites on the electoral rolls wouldn't hurt, either," Colin Fleet said. "The blacks are going to get the vote someday. We won't be able to stop it forever, and they're fifty percent of the population now. These professionals would put us comfortably into the majority for the foreseeable future."

Duncan Baseheart did look at him now, and with respect. Fleet might be a scoundrel and still wet behind the ears, but he obviously had a nice, devious turn of mind. He would have to get over his loathing of the young man; Colin Fleet was going to be as powerful as any of his line.

"What are you doing to make my son so miserable?" Primrose said. She smiled at Carol as she spoke; she loved the girl and she was doing such a great job for the company. Halfway through her year as the Kosmos Girl,

and sales were up fifteen percent in the U.S. "Every time
your name comes up, a cloud comes over his face."

"I'm awfully fond of Jeff," Carol said. "I wouldn't do
anything to upset him. I'm sure you're imagining it,
Aunt Primrose."

"No. There's something that happened between you
two and I won't rest until I get to the bottom of it." She
paused while the waiters cleared the coffee cups from the
table in the Waldorf suite and asked one of them to open
the windows to let out the fug of cigar and cigaret smoke
from the planning session with her marketing and promotion directors. "All the talking, the masses of figures
. . . it was over my head," she said. "It's nice to be alone
with you, Carol. We never get a chance to talk these
days."

The girl laughed. "Nothing goes over your head,
Primrose," she said. "And all your executives know it.
The promotions guy was telling me he never thought
he'd end up working for a woman; now he hasn't time to
think that he is."

"I suppose that's a compliment. But we've talked
enough business today. Let's have a nice glass of sherry,
and you come sit beside me and tell me what's going on."

Carol busied herself getting the drinks, not wanting
to be involved in a heart-to-heart talk with Primrose Odlum. She loved the woman very much, even more so since
she'd learned just how much she had done for them.
Carol had always thought of Primrose as an aunt or a
godmother, someone she could turn to in a crisis if her
mother was not available. But this was different; it was
the fact of who Primrose was that had created the problem. She had tried and tried to put Jeff out of her mind
and her heart, but in the long months on the road the
memory of him had only sharpened. The nights she had
sat in lonely hotel rooms longing to pick up the telephone and hear his voice. . . . She sighed, picked up the
glasses and crossed to Primrose.

"Thank you, my dear. Now sit down and tell me what's
going on. When I mention Jeff, you get the same look on

your face as he does when I speak of you. Have you two had some kind of silly fight?"

Carol shook her head. "There's nothing—"

"Because if you have, I'll be most upset with both of you." She put hand on Carol's. "I'll confess it. I always had this wild dream the two of you would fall in love someday and marry."

Carol spilled some of her sherry as she whirled to face Primrose.

"Marry? But you know who my father was. Sam Fleet. You couldn't approve of your son marrying one of them! Mother told me all about it and I stopped the affair with Jeff. I was heartbroken, but it was the only thing to do."

"Sometimes your mother, much as I love her, is as silly as a teenager. I wish one of you had talked to me about all this." Primrose smiled and touched the girl's cheek, wiping away the tears. "It doesn't matter who your father was. It's who you are, and I've known and loved you all your life. I'd be so happy and proud if you decided Jeff was good enough for you."

Chapter Fourteen
(1860–)

Captain Samuel Smutters studied the young American the purser had assigned to his table; the captain had protested at first that he didn't want some Bible-bashing parson ruining the voyage for him. But the Rev. Henry Bland was like no parson Smutters had ever met. Tall, dark and handsome and quite young; well-traveled and well-spoken; a man who appreciated the good food and fine wines that graced the captain's table. The women guests at Smutters's table all seemed quite taken with the Rev. Bland.

"Your work sounds so dangerous," Mrs. Esme Stewart said, leaning forward, her vast bosom almost dipping in the lobster bisque. "Kidnapping slaves away from their masters! I'm sure all those southerners must want to lynch you."

"Quite right, too," Nathan Baseheart grumbled. "You can't go around interfering with a man's property and expect to be thanked for it. You'll be given short shrift in Bermuda if you start preaching the kind of things you've been telling us."

"I wouldn't want to make any pronouncements about Bermuda until I've seen it myself, sir," Bland said. "I have been told you treated your slaves in a kindly manner, and you were the first colony to free them. How free are they? We shall see. The Odlum family is sponsoring my visit to your colony and I will be guided by them."

"The Odlums! I should have guessed," Baseheart said. He spluttered into his soup and his cheeks flushed red with anger. "That damned family is never content until it's causing trouble."

"And how did they come to sponsor you, Mr. Bland?" Mrs. Stewart asked.

"Their cousin is a member of President Lincoln's Cabinet," he said. "They wrote him asking if there was anyone suitable to muster support in Bermuda for the abolitionist cause in the U.S. and since I'd done a little bit of work for the President he selected me."

"Lincoln's surely not serious about abolishing slavery?" another of the captain's guests inquired. "It would wreck your economy."

"The President may not be as committed to abolition as some of us are," Bland said, "but he is committed to preserving the Union. He will not allow any state to secede, be it over slavery or any other matter. I am afraid there will be a civil war. There is no other way."

"If it does come to such madness," Baseheart snapped, "I can tell you now whose side Bermuda will be on. We will back the South, sir. All our sympathies lie there."

"And the great bulk of our trade," Captain Smutters murmured.

Davis Fleet stood on the deck of his ship and watched the tobacco bales coming up from the Charleston wharf and into his holds; it was a slow process and he was impatient for it to be over. The sooner loading was completed, the sooner they could carry on to New York and Boston, then London and then home. The thought of Bermuda and the young wife awaiting him there caused his heart to ache. Two years since he'd married Pamela Amberley, and he was more in love with her than ever. She had given him a fine son, Horatio, but more than that she'd given him the strength to be a man in his own right, not just a member of the Fleet clan. He knew his mother didn't approve of Pamela—she was "flighty," and although she came from a long line of lawyers there was no real money there. Davis grinned. He doubted there

was any girl his mother would have accepted for him. Old
Honor Fleet thought no one was good enough for her son.

He stretched in the warm sun, felt his own strength.
At least Honor was right about one thing; he had escaped the "curse" of the Fleets. Davis was young, strong
and healthy. Surely, the Fleet fairness of skin, the white
hair and pale eyes didn't make it easy living in a hot climate, but Davis coped. He thought again of Pamela,
damp with passion on the night before he sailed, gripping her long legs around his waist as if she would hold
him in their bed forever, pleading with him to give up
the sea and settle down to his responsibilities as inher-
itor of the mighty Fleet legacy.

He loved the sea and was at least as good a captain as
Smutters, but he knew Pamela was right, knew his
mother, Honor, and father, Jackson, were right. It was
time to shoulder his burden in Bermuda and give up this
happy life on the oceans of the world. To be with Pamela
every night would be wonderful compensation.

"Hurry them along, Mr. Mate," he called. "Those
blasted darkies will have us missing the tide, the pace
they're going."

Henry Odlum refilled his guest's wineglass, pushed
back his chair and lit a cigar. Elizabeth and the children
had withdrawn from the dining room to let the two men
talk of weighty matters. Henry was well pleased with the
man his cousin had selected for this mission to Bermuda.
Bland was a good figure of a gentleman and, judged by
the reaction of both Elizabeth and their daughter, Patience, very appealing to the ladies. That wouldn't hurt
the cause at all.

"I don't know what kind of turnout we'll get for your
first lecture, Mr. Bland," Henry said. "I managed to
mention it in the Assembly, and there are posters all over
town; but the whole issue of slavery is still a most sore
point here. A lot of people didn't want it to end, and re-
sented the British Government making their decision for
them. And there is a great deal of popular support for the
South here."

"We can only do our best," Bland said. He wasn't too worried about his reception; it was enough to just be relaxing in this beautiful place with such kind and generous hosts, away from the tensions of Washington. He knew the severe trials facing America and welcomed this respite before returning to the cauldron. "Tell me," he said, drawing on a fine Havana, "what happened to Bermuda's slaves when they were liberated?"

"Just about what the pro-slavers had predicted." Henry frowned. "Many of them have found no employment, even after all these years. And those who do have jobs are poorly paid. We are trying to improve their education and create more jobs, but this is a small community and the economy has been under a lot of pressure lately."

"The war will fix that. You are ideally placed to get rich off both sides when the conflict begins."

"I wish that weren't so, Mr. Bland, but of course it is. Bermuda has always profited from the misfortunes of others. Our people are merchants first and patriots second."

"Your own excellent house staff, sir—are they former slaves?"

"A long time ago, yes. But my family saw the light many years ago when one of our men, Jubilee, performed a great service for the family. We freed them all and most stayed on in the employment of the family. That, of course, is one more tragedy of the evil institution of slavery. We may have been benevolent masters, but we did not equip these people for a life of freedom. I think we will pay a price for that for a long time to come."

"I doubt we'll do any better in America, but we must try."

Pamela Fleet handed the baby back to the nurse and went and sat by the window with her friend, Liz Benbridge. The two young women sipped their tea and gazed on the beauty of the Great Sound laid out before them.

"My God I'm bored," Pamela said. "It's all right when Davis is here, but the time in between, when he's off on these long voyages, is so hard to kill. And living in this

house, under Honor's watchful eye . . . I swear, Liz, that
woman is just waiting for me to put a foot wrong. Talk
about evil mothers-in-law!"

"It can't be that bad," Liz said. "You've living in the
grandest house in Bermuda, waited on hand-and-foot.
And it will all be yours someday. You're so lucky to have
a husband like Davis, young and strong and clever. He'll
be the greatest of all the Fleets, mark my words."

"But he is a Fleet. Don't you see, that's the problem.
If it were just Davis and me and little Horatio, we'd be
so happy. But as it is, it's as though I've married the
whole damn family and I have to perform to their strange
standards, rather than just please my husband."

"There's not a girl in Bermuda wouldn't trade places
with you."

"I know. It's just I get restless and bored when he's
away. I'm a woman, Liz, and I need love and affection.
Good Lord, Davis will be at sea at least another two
months!"

"We'll have to find things to occupy you, then, or else
you'll be having an affair." Liz laughed at the thought
of it. "Imagine trying to conduct an affair in this incestuous little place! You'd better devote yourself to Good
Works instead. I'm going to the anti-slavery rally on
Sunday. Come with me."

"Mix with anti-slavery rabble-rousers? You must be
joking." Then she smiled. "Old Honor would throw a fit,
her daughter-in-law waving a banner against the practice that made this family even richer. And why are you
going, anyway? I didn't think you cared about stuff like
that."

"I don't, but anything to relieve the boredom. They say
this Henry Bland is a wonderful speaker. And I saw him
on Front Street yesterday. He's handsome as sin. What
a pity he's a reverend."

It was his voice as much as his dark good looks that
captivated her. He seemed to be speaking directly to her,
and the words entered her. Pamela Fleet sat in the sun

at the rally and shivered. Henry Bland had mesmerized her.

"What did I tell you?" Liz whispered. "Isn't he magnificent? I think I'll give money to his cause, no matter how misguided it is."

The rally had not attracted a big crowd, and after it Pamela and Liz joined the small circle of men and women taking tea with Mr. Bland. He knew how to work a group—a smile and a quip for some, a serious word for others. They all seemed enchanted by him. When it was her turn to chat with him, Pamela was tongue-tied.

"I really appreciate it," he said, "a lovely young girl like you giving up a beautiful afternoon to listen to a stranger groaning on about faraway injustices. You have such a lovely island—it must be hard to relate to the problems of the outside world." He dropped his voice as if to impart a wicked secret. "I'm having too good a time here. It makes me feel quite guilty."

She felt dizzy, up close to him like this. His eyes were liquid brown, and she felt he could see inside her. Somehow she found her voice and made it light, and calmly suggested he might like to see more of Bermuda. Perhaps tomorrow, her carriage would pick him up here and they would picnic on the South Shore?

Bland frowned. Warning bells sounded. But what harm could there be in it? She seemed a charming creature, Pamela Fleet, and weren't the Fleets the exact type of family he had to get to if his mission was to be worthwhile?

"That sounds delightful," he said. "I have a free day tomorrow, and my hosts are occupied with their own business. If you're sure I won't be inconveniencing you . . ."

She shook her head quickly. She could see Liz bearing down on them.

"Noon, here," she said and moved away.

A dozen times through the night she had changed her mind. She wouldn't go, or she would take Liz along with them for propriety's sake. But well before noon, on a

magnificent morning, she had quietly organized a picnic
basket and a carriage, keeping well out of Honor's way.
There was nothing wrong with what she was doing, she
assured herself. Just extending typical Bermuda hospitality to a visitor. But she put on her prettiest gown and
tied bows in her hair and sheltered her fair skin under a
broad and fetching bonnet.

He was waiting on Front Street, more handsome than
ever out of clerical garb and dressed in a white linen suit.
He sprang into the carriage and sat facing her as the
driver headed them out of the bustling town toward the
quiet beaches on the South Shore.

"We shouldn't be doing this," he said, gesturing out
the window. "Look at them all, so industrious, going
about their business, and you and I are off sightseeing."
He laughed, but he did feel uneasy about this jaunt. He
had thought to cancel it, but the desire to be with someone young and pretty and bright, to forget his responsibilities for a few hours, had been too great.

They made small talk as the carriage jolted through
the narrow lanes and out into the countryside; they could
each feel a tension between them, and the air in the carriage seemed charged, as before a thunderstorm.

"We'll leave the carriage here and walk down to the
beach, if you don't mind carrying the picnic basket," she
said. They were on a ridge high above the sweep of pink
beaches visible through the foliage. A sandy trail led
them down through the trees and far from the carriage
and driver. Within minutes they were completely alone,
the only sound the birds and the sea.

"It's all so beautiful," he said as they came on to a secluded cove. "I'm glad you asked me to play hooky."

She busied herself spreading rugs while he opened a
chilled bottle of wine. They were still speaking lightly,
about the weather, the views, the variety of birds. They
ate cold partridge and ham, lobster and salads; and an
intimacy, close and hot as the sun overhead, grew between them. Their hands touched and it was like fire.
When she lay back, eyes closed against the bright day,

she knew he would come to her and he did, his lips cool against hers.

Neither thought of stopping; they had already gone too far. Their mouths stayed locked together while their bodies moved closer, in rhythm, and their hearts beat as one. She felt his hand at her breast and strained to meet it; her hips had a movement of their own, lifting up off the sand. And then her gown was up around her waist and she felt the smooth cloth of his suit against her silk-clad thighs. He scrabbled at the buttons constraining him and she opened her eyes for a second and saw his member big and menacing in the bright sun. They both gasped as he entered her, then began to move together, panting and moaning as their passion soared, crashing to a climax; then, without pause, beginning again. They had no sense of time, no idea how long they writhed together on the hot, deserted shore, but at last they fell apart and lay calm in each other's arms. Her ribbons were undone and her hair was plastered to her forehead; the sun burned down on her exposed limbs. She felt wanton, naked, spent. But there was no guilt. She had convinced herself fate had brought this dark stranger to her, a fate that could not be denied.

Henry Bland felt the dizziness in his head subsiding, the near madness he had just felt ebbing away. A great sense of remorse came over him, even as he still gazed with wonder on her beautiful naked breasts. He had betrayed her, this trusting, lovely young woman, just as he had betrayed his cloth. He closed his eyes in shame as he felt his manliness stirring again.

"Don't feel bad," she whispered. "It was my fault. I knew from the moment I saw you that I must have you. I have never done anything like this before. But I'm glad I did." And she pulled his head down to her and cradled it in her bosom.

They spent two idyllic weeks together, stealing time from his duties and her social routine to find secret places in the islands where they could be alone. They made passionate love without speaking of love; they were to-

gether without mentioning the time they would have to
part. But when the news at last arrived that the Civil
War had begun, they faced each other and the truth.

"I love you," she said. "I love you more than honor,
more than life. If you love me too, say it."

He nodded. "I love you, Pamela. I am torn apart by this
but I must be on tomorrow's ship for New York."

"I shall come with you," she said. "I have already
damaged my family irreparably and changed myself for
all time. I have no further function here as wife or
mother. If you will have me, I shall join you in your ship
in the morning."

"It will be hard for you," he said. "You will regret
this." He kissed her. "But I shall make you happy for as
long as I can."

She slipped out of the house at dawn, with only a small
bag and her jewel case. She left a note with her maid to
deliver to Honor Fleet at noon. She looked into the nursery at Horatio sleeping peacefully under the mosquito
net and for a moment she doubted the course she was
embarking on. But her course was set.

Honor was in the front parlor with Samuel Smutters,
checking manifests, when the maid brought the note
from Pamela. She read it and crossed to the window with
it in her hand. She could see the runaway's ship under
sail and heading off down the Great Sound.

"My daughter-in-law, Captain," she said, "is in that
ship in the arms of the Yankee preacher. She has placed
herself in adultery with a reverend. Whatever has the
world come to?"

Smutters came and stood beside her.

"I can go and fetch her back if you like, ma'am," he
said. "I could overhaul that old tub within the day."

"Thank you, Captain, but no. She has left the boy here
and that is all that matters, little Horatio. We are probably well rid of her, though I feel for her poor parents.
And I suppose Davis will be upset at first. No, let her go.
It's probably for the best."

* * *

Davis Fleet's heart was broken when he returned from the long voyage to an empty marriage bed. At first he blamed himself, or his mother, or the crying baby in the sunny nursery. But as his grief turned to mad rage, he placed all the blame on Yankees and the family which had brought one particular Yankee to Bermuda. He put the Fleet shipyards to urgent work, rearming and refitting the fastest vessel in the line. He would not just be a blockade runner for the South; he would go out and actively seek and destroy any ship flying the Stars and Stripes.

"But you are a doctor, Simon. If you must be involved in this dreadful war, at least be so as a surgeon tending to the wounded, like your great-grandfather in the War of Independence." Edith Odlum saw it was too late to change her son's mind; he was gazing out at the ships on the Hudson, and it was clear he wanted to be away with them. "At least wait awhile," she pleaded. "See if you are drafted, and then your father and I can talk with you about what we should do. I would gladly pay a hundred times the three hundred dollars to get another man to go to war in your place."

"I'm sorry, Mother," he said. "The deed is done. I have been offered a commission in the Union Navy. They are desperate for men with sailing skills, and you know how I have always loved boats. There'll be no danger; the war at sea is not as bloody as that on land."

"When will you go?" she asked, admitting defeat.

"Next Monday. I'm to report to a ship in Boston, the *Cooperstown,* which is going on blockade station. It's a very important job." His young face shone with enthusiasm. "The source of supply to the Confederates must be cut off. The worst offenders are those blasted Bermudians: they sail through our blockade as they wish. I think that's one of the reasons I got the commission so easily. They think the Bermudian blood in my veins may help the cause."

"Yes," she said. "I read how Bermuda rallies to the

southern flag while officially staying neutral and continuing to trade with the North."

"The worst of them is this fellow they call the Ghost
of the Gulf Stream," Simon said. "White as a sheet, with
long pale hair, and he is said to sail his sloop better than
any normal man ever could. Two years now and he's a
legend; seven of our ships sunk, numerous others defeated. I pray the *Cooperstown* will engage the Ghost and
his *Deliverance.* Our ship has been specially built for the
purpose, Mother. The Navy sent an architect down to
Bermuda to study their ships and has come up with this
design—light and fast, able to turn on a dime. An iron-
clad would never get near enough to her to fire a shot."

Captain Smutters eased off his boots and stretched out
before the fire; outside the cottage the wind was howling
in from the sea. He was glad the voyage was over. Even
in tempest season, Bermuda was a better place to be than
the cold, dangerous waters around Halifax. He rumpled
his son's head and smiled thanks to his wife as she
handed him a glass of mulled claret.

"You had no trouble, then, Samuel?" she asked. "We
have been hearing the most horrendous tales of great
battles at sea. Davis Fleet's ship returned here for a refit
while you were gone, and everyone went down to marvel
at the scars of war she carried."

"Davis is the one who takes the risks, sails to where
the action is," he told her. "My job is to make money for
the Fleets, so I carry safe cargoes to safe ports."

"You're not a hero like Mr. Fleet?" Jamie asked. The
boy looked disappointed.

"I'm afraid not, son. And I'm also afraid Davis Fleet
will be a dead hero one of these days. He takes such risks,
ignoring all the odds. You would think he had been born
just for war. He is undoubtedly a marvelous sailor, but
the tide is turning for the North and they will not for
much longer let him get away with flouting their blockade."

"I wish it would end quickly, the war," Phoebe Smutters said. "Bermuda is so busy these days! I was in Ham-

ilton the other day and I had to take my life in my hands just to cross Front Street. The traffic and the crowds."

"You're the only one who wishes the war over," he said. "The Fleets must have doubled their fortune since it began, even allowing for the cost of letting Davis play at being a privateer."

Twice in the nine months the *Cooperstown* had been patrolling the blockade line, she had made contact with the Bermudian runner *Deliverance.* And both times *Deliverance,* wonderfully sailed by her white-maned skipper, had run rings around the American. The third time, though, the encounter came in just the circumstances Captain Harry Mannering and his second-in-command, Simon Odlum, had prayed for.

The *Cooperstown* was cruising off the coast of Savannah on a bright, cool morning when their lookout spotted the enemy vessel; it was not until they sailed in closer to the shore that the other ship was identified as the *Deliverance.*

"We've got the bugger this time!" Mannering shouted. "We have the wind on her. There's nowhere she can run to."

As they bore down on the smaller ship, Simon Odlum's pulse was racing; at last they were going to close with this "Ghost" who'd been thumbing his nose at the might of the northern navy for years. As he supervised the priming of the guns, he had time to admire the slim lines of the Bermudian boat; she made their own Bermuda copy look top-heavy. No wonder she sailed like the wind, he thought; for two hundred fifty years those Bermudians had been at home on the Atlantic in just such craft.

"She's beautiful, Captain," he said as the distance between the two ships lessened. "Almost seems a shame to sink her."

"They'll sure as hell not surrender," Mannering said. "So one of us will be on the bottom before the day is out."

Davis Fleet was unlucky this time. If the wind had held he would have made it safely into Savannah despite the big tide running out against him. But he was trapped there and could only ready his guns as the northerner bore down on him. The first shots from the *Cooperstown* were high and whistled through the rigging; the next round fell away to starboard; the third straddled the foredeck and sent splinters of cedar flying through the air. Davis Fleet knew he had the hardest fight of the war on his hands. Still he waited before returning fire, until the enemy was only fifty yards away. Then his well-drilled gunners released a broadside of surprising ferocity, and Fleet took delight in the screams from the *Cooperstown* as the balls crashed into her amidships. There was nothing he liked better than killing northerners.

In the smoke and confusion, with severed limbs littering the deck and a quarter of her rigging gone, the *Cooperstown* was almost lost in the first volleys. Captain Mannering was an early casualty, a flying spar embedding itself in his chest. He died without a sound and Simon suddenly found himself in command and in grave danger of having his ship shot out from under him.

"Pull away, sir, pull away!" the bosun was yelling at him over the din. But if he pulled away the *Cooperstown* would stop in the water as the wind ran out. Then, as soon as a breeze reappeared, the lighter boat would slip away to sea.

"No," he ordered. "Go straight for her with all guns firing."

Both ships were taking heavy damage as they came closer. Simon could now identify the figure on the *Deliverance* directing the battle. He was indeed a man to be feared: tall and thin, long white hair, deathly pale skin. Even through the smoke Simon could see the hatred burning in the man's eyes.

The battle raged another hour, the ships pounding each other from a range of less than twenty yards, but slowly the *Cooperstown*'s heavier guns began to take their toll. *Deliverance* was listing to port; her masts and much of her superstructure was shot away, but still the guns spat out their defiance.

And then she began to settle at the stern, sinking fast into the blue water. In the cockpit the gaunt white figure still shouted commands but it was all over. The victors on the *Cooperstown* decks turned away as the sea closed over the *Deliverance;* already the menacing circle of dorsal fins were slicing through the water toward the men struggling to swim away from their lost ship.

The thrill of victory Simon Odlum felt was tinged with respect for a brave foe, and regret too. He wondered, as the waters turned red and the last survivors died horribly, if there were men of his own blood among the Bermudians. Probably. It was just one more tragedy in a dreadful war.

Chapter Fifteen
(1960–)

Edward Lapin hated making speeches; his slight stutter grew much worse when he was facing a crowd. But tonight's occasion was the pinnacle of everything he'd worked for, and the speech had to be right. He sat in the sun on the deck of his Southampton mansion and went through the words again. He badly wanted to convey to the audience what a struggle it had been from the day, ten years ago, when he had launched Bermuda as an international finance center, to the present and the opening of the new Lapin Worldmoney Headquarters. Pity they'd only been able to snare a junior member of the Royal Family to cut the ribbon, he thought. The project demanded someone much more powerful. And those damned Americans, boycotting the whole thing just because the bank was proving useful to some of the Yanks' biggest tax evaders. He'd pointed out to them that secrecy between banker and client was inviolable and they'd got in a huff, just because one of their nationals had skipped the country with $200 million in fraudulently obtained funds. He went back to the printed pages of his speech but the words were swimming before his eyes; he was glad when he saw Colin Fleet approaching around the pool.

"Don't worry about what you're going to say tonight," Fleet said, dropping into a chair beside him and gesturing to the hovering servant. "A pink gin." Fleet mopped his brow. "God, it's hot. I hate the heat and sun. My skin wasn't made for it." His drink arrived; he drained it and nodded for another. "Anyway, Edward, don't worry about your words tonight. No one will be listening. Just fill them with good champagne and tell them how much money we can save them. That's all they want." He tossed a Telex onto the table between them. "I just got us another thirty-five million from the Mexican connection. The commission will pay for tonight's party and leave some change."

"These Mexicans of yours, Colin," Lapin said, "have put an awful lot of money through the bank. You're sure they're okay?"

"Who cares? It's all money and we take our whack from it as we move it on to the European markets. I never ask questions in this business."

That was the trouble, Lapin thought. No one asked questions. Most of their business was legitimate—even if the governments of their customers didn't approve—but a large slice of it was the funds Fleet brought in. Lapin had an uneasy feeling the bank transfers they received from Mexico had started life as embarrassingly large amounts of cash in brown bags.

"And are you looking after our Royal guest, Colin?" he asked.

"Yes, I stopped by his suite this morning. He's happy as a pig in shit. The poor bugger doesn't get invited anywhere, so he thinks opening the new headquarters is a real occasion." He laughed. "When I left him at the hotel he was just like you are now, boning up on his speech for tonight."

"I do think Buck House could have found someone farther up the scale than him," Lapin said. It still rankled. "But he'll have to do." Thank God his mother wasn't alive to see the insult, sending a chap fifty-ninth in succession to the throne to such an important occasion. Poor old Dimity, always believing she had some special pull with Buckingham Palace. "Out here in the colonies, we have to take what they send us."

* * *

"You must have a nap this afternoon if you want to sit up and watch the fireworks tonight," Primrose said. She took the little girl's hand and led her toward the bedroom. "I promised your parents I wouldn't spoil you or let you stay up too late. At least there's no television to fight about."

"I thought I'd miss TV terribly, Grandma," the child said, "but I'm having so much fun with you, I haven't had time to think about it. I love it here in Bermuda. It feels like it's my real home instead of Boston."

"Well, darling, all your roots are here. It should feel like home. Both your mother and your father were born in this very house. There's a lot of Bermudian history in the name Sarah Odlum Billings."

"My cousins tease me about it," Sarah said. "They say the initials spell something bad. What do they mean?"

"Don't you worry about them. It's a name to be proud of. Now stop trying to keep me talking. It's time for your nap."

"Oh, Grandma, I'm five. I shouldn't have to have a nap like a baby."

Primrose ruffled Sarah's pale blond hair. The love she felt for this child was so great, she hated being parted from her even for a few minutes. She was selfishly pleased that Jeff and Carol were so busy with their careers that they had agreed to let the child summer with her. Poor Jeff, the more successful he got the harder he worked. And Carol, with her talk show on Boston TV, trying to juggle career and motherhood. But they were passionately happy together and doted on their daughter. Primrose was proud of their drive; with the millions Kosmos was worth, neither of them had to work at all.

"Why are they having the fireworks, anyway?" Sarah asked. "Grandma Jane works in a bank and they never have fireworks."

"This is different, darling. The fireworks are to celebrate the opening of a big new building. A titled Englishman, a Duke, has come all the way from England to cut the ribbon. Everyone's excited. It's supposed to be a good thing for Bermuda, creating jobs for lots of people and bringing a whole lot of new money to the island."

"If I lived here I wouldn't worry about money. I'd just sit in the sun all day."

"And take naps," Primrose said. "Come on. I'll read you a story. Then I've got to go to the House of Assembly for a little while. We're having a formal sitting to welcome the Duke to Bermuda."

John Clay swayed and almost fell from his stool at the bar of the Moonshine Restaurant; he'd been drinking rum since mid-morning and was off in a world of his own, muttering to himself, laughing at secret jokes, growling ominously when any of the younger patrons got too close to him. Bob the bartender kept a wary eye on him. Old John was a bit creaky in the joints and he didn't make much sense, but he was still a huge and powerful man and had been known to fell, with one punch from his hamlike fist, fellows half his age. They'd tried barring him from the Moonshine, but Clay ignored the prohibition; it wasn't worth the physical risk of enforcing it. So now they let him sit at his stool until he collapsed in a drunken stupor and could be carried out to the couch in the poolroom at the back of the bar.

"Fucking white bastards," John Clay said. He was having one of his moments of lucidity. "Them and their fucking in-ter-nation-al banking. What does it mean for the black people? Nothing but tears. They steal our houses and give 'em to the new people and force men like me to live in shacks."

Bob figured it wasn't wise to remind Clay he'd been only too happy to sell his cottage to the redevelopment people. The money he'd got had kept him in drink for more than a year.

"It's an insult to us, that's what it is," Clay continued. "All the fuss about opening their new building, some poxy cousin of the Queen coming out here and living it up at our expense. Someone ought to burn their god-damned building down instead of celebrating its opening." He shoved his glass across the wet bar top and Bob refilled it.

"You're not going down to watch the fireworks, then, John?" Bob said. He always tried to keep his remarks as innocuous as possible. You never knew what might set him off.

"Oh, I'll be there all right." The old man chortled. "I have to keep an eye on the bastards. No one else is. Half of our people have sold out. Listening to silver tongues like Mat Youngblood. Jesus, we are our own worst enemies!"

"I guess you're right," Bob said and went back to polishing the glasses.

Allie Youngblood finished setting the table for lunch and listened to her husband's footsteps coming up the neat path to their cottage. She liked it when Mat could get home in the middle of the day; he was so busy with his work in the community, they had few opportunities to be together.

"How was court this morning, darling?" she said, stretching up to kiss him and taking his battered briefcase. "What happened with the Tracys' boy?"

He frowned, and she saw the lines of care etched in his face, the gray in his dark hair. The man was just forty but looked years older. If only he were not so driven. She wondered if they could afford a vacation with her folks in New York. She wanted to get him away for a while, get him somewhere they could relax and forget about the struggles of Bermuda.

"The magistrate didn't listen, didn't want to know," Mat said, bitterness in his eyes. "He gave the kid six months. You know what that means. A boy who's only a runaway now will come out of prison a real criminal. There's no justice for our people here. We have no rights. Even in the Deep South they've felt the winds of change. But not here, not in smug little Bermuda."

She sat him down and brought him a cool glass of lemonade.

"Are you still going to march tonight?" she asked. "I

wish you wouldn't. You do enough for our people in the courts; it's not right for you to take to the streets with a protest banner. You have to work from within the system."

"I'm just about sick of the system, Allie. We have to protest tonight. What the whites are celebrating is another setback for us. International banking hasn't meant a single new job for blacks, except for being a maid in one of their grand houses. Look at the black hospital. It's worse now than it was in my father's day. And the schools—the kind of education they're getting, our children can never expect to be anything more than waiters and maids." He glanced up at her and smiled. "Speaking of school, where's Stephen?"

"He took lunch with him today. He wanted to practice cricket. They've made him captain of the under-eleven team."

"That's good. We might yet see another Youngblood star in a Cup Match. Hell, Allie, I'm sorry I'm always too busy to play with him. I'll try harder." She put the food in front of him and kissed him. "I'll make more time to be with him—and with you," he promised.

"But in the meantime, you're still going to the demonstration tonight," she teased. "Mat Youngblood, when are you going to learn charity begins at home?"

"Come here," he laughed, grabbing her around the waist. "We've got the house to ourselves and I'm not due back in court until two. I'll show you what begins at home." He squeezed her bottom. Arms around each other, they headed for the bedroom.

The Duke of Paddington had been droning on for what seemed like an hour; the audience squirmed in their hard wooden chairs and gazed up into the star-blazed heavens. Edward Lapin, looking down on them from the VIP platform, shared their boredom. At least the Duke's speech was making his own look like a model of wit and brevity. All the friendly white faces in front of him, the fine old names as familiar to him as his own. Somewhere out beyond the perimeter of the invited guests, he could hear the occasional chant from the black protestors, but the police had them well under control. Once the fireworks display began, they'd all shut up, anyway. Nobody could resist fireworks. He glanced at his watch; if the old fool didn't finish speaking and cut the ribbon soon, they would all be late for the formal dinner at the Tropicana.

On the other side of the Duke, Colin Fleet was also letting his eyes run over the audience and farther out, across Front Street to the dark waters of the harbor. His courier from the ship should be preparing to bring the stuff ashore now. It was a great scheme: a suitcaseful of heroin smuggled ashore at the height of the fireworks display when the token Customs force would have their eyes fixed in the same direction as everyone else. Thinking about the drug, he licked his lips. He would keep more than usual of this shipment for himself before sending the rest on to his New York distributors. He really needed the stuff these days. It was the only way he could control the raging in his head or find the energy to go about his business. It was a neat scheme, he thought, congratulating himself again. Bring the stuff in from Marseilles through the island's lax Customs and transship it to New York, where the authorities gave only cursory checks to cargoes from drug-free Bermuda.

He brought his gaze back to the audience. There she was in the front row, Mary Amberley, all dressed in pink linen. He supposed he'd better speed up his courtship. His aunt was making noises about his still not being married. Veronica figured Mary Amberley was the girl to change that situation. Well, she was rich enough and pretty enough, he thought. It was just that he didn't want to be married. Drugs and drink and his male friends— what else did a man need? There were always black whores and willing tourists if he needed to get laid. Colin sighed. He'd hoped Veronica would be dead by now, and the pressure off him. But there she was, right in the center of the front row, a very hearty sixty years old, and looking quite regal.

* * *

Mat Youngblood again cautioned his column of demonstrators not to step out of line. The cordon of police between them and the official ceremony appeared to be
itching to use their batons.

"Just keep walking," he called. "Don't stop or they'll
arrest you for obstruction." He hoisted his placard
higher: "Jobs and houses before banks" it said.

He could hear the Duke's voice floating out over the
crowd. He wished the man would sit down so they could
all go home. He was tired and despondent; the protest
was having not the slightest effect on the comfortable
white crowd.

And at last, to scattered applause and audible sighs of
relief, the Duke finished talking and cut the ribbon on
the great bronze doors of the Lapin Center. The outdoor
lights were switched off and the fireworks began. It was
a brilliant display, organized by a family imported from
France for the occasion. Flares and rockets lit up the
night as bright as day; bangs and screeches forced the
small children and some of the women to cover their ears.

John Clay steadied himself in the branches of the old
mahogany tree across from the new bank building. He
lovingly stroked the barrel of the Lee and Enfield 303
and slowly raised it to rest on a tree branch. The target
was some fifty yards away and lit only by the bursts of
fireworks, but John Clay was confident of his ability as
a marksman. And the Duke was wearing a dazzling
white uniform with red sash. That helped.

No one heard the shot, or if they did, mistook it for part
of the noisy celebrations. It was not until someone in the
front row glanced up at the speakers' platform and saw
the Duke clutching his chest to staunch the flow of blood
staining his uniform that the screaming began. The
rockets went on exploding as frantic people dashed back-
and forward; wild rumors swept the crowd. The blacks
had revolted and were going to kill them all. A crazed
sailor was up the mast of the ship moored at the dock,
picking them off one by one. The police had mutinied.

The crowd pushed back, away from the platform, leaving an empty space of tumbled chairs. Those on the plat-

form had scrambled for the floor. And still the French family happily ignited the display it had so carefully choreographed.

"Lights! Turn on the lights!" Lapin yelled, and at last someone responded and the body of the Duke was revealed, collapsed on the platform, his uniform front soaked in blood, a look of horror frozen on his face. A police inspector ran forward and sprang up onto the platform to check the body. Other police turned on the black demonstrators and began beating them in a fury of fear, anger and bewilderment. Mat Youngblood took a truncheon blow to the side of his head, went down and stayed down, waiting for the hysteria to ease.

In his tree John Clay smiled, revealing his big broken teeth. He pulled the cork from his rum bottle and drained the contents. Then, still clutching the rifle, he passed out and fell gracefully from his hiding place to land, quite unconscious, at the feet of two policemen.

Mat Youngblood handled the defense but it was almost a lost cause. Clay didn't care whether or not he was defended; he felt his action had vindicated a lifetime of repression and was proud, in his deranged way, of what he had done. Youngblood in his summing up tried to explain the forces driving Clay and appealed for mercy. But the court was not interested in excuses; the assassination had gravely damaged Bermuda's reputation. The tourists were staying away; the new businessmen were wondering if they had chosen the right tax haven. There was a sigh of relief when the judge donned the black cap and pronounced a sentence of death by hanging.

The riots on the day of John Clay's execution left every window on Front Street smashed and the street itself lined with burning vehicles.

Primrose watched the rioters from the window of her Assembly office. She could see the tall figure of Mat Youngblood moving about in front of the crowd, pleading for calm, stopping the worst of the violence, keeping the police and rioters from going head-to-head, preventing a total bloodbath.

"The end of an era," she said to her secretary. "It had to end, of course. It was wrong. It is terrible, though, that it ended in death and violence. Now, if we are to have a future, we must address ourselves to the injustices that have been done to these people. They must be given full rights as Bermudians or there will be no more Bermuda."

The next day peace was restored; only forty-odd blacks had been arrested, and there was a tacit understanding among the authorities that they be treated leniently. It was in the interests of all the community that the whole affair be buried as quickly as possible. Colin Fleet and a few of his cronies at first called for the full weight of the law to be applied to the black community, but his aunt firmly disabused him of the idea.

"You are letting your hatred of them get in the way of good business sense," Veronica said. "Unless we get this situation dampened down, we're ruined. Look at the cruise ships—empty. And the hotels. Ever since the assassination Bermuda's been a dirty word in the tourist business. They shouldn't have hanged crazy old Clay—just locked him up forever. The hanging and the riots have set us back another season."

"You'd let those savages get away with mayhem just for the sake of business?" Colin was incredulous. "That's no way to run a country. If they see they are going to be handled with kid gloves, they'll do it again."

"Sometimes you don't think like a Fleet," she said. "Look, as long as we have the numbers we control everything. What's got to be done now, to ensure we keep our majority, is win over a proportion of the blacks. The middle-class ones who own a cab or have their own small business. Someday we'll have to integrate the government, and the way to do it is to isolate the black radicals, picture them as a lunatic fringe which even their own people despise."

She watched him leave her office. Much as she loved him, he was a worry to her. There was something strange about him, a mad desire to strike out at anyone who got in his path. Quite an admirable quality in the old days, but not now, not when a cool head was needed to keep their vast enterprise forging ahead. If Colin would just settle down, she thought, she might hand over control to him. She wanted to; lately she was so often tired and irritable. And lonely. It was so long since there had been a man in her life, and that had been only briefly. If she could just get away—a grand tour of Europe, perhaps. She wasn't really old yet, and she would love to give herself a chance to find some pleasure in her life. Perhaps marriage would straighten Colin out. She would speak to Mary Amberley's mother and see how that affair was coming along.

Veronica crossed to the window and stood looking down into Front Street. Normally this time of the season, it would be packed with tourists buying marvelous bargains from Europe, linen and crystal, cashmere and silver. But today she knew almost every face on the street. The horse cabs were drawn up across from her, their drivers talking lethargically in the shade, the horses dozing, waiting for tourists who weren't there.

Veronica watched Primrose Odlum's tall figure cross Front Street. She had the little girl, her granddaughter, in tow, and the two of them stopped by the horses where the child nervously fed them lumps of sugar. Veronica scowled. Primrose looked so composed, so sure of her place in this society, so happy and proud of the child. The sun caught the little girl's head and her hair gleamed; she looked up at her grandmother and laughed and Veronica imagined the sound. It cut like a knife. The Odlum woman had been through so much, yet she conducted herself like the most contented woman in the world. All right, thought Veronica, she would hurry Colin's courtship along and they would produce grandchildren for her. A little blond girl like that one. She studied the child again. The coloring, the build—she could have been a Fleet. But not the expression, Veronica thought. Fleet children had never laughed or loved so openly.

* * *

"Why did they break all the windows, Grandma?" Sarah asked. The glass had been swept away, but some of the shopfronts were still boarded up waiting for the overworked glaziers to get to them.

"They were upset and confused." Primrose said. "Things like that sometimes happen in small, crowded places. We all have to try to understand the pressures and work to see it doesn't happen again." She squeezed the child's hand. "Now, are you sure you've got presents for everyone back home? There won't be time to shop before the plane leaves tomorrow."

"I've gotten everyone something," Sarah said. "I don't want to shop anymore. Can we go on our picnic now?"

"Of course. It's such a beautiful day, I've just had a great idea. We'll get the basket from the car and hire one of the horse cabs to take us to our picnic."

Sarah bounced around in the open carriage, jumping up to clutch at the brilliantly colored hibiscus and oleander blossoms hanging over their heads as the horse jogged down the narrow lanes. How many journeys like this Primrose had made, the clop-clop of the horse, the crunch of carriage wheels on coral roads, the old black driver singing softly to himself. She smelled again the scents of Bermuda: a hundred perfumes from the trees and flowers, salt on the light breeze, the sharp tang of a sweating horse, the dry smell of sunshine and dust.

So little traffic, just as it had been when she was a girl of Sarah's age. They were passing the old white church where her parents were buried, and she called to the driver to stop. She and Sarah walked through the churchyard, its soft white gravestones surrounded by living flowers. Birds swooped and sung above them in the blue sky; on a day like this it was a happy place and Primrose felt close to her long-departed parents. Sarah touched the gravestones and spelled out the names and dates, then returned to Primrose and took her hand again.

"This is where I want to be buried when I die," she said. "But, Grandma, now's time for our picnic."

They climbed back in the carriage and started up the

rise to the cliff-top fields above St. George's. Their driver
led his horse away to graze on the long green grass, and
Primrose and Sarah carefully spread their rugs and put
out the food they'd packed that morning. Before they ate
she showed Sarah her secret cave behind the wall of
bracken; the child was fearless and went wriggling into
the dark recesses of the cave while Primrose waited at
the entrance.

"Grandma!" she gasped when she emerged, dusty and
cobwebbed. "There're a whole pile of old bones in there.
They look like they were people once. Why aren't they
back in the churchyard like the others?"

"I think they've been there forever, darling. And they
can't hurt us. Just leave them in peace."

After lunch she dozed while Sarah explored farther
afield. A cloud passed before the sun; she shivered and
came awake. Out to sea more clouds were rolling in; it
was early for the tempests but they should be heading
home. Even a little storm would soak them in the slow,
open carriage. She looked around for Sarah and saw her
coming back from the cliff top, accompanied by a large
man. Not their driver; he and the horse were at the other
end of the field and only just starting down toward her.

"Good day, ma'am," the man said as they got closer.
"Your granddaughter and I've been having a most fascinating conversation. She's certainly an Odlum—quite
in love with our islands."

"Hello, Captain Smutters," Primrose said. "Yes, I
don't think Sarah wants to go back to Boston. She doesn't
realize we don't loaf about like this every day. Most times
it's just work, work, work." She realized her *faux pas.*
"Oh, I'm sorry. What are you doing with yourself these
days, Captain?"

"Not too much, ma'am. I can't say I was ready for retirement but now I'm beginning to enjoy it. If and when
the tourists return, I might do a few fishing trips." He
sat down on the grass beside her. "But it's funny how you
discover how little you need. I live on what my garden
and the sea provide. I've got the cottage and my books—
I might just be the happiest man in Bermuda." He

chuckled. "And I'm trying to write about the place. My ancestors were meticulous fellows, like all good sea captains. They kept copious notes, and not just of their voyages. So I'm trying to write this book about how we all got to where we are. I think I'll call it *The Forty Thieves.*"

"Excellent title!" She laughed. "But I think you might have to get it published outside the colony. There are so many skeletons people want kept in their cupboards."

"Like the ones in the cave?" Sarah asked.

"No, dear, it's just a figure of speech," Primrose said. She stood up and waved to their driver. "We must get home, Captain. It looks like rain coming. Can we drop you in St. George's?"

"Thank you, no. I'm only a short walk, and the rain will hold off awhile yet."

"Then you must come to dinner with me one night soon," she said. "My own family always kept accounts of the doings in the colony. There might be something in the family records that could help."

"I'd like that very much," he said. "But I'm not sure it would be wise to open up family diaries. If I ever do finish this book, a lot of noses will be put out of joint."

"So? You forget, Captain. The Odlums are not now, and never were, members of the Forty Thieves."

He tied the cravat carefully and fixed it with a diamond pin, then put on the heavy jacket of his morning suit. It was lucky it was cool and autumnal; a hot Bermuda day could make formal wear a torture. Colin Fleet adjusted the gray top hat and studied himself in the mirror. Not bad, quite dashing, in fact. The fix of heroin had gone right through his veins and his earlier nervousness had vanished. He was quite looking forward to the wedding now, even feeling stirrings of sexual interest. She'd kept him at arm's length through the courtship, but tonight he would show Mary Amberley what it was all about.

"Time to go, Colin," Edward Lapin called from the sitting room.

He placed the hat under his arm and went out to his waiting best man and they walked down the broad stairs

to the front of the house where the car was drawn up. He
was silent during the short drive to the cathedral, gazing out at the familiar landscape, ignoring the stares and
waves from the interested black kids along the way.

The great white church was packed as he and Lapin
entered; he saw all the faces he knew so well, Bermuda's
finest. The Governor, the Premier, the Chief Justice . . .
everyone who mattered was here for this wedding of two
of the colony's most illustrious names. He passed his
aunt in the front pew. She was actually smiling, looking
very happy, a rare occurrence. The old organ thundered
into life as he stood before the altar and listened to the
whispers preceding his bride down the aisle. He glanced
at her when she reached his side; she was a damned good-
looking girl. Pity he didn't feel anything much for her,
but one couldn't expect everything. It was a most suitable marriage.

Mary Amberley wished she had taken an extra Val-
ium. She felt dreadful, awake and crying through the
night before. Her mother had been no help at all, beside
herself with pride about marrying her daughter off to the
last of the Fleet line. Mary had kept to herself the awful
gossip she had lately been hearing about Colin Fleet and
his strange habits, the tales of his insane rages, stories
about his weird friends. Her mother wouldn't listen. According to her, Colin was "charmingly eccentric."

The Archbishop droned on and on, but at last the ceremony was over and they were standing outside in the
sunshine while the photographers took their pictures
and their friends milled about. Mary kept smiling, but
deep inside her was the fear that she had just made the
biggest mistake of her young life.

Across the road from the cathedral, Allie Youngblood
put her hand on her husband's arm and made him stop
a moment.

"Doesn't she look lovely," Allie said. "I hope she enjoys her day."

"She won't have much more to enjoy," Mat grunted.
"Not married to that bastard."

"Hush!" Allie said. "The boy's language is bad enough

already without your example." She glanced back at
young Stephen who was gazing in a store window. The
boy was shooting up fast; his best suit was already too
short at the arms and legs, and she'd only bought it six
months ago. Allie wondered if there would ever be a time
when they could stop worrying about money. For all
Mat's prominence in the black community, his law practice brought in little cash. She looked up at her husband,
handsome in his dark blue suit, and felt the familiar
thrill of love.

"Come on. Stop gaping at the bride," he said. "We're
late already." He was eager to get to the Labor Club and
claim his regular Saturday table. Then the rest of the day
would be spent in political debate, gossip, food and drink,
while Allie and the other wives shopped Court Street and
the children played. He glanced once more at the bridal
party. He supposed he didn't really wish Colin Fleet any
harm; all Mat wanted was for him, his family, and his
people to live in dignity and democracy.

She sat up in bed and looked around the honeymoon
suite of the Tropicana Hotel. The whole hotel, she
thought, could do with a facelift. Perhaps she would
make that one of her tasks, now that she was a Fleet.
Mary fluffed up the pillows around her and checked her
hair and makeup in the mirror of the little gold compact;
Colin was taking his time in the bathroom. She yawned.
It had been a long day of endless toasts and banqueting,
and she was tired and nervous. And she needed to go to
the bathroom. She got out of the bed and crossed the
room. There was no answer to her tap on the door, but it
did swing open to reveal her husband sitting on the edge
of the bath, the sleeve of his silk dressing gown pushed
up and a necktie tight around his upper arm. A syringe
was in his hand and a needle had penetrated a vein.

"Colin!" she said. "What's wrong?"

He stared at her a moment, unseeing. His cold blue
eyes were blank, but as she watched, they came alive.
She did not like what she saw there and took a step back

as he removed the needle, rolled down his sleeve and stood up.

"Dear Mary," he said, "I've kept you waiting." His voice was soft but there was a dangerous catch in it. He saw her sudden fear. "I should have told you about this," he said, indicating the syringe. "It's my little secret. You see, I'm a diabetic. Oh, it's nothing to worry about and scarcely bothers me. I just give myself a daily shot and I live quite normally." He moved past her into the bedroom. "I'll be waiting for you," he said and closed the bathroom door.

When she returned to the bed, the glow in his eyes was even more intense; she took it to be lust and felt a shiver run through her. She switched off the light and slid in beside him, anticipation and fear and the fatigue of the day churning up inside her. She gasped when his cold hand found her breast, but her slowly awakening passion died as he continued down her body, probing at her as if she were just some object he'd found in his bed. If he would slow down, take time to relax her, speak to her of love, kiss her . . . but he was forging ahead without her, hiking up her pretty French gown and forcing her legs apart. He was kneeling between her thighs and she could feel his weapon, huge and hard, forcing an entry. She gasped in pain as he invaded her, and the sound made him force even harder. Her mother had said there would be a little pain, but surely she hadn't meant something like this. When the blood began to flow it was a fraction easier for her, but with every thrust he seemed to grow larger—and farther away from her in spirit. She longed for him to be slow and tender but, biting her lip, she realized she was only a vessel for him. He went on for what seemed like hours, grunting in time with the squeaking bedsprings. He did not notice her tears and stifled moans, and did not hear his own animal sounds; Colin's brain was soaring somewhere in the strange clouds of the drug. His body was a machine locked into another machine. He could not possibly understand the hatred of him that was born in her on their wedding night.

* * *

"The worst thing about getting old," Primrose said, "is realizing you won't be around to see the results of everything you worked for and hoped for. I suppose I'm good for another fifteen or twenty years, but that won't be long enough to know what's going to happen here. Bermuda's only tiny but it's the devil of a place to effect change."

Smutters laughed. "Don't be so sure about that. The changes will come and they'll come fast now. By the time your little Sarah's a woman, this will be a very different country." He looked into his glass of port and sighed. "Although you're right in that it'll be just about too late for us. What a damned waste it's been, the Forty Thieves spending so much effort holding back the inevitable."

"Yes," Primrose said, "a waste of time and lives. I remember my parents so clearly; they thought every day they spent in Bermuda was a privilege and not to be abused. I think they were the happiest people I've ever heard of."

"No happier than me, ma'am. A magnificent dinner and charming company. I haven't talked so much in years." He glanced at his watch. "Good Lord! I've overstayed my welcome. It's almost midnight."

"Nonsense," she said, standing up and refilling his glass. "The one great advantage of being old and on your own is you aren't answerable to anyone else. As long as you're not bored, sit a while longer, stay and tell me some more about your writing. I'm fascinated."

"You could do a better book than anything I attempt," he said, accepting the glass and stretching luxuriously, his polished boots almost touching the grate where the fire now burned low. "You Odlums were at the center of most of the dramas through the centuries, all the passions and hatreds. We Smutters were just bystanders for the most part, seafarers who did as they were told and kept out of the way of the ruling class."

"I think you did quite a bit more than that, Henry," she said. "I've read my own family's notes and I've kept a good ear to the ground myself." She looked fondly at the big man; they had been casual aquaintances for a long time but it was only now, in the late part of their lives, she had got close to him. They dined weekly and she had come to look on these pleasant evenings in her house as the high point of her calendar.

"I know what I would like to do," he said, sitting up, a spark in his dark eyes. "I'd like to leave Bermuda some kind of heritage, something to be used for the betterment of the place. Scholarships for the black kids, maybe, and a library to remind the people of all they've been through. And I know just how to achieve it, too." This was the thing he had sworn himself not to talk about, the dream he had had for years and always repressed because he knew "they" wouldn't let it be achieved. But Primrose Odlum was different; she was a damn strong woman who didn't bow to anyone. He could tell her about his scheme.

"My father," he said, "left me a map. Yes . . ." he grinned. "A good old-fashioned treasure map. He drew it up back at the start of the century, when he was running cargoes for the Fleets. He ran onto a sandspit about a hundred miles west of here. Anyway, in the twelve hours it took 'em to get off, he went exploring and found some pieces of eight and a silver ingot big as a side of beef. He kept the coins and buried the ingot back in the sand. But he said there was a stack more there—he could feel the ingots bruising his feet as he walked about on the sandspit. But he only kept the coins and none of the crew was ever any the wiser about what he'd found. When he got back to Bermuda he did a lot of reading of the old Spanish records and he figured out it was the wreck of part of the fleet that went down in the big tempest in 1622. It wasn't the mother lode in the *Atocha*—she's supposed to be in the Gulf of Mexico—but it probably was from the same fleet, which got decimated in the big storm and spread all over the place. Whatever, the ship my father found had to be carrying treasure worth a few million dollars in today's currency. And she's sitting out there ready to salvage." He fingered the gold coin under his shirt. "I figure it would be a nice thing to go out there and get some of the stuff and use it for Bermuda's future."

"You're an incredible man," she said. She stared at him. "You've never had any real money and yet you've been sitting on a fortune all these years. Why haven't you gone to collect it before this?"

"Because it doesn't belong to me or anyone else. I figure it belongs to Bermuda and finally I can see how it might be used for the good of our country. I wouldn't have raised the matter now except you seem to think as I do."

"How much to go and get it?"

"Quite a lot. Charter an oceangoing tug, a couple of divers. I could probably put it all together for thirty thousand dollars."

"When do you want to start? I'll write you the check now."

"No hurry. Wait until spring, when the tempests have gone. No point in ending up out there in the same resting place as the Spaniard." He drained his glass and stood up. "Now I really have to get on home." Their eyes held a moment and they shared a sense of what might have been between them if it had been a different place. "You're a good woman, Primrose Odlum," he said. "If there'd been more of you and your family instead of the bloody Forty Thieves, Bermuda would be a better place."

"All that's ending now, anyway, Henry," she said. "The old names aren't going to matter so much. Finally it will be what people do. And that's the way it should be."

She saw him out of the house and closed the big doors. She went back to the sitting room and poured herself a nightcap. It was true: Bermuda would be all right eventually, when everyone was given a fair shake. But in the meantime people like her and Henry Smutters had missed out on so much, hidebound by stupid conventions. She moved around the room turning off the lights and looking down at the moonlit waters of the Great Sound. If Richard had lived, if he was with her now, they would have achieved some of what Smutters also cared about. She paused before switching off the last lamp. It glowed on pictures of Richard, Jeff and Sarah. Primrose brushed a tear from her eye. The little girl would carry on; she already loved Bermuda and she would be a real Odlum.

Veronica wasn't going to beat about the bush with the girl. She waited only until the maid had served their tea and withdrawn from the sitting room before fixing her hard blue eyes on Mary.

"You've been married six months," she said, "and still no sign of a baby. What's going on with you two? You look so unhappy. Isn't Colin doing his duty?"

Mary Fleet studied her hands. She wanted to tell this woman it was none of her business, but like all of them she was terrified of Veronica. But she also wanted to tell someone about her fears and the hell her marriage had already become.

"I know how much you want us to have a child," she said. "It was the reason you pushed Colin into the marriage." She said this without bitterness; her own mother would have done anything to see her married to a Fleet and there had been a time when she had liked the idea herself. "I've done everything to ensure we do. My doctor says ... well, he's surprised I'm not pregnant already but figures it's too early to start worrying. He's sure it will all come right in time." Now she toyed with her teacup. "Aunt Veronica, this is very embarrassing but I think it may have something to do with Colin. He's got very strange. And he's taking drugs."

"What do you mean? Drugs! Don't be stupid, girl."

"No, it's true." She stared at Veronica. "Colin hasn't got diabetes, has he?"

"Of course not. He's as healthy as a ... well, he's healthier than most of the Fleet men ever were. What's this nonsense about diabetes?"

"I wanted to believe it. The needles and syringes, hiding himself away in the bathroom. But even someone as dense as I am has to face the truth in the end. Colin's addicted to heroin."

"You're a liar. You're making this up to cover some sin of your own." She felt sick and afraid; she knew there was something wrong with Colin but through all the years she had refused to face it. He was all she had, the only hope of keeping their name going.

"I wouldn't lie about a thing like this. What for? God knows, I want this marriage to work. I know my duty, what's expected of me. My family's been here almost as long as the Fleets. It's not just the drugs, although maybe they're the cause of it, but it's also the way Colin treats me. We don't . . . we don't make love. He treats me as though I'm some kind of whore, to be used and punished. And his rages—I swear sometimes I'm afraid he's going to kill me." She looked up at the older woman. "In the circumstances, it's no great surprise I'm not pregnant."

"You're exaggerating all this. Things will settle down between the two of you. Marriage takes a while to adjust to. And look what you've got—our name, unlimited wealth and influence, one of the grandest houses in the colony. You're the envy of everyone. Look, I know Colin can be difficult, but all men have their faults. We women have to make allowances. I had to marry a man I detested, but I stuck it out and did my duty."

"I think Colin should see a psychiatrist before it's too late."

"Nonsense! I'll talk to him, tell him to be more gentle with you. And if there is anything in this drug thing, well, I'm sure it's just a passing whim. I'll put a stop to it." She forced a smile; she needed to keep the girl on her side. "I'm glad we've had our little talk, and I'll do anything to help you through this difficult time. Just as long as you pull your weight, too."

Mary suppressed a shrug. She was trapped with no way out, at least not until things got very much worse.

Colin lied easily, but she knew he was lying. She listened patiently to his protestations of innocence, nodding sympathetically when he claimed his wife was an immature girl with a dangerous imagination. She let him go on, watched him striding around her study, building himself up to a peak of self-pity. It was only when he was slumped down again in the seat across from her that she reached in the desk and brought out the plastic-wrapped parcel. She stood up and moved close to him.

"I went up to your house this morning, Colin," she said. "I shooed the servants away and went through all your secret places. I found this."

He was suddenly whiter than his normal pallor and his hand twitched as he saw the package she threw down on the desk. He started forward, but she was between him and the desk, swiftly undoing the wrapping.

"Even I know what this stuff is," she said. It was open on the desk now, the brown-white substance dull in the sunlight streaming into the study. She turned suddenly and flung the precious grains in his face; it clung to his skin and his hair, fell on his shoulders like dandruff, scattered around his feet on the burgundy carpet.

He felt himself choking, real pain sweeping his body. That was a quarter pound of pure heroin she'd just flung into the air, heroin he needed, couldn't live without. He fell on his knees and began to scrabble at the carpet, trying to extract the heroin from the thick nap of the rug.

"You weakling." He heard the snarl just before the toe of her pointed shoe caught him on the side of the face. "You're a disgrace to our name." She kicked out at him again, and he had to roll across the floor to escape her fury. She sprang on him then, surprisingly heavy, straddling his chest and pummeling him with her fists. He felt terror at the fury confronting him; he covered up as best he could and rode out the storm of blows. At last she rolled away from him, dragged herself up off the floor and staggered to her desk.

He heard the sound as he lay on the rug, dizzy and confused. It was something he had never heard before; his aunt, the toughest woman in the world, was weeping. It was a desperate, despairing sound, echoing the struggles the women of Bermuda had faced through the ages. It reached him in his heart and he got up and went to her, put his arms around her strong shoulders and held her.

"I'm sorry," he whispered. "I'm so confused. I didn't want to let you down as my father and my uncle did." He

was almost glad it was out in the open now. Veronica
would know what to do. She always had.

The tears had not been part of her plan; they had surprised her as much as they had Colin. It was so long since
she had given way to such an emotion. But now she had
to be strong and ruthless. She shrugged his arm away
and sat back in her chair.

"I don't want your apologies or your promises," she
said. "A common drug addict! You people lie and cheat
and steal to get your loathsome pleasures. There's only
one way to save you from yourself, Colin, and that is by
using force. If you ever touch this drug again I shall turn
you over to the police. You know how strictly we enforce
drug laws. The jail is filled with blacks who merely
smoked marijuana. Imagine what an example they'll
make of you, a Fleet involved with heroin! It would break
my heart to turn you in, but it's already broken so don't
imagine I won't do it." He started to speak, but she held
up her hand.

"No. Just shut up and listen to me. I'm going to arrange for a psychiatrist and an addiction specialist to fly
down here from New York and lock themselves up with
you for as long as it takes to cure you. At least money
buys privacy. No one will know what's going on behind
the walls of your house. And you will cooperate, Colin.
It's the only chance you have." He nodded, still too
shaken to understand all she was saying. "By tomorrow
there'll be three male nurses watching you around the
clock. We'll put it about that you're suffering some mystery illness." She stood up and had to clutch the edge of
her desk; her head was swimming and she feared she was
going to faint. "Get over to your office now and tidy up
anything that needs doing. This is going to be a long
process."

Dr. Denton was grave, for all the good news he seemed
to be giving her.

"He's detoxified now and there's no reason he should
return to heroin dependency," he said. "All he needs is
the willpower to resist. We can prescribe a course of

chemicals that will make it easier for him, a crutch, if
you like, for the next year or so. It helps being rich," he
added. "There are so many diversions. But of course, so
many temptations, too." He sighed. "There's something
else. I did all the blood tests as a matter of routine. I
wasn't looking for it and it came as a shock." He hesitated and saw the impatient jerk of her head. "Your
nephew is suffering from congenital syphilis. The prognosis is not at all good. The disease has been undetected
in his system from birth and it is only a matter of time
before its gravest effects begin to show. Already, the irrational rages occur. They are a symptom. I take it his
parents were married here in Bermuda." She nodded. "A
pity. In the U.S. there would have been tests, the disease
would have been detected and the child not harmed."

"There is no cure?" She kept her voice flat; she was not
going to let this fussy little man see how gravely she was
shocked.

"No, ma'am. His life expectancy is not much past fifty.
But before that there could be bouts of quite irrational
behavior. To be blunt, insanity."

"What about his children?"

"He is, mercifully I think, sterile. It sometimes happens in these cases."

She thanked the doctor and saw him out of her study,
then went to stand by the window. She fought against
the grief, trying to hold it off. But even her great strength
was not enough and silent tears flowed down her cheeks.
Outside the window was a brilliant blue spring day; in
Veronica's heart was the beginning of her darkest winter.

Henry Smutters had spent the winter preparing for his
expedition. He had made one solo trip, sailing his old
ketch out to the sandspit to make sure the wreck was still
there. He'd gone over the area in a rowboat at low tide
and the metal detector had gone crazy. The two young
black divers he hired for the spring trip were sworn to
secrecy, but nevertheless, when the stout little tug and
its crew of six finally set sail, St. George's was buzzing

with stories about "Cap'n Smutters's Treasure Hunt." Smutters stood in the wheelhouse, puffing his pipe and humming to himself as they passed the breakwater. It was a great feeling to be in command of his own ship again. He grinned at the memory of Primrose, eager to come along on the voyage, hard to convince it was no place for a woman.

It was a fifteen-hour journey to the site. The old diesel engine pushed them easily through the flat seas. They dropped anchor in the dark on the edge of the sandspit, prepared a meal and settled down in the cramped quarters. Before he slept, Smutters thought of his father, sixty-odd years before, aground in these same waters, finding the treasure and then returning it to its resting place. It was right to recover it now, Smutters thought, and use it to make Bermuda a better place.

The morning was pale and calm. As the tide ran out they could see the sand glowing just below the surface of the water. It was so shallow there was no need of diving suits; his men could use them later if they had to dig far below the spit, but for now they snorkeled around the area looking for traces of the treasure. By mid-morning they had recovered forty-two silver pieces of eight, ten gold doubloons and a bar of solid silver weighing close to a hundred pounds.

"Jesus," Smutters whispered as he looked at the treasure laid out on the deck in the sunshine. He was awed by it, and wondered again if he was right to disturb it. The divers and crew seemed to feel the same awe; there was no jubilation. Too often in Bermuda's history, treasure had led to tragedy.

They dived at each of the next four low tides and the booty on the deck mounted. There was a ten-foot-long chain of soft yellow gold links; a dozen uncut emeralds; more silver and gold coins; and a collection of well-preserved silver cups and plates.

"It's enough," Smutters said at the end of their third day on the spit. "We'll sail for home in the morning." He broke out the rum that evening and they celebrated well past midnight. They weren't a bad bunch, his men, and he figured he could trust them for now. Later, of course, there would be a temptation to return to the wreck, which was why Smutters had done all the navigation himself, and had brought them to the site by a roundabout route. He was sure none of them would be able to find this spot again without his guidance.

The treasure was stowed belowdecks in a compartment forward of the engine; Smutters secured the hatch with a heavy chain and a massive brass padlock. The treasure would have to stay aboard until Primrose Odlum decided what to do with it; Smutters did not trust the wharf rats of St. George's not to attempt to pilfer his cargo. He kept a pocketful of coins to give Primrose.

She arrived at the wharf an hour after they berthed. Already rumors had spread. A knot of people were standing around watching the tug, and Primrose had to push her way through. Smutters helped her up to the wheelhouse, and there, on the chart table, spread the coins before her.

"They're beautiful, Henry," she said. Even with only the basic cleaning he had given them, the gold and silver glowed in her hands. She felt the weight of them, the solidness, the history. She listened as he described the rest of the haul and they tried to estimate its worth. They agreed there was more than enough to give the best pieces to the local museum and sell the rest to set up a scholarship fund for promising young Bermudians.

When the reporter from the *Gazette* arrived, Primrose and Smutters took turns describing their vision. Primrose said she hoped a committee of Assembly members would be set up to administer the fortune; Smutters told them how his father had found the wreck and left it lying in peace until the day the treasure could be used to benefit Bermuda.

When Colin Fleet read the story the next day, he immediately called his lawyers.

"Of course it belongs to the Fleets," he said when the senior partners from Amberley & Benbridge were settled in his office. He slapped the copy of the *Gazette* on his desk. "Smutters admits it. His father found the wreck while on a voyage for the Fleets."

The lawyers shifted uneasily.

"You've probably got a point in law, Colin," Eric Amberley said. "But are you sure you want to win? Primrose Odlum says they're not out to keep it for themselves. It wouldn't look good, your claiming it for yourself. It's not as if you needed the money—"

"I don't give a damn how it looks. And it's not the money. The stuff belongs to my family, it's part of our heritage. I might even build a new museum to display it. But it's mine and I'll decide how it is dispersed. I want you fellows to go into court and get a writ of sequestration or whatever you need. I'm damned if I'll sit back and let this treasure be flogged off to provide educations for shiftless blacks. Just do it!"

The court battle attracted more attention in the community than had the treasure itself. Most of the residents were rooting for the Odlum lawyers, but there was a general feeling the Fleets would triumph. The Fleets always got what they wanted. Through the three days of preliminary hearings Henry Smutters lived on the tug, fiercely rejecting the sheriff's suggestion that the treasure be removed to a safe place until the court decided its fate. Primrose found him on deck, big and menacing, a shotgun at his side, when she made a late-evening trip to St. George's.

"We're going to lose, Henry," she said. "My fellows say the court will announce it tomorrow. Damn the Fleets! How long will they run this colony like a fiefdom? You and I just wanted to do something nice for the country and we're going to be ripped off." There were tears of rage in her eyes. "I even went so far today as to call Veronica Fleet. We've hardly spoken in fifty years. I begged her to persuade Colin to drop his action. All she said was that anything Colin desired mattered to her, and she hung up on me. The way she talked, you'd think her bloody nephew was some tragic orphan who deserved special coddling."

"So when the court gives its decision they'll come and

seize all this," Smutters said, banging on the deck with the stock of his gun. "It won't be used for the purposes we intended, but end up in safe glass cases to be looked at by the Fleets and their friends."

He stood up and peered out into the velvet night. Across the square the tavern lights gleamed; laughter and singing came in on the breeze.

"You wanted to come along with me before," he said. "Now's your chance. I think it's a perfect night for a brief cruise."

They let go the mooring ropes and the tug drifted out into the harbor; he did not start the engine until they were in the shadow of the breakwater, so no one heard them leave.

"This will do," he said after an hour. They could just see the lights of the houses on the high points of the island. He could fix his position from the lights. He put the engine into neutral. "If you'll take the wheel, Primrose, and keep her nose into the swell, I'll get the stuff out and over the side."

She stood there for another hour, listening to him bumping about belowdecks. Then she heard the soft splashes as the precious cargo went over the side.

"That's done," he said, returning to the wheelhouse. He revved the engine and turned the boat for home. "If Fleet wants the treasure, he'll have to go find it." He laughed. "But just between you and me, it's lying in only fifteen feet of water. When all the fuss dies down, we can come and retrieve it, do what we set out to do. The coins I gave you, hide them somewhere. Tomorrow when the sheriff comes I'll show him the empty boat and tell him the whole thing was a joke, that there never was any treasure and we staged it all to make the Fleets look silly." He laughed again. "You don't win many rounds with the Fleets; I'm really going to enjoy this one."

Chapter Sixteen
(1972–)

Stephen Youngblood's head rang from the sacking he'd just suffered. He moved back to the line of scrimmage; now he could hear the Harvard crowd exhorting his team to one more effort, and the Princeton supporters jubilantly counting down the last seconds on the clock. No signals to call, no time. It was the play they always hoped they wouldn't have to use; "desperate and deep" the coach called it. Stephen took the snap and moved back three paces. His guards were holding; heaving and grunting against the heavier Princeton men, but holding. The autumn light over the field was crisp and clear with just a hint of blue wood smoke. He could see the empty end zone forty-five yards away but no one free between him and it. Stephen pumped his arm twice and waited, dancing on his toes. And then a raised arm as Bill Rollins broke free into the open. Stephen rifled the ball out over the players milling in front of him. It seemed as if the world had stopped. Silence in the stands as the pigskin soared above the turf on its way to the moving target and all the players, apart from the two desperately pursuing the sprinting Rollins, standing still to watch. The ball wobbled once as it came to the end of its flight and Stephen felt his knees trembling. He'd underpitched it and the game was lost. But somehow Rollins, in full flight, reached down to his boot tops and gathered it in in one big hand, shrugged off a tackler and went sprinting into the end zone.

They never got to take the point-after; the delirious home crowd invaded the field and swamped their heroes. Stephen was pummeled and pushed and lifted onto the shoulders of his teammates to sit above the surging masses, his eyes blinded by tears of joy. At the sideline he managed to scramble down and into the arms of Bill Rollins.

"Great pass, Steve," the big, blond receiver gasped, hugging him. "It was right on the button but I made it look harder. Had to do a little showboating to mark our last appearance for the old school." He punched Stephen on the shoulder. "Jesus! I wonder if we'll ever have another day in our lives like this."

In the locker room there was even more pandemonium as beer and champagne sprayed over the exhausted, exhilarated young men, and the glory of what they'd achieved was realized fully. Stephen's head was spinning and he forced a way through the ruckus to sink down on a bench in the corner. It was all and more than he could have hoped for, the grand finish to his glory days at Harvard. But even in this moment of triumph he knew the serious business of life was only just beginning. He shook his head. Just being there still sometimes seemed like a dream. The mysterious "scholarship" to prep school, then college, provided by Captain Smutters, in much the same way as the old seaman had sent Stephen's grandfather off to a new life in America. Then the burning desire to succeed, to show the captain and Stephen's own family their efforts had not been wasted. The Law Review, the academic honors, social and sporting success—he supposed he had done what was expected of him so far, but it was how he spent the rest of his life that would count. He got up from the bench, stripped and plunged under a hot shower while his teammates partied on. He suddenly felt a need to be by himself.

Dressed, he slipped out of the locker room and into the cool dusk. He started walking, thinking he might spend a quiet hour in Langdell Hall with the books. Tonight he

would join the celebrations, but for now he felt he owed
his benefactors some kind of gesture. He grinned as he
strode along; Stephen was already wise enough to recognize the conflicts in himself between the high-spirited
youngster and the hardworking scholar. Harvard had
been good that way. He'd expected to be thrown against
rich and privileged students looking out only for themselves, had anticipated prejudice, to be patronized for his
provincial background. But Harvard had given him his
chance and taught him he could be anything he desired,
if he was capable.

He passed a couple walking under the trees and heard
the man's voice call to him. He thought he heard a trace
of Bermuda in the words.

"Stephen Youngblood. Excuse me, young man, but I'd
be honored to shake your hand."

He stopped and turned around as they approached him.
A tall, strong man in healthy middle age and a girl, teenaged, her blond hair and fair skin gleaming in the dusk.

"Congratulations, Mr. Youngblood," the man said. "If
Princeton had to be beaten, I'm consoled by its being a
fellow Bermudian who did it." He held out his hand. "I'm
Jeff Billings and this is my daughter, Sarah. We're Odlums. My mother knows your family well."

The girl was stunning. Stephen tried to keep his eyes
off her as he exchanged polite comments with her father
about the game and how well Princeton had played. He
had seen the girl before, during summers at home in
Bermuda. But she'd just been a gawky girl glimpsed over
the walls of the Odlum mansion, another of the whites
who could have been living on a separate island for as
much as they mixed with the black population.

"Would you join us for coffee, or a drink?" Mr. Billings
asked. "My car's just down here and we can go somewhere nearby. I won't keep you long. I guess you've got
a big night celebrating ahead of you."

"Sure, I'd like that, sir," he said, all thoughts of the
law library forgotten. From the backseat of the Cadillac
he studied her profile as they eased through the leaf-
strewn streets; she was more beautiful than pretty, still

not completely formed, a softness around the jawline and cheekbones that would soon vanish and reveal strength and purpose. He was caught staring at her when she swung around to speak to him.

"I told Daddy if anyone was going to upset his team it would be you," she said. She laughed. "I saw you play in Cup Match three summers ago. You bowled like a demon! So I figured you'd be able to throw the ball where it had to go."

"You've been to a Cup Match?" he said. It seemed so far away, the green grass and golden sun of the old cricket pitch, a different world from Cambridge in the fall.

"I've been to lots of them," she said. "I'm training to be a Bermudian. I've spent every summer there for the last twelve years." She laughed again. "Daddy slipped into the trap of being a Bostonian lawyer but it's not going to happen to me. After college I'm going home to where my heritage is."

"And her mother and I are pleased as we can be," Jeff Billings said over his shoulder. "Sarah's right when she says I got trapped but, hell, a man's got to make a career for himself and there wasn't room for me in Bermuda. Sarah, though—"

"Daddy, you are a male chauvinist pig," she yelled. She stuck out her tongue at him and Stephen thought how young and unaffected she was. "You think it's right for Bermuda's menfolk to go away and make their fortunes, but since women don't really *do* anything, they might as well sit around in Bermuda. Well, you just wait! It's always been the women who have provided the strength and leadership in Bermuda and it's going to be even more so in the future. My grandmother—"

"I know what your grandmother's achieved," Stephen said. "She's been a good friend to everyone in the colony, Miss Billings, but especially to the black people. If there'd been a few more like her we wouldn't be in the mess we're in now."

"Call me Sarah. What do you mean, we're in a mess? I think it's just the most fantastic place, so gentle and beautiful."

"That's only on the surface, the white surface," her father said quietly. "Stephen's people have the vote now, and officially there's no color bar anymore. But there are still terrible imbalances between the races. The blacks have so little political power or wealth. It would be an injustice anywhere, but in a tiny community like Bermuda it's a tragedy. Until the entrenched old white families are willing to see that we're all Bermudians, there's going to be the potential for terrible trouble." He steered the car into the parking lot of a roadhouse. "I'm cold and thirsty. Let's go drink something hot with rum."

Stephen accepted the invitation to lunch at the Billings' home in Boston the next day. After they dropped him at Kirkland House he stood in the dark and watched the red tail-lights of the limousine vanish. He shook his head in bewilderment as he realized he had quite forgotten about the day's triumphs since he'd met the Billings. And he wanted tonight's celebrations to speed by so it would be tomorrow when he would see her again. It was stupid; she was just a kid. And, anyway, she was white and a member of one of Bermuda's most prominent families. But he couldn't help thinking about her blue eyes and glorious hair, and that pert, pink tongue sticking out at her father.

A bunch of students came up the steps past him.

"Hurry up, Steve," one called. "The party's starting. It's our night to howl."

Sarah found it hard to sleep. She tossed and turned in her cozy bed in the little room at the top of the old house on Beacon Hill. It was unfair; if she were older, smarter, more sophisticated, he might have taken some notice of her. But what chance did she have with all the girls who'd be pursuing Stephen Youngblood, Harvard hero? She imagined him at the victory party, the elegant, clever women draped on his arm. Maybe tomorrow at lunch she'd be able to make an impression on him, wear something daring, say something witty, charm him. She finally fell asleep, dreaming of him standing tall on the football field, his light copper skin gleaming.

* * *

A white maid opened the door for him and Stephen
suppressed a grin. Quite a reversal of the roles in Bermuda. She showed him into a tall, book-lined library,
leather chairs and old wood and the Sunday sunshine
streaming in from the cobbled street outside. He had only
a moment to admire the gracious room before Jeff Billings, casual in flannels and a tweed jacket, appeared and
greeted him.

"Good morning, Stephen. I'm amazed you could make it
on time. I guess you had quite a party last night." He
moved to a silver tray sitting on an oak sideboard. "I already made us bloody marys. I figured you could use one."

"I sure could, sir. I usually don't drink much but I
broke the rules last night."

Billings brought him the drink and gestured for him
to sit down.

"The ladies will join us shortly," he said. "But first I
wanted to have a talk with you. We were talking about
Bermuda last evening, about how difficult it is for a man
to make a career unless he's inherited one of the old family businesses. I've been thinking about your future,
Stephen."

Stephen sipped the drink. It was strong and spicy and
cleared the clouds from his brain. He decided to say
nothing for the moment.

"Stephen, you could have a very big future in law here.
I've been reading all about you in the *Globe* this morning. Top grades, top sportsman . . . just the kind of young
man the law firms want to recruit. I suppose the Wall
Street headhunters have been after you?"

"There have been a few approaches, sir," he grinned.
"Being black doesn't hurt, either. Equal Opportunity
and all that."

"Well, what I'd like you to consider is my firm, here in
Boston. We're just about as big as most of the Wall Street
outfits but we like to think we have more to offer. Higher
standards and a better way of life, plus more diversifi-
cation than a young man could get as a Wall Street associate. We're not a factory, which they usually are. And

I'd dearly love to have a fellow Bermudian on the staff.
I think we'd spring for about $25,000 a year to start and
throw in an apartment and a car. Does that sound good?"

"It's very generous," Stephen said. "And I'm flattered
you'd make me such an offer. But I couldn't accept. In a
lot of ways I'd love to stay here but I feel my duty lies
back in Bermuda. The next decade is going to be one of
big changes and the people are going to need all the
professional guidance they can get. Apart from my
father, all the legal guns are in the hands of the Forty
Thieves. So, next summer, I'm going home to stay. I have
to do what I can."

"I figured you might say that," Billings said. "But it
was worth a try." He stood up and clapped the younger
man on the shoulder. "Actually, I'd be disappointed if
you'd decided on anything else. We'll have to see what
work we can channel to you and your father. We're doing
quite a bit of trust business down there. There's no reason Amberley & Benbridge should get it all. They don't
need it and you do, with all the *pro bono publico* stuff
your father's doing."

"Anything would help, sir. Daddy hasn't exactly been
getting rich." He was relaxed, now that business had
been disposed of. And he was anxious to see Sarah.

A moment later the door opened and there she was,
even more beautiful and fresh than he remembered. And
right behind was someone who could have been her twin.
He struggled to his feet.

"Mr. Youngblood," the other woman said, coming forward and holding out her hand. "We're delighted to have
you here. I'm Carol Billings, Sarah's mother."

In the sunlight he could see she was probably about
forty but with the same fine skin and dazzling blond hair
as Sarah.

"Of course!" he said. "You're the Kosmos Girl. You
were everyone's pinup in Bermuda. I've seen the magazine clippings."

She laughed. "That was years ago. Primrose is much
more sophisticated in her promotions these days." She
studied him, her head to the side. "Actually, Jeff, you and

your mother ought to look at Mr. Youngblood as the model for the new men's line."

"Stephen's too serious for that kind of thing, honey," Billings said. "He's going home to set the country right."

"Good," Carol said. "It needs a bomb under it. I get so mad when I see the unnecessary frictions down there. Some of the old families are like plantation owners—when are they going to realize it's all one country? Bermuda will stand or fall as one people."

"Let's go into lunch," Billings said. "We can reform the politics of Bermuda just as easily over a good meal."

"No politics, please," Sarah said with a sigh. "When I talk about Bermuda, I like to mention the beautiful part of it."

But they did talk politics and Sarah joined in. He realized she was much brighter than she pretended to be, although he found it hard to listen to her words while watching her face.

"What about the long term?" Billings asked him when they were all settled back in the library with coffee. "How do you see Bermuda's political future?"

"Independence," Stephen said. It was as simple as that, and as he spoke the word he felt a thrill run through his body. All the political debate with his father and other black leaders over the years; in the end it boiled down to independence from Britain and anyone else. "I think we have to cut the formal ties with England," he said, "and make a fresh start as our own nation. It's the only way to wipe out the sins of the past; create a new country comprising black and white Bermudians—all equal."

"The Forty Thieves wouldn't like it," Sarah said. "They wouldn't be able to get their knighthoods from the Queen if you weren't a colony anymore."

"There'd be far greater rewards," Stephen said. "As long as we're a colony, the old attitudes remain, no matter how many cosmetic reforms are made. But when we're a real country of our own, we'll be able to make the decisions for all the people."

"A very small country," Billings said. "Aren't you afraid we could step out of one sphere of influence and into another? And what about defense? How would we be without Britain to protect us?"

"I don't see any problems there, sir. The Americans will go on leasing their base and the Canadians would be happy to sign a defense treaty with us. Sure, we're only a little rock out in the Atlantic, but we're strategically very important to North America. I see us being friendly to everyone and subservient to no one."

"The whites won't go for it," Billings said. "They've everything to lose and nothing much to gain."

"They'll have to go for it eventually," Stephen said. "Apart from anything else, I figure Britain's going to want to cut the strings one of these days. She's not interested in having colonies anymore, not when they don't make a profit for her. But the big push for independence will come from moderates, both black and white. What's happening now is you've got a dangerous fringe of Black Power advocates on one side and an element of white reactionaries on the other. In the end the middle ground will see our future as one nation." He smiled. "And if we do it right, if we learn from the lessons of others who didn't, it will only be good for Bermuda. It won't alter tourism, or international banking, but it will give us the chance to move into new fields where, at the moment, Britain doesn't want us to go."

They talked on late into the afternoon; the sun was setting as the family saw Stephen to his car. Sarah was going back to William and Mary in Virginia in the morning, and as Stephen watched her in the fading light he felt a real ache. But at least she had a few words of hope for him.

"I guess we'll see each other at home next summer," she said. "You'll have to come up to the house. Grandmother will adore talking revolution with you."

Hardly anyone remarked on the change in Colin Fleet anymore; for ages now he had been calmer, more reasonable than the Fleet they remembered. Only Colin himself knew what an effort it took to face the world while under sentence of awful death. After the doctor had told

him of his terminal condition, he wept tears of rage and
mortification. Then, with all the determination of a
Fleet, he had set about ensuring his final years were
worthwhile ones. If there were to be no more Fleets, then
he would make sure this last generation left its mark in-
delibly on Bermuda. He read the winds of change and determined their course must be altered; Bermuda in the
future would need a far more conservative leadership
than it now had, and Colin began to gather around him
like-thinking men. He tidied up his financial affairs, ex-
punging from the records his more dubious money dealings, removing his vast profits and setting the proceeds
aside to fund a new Conservative party.

In his personal life he became distantly polite to his
wife; Mary welcomed the relief from the savage sexual
assaults. She knew nothing of his disease and he told her
it was the medication he was taking that had changed
him. He was cured, he said, of drug addiction, but the
price of the cure had been his libido. She accepted this
and settled into the indulged life of Bermuda's young
matrons. She did not miss a normal marital life because
the one she had known had been so awful.

It was Veronica who suffered the most. She still presented a stern face and strong will, but her hopes had
been shattered. She had given up much for the cause of
continuing Fleet dominance in Bermuda and it was all
for nothing. Sometimes it seemed to her the decline and
fall of the Fleets was everywhere. When she had to pass
the crumbling pink palace on the way to the airport, she
averted her eyes; but she could not erase the memory of
her mean, mad brother and the gruesome legacy he had
left his son. The only thing Veronica had to sustain her
was pride. And hate. She knew it was irrational, but
daily her hatred of the Odlums grew. It was all their
fault, all the things that had happened to the Fleets. The
Odlums flourished and were happy, even if they never
had commanded the respect and power that had accrued
to generations of Fleets. She heard about Primrose Odlum being thick as thieves with Henry Smutters and she
cursed both of them. She had had Smutters to herself a

long time ago, but he was only a sea captain, not of her class. He wasn't even of Primrose Odlum's class, come to that, and it was just more proof of how common the Odlums truly were.

Primrose never felt the waves of hatred flowing in her direction from Veronica. If she had, she was too content to care. She had her summers with Sarah, and she was overjoyed to see that—as the girl matured through college—her love of Bermuda grew. It was now accepted that Sarah would make her life in the colony after graduation; her parents approved and, indeed, were making their own plans to retire there within a few years. Primrose watched the attraction between her granddaughter and Stephen Youngblood develop. She could understand the young lawyer's trepidation; Bermuda hadn't changed *that* much. She ached for Sarah, so obviously in love, unable to understand why her chosen one did not display more than friendship toward her. Sometimes Primrose had the urge to take the two young people aside and talk to them, but Henry Smutters wisely counseled her to wait and let events run their course.

"They'll speak their hearts soon enough," the captain said. They were drinking iced lemonade on the lawn overlooking the sound and planning their next dispersal of funds from the hidden treasure trove. So far, apart from Stephen's education, they had paid for four young Bermudians to study medicine in the U.S. and had equipped the black hospital so handsomely that some whites now sought treatment there. "It's going to be hard enough for both of them," Smutters continued. "Stephen's people—the radicals, anyway—won't like him being involved with a white girl, even if she is an Odlum. And it will hurt him politically. His New Alliance party has to win both the black radicals and the black conservatives if they're ever going to take power. And I know you don't give a damn, but Sarah's being involved with a black, even if he's mixed blood, will cause her a lot of social strife in the white community. Don't hurry them. It's going to be a very difficult affair."

"I know you're right, Henry," she said. "But I hate to

see anyone waste the chance of happiness. We never know how much time we have, so we ought to be grabbing at every minute." She studied him in the sunlight. "I've had a wonderful life but I still missed out on a lot by waiting, delaying. I don't want Sarah to waste a moment."

"She's only twenty-one," he said. "There's plenty of time." He picked up a sheaf of papers lying on the grass. "Now what about the Hoxton kid? His teachers say he could make it as a physicist but the parents can't afford to send him to M.I.T. and there're no scholarships. You reckon we ought to send him?"

"Sure." She nodded, and then she laughed. "My God, I'm a spoiled old woman. I pretend I'm in this with you because I want to do good. Actually, Henry, I'm having fun. If I were genuine, why, I'd fund all these things myself. There's enough money to do it. But I like our secret trips in the ketch, digging up a few more bits and pieces of treasure and using it as we see fit. Poor Colin Fleet. He'll never enjoy his life as much as I'm enjoying mine these days."

"Nor mine." Henry Smutters meant it. His latter years of involvement with Primrose had been the high point of his life. If he hadn't been so old, and such a confirmed bachelor . . .

Sarah looked up from the electoral rolls and wiped her forehead with the back of her hand, leaving a smudge of blue ink. It was the hottest time of the day and there was no air conditioning in the cramped Court Street offices of the New Alliance party. She saw Stephen filling the doorway, his white suit crumpled and his dark hair plastered to his scalp.

"A tough morning in court?" she asked. "I already heard they threw out your petition. What's next? The Privy Council?"

"I suppose so. But it grates on a republican like me, having to appeal to the Queen's private court to establish one man, one vote." He slumped in a chair and grinned at her.

"But we'll win, of course. The Privy Council's all for giving us darkies a fair shake these days."

"Don't joke," Sarah said. "We're talking about giving *all* Bermudians a fair shake. I'm getting bored with your playing up this black thing." She was tired and hot and heartily sick of doing the drudgery while everyone else in the party was at the barricades. "Sometimes I think you're as bad as the rest of them."

He came out of his chair and stood by her desk. She looked up and saw the anger flashing in his soft brown eyes, heard the deep voice that had made him Bermuda's most charismatic speaker.

"Bored?" he said. "Yes, I can see how someone like you would get bored with our work here. For you it's just a way of filling in your summers, playing at politics. For me it's the only future my people have."

She felt her own rage subside into quiet panic. It sounded as though he was going to send her away, when all she wanted was to be near him, no matter whether he paid her any more attention than he did the rest of their small staff.

"I'm sorry," she said. "It's the heat and the frustration, feeling we're not making a dent in anything."

"I'm sorry, too. I didn't mean to snap at you. We need people like you and your grandmother if we're ever going to put a consensus party together. I forgot who you were for a moment." A tiny breeze came through the office and lifted the papers on her desk. Stephen reached down to prevent them blowing away and his hand touched hers. There was a current running between them and they both felt it.

"I wish you could forget who I am," she said, close to a whisper. His hand was now firm on hers, drawing her up. "I wish we could both just forget the tensions of this place and be ourselves for once." She was standing close to him, the strength and maleness of him overwhelming her.

He put out his other hand, tentatively, and pushed a damp lock of blond hair off her forehead. He took a half step forward and bent his mouth to her lips, and for the first time, they kissed. Outside in Court Street traders shouted their wares, cars honked in the busy traffic and angry little mopeds buzzed back and forth. They heard none of it; they were in a tight embrace, releasing all their long-pent-up love. It was the moment they had both dreamed about but never expected to realize.

"Do you know what you're getting yourself into?" he said, reluctantly breaking the embrace. "Do you realize where we are?"

"Yes," she said. "I'm not afraid. I've known what I wanted since the day I met you."

The editor of the *Royal Gazette* flipped through the sheaf of photographs. The most notable feature of the pictures was who wasn't in them. An Odlum marrying in Bermuda normally would have brought together most of the colony's leading citizens except, of course, representatives of the Fleet family. But for this wedding, only the immediate families of the bride and groom would be in attendance.

"I'm buggered if I know what to do with it," the editor complained to his staff. "Of course it's big news in Bermuda. But if I play it the way it deserves, front-page, the Establishment's going to come down on us like a ton of bricks."

"Maybe if we just tucked it away in the social pages?" his assistant suggested.

"No. It's all or nothing." He flicked through the photographs again and extracted one. "This is the shot to go with, if we go. Bloody young Michael's overdeveloped it and made Stephen look black as the ace of spades and the Odlum girl white as snow. What a contrast!"

"You can't, Ian," his assistant said. "It'll stir people up even more than they are now. That picture is so . . . so black and white!"

Ian Padgett sighed. "That's what Bermuda's about, black and white. It's time we faced the fact. Do you know, about fifty years ago, the *Gazette* actually apologized for being duped into running the report of a marriage between two black people? In those days—and until pretty recently—we tried to make nonpersons out of our blacks.

Those days are gone. We can't pretend half the population doesn't exist. Bugger it, put the picture on Page One."

Veronica Fleet studied the *Gazette* as she took her morning coffee. While some of the other *grandes dames* of Bermuda society were that morning consumed by outrage and anger at what had been presented to them in their newspaper, Veronica felt only an awful inevitability about it. Her world was changing and this was one more symptom of change. And of course an Odlum would be at the vanguard of change. The blasted Odlums had never conformed to Bermuda's ways. Veronica held the paper closer and looked at the bride again. So fair and beautiful, so familiar. Of course she remembered the girl's mother, the one who'd been the face of Primrose Odlum's company. She'd looked the same. Could have been a Fleet, with those bones and that coloring. And as for the husband, Stephen Youngblood, somewhere well-buried in the family records there'd been a black by-blow of that name. A small, bitter smile crossed Veronica's face. How ironic, if that was the last of the Fleet blood, the few drops in a black man's veins. A black who was pushing the heresy of independence from Britain. Veronica wondered if Primrose Odlum was feeling any shame today. Probably not; her family had never given a damn what people thought of them. And even though the fellow was a radical black, he was also some kind of football hero, handsome as sin and professionally qualified. Veronica realized she actually envied Primrose. Primrose would have her line continued, no matter how tarred. And all Veronica had left was poor, sick, doomed Colin. She put down the paper and frowned at her cold coffee. No use raging at what might have been; her name had decided her course in life and she could not have changed it.

Veronica Fleet rang for her car and, as she had done almost every day for the past sixty years, prepared for the short trip to her office on Front Street. Running the empire was all she'd ever wanted to do; now it was all she had to do.

* * *

"The worse part of it," Amberley was saying, "is that the marriage will deliver both funds and respectability to this blasted New Alliance." He was taking an early lunch in the club with his son-in-law. The Odlum girl's marriage was the only topic of conversation among the members.

"Respectability?" Colin Fleet asked. "How can you say a nigger marrying a white woman is going to make 'em respectable? I thought the affair would finish him politically."

"For people like us, yes," Amberley said. "And for some of Youngblood's more radical followers, who'll see it as a sellout. But a lot of moderate whites and blacks won't be too offended. I'm afraid a lot of our fellow Bermudians are changing, Colin. If Youngblood's got the Odlum fortune behind his party through marrying the granddaughter, we are going to have a real struggle on our hands. I think it's time we put some more money and effort into the Conservative Party if we're going to save Bermuda. The existing parties have done their dash. Youngblood's eventually going to win over most of the liberals, so we must muster all our strength to hold the line." The waitress brought dessert and the two men fell silent, each looking around the big, sunny dining room, remembering how many events of importance to their colony had been decided in this exclusive club.

"I suppose you're right," Colin said finally. "In the old days, if a disgraceful thing like this had happened, we'd have burned his house and kicked him off the island. Now we have to attack him on the hustings. I liked the old days better."

"We all did. You'll take brandy with coffee? Good. Now tell me, how's my daughter? Her mother and I scarcely see her these days."

Colin shrugged. "She's still gadding about Europe," he said. "Mary seems to find Bermuda too small. She's due back next month, I think."

"You should insist she spend more time here, Colin," he said. "It doesn't look right."

"Mary doesn't give a damn how things look." His head was aching again; if he wasn't careful the rage would come

to the surface. He could not afford to have any more violent
quarrels with his friends and associates. Colin made a
great effort to control himself. "It's not her fault, Eric.
When your daughter was told she couldn't have children,
it was a terrible blow to her. As it was to me. We make the
best of our lives." He drained his cognac and it dulled the
ache. Mary would be back for a while, when she was fully
over the latest abortion. At least she was discreet about
her lovers and had not shamed him in his own country.
And the longer she was away, the less time they had to
fight. But it was unfair, the way everything had gone
wrong with his life. Someone would pay.

They honeymooned in Acapulco, made glorious, passionate love several times a day and found new depths in
their devotion to each other. Away from Bermudian politics, Stephen allowed himself to relax for once, delighting
in her company. Sarah was so vital and alive, so beautiful.
She took his breath away when he first saw her in the
morning, or when he watched her walk across a room. For
her part, what had begun as a schoolgirl crush had deepened to adult love and was now an enduring feeling of
rightness. They were right for each other. Sarah supposed
there had been a time when the rebel in her had enjoyed
their differences, had liked the notoriety their love affair
produced. But all that was past; his bronze coloring, his
pride, his political passion were just part of the makeup of
the Stephen Youngblood she loved. She was no longer
making a gesture to the world; she only wished the world
could be as happy as she was.

"Five more days of this," she sighed as Stephen lay beside her, the water from the pool glistening on his hard-
muscled body. "I don't want to leave, but at the same
time it will be good to get home and resume real life."

"Real life!" He laughed. "Darling, Bermuda's not
about real life. It's a fantasy island for most of the people
who live there, a beautiful, bountiful place where the sun
shines every day and living's easy. I don't want to disturb Bermudians' happy dreams, but I'm going to have
to. We can't drift on like we've been doing for all these

centuries. It's time we became a modern, independent, fair nation."

She made a face at him.

"I know, Stephen. But the need for change at home surely doesn't mean we have to lose the good things of life there, does it? Do I have to pretend I'm not rich to fit in with our political ideas? Can't we enjoy life even while changing it?"

"Sure," he said. "As long as it's a fair society, I guess some people are going to be fairer than others." He bent and kissed her. "And you are the fairest of them all. My poor little rich girl."

"I can buy us the house, then?" It was something he'd refused to discuss before their marriage; Stephen seemed perfectly happy to go on living in his cramped apartment. He wouldn't even look at the lovely old cottage she'd found in Devonshire Parish. "It's something I want for both of us, Stephen, and for the babies when they come."

"I guess I couldn't stop you if I tried." He hugged her. "And why should you be penalized just because I chose politics instead of a lucrative law career? So long as I don't become a kept man."

"I'd keep you if you'd let me. I want to keep you forever." She looked at him and the love swept over her. "It's going to be tough, isn't it, Stephen? And dangerous. A lot of people don't like what you're trying to achieve in Bermuda. Please be careful."

Primrose and Jane Bellowes sat on the wide, shaded balcony looking out over the water and watched their adult children walking up the garden toward them.

"My God, they're still a handsome couple," Primrose said. "It would have been a tragedy if they hadn't married. And they so nearly didn't."

"Don't rub it in," Jane said. "I thought I was doing the right thing, telling Carol who her father was and what it meant for a Fleet to be involved with an Odlum. Thank goodness you stepped in and showed us some good sense."

"Jeff knew what he wanted. He wouldn't have let an old family feud stand in his way," Primrose said. "And he was right. Look at them, married more than twenty-five years, and still as much in love as teenagers."

"Yes. If Sarah can be just as happy, I'll be content." Jane looked at her old friend. "Does Sarah know about her Fleet bloodline? I never got around to asking Carol if she'd told her. It just didn't seem to matter anymore."

"I don't think she knows. She's never asked me who her grandfather was. It's best to leave it buried. Names! They've caused so much heartbreak and bloodshed in these islands. I'd hope we have all grown out of that kind of thing."

"What kind of thing?" Jeff demanded, hand-in-hand with his wife, bounding up the steps from the garden. "What are you trying to change now, Mother?"

"Bermuda," she said wryly. "Just trying to drag us into the twentieth century."

"Leave that to the young ones," Jeff said. "You've fought all your battles. You should be sitting back and enjoying life."

"I'm not that old. I'm not ready for the scrap heap. If you must know, for the next election I'm going to stand as a candidate for Stephen's new party. At least he doesn't think I'm all washed up." She grinned mischievously. "I figure I can carry this ward for the New Alliance. Can you imagine the upset that's going to cause some of our neighbors? To be represented by a crazy old woman who's a member of that dangerous radical party?" She caught the look Carol and Jeff exchanged. "Well, what's wrong?"

Carol came and sat beside her; Jeff remained standing, apparently studying a small boat beating up the sound against the afternoon breeze.

"You know we had no reservations about Sarah marrying Stephen," Carol said. "He's a fine young man and they're very much in love. The color aspect isn't important. To us, they're both Bermudians. But since we've been here this time, Jeff and I have been listening to what the people are saying."

"And I'm afraid there are not many as liberal as you, Mother," Jeff said.

"Oh, they'll come around," Primrose said. "We Bermudians always do a lot of shouting, but in the end most of us show good common sense."

"We're worried," Carol said. "There's a lunatic Black Power fringe who are opposed to everything Stephen is for, who actually want the whites out of Bermuda! And at the other end of the scale you've got the Fleets and their associates who don't want to share power and who certainly don't want independence from England."

"They're just going to have to get used to independence," Primrose said. "Apart from anything else, Britain's tired of supporting us. She doesn't want colonies anymore. Watch how willing she is to get rid of Hong Kong."

"We understand all that," Jeff said. "But we don't want our only child being right at the center of what's going to be a dangerous situation."

"Oh, Jeff," Primrose said. She laughed. "With that child's bloodlines, wherever else do you think she'd be but in the center of things? But please don't worry. I'll see she doesn't come to any harm."

"It shouldn't be your responsibility," Jeff said. "Another five years, and Carol and I will be ready to come home here and semi-retire. But we can't do it yet, no matter how much we want to. We've each got a career to finish out, and someone in the family has to keep an eye on Kosmos in the U.S."

"We hoped—we still hope, I suppose—Sarah would have shown an interest in Kosmos," Carol said, "instead of getting mixed up in radical politics. It would have been so much better for her."

"No." Jane had been silent through the conversation, but now she faced them. "No, Carol, it wouldn't have been better if she'd taken the safe way out. Primrose taught me a long time ago life has to be faced. I'm glad Sarah hasn't chosen the easy options. I guess she and Stephen will run into a lot of unpleasantness, even danger, but it will be worthwhile. It's like Bermuda: the occasional tempest is the price you pay for living in paradise."

Chapter Seventeen
(1986–)

Barry Brock chomped on his unlit cigar and glared at his secretary.

"Explain to me," he said, "why I am seeing some turkey from Bermuda. I am a very busy man, the hottest political consultant in the whole fucking nation, and you schedule some nobody from nowhere. Why?"

"Because the Governor asked me to. This Fleet man looked after the Governor when he was down there on vacation. Fleet runs one of the political parties in Bermuda."

"A political party in Bermuda. Shit! I'm into bigger things, Agnes."

"Sure you are, Barry. But we need to pay the bills, and Colin Fleet is rich as sin."

"He'll need to be, he wants to talk to me. Okay, I'll see him, but not this minute. Give him a cup of coffee and keep him happy. I've got some calls to make. I've got six senators wanting me to handle them and you've scheduled a nobody from Bermuda."

"Yes, Barry." She sighed and went out into the plush foyer where the tall, pale man was sitting leafing through an old copy of *Time.* "I'm so sorry, Mr. Fleet," she said. "Mr. Brock has been delayed at City Hall. The Mayor's got some crisis. But I'm sure he won't be too long."

Colin Fleet shrugged. He didn't like and wasn't used

to being kept waiting, but he was in foreign territory, and he realized the Fleet name did not give instant access to power brokers outside Bermuda. And he needed Brock: Brock was the best in the business. The Conservative Party had been Colin's obsession for so long now that a few minutes waiting didn't matter.

He continued to look through the magazine; he had read it weeks before, of course, because it contained a few inches on Bermuda's situation. "Politics in Paradise" was the heading, and the article was accompanied by a picture of Stephen Youngblood. It made Colin's head ache, just looking at it; that smug, smiling black son-of-a-bitch being lauded as the political future of Bermuda. And the crap they'd written about Black Power and the waning influence of the Forty Thieves. Only a one-line mention of Colin's party. Well, he'd show *Time* a thing or two. There was a year to the next election, and by the time it came around they'd be writing about the Conservatives as the saviors of all that was good and proper in the colony. He had sacrificed much for the party and he expected recognition for it; the party's success would be his legacy to Bermuda, one crowning achievement after his disappointing life. He would show them, the ones who sneered at him behind his back, gossiped about his tramp of a wife. Some of them seemed to think he was like his father's house, the Pink Palace, a crumbling, empty shell. Well, they were in for one hell of a shock. Colin Fleet was going to leave his mark on Bermuda.

Agnes Muir looked up from her desk when she heard Fleet chuckle to himself. She ducked her head again when he fixed her with his pale blue eyes. She shivered; he looked like a ghost. She hoped the Governor hadn't fobbed off a wacko on them. The light on her console blinked and Brock's gravelly voice told her to send the client in.

Brock was tall, but when he stood up to shake hands, the visitor towered over him. And the stranger's hand was cold, as cold as his eyes.

"Sorry to keep you waiting, Mr. Fleet," he said. "But when the White House calls, I jump."

"Your secretary said you were at City Hall."

The two men stared at each other across the desk. Brock ran a hand over his bald head; he didn't need this kind of aggravation.

"All right, Mr. Fleet, get to the point. I'm busy. What is it you want?"

Fleet reached into the inside pocket of his blue pin-striped suit and withdrew an envelope. He slid it across the desk and nodded to Brock to open it.

The bald man slit open the envelope and examined the yellow form inside. It was a cashier's check, drawn on the Bank of Lapin & Son, made out to Barry J. Brock in the sum of one million U.S. dollars. He placed it carefully faceup on the desk in front of him.

"Now," Colin Fleet said, "do you think you've got time to talk to me? If we talk and if you agree to do what I want, that check will be deposited in a Bermuda account for you. It will be tax free if you wish. Your IRS need never know about it."

Brock punched a button. "Hold all calls, Agnes," he said. And then he settled down to listen as Colin Fleet explained to him the intricacies of Bermuda politics.

"And you figure the existing parties will be swamped by the New Alliance and the Conservatives?" he said when Fleet was finished. "Why? They've done okay for the past twenty years or so, haven't they?"

"They are irrelevant now because they're too middle-of-the-road. The next election will be fought on Bermuda's future, whether she is to be led by responsible people and remain a member of the British Commonwealth, or be taken over by the blacks and socialist republicans."

"This Youngblood character. You say he's married to a rich white woman. Surely that's going to cost him votes?"

"It should," Fleet said. "But unfortunately a lot of the people are color-blind these days. And besides, Youngblood and his wife present themselves as model citizens, devoted parents, moderate in everything. And as for her being an Odlum and rich . . . I must say, Mr. Brock, that being rich has never been a handicap in Bermuda. Even a lot of the blacks see themselves as capitalists these days."

"Why does this all matter so much to you?" asked Brock, touching the check.

"Bermuda has been my family's home for almost four hundred years, Mr. Brock. I will not see it turned over to the riffraff. And independence would be a disaster for the things we cherish. What I want you to do is come down, study the situation and advise my party. This is an election we must win and I'm told you're a man who creates winners."

"It's going to be tough to find the time, Mr. Fleet." He touched the check again. "But your price is right. All right, I'll take it on. I'll put a couple of my best people at your party's disposal and make as many personal trips as I have to." He stood up and put out his hand. "We've got a deal."

Stephen wrapped his arms around her and held her tight in the dark of their bedroom; it was here, at the end of the long, hard days, that they both found sanctuary and love. Sarah snuggled closer to him and sighed with pleasure as she felt his warmth and strength.

"We're so lucky, darling," she whispered. "No one's supposed to be this happy."

"You're a brave girl," he said, "putting up with all you do for the sake of our politics. And still you can say how happy you are. Sometimes I wish I hadn't dragged you into this."

"You didn't drag me into anything. I want to share your life and if it's politics . . . well, I happen to agree with them, anyway. It's some of our fellow Bermudians we're going to have to drag—kicking and screaming—into the modern world." She sat up, and a shaft of moonlight caught her bare breasts. He shivered at the beauty of her. "Those bitches at the Oceanic Club blackballed me again." She laughed, but he thought he detected bitterness. "I don't know why I let the girls put my name up for membership. I'm no clubwoman frittering her life away with tea and tennis. I guess I thought if I did join I might be able to win a few of the so-called ladies over to our side. But their minds are closed, Stephen."

"Yes," he said. "A few of them, at both ends of the social scale, are blinded by old hatreds. We've just got to go on working under the assumption there are enough sensible people in the middle ground."

Somewhere out in the night they heard the whine of a motorcycle coming down the hill on the road past their house. They waited in silence as it got nearer; several times in the past months young black hooligans had thrown bricks and stones at their windows. The motorcycle went by the house and its noise faded. They relaxed.

"At least the children haven't been affected by all the tension," Sarah said. "Jonas can't wait to start school, so I guess he's not expecting any hassles from the other kids. And Alice is too young to understand the situation."

"I hope it'll be resolved before either of them has to face things," Stephen said. "If we can win next year's election and put our policies to work, the situation will be easier. Once they see we're not ogres, dedicated to destroying their way of life, most of them will come around. It's in the beginning there's danger. People are scared and they respond to any rumor, any crazy idea." He pulled her close to him again and their bodies merged. "I don't suppose there's any point in me suggesting yet again that you and the children go live in the U.S. until after the election?" He felt her head shaking. "Oh well, it was a dumb idea anyway. I couldn't cut it without you here. And you are just about the party's greatest asset, you and your grandmother."

"Stop talking politics," she said, her voice husky. "Just be quiet and I'll show you what kind of asset I really am."

Barry Brock stayed on the fringe of the crowd milling around the flatbed truck. Brock was dressed like any other tourist on this hot night, in slacks and a casual

shirt, and no one paid him any heed. He had come to
study the enemy, and already he knew he had a real political fight on his hands. Youngblood, mounted on the
truck, had the crowd firmly in his grasp. The voice that
rolled over them was rich and resonant; the words were
forceful and well-thought, promising a new and better
deal for all the people of Bermuda. Brock wondered if he
might not have picked the wrong side. Youngblood was
a dream candidate anywhere; a handsome, light-skinned
orator, the lilt of the West Indies in his speech, his strong-
boned face showing the unique Bermudian blending of
black, white and Indian blood. It was, indeed, the face of
the new Bermuda, Brock thought. Except that he was
being paid a fortune to see it didn't succeed.

Brock glanced at his watch and started back along
Front Street to his hotel; he was expected at a cocktail
party Fleet was giving to introduce him to the Conservative leaders and a few other notables they hoped to attract to their ranks. God, he'd had a lot of desperate
clients in his career but Fleet was something else. Nothing mattered except beating Youngblood's party. It was
worse than a crusade, as if this election was the culmination of his whole life's work. And that aunt of his, the
way Veronica Fleet had taken him aside and told him
not to spare any expense or effort to see Colin's party was
successful. He had a blank check, she told him. Just come
to her for anything he needed in the forthcoming battle.
They were probably a little crazy, the Fleets and their
associates, Brock thought. They'd have to be, all the in-
breeding down through the centuries.

He walked through the faded foyer of the Tropicana to
the function room where they were waiting for him, nodding and smiling as if he were some kind of savior. He
was used to the treatment, to being the kingmaker, and
he wouldn't let them down. Barry Brock was a winner.

"This must seem like schoolyard politics to you," Evan
Jones said. "I mean, getting three out of three senate
candidates home last time—I'm quite amazed a man of
your skills, so in demand at home, could make time for
poor little Bermuda."

He glanced at Jones over the rim of his glass. The big black man had a wide-open face and friendly smile but Brock had been well briefed on him. Evan Jones was a Cabinet Minister in the current regime, one of the black middle class, politically moderate and very intelligent.

"I'm here because I believe in what the Conservatives are about, Mr. Jones," he said. "I hope leaders like you will come to believe in it, too."

"Oh, I'm keeping my options open, Mr. Brock." The smooth and easy smile was there but the eyes were calculating. "The Conservatives have spoken to me about joining their ticket. So have the New Alliance people." He laughed. "Why, they said I could be our first Ambassador to the United Nations after independence. Wouldn't that be a nice ending to my career."

"But you'd be a member of the Cabinet with the Conservatives, in a position to guide Bermuda to an even greater future."

"We'll see, Mr. Brock. There is plenty of time before we have to decide our positions. In the end I'll do what I think is best for my country. As I'm sure everyone in this room will do. The one certain thing is that my own current party and the existing opposition have run their race and now we must decide which of the two new extremes we will support. An exciting time, Mr. Brock."

Primrose felt the tug on the rope and began to turn the winch; she could see down through the blue water almost to the bottom. Slowly the net at the end of the rope appeared, a pair of curious parrot fish following it. And there was Henry Smutters drifting up to the surface, his mane of gray hair swirling in the gentle current. She winched the net just clear of the water and waited for Henry to climb the rope ladder and help her bring the cargo inboard.

"Getting far too old for this caper," he said as he struggled over the rail and stood wheezing as the water ran from his scarred body. "I think it's a good thing that's the last of the treasure." Together they grappled the net up over the rail and onto the deck; the barnacle-encrusted silver bars and gold coins lay there looking like nothing of value. "A good haul, though," he said. "Certainly it'll fetch enough on the U.S. market to hire Stephen's party their own 'expert,' if that's what they want to do."

"Are you sure you want to give the last of it away?" Primrose asked. "I mean, you found the treasure and you've never had any benefit from it. Surely there's something you want for yourself."

"Hell, no, Primmy. There's nothing an old codger like me needs. We've had fun with our secret hoard, haven't we, and that's all that matters. And if the last of it helps beat Colin Fleet and his racists, well, that's a nice ironic touch."

"I'd still like to see you do something for yourself. I've got so much money it's sinful; I can finance the New Alliance party for anything it needs."

"No, Primmy. You've done enough already. And it's kind of appropriate this stuff goes toward securing Bermuda's future." He shivered and wrapped his arms around himself, although the day was hot and bright. "Feels like there's a change coming on," he said, studying the empty horizon.

"I'll go below and make us some tea," she said. She bustled around the tiny galley and returned to the deck with two steaming mugs. "This will warm you . . ." She stopped in her tracks. Henry was slumped in the cockpit, his arms locked across his chest, deathly pale beneath his tan. She dashed forward to kneel beside him, clutching his hands.

"Sorry, Primrose," he whispered. "I reckon my heart's gone for good this time." He rallied for a moment. "How about you put a slug of brandy in the tea and see if it does me any good. Too late to do me any harm."

She fetched the bottle and poured a generous measure into the mug, then held it to his gray lips, her other hand supporting his head. She could feel the strength running out of him, the great, powerful body becoming a dead weight.

"You just lie here and I'll sail us back to St. George's,"

she said. "We'll get you to a doctor and have you all fixed up in no time."

"Don't go," he said. With a supreme effort he opened his eyes and gazed on her. "I'm done for, Primrose, and this is the way I want it to be, at sea with my own boat under me. Just stay by me, please, and dump me over the side when the time comes." He kept his arms locked across his chest, trying to contain the pain. There was no surprise, or regret. Henry had known for the past ten years he was living on borrowed time. He was just grateful it had been such a full life. And that he had known this woman.

"Primrose," he croaked, fighting the massive spasm in his chest, "one last thing. You're one helluva lady. Please, would you kiss me?"

She put her lips to his, already cold as marble, and held him against her as the seabirds wheeled over them and the ketch gently rocked in the warm sea. She was crying, but he did not feel the tears that fell on his face. She stayed holding him for another half-hour, not wanting to release her grasp on the things he had come to mean to her. Their long and pleasant evenings of books and conversation, their shared adventures and history, their delight in defying the conventions of their tight little society.

"Oh, Henry," she whispered, "what a pair of silly old scallywags we were. But wasn't it fun?" The sun had shifted into the west and dried her tears: it was time to move. She never considered denying his request, but went below and found a sailbag big enough for him. It was a struggle, but she managed to wrap him in the bag and then tie it securely. Straining under the burden, she rolled him out of the cockpit to the edge of the deck before unhooking the safety rail to clear a path for him. Gently, softly, she spoke the Lord's Prayer, patted the canvas that enclosed him, then sent it falling into the sea to rest in the spot where they had for so long concealed their treasure.

By the time she had lugged the last of the precious cargo belowdecks, Primrose was exhausted. But she kept going, not wanting to face the loss she had suffered. She winched the main up, and the ketch responded instantly, leaping to the evening breeze. She stood at the helm and headed for Bermuda. Just once she glanced back. "Good-bye, old friend," she said.

Barry Brock surveyed the leadership of the Conservative Party sitting around him at the boardroom table in the Fleet building. Lapin, their choice for Premier; Amberley; old Baseheart; Colin Fleet. They had the wealth and the power and the sure knowledge they were born to rule. Brock wondered if it would be enough.

"Gentlemen," he said, "we've done our polling and we've talked to people. A lot can happen in the next nine months, but at this stage I'd have to say you're a whisker in front of the radicals." He watched their satisfaction spread around the table. "But I have to warn you: this independence idea is gaining a lot of support. It could turn things right around. A lot of people, white as well as black, feel colonial status has worked against them. They perceive the current system as being there for the benefit of the Forty Thieves." He grinned as he said it but got only scowls in return. He hurried on. "The best thing that could happen from our point of view would be more trouble with the blacks. A general strike, noisy demonstrations, a bit more heat from the Rastas and the Black Power fellows. Anything like that will swing white support solidly behind you. And it will get enough of the black moderates into your party. Evan Jones, he's a key element. He won't say which way he's going at present, but I think he's genuinely concerned about law and order. I'd love to see him on our ticket."

Colin Fleet listened to Brock as he went through the electorate ward by ward. The man knew what he was talking about and Colin figured his money had been well spent. Stir up the blacks, eh? Sound common sense there. In the old days they could have achieved it easily, send out the night riders and flog a few niggers to start riots all over the islands. It had been so much simpler then. He felt his anger rising, and with it the early warning of another blinding headache. He took two pills from his breast pocket and washed them down with water. No one at the table even glanced at him; they were used to Colin and his "dicky heart." It was a lousy way to live, though, always popping pills to keep himself in check. Still, he'd got past fifty now, which was a longer span than the doctors had given him. And he'd last a good few more years, at least long enough to see Youngblood and his backers, the Odlums, defeated. He looked around the table and exchanged glances with his father-in-law; old Amberley looked away quickly. Colin wondered how much he knew of the marriage. Did Mary confide in her parents, tell them how ugly her domestic situation had again become? Probably not. Even half the truth would cast her in as bad a light as him. Now Brock was talking about the need to make the party nominating convention a big production, a vehicle to show off the Conservatives as the rightful leaders of the country. Well, that was all well in hand. They would stage the show at the Tropicana, fly in the British Prime Minister as keynote speaker—if her government could last out until then. Pity they couldn't publicly boast about Lapin's pedigree—that would clinch the election, running a Royal bastard for Premier. The Tropicana was looking pretty faded these days. He wondered if they shouldn't give it a facelift for the convention. But it was all too much of an effort for Colin. These days he found he could only concentrate on one thing at a time; winning for the party was taking all his attention right now, and the family business had to wait its turn.

"So there you are, gentlemen," Brock said, gathering his charts and graphs. "It's winnable but it will be close. What you need is something to put the fear of God into the undecided voters."

Colin stood at the window, looking out over Front Street to the docks, as the others filed out of the boardroom. In a moment he would stop by his aunt's office and pass the time of day with her. Incredible old woman, tough, indestructible. He sighed. The scene before him was so familiar, like a photo from a family album. God, he loved this place and hated those who would change it.

Veronica was speaking on the telephone when he entered her office; she waved him to a chair. She let the party at the other end ramble on while she studied Colin. He looked in good shape: pale, tall and slim. There was still time, Veronica thought, time for her to realize her only desire. Ever since the doctor's verdict on Colin had been so brutally delivered to her, Veronica had been consulting the world's leading experts on infertility. She gave millions to their clinics, and all were desperate to please her. If Colin could only sire a son, she could live with the risk of him passing along his disease. After all, it was controllable. And it would be infinitely better to have a sick Fleet than no Fleet at all. She'd even settle for his fathering a daughter. It wasn't the name that mattered so much as the bloodline. Right now she was in contact with a doctor in Melbourne, Australia, who was reporting great success with supposedly infertile men. If his results checked out, she would have Colin fly down there. He wasn't getting any younger and neither was she; she wanted this grave matter settled as soon as possible. She put down the telephone, stood up and kissed her nephew.

"A satisfactory meeting?" she asked.

He nodded. "Brock knows his stuff. I'm glad we bought him."

"I saw Mary at the club yesterday," she said. "She's looking well. Travel agrees with her. But I want her to stay home for a while now. There's this new doctor I've found, and if he can do what he claims, then we'll need your wife on standby."

Colin scowled. "She does as she pleases. I can't control her. And really, Veronica, I don't believe any of these quacks of yours are suddenly going to come up with a solution to my . . . my problem."

"I still have faith," Veronica said. "Every year there are new breakthroughs. I'll speak to Mary myself. She'll do as I tell her or we'll find you a new wife. I don't think Mary would enjoy not being able to live like a Fleet. Do you know how much she's spending on these grand trips of hers?"

He shrugged. "I don't care. It's such a relief to have her out of my hair. God, she's a bitch."

"But very fecund. We know that. And she's from good stock. But her childbearing years are running out. Oh, God, I pray this new doctor will hold the key, Colin."

"Don't get your hopes up," he said. He felt some affection for his aunt, so single-minded, so ready to crush any opponent. Her determination to solve his problem no longer embarrassed or irritated him. He saw it as an old woman's foible and he figured he owed her enough to go along with it. "We've been disappointed many times before."

"I've got a feeling it's going to be different this time," Veronica said. "I want you both ready to fly to Australia if this clinic checks out."

"Australia!" He laughed. "I haven't got time to be dashing off to Australia. We've got the political fight of all time on our hands."

"I thought you said Brock had it under control."

"No. I said he knew his stuff. He figures either side could win, and we need the blacks to cause enough trouble to frighten the swinging voters into our camp."

"Then we'll have to see the blacks do play up. I will not sit back and see my country taken over by those people. It's a disgrace. A black man, married to an Odlum. The two representatives of the ugly side of Bermuda." She was striding about the big office, tall and strong, the years falling from her. "I can't believe it has come to this, that people would actually take Stephen Youngblood seriously. And the very idea of independence! It must not happen, Colin."

He put a hand on her shoulder. Their pale eyes locked. "It won't happen, Veronica. I promise you it won't happen."

The week before the convention, Colin Fleet flew out of Bermuda. He was sorry to miss the event, he told the *Gazette,* but he had important fund-raising tasks in the

U.S. The convention would get along just fine without
him, he added.

In New York he checked into an anonymous downtown hotel, using the false name that had served him
well in the past, and began to put his grand plan into action. First he called the old contact number, the freight
company in Brooklyn. Despite the years since he had
used it, it was in service and the man called Camperi was
there.

"A long time, Mr. Tempest," Camperi said. "I figured
you'd gone out of business."

"I had," Colin said. "But now I need some things done.
I'll pay very well for your services." He paused. "Can we
talk on this line?"

"Sure," Camperi said. "It's clean. We check every
week. How do you think we've stayed in business so
long?"

"Good." He held the written list in his hand and read
it through to Camperi. He admired the gangster's cool
professionalism; no questions asked, no difficulties
raised.

"I can do that for you, Mr. Tempest," he said. "Leave
the package with the tickets, the cash and the instructions at your hotel desk. One of my boys will collect it
tomorrow."

Colin felt a rush of adrenalin, now things were under
way. And he felt the old desire, stronger than ever. To
hell with pills; heroin was more pleasurable and kept
him under just as strict a control.

"One other thing," he said. "For my personal use. Say
a thousand dollars of the best stuff you've got?"

"Done, Mr. Tempest. My boy will leave it at the desk."

"And I'll include the grand for you in the package.
Thanks for everything."

"No trouble. Say, you're not thinking of getting back
into business are you? The quality of your product was
always tops. And you wouldn't believe the prices we're
getting these days. I'd be very pleased to work with you
again."

"Maybe. We'll see after this is tidied up."

Colin left his hotel in late afternoon and walked uptown to the Grand Central airlines ticketing offices. The
summer heat was oppressive, but at least the streets
were not too busy. He hated crowds. They brought on the
headaches. Tomorrow, though, when the heroin arrived,
nothing would bother him. Anticipation. Almost as good
as the drug itself.

The girl behind the Eastern desk was pleasant and efficient. She sold him the two tickets in the names he gave
her, explained Bermuda's entry requirements—no pass-
port needed, just proof of U.S. residence—and accepted
his cash.

Then he walked toward Times Square, to the address
given in the Yellow Pages for the Outrageous Costume
Shop. The young man behind the counter was untrou-
bled by his request to purchase a nun's complete outfit;
his only query was whether Colin wanted the habit of
any particular order. He paid for his packages and moved
along the street to a lingerie shop; again the woman
serving him expressed no surprise at his request for gray
pantyhose, plain white knickers, singlets and bras to fit
him. God, he thought, this is one sick town when a six-
foot-four transvestite nun attracted no comment.

A rosary and a Bible and a cheap but serviceable suit-
case; a pair of heavy horn-rimmed dark glasses; plain
black square-toed shoes; a cheap toilet case filled with
unscented soap, toothpaste, toothbrush and Tampax.

Back in his room Colin poured himself a large Scotch
and surveyed his purchases; everything had a suitably
modest look to it. No need of a wig; the headdress would
cover that. He drained his glass. His head was pounding,
but he was damned if he was going to take any of the
pills. He was sick of leading a life of semi-sedation. No,
the Scotch would get him through the night and in the
morning the heroin would be there. He put through a call
to the South Shore Cottages in Bermuda; he knew they
had vacancies, had checked before he left Bermuda. It
was a new, low-key operation, almost designed not to appeal to the regular run of tourists. The night manager
sounded pathetically grateful to accept his reservation

of two cabins for five days. Finally, he took a large envelope from his case and put one of the air tickets, a sheet
of instructions and eleven thousand dollars inside,
sealed it and addressed it to Camperi.

He slept lightly that night, eager for the day and the
next stage of his adventure.

Colin settled himself in the window seat of the Eastern flight; a good hit of heroin before leaving his hotel
that morning had given him supreme confidence. He
didn't feel awkward or uncomfortable in the strange
garb. He let the rosary drape across his long, slim fingers
and moved his lips silently. The perfect picture, he
thought, of a nervous nun. He did not look around as the
seat next to him was occupied, and it wasn't until they
were in the air, turning left out of JFK then banking to
the right for the run to Bermuda, that he stole a glance
from behind his dark glasses at his companion. Camperi
had chosen well; Homer Davis was a thin, respectably
dressed young black man. A teacher, maybe, or a clerk.

They completed the flight in silence, neither taking
food nor drinks, and Colin followed his hired hand to the
Customs line. He needed to be able to observe anything
that went wrong at this vital stage. Homer Davis went
through the line that was having its bags opened while
Colin was waved to the no-inspection gate. He lingered
long enough to see the Customs inspector nod and slap
a bright red "Passed" seal on his man's case.

Outside the Customs area, in the bright sunshine, a
crowd waited to welcome family and friends; Colin kept
his head down and headed for the taxi rank. He slowed
until Davis was alongside him, then turned his head and
spoke quietly.

"We're both staying at the South Shores Cottages," he
said. "We'll share a taxi."

Davis started slightly but nodded. His instructions
had said contact would be made here, but he hadn't expected it to be a fucking nun, the one who had occupied
the seat next to him. He felt better about the job; the people organizing it seemed like real professionals. They

were silent on the trip to the South Shore, but the driver made up for them, extolling the virtues of his lovely island. The nun went ahead of Davis to the check-in and was given her room key; Davis stepped up and was allocated the room next door.

The complex was obviously still getting its act together. The receptionist couldn't raise a porter, but she insisted the nun couldn't carry her own bag down through the garden to the secluded cottage. Davis grabbed the opportunity to establish a casual relationship.

"We're right next door," he said, swinging her case under his arm. "I'll carry the sister's bag for her."

Colin Fleet strode down the narrow, flower-bordered path to the cottages, Davis trailing behind him. He felt better than he had in years, a heady sense of excitement, partly from the drug working in his system and partly from how his plan was working every step of the way. He stopped at the door to his cottage, nodded thanks to Davis and handed him a dollar wrapped around a note. Then he entered the cool gloom of the cottage and unpacked his meager luggage.

An hour later he was sitting on a deserted bench in the cottage's grounds looking over the sweep of pink beaches toward the big tourist hotels. Davis appeared a minute or so after him and sat a respectable distance away on the bench. They were quite alone.

"You've read my instructions," Fleet said. "Have you any questions?"

"How do you know this Youngblood guy will agree to see me tomorrow?"

"You've got a convincing story to tell him over the telephone," Fleet said. "And it's no great effort for him to spare you a few moments. He always spends an hour in the middle of the day taking tea and talking to anyone who wants to see him. Always the same table on the Town Square."

"And after that I don't see you until the night, right?"

"Yes, you can just relax and have a couple of days' holiday. Be a tourist and don't do anything to draw atten-

tion to yourself. If you have to contact me, I'll be staying
close to my cottage the whole time. But there won't be
any need. I've spelled out everything in all the material
I sent you through Camperi. What you can do now,
though, is go up to the minimarket and buy me two bottles of Johnnie Walker Black, some cheese and biscuits
and salami. This place provides breakfast and dinner to
the cottages, but I don't want to go out for lunches."

Davis was back at the door of Fleet's cottage with his
shopping within the hour. It wouldn't have meant anything if he had been observed: just a helpful young man
looking out for an elderly nun. Alone again, Fleet poured
himself a Scotch and settled down to wait. He could have
been out in the sunny courtyard, but the dim light inside
suited him better; the Fleets had always had to avoid
strong sunlight. The waiting did not upset him; the heroin was there to transport him into a world of his own if
required, but the anticipation of justice and revenge was
enough for now.

Stephen Youngblood pushed back the Panama hat and
wiped his forehead with a big handkerchief; one P.M. but
it was so hot the usually bustling square was almost deserted. For once there hadn't been the string of suppli-
cants waiting by his table to seek help in one form or
another. He was sorry he'd agreed to meet the man from
New York. Otherwise he could have gone home to Sarah
for a while. Except Sarah was at a women's action meeting on the other end of the island. They had little time
to themselves these days, and it would only get worse as
the election got closer. The election. He'd never expected
it to be easy, but the Conservatives seemed to be doing
everything right these days. The colony was beside itself
with excitement about the visit of the British PM. Suddenly people Stephen had counted on to support independence were waving British flags. The Conservatives
couldn't have picked a better keynote speaker.

He looked up as a shadow passed between him and the
sun. He saw a small, neat young black man standing a
foot from his table.

"Mr. Youngblood, sir? I'm Nat Bell. I called you yesterday."

"Sure, Mr. Bell," Stephen said. "Sit down and have something cool. I'm sorry Bermuda's decided to turn on one of its scorchers for you. It's not often like this."

"It's very good of you to see me at such short notice and without an introduction," Bell said. "I hope you won't think I've wasted your time."

"You said you had some papers, some evidence, that would help the New Alliance. If you have, you won't be wasting my time. We need all the help we can get."

The waitress placed a fresh jug of iced tea between them. Bell rummaged in the airline bag slung from his shoulder and placed a bulky brown envelope on the table.

"What it's about, Mr. Youngblood, is some material we turned up when we were looking for something else. You see, I'm attached to a research group set up to keep an eye on the more extreme right-wingers in the States. We monitor where their funds come from, that kind of thing. Anyway, from these reports you'll see there's been a flow of funds to Bermuda's Conservative Party. Here, have a glance at them." He pushed the envelope to Stephen, who opened it and began to read.

There wasn't much that surprised him: a list of cash contributions from individuals and organizations around America sent to the Conservatives. Not big amounts and no startling names. He considered what use he could make of them. He did not notice the old, tired nun who plopped into a seat three tables away.

"I'm sorry, Mr. Bell," he said finally. "It's interesting reading, but of not much use to us." He carefully placed the papers back in the envelope and handed it across the table. He did not hear the nun's camera click. "I appreciate your interest, but I guess you don't know our electoral laws are different from yours. Why should you? The thing is, unlike the U.S., it's not illegal for foreigners to contribute money to political campaigns here." He stood up. "I'm sorry it's been a waste of your time. I just hope you'll have a nice vacation here, anyway, and if I or the

party can help you, please call on us." He held out his
hand and Bell shook it warmly.

"It's your time that's precious, Mr. Youngblood," he
said. "Good luck in the election. I'll be rooting for you."

Stephen nodded and started across the square, heading back for his office. It was so hot; he had to fight to
suppress the irritation this wasted meeting had roused
in him. From the corner of his eye he saw a nun slumped
in the shade of a green and white Perrier umbrella. Stupid time for her to come to Bermuda, all bundled up in a
habit in the height of summer. At least in his white linen
suit Stephen was dressed for the climate. Poor American
nuns, he thought. Every year a few dozen of them came
down to visit their sisters in the local convents. They
were a common but incongruous sight, fluttering
through the streets trying not to sweat, surrounded by
scantily dressed holidaymakers.

Fleet was proud of himself; through three days of
waiting, most of it cooped up in the cottage, he had remained calm. No blinding headaches, no irrational
rages. The heroin and whiskey had helped, of course, but
he liked to think it was the overpowering sense of rightness about the course he had chosen that was keeping
him steady. And now the night, the time of truth, had
arrived. He gathered his things and walked up through
the dark garden, skirting the office and restaurant, and
out to the road. The Hamilton bus arrived within minutes and he climbed aboard, handing the driver the correct fare. There was a handful of tourists on the bus, and
some nodded and smiled at him as he made his way to a
rear seat.

He got off halfway down Front Street, and from there
could see the big crowd gathered outside the Tropicana
waiting for a glimpse of the British Prime Minister. He
crossed over and headed up Burnaby Hill and through a
series of deserted lanes to reach the rear entrance of the
Tropicana. He used his master key to open the heavy
door and waited there until Homer Davis emerged from
the dark of the reserve across the laneway. Silently Da-

vis followed him down into the bowels of the old hotel, Fleet moving surely through the black corridors he had known since childhood. It wasn't until they were in the big, disused cellar that he switched on his flashlight.

"Do the slogans first," he whispered to Davis. "I'll listen for anyone."

Fleet watched by the torchlight as Davis brought two spray cans from his flight bag and began working on the faded whitewash of the walls. "Black Power!" "New Alliance Rules!" "Drive out whites." "Unite with IRA." "Fleets=Slavemasters."

He stepped forward. "That'll be enough," he told Davis. "Now do whatever it is you do with the petrol." He settled back to watch again as Davis packed gas-soaked cotton wadding in under the tinder-dry rafters of the cellar and made a big pile of old debris in one corner. He wondered if the five-gallon can of gas would be enough for the job, but Davis obviously knew what he was doing. He finished splashing the fuel around and crossed to stand by Fleet.

"Whenever you're ready," he said. "Just one match in the corner and up she goes."

Fleet reached into the sleeve of his habit and clutched the blackjack resting there. He let the torch slip from his fingers, and as Davis leaned forward to retrieve it, he struck the man hard and fast, just behind the ear. Davis slumped to the floor without a sound. Fleet moved swiftly. He took a big green garbage bag from beneath his skirt and pulled it over Davis's head and shoulders. Next he took the little red smoke signal, bashed off its cap against the wall and pushed it up under the garbage bag. Even in unconsciousness, Davis started to jerk about as the smoke reached his lungs, but Fleet lay across him and held him down until all movement had ceased.

He removed the smoke bomb and stubbed it out on the floor; then the garbage bag came off and he checked again that Davis was dead. He wrapped the bag and the burned-out smoke signal together and placed them back in his sleeve. Davis was heavy and Fleet was breathing

hard by the time he got the body to the rear entrance.
Working in the dark he put the envelope in the pocket of
Davis's Windbreaker. He could feel the $5000 in notes
crackling inside the envelope and he wondered if he need
be so generous. But it was worth it. Fleet pushed the body
into a corner just outside the door, arranging it in what
he thought was the right pose for a man dying of smoke
inhalation and desperately trying to reach fresh air.
Then he hurried back down into the cellar, threw a
match into the soaked debris in the corner and ran
soundlessly back up to the rear entrance. He was two
blocks away and turning into Front Street before the first
nervous shouts were heard and the first smoke began
sneaking from the old hotel.

Edward Lapin slumped back in his office chair and
looked at the dinner-suited men gathered around him
drinking brandy. The first shock had worn off now, and
they were almost jovial, comparing stories of their bravery, wearing the singes on their jackets and the ashes in
their hair like badges won on a battlefield.

"It could have been worse, a lot worse," Lapin said. "If
they hadn't got the Prime Minister out . . . but, damn it,
it's still a terrible tragedy for Bermuda. And the Fleets,
of course. I suppose someone should track Colin down
and tell him what's happened."

"He'll not be too upset," Eric Amberley said. "The
Tropicana was about due to be replaced, and you can be
sure Colin had it well insured. Anyway," he added, "we
don't know where to reach him. He's somewhere in the
northeast. Time enough to tell him when he returns next
week."

"He'll need insurance," Lapin said. "Four tourists
killed and a dozen injured! All of them Americans, and
you know how the bloody Yanks sue at the drop of a hat."

He stopped talking. The boardroom doors had opened
to reveal the Police Commissioner, red-faced and rumpled, his glittering uniform stained with smoke and
water.

"One of you get Farrell a drink," Lapin said. "The poor

chap looks done in." He glanced out his office windows,
down the street to the Tropicana. The fire units were
rolling in their hoses and there was no more smoke or
flame to be seen. "It's all over then, Frank?" he asked
the Commissioner.

"Yes. But it's worse than we thought." The Commissioner clutched at his brandy. "We found a body, black—
dead of smoke inhalation, by the look of him. And in the
basement, all these slogans. It was arson, the work of the
Black Power maniacs. It's going to be dreadful publicity
for Bermuda."

"Arson. The blacks," Amberley mused. "I suppose it
is going to damage the tourist trade. But," he added,
toasting Lapin, "look on the bright side. The New Alliance and all this talk of independence is done for. Edward, you're going to be the next Premier."

Fleet was already safely in his rented cottage, toasting himself with Scotch preparing another injection of
heroin. Now that it was all done, he felt released,
cleansed. Tomorrow he would board the afternoon flight
for New York and return to normalcy. He got up and
fetched the photographs from their hiding place behind
the air conditioner. Mustn't forget to mail them before
boarding the plane.

The blacks gathered in Court Street and the back alleys of St. George's, swapping rumors and fears, waiting
for the tied bundles of *Royal Gazettes* to be delivered and
confirm the stories sweeping the island about what had
happened last night. The *Gazette* was late—special edi-
tion on the tragedy had not been put to bed until five
A.M.—but it was worth the delay. It was all spelled out
there: the death and destruction the arsonist had
wrought; the slogans sprayed around the basement of the
Tropicana; the picture of the dead face of the black man
who the police said had set the blaze. Some of the more
radical young blacks were thrilled by it all, the idea of a
violent strike against the hated white oppressors. But
most of the black community knew it could only mean

more trouble for them. The marijuana dealers buried their stocks and retired to their homes for the day; even the shopkeepers decided not to open for the present. They knew the police would come calling this day.

Stephen Youngblood had been up all night, gathering news from his followers. At first it had seemed just another tragic hotel fire, damaging to the community but no more. Then the whispered report from a black constable that a black had set the fire, a black who, apparently, was a fervent supporter of the New Alliance.

"My God," Stephen said, slumped at the desk in his study, head in hands as the dawn broke. "What have we done? I only wanted to show my people a political way to shape their own future. Instead, politics has driven one of them, at least, to murder and madness. Maybe people like Fleet are right, maybe we're not ready to run this country."

"Don't talk like that, Stephen," Sarah said. She put fresh coffee in front of him. "Even if it did happen the way you've been told, if it was some insane Alliance supporter, we can't be held responsible for it."

"Yes, we can. And we will be. The party's finished, of course. The Conservatives will walk in; there'll be a terrible new wave of racial hatred; and Bermuda will suffer some more. I should have left well enough alone."

She sat with him and remained quiet. There was no point trying to buck him up now. All she could do was be with him until he overcame this sense of desperation.

It was eight A.M. when the maid, who had been keeping the children quiet in the nursery wing of the house, appeared with the *Gazette*. Hoping for facts instead of rumor, Sarah spread the paper in front of Stephen and sat beside him. But the facts were even worse than they had feared. Suddenly she shared her husband's sense of hopelessness, despair and foreboding.

"I know that man, I know him." Stephen's hand was touching the front page, the picture of the corpse found behind the Tropicana. "He came to see me a couple of days ago in the square, wanting to give me information about the Conservatives. I sent him away."

"Is he a Bermudian?" she asked. "The paper says they don't know who he is yet."

"No. An American. He gave me his name when he called for the appointment. It'll be written down in my diary, at the office."

"You'd better call the police at once," she said. "Tell them . . ."

"You don't understand the way it is," he said. "Today they are going to be looking for scapegoats, for conspirators, spreading their nets wide to entangle as many troublemakers as they can. They will use this outrage to put as many of us as possible out of action. I'm not volunteering anything."

"You're a lawyer, Stephen. You believe in the law, in upholding it. Surely that includes helping the police."

"You don't understand," he said again. "The color of your skin, the strength of your money, the illustriousness of your lineage—of course you would go to the authorities in a situation like this. But I'm black and powerless. I know when it's time to lie low."

She didn't think about it. She swung her hand and caught him in a stinging blow on the cheek.

"You have no right to speak of me that way," she said. She was angry enough to hit him again, and she forced herself up and away from the desk. "Even if you think, after all these years together, I don't have an inkling of what oppressed people suffer, at least acknowledge what my grandmother had tried to do. Damn it, Stephen, sometimes you are as racist as any one of the bloody Fleets!"

He stood up and his hand came out at her, encircling her and pulling her close to him. He bent his head and rested it on her shoulder and held her tight.

"I'm sorry," he whispered. "I've never doubted your understanding and your concern. It's just that I'm very afraid for myself and all of us. I think you should take the children away for a while."

"No," she said, consoled. She kissed him. "No, our

place is here with you. It wouldn't be right to run away. And, anyway, there's nothing to flee for."

Colin Fleet settled into the suite at the Regency. It felt odd, to have reverted to his own clothes and name. He had enjoyed the anonymity his disguise had afforded him. Perhaps he would try a new identity again sometime. But now he had to tie up the loose ends. He called Edward Lapin's private number.

"Edward? Colin. I've just checked in here in New York and saw the *Post*. It's terrible, a tragedy like that in our hotel. And the paper says some mad black did it." He listened for a moment. "No, I think that would be in the worst of taste, Edward. Everyone will link the New Alliance with this outrage, anyway. No need for our chaps to play it up. Look, don't make any hasty moves. I'm booking myself home tomorrow. We'll talk about it in my office tomorrow evening. Okay?"

The photographs, in a neatly typed envelope, arrived on Commissioner Farrell's desk the next morning. There were three of them, all in clear focus, and they showed the dead arsonist sitting at a table in St. George's town square with Stephen Youngblood. In one, the two men were talking intently; in the second Youngblood was handing a package to the arsonist; in the third they were shaking hands. Farrell spread them out across his desk and sat back. It was the link he had been looking for, but the one which he wasn't sure he had wanted to find. The whole community, black and white, was already in an explosive mood: Farrell could not guess how extreme the reaction would be if a direct link was established between the dead man and the leader of the New Alliance. He sipped his tea and thought about it. Perhaps he would ignore the photographs and settle for what he had—a single madman, destroyed in the act of arson. It was so much neater and safer. But there was the matter of the $5000 found on the corpse to be explained. The reporters were already beginning to demand explanations of where it had come from. Farrell pushed the pictures together and rang for his Chief Inspector.

"Bring in Stephen Youngblood," he said. "Don't make too big a fuss about it. I only want to question him."

Stephen saw the police car stop outside his office and watched the Chief Inspector coming up the walk. He guessed they were coming for him and put on the jacket of his suit. The police officer was polite but told him nothing, leading him back to the car through the small and curious crowd that had already gathered. Stephen glanced into some of the faces: desperation, resignation, despair was what he saw. Something terrible had happened at the Tropicana, and now the blacks and their leader must pay for it. He wanted to tell them to cheer up, not to be afraid, but the words were not there. He felt as despondent as any of them.

Farrell waved him to a seat and dismissed the Chief Inspector.

"Sorry to trouble you, Stephen," he said. "But these photographs came in the morning mail." He took them from the envelope and pushed them across the desk. "You'll recognize yourself, of course, but can you tell me who's the man with you?"

"It looks like the picture of the dead man in back of the Tropicana," Stephen said after a minute. His mind was racing. He'd been set up. The lawyer in him screamed for caution, calm; the man he was fought back rage that someone had gone to so much trouble to damage him.

"It is," Farrell said. "If you care to have a look at the guy in the morgue . . . you can tell better than the picture they had in the *Gazette*. It's the arsonist." He sighed. "Do you want to tell me what you were doing with him?"

"He called me the day before, said he was down from New York and had some information helpful to the party. I told him he could see me in the square, like anyone can. What he had for me wasn't of any use, just a list of U.S. contributors to the Conservatives. I thanked him and left."

"You didn't give him any money?"

"No."

"Will you let us take your fingerprints?"

"Not unless I'm charged with something."

"Okay, Stephen, I'm charging you with being an accessory to murder and arson."

Among the prints they had managed to lift from the envelope containing the $5000 was one partial set which matched Stephen's. With the photographs, Farrell knew, it would be enough to convict Youngblood in a Bermuda court. He paraded his suspect before the magistrate, bail was refused and Stephen was led off to the cells.

"I can't see him until tomorrow," Sarah said. She was close to tears, at the end of a terrible day. She only stopped herself from crying for the sake of the children; they were clinging to her, sad and frightened. The news of the jailing of their father had swept the island and quickly reached their ears. "What am I going to do, Primrose? The whole thing's insane."

"Try and be calm," Primrose said. "We know Stephen had nothing to do with this terrible affair. The truth will come out in the end."

"Not in this damned place, it won't!" Her voice was shrill with worry. "I talked to my friend at the *Gazette.* She says Farrell's convinced they've got the whole thing wrapped up. And most of the people in Bermuda agree with him. The investigation's over. They've got a body and a scapegoat, so what else do they need?"

"Your father will be here on tomorrow's flight," Primrose said. "Stephen needs a good lawyer and I wouldn't entrust his case to any of the locals, not with the mood this place is in." She moved from her chair and took Sarah in her arms. "Don't fret. We'll find a way out of this mess. We're Odlums, remember. They've tried to do things like this to us before."

Jeff Billings saw his mother and his daughter waiting for him as he came through Customs. Arriving back in Bermuda had always been a happy occasion, but this flight had seen him doom-laden. The evidence against his son-in-law was circumstantial, for sure, but Jeff knew how difficult it would be to convince an emotion-charged jury of this.

"Thanks for coming, Daddy," Sarah said when they were seated in the car. She sounded calm, but he could see the dark shadows under her eyes. "I thought we'd go straight to visit Stephen," she said. He nodded.

It was not a happy meeting. Stephen was alternately angry and fatalistic.

"It's such an obvious setup," he said. "Anyone can see that. But that Irish idiot of a Commissioner won't do any more investigating. Those bastards have stitched me up beautifully." He made a fist, as if to strike the wall of the interviewing room. "Shit! I was a fool to think it would have been any different. I was a threat to them, so they've got me out of the way."

Jeff let him run on, and shook his head when Sarah tried to speak. Finally, when Stephen had slumped back in his chair, Jeff began. "Everything you say sounds right, Stephen, but it doesn't help our case any. I don't know where to start, but just remember we have good and powerful friends. We'll find the truth in this."

Veronica hugged her secret to her and let Colin talk. She was pleased to see her nephew so elated, so confident; her own news could wait.

"So I cut short the fund-raising trip," he was saying. "Well, with the trouble the New Alliance is in, there's no need for us to raise any more money. We'll win the election by default."

"I'm almost sorry it had to be this way, though," Veronica said. "It's terrible for Bermuda, all this Black Power nonsense. And the deaths. The cancellations are coming in now and we're going to lose another tourist season."

"It doesn't matter. We'll more than make it up in the long run. Now the colony is secured for all time. The blacks won't make another grab for power in a hurry." He lit a cigaret and lay back in his deck chair. "It didn't hurt us, either, the fire. The old place was due for a major facelift, and the insurance will pay for that, with change.

I couldn't be more pleased with the way things have worked out."

"I must be getting old," she said. She frowned. She *was* getting old. "But I feel kind of sorry for Primrose Odlum. I mean, the disgrace . . . sure, she brought it on herself, but it must be awful to have your family involved in a sordid affair like this."

"They did bring it on themselves," Colin said. "From the day they began to take on airs, to believe they were as good as anyone else, the Odlums were heading for trouble. I don't feel a damn thing for them. They've brought nothing but grief to our family, and I'm not going to sit here pretending to feel any sympathy for them now that justice has been done at last."

"I suppose you're right. It's just that, these last couple of days, I've been feeling kindly toward the whole world." She watched him, sitting back in the sunshine, so happy for once. Her news would make him even more content. "The Melbourne doctor I told you about, Colin, the fertility man. I sent him all the details and I got a reply two days ago. He says he can make you a father! He's certain. And the other thing . . . the nasty thing . . . he says it can be screened out. There's a new treatment called gene therapy. They'll give you a gene transplant." Her pale face was glowing with joy; she wished Colin would be a little more enthusiastic. "Don't you see? There'll be a new line of Fleets to carry on. It's all I ever wanted."

"I know how much you care about that," he said. "I guess I do, too. It's just that I reconciled myself along ago it could never be. Are you sure this fellow's not just another quack, squeezing you for money?"

"No. This is the best clinic in the world. I want you and Mary to fly down there and put yourself in his hands."

"I can't," he said. "At least, not right now. I must stay here and see the election through. It's going to be the proudest moment of my life, seeing the Conservatives elected and Bermuda saved." He saw her disappointment. "Look, Veronica, right after the election we'll go and put ourselves under the care of your miracle worker. Okay? A few months won't make any difference."

"Two weeks, Daddy! Two weeks he's been in that damned prison and nothing's happening. You're the hotshot Boston lawyer. What are you doing for Stephen?" Sarah knew she was being unfair, but she was weighed down with frustration and heartbreak. She was beginning to hate Bermuda, for moving so slowly, for being so complacent. Surely if they were in the U.S., or even England, Stephen would have been out of jail by now and home with her and the children. What harm could it do? The party was in tatters; whoever had wanted to ruin Stephen had certainly succeeded.

"I know how you feel," her father said. "You're entitled to be bitter. But all our applications have been refused. The courts accept the police case. I think you're going to have to face it, darling. Stephen's going to be convicted, no matter what I or any other lawyer argues for him."

"Surely, Jeff," Primrose said, "we don't have to accept this. We know Stephen didn't do it. Shouldn't we be out proving he didn't, instead of sitting here despairing?"

"I'm doing my best, Mother." He kept the anger in check. "The police think they have an open-and-shut case. They're not bothering to work too hard on it. They've established the arsonist was an American and he traveled here on false papers. You know how easy that is to do. The place he stayed knew nothing about him. It's new, the South Shore Cottages, and they didn't even keep a record of who made the booking. The money he had on him isn't traceable, and Stephen's prints are all over the envelope it was contained in. Damn, I'm sorry, but if I was the police prosecutor, I'd be pretty complacent, too."

"I guess we'll have to do the police's work for them," Sarah said. "Go out into the streets and find the truth. Someone must know."

"It's not that easy," Jeff said. "And you don't know what you're looking for." There was a tenseness between the three of them. He wished he could ease it, but he would not give them false hope. "I'll fight Stephen's case through all the courts. That's all we can do."

"But," said Primrose, "it won't do any harm if Sarah and I start asking around. We feel we've got to do something, Jeff."

In other circumstances, Primrose would have enjoyed the task she had set herself. She loved talking to people and understood her fellow Bermudians. She knew their unhurried, roundabout way of speaking, realized that casual chat produced more information than direct questioning. So when she approached the receptionist at the South Shores Cottages it was as a potential client, rather than as the mother-in-law of the accused.

There was to be an Odlum family reunion, she explained, with too many visitors to accommodate in her own house. She wondered if the cottages would be a suitable place for the clan to put up in.

Indeed it would be, the girl assured her. She took Primrose on a quick tour of the cottages, explaining how new the place was, which was why it was largely unoccupied at this stage. The inspection over, Primrose and the girl took tea in the little reception lounge.

"I guess that's why that terrible man, the one who burned the Tropicana, stayed here," Primrose said. "Quiet and out of the way, where he wouldn't be noticed."

"He did seem a quiet little man himself," the receptionist said. "I remember checking him in, and he wasn't at all fussed with the way things were. I mean, the porter hadn't showed up for work. You know how it is when you're just starting up. But he wasn't like some of those New Yorkers, all pushy and complaining. He even carried the funny nun's bag down to her cottage."

"The 'funny nun'?"

"That's what I called her. She checked in just ahead of the ... the arsonist." The girl sipped her tea and frowned. "Oh, I hope the fact that awful man stayed here

isn't going to hurt our reputation. How were we to
know?''

"Of course, dear," Primrose soothed. "No one can
blame you for your guests. I mean, there you had a nun
staying at the same time as him. What a contrast!''

"Yes," the girl said. "Why, he even did some shopping
for her. She almost never budged from her cottage.
That's why I thought of her as funny. Fancy coming all
that way for a holiday in beautiful Bermuda, then not
seeing any of it. And of course she never got out of her
habit, so she didn't get any sun. She was just as pale the
day she checked out as when she arrived.''

"Poor thing. I always feel for the nuns in this climate.
You'd think they would be allowed to dress for it. When
did she check out?''

"The day after the fire. At that time we still didn't
know about the man, that he'd been staying with us. I'm
glad she never knew, either. It would have been such a
shock for her, wouldn't it, to learn she'd been living next
to a killer.''

As Primrose was driven home she went over what the
girl had told her. Not much, really, hardly anything
more than they had already known. The nun might be
worth talking to, though. She'd at least had personal
contact with the arsonist. Primrose had got her name
from the register. Sister Mary Leo. But the only address
she'd given was "New York, NY," which wasn't any
help. What a shame Bermudian hotels didn't copy their
European counterparts and insist on full details and
documentation from their guests. There might be
hundreds of nuns with that name in New York.

Sarah was making even less progress. She was trying to
determine who had taken the incriminating photographs
of Stephen and sent them to the police. Her father had been
allowed to examine the prints, and had told her they had
been made at Bermuda's central photo lab, rather than at
one of the instant-print shops. So there was no order number on the prints; no way—without the negatives—to establish who had put them in. The manager of the photo lab

was sorry he couldn't help her. The police had sought the
same assistance, he said. But thousands of rolls of film
came in every day from more than fifty outlets all over
Bermuda. Impossible to trace, he said.

She tried, anyway. A half-dozen drugstores along
Front Street couldn't help. She didn't even have copies
of the prints to show them. They were "evidence," according to the police, and would not be produced anywhere except in court.

Finally Sarah drove to St. George's. She sat at Stephen's table on the square and ordered a lemonade. The
waiter brought it and smiled sadly at her.

"We're all missing Mr. Stephen very much," he said.
"We count the days until he's back at this table, helping
all the people. Don't you worry, missus, he's going to be
all right."

She glanced wearily around the square, now thronged
with tourists posing in the stocks and by the ducking
stool, clowning for the folks back home. She noted the
big "Agfa" sign on the drugstore. It was a long shot, but
surely if the pictures had been taken here, you might put
them in for processing to the nearest shop? Sarah finished her lemonade and walked across to the drugstore.
Inside it was dim and cool; a fat black woman behind the
counter looked up at her.

"Hello, Mrs. Youngblood," she said softly. "I'm real
sorry about what's happened. Hope it'll all get straightened out. He's a good man, your husband, and we need
him."

Sarah smiled her thanks.

"I doubt you can help me," she said, "but it's worth a
try. A couple of days before the fire someone took pictures
of my husband sitting at the table over there. I thought
maybe they brought them in here for processing."

"Yes, ma'am," the woman said.

Sarah's heart stopped, restarted. Was the woman only
saying yes, or did she mean yes the pictures had gone
through her shop?

"Yes," she said again. "I saw some nice pictures of Mr.
Youngblood." She chuckled. "Don't think I'm a snoop,

but often I go through the photos before the customers
come in to collect them. It's a hobby of mine. I like to see
what interests the tourists, what kind of pictures they
take. Those stocks out there, everyone gets his picture
taken in them. So this day, I thought it was a nice change
for a tourist to have some pictures of your husband, the
next premier." She stopped abruptly, embarrassed. Because Stephen Youngblood was in jail instead of on the
campaign trail.

"Pictures of Stephen with another man?"

"I guess there was someone else in the picture, but I
didn't look too closely at him. It was a real good likeness
of Mr. Youngblood, though."

"And do you have the name of the person whose pictures they were?"

"No, ma'am. We don't take names, we just give the
customer a docket."

Her heart gave another lurch. The hope had gone.

"But I'd recognize her anywhere," the woman said. "I
felt sorry for her, dressed so heavy in the heat and the
same time so pale in the face. She was a nun; a big, tall
old nun."

"Don't you see, Daddy?" Sarah was almost shouting.
"This nun stayed at the same place as the arsonist, then
took the pictures of him with Stephen. It was a setup. All
we've got to do is find the nun and Stephen will be
cleared."

Jeff ran a hand through his thinning hair and looked
at the two excited women facing him in the drawing
room. If only it was so simple.

"You've both done very well with your sleuthing," he
said. "But it doesn't really help Stephen. As far as the
police are concerned, they've got the pictures and the
fingerprints. They don't care about a mystery nun who
might or might not have played some part in this."

"But if we find her," Primrose said, "and discover who
she was acting for—"

"Mother, you saw the register. 'Sister Mary Leo, New
York, NY.' " Jeff raised his hands in a gesture of help-

lessness. "If she was involved in setting Stephen up, you can bet she wasn't a nun. She'd have come and gone on a false identity. How could you track her?"

"Through the arsonist," Primrose said. "Sometimes you lawyers can't see past your law books. Good God, Jeff, you boast about what good and powerful connections we have. Let's put 'em to work. The Bermudian police didn't get anywhere with establishing the arsonist's real identity. They haven't got the muscle in the U.S. and they don't really care who he was, anyway. They have his body and that's what matters to them. But now we've made the connection between him and the nun, we've got to find out all about him."

Jeff thought about it, and suddenly the women's excitement spread to him. Chester's boy was Under Secretary at HEW. He'd surely have enough pull to get the FBI to lend an unofficial hand. And get Customs to pull the nun's departure card from their files. There might be some more information on it, and certainly it would be made out in her handwriting.

"You're right," he said. "I'll fly up to Washington tomorrow and get things moving."

In the end it wasn't so hard. The FBI had some very good undercover men in Brooklyn, and armed with a picture of Homer Davis they soon established he was a skilled arsonist named Benny Lee Powers who hadn't been seen on the streets for a month or so. Benny Lee sometimes worked for a guy named Camperi who was quite well known to the Bureau. Camperi, who didn't want any trouble with the feds, was willing to admit off the record that he had put Benny Lee, aka Homer Davis, in contact with a "Mr. Tempest." The desk clerk at the downtown hotel gave them an excellent description of "Mr. Tempest," who, tall and pale with flowing white hair, was hard to forget. "Tempest's" handwriting in the hotel register matched that of "Sister Mary Leo's" Bermuda Customs card.

"And that's as far as we've got," the FBI man said as he laid down the file on Chester Odlum Jr's desk. "A tall,

pale man, almost an albino. But maybe he was wearing
a wig, or his hair was dyed white. Sorry, but all we've got
you is a lot of information and no solution."

Chester glanced at Jeff Billings, who quickly shook his
head.

"Well, thanks anyway, Dave," Chester said. "It was
worth trying and maybe it'll help us some way." He
shook hands with the FBI man who nodded to Jeff and
left them alone.

"It has to be him," Jeff said. He spoke softly, the en-
ormity of it almost too much for him. "The Fleets and the
Odlums again. Oh, Christ, won't it ever end?"

There were plenty of samples of Colin Fleet's handwriting available; a rich and powerful man like him was
always signing documents. The three most respected
handwriting analysts in the U.S. confirmed that the sig-
natures of Sister Mary Leo, Mr. Tempest and Colin Fleet
were all written by the same person.

"So let's go to the police right now," Sarah said. "I
want Stephen out of jail and that bastard in."

She looked at her father and grandmother, wondering
why they weren't already in action.

"I don't think that's the way to do it," Primrose said.
"We don't want a trial if it can be avoided. Colin's obviously insane. We've all suspected it for years. I shall
go and see his aunt tonight and put something to her.
Jeff can go and talk to the Governor and Commissioner
Farrell unofficially and I'm sure they'll release Stephen
at once." She looked at Sarah fondly. "I know you want
to hurt this man for what he's done, dear, but please be
patient. Revenge has never done anyone any good in
Bermuda. We'll handle this in our own way."

Primrose told her driver to wait with the car by the
gates; she preferred to walk up the long drive to the Fleet
mansion. She'd phoned ahead and, despite the cold reception, had insisted she see Veronica that night. The
house loomed large in front of her, lights gleaming in the
dusk, and she was panting slightly when she reached

the top of the drive. But her old legs, she thought proudly, were still holding up pretty well.

The maid admitted her and she stood in the broad entrance hall lined with portraits of Fleets, decorated with exotica gathered on a thousand voyages around the world. How strange that she had never before set foot in this house, strange that two of the oldest families in a small community could have had so little to do with each other. Primrose straightened as she heard the footsteps, and then the two of them, old, erect and proud, were facing each other.

"Good evening, Veronica," she said. "I'm sorry to intrude on you like this but what I have to say is of vital importance to us both."

"Come in here," Veronica Fleet said, leading the way into a small sitting room. She hesitated a moment and then civility overcame hostility. "Would you like a glass of sherry?"

"Thank you." Primrose settled in a chair and waited until the maid had served them and left the room. "It's been a long time, Veronica. Remember when we were almost friends? At school, my goodness, sixty-odd years ago."

Veronica nodded impatiently.

"All right," Primrose said. "I won't waste your time with old memories. I want you to know that what I'm here to tell you gives me no pleasure, only sadness. I have no hatred for you and your family." She sipped her sherry and began, as gently as she could, to tell Veronica what had been established about Colin's actions. The other woman flinched at one point and a grayness crept in under her pale skin, but she said nothing.

"So," Primrose concluded, "my son is meeting with the Police Commissioner now, and I expect they will also talk with the Governor. There is no need for any of this to become public. Enough damage has been done to Bermuda already and nothing will be served by Colin's standing trial. The Governor can sign a secret order committing Colin to the psychiatric hospital. He's not well, is he?"

Veronica nodded.

"He'll not be allowed to leave, ever," Primrose said. "But it is better than a trial and execution. Do you agree?"

"When? When would it have to happen?" Veronica asked. "I want him to go to Australia—"

"No. If we're going to do this, it must happen tonight. Any delay and the truth will begin to come out. You know how hard it is to keep a secret in Bermuda. This way Colin will be comfortable, well cared for, the family name will be intact and he won't be able to harm anyone else."

"Is that all you want?" Veronica's voice was flat in defeat.

"The police will issue a statement saying the fire had nothing to do with Stephen or the New Alliance. And you'll instruct Edward Lapin to announce that he believes some fanatical U.S. supporters of the Conservatives were behind the outrage, in an effort to discredit the Alliance. He'll apologize on behalf of his party."

Veronica nodded again and Primrose got up to leave. For a moment their eyes met and the two old women shared a bond of history and pain.

"You realize this is the end of the Fleet line," Veronica said. She was almost whispering. "Tell me one thing, please. I have seen your daughter-in-law, and your granddaughter. They haunt me. It's as if they could be of our blood. And Sam was involved with the Bellowes girl, back before the war. Can you give me some hope, tell me what I suspect is true?"

Primrose shook her head. "Forget it, Veronica. It does no good. Old names, bloodlines, feuds and fears . . . all we are are Bermudians. All distant cousins. There's no need to take it further than that."

Election Day, the last Saturday in October, a chill in the air and low, dark clouds gathering on the horizon. . . . Primrose had driven around the polling places and watched them streaming in to vote. No one could be sure of the outcome; Stephen's interrupted campaign had never really got back on the rails and there was confusion and doubt about both parties throughout the electorate.

Late in the day Primrose drove to St. George's and left her car in the town square. Knots of people stood around awaiting the poll results. There were few tourists to enjoy the beautifully restored square. Primrose moved around it slowly, touching the gleaming stocks where the first Sarah Odlum had been punished. The long-dry Fleet Fountain, paid for by the shooting down of Jonas Odlum. The ducking stool, where Prudence Odlum had perished while an ignorant mob howled from the dock. The tourists saw quaintness here; Primrose saw bloody, turbulent history.

She walked slowly out of the square, up through the narrow, winding lanes and on to the grassy slopes leading to the cliff tops. She rested on a rock and gazed out over the bountiful sea. There had always been enough for all of them in this beautiful place, but some would never be satisfied. The clouds were moving fast now, obscuring the setting sun. The wind was rising and the first drops of cold rain began to fall.

Primrose's legs were too tired to hurry down the hill to her waiting car; instead she crossed the field to the bracken-covered entrance to her secret cave. Inside, it was dry as dust and welcomed her. Already the storm was threatening to become a tempest, but it could not reach her there. She was safe, safe as the bones of three sailors resting in the back of the cave. She dozed as the lightning flashed outside, and she dreamed, hearing the voice of Sarah Odlum calling to her down through the ages. It would be all right now, Sarah Odlum told her. Bermuda was in good hands.

The strong beam of the flashlight woke her.

"I thought you'd be here," Sarah Youngblood said. "Come on our, Grandmother, the tempest has passed. And it's time for the victory party. Stephen's ticket swept the polls." She reached out a hand to help Primrose up. "A new era starts tonight," Sarah told her grandmother.